A FOLLY BEACH MYSTERY COLLECTION IV

BILL NOEL

Copyright © 2022 by Bill Noel

All rights reserved.

No part of this book may be reproduced in any form or by any electronic or mechanical means, including information storage and retrieval systems, without written permission from the author, except for the use of brief quotations in a book review.

ISBN: 978-1-958414-18-7

Enigma House Press

Goshen, Kentucky 40026

enigmahousepress.com

Other Folly Beach Mysteries by Bill Noel

Folly

The Pier

Washout

The Edge

The Marsh

Ghosts

Missing

Final Cut

First Light

Boneyard Beach

Silent Night

Dead Center

Discord

A Folly Beach Mystery COLLECTION

Dark Horse

Joy

A Folly Beach Mystery COLLECTION II

No Joke

Relic

Faith

A Folly Beach Mystery COLLECTION III

Tipping Point

Sea Fog (Coauthored with Angelica Cruz)

Mosquito Beach

Pretty Paper (Coauthored with Angelica Cruz)

TIPPING POINT

A FOLLY BEACH MYSTERY

Copyright © 2021 by Bill Noel

All rights reserved.

No part of this book may be reproduced in any form or by any electronic or mechanical means, including information storage and retrieval systems, without written permission from the author, except for the use of brief quotations in a book review.

Cover photo and design by Bill Noel

Author photo by Susan Noel

Enigma House Press

Goshen, Kentucky

www.enigmahousepress.com

1

Two extraordinary events occurred this morning. First, Charles Fowler convinced me to accompany him on a kayak adventure through the waterway as it weaves through the salt marsh separating Folly Island from the rest of South Carolina. The trip was extraordinary because of my fear of water, something there's no shortage of on a kayak ride. By fear of water, I'm not talking about panicking over taking a shower or getting caught in an occasional rainstorm. My fear, or as I refer to it in less-dysfunctional terms, extreme caution, involves water containing three-and-a-half-percent salt and in my mind roughly twenty percent sharks gathering to savor me for lunch.

I agreed to go because my friend said we'd rent a double kayak, plus he'd been kayaking many times on the same body of water. Nothing could possibly go wrong, or so he said. We'd paddled a couple hundred yards before he revised his kayaking experience saying this was the third time he'd been in one, but he'd thought many times about renting a kayak. I considered smacking him with my paddle or using my novice skills to turn the kayak around then head to shore. Either option would've capsized the vessel depositing me where the sharks were drooling over my meaty body. Falling for his story was on me since in the decade I'd known Charles, I couldn't recall him mentioning kayaking. He was also a master embellisher.

A few hundred yards later, I was feeling more comfortable using the fiberglass paddle, even started enjoying the scenery. It was early March, so the marsh grasses were beginning to change from winter brown to spring green. A handful of puffy cirrus clouds dotted the sky, the temperature a perfect seventy-two degrees. Large homes with walking piers ending at the river were to our right, where I recognized the residences of a couple of my friends. Even if I hadn't, Charles shared the name of the home's owner, who else lived in the house, including their pets. I became less comfortable when he insisted we take one of the tributaries branching to the left where the waterway narrowed. No manmade objects were in sight. The oyster-lined, eight-foot-wide passage appeared to become narrower with each paddle stroke. We came close to capsizing when a dolphin playfully arched out of the water close enough to splash me as it reentered the shark habitat. Charles thought it was way funnier than I had.

The only sounds I heard for the next fifteen minutes were a couple of terns laughing at me for believing Charles's story about how many times he'd been kayaking. I was beginning to relax, enjoy the marsh grasses, birds, and especially the dolphin gliding beside us.

Then the second extraordinary event occurred. My enjoyment of nature abruptly ended when the pleasant sound of the birds was drowned out by the roar of an airplane engine. It didn't take an aeronautical engineer to know the small, single-engine plane was in trouble. Its left wing dipped toward the water. It couldn't have been more than a hundred feet off the ground, or more accurately, the water. The plane was losing altitude and heading directly at us.

I didn't know if the pilot would or could gain altitude. It wasn't more than fifty feet from the marsh grasses when its nose pulled up. It still looked like it was going to crash. The deadly projectile was heading toward us when its front wheel caught in the thick marsh grasses, bounced once, then skipped across the narrow waterway. The aircraft continued in our direction. My fear of sharks was replaced by terror. I was about to be decapitated by the propeller with no time to paddle out of its way.

I screamed for Charles to bail out of the kayak. I did the same. We hit the water at the same time the plane's twisted landing gear filled the space our heads occupied seconds earlier. We were out of the overturned kayak in time to see the prop slam into the dense marsh three feet above the water. The nose of the aircraft burrowed in the pluff mud. The plane flipped and skidded, ripping a path through the grasses, before coming to a stop upside down and fewer than a hundred yards from where we were standing in waist-deep water.

The near silence that followed was eerie and consisted of a flock of birds squawking and Charles splashing around trying to find his paddle and Tilley hat. I managed to hold on to my paddle, but my hat was floating behind me. I grabbed it and my next thought was how we would get to the plane. It was high tide, the marsh grasses along with the island of mud was a few feet higher than the water, so I could only see the upside-down landing gear. It would've been impossible to walk through the mud without slicing our legs open on razor-sharp oysters along the bank before we'd sink knee-deep in the mushy surface. The waterway we'd been navigating meandered close to the plane.

Charles found his paddle and after what seemed like forever, we managed to climb back in the kayak, turned it around, then paddled to within six feet of the wreck. The right wing was above water and wedged into the side of the mud wall. That was all that prevented the cabin from being under water. Smoke was coming from the cowling, but there were no flames. That's when I heard banging sounds from inside the partially submerged fuselage.

Charles climbed out of the kayak to hold it stable while I gracelessly exited the vessel. I slogged through water and mud before grabbing a wing strut where I pulled myself up enough to see in the side window. Four men were in the cockpit, three upside down, held in place by seatbelts and shoulder harnesses. One was struggling with his harness; the other two, the pilot and the front seat passenger, were unmoving. Blood dripped from their heads. The cowling was mangled, the windshield shattered. Their heads had slammed into the upper section of the instrument panel. The fourth passenger had managed to get his restraints unhooked and knelt on the roof. He began shoving the unconscious man out of the way while ramming his shoulder into the door. It didn't budge.

Movement inside the cabin combined with my weight on the inverted wing dislodged part of the plane from the mud. It started tilting toward the water. If it slid much more, the cabin would be submerged.

We had to get the passengers out, and fast.

2

The top of the door was wedged in the mud with the weight of the plane pressed on it making it impossible to open. I yelled for Charles to go to the other door to see if the situation was better. The backseat passenger who'd struggled with his harness got it unhitched before Charles waded around the plane. The passenger fell, landed hard. His impact rocked the plane enough that it slid closer to the tipping point which would drown anyone who'd survived the crash. The man pushing the door turned to help his friend. Charles yelled the pilot's door may open but he'd need help.

The tail was sinking, the rest of the deathtrap not far behind. The men inside the aircraft were attempting to unbuckle the unmoving front seat passenger.

"Stop moving!" I yelled, hoping to keep them from rocking the plane.

I grabbed the strut then slid off the wing and splashed to Charles who fought to open the stubborn door. My thigh scraped the side of the pluff-mud island as I moved beside him and wrapped my hands around the edge of the door. Charles managed to force it open a few inches. Both of us pulled. Nothing. One more yank and it swung open a couple of feet. The plane groaned then slid six inches toward deeper water.

The pilot, still strapped in his seat, blocked the escape route for the others. If we tried to free him, the movement could hasten the plane's slide. If we left him suspended, there was no way the others could get out. The choices were bad and worse. I opted for bad.

"Charles, can you hold the pilot in place while I unbuckle his shoulder harness?"

"I'll try."

Neither the pilot nor the front seat passenger had shown signs of life. From the unnatural way their heads were twisted, I didn't hold out hope.

"The plane's not going to stay where it is if there's much movement or weight shift."

"What are we waiting for?" Charles said, as he knelt under the pilot and pushed up.

It took three tries before I unhooked the restraints. The pilot's dead weight fell on Charles. He stumbled yet managed to lower the pilot. With help from the rear seat passenger, Charles and I dragged the pilot out of the aircraft and carried him through the water to where we could lay him on the mud. The other rear seat passenger scampered out behind his friend. He grabbed his shoulder cursing it was broken. It may be, but he was alive, climbing out under his own power. One unconscious passenger was still strapped upside down in a plane which was slipping with each passing second. The water was rising in the cabin and inches from covering his head.

There wasn't time to worry about him getting hurt if we unhooked his harness. Charles slid underwater then surfaced on the other side of the man. He pushed him up while I unhooked the harness. The man flopped down in the water filling the cockpit. I dragged him out of the wreck.

The plane creaked then slid the rest of the way into the murky saltwater before we reached the muddy, cordgrass covered plot of land.

We'd maneuvered the last man out toward a safe resting place when I heard the thump-thump sound of props. I looked up and saw a distinct orange and white Coast Guard helicopter swooping toward us. Someone must've seen the plane go down and called for help.

The man who'd helped his fellow passengers out of the plane collapsed beside the pilot. The one with the injured arm sat in the mud staring at the mostly submerged aircraft. Both appeared in shock.

I gasped to catch my breath as a Coast Guard crew member was lowered from the air-sea rescue chopper hovering directly over us. The rotor's turbulence had the marsh grasses swaying like they were in a hurricane. Seconds later, I heard another engine and saw a black jet ski moving around the mostly sunken plane. The wave runner had OCEAN RESCUE in yellow on the front and was manned by a member of the Folly Beach Department of Public Safety. We weren't in the ocean, but I wasn't about to complain.

I met the officer on the wave runner who asked if everyone was out of the plane. I told him yes then pointed to the two unmoving passengers. Folly Beach police officers doubled as firefighters; most were trained EMTs. He rushed to the closest passenger while the crew member from the helicopter was bent over the pilot. Charles was with the police officer and the unmoving passenger.

I walked to the other two passengers who'd scooted close to each other. Both were dressed in bright-colored polo shirts, one in Kelly green slacks, the other in bright-red shorts.

I knelt between them and asked what happened.

The man in shorts shook his head, the other said, "No idea. We were headed to Myrtle for a golfing weekend. Took off from Charleston Executive Airport." He pointed at the man being attended to by the Coast Guard member. "Gary, the pilot over there, was in the plane when we arrived. We were running late. We threw our clubs in and took off. Oh, I'm Tom, by the way. Thanks for saving us."

"I'm Chris Landrum," I said before pointing at Charles. "It's fortunate my friend, Charles Fowler, and I were nearby."

"Sure was," said the man in the Kelly-green slacks, grimacing while holding his shoulder. "I'm Richard."

"You took off, then what?"

Richard said, "Gary didn't say much. He had a cold, all stopped up, cranky. He was also mad because we were late. He's anal like that. It was my fault, so I apologized. It didn't help." He shook his head. "We take these golf outings three times a year. Gary, Tom, and I live on Folly, so each time we head out, Gary goes out of the way to fly over our houses. It's neat seeing Folly from the air. We took off then turned this direction. It's a beautiful day. Gary said it should be a smooth flight." He looked at the still-unmoving pilot. "Suddenly he turns chalk white. The plane starts down. He didn't say another word. None of the rest of us knew anything about flying." He slowly shook his head. "A couple of us screamed, not sure who. Umm, that's all I remember until you helped us out of the plane. We didn't …" He stopped, grabbed his shoulder and winced.

Tom said, "You okay, Richard?"

Richard was in pain. He continued holding his shoulder. "I will be."

Tom said, "Good. Back to your question, I couldn't see Gary well, but he glanced back once. From where I was in the back seat it looked like his eyes glazed over. Then he turned, stared straight ahead. I could be mistaken, but it seems his head flopped forward seconds before we hit. Mark pulled up on the yolk, the steering-wheel looking thing in front of each front seat. It must've brought the nose up. That kept us from nosediving into the marsh. It saved our lives." He glanced at Charles and the police officer bending over the lifeless passenger. "Some of our lives." He lowered his head then whispered, "Mark's a hero."

Their stories were interrupted when Charles waved me over.

He removed his soaked hat and held it over the Naval Academy blue logo on his long-sleeve T-shirt. "He's gone."

The Coast Guardsman went over to the police officer and the deceased passenger. The two conferred as Charles and I slowly walked to the group. The Coast Guardsman then radioed the chopper, said there was nothing they could do, to send the harness down for him.

The police officer watched the Coast Guard copter retrieve its crew member and moved close to Charles and me, so we could hear over the sound of the rotor. I'd seen him around town but didn't know his name.

Charles said, "Chris, you know Officer Lane, don't you?"

Charles had lived on Folly thirty-five years and knew many of its residents. I had been there a decade and knew several people, but nowhere near as many as my friend.

"Don't believe I do."

We shook hands, he pointed to the pilot, then sighed.

The sound of an outboard motor got our attention as a white boat with Charleston County Rescue Squad on its side approached. It eased against the side of the elevated marsh mud. Two members of the volunteer rescue squad exited as the air filled with the thumping sounds of two approaching helicopters. They were marked with the logos of Charleston television stations and began circling the downed aircraft like buzzards preparing to descent on an animal's carcass.

Charles and I greeted the members of the rescue squad. The taller of the two asked if we needed medical assistance. I told him no, although I was feeling a sharp pain from a foot-long scratch on my thigh from when I scraped it on an oyster shell as I was helping Charles open the door. I pointed to the plane's surviving passengers and the paramedics headed their way to see if they could help.

The television choppers continued circling. They were so loud I didn't hear two more boats approach until the familiar voice of Cindy LaMond yelled my name. Cindy, Folly Beach's Director of Public Safety, was in the smaller of the two boats. The other watercraft held two more members of the rescue squad. Charles went to meet their boat while I helped Cindy out of hers.

I'd known Cindy since she moved to Folly several years ago to join the police department. She was in her early fifties, a five-foot-three bundle of energy, with a quick smile, and an irreverent sense of humor. She became Director of Public Safety, commonly called police chief, three years ago after her predecessor ascended to the position of mayor. Cindy is also married to Larry LaMond, another friend who owns Folly's tiny hardware store.

She glanced at the downed aircraft, then toward the others gathered near the scene, before saying, "Chris, what are the odds on you going anywhere without attracting a disaster?"

Cindy had exaggerated, although some would call it slight, at best. Since I moved from Kentucky, I'd stumbled across a few horrific situations. As unlikely as it had been, with the help of some friends I'd been involved in solving murders. What made it unusual was neither I nor any of my friends had worked in law enforcement, quite the opposite. Before retiring, I'd been employed in the human resource department of a large healthcare company. Most of my friends had equally unexciting careers.

"Cindy, Charles and I were—"

She waved her palm in my face. "Don't try to explain. Tell me what in the hell happened."

I described the crash and what the survivors had shared about the pilot losing consciousness. She told me not to leave, as if there was a chance of that happening, before she walked over to the rescue squad staff, talked briefly before stepping away from the group, then calling dispatch. I wasn't close enough to catch all her conversation but heard her mention the National Transportation Safety Board and the Federal Aviation Administration. Officer Lane stood a respectful distance from his boss until she finished her call, then cornered her as she approached the airplane.

Charles moved to my side and said, "What now?"

"Good question. Let's ask Cindy if there's anything we can do to help."

Cindy finished the conversation with her officer, shook her head, and said, "You two look like you've been mud wrestling."

Charles glanced at my soaked, mud-caked cut-off jeans and brown T-shirt, smiled at the chief, and said, "I won."

I ignored him. "Cindy, anything we can do to help?"

She looked at the plane then to the group of rescue workers huddled with the two survivors. "One of the rescue squad boats is going to take those two to an ambulance waiting at the dock. I suspect the one holding his shoulder and moaning will need more attention than the other guy. But, hey, I could be wrong. I dropped out of medical school. Wait, I never went to medical school. Anyway, I'll need to stay until the coroner arrives. I'm also waiting for a call back from the FAA and the NTSB. Somebody from the FAA will probably get here later today. The NTSB guy has to come from their field office in Atlanta. It'll be tomorrow at the earliest."

Charles said, "So, there's nothing we can do?"

Cindy glared at him. "Did I say that?"

"Umm, no."

"You two disaster magnets are going to hop in your cute little kayak and paddle back to wherever you got it. If you don't stumble across another plane crash or a hostile submarine peeking its periscope out of the marsh, you're going to go to a quiet place to write down what you saw, everything from when the plane headed your way until the cavalry arrived. When you're done, drop it at my office."

Charles let out a loud sigh before saying, "I hate homework."

Cindy wisely skipped over his comment. "Do either of you know the three guys who live on Folly?"

"I don't," I said and turned to Charles.

"I've seen Tom Kale around town. He's got a white poodle. Cute little thing, name's Casper. I introduced myself to him once, the guy, not the poodle, although it did lick my face when I knelt to pet it."

That didn't surprise me. I've suspected Charles thought more of dogs than he did of people. That was saying something since he's the best I've ever seen in getting along with almost everyone.

Cindy shook her head. "Other than having a dog named after a damned ghost, do you know anything else about him?"

"Not really. We didn't say much. He seems like a quiet guy."

"Neither of you know the other two who live here?"

We shook our heads.

"Hmm, that's unusual. Charles, I thought you knew everybody."

He sighed. "They must not have dogs."

Cindy rolled her eyes.

I was tired, sore, traumatized, and had heard enough canine talk. "Charles, ready to go?"

"Almost. Got another question for Cindy."

She rubbed her temples. "What?"

He pointed to the plane. "How're you going to get that out of here?"

"I'm not. It ain't flying out. I'm no expert since it's not a regular occurrence having an upside-down airplane in the marsh. I imagine someone'll have to get an aerial crane helicopter to haul it out. Nothing will happen until the NTSB and FAA clear the scene. Now get out of here. Let me start taking photos for the feds. The tide's starting to go out. I don't know what the plane will do when we reach low tide."

Charles looked down at his mud splattered red swim trunks, and said, "Cindy, one more—"

She pointed to the kayak. "Scat!"

3

I was knocking on the door to my seventieth birthday, Charles a couple of years younger, so by the time we returned the kayak, a nap sounded more appealing than as Charles put it *doing homework*. I also knew our memories about what happened would never be better than now, so I told him we should go to my house to write our recollections. He mumbled something about he'd rather stick chopsticks up his nose and didn't think he would be at his homework best if he looked like he'd spent the afternoon in a pigpen. He was right about the second part of his gripe. I agreed to drop him at his apartment so he could shower. I'd pick him up in a half-hour to complete our assignment. I could've told him to come to my cottage, but that would've given him a reason not to show.

Thirty minutes later, I'd gone home, taken a quick shower, dumped my mud-covered clothes in the hamper, spread an antiseptic cream on my scratched thigh, and drove back to Charles's apartment in an ancient building on Sandbar Lane. In true Charles style, he was outside leaning against the building as I pulled in the gravel lot. He looked at his wrist where most folks wore a watch. He didn't wear one, which didn't stop him from glaring at me as he walked to the car.

He pointed a gray, legal pad at me. "You're late."

When I'd dropped him off, I said I'd get back as quickly as I could. In his mind, I'd taken longer than *as quickly as I could*. "You're late," was one of his often-used phrases. Over the years I'd learned to ignore it. I again took that tactic.

Charles leaned his head back and closed his eyes during the short drive from his apartment to my cottage next door to Bert's Market on East Ashley Avenue. I would've done the same if I wasn't driving. We were too old for the day we were having.

We decided to write our recollections separately, then compare once we finished to iron out discrepancies. Over the years, Chief LaMond had beaten into my head how witness descriptions were suspect under the best circumstances. It wasn't unusual for three people to see a robbery then give the police three drastically different descriptions of the robber.

I asked Charles if he wanted something to drink before we began. He said water, so I grabbed two bottles from the refrigerator as he went to the spare bedroom I used as an office. He plopped down in a secondhand chair in front of a table to start writing. He looked like a student preparing to answer an essay question on a test, a very old student. I settled in front of my computer. My handwriting was so poor that not only was it illegible for anyone else to read, I couldn't decipher it. Keyboarding was my lone readable option.

"What kind of plane was it?" Charles asked before I started.

"It said Cessna on the side."

"What model Cessna?"

"Charles, I don't have a clue. I was sort of busy. Why?"

"Want to make sure I'm accurate."

"Did you see any other upside-down Cessnas out there? I think the NTSB will know the one you're talking about."

"No need to be touchy."

I sighed.

Ten minutes later, Charles said, "Would you call Richard's slacks Kelly or Crayola Green?"

I lifted my hands off the keyboard and rubbed my eyes. "Charles!"

"Just asking. I'll go with Kelly."

"Excellent choice," I said, not attempting to mask sarcasm.

Miraculously, the next thirty minutes passed without more questions. The streak was broken when he said, "What do you think happened to the pilot?"

"Don't know. I suppose they'll have to wait for the coroner's report. From what Tom said, it sounds like he had a heart attack or a stroke."

"He was in his forties. It seems strange."

I shrugged. "All I know is it's fortunate two of them are alive."

"Fortunate we are, too."

He was right. I started to agree when the phone rang.

"Is this Chris Landrum?" asked an unfamiliar female voice.

"Yes."

"Good. I'm Kylee Loftus with the *Post and* Courier. I'm following up on the fatal plane crash near Folly Beach."

It'd been fewer than five hours since I witnessed the crash, so I wondered how Charleston's daily newspaper learned my identity.

"How'd you get my name?"

The reporter hesitated before saying, "I was talking to one of the men from the Rescue Squad. He gave me your name, number, and that of a Charles Flowers who was with you."

"It's Fowler, not Flowers."

"Oh, thanks for the clarification, Mr. Landrum. Could I ask a few questions?"

My preference would have been to hang up, instead I said, "Not many. This has been an exhausting day."

"I can appreciate that, sir. I won't take much time."

"Go ahead."

"I was told you saved two of the passengers from drowning. Tell me about it."

"Charles and I did what anyone would've done under similar circumstances. We were nearby and helped them out of the plane. I'm only sorry we couldn't have done anything for the other two."

Ms. Loftus said, "That's not what, umm," I heard her shuffling papers. "Mr. Haymaker, one of the survivors, said. He told me if you hadn't helped at significant risk to your safety, he wouldn't be alive."

I repeated what I'd said about doing what anyone would've done, so she changed the subject. "Prior to the crash, did you know any of the men in the aircraft? My understanding is three lived on the island where you reside."

Charles had scooted closer as he motioned for me to put it on speaker. I did, and he leaned closer to the phone.

"No, Ms. Loftus, I didn't know the men."

"So, you and your friend risked your lives for strangers."

"You think if we didn't know anyone in the plane we wouldn't have helped?"

"No, no, sorry, Mr. Landrum. That's not what I meant. I was trying to put a lead on the story. Two men heroically risking their lives to help strangers has a positive ring to it."

I was tempted to hang up, but instead repeated what I'd said twice about doing what anyone would do. She must've figured she wasn't getting anywhere trying to put hero in front of our names. She thanked me for talking to her. She started to hang up. I stopped her figuring since she'd already managed to find me, she might have information about what caused the crash. I said, "Let me ask you a question. Do you know what caused the pilot to collapse?"

"Nothing official. The first responder with the Rescue Squad said it looked like a heart attack. Understand though, he was guessing."

She thanked me for talking with her and asked if she could send a photographer to the house to get my photo for the paper.

"No."

"But—"

I cut her off with another, "No."

She took my less-than-subtle hint, again thanked me for talking with her, and ended the call.

Charles took the pen that he'd been writing his description of the event with and pointed it at the phone. "At least you got my name corrected."

4

Minor discrepancies existed between the narratives. The variations were where we were on opposite sides of the plane, and when he took credit for having us bail out of the kayak to prevent multiple decapitations. It wasn't worth debating, so I let him keep his memories. I dropped him at his apartment, illegally parked in a yellow zone in front of the police department, and scampered, okay, walked to the reception area. I was told Chief LaMond was still at the crash site, then handed our reports to one of the officers who said he'd give them to her when she returned.

My energy tank was running shy of empty by the time I got home. There was little food in the house, a common occurrence, yet I managed to scrounge up two slices of stale bread and a jar of peanut butter then using all my culinary skills, slathered peanut butter on the bread. I ate most of the sandwich before falling asleep in the recliner in the living room. I'd turned the television on to watch stories of the crash on the two stations that had aerial coverage. I slept through whatever was reported.

The phone jolted me awake. I couldn't imagine having slept too long until I realized the morning sun was filtering through the slats in my window shade.

"Chris, this is William. I know you're an early riser, so I trust I didn't awaken you."

William Hansel had been a friend since my first week on Folly. We'd also been next-door neighbors the first few weeks until an arsonist torched my rental house. Torched with me in it.

"Good morning, William."

I didn't tell him I'd been asleep and didn't dare ask what time it was.

"I saw on the morning news about an aircraft incident which occurred yesterday taking the lives of two gentlemen."

William, unlike most of my friends, spoke with the demeanor of a college professor lecturing his class. That was understandable since he was a professor at the College of Charleston and had been for many years.

"It was terrible."

"Correct me if I'm mistaken. From the angle shown by the camera on the news helicopter, it appeared you and your colleague Charles Fowler were near the inverted aircraft, the first responders tending to the injured, and to the unfortunate gentlemen whose lives were lost in the tragic occurrence."

I warned you he spoke like that.

I gave him an abbreviated description of what'd happened.

"As I suspected. The reporter gave the names of the deceased victims yet didn't divulge the monikers of those who were at the scene of the misfortune."

"William, I appreciate your concern."

"Yes, of course, Chris. The news story not only showed two of my friends at the scene. But, how best should I say it, I am also acquainted with Mr. Tom Kale, one of the survivors."

"Oh. He said he lived over here. Is that how you know him?"

"To a degree. As you and I have lightly touched on over the years, there are a minuscule number of African Americans residing on Folly."

"Yes," I said, wondering where he was going with the story.

"And, I am certain you noticed Mr. Kale shares my racial human categorization."

"You're both black?"

William chuckled. "Yes. Additionally, you may or may not know Mr. Kale is a stockbroker by trade."

"All I knew about him was he survived the crash, and thanks to Charles, knew he has a poodle named Casper."

"I didn't know he possessed a canine."

"I can understand that."

"Chris, as you are aware, I'm not a wealthy man. I live by modest means thus keeping my expenses to a minimum. With that said, I have been able to accumulate a tidy sum of money to tide me over in retirement."

William had turned sixty-six a few months ago and shared plans to retire in the next two years.

Not knowing what to say, I gave a benign, "Yes."

"For the last five years, I have been investing utilizing the services of the brokerage firm in which Mr. Kale is a partner. I began working with his wife, Alyssa, then the Kales divorced a year ago, highly contested, I regret to say. Tom took over my account after Alyssa left the firm."

"Do you know him well?"

"Not much beyond his professional talents. He lives in a large house past the Washout. I seldom saw him in town. Most of my contacts took place in his office in Charleston. Truth be told, I knew Alyssa better. She seemed to always be concerned about my portfolio. She would contact me whenever adjustments were needed."

"Why didn't she take your portfolio with her?"

"I wish she could have, being as easy as she was to work with. It was prohibited by her contract, thus I remained with the firm. Mr. Kale, Tom, was always nice and appeared interested, but didn't have the personalized touch his wife exhibited. All, neither here nor there. I simply wanted to make sure you were okay and to share I knew one of the survivors. I'm certain you're busy, so I'll let you go."

William was overly generous saying I was busy. I wouldn't put retirement among the high-stress, demanding professions. I thanked him for calling and suggested we should have lunch soon. He said he would like that. Of course, he used multisyllabic words to express it.

I pushed out of the recliner, realized my neck was sore from sleeping in the chair, my back ached from yesterday's rescue, and my thigh stung from the encounter with the oyster shells. I was also starved. Unless I wanted another peanut butter sandwich, I'd have to leave the house to eat. I wasn't ready to encounter a restaurant full of people, so I headed next door. Bert's Market was a Folly icon, sold everything from beer to banjo strings, and prided itself on never closing.

Mary Ewing, a mid-twenties, single mother, greeted me. I'd met her a couple of years earlier when she was homeless and raising two young children while squatting in vacant rental houses. I introduced her to Preacher Burl Costello, minister of First Light Church, who helped her find more appropriate housing and the job at Bert's.

"Chris," Mary said, "I saw your name in today's newspaper. Did you and Charles really see that plane crash then save two men?"

I nodded.

"Wow, you're heroes. To think, I know both of you."

I repeated my story that we were in the right place at the right time doing what anyone would do under similar circumstances.

"You're still a hero. You know something else? I knew the pilot, well, I didn't really know him. He came in a few times."

"Know anything about him?"

She lowered her head. "I hate to talk bad about the dead. He, umm, he wasn't a nice person, not nice to me anyway."

"What do you mean?"

"He's a lawyer. Nearly every time he came in, he bragged about living in a big house on the beach. I think it was past the Washout. It seemed strange. Most folks treat all of us working here like we're friends. He was, how shall I say it, standoffish, snooty. Who talks about how big their house is or that it's oceanfront when all they're doing is buying a six-pack of beer?"

"That's strange."

"Not only that, I didn't like how he treated his wife. It was sort of like she was, umm, what's the word? Got it, she was subservient to him. She walked behind him like she was property. Sorry to ramble. He struck me as not being nice."

I'm glad Mary didn't like speaking poorly about the dead. No telling what she would've said.

"Thanks for sharing."

"I'm sorry he's dead, sorry for that other man who was killed. Enough about that, what can we get you?"

I thanked her again, said I knew where I could get what I needed, and headed for the cabinet holding pastries. I grabbed a cinnamon Danish and a newspaper from a nearby shelf. It would've been hard for Mary to have missed the story about the crash since there was a photo of the upturned airplane taking up most of the space above the fold. I drew a cup of complimentary coffee from the large urn then took my purchases to Mary who'd moved behind the counter. She took my money, grinned, and repeated, "My hero."

I tapped her on the arm, returned her smile, then headed home.

5

The newspaper article filled several blanks about who was on the plane and their background. The deceased pilot, Gary Isles, a married, forty-three years old, was partner in Chapel Smyth & Isles, a law firm founded by his father. Gary had been a pilot nine years. Mark Jamison, age forty-five, the other man killed, owned a trucking company, MJ Transport and Logistics, and was in a relationship with Kevin Robbins. The survivors were Richard Haymaker, thirty-nine, a Charleston stockbroker, and Tom Kale, age forty-seven, also a stockbroker, a fact I'd learned from William. The men were avid golfers. Over the last couple of years, they'd flown to popular golfing destinations in South Carolina and Georgia. The story was vague about the cause of the crash although it hinted that most likely it was the result of a medical crisis with the pilot rather than mechanical. The plane was a 2006 model Cessna 182 Skylane, a fact meaning nothing to me, but would meet Charles's penchant for trivia.

Charles and I were mentioned as residents of Folly Beach who had assisted the passengers out of the aircraft. Tom Kale was quoted as saying, "If those guys weren't there, Richard and I would've been goners." The story ended by referring readers to the newspaper's website for updates, a frequent practice of newspapers, radio, and television stations in this age of instant information.

I turned on the computer, entered the paper's website, to find the story had been updated three hours ago, although all that was new was the coroner's office wouldn't be able to determine cause of death until the toxicology tests were complete which could take several days. An employee of Atlantic Aviation, the company providing fuel and other services at the Charleston Executive Airport, who knew the pilot, said Gary was an excellent pilot, kept his aircraft in peak condition, and with the perfect weather the day of the crash, couldn't imagine anything going wrong unless something happened to Gary.

Another nap filled my afternoon. Apparently, assisting men out of the plane was exhausting for this near septuagenarian. I woke up and realized that hunger must also be a byproduct of my recent activities. I called Charles and we agreed to meet for supper at The Washout, one of Folly's larger restaurants. It was located on Center Street, the center of commerce on the island, and three blocks from Charles's apartment. I carried a few extra pounds—if twenty could be defined as few—on my five-foot-ten-inch frame and knew I needed more exercise than I'd been getting, oh, let's say, the last thirty years. The weather was still pleasant, so I walked the six blocks.

Charles was seated on the outdoor patio and sipping a beer when I arrived. He waved. "Yo, hero, come join me."

He wore black shorts and a maroon long-sleeve T-shirt with a strange looking logo with Erskine Flying Fleet under it.

I slid into the booth and avoided looking at his shirt, in hopes he wouldn't need to tell me about it. His T-shirt collection was only surpassed in quantity by the collection of books filling his tiny apartment.

He tapped the logo. "Flying Fleet, get it? Remind you of when we became heroes?"

I waved for the server and ordered a glass of chardonnay, again, to draw attention away from Charles's shirt.

"Did you know Erskine College is in a place called Due West, South Carolina? Can you believe that?"

Not only didn't I know its location, I didn't know there was an Erskine College.

I mumbled, "Interesting."

"Yep. Been waiting years for a good time to wear it. By the way, did you know a 2006 Cessna 182 Skylane like the one we heroed the guys out of cost more than a quarter million dollars? Used! Like a dozen or so years old. Two-hundred fifty-thousand bucks."

That was two things I learned in the last two minutes.

"You know that how?"

"The guy on the TV said the upside-down plane was a Cessna 182 Skylane. Who wouldn't wonder what one costs? Used my handy-dandy laptop computer to ask Mr. Google what he knew about it. Found all sorts of stuff about the plane, most of it I didn't understand. They had the nerve to call it a light utility aircraft. Sure as heck didn't feel light when we were trying to lift it out of the mud to get the door open." He sighed. "Gary Isles must've had a pot load of money to be flying around in that expensive of a plane. Used."

I nodded, the safest response to most anything Charles says. "The paper said he was a partner in a big downtown Charleston law firm his father founded. He could afford it."

The server, Dennis, according to Charles, returned to the table with my drink and asked if we were ready to order. We each ordered fried seafood baskets, negating the calories burned on the walk over, then continued our—Charles's—discussion about the ill-fated plane. I zoned out when he started telling me about the twenty-six variants of the Cessna 182 since its debut in 1956. I rejoined the conversation when he said he wondered if we knew anyone who knew the two men who lived on Folly other than Tom Kale.

"Don't know about the other two," I said. "William called to tell me he knew Tom Kale. Tom and before that, his wife, Alyssa, were William's stockbrokers."

Charles leaned toward me. "When were you going to tell me?"

My friend considered it a personal affront if I learned something he may have interest in and didn't share it with him immediately. Immediately meant immediately.

"I just did."

"What time did William call?"

"Earlier," I said, hoping it was vague enough.

"Tell me everything he said."

I'd made it through retelling most of my conversation with William when our food arrived.

Charles attacked his flounder like he hadn't eaten all day, which could've been true.

He took a sip of beer, belched, then said, "Did William know Casper?"

It took me a few seconds to remember that Casper was Tom Kale's poodle.

"No."

"Wonder how Richard Haymaker's shoulder is," said Charles, a man who could change subjects on the head of a pin.

"Don't know."

"Think we should call to see?"

"No."

"How're we going to find out what went wrong, to find out how the guys are doing if we—"

My phone rang before Charles could lead me farther down Nosy Street.

Cindy's name appeared on the screen. "Good evening, Chief LaMond."

"If you say so. From my bloodshot eyes, it don't look so good. Of course, I have a job where I'm responsible to every citizen of this fine city, and you're, well, you're worthless and retired so everything looks brighter to you than it does to me."

"Cindy, did you call to remind me of my worthless status?"

"Nah, that was extra, no charge. I called to give a preliminary report on the untimely death of Mr. Gary Isles. The coroner won't issue a full report until the tox screen analysis is back in a few days. What he can say is the deceased pilot's heart appeared to be in excellent shape—excellent for a dead guy."

"So, it wasn't a heart attack?"

"That's what I said, pay attention."

"Is the coroner ruling out natural causes?"

I heard an audible sigh. "Not completely, but close."

I stared at the phone then said, "That mean he was murdered?"

I thought Charles was going to twist his shoulder out of the socket flailing his arms around. He wanted me to put the phone on speaker so he could hear. It was too late.

Cindy said, "Could be," as she hung up.

I hit end call, although it was already ended, then received a glare from my friend, before he said, "Was he?"

"Was he what?"

"Murdered?"

I shared the rest of Cindy's conversation and watched Charles get more agitated. Dennis made the mistake of returning to the table to ask if we needed anything else. I suppose that was what he was asking.

Charles interrupted before Dennis finished the question. "Another beer. Quick."

Dennis looked at me, so I nodded and pointed to my near-empty wineglass. I figured I'd need more before Charles calmed.

"Chris, we've got to figure out who killed those men, honest we do."

"Hold on, Charles. Nobody knows if the crash was anything but an accident. All Cindy said was the pilot appeared in good health. And, my friend, even it was something other than an accident, we have no reason to get involved."

"No reason? You've got to be kidding," Charles said while he waved both arms over his head. "That plane all but knocked on our door screaming help us. We saved two, now we have to help the other two. Got to find the dastardly person that killed them."

There was no arguing with Charles once his mind was set. I sipped the wine Dennis deposited at the table while Charles was in the middle of his proclamation.

I watched Charles take a gulp of his second beer, then said, "Tell you what, let's take some time away from what happened and see what, if anything we learn in the next couple days."

I'd expected a fight about my suggestion. Charles agreed which proved he was exhausted. I knew I was, both exhausted and hurting from head to toe from our peaceful kayak ride.

6

I called Charles three times the next day to be rewarded with voicemail. He'd purchased a cell phone a couple of years back when he and his then girlfriend moved to Nashville. As the old saying goes, should go, you can lead Charles to a cell phone, but you can't make him carry it. On the third try, I left the message that I saw in the paper where Mark Jamison's funeral will be tomorrow. I asked if he wanted to go. Charles had never passed up an opportunity to be nosy, so I knew the answer. My message was a formality.

He returned the call around sunset. As only Charles could do, he asked why I hadn't invited him sooner. As only I can do, I ignored the question and told him what time I'd pick him up. I'm certain somewhere in his mumbled response, he thanked me.

Next, I called Chief LaMond and was rewarded with, "Why in a heifer's hoof print are you harassing me while I'm having a romantic, candlelight supper with my charming, sexy spouse?"

"Whoops. Sorry, want me to call back?"

"Crap no, why wouldn't I want to be interrupted? Besides, the Chef Beef Boyardee I slaved over for seconds is getting cold. I repeat, what're you harassing me about?"

"I saw where Mark Jamison's funeral is tomorrow. I was

wondering if you knew anything more about Gary Isles' autopsy or when his funeral will be."

"And you're wondering this because you're a funeral junkie who doesn't want to miss a chance to smell the chrysanthemums? Oh, wait, I forgot, you're a guy, so you don't know the difference between a chrysanthemum and an Iranian bum."

That kind of comment reminded me why Cindy was one of my favorites. I chuckled, then said, "No. Charles and I were there when the men died, so I wanted to attend to express sympathy to their families."

"That'd be touching, if it wasn't a crock. You want to learn all you can about them in case the accident wasn't an accident. Then, you and your faux-detective friend can start meddling in police business."

In the recesses of his lopsided imagination, Charles thought he was a private detective. No training, no law enforcement experience, no license, no problem. He claimed to have read every private detective novel written making him qualified to carry on the legacy of Philip Marlowe, Sam Spade, and Sherlock Holmes. The frightening thing was that over the years, we'd stumbled on several murders, and through actions resembling Wile E. Coyote more than Sam Spade, we'd caught some killers.

"Cindy, all we want to do is pay our respects."

"And dear hubby sitting here staring at me thinks I look like Jennifer Lawrence."

"Of course not," I said. "You're far prettier."

"Nothing like BS with Beefaroni. No."

"No what?"

"Don't you remember your question? No news on the autopsy. No news on Jamison's funeral. Here's an answer to a question you didn't ask. The NTSB guy unofficially told me at first glance he couldn't see anything wrong with the plane. Nothing other than it was plopped upside down in the marsh. He's talked to the two survivors who said everything appeared normal until the pilot collapsed. Nothing official will be released for months."

"Thanks, Cindy. Now get back to your romantic supper."

"Right. Larry's done got bored and is in the living room watching reruns of *Rehab Addict* on the DIY Channel."

* * *

The funeral home was off Greenwood Road in North Charleston, some twenty-five miles from Folly. As anyone who knew Charles could've predicted, we arrived thirty minutes before the service. What I wouldn't have predicted was the number of mourners gathered around the entrance to the Colonial style, red-brick building. I recognized Richard Haymaker from the crash but hadn't realized how tall he was. At roughly six-foot-two, he towered over most of the others milling around. He was talking with an attractive blond, who, at five-foot-eleven, was taller than any of the women in the group.

Richard, wearing an expensive-looking, dark-gray suit, navy and white striped tie, and polished dress shoes, looked drastically different than how we'd seen him at the crash site. His arm was in a dark-blue sling, color coordinated with his tie. Charles and I approached the couple. Richard glanced at us and his expression changed from disinterest, to recognition, to a radiant smile.

"You're Chris and, umm—"

"Charles," my friend assisted.

Richard's right arm was in the sling, so he shook with his left hand, an awkward move. "Yes. Sorry I forgot. The other day was quite traumatic."

Charles said, "How's the arm?"

"I'm fortunate, only minor damage. The worst part is keeping it in this stupid sling. Allow me to introduce my wife, Charlene Beth. Charlene, these are the men who saved Tom and me. If they weren't there, we'd have drowned."

Charlene Beth, who'd been standing a step behind her husband, stepped forward, smiled, shook Charles's hand, reached for mine, and said, "Richard hasn't stopped talking about you, about what you did. Thank you so much. You'll never know how much your heroic act means to me."

"Me, too," said Richard, as he put his arm around his wife to pull her close.

She kissed his cheek.

I said, "We're sorry we couldn't have done anything for the other two."

Richard looked at the funeral home entry and lowered his voice. "I feel guilty standing here with such a minor injury, while my friend Mark is in there. So sad."

The group started entering the building so I suggested we should go in.

"Would you join us?" Charlene Beth said as she moved toward the door.

I said, "We don't want to infringe on your privacy."

Charles took a step closer to Richard's wife, and said, "Sure."

Those gathered appeared to be in two groups. There was a smattering of men wearing dress shirts and ties. A couple of the shirts were creased indicating they were right out of their packaging and the men were fidgeting with the knots in their ties as if they were being strangled. My guess was they worked at the trucking company Mark Jamison owned and were uncomfortable. The larger group seemed at home in suits.

We followed Richard and Charlene Beth to the third pew in the chapel while organ music playing a song I didn't recognize wafted through the room. In front of us was an impressive mahogany coffin resting on a cloth-covered bier surrounded by flower arrangements. The row in front of us was empty, but there were three people in the first row. The youngest of the three was in his mid-forties, well-dressed and had his head bowed. Beside him sat a white-haired lady, probably in her late sixties along with a balding gentleman roughly the same age.

Charles, seated beside Charlene Beth, asked if she knew the front-row attendees.

"The younger guy is Kevin Robbins. Mark was gay, you know. Kevin was his spouse. They'd gotten married in Florida a while back. I don't know for certain, but guess the others are Mark's parents."

She leaned close to Richard and said something. He replied, and Charlene Beth turned back to Charles to confirm the identities of the couple as Mark's parents.

The music turned more recognizable with the organ playing "Rock of Ages," followed by a minister eulogizing the life of Mark Jamison, attempting to convince those congregated he's in a better place. The short service ended with "Amazing Grace," and the minister inviting those gathered to join the procession to the cemetery. It was also followed by what I would characterize as a dignified stampede of the trucking company employees heading to the exit. I asked Richard and Charlene Beth if they were going to the cemetery, Richard said they'd said their goodbyes to Mark last evening at the visitation.

"I have to get to a meeting with a potential homebuyer," Charlene Beth added.

We were waiting for those going to the cemetery to leave the funeral home when Charles pointed to a couple at the back of the room. "Isn't that Tom Kale?"

Tom had been seated behind us, so I didn't see him until now. He was in a black suit. His hair was slicked back, and he had a sad expression on his face. There was a woman approximately his age leaning close to Tom.

"Is that his ex?" I asked.

Richard made a grumbling sound and said, "No. She's one of his current flings. Think her name's Nicole, or some cutesy name. His wife, his ex-wife is Alyssa, a nice lady."

I remembered her name from William telling me, and that she'd been his stockbroker before the Kales' divorce. I gathered Nichole wasn't one of Richard's favorite people.

The funeral procession pulled out of the parking lot as Charles and I made it to the car.

Charles watched the black Chrysler hearse turn left on the street, then said, "You know how many funerals we've attended since you moved here?"

I didn't and wasn't ready to start counting. "How many?"

"I was hoping you remembered. It's a bunch."
I shook my head, "Way too many."

7

Folly's Fourth of July fireworks had nothing on the light and sound of the thunderstorm that visited overnight and continued as I was awakened a third time by thunder shaking my cottage. The clock indicated it was a little after sunrise, although all I saw outside was coal-black sky and a torrential downpour illuminated by lightning's blinding bolts of pure energy. Two inches of rainwater covered most of my front yard, so I knew several of the city's lower-elevation areas would be flooded, a regular occurrence because of the island's mostly flat, near sea-level topography. This would be an ideal day to stay home to do, umm, whatever a retired bureaucrat would do. I was selfishly thinking how fortunate it was that the torrential downpour waited a day after Mark Jamison's funeral.

I brewed a pot of coffee then settled in the kitchen to enjoy not having to be anywhere when the phone rang.

"Ready to go kayaking in the marsh?" Charles said, in way too cheery a voice.

"Good morning, Charles," I said, in my ongoing attempt, ongoing failing attempt, to bring civility to telephone conversations.

"Good morning? What window are you looking out? Ain't nothing good about there being enough water out there to float the Ark."

"So, we're not going kayaking?"

"If you turn on that contraption called a television the only kayaking you'll see will be down the middle of the market in Charleston."

Charleston was notorious for flooding during heavy rains especially at high tide. A century or so before I was born, the city infilled creeks and marshes making development possible with flooding an unintended consequence. A dozen or so times since I lived here, the local media would show kayakers paddling through the Historic City Market located fewer than ten miles from my house. It made a great visual, while being a major headache for vendors, shop owners, not to mention tourists who had to wade through foot-deep water to cross the street.

During mornings like today, Folly didn't attract the video crews from television stations or reporters wielding cameras but flooding still could do a lot of damage for the barrier island residents.

Another flash of lightning lit the sky. I said, "Would it be asking too much to ask why you disturbed my peaceful morning coffee if we weren't going kayaking?"

"You're no fun."

I agreed.

"Anyway, I was in the bar at Loggerhead's last night, casually asking around if anyone knew the guys on the plane. Mark Jamison's funeral was fresh on my mind. I was confused how three of them could live on Folly with me only knowing one, plus cute fuzzball Casper."

Charles didn't do anything *casually*, so if he was at one of my favorite restaurants asking around, he was on a mission.

"Did anyone?"

"Glad you asked. Yes and no."

"Meaning?"

"Denver, a guy at the bar, not the city, said his wife was friends with Kelly."

"Kelly?"

"Gary Isles' wife. Keep up. Can I finish?"

I didn't respond so he figured he could. Besides, I couldn't have stopped him.

"Denver's wife, I believe her name's Tessa, told hubby, who told me, Kelly is one pissed-off spouse."

"Why?"

"Gary was a hotshot in that three-name law firm his dad started. Remember that from the newspaper?"

I said I did.

"Pissed-off Kelly worked in the firm when she and Gary got hitched. Had to give up her lucrative career to become a happy homemaker."

"Why'd she have to quit?"

"Denver's an electrician and no expert on law firm etiquette, although he says his wife is an expert on everything."

"And?"

"Chris, it's pouring down outside, you have nowhere to go, so chill. I'll get the story out if you stop interrupting."

Charles was a master interrupter, so I figured he knew one when he heard one. "Proceed."

"Denver's wife told him Kelly told her the three-name law firm was so hoity-toity, only working for the most prestigious businesses and individuals, that their attorneys' spouses weren't permitted to work. They had to look rich, act rich, appear like we were living in the 1930s. I added that last part."

"Thanks for the history lesson. Now what's so important you had to interrupt my morning coffee?"

"Oh, did I forget to mention pissed-off Kelly told Denver's wife she was so unhappy that at times she'd like to bash in his head?"

"You think she had the power to wiggle her nose causing her husband to pass out and crash the plane killing him, Mark, and nearly killing the other passengers because she couldn't work?"

"I don't have it all figured out. That's my working theory. Aren't you glad I called so you could cypher out the details?"

His last statement was punctuated by a rolling thunder vibrating coffee in my mug.

"Did Denver, the person and not the city, tell you anything else?"

"He knew my landlord, said if he wasn't careful, the electrical system in the building could start a fire. Said it hadn't been updated since Tyrannosaurus Rex stomped down Center Street."

"Anything else about the pilot or his wife?"

"No. Isn't that enough to cypher on?"

"Charles, you know there isn't anything saying the crash was anything other than a tragic accident resulting from the pilot's collapse."

"We'll see. Remember, you heard it here first. Pissed-off Kelly has a motive for bumping off hubby. Heck, she even confessed—sort of—she'd bash in his head. The ground did it for her. You need to tell Cindy."

"Why can't you tell her?"

"She thinks I'm a nut. She trusts you. For some reason, the chief thinks my wonderful, innate, level of inquisitiveness, is a bad thing. As President Jefferson said, 'Good qualities are sometimes misfortunes.'"

It wasn't accurate that Cindy considered Charles a nut, although I knew what he'd meant. He's been known to not quite jump off the deep end but would step in water deeper than normal people should venture. I didn't see the motive he saw. I didn't think Kelly's remark about bashing in her husband's head amounted to a confession. What I knew was unless I shared this with the Chief, Charles would pester me until the end of time, if not beyond.

"Okay," I said.

"Okay, what?"

"I'll tell her."

"Really? I figured you'd call me nosy, crazy, claim my imagination was working overtime. Again."

"All true. I'll tell her anyway."

"You're a pal."

I said, "You're welcome."

I no sooner set the phone on the table, poured my cold coffee out, refilled my Lost Dog Cafe mug, and figured out what I was going to say to Cindy, when it rang again. What did Charles want now?

If he wanted something, I wasn't going to learn it. Cindy said, "Are you out playing in the rain?"

"Good morning, Cindy." One more effort to resurrect phone courtesy.

"What's good about it? You think I'm cuddled in my flannel PJs with cute dolphins frolicking all over them? For your information, I've been out with the fire department since four this morning rescuing a carload of citiodiots from Boston who thought their Chevrolet Impala was a boat and tried to float through eighteen inches of water covering the street out by the County Park."

I stifled a chuckle. "Citiodiots?"

"Idiots from the city, my dear unenlightened friend."

"You called to tell me about the rescue?"

"No. I called to tell you the coroner called while I was watching the Impala wash down the street. I figured I'd tell you what he said before you called to pester me about it."

"He said?"

"Preliminary lab results are back. The late Gary Isles left this earth before his plane returned to earth. It appears a form of cyanide ended his life."

"He was murdered?"

"Yep."

Cindy didn't know much more than she'd already shared. She didn't know how or when Gary had ingested the deadly poison, wasn't sure how long it would've taken from when he ingested it to when death occurred, and most importantly, didn't know who'd poisoned him.

I thanked her for sharing what she did know before she added the coroner released Gary's body to his wife and she was having him cremated and there'd be a private funeral with only immediate family invited. I wondered if it was being held privately as Kelly's snub to Gary's three-name law firm, Chapel, Smyth, & Isles, the firm that made her quit. I managed to slip in Charles's theory in the conversation. The Chief responded in a professional, inquisitive manner. She laughed.

I could tell Charles I'd shared it with the Chief.

8

By noon, the torrential rains had moved on to soak Georgetown and I realized I hadn't eaten since late yesterday. It had also been a few days since I'd talked to Barbara Deanelli, but even then, it was a brief conversation letting her know what'd happened in the marsh. She owned Barb's Books, a used bookstore on Center Street in the building previously housing Landrum Gallery. It's no coincidence the now defunct photo gallery shared the surname I'd been using since birth. Opening a gallery had long been my dream which became reality after I retired. It turned out to be more of a nightmare after losing money each year it'd been open. I gave up on the dream three years ago and the store stood vacant until it morphed to a bookstore. Barb and I've dated the last two years.

To meet my need for nourishment combined with a conversation with someone other than Charles, I walked two blocks to Center Street, location of most of Folly's restaurants and only used bookstore. The walk was challenging since I had to weave around large puddles, and at one low-lying spot, crossed the street to avoid becoming waterlogged.

Snapper Jack's restaurant was in a multi-level building on the corner facing Folly's only traffic light. The rain had taken its toll on fair-weather vacationers, so the colorful building was three tables shy of empty. The hostess told me to sit anywhere, so I chose a bar-height round table by the closed garage-style door facing Center Street. A server I hadn't seen before greeted me. I ordered a fish sandwich, coleslaw, and water. I plopped my elbows on the table and thought about what Charles had said about Gary Isles' wife, now in the context of Cindy's revelation about the poisoning. Was it possible her anger escalated enough to risk killing three others to get rid of her husband? It seemed unlikely, yet if Gary was poisoned, someone was responsible. Then, my thoughts drifted to wondering if Gary was the intended victim. It could've been any or all the men. Yes, it was terrible two people perished in the craft, and it wouldn't have taken much for it to have been all four.

Food arrived redirecting my thoughts to my stomach. I was hungrier than I thought. More vacationers began venturing out of their dry houses, hotel rooms, or condos. The dining room was filling. Thirty minutes later, I'd finished lunch, walked a block and a half, entered Barb's Books, where I was greeted with a smile from the proprietress. Barb was a couple of years younger than me, at five-foot-ten, the same height. I was on the upper end of average weight for my height, okay, upper, upper end, while Barb was thin. She wore one of several red blouses and because of the marginal outdoor temperature had on tan khaki slacks instead of shorts she often wore.

None of the vacationers who'd ventured out were in the store, so Barb moved from behind the counter to give me a peck on the cheek. Her hazel eyes and endearing smile made the walk to the store worth every step.

"To what do I owe the pleasure of a visit?"

"I haven't seen you in a few days."

Barb nodded. "I suppose it kept you busy saving two men and handling the adulation you've received. Fame is time consuming. Want something to drink?"

"I don't know about fame, but sloshing through the marsh, prying a door open in the mud, and putting up with Charles was exhausting. I still hurt from the rescue. What's on the drink menu?"

I followed Barb to her office in back of the store. When I occupied the building, the back room was more of an above-ground man's cave. The office/storeroom had been furnished with a yard-sale table, mismatched chairs more at home in a condemned trailer park, and a full-sized refrigerator stocked with beer, wine, and an occasional soft drink. It was often the hangout for Charles, and a few other friends who were staying busy solving the problems of the world while gossiping about whatever was happening locally. The current drink menu included wine and bottled water. I chose water so Barb grabbed two bottles from the apartment-size, black refrigerator and set one in front of me on the glass-top desk. Classical music was playing from a portable Bose sound system. Night and day was the only way I could describe the difference in the room since I'd lost money in it for years.

She sat in her black, Herman Miller Aeron Chair and took a sip of water before rolling the high-tech-looking chair to where she could see if anyone entered the store. I recalled sitting at the same spot in my yard-sale chair which wouldn't roll anywhere while hoping someone would enter.

I watched her glance toward the front of the store, and said, "Have you heard anything about the plane crash?"

She jerked her head toward me. "Is that what prompted this visit?"

"No. Just curious."

She squinted then glared at me. Her stare reminded me of an attorney in a courtroom homing in on a hostile witness, a look she'd perfected during years as a successful defense attorney, a profession she'd given up when she moved to Folly. That's a story for another time.

Her expression remained unchanged. "Hmm, curiosity?"

I was saved by the bell—the bell over the front door announcing the arrival of a potential customer.

Barb slid the chair back to the desk, stood to greet whoever entered, and said, "To be continued."

No doubt, I thought. Barb hadn't been on Folly that long, but knew firsthand how I, with a few of my friends, had a penchant for getting involved in police investigations that were none of our business. In fact, she'd been the recipient of our help when someone from her past attempted to have her killed. She benefitted from my involvement but didn't like it. She didn't hesitate sharing her opinion.

Barb was gone several minutes, so I finished my water and walked to the front of the store to see if she was still with a customer.

She smiled. "Chris, you know Virgil?"

Barb was talking to a man in his early forties. He was my height, much thinner than I, with slicked-back, black hair. He wore sunglasses so I couldn't see his eyes.

I said, "I've seen you around town, but we haven't met."

The man smiled, shifted three books to his left hand, shook my hand, and said, "You can't say that again. I'm Virgil Debonnet. Your last name is?"

"Landrum."

"Virgil," Barb said and waved her arm around the room, "Chris had a photo gallery in this space before it became a bookstore."

Virgil reached to shake my hand again. "Cool. I'm an amateur photographer. I used to be in it big time, until, umm, until I wasn't. Had a Leica M camera, three lenses."

I never could've afforded Leica cameras, but knew they were among the best made. The equipment Virgil mentioned would've cost upwards of ten-thousand dollars. I also noticed the frayed cuffs on his long-sleeve, button-down, white dress shirt. He wore it untucked over navy blue chinos.

"Great cameras," I said. "What happened to it?"

"My ex has it." Virgil chuckled. "Doesn't really have the camera. She needed some lucre according to the divorce decree, so I pawned it. But, hey, that's neither here nor there. How come this is a bookstore, not a photo gallery?"

I just met Virgil and thought my answer was neither here nor there, also known as *none of your business*. I said, "I decided to move on."

Barb could tell I was uncomfortable with the direction of the conversation. "Virgil's one of my regulars."

"Regular visitor," he said as he chucked, a second time. "Seldom buy anything. I remember back in the day when I had a floor to ceiling set of bookshelves chock full of classics plus books on everything imaginable. The ceiling was fifteen-feet high. Had one of those ladders on rollers to reach all of them. Ah, the memories."

His mouth smiled, but with the sunglasses covering his eyes, I couldn't tell if he meant it. Do I ask what happened? Charles wouldn't let Virgil's statement go unexplored. That was enough reason for me to let it go.

Before I changed the subject, Virgil's head jerked in my direction. He snapped his fingers. "You're the guy who saved the men from the plane crash?"

I gave him my well-rehearsed comment about being nearby and doing what anyone would've done.

Virgil gave me an exaggerated bow then shook my hand again. "Not often one gets to meet a real-life hero."

When he bowed, I saw he wore scuffed, black Gucci loafers. The top of the shoes looked like they had many miles on them while the soles appeared new.

"Virgil, do you live on Folly?" I asked to move past a discussion about the crash.

"I do."

Dare I ask where?

Barb came to my rescue. "Virgil lives in an apartment a few blocks out East Ashley Avenue."

"Close enough to walk here and pester this sweet lady." He grinned.

I returned his grin. "Do you work over here?"

He laughed and shook his head. "I'm between jobs." He laughed louder. "Been between them a long time."

I said, "What kind of work do you do?"

"I know Charlene Beth Haymaker. She's the wife of Richard, one of the guys you saved."

I didn't detect the answer to my question in there. What I did detect was Virgil avoiding the question.

"Have you known her long?"

"A year or so. She handled a real estate transaction for me. After it was over, she and Richard took me to supper to celebrate. Nice couple. In fact, Richard found the tiny-tiny apartment where I'm currently residing." He glanced at his watch then continued, "It was great that you saved him. Too bad about the guys who didn't make it." He again looked at his watch. "Whoops, gotta be going. Barb, I'll get these the next time I'm in." He handed Barb the books he'd been holding, said it was great meeting me, then waved to us over his shoulder on his way out.

I watched the door close. "What's his deal?"

"He's in three or four times a week. Looks at books, seldom buys any. Occasionally he comes in later in the day, smells like he's spent some time, perhaps a lot of time, in one of the bars. Never causes trouble even if he's been drinking. I get the impression he's bored."

"Know what he did for a living?"

"I figured you caught his non-answer."

I nodded.

Barb looked at the front door. "It's funny. I asked him the same thing the first couple of times he was in. He gave me the same answer he gave you."

"None."

Barb smiled. "I stopped asking, although from a couple of remarks he's made, I get the impression he came from money."

"Remarks like the floor to ceiling set of bookshelves, the fifteen-foot high ceiling in his house?"

"Exactly," Barb said. "He also knows a lot about the stock market and international trade, topics that aren't often discussed by the less-fortunate."

"He now lives in a *tiny-tiny* apartment on East Ashley Avenue. Does he always wear sunglasses?"

"Don't know about always. He's had them on every time he's been in."

"Interesting gentleman," I said. "Before Virgil came in, we were talking about the plane crash."

"The one you're nothing more than curious about?"

I nodded knowing I'd be risking the ire of Barb once I told her what I'd learned from Chief LaMond. Regardless, I'd rather her hear it from me than from someone else.

"Cindy LaMond told me what caused of the pilot's death."

Barb frowned. "Let's hear it."

"The preliminary lab results indicate cyanide poisoning. He was dead before the plane hit the marsh."

Barb took a deep breath and stared at the wood floor. After an awkward pause, she looked up. "Murdered? You're going to stick your nose in the middle of it, aren't you?"

I shrugged and started to halfheartedly deny I would get involved, when my phone rang. I didn't recognize the number, so was going to let it go to voicemail when another customer entered the store.

Barb pointed to the ringing phone. "Go ahead, get it. I've got a real customer."

"Is this Chris Landrum?" asked an unfamiliar voice.

I said it was.

"This is Tom Kale. I don't know if you remember. I was one of the men you and your friend pulled out of the plane."

"Of course, I remember." How many crashes does he think I witness in a normal day, although he may think I remembered the crash but not his name?

"Good. Richard, the other man you saved, and I are putting together a reception to thank you and Charles Fowler for your heroic efforts. To thank you for our lives. Would you be available Saturday evening?"

"Yes, although you don't have to thank us."

"Good. I tried Fowler's number a couple of times and he didn't answer. Think you could get with him to see if he's available?"

I told him I could, then would let him know if Charles was available. I didn't tell him but knew there was a 99.9 percent chance Charles would be free. Tom gave me the address and time then ended by saying we could bring spouses or dates.

Now all I must do is invite Barb without it appearing that I was sticking my nose in the middle of a police matter.

I reached Charles the next morning. As could be predicted, he said nothing could keep him away. Barb said she would go if I promised not to leap off the cliff of curiosity into an amateur investigation of who killed the pilot. I told her I had no intention of getting involved. It didn't appear to completely satisfy her, although enough for her to agree to be my date.

9

Tom Kale's house was three miles from the center of town on East Ashley Avenue. The large, two-story, pale yellow elevated structure's front door faced the street, its back yard the Atlantic Ocean. Four vehicles were parked on the oversized driveway. To no surprise, one of them was always-early Charles's Toyota.

Barb leaned toward the windshield and craned her neck to look at the tall structure. "Almost as large as your mansion," she said with tongue firmly planted in cheek.

"My back yard's not flooded," I said with a straight face.

"I see Charles is here."

"Of course. He's been here twenty minutes or so."

Barb continued to gaze at the McMansion. "Thirty minutes early?"

I nodded then walked around to open her door.

Tom Kale greeted us at the front door, carrying a white poodle. He was wearing blue shorts and a yellow polo shirt that contrasted nicely with his mocha colored skin. He looked far better than when I'd seen him at the crash.

"Glad you could make it," he said as we shook hands.

I introduced Barb. Tom said he hadn't made it to the bookstore yet but planned to soon. Barb graciously said she looked forward to it.

Tom then introduced Casper, who licked Barb's hand but didn't say anything about wanting to visit the bookstore.

"Let's go to the deck," Tom said. "Your friend Charles and his date are already here."

The house's interior could be featured in *Charleston* magazine. The white-washed plank flooring held a large, off-white cushioned sofa and three light-blue chairs. I didn't have time to look closely, but two large paintings of the dunes appeared to be originals. Tom led us up the inch thick, green tinted, glass stair treads to the top floor.

Our host beamed as he said, "This floating staircase system is what sold me on the house. Amazing, isn't it?"

Barb said, "Amazing."

I nodded instead of saying ostentatious.

The stairs opened to an office with a laptop and two computer monitors on a granite top supported by chrome legs. The desk overlooked the ocean. Each monitor was forty-three inches bragged Tom. I wondered how anyone could get work done with the expansive view of the coast. French doors were beside the window. Several people were on the deck.

Tom motioned out to where Charles was standing beside Laurie Fitzsimmons. Laurie was five-foot-three inches tall, petite, and ten years younger than Charles. He and I met her nine months ago after Anthony, her husband, had been murdered while the couple was treasure hunting at the end of the island. Laurie was a retired drama teacher from Jacksonville, Florida. She and Anthony had moved to Folly weeks before his death and didn't know many people here. After Anthony's death, she latched onto Charles and they'd met to share meals a half-dozen times. According to Charles, they were friends, nothing more.

Barb, Laurie, Charles, and I shared hellos, then Tom said he wanted to introduce Barb and me to the others. He escorted us to Richard Haymaker and his wife, Charlene Beth. I remembered both from Mark Jamison's funeral, but Barb hadn't met them. Richard said it was nice meeting Barb, and Charlene Beth said she'd been in the bookstore a couple of times. Barb didn't appear to remember until

Charlene Beth said her two-year-old twins had been with her. She apologized for them making a playroom out of one of the chairs. Barb's face lit up. She said she remembered yet compared to many kids who ventured in, how well-behaved the twins had been. Charlene Beth said yes, that would've been memorable since it was rare. Richard still wore the sling, so I asked how his shoulder was doing. He said the doc told him to wear it a few more days, but the pain was minimal. I told him I was glad. Charlene Beth said she was too. He was being a baby acting helpless. Richard gave her a dirty look but didn't comment.

A college-age woman wearing a white waiter jacket moved beside us and offered a choice of white wine, beer, or sparkling water. Richard and Charlene Beth already had drinks, Barb said white wine. I followed suit. The young lady left, and Richard thanked us for coming. He said this reception was the least he and Tom could do to thank us. I skipped my *we did what anyone would've done* story.

Tom left to greet a newcomer. She was five-foot-five, marathon-runner thin, with brown hair, and a beautiful smile. She hugged Tom and glanced around the deck.

Charlene Beth leaned close to whisper, "That's Kelly, Gary Isles' widow."

Tom kept his arm around Kelly's waist as he escorted her over.

"Chris, I'd like you to meet Gary's widow, Kelly. Richard and Charlene Beth are Kelly's friends."

From the tone Charlene Beth used when she whispered who Kelly was, I hadn't detected much friendship.

Kelly said, "Chris, I apologize for being late. I was talking to Gary's cousin in Montana." She shrugged. "Time got away. Tom told me what you and your friend did to save his and Richard's life. I only wish Gary was here to say the same."

Tom's arm returned to Kelly's waist. "Chris, Kelly lives three houses down." He pointed east. "If you lean over the balcony, you can see her place."

I took his word for it. By now, Charles and Laurie had joined us. Tom repeated the introductions for their benefit. The caterer returned with our drinks and asked if anyone else needed anything. Tom ordered a glass of wine for Kelly. Richard said he could use another.

Charles turned to Kelly. "Did I overhear that you lived a couple of houses that way?" He pointed the direction Tom had indicated.

Kelly said, "Three houses over. Gary's father owned the house. My husband inherited it when his dad passed away a few years ago."

Tom added, "Gary was an attorney in the firm his father founded."

"I worked there until we married," Kelly said.

Charles moved closer to Kelly. "Why'd you leave?"

Only Charles could get away with asking that kind of question. He'd already learned why from the electrician, so he wasn't asking out of curiosity.

Kelly looked toward the beach before saying, "They have a policy that spouses of members of the firm don't work, female spouses, that is. They're old fashioned. Think it looks bad on the firm if the 'little women' must make money. Damned stupid policy. Anyway, that's why."

Barb said, "That's not unusual in some of the older law firms. It was that way when I was practicing law in Pennsylvania."

Kelly's eyes opened wider. "Oh, I thought you had the bookstore. Do you still practice?"

"No, I retired to the leisurely life of running a bookstore when I moved here."

Few people on Folly knew the circumstances of why Barb had left Pennsylvania and the law. She wanted to keep it that way.

I said, "Tom, you have a lovely house. I think I'm speaking for Charles when I say we appreciate you having this gathering."

The caterer returned with Kelly's drink plus a tray of finger foods. Each of us took a couple of whatever the little things were, and the discussion drifted to the perfect weather. Three seagulls were doing flybys in hopes we would share our bounty.

The conversation remained polite and benign until Richard said, "Kelly, have you heard if poor Gary had a heart attack, or what happened to him?"

She lowered her head. "No, sometimes things just happen."

Charles said, "Could someone have hurt him on purpose?"

Kelly looked at him like she hadn't seen him before. "What do you mean?"

"Oh, I don't know. Like a gunshot, poison, or something."

Charles was fishing since he knew Gary had been poisoned.

Kelly continued to stare at Charles. "Why would you even say something like that?'

Tom moved closer to put his hand on her shoulder.

I made a mental note to ask Cindy if the police had told Kelly about the poison. If they had, why was she acting confused?

"I was wondering," Charles said.

Laurie patted Charles on the arm. "Why don't we talk about something else?" She whispered, "Please."

Her husband's murder was still raw on her nerves. It was clear that Tom and Kelly were uncomfortable with the conversation.

"Tom," I said, "we have a mutual acquaintance. William Hansel has been a friend for several years. He told me you're his stockbroker."

Tom smiled. "Yes, William is a wonderful man. My ex-wife was his broker until she changed firms. I inherited William's portfolio. How do you know him?"

I gave him an abridged version of how we'd become acquainted. The story was interrupted when Richard, who was standing on the other side of the balcony with Charlene Beth, raised his voice and said, "No wonder you're gaining weight. How much more can you stuff in your mouth?"

Charlene Beth looked toward us. Her face turned red. She slammed her wine glass down on a nearby table, turned, and scampered through the French doors. Richard mumbled a profanity, came over to us, and said, "Charlene Beth isn't feeling well, so we'd better be going. Charles and Chris, thank you again for what you did. I hope to see you soon."

He whispered something to Tom then followed his wife off the deck.

The Haymaker's rapid departure put a damper on the festivities.

Tom tried to keep everyone cheered by plying us with drink and a few humorous stories about his clients. I'm certain in stockbroker circles the stories would've been funny, but stories involving words like puts, calls, IPOs, and my favorite, although I had no idea what it meant, Fibonacci retracement, didn't tickle my fancy.

Even Charles, the ultimate trivia collector, began to yawn. I thought it was time for the honored guests to bid farewell. Tom and his neighbor, Kelly, walked the four of us to the door and thanked us for coming. Kelly said she was going to stay to help Tom clean up. I thought that was the role of the caterers and wondered why Kelly felt the need to tell us why she was staying. Charles gave me a sideways glance when she said it, so I knew I'd hear more from him about it.

10

The next morning, I left a message for Chief LaMond to call. After two hours, I wondered if she'd received it. My wondering ended when the phone rang a little before noon.

"You buying lunch?" the Chief asked as a preamble.

"Where and when?"

"The Dog. Now."

"Fifteen minutes," I said.

"Good."

The strange thing was we both understood the conversation. I drove six blocks to the Lost Dog Cafe, a half block off Center Street behind the Folly Beach branch of the Charleston County Public Library sharing a building with the community center. Rain was in the forecast, so I rationalized that as reason for driving instead of walking, the heart-healthy approach, the one I should be taking. Granted, there wasn't a cloud to be seen, yet all it took was the word rain to convince me not to walk.

The Lost Dog Cafe, shortened to the Dog by most, was my favorite breakfast spot. I'd spent more time in the restaurant than in my kitchen, not surprising since unlike my kitchen, there was always food there. It was also the workplace for Amber Lewis, one of my favorite

Folly residents. We'd dated when I first moved to Folly. Since then we'd remained friends, something many people couldn't say after a breakup.

Cindy LaMond's Ford F-150 was parked across the street in the parking area reserved for customers and employees in an adjacent building. Parking in a lot marked *For customers only* was one of the perks of being Folly's top law-enforcement official. I would've been towed if I'd tried, so I drove past the restaurant before I found a spot a block away.

Amber greeted me. She just turned fifty, was five-foot-five-inches tall, with auburn hair tied with a rubber band. Her wide smile accented her dimpled cheeks. She pointed to a table in the center of the room where Chief LaMond sipped coffee and stared at her phone. I exchanged a couple of pleasantries with Amber, asked about Jason, her twenty year old son, and said I'd appreciate a glass of water once I joined the Chief.

Cindy looked up from her phone when I pulled out a chair facing her.

Instead of saying something normal like "Good morning, handsome citizen," she said, "Did you know the estimated median household income on Folly is just shy of a hundred grand?"

"Somehow that'd slipped past my demographic database. How and why do you know that?"

"That world-renowned statistician Dr. Google told me."

Amber interrupted the stimulating, meaningless, conversation, when she set a Ball jar of water in front of me and asked if I wanted to order.

Cindy answered for me. "Give him a few minutes to see what the cheapest thing you have on the menu is and put it on my check."

Amber moved to a table behind us and I said, "Okay, that answers where you found that enlightening statistic. How about why?"

"My highly-efficient staff gave me a report this morning where I learned roughly two-thirds of our fine citizens owe the city parking ticket fines. I figured the average resident must earn about four hundred dollars a year and couldn't afford to pay the tickets."

I got over the shock she was buying lunch. I didn't dare mention her vehicle was illegally parked. "Do I detect sarcasm?"

"Absolutely." She smiled. "It's one of my endearing qualities."

"Endearing, I'm not sure, although I agree you do sarcasm well."

Amber returned to ask if I was ready to order.

I said, "Hot dog with kraut."

Cindy interrupted, "That the cheapest thing you have?"

Amber said, "A cup of soup is less."

Cindy sighed. "Give the growing boy the hot dog. He's almost worth it."

"Sometimes," Amber said.

"Enough of the lovefest," I said.

Amber laughed as she left to put in the order.

Cindy watched her go then said, "Where were we?"

"You were bemoaning a pile of unpaid parking tickets."

"Enough of that. Guess where I was this morning?"

"Applying for one of those four-hundred-dollar-a-year jobs?"

"Funny. Although for the hours I spend on this one, it's tempting."

"Cindy, where were you this morning?"

"Thought you'd never ask. I was out in the marsh watching one of those big-ass helicopters picking up the plane that nearly decapitated you. They had to fly the big-ass helicopter in from out of state. Would you believe there aren't any in South Carolina?"

"Not enough marsh plane crashes to justify one?"

"Funny. You know they use them for humongous construction jobs or to replace HVAC units on super-tall buildings."

I ignored her comment. "So, you invited me to lunch to tell me about the plane being moved?"

"No. Guess who was at the plane-raisin'?"

I looked at her and rolled my eyes.

"Okay, you couldn't guess it anyway. Aaron Cole."

I shrugged.

"He's a field investigator from NTSB's office in Atlanta. Seems like an okay guy, a tad stuffy for Folly, but I suppose not everyone can be as wonderful as those of us here. The NTSB on the back of his black

T-shirt was about the size of that Hollywood sign in, well, in Hollywood. I bet the guys on the space shuttle could read it. I asked him if I could have one to give Charles. The stuffy part of him said no. He didn't even ask who Charles was."

My second cheapest item on the menu arrived and I took a bite while Cindy was winding down about the field agent's shirt.

"Did he say anything about the crash?"

"Nothing he hadn't said before. It'll be weeks before they issue a final report on the cause. He did say while nothing was official, he hadn't seen anything unusual about the plane other than it was upside down in the marsh, not a normal hangout for airplanes. Since the pilot died of a lethal poison, the cause of the crash seems obvious." She shook her head. "There's one thing that upset the investigator, me too. Someone had been in the plane. Absconded with everything that wasn't attached. Wait, that's not true. They tore the radio out and took the golf clubs, luggage, no telling what else. Aaron looked at me like it was my fault. I told him I couldn't have had someone camping out there twenty-four-seven until he arrived."

"What'd he say?"

"Cross between a growl and a profanity. He finally calmed and said he understood. The bad thing is if there was evidence of how the pilot was poisoned, it was gone."

I nodded. "I'm glad you mentioned poison. When did you tell Gary's widow about what happened?"

"I didn't. Detective Callahan broke the news to her the day I told you."

Detective Michael Callahan is with the Charleston County Sheriff's Office, the office charged with investigating major crimes on Folly. Cindy's force is lean and not equipped with a staff to investigate murders. The Folly Beach Department of Public Safety and the Sheriff's Office cooperate with each other, but occasionally the cooperation is challenging since the Sheriff's Office treats the Folly Beach department like a stepchild, not always forthcoming with information. I'd become acquainted with Detective Callahan four years ago after I stumbled into a murder investigation he was conducting. He had the reputation for being one of the best detectives in the department, so I was glad he caught the case.

"That's interesting," I said.

"Why?"

"Last night, Charles and I were talking with Kelly Isles, Gary's widow. She acted like she didn't know the cause of her husband's death."

"Whoa, nosy one. Why were you two vagrants talking to Ms. Isles?"

I told her about the gathering at Tom Kale's house and who was there.

"Please, please don't tell me the two of you are sticking your nosy noses in police business."

"Of course not. We thought it was kind of Tom and Richard to invite us, so we graciously attended."

"The only part of that I believe is Tom and Richard invited you. With my suspicion noted, you sure Kelly didn't know her husband was poisoned?"

"I couldn't say if she knew or not, although she gave the impression she didn't."

"Makes one wonder, doesn't it?" Cindy took a sip of Diet Coke as she looked around the room. "I'll let Detective Callahan know."

"Good."

"Now I have another question. Why was Gary Isles' widow there?"

"She lives a few houses past Tom Kale's McMansion. She said even though we couldn't save her husband and Mark Jamison, she wanted to thank us for saving the other two. I don't know how friendly Tom had been with Gary, but he seemed quite friendly with Kelly. She stayed at Tom's after everyone else left."

Cindy lowered her head then glanced up at me with her eyes at half-staff. "Think there's something going on between them?"

"All I know is they were a tad too friendly with each other."

"Hmm," Cindy said then took another sip. "I suppose I'd better mention that to Detective Callahan."

"Another good idea."

She nodded. "What's the deal with Charles and widow Laurie?"

"Don't know if there's much of anything. They've gone out to eat a few times. She enjoys his company. He doesn't say much about her."

"Hmm," Cindy repeated.

We finished lunch on lighter notes. Cindy wondered how many photos of dogs adorned the walls. I said there were as many as there were residents of the island. The chief speculated the dogs would pay their parking tickets quicker than many of the human residents. I didn't dispute her analysis before she said she needed to get back to the office to pester her staff.

"And call Detective Callahan to tell him about Kelly and the interesting relationship between Gary's widow and Tom Kale."

She sighed then headed to the door.

11

I wanted to tell Charles about my conversation with Cindy, and to follow in his footsteps by being nosy about his "date" with Laurie. I left two messages before figuring out he'd probably left the phone in his apartment. Instead of waiting at home for his call, I walked three blocks to Cal's Country Bar and Burgers, commonly called Cal's for a couple of reasons. First, most of us are too lazy to say its full name. Second, the quality of the bar's burgers didn't deserve being included in the name, a fact even its owner doesn't dispute. Fortunately, Cal's is a great country music bar. It's owner, Cal Ballew attributes its success to its vintage look, often confused with old and worn out by those who step through its door the first time.

I stepped through the paint-peeling front door for nowhere near the first time. If I didn't know what year it was, I would've sworn I was sauntering into the 1960s. The walls were painted dark green with other colors peeking through the chipped paint. There were a dozen tables, a long wooden bar along the right side of the room, with a tiny, elevated bandstand along the back wall bookended by restrooms.

A Wurlitzer jukebox, a relic of the 1960s, was on the corner of the bandstand playing George Jones's classic, "He Stopped Loving Her

Today." Three tables were occupied, two with couples, the third with four patrons. Empty beer bottles exceeded the number of customers at two of the tables. Behind the bar, illuminated by neon beer advertisements, Cal was multitasking by singing along with George while drying a wineglass.

Cal saw me, waved me over, pointed the wineglass at me. "Knew you'd be coming. Was getting it ready for you. White?"

I'm glad one of us knew I was coming, although he did have the drink right. I'd known Cal eight years, including a year before he'd taken over the bar after its previous owner killed a local attorney and is now residing behind bars, the steel kind. Cal had been a country-music singer before most Americans were born. He'd travelled the South forty-plus years singing at any venue that'd have him while living out of his 1971 Cadillac Eldorado. Folly was his last tour stop and where he made a career change from traveling musician to bar owner. He kept his voice in shape by performing on weekends.

"Haven't seen you in a while," he said, as he handed me the glass then tipped his sweat-stained Stetson my direction.

Cal had lived about a hundred years during the seventy four he'd been on earth. His spine curved forward from leaning over to sing in a microphone nearly every night of his life.

"Missed being here," I said then took a sip.

John Wesley Ryles' haunting version of "Kay" filled the air, as Cal said, "Hear you and Charles saved a couple of guys in that crash out in the marsh. How do you and your shadow manage to be at every disaster? Hell, I hear you were at this one before it was a disaster?"

Cal received my speech on *we did what anyone would have done*. I tried to change the subject as I looked around the room before saying, "Light crowd."

"It'll have to pick up a heap to be light. It'll take more than this to keep the old jukebox spinning ole George, Johnny, or memories from the rest of my buds."

Cal had recorded "End of Your Story," a song he'd penned, which became a regional hit in his home state of Texas while reaching number seventeen on the national country charts. That was the peak of his musical career. In 1962. That didn't stop him from telling anyone who'd listen he'd been friends with Hank Williams Sr, George Jones, Johnny Cash, Patsy Cline, and Willie Nelson. Four of the five are residing in hillbilly heaven and unavailable for confirmation. To my knowledge, the fifth, Willie Nelson, has never been to Folly Beach. True or not, Cal spins some interesting stories about his escapades with the music greats.

Cal wasn't to be distracted. "What caused the plane to crash? Rumors flying around here, pardon the pun, are it ran smack-dab into a squadron of pelicans. After chopping up a couple, the propeller broke. I heard the pilot intentionally crashed it so his wife could collect his life insurance. Oh yeah, I also heard but didn't take it too seriously, it was shot down by a terrorist with one of those handheld surface-to-air missile things. Figure you'd know the skinny since you were there."

Before I shared the "skinny," two people entered. Charles spotted me and made a beeline to the stool next to me. He wore a navy and light blue Roger Williams University, long-sleeve T-shirt, red shorts, gray tennis shoes, and his canvas Tilley hat. He pointed at his chest. "It's in Rhode Island."

I nodded like I cared.

"Got your message. Instead of calling, figured I'd check out a few bars and would find you. Did you know you're not at Planet Follywood, the Crab Shack, or Rita's?"

Can't slip anything by my friend. I nodded a second time when Cal returned from getting a beer for the other man who entered with Charles. He'd sidled up to the far end of the bar.

Charles knew Cal's beer selection numbered three, so he said he'd have whatever the other guy was having. Cal turned, pulled a bottle of Budweiser from the cooler, set it in front of Charles, leaned across the bar then whispered, "Either of you know who that is?"

Charles and I pivoted toward the stranger who looked to be in his fifties, tall, maybe six-foot-two, overweight, not bad looking except for the long, straggly black beard that could house a family of mice. I told Cal I didn't recall seeing him before. Charles said, "Me either. Why?"

"Something strange about him. He came in last night. Sat at the same spot, sipped on three beers for a couple of hours, didn't say anything except 'another beer' and 'check.' I could be imagining it but had the feeling he was staring at me when I wasn't looking. Strange."

That was all it took for Charles to grab his drink, hop off the stool, walk over to the man, and take a seat.

Cal turned away from Charles and his new friend. "When's this ole, washed-up, country crooner going to learn to keep his mouth shut around Charles?"

Never, I thought. I knew the rumor about a surface-to-air missile shooting down the plane wasn't true but was certain Charles was a surface-to-surface missile when he wanted to find out something. Sammy Smith was singing "Help Me Make It Through the Night" while I was trying to distract Cal from worrying about what Charles was saying to the stranger. I was partially successful, which didn't stop Cal from glancing over at the newcomer like he thought he was going to pull out a gun and shoot up the place. I was glad when one of the tables of drinkers waved for Cal to bring refills. The group at another table asked for their check.

Charles's new acquaintance patted him on the back before heading to the door. Cal was back in front of me when Charles returned with a smile and message for Cal to put the stranger's beer on my tab. Charles was generous with my money.

Charles ordered another beer then said, "Okay Cal, what do you want to know?"

Cal looked at the door where the stranger had exited. "How about who he is?"

"Name's Junior Richardson, says he's from Arkansas."

Cal said, "Name's really Junior?"

Charles smiled. "Didn't figure he'd show me his driver's license. We'll have to take his word."

I said, "What else?"

"He was passing through. From what he's seen the few days he's been on Folly, said he may settle here. He's been impressed by how laid back everybody is. He thought some of the street names are out of place. Silly him. He didn't think Arctic, Huron, or Erie should be streets in the South."

He wasn't the first to wonder that, so I didn't comment.

Cal said, "Why's he been staring at me?"

Charles took a sip of beer, then stared at the stool Junior vacated. "That's a question I couldn't figure how to slip in the conversation. He seemed like a nice guy. Looks like the kind of person who'd fit in."

I asked, "Did he say what he does for a living?"

"He was vague when I meandered down that path. Garbled something about the food industry, owning restaurants, then threw in retired. If I had to guess, I'd say he does nothing." Charles rubbed his chin. "I'm not done getting the scoop on him."

That, I didn't doubt.

12

Mel Evans called the next morning. It surprised me since he calls slightly more often than wild kangaroos hop past my house. I'd met Mel, affectionately or not so affectionately known as Mad Mel for reasons obvious to anyone who met him, five or so years ago through a mutual friend, Dude Sloan. Mad Mel had pulled me out of a jam at that time. I, along with Charles, had managed to prove him innocent of murder three years ago. I masked my surprise and asked what I did to deserve a call.

"Haven't seen you in a while. I like to keep contact with a few straight people to reinforce how stupid all of you are."

"Generous of you," I said and chuckled. "Now, what's the real reason?"

"Gotta take a boat load of freakin' left-wing, brainwashed, snivelin', college brats on one of my world-famous marsh tours at fourteen hundred. Checking to see if you were free for lunch."

Mel was a retired Marine who operated a marsh tour business out of Folly View Marina just off the island. He specialized in taking groups of students, a.k.a. freakin' left-wing, brainwashed, snivelin' college brats, on excursions to remote areas of the marsh so they could drink beer while partying to their hearts' content and bladders' discontent. Unlike other marsh tour operators who specialized in educational excursions, Mel knew as much about the flora and fauna of the marsh as I did about the heart rate of a camel. Mad Mel had found his niche.

We agreed to meet at Rita's at twelve hundred in Mel-speak before he decided he'd talked long enough. He hung up on me. Rude was another of his charming qualities.

To kill time before meeting Mel, I Googled Junior Richardson in what I suspected would be a futile search. As is often the case, Google exceeded being helpful by showing more than twenty-million references to the name. I narrowed it down by adding Arkansas, which proved to be equally unsuccessful. I don't know why I'd hoped to find him. First, I doubted his first name was Junior. Second, even though Charles said he was from Arkansas, he didn't say that's where his restaurants had been, or even if he'd owned restaurants.

I abandoned the Internet search when it was time to head to Rita's. The restaurant was two blocks from the house and sat on a prime spot of Folly real estate across the street from the iconic Edwin S. Taylor Folly Beach Fishing Pier. The temperature was in the upper sixties but with the outdoor seating area in the sun, it would be comfortable. Mel didn't have Charles's proclivity—obsession—for being early, so I figured he wouldn't be here and requested a table on the patio.

I heard the rumble of Mel's retro-styled, black Chevy Camaro before I spotted it rounding the corner and parking on East Arctic Avenue. Even if I hadn't seen him park, it would've been hard to miss the six-foot-one, burly, tour boat operator as he ambled across the street, holding out his hand to stop a car from hitting him. He was wearing his constant frown along with leather bomber jacket with the sleeves cut off at the shoulder and woodland camo field pants sheared off at the knee. His frown almost broke when he saw me seated at a table at the side of the patio.

"Suppose you're going to whine, scold me for being two minutes late," he said as he removed his camouflaged cap with Semper Fi on the crown and dropped it on the table.

I smiled as he plopped down in the chair. "It's good seeing you, Mel."

He shook his head. "Add salt. You're too damned sweet."

I continued smiling. "How many are you taking out this afternoon?"

"M5 will be cluttered with fifteen freakin' morons."

M5 was shorthand for Mad Mel's Magical Marsh Machine, the name printed in nine-inch-high letters on the side of his twenty-five-foot-long Carolina Skiff.

"You ever thought about being nice to the students, you know, your paying customers?"

"Hell no. What's this I hear about you trying to get your head sliced off by a damned aircraft?"

Good, I'm getting to the reason for the lunch invitation. I gave him my explanation of what we did plus my well rehearsed it wasn't anything different than what anyone else would do.

"Bet he was a freakin' Air Force pilot. Couldn't even land the plane on dry land."

According to Mel, there was only one true branch of the military, the Marines. I told him I didn't know, then he mumbled a couple of more profanities. I added that the pilot had been poisoned, was dead before the plane crashed.

"Excuses, excuses," he mumbled. He waived a server over and ordered a cheeseburger plus two beers. I ordered a fish sandwich and a Diet Coke. Mel looked at me like I'd ordered a glass of Kool-Aid and a Twinkie.

The server left. I said, "By any chance, did you know Mark Jamison, one of the men killed in the crash, or possibly Kevin Robbins?"

Mel waved his fork at me. "Crap, Chris. I'm gay so you think I know every gay person? Hell, I've never met Barry Manilow, Anderson Cooper, Leonardo da Vinci, or most of the other gay dudes and dudettes in the world."

I didn't point out he couldn't have known Leonardo da Vinci. "Mel, I'm asking since they lived in Charleston."

Our drinks arrived.

Mel took a gulp of beer, mumbled something I couldn't understand, then said, "Know both."

"Elaborate."

"Let's see. If the newspaper's correct for a change, Mark Jamison's dead. Kevin Robbins ain't." Mel grinned, or what passed as his effort at a grin. Smirk would be a better description.

I sighed, "Anything else?"

"Met them in Connections. For you narrow-minded straight folks, that's a gay nightclub in town. I talked more with Mark since we both have businesses. Caldwell got to know the other guy better. He's a grocery store pharmacist on the other side of the Cooper River, maybe in Mt. Pleasant."

Caldwell Ramsey is Mel's significant other who made up for Mel's lack of political correctness and civility.

"A pharmacist?"

"Ain't that what I said?"

"Yes. I was thinking …" I didn't finish the thought.

Mel took another bite. "Spit it out. Thinking what?"

I hadn't realized I'd said it out loud.

"If Kevin Robbins is a pharmacist, he'd know poisons."

"Aha! Don't say it. You're sticking your pasty-white nose where it don't belong."

"Curious, that's all."

Food arrived; Mel took a large bite of burger. With part of the meat oozing out of the side of his mouth, he said, "It's a wonder as much crap as you keep spouting out of that mouth you don't have a flock of flies circling your head. Mark my words, you're playing cop."

He guzzled the rest of his first beer.

"How well did they get along?"

"Do I look like a freakin' head shrink? They talked; they drank. I didn't notice them making google eyes at each other if that's what you mean."

Not exactly, I thought. "Did they argue about anything?"

"Mark was pleasant. He wasted too much time talking about how poor business was, how much little companies struggled. My business is doing just fine, thank you. I ignored most of what he said. If I wanted a lesson in economics, I'd subscribe to *Forbes*."

"Think his trucking business was in trouble?"

"He never said it, but I wouldn't be surprised."

"Anything about Kevin Robbins?"

"Let's see," Mel said then glanced at his watch. "Don't recall hearing him say he was going to poison his lover. Gotta head out to play nice with the left-wing, brainwashed college brats."

"Nothing else about Mark or Kevin?"

"Caldwell spent more time talking to Kevin. I'll see if he recalls anything. Will let you know."

Mel waved to the server and asked for his check. It was one of the few times whomever my dining partner was hadn't stuck me with paying. There was hope for Mel yet.

He finished his cheeseburger, washed it down with beer, paid, and before leaving the table, said, "Try not to get yourself killed while you're not sticking your damned nose in someone else's business."

13

The unseasonably warm weather had headed south, with the temperature now in the low sixties, normal for early-March. It was sunny and the perfect day for a walk, so I grabbed my Nikon, Tilley, and headed a block to Arctic Avenue then toward the Tides, Folly's nine-story hotel standing where Center Street terminated at Arctic Avenue. Each room overlooked the ocean with a spectacular view of sunrise and the Pier. Over the years, I'd become acquainted with several Tides's employees, so I walked through the lobby to see if any were working. A large group was checking out, so members of the staff were scurrying around helping with paperwork and luggage.

I left the hotel to walk to the beach access walkway bisecting the hotel's parking lot and the large Charleston Oceanfront Villa's condo complex where I saw someone I thought was Virgil Debonnet. He was leaning against the wooden railing on the ramp leading from the walkway to the beach. The breeze coming off the ocean was strong. Virgil's hair that had been neatly slicked back when he was in Barb's Books was whipping around the front of his face. I wasn't certain it was Virgil until I recognized the resoled Gucci shoes. He was drinking something from a brown paper bag, something I'd wager wasn't sweet tea.

Virgil was focused on the Pier to our left and didn't notice me moving beside him.

"Hey, Virgil. Nice day, isn't it?"

His head jerked my direction. "Umm, yeah."

His eyes were hidden behind sunglasses and I couldn't tell if he recognized me, so I said, "I'm Chris. We met in Barb's Books."

He nodded. "Oh, sure. Barb tells me you two are an item." He took a drink of whatever he had in the paper bag. "I'd offer you some, but it's illegal drinking this at the beach. Wouldn't want you to get in trouble."

"That's okay."

"Good. I don't have enough to share. Before you get the idea I'm an *arfarfan'arf*, I consume no more than a dozen adult beverages a day." He laughed as he tapped me on the shoulder.

"You're not an arf what?" I asked, channeling the inquisitive mind of Charles.

"*Arfarfan'arf*, my good man, a Victorian term for a drunkard."

I wondered why I'd asked in the first place. "Oh."

"Sorry to wax erudite. Couldn't help it. My ex has a degree in English, not the helpful kind of degree that helps you conjugate verbs, but one that made her act superior to all of us lowlifes who don't speak Victorian."

And there he was speaking Victorian to me. He'd already forgotten his discussion about Barb and me.

"The other day you said you were between jobs. What kind of work did you do?"

"Isn't that a bit forward to be asking someone you don't know and simply found gandering at the deep blue sea?"

"Sorry if I offended you. I was thinking if I heard of anything in your field, I could let you know."

Virgil laughed. "Just teasing. I had a semi-stellar career as a stock market analyst." He looked around the ramp only the two of us occupied. "Truth be told, I made my money the old-fashioned way. I inherited it." He laughed. "Anyway, my father, who art probably in hell, had been part of Charleston's old money. He made a fortune in shipping, boats bringing stuff from the old country to the good old US of A, not UPS." He paused as he looked at a couple walking hand-in-hand on the beach.

"Interesting," I said to let him know I was paying attention.

"He left me one of those stately mansions overlooking the Battery, you know, the ones tourists ogle over, the ones carriage tour guides spend way too many words talking about. Yes sir, life was grand."

To ask, or not to ask. Why not? "What happened?"

Virgil chuckled. "My stock market analytic skills failed to exceed my fortune. Well, that's not all that caused my, let's say, downsizing. Gambling, like with bookies plus junkets to Vegas, also gambling big on stocks, and, oh well, why not say it, an illegal substance or two, led to me, umm, to me standing here with absolutely nowhere to go or anything to do, nor with the resources to do it." He laughed. "Is that a sad story, or what?" He took another drink.

I started to say I was sorry, but sorry for what? Instead I looked at him and nodded like I understood.

"Know why my wife left me?"

I shook my head.

"She said poverty wasn't in her genes. When my platinum American Express card got shredded, she shredded our marriage license. Being smacked in the face by broke was her tipping point. Go figure."

One of the amazing features of Folly was the wide range of residents, and those living here without a residence. It was no accident the island was labeled *The Edge of America*. Homeless men and women coexisted with the wealthy. People who thought Barry Goldwater was a screaming liberal coexisted with people who'd supported Bernie Sanders. While there were constant disagreements about, well, about everything, most of the people on Folly whom I'm acquainted with would defend to their death the rights of those with whom they held strong disagreements.

I'd only met Virgil twice, yet figured he'd fit in quite well. His positive attitude was welcomed and appreciated. I hoped it wasn't a result of what was in the paper bag. He seemed to take his situation in stride, had a much better attitude than I would if I'd lost a fortune.

I told him I was sorry about losing his wife. He said he was sorry that he'd lost someone who'd constantly criticized him for how he'd dressed, who he chose as friends, how terrible he'd treated her silver-spoon-in-the-mouth relatives. He said it didn't take long to realize how little he missed her.

He shook his head and added, *"C'est la vie."*

I wasn't fluent in any foreign language, was moderately fluent in English, and knew he wasn't speaking Victorian, and said, "True."

He nodded at my camera then turned toward the Pier. "Think anyone ever took a photo of it?"

I thought I detected a grin on his face, although it was hard to tell under his sunglasses.

I chuckled. "A zillion, give or take."

"Did I ever tell you about my Leica?"

"You mentioned it when we were at Barb's," I said, wondering how many conversations he thought we'd had.

"Loved that piece of incredible German technology. Did I also tell you I knew the Haymakers? A fine couple, they are."

I was beginning to wonder if my new acquaintance was operating on all cylinders. I was also glad he didn't have enough of his drink to share with me.

"You mentioned that."

"Did I tell you how we met?"

"Yes."

"Ah, I now recall. I told you about them because you saved Richard and that other guy in the plane. So sad about the others. So sad." He bowed his head like he was praying.

I remained silent wondering why he felt the need to talk about the Haymakers.

Virgil lifted his head, glanced at the Pier, then turned to me. "Did I tell you the circumstance of how I met Charlene Beth and Richard? Whoops, just asked that, didn't I?"

"Yes, and yes. It was something about her handling a real estate transaction."

"Ah, I gave you the sanitized version. Suppose that wasn't unusual

75

since I'd only met you seconds earlier." He patted me on the arm. "Now that we're good buddies, I'll share, as that old geezer used to say, the rest of the story."

Good buddies, I thought, then nodded for him to continue.

"Did I mention I had one of those mansions on the Battery?"

Not quite five minutes ago, I thought. "Yes."

"It appears in this country when one becomes unexpectedly broke, even though one's domicile is paid for, there still are taxes to be paid, and those in charge expect them to be paid each year. Who would've guessed? Anyway, not only was I without money, a condition I could've recovered from, if I hadn't been a couple of million dollars on the underside of broke, the house had to cease being in my name, a name I regret had lost its luster."

"Two million dollars in back taxes?" I said.

Virgil shrugged. "Not all taxes. A half-dozen companies thought they should be paid money I owed them."

"That's too bad," I said.

"Not really. I'd been a *zounderkite*, got what I deserved."

"A what?"

"Oh, sorry. Another Victorian word my ex called me on numerous occasions. Means a complete idiot."

"Oh."

"Anyway, it's water under the dam, or is that water over the bridge? Doesn't matter, it's gone, so here I am, happy as a lark, enjoying an adult beverage, talking with a new friend. Umm, did I mention, happy as a lark?"

I said he had.

Virgil shook his head and laughed. "Charlene Beth and Richard took me to the Peninsula Grill, treated me to a magnificent supper to 'celebrate' my freedom from home ownership." He laughed again. "It really was a sympathy meal although they were too kind to put it that way. Did I mention Richard helped me find the apartment I now call home?"

"Yes."

"Did I tell you how lovely Charlene Beth is, how adorable her twins are?"

That was something he hadn't mentioned, and I told him so.

"Well, she is, they are. If I had more money and less integrity, Richard had better look out." He slapped the side of his head. "I'd better stop while I'm ahead. Besides, I'm beginning to repeat myself. Let's end this chat to continue it another time. I would give you a card with my name and phone number, but while my name is unchanged, I left my phone in the apartment. I don't recall the number."

I watched my new "friend" turn, nearly trip over his own feet, then stagger up the walkway to the sidewalk behind the hotel and condo complex. I then took a photo of the Folly Pier. Photo number zillion-and-one.

* * *

AFTER FINISHING my Folly-like conversation with Virgil, I headed up Center Street to Barb's Books. I hadn't talked with the lovely store owner since the gathering at Tom Kale's house. I held the door open for a smiling customer who was leaving carrying a bag holding several books.

"Looks like you've had a profitable morning," I said as Barb greeted me with a kiss.

She waved toward a bookshelf along the left wall. "I didn't even know I had three books on pottery. Now I have none." She turned to me. "What brings you in?"

"Thought it was a good day to visit the most fetching bookstore owner on Folly."

Barb rolled her eyes. "Only bookstore owner."

"Most fetching even if there were a hundred bookstores."

"With the bull out of the way, what brings you in?"

"I'm curious about your reaction to Tom Kale's party."

"Wondering when you'd ask. I thought it was nice of him and Richard to have you and Charles over. They didn't have to do anything. Something bother you about it?"

"Not really," I said and asked if she had any coffee in back.

Barb led me to her office where she had a Keurig coffeemaker. We each brewed a cup then she moved to the doorway, so she could see if anyone came in the store.

"I was surprised to see the pilot's wife," Barb said.

"She lives close, so I suppose she wanted to thank us for trying to help the guys in the plane."

Barb slowly nodded. "I get that. What struck me unusual was how she didn't appear too distraught over her husband's death. I also had the impression she was irritated by Gary's law firm's policy against spouses working. As I told her, it's rare but not unheard of, but I see how it'd bother her since she was an attorney who'd worked at the same firm. Don't get me wrong, it's only an impression."

"I didn't catch that, but it seemed she was closer to Tom than a three-houses-away neighbor."

Barb smiled. "I was wondering if you noticed. Curious, isn't it?"

"Speaking of curious," I said. "This morning I had a strange conversation with Virgil Debonnet."

"That's redundant. Where'd you see him?"

"He was on the walkway to the beach beside your condo building."

"Why strange?"

"He was standing there looking at the Pier while drinking something out of a paper bag."

Barb smiled. "Gatorade?"

"Hardly. He started telling me his life history. How he'd been wealthy, had a big house at the Battery, how he'd lost everything because of bad luck and bad choices, about losing his wife, on-and-on. This was only the second time I'd talked with him. Remember, you introduced us? Don't you find it weird he'd be telling all that to someone he'd just met?"

Barb took a sip of coffee and said, "Virgil's a talker. He'd told me everything he shared with you. He doesn't hide much. To be honest, I find his self-deprecating humor refreshing. We all would be much better off if we took ourselves less seriously."

"I agree, although it still struck me as unusual."

Barb laughed. "To quote the guy who's standing in front of me, 'On Folly, unusual is usual.'"

I returned her laugh. "You do listen."

14

"I've been thinking," Charles said as we walked up the steps to the elevated, diamond-shaped, upper-level of the Folly Pier.

"Dare I ask?"

Charles had called on my way home from the bookstore to ask if I could meet him on the Pier. I knew not to ask why. He'd tell me when he was ready. I had nothing else to do so I agreed to meet.

"Been thinking about the crash," he said as he sat on a wooden picnic table with a view toward the beach.

I joined him on the table. "What about it?"

"Wondering how we're going to figure out who poisoned Gary." He glanced sideways at me, probably because he expected me to say it was for the police, not us to figure out.

I didn't want to be too predictable. "Why should we get involved?"

He twisted around and faced me head-on. "Have you already forgotten how someone poisoning poor Gary nearly got us decapitated? How much more involved can we be? Yep, we've got to figure it out."

I sighed. When Charles is on a mission, it'd be easier to stop a speeding locomotive with a toothpick. Also, a few things about the crash were bothering me. First, if someone wanted Gary Isles dead, why choose a method that most likely would've killed the other three men?

That must've been on Charles's mind as well when he said, "Think Gary was the person the killer was after?"

"If he was, why kill the others?"

"Exactly. I think one of the passengers was the intended victim. Poisoning Gary and crashing the plane was a clever way of doing it without giving away who was supposed to die."

"It could've been more than one," I said as I looked back at Pier 101, a restaurant on the structure.

Charles said, "Or all four."

"If Gary hadn't taken the extra time to buzz Folly, the plane would've been at a higher altitude when he collapsed. The crash would've killed all of them."

Charles removed his Tilley and ran his hand through his thinning hair. "The killer could've targeted one of the people in the plane, two of them, three of them, or all four."

I agreed.

"See," Charles said, "it's too complicated for the police to figure out. That's why we need to."

Charles logic at its best.

"How do you propose we do that?"

"Coming up with a list of likely suspects would be a good place to start."

"First," I said, "let's eliminate Richard and Tom. They were fortunate to survive. Who would gain the most by the death of one or more of the group?"

Charles returned his Tilley to his head then leaned back on the bench. "You're always telling me the top motives for killing are love, money, or revenge. So, what about love?"

"Charles, that's impossible to answer unless we know the intended victim. If it was Gary, I suppose Kelly could be guilty. She's probably the beneficiary of his estate. This morning I was talking to Barb who told me she detected resentment at the party when Kelly was telling us about having to leave Gary's law firm."

"Kelly didn't seem too distraught about his death."

"That too," I added. "Yet, it could only be her if Gary was the person the killer was after. Add to that, others we don't know who could've wanted Gary dead."

"Okay, what if it was the gay guy, what's his name?"

"Mark Jamison," I said. "I don't know anything about his relationship with his spouse, Kevin Robbins, but Mel told me that Robbins is a pharmacist. Who better to know poisons?"

"Chris, you're giving me a headache. Too many options, too much information."

I nodded toward Charles. "You're the one who decided we needed to do something."

"Yeah. You're the one who's supposed to talk me out of it."

I smiled.

Charles said, "What do we know about Richard Haymaker?"

"Not much."

"At the party he was on his wife's case about gaining weight."

I smiled. "If every woman who's been told by her husband she's gaining weight killed him, the male population would be cut in half."

"True," Charles said. "Suppose we need to find a better motive to accuse Charlene Beth of sabotaging the plane. What if Tom Kale was the intended victim?"

"We know less about him than the others. He has an ex-wife. William told me she'd been his stockbroker before their divorce. When she left the firm, Tom took over William's portfolio."

Charles looked at the hotel and then at a group of surfers patiently waiting for the perfect wave. "At the party, he seemed mighty friendly with Gary's grieving widow. What if some hanky-panky is going on? That'd be a reason for the widow to want her hubby dead."

"But if she poisoned Gary, the odds were high Tom would've been killed in the crash."

"Picky, picky."

Something came to me that I hadn't thought of. "Virgil Debonnet."

"Huh," Charles said, for good reason.

"I ran into him this morning at one of the walkovers to the beach.

Interesting guy. He was telling me Charlene Beth handled the real estate transaction when he sold his house in Charleston. She and Richard had taken him to supper after the closing."

"Dang," Charles interrupted. "You've figured it out. Virgil killed Gary to crash the plane to kill Richard because he had the nerve to feed him."

"May I finish?"

He motioned me to continue.

"Virgil was telling me how lovely he thought Charlene Beth is, called her twins adorable. He said if he had more money and less integrity, Richard had better look out. It's a stretch, but that could've been a motive."

"About as weak a one as possible. I think Charlene Beth is a fine-looking woman. Think I poisoned Gary?"

"Charles, we're throwing out ideas."

"Good, cause I'll throw that one out."

I conceded he was probably right.

"That covers love," Charles said. "What about money or revenge?"

"I don't know about you, but I don't know enough about the cast of characters to know if there's a reason for any of them wanting revenge. Do you?"

"No. How about money?"

"Kelly would inherit Gary's estate which should be substantial. Charlene Beth would get Richard's. Since Tom was divorced, I don't know what'd happen to his estate."

"What about Mark Jamison?"

"Don't know. Guess he'll get it if they were married."

Charles stood, looked over the railing, then mumbled something I couldn't understand. I moved next to him and asked him to repeat it.

"Remember in the past when you got me stuck in the middle of trying to catch a killer?"

"I'm fairly certain it was the other way around."

"Whatever. My point is there was one dead person—one, not two, not almost three or four. Our only problem was figuring out who killed one, I repeat, one, dead guy. Even then, it was hard. If memory serves me correctly, it nearly got us killed a time or two."

I nodded. "Now, no one knows who the intended victim was. Or intended victims."

"You got it. That's the problem."

"Let me add another unknown to the equation. We know the pilot was poisoned. I don't know much about it, but from what I've heard, cyanide poison is quick acting. If swallowed it can cause almost immediate unconsciousness. How'd he get the cyanide? If he ingested it on the plane, where did it come from. I've also heard it has an almond smell. Wouldn't he have noticed something wrong if he'd drunk something with it in it?"

Charles nodded. "When we rescued the guys, one of them said Gary had a cold. That could've kept him from smelling the poison."

"Yes, I believe it was Richard. That could explain why he didn't notice it. That still doesn't explain what it was in, or if it was in anything. Cyanide can also be inhaled, although if that happened, the others on the plane would've been drugged."

"Either of the guys mention drinks on the plane? I didn't see anything, although we were sort of busy saving people."

I thought for a moment. "No one said anything. I didn't notice a cooler or drink containers on the plane."

Charles said, "Cindy told you someone stole everything before the plane was hauled out of the marsh. It could've been the person who poisoned Gary. If there was evidence on the plane, it would've been smart for the killer to steal it before it could be found."

"True, although that seems remote. It was a few days after the crash before the plane was removed. Cindy or someone from the Sheriff's Office could've found it long before the theft."

Charles pointed at my phone. "Call Cindy. Ask if anyone from her office, or from the Sheriff's Office, or the NTSB found where the poison came from, or if they asked the survivors if they had any idea."

"Charles, how do you propose I ask her without looking like I'm nosing in her business?"

"You're the smart one. You'll figure it out. Put her on speaker. If I think of anything you should say, I'll use sign language to tell you."

I exhaled. "Sign language?"

"Oh yeah, I forgot. You don't know sign language."

I rolled my eyes. "Neither do you."

"You certainly know how to shoot down a great idea. Okay, I'll whisper wisdom in your ear."

I smiled as two girls about ten years old rushed to the railing, squealed, as they pointed to a couple of dolphins frolicking in the waves near the Pier. Their parents moved beside them, joining their girls watching the graceful aquatic mammals doing their thing.

Charles elbowed me. "Don't get distracted. Remember, you're calling the Chief."

I didn't know what I was going to say yet knew unless I called, I'd suffer more from the mouth of Charles.

Cindy answered on the third ring. "This is Chief Lamond. How may I help you?"

The polite answer told me she was with someone and couldn't talk. I asked her to call when she had a free minute. She said she would then ask for my number, the number she had, the one appearing on her phone's screen.

"What could be more important than talking to you?" Charles asked, sighed, then said he had to make three deliveries for Dude. If Cindy called when he wasn't with me, I should take notes, so I could tell him everything she said.

It was my turn to sigh. I told him I'd let him know. I didn't mention I wouldn't have notes.

Charles barely had time to get off the Pier when Cindy called. "If I promise not to have you arrested for pestering a police chief, will you buy me a beer at the Surf Bar?"

"When?"

"Five minutes."

"I'm on the Pier. It may take me a little longer to get there."

"If you're planning on jumping, go ahead. I'll buy my own beer."

"See you at the Surf Bar."

15

The Surf Bar is a popular hangout, especially for locals, and, as implied in its name, surfers and the younger crowd. Cindy is at the average high-end age of the bar's clientele. I'm the grandfather's age of many of its customers. Regardless, most regulars are accepting of any age visitor, more importantly for the Chief, the bar is directly across the street from Folly's Department of Public Safety.

Cindy was at the bar staring at her beer. When I took the stool next to her she held up the beer and said, "Don't worry. They said they'd wait so you could pay."

I thanked her for her allowing me to buy. Before I could order, the bartender set a glass of white wine in front of me. Cindy smiled saying I could pay for my drink as well.

"Rough day?" I said, figuring it must be considering her drink was half gone.

"Once upon a time, many moons ago, traffic didn't get bad until around Memorial Day. Our fine citizens didn't start bitching about how bad it was until, oh, let's say, the holiday weekend." She took another sip and continued, "Then something happened. Perhaps it was global warming, or word got around that Folly was a cool place to hang out, or those same fine citizens who are now bitching were younger and more tolerant, or no telling what else." She shook her head then took another drink.

"And?" I said to break up her monologue.

"Even though horologists tell us it's mid-March, and the meteorologists tell us the average high this time of year is still in the sixties, flocks are already arriving. They're driving, parking everywhere. Car clutter."

I was stuck on the first part of her sentence.

"Horologists?"

"Thought you were smart. They're folks who're obsessed with time, even study it, if you can believe that. True, most of them study time measured by clocks, but the oldie-goldie horologists are still hung up on the calendar." She grinned as she leaned back on the seat.

"I'm impressed."

"Don't be. I saw it in a magazine this afternoon. Been waiting three hours to drop it on somebody."

By now, I'd forgotten what she'd been talking about. I didn't have to remember, she said, "Why the call?"

"Charles and I were talking about—"

Cindy waved her hand in front of me, then waved for the bartender, who was quick to respond.

"Another beer. I'll need it." Cindy turned from the bartender to me. "I'll warn you now. I may retract my offer not to arrest you. Go on."

"We were thinking about the crash, wondering since the pilot was poisoned, how it was administered."

"Um, hum," Cindy responded, saying nothing.

"Do you know how cyanide got in his system?"

She took a sip of her second beer, glared at me, before saying, "Chris, you're incorrigible."

I smiled, hoping to get her to do the same. "Did you read that in the magazine?"

She shook her head. "All the damned cars cramming the island, not even one of them ran over you on your way here."

"So, you know how it got in his system?"

"Chris, if you weren't so nice, on a rare occasion lovable, I wouldn't be letting you bribe me with drink. I'd have my guys pack your stuff up then escort you off island." She looked around to see who was in hearing distance, lowered her voice, and said, "In a rare moment of cooperation, Detective Callahan let me sit in on his interview with Tom Kale. If Callahan's boss, the Sheriff, knew, he'd probably boot Callahan down to corrections officer strip-searching drunks."

She took another sip, so I said, "Learn anything?"

"Kale said Gary had a cooler. He offered each of them a drink when they were ready to take off. Mark Jamison grabbed a bottle of Mountain Dew. Richard and Tom didn't take anything."

"What about Gary?"

"That's where it got interesting. Tom said Gary took a screw-top bottle of an energy drink. Detective Callahan asked if Gary drank from it. Tom said yes, he opened it after they were in the air heading this way. Callahan asked if Tom knew what the drink was. He said he didn't know because he was distracted trying to see Folly and his house."

"How long after he took a drink did he collapse?"

"Tom said it seemed more like seconds rather than minutes. That's consistent with what the coroner said about how fast cyanide works."

I said, "Did anyone else on the plane have access to the cooler before Gary took out his drink?"

"Tom said no since Gary took off as soon as the others arrived."

"I don't suppose he had an idea who would've had access to the cooler before they arrived."

"Nope. Let me tell you what I do know. Fries are good with beer." She once again waved for the bartender, ordered fries, adding for the employee to bring her another beer with the fries.

I told her I didn't need anything else, then turned to Cindy, "If whoever put the poisoned drink in the cooler meant for it to go to Gary to crash the plane, he or she must've known which drink Gary would take. The one Mark chose didn't have poison in it, and probably neither would the ones the guys in the back seat may've selected."

"Correct, Mr. Faux Private Eye. That's why the real detective and I left our interview with Tom and drove out to the rich end of the island. We knocked on Kelly Isles' door and had a pleasant conversation with her."

"I don't suppose she confessed to poisoning her spouse?"

Cindy stared at the bartender like that would speed up the delivery of her fries and third beer. It didn't, so she turned back to me. "Do you think if she confessed, I'd be wasting time sitting here talking about interviewing Tom Kale?"

"Sure, because I'm nice, lovable."

"Correction, I said lovable on rare occasions."

The fries and Cindy's drink arrived before I could dispute her correction. She grabbed two fries, stuffed them in her mouth, then mumbled, "Dear, sweet, widow Isles invited us in, grabbed a box of Kleenex off a table by the door, before ushering us to the living room where she lowered her head, did a passable job appearing grieved, patted her eyes with a Kleenex, before asking how she could be of assistance."

"Cindy, you said that like you're doubting her sincerity."

"Neither yes nor no. It was over the top, making me suspicious. Detective Callahan expressed sympathy for her loss then asked about the cooler. The widow Kelly said she had no idea what was in it. Her story was Gary always filled it before heading out to play golf. She didn't know he had it on the plane, had no idea who else may've had access to it before taking off."

"Did you believe her?"

"Something about it didn't feel right. I can't put my finger on what."

"What did Callahan think?"

Cindy grabbed two more fries, dipped them in catsup, and studied dollar bills attached to most every surface in the building while she chewed the fries. I took a sip and waited.

"If our fine citizens didn't stick their money all over this place, they could pay their parking fines."

I rolled my eyes. "Callahan, Kelly's story?"

"Guys are swayed by a sob story or a tear, especially if the sober is attractive," Cindy said. "Callahan said Kelly's story sounded sincere. He pointed out how sad she must be, that her story about the cooler made sense."

"Anything else you can share?"

"Crap, Chris, I shouldn't have shared what I did. Now, let's either change the subject or let me arrest you for harassing the police chief."

I smiled. We started talking about the weather, how crowded the bar was getting, and I asked how her husband Larry was doing. She finished her third beer, the fries, and said she had to get home to see what TV dinner Larry wanted for supper.

"One more thing, Cindy. Was the cooler in the plane when it was hauled out of the marsh?"

"Gee, Chris, why didn't we professional law enforcement officials think of that?" She shook her head. "It wasn't there. Callahan thinks it was taken by whoever stole the rest of the stuff out of the aircraft."

"And the bottle Gary drank from?"

"Gone."

Convenient, I thought. I didn't share that with the professional law enforcement official who was now standing to head home to heat a TV dinner.

16

The phone rang as I was sipping coffee and standing on my screened-in porch watching a line of sleepy commuters drive by on their way to work.

An equally sleepy, barely recognizable voice said, "Good morning, Kentucky. Didn't wake you, did I?"

I couldn't recall talking to Cal this early in the morning since he normally doesn't leave his bar until after midnight. I knew it was him since he referred to me by my state of birth, a habit the crooner occasionally resurrects.

"I was on the porch watching traffic go by. What's up?"

"What're the chances you could mosey over to my apartment?"

"When?"

"Now?"

I'd never been to Cal's apartment. Something was up. Although I'm nowhere near as curious as Charles, Cal had my attention.

"I'll be there in fifteen minutes."

"Super. I also invited Charles. Whoops. He's knocking. See ya."

Cal's place was three blocks from his bar and located in a concrete-block building that had been divided into a duplex about the time of the Revolutionary War. The north side of the building was covered in mildew and looked like it'd been painted green as opposed to the off, way off, white of the other sides. Charles answered the door like he'd invited me and said, "Cal's fixing us breakfast."

The room's furnishings were sparse. There was a brown recliner tilted in its reclined position and listing to one side. It faced a twenty-seven-inch JVC television that I knew from having one years ago weighed as much as a cruise ship. The dark-green carpet was threadbare yet clean. To the left of the television, there was a laminate, three-shelf bookshelf that held two rows of record albums with an empty top shelf.

Cal appeared, saw where I was looking, and said, "Used to have a record player there but it died a while back."

I didn't have time to check-out the rest of the room, which wouldn't take long since the apartment was so tiny it'd make a telephone booth look like the Biltmore House.

Cal straightened his Tammy Wynette, faded-blue T-shirt, before continuing, "Thanks for moseying over." He handed Charles and me a paper plate with a slice of toast slathered with butter and red jam made from some unknown fruit. "Thought I'd better feed you breakfast after screwing up your morning."

I took the *breakfast* as I looked for somewhere to either sit or to set the plate.

Cal followed my gaze. "I'm not used to visitors. Suppose we'd be more comfortable in the kitchen."

The kitchen was tinier, if that was possible, than the living room. A round, vintage, pub-sized Coca Cola table with one chair filled the room.

Cal pointed for us to set our plates on the table. "Best piece of furniture I have. It's a classic." He chuckled. "Like me."

He asked if we wanted something to drink, followed by saying that the choices were beer in the green refrigerator and water.

"Jadeite green," trivia collecting Charles said as he pointed at the refrigerator that also had to be a classic.

"If you say so," Cal said as he made a tipping motion where his

Stetson would normally reside. His straggly white hair was Stetsonless.

I declined the beer saying water would be fine.

Cal turned to the dripping sink. "Good, got plenty of it."

What he didn't have was an explanation of why he'd summoned us. Cal rooted through the cabinet, found two glasses, wiped a smudge of something off one, and delivered our water. He started talking about the weather and how slow business was the previous night. He appeared to want to talk about anything but the reason we'd been summoned.

Charles would have none of it. "Cal, good buddy, I appreciate the fine breakfast, chance to visit your abode, but why're we here?"

Cal plopped down in the chair that went with the Coke table while Charles and I rested in the two card table chairs Cal dragged to the kitchen from the back porch.

He took a deep breath, looked in his water glass like he was trying to find the next words, and said, "The guy you met in the bar came back last night."

That didn't narrow it down much, but Charles did when he said, "Junior Richardson from Arkansas?"

Cal pointed his forefinger at Charles and winked. "That's the one. Know what he asked me?"

Charles told him he didn't know. I shook my head.

"The boy was on his second beer then motioned me out from behind the bar, asked me to hop on the stool beside him. There were only two other guys in the place, so I sidled up beside Junior. He then gasted my flabber when he said, 'Cal, know where you were this date fifty-seven years ago?'"

Not a normal question to ask a bartender you hardly knew, I thought. "What'd you say?"

"Looked at him like I'd look at a red stoplight. Told him I couldn't tell you where I was Thursday. Asked what he was talking about."

"Cripes, Cal," Charles muttered. "Spill it. What was he talking about?"

Junior sat up straight, ran his hand through his beard and said I was getting hitched to Jasmine Folkstone." Cal shook his head. "Now that was a blast from the past. Remember a few years back when I told you I'd been married a few times?"

I said I remembered.

"Jasmine was *numero uno*."

Charles leaned toward Cal. "How'd Junior know?"

Cal shook his head, looked at me, then at Charles. "Suppose because he's my son."

Charles jerked back. "He's what? Didn't you tell me you didn't have kids?"

Cal rubbed his hand through his hair getting most of it to go the same direction. "Didn't know I did. Was hitched to Jasmine six months. Got married in sixty-two, the year I had my hit record. She was from Fulton, Arkansas, a town about the size of my bar. Charles, you being a trivia collector will like this. Fulton was named after Robert Fulton the steamboat inventor. Anyway, I'd been on the road a couple of years, figured it was about time to settle down. Met Jasmine, sort of fell in love, got hitched. The problem was there was only one place in Fulton for me to sing. I tried to make it work. Honest to God, I tried."

"And failed," Charles said.

Let Cal tell his story, I wanted to say.

"Yes, Charles, I failed. Jasmine was a nice gal, but I had, what's the word, wanderlust. Settlin' down wasn't my thing. Besides, I had to get to other cities to promote my record. I tried to explain it to Jasmine. I was as successful as grabbin' a beach umbrella and flying it to Uruguay. We didn't depart on kissy-face terms."

I said, "You didn't know she was pregnant?"

"Nope. Last I heard from her was a year later when she found out I was staying in a flea-bag motel near Nashville. Sent me divorce papers to sign. Not a word about a kid, no sir, not a word. Hell, not even a syllable."

I said, "How do you know Junior's telling the truth?"

"That's a fine question, Kentucky. I asked him the same thing. The first hint was when he told me his real name was Calvin Richardson. Claimed his mom named him after his dad. He pulled a wallet out of his britches, slid out a folded, old black-and-white photo of Jasmine holding a baby. The kid didn't have a beard like Junior, but Junior, umm, Calvin, said it was him. When he was old enough to understand, his mom told him his dad was a soldier, that he was killed in Vietnam."

"Cal," Charles said, "a picture doesn't prove you're the dad."

"Same thing I said to him. He said that was true but said he'd take a blood test if I wanted."

Charles said, "What'd you say?"

"I've been around the block a time or two, pretty good at figuring out when someone's lying. I don't doubt Junior, Calvin, is being square with me. Guys, I'm a dad at the ripe young age of seventy-four, yes I am."

"Cal," I said, not wanting to get in a semantic argument about when he became a father, "if Jasmine told him his father died in Vietnam, how'd he learn about you?"

"Jasmine died five years ago, lung cancer. Heck, I remember her chain-smoking Kool menthol cigarettes from the time she had her first cup of coffee until climbing in bed at night. It's a wonder she made it as long as she did. Bless her soul."

Cal stared into space until Charles interrupted his memories. "Junior learned about you?" He made a move-along motion with his hand.

"After Jasmine passed, Calvin Jr. was going through her stuff. He found a promotional picture of me, one of those record companies send to radio stations along with records. Junior said I almost looked handsome back in those days. He also found newspaper clippings about me at shows in Arkansas, some in Texas. The tipping point was when he found his birth certificate. In the space for father, it said Calvin Ballew."

This was coming from so far out in left field that I was at a loss of words. Charles wasn't.

"How'd he find you?"

"Said it wasn't easy. It took him three years of surfing the Internet, going through old newspaper clippings in Little Rock. The boy even took a trip to Nashville to look through newspaper morgues. He finally found something on the Internet about when I took over the bar a few years back. Persistent fellow, I'll give him that."

"Congratulations, Dad," Charles said. "What's your baby boy want?" He drew a dollar sign in the air with his forefinger. "Money?"

Cal stood and looked out the back door. "Same question I asked, except for the baby boy and money part." He laughed although I didn't see anything funny about his recent discovery.

Charles said, "Well, what'd he say?"

"Look around you. Do I look like I live in a mansion overlooking the ocean? Hell's bells, I have a breathtaking view of a commercial dumpster." His laughter turned to a chuckle. "It ain't a breathtaking view but is breathtaking to my nose. Money. If that's what he's looking for, he's barking up the wrong family tree."

"Cal," I said, then repeated Charles's question, "you asked Junior, umm, Calvin, what he wanted. What'd he say?"

"Said all he wanted was to meet his old man. If it's okay with me, he'd move to Folly."

Cal had returned to his view of the dumpster. Charles said, "What's he do for a living?"

"Said he owned a chain of chicken restaurants in Arkansas. Twern't no KFC, but he made a good living, then sold the chain to track down his fathe—umm, to track me down. He's not starvin' for money if what he said is true."

"You believe him?"

Cal shrugged. "Suppose so. He said the only reason he was here was to get to know me better."

"How do you feel about that?" I asked.

"Strange, odd, weird."

Charles said, "You honestly believe him?"

Cal rubbed his hand through his hair, again, blinked twice, then said, "Yep."

I said, "What happens now?"

"He said he'd stop in tonight, so we could shoot the breeze. That's why I wanted to talk to both of you. Can I handle having a new son, new even if he's fifty something years old?"

Charles nodded. "Teddy Roosevelt said, 'Believe you can and you're halfway there.'"

17

Cal said how much he appreciated us coming, yawned, then hinted that he needed to get some shuteye before opening the bar. After leaving, we agreed that Cal's well-intended breakfast did little for our stomachs. A trip to the Lost Dog Cafe would meet that need.

The restaurant was near full. The only vacant table was a four-top in the center of the room. Amber was quick to greet us with a mug of coffee and asked if I wanted to order a bowl of fresh fruit parfait. I said her sense of humor was outstanding. She told me the same was becoming true for my stomach. Charles leaned back taking it all in with a smile. I sucked in my stomach and said I'd have French toast. Amber said she'd wasted time asking.

Charles waved a hand in her face. "Yo, Amber, I'm here, too."

She smiled. "Of course, you are. That's why I put that mug in front of you."

He got around to ordering pancakes. Amber left the table mumbling something about Pillsbury Doughboys.

Charles sipped coffee, looked around the room, and said, "Can you believe Papa Cal?"

"I can't think of many things more shocking. He seemed to take it in stride."

"I hope Junior isn't running a scam. Cal can be naïve about things, even if he's in his mid-seventies and according to him, been around the block a time or two."

I didn't have a chance to respond. Virgil Debonnet was standing beside our table alternating between looking at me and the empty chair.

I took the hint asking if he wanted to join us.

"If you don't mind."

Charles said, "Not at all. We'd love to have you."

I thought Charles was being overly friendly to someone he'd never met. Virgil sat and introduced himself to Charles, who said he'd heard lots of good things about Virgil.

"That's nice," Virgil said. "I've also heard a few things about you."

I noted he omitted the word *good*.

Charles asked what Virgil had heard.

"You and Chris have a reputation around here. I've heard from more than one person you are killer-catchers extraordinaire."

Charles smiled like Virgil had crowned him king of Monaco. "I don't know about extraordinary, but in all modesty, I must say we've been successful."

I wanted to move off that subject. "Virgil, any luck finding a job?"

He smiled. "No, but that brings up something I wanted to talk to both of you about. Word around town is that you're trying to find out who offed the pilot."

"No," I said. "The police have it under control."

Charles interrupted, "Chris, let Virgil talk."

I motioned our guest to continue.

"Chris, do you remember I told you about working with Richard and Charlene Beth on the sale of my house?"

"Yes, plus how Richard helped you find your apartment."

"What I didn't tell you was I know the other survivor's wife, umm, Tom Kale's wife, ex-wife, Alyssa."

I asked, "How do you know her?"

"She's a stockbroker. I ran into her at a couple of social gatherings of people in that business."

Charles leaned closer to Virgil. "Think she poisoned the pilot to kill her ex?"

"That was before the crash. She didn't mention planning on killing him while we were standing around at a cocktail party sipping vino." Virgil chuckled. "I would've remembered her saying she was going to bump off the pilot."

Amber returned with our food and asked Virgil if he wanted anything. He looked at our plates but said water would be all. Charles, generous Charles, told Virgil if he wanted something to eat, I'd buy. He hadn't gotten the last of the sentence out when Virgil interrupted and asked Amber for a menu, studied it, then ordered a breakfast burrito.

I imagined snarling at Charles, but instead said, "Virgil, did Alyssa say anything to indicate she was unhappy with her husband?"

Virgil smiled. "I thought you said you're not trying to catch the killer?"

Charles turned to me. "Yeah, Chris."

I said I was curious, nothing more.

Virgil rubbed his chin. "Now, let's see. She didn't say she wanted him dead. What she said was their divorce was filed a year ago, it was acrimonious, they were still fighting over everything including their poodle. I believe it's named Casper."

"There you go," Charles said. "The ex had a reason for bumping off her husband."

I took a bite of French toast as Virgil picked up his knife and pointed it at Charles, then at me. "Want to know what I was thinking last night?"

I was tempted to say no, but knew it'd be rude. I told him to continue.

"I was thinking several things. For example, I know two spouses of the guys plus one of the men in the plane that tried to be a boat. Then, I was thinking if I saw you two today, I could give you what you detectives call a clue, that being Alyssa Kale had motive for wanting her husband gone, dead gone. Then, I was thinking it'd be nice if I still lived in the mansion overlooking the Battery." He shook his head.

"Ignore that thought. Was feeling sorry for myself." He took a deep breath. "That leads to my biggest thought."

His breakfast burrito arrived along with coffee refills for Charles and me. Before he had time to chew the first bite, Charles said, "What was your biggest thought?"

Virgil put his finger to his lips which I figured meant he'd wait until he finished chewing before answering. That proved he had more couth than either Charles or me, or for that matter, most of my friends.

The aroma of bacon was strong as Amber delivered an order to the table beside us.

Virgil glanced at Amber, swallowed, then turned back to us. "I'm between jobs, have time on my hands, so I thought I could join forces with you to find out who killed the pilot and nearly took the life of my friend Richard. We could be the crime-fighting dynamic trio."

Dynamic trio! I felt a headache coming on caused by the man sitting beside me, a man who was eating breakfast I was paying for.

"Interesting idea," Charles said as he poured more syrup on his pancakes. "What makes you think you could help?"

A question asked by Charles, the person who thought he's a private detective because he's read a plethora of detective novels.

"Good question," Virgil said. "It's easy to see why you're a successful detective."

Charles beamed. I turned my head, so Virgil wouldn't see me roll my eyes.

Charles said, "Thanks."

Virgil continued, "I confess I'm nowhere near as good as you, not close by a kilometer. I haven't had formal investigative training, although I've watched every episode in the Masterpiece Theater Mystery series. I've been a fan of NCIS since there was only one of them. And don't forget, I know some of the players involved in the tragic event." He gave a short nod.

Was he waiting for applause?

I said, "Virgil, that's a good thought, but I don't think—"

He waved for me to stop, looked at the nearest table, then whispered, "I forgot to mention, everyone knows Sherlock Holmes was a druggie, something he and I had in common before I cleaned up a while back. That could be a big help to us."

I didn't waste time reminding him Sherlock Holmes was fictional.

Charles said, "That gives us something to think about."

Virgil clapped his hands. "That's all I can hope for. I won't push. With that out of the way, tell me what brought each of you to this enchanting island."

I was glad to change the subject and gave a brief synopsis of my move to Folly, Charles did the same. Virgil shared he found many of the residents to be friendly, much friendlier than his neighbors South of Broad in Charleston. I'd never lived in a mansion overlooking the Battery, so I couldn't compare.

We stayed off the topic of becoming the dynamic trio until Virgil finished his burrito. He said he didn't want to be a *rakefire* and would leave.

Of course, Charles asked what a *rakefire* was and Virgil enlightened us with another lesson in Victorian-speak. For the record, *rakefire* was someone who overstays his welcome.

My headache increased.

18

"What a morning," Charles said after Virgil left the restaurant. "We learn Cal's a pop and our dynamic duo can become a trio. Yes sir, what a morning." He took a sip of coffee, clasped his hands behind his head, then leaned back bringing the front legs of his chair off the floor.

"Charles, how many times do I have to tell you we're not a crime-fighting duo, dynamic or otherwise?"

After a slight nod, he said, "Thirty-seven."

I told him it'd exceeded thirty-seven years ago. He agreed it may be true, but for me to look at our track record then added our success rate would be the envy of many honest-to-goodness, real detectives. I reminded him we knew near nothing about Virgil Debonnet, that he could've poisoned Gary Isles.

"Chris, you're always telling me some of my ideas are half-baked, if that baked. Throwing Virgil in the suspect pool is less baked than some of my ideas. What's his motive? If he did it, why would he be trotting over to us in his Gucci loafers to offer to help us catch him? Your idea doesn't make a lick of sense."

"I don't think he did it. I was pointing out how little we know about the man. With that said, I wouldn't rule him out. He's overly interested in the crash. As he said, he knows three folks directly or indirectly involved with it."

"Using your logic, Chris, we could've poisoned Gary. We know four people involved. That's more than Virgil knows."

"Charles, I should've said Virgil knew three of them before Gary was poisoned. We met the four we know after the crash."

"I'm confused. Are you saying Virgil did it or not?"

"Probably not, although probably leaves a possibility."

I was so intent on explaining myself that I didn't notice Cindy LaMond approach.

She said, "What in holy hamsters are you mumbling about? Probably, possibly, poop."

"We were—"

"I don't want to know," she said. Without any gestures or hints, she took the seat Virgil vacated. "Yes, I'd love for you to buy me coffee."

Amber must have seen Cindy enter. She was quick to see what the Chief needed.

Charles waited for Amber to return with Cindy's coffee, and said, "Do you know Virgil Debonnet?"

"Would that be the Virgil Debonnet who just met me in the parking area, the one who told me I looked as lovely as a Gainsborough painting on this fine March day? Hell, I don't know a Gainsborough from a Gaines-Burger but figured it must not be too bad for him to claim the top-cop looked that way. That the Virgil?"

I said, "Yes."

Cindy nodded slowly. "Most of the people I know are ones I've gotten to know over the years, or ones we arrest, where I get a quick dose of getting to know them. Virgil doesn't fall in either group. He'd gone out of his way to find ways and places to talk to me. I gather he hasn't been on Folly long. If he can be believed, he used to be among the wealthy who have their domestics fold and gently place their underwear in dressers costing more than my annual salary. Because of bad luck and bad habits, he now hangs his tighty-whities outside to dry while he lives in an apartment that's not as big as his walk-in closet from days gone by."

I said, "He told you all that?"

"That and more. He may wear his tighty-whities inside his britches, but he wears his deepest secrets on his sleeve."

Charles said, "Could he be hiding something?"

"Who isn't?" Cindy said. "You thinking about something in particular?"

"Not really," Charles said.

Cindy's focus narrowed. "Hmm. Mind if I don't believe you?"

Charles shrugged.

She took a sip, then said, "The only thing I see a problem with is his drinking. I suspect the only thing that's keeping it from getting out of hand is his state of broke."

I said, "I had that impression."

"Are you going to tell me why you wanted to know about him?"

I smiled. "I met him in Barb's. We've talked a couple of times since then. I thought he was an interesting fellow, so I wondered what you knew about him."

"Now that your vague brush off is out of the way, are you ready for me to tell you why I'm here?"

I said, "I thought it was because we were fascinating, handsome, charming men."

Cindy shook her head. "Add delusional."

"Chief," Charles said, "I want to know."

She turned to Charles. "Thank you. I got a call from Detective Callahan this morning. He'd talked with Aaron Cole, the NTSB investigator. Everything is still unofficial. Seems NTSB folks can't sneeze without waiting six months until an official sneeze report is finished. Anyway, Cole told Callahan there is still no indication anything was mechanically wrong with the plane. That wasn't news. He said it was fortunate any of the passengers survived. The flight to Myrtle Beach takes less than an hour. If the plane had ascended at its normal rate, it could've been at roughly seven-thousand feet when Gary took his last breath. The odds on anyone surviving would have been plus or minus zero. The Folly flyby saved Haymaker and Kale."

That wasn't anything we didn't know or suspected, so why did

Cindy come to share that with us? She already said it wasn't because we were fascinating, handsome, or charming.

"Cindy," I said, "did Callahan have anything else?"

"Yesterday, he interviewed Richard Haymaker and Tom Kale."

I said, "Isn't this the second or third time he's interviewed them?"

"Third. We now know the pilot took cyanide and it's a quick-acting poison, so Haymaker and Kale were with him when he ingested it. Remember, I told you Kale said Gary drank from an energy drink."

I nodded.

Charles leaned closer to Cindy. "Don't suppose either of them confessed to killing him?"

Cindy shook her head. "Charles, can you think of one reason either would've had to poison the pilot which would result in a quick trip to dead for all of them?"

"Just asking."

I waited for Charles to give a reason, which he didn't, so I said, "Did Callahan learn anything new from the survivors?"

"No. They were in back of the plane, more intent on seeing their houses than anything going on in front."

Cindy still knew something she wasn't sharing. "Cindy, what else did Callahan tell you?"

"Has anyone told you you're getting as pesky as Charles?"

"There's hope for him," Charles interjected.

Cindy ignored him. "It's a gut reaction on Callahan's part. He said Kale seemed overly concerned about dead Gary's wife, Kelly. He said it was nothing he could take to court."

I said, "Like what?"

"Callahan didn't go into detail, other than Kale's voice got softer when he talked about poor, poor Kelly. Said Kale almost broke into tears when talking about her. Nothing else."

I reminded Cindy how comfortable Tom Kale had been with Kelly at the reception he and Richard had for Charles and me.

Cindy said, "They live close to each other; their husbands were friends."

"True, but I had the impression they were closer than most neighbors."

"That's consistent with Callahan's comment."

I said, "It still doesn't make sense either is responsible. Tom could've been as dead as Gary, and Kelly would've lost Tom and her husband. Cindy, she knew Tom was going with the group, didn't she?"

"Yes."

Charles said, "Did Callahan say anything else?"

"Yes, Charles. He said if I run into nosy, busybody, troublemaking Charles Fowler, to cuff him and throw him in the clink."

Charles's mouth opened wide and he took a deep breath. "He didn't say that."

"He should have," Cindy said, stood, and headed to the exit.

19

"Is this the Chris Landrum who tried to balance a damned airplane on his head while he was cavorting with dolphins in the marsh?" boomed the loud voice of Bob Howard soon after I made the mistake of answering the phone before inserting earplugs.

One of my first memories when I arrived on Folly Beach eleven years ago was meeting Bob, then a realtor with Island Realty, which, as he was prone to say, was *the second largest of the three very small island Realty firms*. If you picture the ideal realtor, Bob would be absent. He was loud, boorish, profane, opinionated, politically incorrect, and dressed street-person chic. Despite traits that would be the antithesis of anything found in a realtor handbook, Bob had been successful for decades. He and his wife, Betty, lived in one of the more prestigious sections of Charleston.

Bob had helped me find a vacation rental, then an inconsiderate killer torched the rental with me in it, Bob found the house I now call home and for reasons way more complicated than I can articulate, we'd become friends.

"That's old news, Bob. Did you crawl out of a cave?"

"Betty and I just got back from a damned cruise to some freakin' backward islands in the middle of nowhere."

"Sounds like you had a wonderful time."

"Damned right I did. Betty told me so. Enough about my trip to ecstasy, or whatever the damned islands were called. What happened to you and your shadow?"

I gave him the abridged version of our fateful kayak trip plus a little about what I'd learned since the crash.

"Let me guess," Bob growled. "You nearly got your head chopped off, so you and your quarter-wit friend feel a lunar pull making it your calling to catch whoever killed two men and nearly killed their golfing buddies."

"Bob, it's in the able hands of the Sheriff's Office with the assistance of the Folly Beach Department of Public Safety."

"So, there's no need for me to tell you how I know the spouse of one of the survivors?"

"Who?"

Bob laughed. "Gotta get to Al's. If you stop by for a cheeseburger, I might have time to share the skinny on ... whoops, guess you'll have to wait."

A year and a half ago, Al Washington, a close friend of Bob experienced near-fatal health issues and sold Bob his bar. He knew as much about running the business as I did about conjugating the verb to belch in Hungarian, but his friend needed him, so Bob was there for him.

I parked in front of Al's. Bob's purple PT Cruiser convertible, the vehicle he'd had since I met him, was taking up two spaces in front of me. He'd told me he takes two spaces so no stupid, terrible driver would accidentally scratch his classic mode of transportation. A few years back, I told him taking two spaces was a trait of a stupid, terrible driver. My observation was met with a gaggle of profanities, so I never mentioned it again.

The first person I saw when I entered the paint-peeling concrete block building Al's shared with a Laundromat was the former owner seated on a wobbly, wooden chair beside the door. Heart problems and arthritic knees limited mobility for the eighty-two-year-old but didn't stop him from appearing each day to serve as greeter.

Al saw me and pushed up from the chair, smiled showing his coffee-stained teeth, and wrapped his bone-thin arms around me.

"Mr. Chris, it's good to see you. We've missed you around here."

I told him it'd been too long and asked how he was doing.

From the jukebox, Vern Gosdin was singing "Chiseled in Stone" as Al started to answer. Both Vern and Al were drowned out by Bob yelling, "Old fossil, stop pestering the poor boy. Let him get over here and spend money."

Two tables of diners glared at Bob. He motioned for them to mind their own business then pointed to the seat opposite the new owner. His polite way of saying he'd loved to have me join him.

In addition to Bob not knowing anything about a restaurant other than spending many hours in them stuffing his face, he was marshmallow white. That wasn't a big deal most of the time but considering Al and roughly ninety-nine percent of his customers were African American, it rose to significant proportions. Bob prided himself as being an equal-opportunity offender, so tensions were occasionally elevated. While he wouldn't admit it, that was one reason Bob had encouraged Al to remain involved in the restaurant.

"Shut your trap, you old tub of lard," Al responded.

The other diners didn't give Al a standing ovation but didn't hide their laughter.

Country crooner Vern Gosdin was followed by The Supremes with "Where Did Our Love Go."

I sat across from Bob in the booth that everyone knew was his because he'd attached a brass plate on it that read *Bob's booth. WARNING: Sit at your own risk.* He held his chubby hands over his ears while mumbling something about that damned music being the death of him. For years as an outward sign of the two men's friendship, and to the consternation of his other customers, Al had salted his jukebox with Bob's country favorites.

Bob, at six-foot-tall carrying the weight of someone a foot taller, barely folded into the booth. He was in his normal attire of a Hawaiian flowery shirt and black shorts he wore because he said black made him look slim. He looked as slim as a rhino, an observation I'd keep to myself.

"Who ran the restaurant while you were on your luxury cruise?"

Bob pointed toward the kitchen. "What's his name back there and old fart Al chipped in managing to keep the place from burning down from a grease fire."

Lawrence was Al's cook. Bob knew his name as well as he knew his own. Given the choice of a compliment or an insult, Bob always leaned negative.

"I see it survived."

"Don't tell him I said it, what's his name does a fantastic job. I'm thrilled to have him."

Okay, he doesn't always lean negative.

"Bob, you said you know one of the—"

Bob interrupted and yelled in the direction of the kitchen, "Get this scrawny honkie a cheeseburger and a glass of our finest jug wine."

I waited to see if he would yell anything else. He didn't, and I said, "You said—"

"Alyssa Kale," Bob interrupted, again. "The person you were taking too long to ask about."

"You know her?"

"Isn't that why you're here?"

"That, getting the best cheeseburger in the country, and to see you and Al."

"Yeah, right," he scoffed. "Alyssa is my stockbroker. I inherited her after Jordon had the audacity to up and die instead of managing my portfolio."

"What do you know about her, other than she had to have thick skin to put up with you?"

"You want to know this because you are not, with a capital N and O and T, getting involved in what happened to the plane?"

"It's because I met her husband so was curious about his wife."

"Ex-wife," Bob said. "She was quick to point that out during our first meeting. She's about as opposite from her predecessor as can be.

He was laid back, would shoot the breeze as much as shoot stocks, had an awesome body like mine."

I couldn't help interrupting. "Awesome body?"

"Do I detect doubt?"

"Of course not, Bob. How is Alyssa different from Jordon?"

"Let's see. He's white, she's black; he had an ample body like mine, hers is petite; he's laid back, she's wound tighter than a girdle on a four-hundred-pound woman; oh yeah, he's dead, she's not. That's not what you really wanted to know. The main thing I got from her is she's two steps past royally pissed at her ex."

"Why?"

"I didn't ask. I was more concerned if she was recommending I sell my Apple stock than her pissed level with Tom Kale. Tell you what, if you want I'll set up a face to face with her and say something like, 'Alyssa, tell me why I should sell a hundred shares of Microsoft and why you poisoned the pilot.'"

"You're always thinking, Bob. Not a bad idea, although I doubt it'll work. Did she say anything else about her ex?"

He shook his head. "I'm not as good a detective as you and your fractional-wit sidekick."

Lawrence delivered my cheeseburger and wine, Patsy Cline's haunting voiced filled the room singing "I Fall to Pieces," and three customers at the next table moaned in unison.

"Bob, while we're talking about the crash, do you know Charlene Beth Haymaker?"

"By reputation and rumor," Bob said, as I took a bite of the cheeseburger.

I wiped catsup off my lip then said, "Elaborate."

He spelled *NOT* with his forefinger on the table as he said, "Getting involved."

I got the message. It didn't stop me from repeating, "Elaborate on reputation and rumor."

"Charlene Beth is one of the new wave of realtors. That's one of the reasons I retired from that life, why I started living the dream of running a dilapidated, dying bar. Charlene Beth." Bob hesitated, and said, "Have I told you how much I hate people who use two first names?"

"I've heard seven hundred other things you bitch about. That's a new one."

"Add it to the list. Wouldn't Charlene do? How about Beth, a perfectly acceptable name? Why clutter up speaking by using two names when one will do?"

I pointed to Bob's phone. "Call her and ask?"

Bob tilted his head. "You being a smart ass?"

"I am. With your most recent pet peeve out of the way, new wave of realtor?"

"They do everything on the Internet." He picked up his smartphone. "If someone took this away, they'd be dead in the water. They're showing out-of-town clients homes with live chat thingies. They walk through a house, talk about every damn room while they point their damned phone camera at it. The client asks questions. Hell, some of their clients buy a house without stepping through the door. After that, all the paperwork is done in bits and bytes. Robots will be doing all of it before the sun sets. Chris, it ain't right."

I figured that qualified as the reputation part of Bob's comment about Charlene Beth. I said, "Rumor?"

"The word in Realty circles is she's having an affair with Walter Middleton Gibbs."

"Who's he?"

"Who's he? Chris, I continue to be shocked by your ignorance. Walter's old, old, old money. His ancestors were in Charleston so long ago the town was named Chuckie."

I smiled, hoping that was a joke. "Think the rumor's true?"

"Hell if I know. If it is, and if you were not not trying to figure out who poisoned the pilot, two-named Haymaker could be what you detectives call a suspect. She could've bumped off the pilot to crash the plane killing her loving husband."

I ignored his comment about me being a detective. "Know anything else about her?"

"Not a thing."

I figured Bob had shared all he knew about Alyssa Kale and Charlene Beth Haymaker, so I leaned closer to him. "How's Al?"

Bob lowered his head. "I'm afraid he's as good as he's going to get. On the positive side, that's a hell of a lot better than he was when I bought this trillion dollars in debt dump. I worry about him." Bob raised his head, looked at Al, then in a voice about the level of an Indy 500 race car, yelled, "Old man, get your scrawny, ancient ass over here!"

The customers who'd moaned at Patsy Cline's singing turned to Bob and looked ready to leap over the table to show him where he could take his far-from-scrawny rear.

The equal opportunity offender smiled at them as he yelled for Lawrence to take them another round. On the house. Bob never apologized with words but with deeds.

Al arrived at the table after what appeared to be a painful walk across the room. He sat beside me and for the next hour Bob and Al shared insults, humorous stories about Bob's encounters with customers, Al's family, and some of the best cheeseburgers known to man.

I left Al's with a full stomach plus a head full of questions about who poisoned Gary Isles. This was the second time that I'd heard about Tom and Alyssa Kale's divorce. William had said it was highly contested. Bob was less civil in his description by saying Alyssa was highly pissed with her ex. Contested divorces weren't uncommon, but the vast majority didn't end in one spouse killing the other. Was this the exception?

Then what about the rumor that Charlene Beth was having an affair with one of Charleston's leading citizens? If true, could she have orchestrated the crash? Of course, she could have, although if everyone who has had an affair killed their spouse, we wouldn't have to be worrying about overpopulation.

All I knew for certain was someone killed Gary Isles which led to the death of Mark Jamison.

20

The next two days were uneventful. I spent them doing the routine, aka boring, activities of living alone. The highlight, or to me, lowlight, was my bimonthly trip to the Harris Teeter which I looked forward to as much as I would look forward to prepping for a colonoscopy the same day I was having a root canal. Most of my often-meager grocery shopping took place next door at Bert's Market instead of traveling the extra two and a half miles to the large, chain store. The grocery shopping safari combined with a day of cleaning floors helped keep my mind off the crash.

That streak ended when I answered the phone to the aristocratic voice of Virgil Debonnet saying, "Is that you, Christopher?"

I admitted it was while wondering how he got my number.

"Good, this is Virgil Debonnet. I hope you don't mind me calling. Mary, the lovely young lass at Bert's, gave me your number. I told her we were friends and I misplaced the way to get in touch with you. Folks in Bert's are better than Google. They know everyone and everything while selling you a headache remedy at the same time. A true blessing. Anyway, I bet you wonder why I'm calling."

Definitely, I thought. "It entered my mind."

"I've acquired some information that'll help you, your fellow detective friend, and me as we search for the dastardly person who poisoned the pilot of that ill-fated aircraft. Let's get together so you can hear what I've learned. We can plan our next move."

I was curious enough to ignore his comment about my "fellow detective friend," or about the three of us searching. "I suppose. Have you tried to contact Charles?"

"No. Mary didn't know his number. Could you see if he's available?"

"If he is, where and when do you want to meet?"

"Umm, my finances are a bit tight this month, so I'd rather not meet at a restaurant. How about gathering at the end of the walking pier adjacent to the little park by the bridge? I don't know its name. It's where they have outdoor art shows."

"The Folly River Park. When?"

"Sooner the better. We don't want a killer roaming the streets longer than necessary. How about this afternoon if you all can fit it into your schedule?"

"I'll call him then let you know."

Virgil gave me his number then added he'd be on pins and needles waiting for my answer. I wondered how he would've said that in Victorian.

Ten minutes later, I'd called Charles, and got Virgil off pins and needles when I told him we'd be there.

I arrived at the park at two-thirty since I knew Charles would arrive early. He didn't disappoint. He was standing at the railing overlooking the Folly River as I made my way out the narrow foot pier. Charles was wearing dark-green shorts, a Tilley hat, tennis shoes looking like they'd survived a long hike in pluff mud, and a long-sleeve, green T-shirt with Johnson State on the front below a strange-looking, cartoonish creature.

"What's so all-fired important that Virgil took me away from reading a biography of Calvin Coolidge?"

I smiled and thought how little it would've taken for me to stop reading the biography. "Don't know. We'll have to wait and see."

We didn't wait long. Virgil headed toward us with a smile on his face and Gucci shoes on his feet. In between, he wore a short sleeve, wrinkled button-down white dress shirt, and gray dress slacks thinning in the knees.

He pointed at Charles's T-shirt. "That a weasel?"

"It's a Mustelidae, same family but not a weasel. It's a badger, the mascot of Johnson State College in Vermont."

"Oh," Virgil said, a common reaction to Charles's T-shirts. He turned to me, "Thanks for pulling this meeting together."

We sat side by side on the wood bench and watched traffic cross the river.

"Virgil, Chris told me you have something to help us catch the person who killed the pilot."

Virgil took off his sunglasses momentarily and wiped his brow. It was the first time I'd seen his green eyes. He returned the glasses to his face. "After we agreed to work together on catching the killer, I sort of accidentally ran into Richard Haymaker and Tom Kale."

I saw my reflection in his sunglasses as I said, "Sort of accidentally?"

"I'd been looking all over for the survivors or their significant others. The extent of my detecting is rather limited since my only means of transportation is an old scooter I bought from a guy working at the Tides. Did I tell you I used to have a Jaguar, the car, not the animal?"

"No," Charles said.

"Anyway, back to the subject, do you know how many times I went in restaurants, stores, up and down Center Street hoping one of them would appear?"

That was the kind of question Charles lived for. He said, "Nineteen?"

"Shoot, I don't know. Could be. It was a lot. It finally paid off two days ago when I saw Tom getting gas at Circle K. I walked up to him and said, 'Are you Tom Kale?' He kept pumping gas as he looked around to see if I was part of a band of roaming marauders fixing to steal his money or his car. He didn't see any but looked at me like I was a stranger."

Charles said, "Had you met him?"

"Nope, I was a stranger. I covered by saying I'd heard he was one of the crash survivors. The person who told me described him. Told him I wanted to say hi. Wanted to say how glad I was he was among the living."

Charles said, "How'd he respond?"

"Said he was fortunate. I asked if he'd heard how come the plane crashed. Course I knew the answer."

Charles gave what I knew was a nod of frustration. "Kale said?"

"He hemmed, hawed, and looked at the pump like he wanted it to spew petrol faster so he could get out of there." Virgil hesitated, looked at Charles, and said, "Then he said Gary, the pilot, was poisoned. I acted shocked. 'Wow, who would've poisoned him?' Tom looked at me, said he didn't know. I think he was fibbing."

I asked, "Why?"

"His eyes got all shifty, he wouldn't make eye contact. Isn't that a sign of lying?"

"Not necessarily," I said. "Did he say anything that seemed out of place?"

"He jumped right to saying how bad he felt for Gary's wife, Kelly. Now you can take this with a grain of salt, heck, maybe a shaker full, but the way he said her name, I took it they were closer than friends, if you know what I mean."

That's consistent with what I felt after seeing Tom and Kelly together at Tom's reception.

Charles swiped a bug away from his face then said, "Do you think Tom and Kelly are having a thing?"

"Charles, I've already told Chris this, but one of the reason's I'm living in an apartment the size of a wasp nest instead of a mansion is because I managed to lose a Fort Knox load of money gambling. For that reason, I'll refrain from saying if I was a betting man, I'd put money on it."

I said, "Does that mean you think Kelly poisoned Gary so they could be together?"

"Wouldn't rule it out."

I would. If Kelly poisoned Gary, there would've been an excellent chance Tom would've been killed in the crash. I pointed that out to Virgil.

"That's something to think about," he said as he once again removed his sunglasses while wiping his brow. He returned the glasses to his face before continuing, "There's something else. Not only did I accidentally on purpose run into Tom, I saw Richard Haymaker in Bert's. I already knew him, so I didn't have to use the ruse I used on Tom. He was buying milk for the twins. He said they were driving Charlene Beth crazy. He wondered if he should get some tranquilizer to put in the milk to calm the kids and his wife's nerves. He was joking. Anyway, he asked how I liked the apartment, liked living on Folly. I told him the apartment was good, Folly was fine, blah, blah, blah. It didn't get interesting until we started talking about the crash. Know what he said?"

We said no.

"Get this, Richard told me Gary was poisoned, no news there, but he said the poison was in Gary's drink, that someone must've put it there before Gary put the cooler on the plane. Here's where it gets interesting. He said the cooler had been in the hangar at the airport and he knew several people were in there."

"How'd Richard know that?" I asked. "My understanding is he, Mark, and Tom arrived late, with Gary and the cooler already onboard."

"Richard told me Gary told him it was busy that morning, that he was surprised to see someone he thought he recognized in the lot."

"Who?"

"Didn't say. He started talking to the air traffic controller." He shook his head. "Gary didn't say anything else about it before he dropped dead."

I said, "Did Richard say if he saw anyone familiar when he arrived?"

"Holy moly, I'm going to be a good detective," Virgil said, before fist bumping me. "That's the same question I asked him. Near word for word."

Charles looked at Virgil like he was ready to fist bump him in the head. "Did he?"

Virgil said, "Did he what?"

Before Charles went for Virgil's throat, I said, "Did Richard say he recognized anybody at the airport."

"No."

That was an indication Virgil was becoming as good a detective as Charles.

"Learn anything else?" I asked.

"To be as good a detective as you two, I'll have to learn how to be sneaky asking questions. You know, so the other person doesn't know what I'm doing. Don't think I'm there yet."

Charles frowned at Virgil. "Did you learn anything else or not?"

"That's all," he said. "Knew you'd want to hear about my conversations with both survivors. What's our next step?"

For him to step off the pier into the river was my first thought. I held my tongue, thanked him for sharing what he'd learned. I also hinted I'd tell Chief LaMond, although I had no idea what he'd said worth sharing.

"That's a good start. Give me a holler if you think of anything else I can do to help catch the killer."

I said I would, leaving out when hell freezes over.

"I've taken up enough of your time." Virgil started walking away. He stopped, pivoted, then said, "I've been thinking. Nobody knows who the killer wanted dead. If Gary or Mark weren't the target, it's Richard or Tom."

"Yes," Charles said, showing more interest than irritation with Virgil.

"So," Virgil said, "seems somebody desperate enough to crash an entire airplane to kill someone is mighty desperate. If the person he or she wanted dead is Richard or Tom, they'll try again." He put his hand up to eye level, palm facing Charles and me. "That's only my theory. I'm not a great detective like you."

That was about the only thing Virgil had said that made sense, that is, until he got to the part about us being great detectives. I told him I agreed that Richard or Tom could be in danger.

"When you're talking with the Chief, you better ought to let her know." He walked away.

21

We remained on the pier. Charles appeared more fascinated with a fishing boat as it passed under the bridge than talking. He hadn't spoken for fifteen minutes, rare for my friend, so I asked what was bothering him.

Charles shook his head like I'd awakened him from a trance then looked in the direction that Virgil had gone. "Here I am, a detective, now look what happens. I've been so caught up in how Richard and Tom survived the crash I didn't consider one or both could be in danger. Then Virgil comes along, figures it out."

During my many decades on this earth, I'd never been able to explain how televisions get a picture into my living room, how we can be heated by a sun that's 92.96 million miles away, or why God created mosquitos. I have also never been able to explain to Charles he is not, never has been, never will be a private detective. Like my other unexplainables, I'd stopped trying.

"Charles, Virgil could be right. There's no way to know if anyone else is in danger. Virgil was stating the obvious, something we knew."

He slowly shook his head. "That's my point, Chris. I didn't think about it. How stupid can I be?"

I didn't want to say anything that'd send my friend further down the rabbit hole. Heather, his long-term girlfriend, left Folly a year ago leaving Charles a note asking him not to try to find her. He'd planned to propose the next day. Since then, he's been moody, more negative, less inclined to find the good in everyone, something that'd been one of his most enduring qualities.

"Charles, it may not have been something you'd given a lot of thought to, but we knew it was a possibility."

He looked at the deck. "If you say so."

"Charles, I'm going to let Cindy know what Virgil said about someone being at the airport Gary recognized. Want me to call her now or later?"

He nodded toward the pocket holding my phone.

"Hi, Chief. How are you this lovely day?"

"It's not bad for a change. What are you going to say to ruin it?"

"I'm with Charles—"

"That's the perfect recipe for ruining my day."

I put the phone on speaker and said, "Two things. First we were wondering if you or Detective Callahan learned anything new about the crash?"

"Yes. What's the second thing?"

Charles leaned close to the phone and said, "Whoa, Chief. Yes what?"

"Hello to you too, Charles. I'm glad you haven't lost your hearing in old age. Where are you?"

I told her. She said for us to stay put, she'd see us in ten minutes. I took it as a sign she had more to share, not that she was excited about seeing us.

A handful of minutes later, the Chief's pickup pulled in a parking space at the edge of the park.

Before she made her way to the table we'd moved to, Charles said, "What've you learned?"

She sighed. "Move over. Let these tired but much younger than your legs get a break."

Charles scooted while repeating his question.

"You didn't hear this from me. Callahan told me Tom Kale has a two-million-dollar life insurance policy."

Charles whistled.

"Hubby better not ever get that big a policy," Cindy said. "I'd bump him off in a heartbeat. Whoops, that's the second thing you didn't hear from me."

Cindy and Larry are the happiest married couple I know. She was teasing, I hoped.

"Cindy," I said. "Tom was divorced so who's the beneficiary?"

"Excellent question. He hasn't changed the beneficiary. It's still his ex, Alyssa."

Charles shook his head. "That's a humongous motive for her to poison the pilot."

"Guys, we have motives out the ear." She raised her forefinger. "Gary Isles' wife has a burr up her butt about him not letting her work. He had big bucks, most likely a large policy." She raised another finger. "Richard's wife Charlene Beth … Have I told you how people with double first names irritate me?"

I told her how Bob Howard had the same problem.

"Then, never mind. I don't want you to confuse me with your realtor friend. Anyway, Charlene Beth doesn't seem torn up about Gary and Mark being killed. When I was talking to her she tried to look lovey-dovey, cooing about how great it was Richard survived. She was as sincere as a used car salesman. Granted, that ain't much of a motive, but in my eyes it's a glimmer of one. Then add Alyssa Kale's two-million-dollar motive." She shook her head. "Mark Jamison is the only person on the plane who didn't have someone with a motive to kill him, or someone we didn't know about."

"Let me add something to Charlene Beth's possible motive." I shared what Bob Howard had told me about the rumor that Charlene Beth was having an affair.

"Interesting, I'll share that with Callahan," she said. "One of these days I'll give you a Deputy Dog detective badge."

Charles waved his hand in Cindy's face. "Me, too?"

She put her hand over her face and mumbled. "Why not?"

"What next, Chief?" I asked.

"Crap on a cupcake, Chris. We don't even know the intended victim."

I'd nearly forgotten the main thing I wanted to tell her.

"You know anything about Virgil Debonnet you didn't share with me in the Dog?"

Cindy looked at me like I was trying to trick her. "Other than he's the millionaire who slipped to a dollaraire?"

I said, "Anything else?"

"Not much. He's not been arrested. He's not been in any trouble I'm aware of. He does strike me as odd. If I was rich, yes, I'm dreaming, and lost it all, I'd be a holy terror, mad at the world, sucky miserable. Not Virgil. He's nonchalant about his new state of poverty. I wouldn't say he's happy about it, but he ain't outwardly pissed. Odd."

I agreed.

She said, "What about him?"

I shared what he'd told us about the pilot seeing a familiar person at the airport and Gary was the only one of the four on the plane who had access to the cooler.

"How is it you know Virgil enough to be sharing information about the plane and its passengers?"

I told her how he'd approached me saying he wanted to be a detective, how he could join Charles and me to find out who killed the pilot.

Cindy frowned. "Odd and delusional."

A voice from Cindy's radio disrupted our conversation. "Chief, we've got a 10-57 in the three-hundred block of East Huron. We're rolling police and fire."

Cindy keyed her mic. "Donna, speak English. You know I'll never learn all those codes."

"Sorry, Chief. Hit-and-run. Car versus pedestrian. That's all I know."

Cindy thanked the dispatcher for the translation then told us she had to go.

Charles yelled to her as she headed to her vehicle. "Let us know what happened."

"Big N. Big O."

He turned to me. "Should we follow her?"

"You want to jog after her truck?"

Sirens began filling the air. The three-hundred block of East Huron was four long blocks from our location. After considerable back and forth, I agreed we could walk that way to see what happened. Besides, I couldn't have convinced my friend not to go, and the walk would do me good.

22

East Huron is a narrow residential street a block from houses backing up to the Folly River. Many of the structures predated Hurricane Hugo that devastated the island in 1989. There were no sidewalks, so we moved off the road three times to allow emergency vehicles to pass. A patrol car had the road blocked at the intersection of Third Street East and Officer Allen Spencer was detouring traffic onto the perpendicular street. I'd known Allen since I arrived on Folly. He was new to the force at the time, so we had several conversations about Folly's character and characters.

I asked what happened.

"Don't know much. I was third on the scene, asked to stop traffic. Apparently, a man was walking east on Huron and struck from behind."

"What's his condition?"

"Bad, I think."

To echo that opinion, a Charleston County ambulance, siren screaming, pulled up behind the cruiser. Allen rushed to move his car so the emergency vehicle could head to the hospital. We waited for the officer to once again block the road. East Huron was a lightly travelled street, so Allen had little to do except talk.

"Anybody see it happen?" I asked.

"Don't know. Our guys are canvassing the houses to see if anyone saw anything."

"The driver skedaddled?" Charles said.

Allen nodded.

I pointed in the direction of the multiple emergency vehicles. "The Chief back there?"

"Yes, but if I were you, I'd stay clear. You know how she gets at scenes where bad stuff happened."

"Good point, Allen. I'll get with her later."

A car pulled up to the cruiser. The driver said he lived two houses down and needed to get home. That was well before the scene of the incident, so Allen moved his car to let the resident through. Charles and I headed toward the center of town where I would turn left to go home. Charles stopped before going the other direction to his apartment. He said, "So when are you going to call Cindy?"

I told him I didn't know but it wouldn't be until much later to give her time to do her thing at the scene.

"Okay," Charles said, "Call me in an hour with what she told you."

Only Charles would interpret "much later" as an hour. I limited my response to, "Okay."

***

I DIDN'T HAVE to call Cindy since she called at seven-thirty that evening. It was the third call I'd received. As anyone who knows him could've guessed, the first two were from Charles wanting to know why I was taking so long to call the Chief.

"Good evening, Cindy."

"You're not going to believe this," she said as a nonsensical, although typical opening by my friends.

"Try me."

"Know who got hit?"

I'd been home since leaving Charles, so I hadn't heard anything about the hit and run. "Who?"

"Who were we talking about when I got the call?"

I drew a blank, then it struck me. "Virgil."

"Bingo."

"Is he alive?"

"Barely."

"What happened?"

"He was walking out East Huron, then he was flying through the air over East Huron, vehicle propelled. Don't ask, we don't know what kind of vehicle, nor do we know who was driving."

"Nobody saw it happen?"

"I suppose the driver did. No one else we've found. None of the residents were outside, no other cars were driving by. Crap, there wasn't even a nosy grandma sitting in a rocking chair staring out her window like you see on television shows. All we know from seeing the condition of Mr. Debonnet is that somewhere there's a vehicle with a serious dent in its front end."

"Could you tell if it was an accident or if he was hit on purpose?"

"It looks like he was on the edge of the road, so I wouldn't rule out intentional."

"You said he was barely alive. What'd that mean?"

"The EMTs who hauled him off said he was breathing, but from the number of broken bones, suspected internal injuries. His age plus apparent good physical condition could help him, although I wouldn't put money on it." Cindy paused, and I heard someone speaking in the background. She returned to the phone. "Larry's here so I have to play housewife. As you know, I'm as good at that as I am at wrestling alligators."

"One more thing," I said. "Does anyone know Virgil is in the hospital?"

"Other than the person who sent him flying?"

"Yes."

"Don't think so. He had a wallet on him, but no next of kin or emergency contact was listed. You told me he knew the Haymakers, so I contacted Charlene Beth."

"And?"

"She checked her records but couldn't find contact information on his ex-spouse. She thinks the ex moved back to Boston, or some other snooty city, but didn't know anything else."

"Will you call me if you learn anything about his condition?"

"Chris, you know I live to keep you informed."

She was being sarcastic. I thanked her anyway.

Now to call Charles.

23

I spent the next two days working on taxes, an annual event where I'm traumatized by how much money the government wants, no, demands, this aging, retired, non-producing member of society to send them simply for existing. To show how traumatizing the exercise is, I stopped twice to clean the house which, next to swimming with the sharks, is one of my least favorite activities. Charles had been surprisingly quiet. Since I called him after my talk with Cindy, I hadn't heard from him.

The person I did hear from with two calls was Cal, more calls than I'd received from him in the last five years. He vacillated between being thrilled having his middle-aged son in his life and overwhelmed by having Junior here. Cal needed a willing ear to listen to his varied emotions and reactions. I'd become that ear.

I spent little time thinking about the plane crash because if I had I'd have been lost in a maze of confusion. Who was the intended victim? Without knowing that, how could anyone determine who poisoned the pilot? Then, if Richard or Tom, the two survivors, had been the person the killer was wanting dead, was one or both in danger? Finally, how did Virgil fit into the equation? Or, did he? Was his near-death experience a result of talking to Richard or Tom? Or, was it simply a tragic accident caused by someone not paying attention then panicking after hitting him?

A call from Cindy didn't answer any of the questions although it was encouraging about Virgil. His condition had improved. Unless something unexpected occurred, he'd live. She reported he had more broken bones than if he'd fallen from a satellite, an exaggeration I suspected. He was lucid enough to tell her he'd been minding his business while strolling down the road when clobbered. He saw nothing except his life flashing before his eyes. She ended by telling me not to visit him, especially to keep my buddy Charles from invading the hospital. I assured her I'd wait until she said it was okay to visit. I wisely didn't comment on my ability to stop Charles.

Another day passed, then I received a hushed call. "Chris, this is Cal, Sorry to whisper. Can you hear me?"

"Yes. Why are you whispering?"

"Don't want Junior hearing. He's poking around somewhere."

"What's up?"

"Think you can stop by the bar this afternoon around two?"

Let's see, finish my taxes, do more cleaning, or visit Cal's?

"I'll be there."

The weather was nice, so I walked. I was a few minutes early when I saw Junior leaving through the side door. I waited until he was out of sight before going in.

Johnny Cash's version of "Ring of Fire" was playing, the lone customer was leaning on the bar staring at a half empty bottle of Budweiser. Cal was at the jukebox punching numbers. I smiled at his sartorial splendor. He wore his Stetson, a green and red striped polo shirt, and blue jogging shorts. He saw me, pointed to the table farthest from the bar, and asked the customer if he needed anything. The customer looked content staring at his beer as he told Cal he'd yell if he needed another.

Cal plopped down on the chair opposite me so hard I was afraid it'd collapse. It didn't, so I said, "You okay?"

From the jukebox, another Cal, Cal Smith, started telling a story about being a "Country Bumpkin."

He glanced at the customer and leaned closer to me. "No."

That much I could tell. "What's wrong?"

"Junior."

"What about him?"

"Don't get me wrong, pard, it's wonderful having him around. I'm still adjusting to having an offspring. Junior found himself an apartment, so he didn't have to bunk in my hole in the wall. If he had, one of us would be dead by now."

I still hadn't heard what was wrong. "What's the problem?"

Cal waved his arm around the room. "Remember when I took over this place?"

How could I forget? He'd been performing here when it was GB's. The owner, Gregory Brile, then rudely murdered a local attorney resulting in an all-expense paid, thirty-year, vacation in prison. Cal, who knew as much about running a bar as a housefly knows about driving a Mack truck, took over, stumbled through learning pains, and now managed running a profitable business.

"Sure."

He sniffed. "Take a whiff."

I followed his lead.

He smiled. "Smell stale beer and burgers?"

I said I did.

"See the classic, raveling carpet? How about these table and chairs? Do they ever have stories to tell." He patted the back of the chair next to him. "How about that old Wurlitzer? Listen to old George moaning about how 'She Thinks I Still Care.'"

Somewhere in there was a reason for me being here. Unlike Charles, I waited for Cal to share what it was.

"Chris, my friend, this here is the quinty, umm, what's the word?"

I guessed, "Quintessential?"

"Yeah, that's it. Cal's is the quintessential country music bar, yes, it is."

"Let me guess," I said. "Junior owned a chain of restaurants. He knows more than a thing or two about the restaurant and bar business." Cal nodded so I figured I was on the right track. "He thinks you ought to change some things."

Cal looked at the ceiling then back at me. "Some? Hell, he wants what those TV shows call a total makeover." He turned and pointed toward the tiny kitchen. "He wants to knock out a wall, enlarge the kitchen, expand the menu. Chris, can you see us selling chicken cordon bleu or steak with bacon on it?"

I choked back a smile. "No."

"That's right. He wants me to mosey over to the bank, borrow money, buy new tables and chairs." He shook the tabletop. "Get this, he wants me to start selling craft beer. I don't even know what it is."

"What'd you tell him?"

"Here's the biggy," Cal said, ignoring my question. "Junior wants me to put some new songs on the jukebox. By new he don't mean old songs that ain't on the jukebox, but that country crap youngsters listen to nowadays. Can you believe that?"

If Cal hadn't heard a song before 1980, it wasn't on his Wurlitzer.

I tried again. "What'd you tell him?"

"Chris, the only thing we agreed on was the walls could use some paint."

The paint-chipped walls hadn't received attention in twenty years. They were dirty, coated with aromas of food, and dried beer.

"It's good you could agree on that. What about the other stuff?"

"Told him I'd ponder it. Didn't tell him I'd pondered it for about three seconds after he brought it up. Rejected the hell out of them. Haven't worked up the nerve to tell him. He's my kid so I don't want to discourage him."

"Cal, he's not a little boy, he's in his fifties. This is your place. The quicker you get it over with the better."

"I know. Needed someone I trust to tell me. Thanks, pard." Cal snapped his fingers. "I'm being inhospitable. Let me get you a glass of wine. I think I could use a Bud myself. I'm plum out of craft beer."

He smiled, a good sign I thought, as Roger Miller sang "When Two Worlds Collide."

Cal slid another Budweiser in front of his customer at the bar before returning with my wine and his non-craft beer.

"Figured out who snuffed Gary Isles?"

I would've rather talked more about Junior than the plane crash.

"No."

"Want to know what I heard?"

I channeled Charles. "Sure."

"I hear Tom Kale's ex, Alice, is pissed that her ex survived."

"Her name's Alyssa," I said, continuing to channel Charles. "Who said that?"

"Denton, a semi regular. He has a few, quite a few, bucks. He's heavy in the stock market. Seems that Alice, umm, Alyssa is his broker. He was talking to her the other day. He told her he was glad Tom survived. Know what she told him?"

I didn't.

"She said, 'I guess.'"

"That's not enthusiastic but doesn't mean she's pissed."

"Denton said it was how she said it. He was surprised. Anyway, I figured you'd want to know since no matter how many times you claim it ain't so, you're trying to figure it out."

I took a gulp of wine, changed the subject, and didn't give another thought to the plane crash until Cal said something about a group of locals who'd wandered in recently who were becoming regulars. I didn't recognize the names until he said Virgil.

I stopped him mid-sentence. "Virgil Debonnet?"

"I'm not big on last names. There've been a few times I couldn't remember mine. If he's to be believed, he was rich, now he ain't. I figured you'd know him or knew about him since you know about all the bad stuff that happens here. He's the guy smacked by the car."

"That's Virgil Debonnet. What do you know about him?"

"Just told you."

"I meant anything other than he used to be rich and was victim of a hit-and-run?"

Cal took a sip of beer, looked to see if his bar customer needed anything, then said, "Now that I think about it, there is something you might be interested in. The night before he was hit, he was here talking to a gaggle of guys. I heard him say something like he was figuring out who caused the plane crash." Cal paused then nodded like that was all.

And Cal didn't think that was important enough to mention first?

"Did he say he was figuring out who caused it or was trying to figure out who?"

"Ain't that the same thing?"

"Not exactly. If he said he was figuring it out, he may have a good idea who it was."

Cal removed his Stetson and scratched the back of his head. "I don't know anything about them puny differences. Besides, I was behind the bar trying to get a customer to pay his tab. I wasn't concentrating on everything Virgil said."

"Remember who he was talking to?"

"Nope. It was that group of new customers."

"Remember anything else he said?"

"No, but he must've been saying something funny. Guys around him kept laughing, patting him on the back. One of them picked up his tab. I hope he gets okay. I like customers who make people laugh, make people feel good." He rubbed his chin. "Could be because I'm a fossil, but it seems folks used to have a better time in the old days. Now everybody's all serious, uptight, griping about everything. Gripe, gripe, gripe."

Four men entered the bar and Cal said, "Gotta get back to work. Thanks for kicking my butt into action. I'll tell Junior I love him, but to get his nose out of my business."

I wished him luck.

I left Cal's with Eddy Arnold singing "Make the World Go Away."

24

Five more days passed before Cindy let me know Virgil had improved enough to have visitors. Fifteen minutes and a phone call to Charles later, he and I were on our way to the hospital on the outskirts of downtown Charleston. A helpful nurse told us where we could find our new friend but encouraged us to limit our visit. She shared he was doing much better than when he arrived but wasn't ready to run a marathon. A glance in his room told me he not only wasn't ready to run a marathon but wasn't ready to sit without the aid of a forklift. *Mummy* was the word that came to mind. Except for a few square inches of actual Virgil, his body was wrapped in either gauze or a plaster cast. His left leg was elevated and held in place by a gadget suspended from a stainless-steel bracket. I barely recognized him, not just because of the white covering, but because he wasn't wearing sunglasses. He was in a double room in the bed closest to the door. The curtain was pulled so I couldn't see if he had a roommate.

Virgil's eyes were closed. I moved closer to the bed and whispered, "Virgil, you awake?"

He blinked several times, probably because of the non-sunglasses unfiltered light. He said, "Hey, Chris, how're you doing?"

An interesting question considering his condition. "Fine." I tilted my head, something I doubted Virgil could do, toward Charles. "You remember Charles, don't you?"

Virgil's head didn't move, but his eyes shifted in Charles's direction. "Hi, Charles. What brings you two to this cheery place?"

I told him we'd come to see him, he said he was honored, and for us to pull up chairs. There was one chair on Virgil's side of the curtain, so I motioned for Charles to sit. Virgil told me to grab a chair from the other side of the room, adding the man over there hasn't had a visitor for days. The chair was going to waste.

I maneuvered the chair to Virgil's side of the room then asked how he was doing.

He smiled. "Know how many places itch every day, places you can't scratch because of this clunky cast?"

I knew what he meant and nodded. Charles, the collector of all things trivia and unimportant, said, "How many?"

"A bunch."

I hoped that was good enough for Charles. In case it wasn't, I asked Virgil if he knew how much longer he'd be in the hospital.

"The docs said I was better than I look with all this crap wrapped around me. They also said I was lucky. I asked how much worse I could look if I wasn't lucky. One of them, think he's from India, gave me a lengthy answer in medical gobbledygook. I understood two of the hundreds of words he spewed. A doc from around these parts tapped on the cast on my leg and said that if I was worse, I'd be all spiffed-out in a suit, resting in a coffin. That I understood."

"Virgil," Charles said, "I believe I heard Chris ask how much longer you'd be here?"

"If I knew, I wouldn't have hopped over to talking about what the docs said. My friend, I don't know."

I remembered Cindy had said he hadn't remembered anything about being hit. That was more than a week ago when he'd told her. Was more coming back to him?

"Virgil, tell us what happened."

He blinked a couple more times. "Can't tell you much. I remember talking to you in that park, then heading out Huron. I haven't been on

Folly long, but long enough to know many roads are narrow, there aren't many sidewalks. To be safe, I walked as far on the edge of the road as possible. Ha, see how much good that did? Anyway, speeders can be a problem. I'd heard that more than one person had been killed walking along the streets."

Charles interrupted, "That's true. Chris was with someone who—"

"Charles," I said, interrupting the interrupter, "let Virgil finish."

"Sorry. Go ahead, Virgil."

"I'm afraid I can't add much. The car, truck, bus, boat, train, whatever hit me from behind. I never heard it coming. Smack! The next thing I remember was waking up somewhere in this building with lights the size of searchlights glaring down at me."

"You're fortunate to be alive," I said, stating the obvious. "Do you think the vehicle hit you on purpose?"

"Don't know. I was on the side of the road so whoever it was had to be drunk, texting, or falling asleep and weaved over to where I was. I heard he didn't have the courtesy to stop."

"Or intentionally ran you down," Charles added.

Virgil hesitated, then said, "Why? I don't know many folks on Folly. I'm not having an affair with anyone's wife. I'm not working for the IRS, not working at all, for that matter. Hell, I think I'm a pretty nice fellow."

A pretty nice fellow who's been asking questions about the plane crash, I thought. "Virgil," I said, "Cal told me you were in his bar talking to a group of men about how you either were figuring out or had figured out who poisoned the pilot. What was that about?"

"Don't remember saying anything like that. Heck, I don't even remember being in Cal's. My memory is sort of fuzzy these days. Think it's the drugs they're pumping in me."

I said, "Do you remember much that was said when you talked with Richard and Tom? In other words, could they have thought you were questioning them about the crash?"

"You mean like I suspected one of them of the poisoning?"

I nodded.

"Nah, that's what I was trying to figure out, but I was sneaky about how I was beating around that bush. They wouldn't have figured it out."

I wasn't sure about that. "Had you talked to anyone else about the crash?"

"Chris, I may be drip-drip, getting drugs, drip-drip into my body, and may not be catching what you're hinting at. Are you saying one of them tried to kill me because I was getting close to learning who killed the pilot?"

"Yes."

"Wow, umm, wow. That's scary."

"Virgil," I said, "it's a thought. It could also have been nothing more than an accident."

He laughed, something I couldn't imagine doing if I was in his condition. "Suppose I should be happy if someone did all this by accident."

Charles smiled. "You bet."

"Virgil," I said, "we'd better be going. The nurse told us to keep our visit short." I stood; Charles followed suit.

"Oh," Virgil said, "speaking of the crash, I nearly forgot, the day before I got smacked, I ran into Kelly, you know, Gary's wife, at Bert's. One of the clerks pointed her out. She was buying a package of bologna. I sidled up to her and told her how sorry I was about her loss. She gave me a funny look like she didn't know who I was. Natural, I suppose, since she didn't know who I was. I introduced myself then told her again how sorry I was."

"That was nice of you," I said, wondering how he remembered that but not his conversation in Cal's.

"Yeah, I told her it was terrible about what happened, that I was working on helping find out who poisoned her husband. I figured that'd give her hope."

I figuratively rolled my eyes. If Virgil had been that obvious with Richard, Tom, or others, it was becoming clear his accident was no accident.

I asked, "What did she say?"

"She smiled and said that was nice. She asked me to remind her what my name was then wanted to know if I lived on Folly. I told her. She said she was glad to meet me. I think I cheered her up."

And if she happened to be the person who poisoned her husband, he'd given her a reason to run him down.

We told him we were glad he was doing better. On our way to the door, Virgil said, "Before you go, would you check and see if my Guccis are with my clothes? We've been together for a lot of shoe leather."

They were. He exhaled a sigh of relief.

25

Caldwell Ramsey called the next morning to ask if I could meet him for lunch at Planet Follywood. It was the first time he'd invited me to lunch, so I was intrigued enough to say, "What time?"

Planet Follywood was one of the island's more established restaurants. In addition to good food, it was known by many as the restaurant with a large, painted mural covering an exterior wall with images of famous entertainers ranging from Elvis, Marilyn Monroe, Sammy Davis Jr., to John Wayne. I walked to the Center Street restaurant and was pleased to see Caldwell seated at a table along the side of the room. He wasn't hard to spot since he was six foot six-inches tall and African American, both traits in short supply on Folly.

He saw me enter, stood, and said, "Chris, glad you could make it."

Caldwell was in his mid-fifties, trim, his short, black hair had patches of gray sprinkled in. He'd played basketball for Clemson in the eighties and looked like he could still compete.

"Thanks for the invitation. Why didn't Mel come with you?"

Caldwell laughed. "He told me he's sick of talking to you, that he'd rather watch soaps."

I chuckled knowing that wasn't true. "Tell him I said the same."

"Good. With the love messages out of the way, let me tell you why

I asked you to lunch. I was nearby meeting a couple wanting to open a bar. They wanted my advice on what kind of acts they should hire to play weekends."

Caldwell was a music promoter and worked with several bars and concert venues.

"It's not on Folly, is it? There are enough bars here."

"No, it's three miles up Folly Road. Besides, I don't know if they have the capital to pull it off. Anyway, that's not why I called."

A server appeared to ask if we wanted drinks. Caldwell said beer, I chose iced tea.

He watched her go then said, "Mel told me you were asking about Mark Jamison's significant other."

"Kevin Robbins."

"Yes. I would've gotten back with you sooner, but I was in Atlanta at an event planners' meeting for a week after the plane crash. To be honest, I was so busy when I got back, I forgot Mel wanted me to talk to you. Sorry."

Caldwell was as opposite Mel as two men can be. The word sorry wouldn't leave Mel's mouth unless he was threatened with severe bodily harm. Even then, it would be surrounded by profanities.

"That's okay. Mel said you knew Kevin fairly well."

"Wouldn't go that far. We spent several hours together at Connections, a bar in Charleston. Mel kept getting into pity-party discussions with Mark bemoaning how bad business was. Mark owned a trucking company. When they went on a tirade about poor business, I was left talking to Kevin. I never saw or talked to him outside the bar. Mel said you were butting in police business. He didn't say it that politely."

"That I figured, but I'm not butting in. I'm curious about what happened."

"I doubt I can offer anything helpful."

"Did Kevin and Mark get along?"

Our drinks arrived. Caldwell ordered a chef salad, one reason for his trim physique; I asked for the American burger, a reason for my not-so-trim physique.

Caldwell asked me to repeat the question.

I said, "Did they have problems you heard about?"

"I don't know if it was a problem as such. Kevin makes good money as a pharmacist. Whenever Mark started talking about the trials and tribulations of his trucking business, Kevin would throw in something about how Mark should find something to do that had a steady paycheck. He wasn't mean when he said it, but if I heard it once, I heard it a dozen times. I don't know about Mark, but I would've been pissed listening to it over and over."

"How did Mark react?"

"He changed the subject. That's when he and Mel huddled and griped to each other leaving me with Kevin."

"Was Kevin covering most of their expenses?"

"I don't know about their living expenses, they have a house north of the city, but he always picked up the tab in Connections."

"Could Kevin have been angry enough with Mark to poison the pilot hoping the crash would kill Mark?"

Caldwell looked toward the exit then down in his beer before saying, "I've given a lot of thought about it since Mel said you were asking. Kevin's a pharmacist, so he'd know how to poison the pilot. He was often irritated with Mark. I don't know if this means anything or not, one night after a few drinks they were carping about something when Mark said something like, 'You'd be better off with me dead.'"

"What'd he mean?"

"Nothing was said then. I remember another night they were talking about something called a key man insurance policy he had through the company. I don't know if that's what he meant."

From working in a human resources department, I knew a key man policy was often taken on top-level executives by a company listing the business as beneficiary in case something happened to the valued, or key employee. In this case, the trucking company, MJ Transport, would get the proceeds from the policy.

"Caldwell, do you happen to know what happens to the trucking company now that Mark's gone?"

"Kevin would get it since they were legally married. I know they'd worked with an attorney on all that stuff because one night Kevin complained about paying the lawyer. Chris, do you think that was enough to kill an innocent man over?" He glanced in his beer. "It could've been three innocent men?"

"Don't know."

Food arrived, and Caldwell suggested we talk about something more pleasant. I switched to asking him about business. He shared a couple of humorous stories, one about a band from California a competing promoter had scheduled for a couple of Charleston venues and how the band had flown to Charleston, West Virginia, instead. After the promoter finally caught up with them, the lead singer said all he knew about Charleston was it's a dance. He didn't know the difference between Charleston, West Virginia and our city. The venue's owner is now booking acts through Caldwell.

I asked how Mel was doing. Caldwell said he was as bad-tempered, cranky, and boorish as ever.

"So, he's doing fine."

"Couldn't be better. In fact, I'm meeting him after lunch. We're going shopping."

"He need more camo pants?"

Caldwell laughed. Woodland camp field pants were to Mel as shorts were to most everyone on Folly in the summer. "I think twenty-three of them is enough. No, he lost his Semper Fi cap to a brisk wind on the marsh the other day."

"Good luck finding one like it," I said, then saw Charles waving for me at the entry. I told Caldwell I'd be back and walked over to Charles.

He looked at Caldwell, turned to me. "How much longer are you going to be?"

"Not much. Why?"

Charles tapped his temple with his forefinger. "My head's about to explode about the plane crash. Figured we needed to talk it out. Tell you what, I'll be on the Pier. Head that way when you're done."

Charles hadn't come in and interjected himself in my conversation with Caldwell, so I knew his head was truly spinning. I said I'd see him at the Pier.

26

I found Charles on the far end of the Folly Pier leaning back on a wood bench shaded by the diamond-shaped second level of the iconic structure. His Tilley was pulled down over his eyes. His head exploding hadn't kept him from napping. I joined him on the bench and watched three fishermen tending to their fishing gear while carrying on an animated conversation.

Charles jerked his head up knocking his Tilley to the deck. He picked it up, returned it to his head. "Woah, how long have you been here?"

"Not long. Enjoy your nap?"

"Pondering, not sleeping."

"If you say so. Tell me about your head exploding."

He glanced at the fishermen then at the deck. "Chris, remember the last few times we've helped the cops?"

"Of course."

"What'd they have in common?"

I smiled. "Other than nearly getting me killed?"

"Something more important."

"I thought that was important."

He rubbed his chin. "Other than that, what did they have in common?"

"You tell me."

"Everyone knew who the killer kilt."

I nodded. "Now we have two dead bodies, four potential victims."

He used his Tilley like a fan and waved it in his face. "Chris, how in red, white, and blue blazes are we supposed to learn who the killer is if we don't know who was supposed to be killed?"

I didn't offer we'd already talked about that plus we weren't supposed to help catch anyone. Another reason I didn't tell him was because I hated to admit it, but I agreed. We were there when the crash occurred. It came close to adding us to the list of bodies. Now Virgil was nearly killed. Granted, he's not a close friend, but someone who's latched onto us, who's taken an interest in the crash. I also reminded myself he was a suspect until he was run down.

"Charles, I suppose the most logical intended victim was the pilot, Gary Isles. It was his cooler the poisoned drink was in. Regardless of the results of the crash, Gary wouldn't have survived."

"If it was him, the best suspect would be his wife, so what would've been Kelly's motive?"

"It's possible that she resented him for having to leave the law firm because of its rule about wives of their attorneys working there. I know it'd irritate me. Or, it simply could've been for his life insurance."

"Yeah," Charles said, "another thing, and it's mere speculation on my part, but remember how close she was with Tom Kale at the party they had for us?"

"Sure, but they were neighbors, well, almost neighbors, and she'd lost her husband. Maybe Tom is a sensitive guy who wanted to comfort widow Kelly."

"My gut tells me it's more."

I said, "Charles, we've been over this. If she and Tom were having an affair, why would she have poisoned her husband when she knew Tom would be in the plane?"

"True." Charles nodded his head left, then right. "Okay, let's say

Kelly did it because she resented not being able to work for the snooty law firm or for the insurance. Why would she endanger the lives of three others if all she wanted to do was to bump off her husband?"

"It seems unlikely. She would've had numerous chances to kill him over the years. I'm leaning toward eliminating Gary as the intended victim."

Charles said, "One down, three to go. My head's still exploding. What about the other guy who didn't survive?"

"Mark Jamison," I said. "Let me tell you what Caldwell shared." I proceeded to give him the highlights of the luncheon conversation.

Charles glared at me. "Why didn't you say that before you started talking about Gary Isles, before letting me go off on a tangent about him being the intended victim?"

"Charles, have you ever stood in a field and tried to stop a charging buffalo?"

"Can't say I have. Why?"

"If I started with telling you what Caldwell said, you'd be like that buffalo. I wouldn't have a chance to slow you much less stop you long enough to talk about the other possible killers."

"I'm confused. Are you saying that because Mark's spouse, Kevin, had an excellent motive for wanting Mark dead, Kelly didn't do it?"

"No," I shook my head. "I'd put Kevin near the top of the list, but not there alone. If I told you what Caldwell said, I was afraid it'd cloud our, your thinking."

"You don't give me much credit." He sighed. "You're right though. I suppose you want to talk about the others on the plane as the possible target."

"Yes. Let's take Richard Haymaker next. Who could've wanted him dead?"

"His wife."

I said yes before telling him what Bob Howard had told me about Charlene Beth, how much he hated double first names, about her alleged affair with Walter Middleton Gibbs.

Charles grinned then said, "So you think she tried to kill her husband because Bob Howard has a thing against double first names?"

I rolled my eyes. "If she's having an affair, she may've wanted her spouse out of the way."

"Okay, so let's add Charlene Beth to the list. What about Leroy Jethro Gibbs, the guy she's supposed to be having the affair with?"

"It's Walter Middleton Gibbs. Leroy Jethro Gibbs is a character on *NCIS*."

"Whatever. It's a three-word, snooty-sounding name. Can we add him to the list?"

"It's your list. Let's talk about Tom Kale. Who'd have a motive to want him dead?"

"The only person I know of is his stockbroker ex-wife, Alyssa. Didn't you say she didn't seem too happy he survived?"

"Yes. Their divorce was highly contested, with the financial part still not finalized."

"A dead Tom Kale would finalize it. Sounds like motive to me."

"No argument there," I said. "Let me throw something else out. What if the killer is Virgil?"

"The Virgil who's in the hospital looking like a mummy with his appendages propped up in the air?"

"Yes."

"You think he poisoned the pilot, killed two people, then ran himself down to make it look like someone wanted him dead?"

"No. What if his accident was simply that, having nothing to do with the plane crash? It's bothered me how he's wiggled his way into our lives wanting to help catch the killer. Why would he do that?"

Charles hesitated, then said, "To learn what we know about the murder; to know if we're getting close to him as a suspect?"

"Yes. What other reason would he have to get involved?"

"He finds me charming, personable, an outstanding detective. He wants to learn from the best."

That earned a second eye roll. "I'll stick to my first reason. He wants to see what we know."

"For sake of argument, I'll add him to the list. Anyone else?"

"Our problem is we know little about the passengers. There could be, and probably are, others who had a motive for poisoning the pilot."

Charles blinked twice and put his forefinger in the air. "So, our suspects are Kelly Isles, Kevin Robbins, Charlene Beth, Walter Middleton, not Leroy Jethro, Gibbs, Alyssa Kale, and Virgil Debonnet. Oh yeah, to make it so much easier for us to figure out, add countless others we don't know about. That cover it?"

I nodded.

"That's four potential victims, five counting Virgil, six suspects we know about, plus a cast of thousands of others. See why my head's exploding?"

"Yes," I realized I shared that condition.

What I couldn't say was how we were going to learn the identity of the intended victim. Unless we did that, there was little chance of learning who poisoned the pilot.

We sat and stared at the breaking waves for thirty more minutes before deciding that there were no answers coming to us. We'd be better off in air-conditioned comfort.

27

Charles headed to his apartment and I was on the way home when I received a call from a number I didn't recognize. I was tempted to let it roll to voicemail until I realized it may be Virgil.

Wrong.

"Chris, this is Tom Kale. Did I catch you at an inconvenient time?"

I told him no. I didn't share that his civil, thoughtful question was out of character for any of my friends.

"Could I impose on you to stop by the house?"

"When?"

"Within the hour if possible. I must attend a meeting in Mt. Pleasant and will need to leave in a couple hours."

I asked if fifteen minutes would be too soon. He said no.

A black Range Rover with temporary tags was parked in Tom's drive. I parked behind the impressive vehicle and Tom greeted me with a smile with Casper cradled in his arms. The stockbroker wore gray dress slacks and a white, button-down dress shirt. I felt underdressed in my tan shorts and orange polo shirt, yet despite my appearance he motioned me in as I made cooing sounds while Casper licked my cheek.

"Let's go to my office."

I followed him up the stairs as he remarked how the floating staircase was the main reason he bought the house. He'd told me the same thing the day of the reception. He pointed for me to be seated in front of one of the computer monitors, set Casper on the floor, then took a seat at the other monitor. I was again impressed by the expansive view of the coast, and curious about why I'd been invited.

"Thanks for coming," he said, not giving anything away.

I remained silent. It was his show.

"Chris, I've heard some disturbing news." He glanced out the window as his smile turned sour. He gripped the arm of the chair then turned to me. "It's come to my attention you and some of your friends have been nosing into the cause of the crash." He glared at me. "I find that inappropriate."

"Tom, Charles and I have—"

Tom waved his hand in my face. "I'm not finished." His grip on the chair with his other hand tightened. He continued giving me a menacing look. "You've accused my ex-wife of poisoning Gary in an effort to kill me." He slammed his other hand down on the chair arm. His mood change and action startled me. I remained silent. He continued, "That's ludicrous." He took a deep breath. "Then your friend Debonnet starts harassing my acquaintances spewing accusations about me and of all people Gary's widow. Where in the hell do you all get off butting in, sullying Alyssa and my name?"

I was shocked. He reminded me of one of those creatures in the movies that morphs from a friendly, cuddly animal to a fanged demon devouring its prey.

"Tom, I don't know what you've heard. I'm not doing anything to cause harm to you or your ex-wife. When my friend Charles and I learned Gary had been poisoned we were curious about what'd happened. You may not know, but I'm friends with Chief LaMond. I talked to her about the investigation."

I didn't think it was possible, but his glare turned more menacing. I continued, "I'm sorry if you think we're overstepping. I would've thought you'd be anxious for whomever poisoned Gary to be caught. Two people were killed. You and Richard are fortunate to be alive."

He wiped his hand over the granite desktop like he was removing dust and looked out the window before turning back to me. "Don't play me for an idiot. I've heard how you and your friends interfere with police investigations. What happened out in the marsh is none of your business. Period."

He pounded the arm of the chair once more, stood, and jerked open the door to the patio. I remained in my chair as he walked to the outdoor railing. I was about to join him when he pivoted and returned.

I wanted him to get it out of his system, so I remained silent as his glare returned. He continued where he'd left off, "What about your friend Debonnet who's going around telling everyone he's working as an assistant detective for you and your buddy? What in the hell is an assistant detective? Why is whatever happened his business?"

"Tom, Virgil is a new acquaintance who offered to talk to some people to see what they knew about the crash. He told us he'd dealt with your ex. He may've said something to her."

He stomped his foot on the floor. "He said something to Alyssa, crap. He nearly pounced on her, accusing her of killing Gary and Mark." He shook his head. "Alyssa and I have had a challenging time settling our divorce. She doesn't need someone harassing her."

I was floored by his level of anger. What's with him defending Alyssa? From what I'd heard, their divorce was contentious. Did he have something to hide? Did he know she had something to hide?

I took a deep breath to calm my voice. "Tom, when that plane nearly killed Charles and me, it became our business. We've done nothing more than ask questions. As for Virgil, I hardly know him. We've talked maybe four times. He did express interest in the crash. Since he'd worked with Alyssa, he said he was going to talk to her. Nothing more."

"That's not what—"

My turn to interrupt. "Are you aware that someone tried to kill Virgil?"

His scowl softened. "When? How?"

He was either surprised or a good actor. I shared the details of the hit-and-run. Tom asked if Virgil was going to be okay. I told him the doctors thought so. Tom loosened his grip on the chair.

He said, "That's too bad. It still didn't give him the right to pester Alyssa."

He looked at his watch and I knew he'd have to leave soon. "Tom, I understand how you may be displeased about the way Alyssa has been treated, but aren't you concerned about who poisoned Gary, killed Mark, and if it hadn't been for luck, killed you and Richard?"

He rubbed his hand across his face as he looked at the floor. "Sure I am. It doesn't make sense." He stared at me. "I may be overreacting about you and your friends. I suppose I must take my frustration out on someone." He shrugged. "That was you."

A meager apology. "We all know Gary did, but there was a good chance all of you would have perished in the crash. If Gary wasn't the intended victim, do you have a guess who it could've been?"

He didn't answer for several seconds. Finally, in a lower, less hostile tone, he said, "That's all I've thought about since you dragged us out of the wreck. My first thought was it was me. I know Alyssa can be, well, can be vindictive, or hard to get along with, but for the life of me, I can't see her doing something like that." He bit his lower lip. "I've known Richard for years, socialized with him and Charlene Beth at conventions. Richard is liked by all. I can't see anyone wanting him dead." He paused then looked out the window.

"What about Mark?"

"Chris, I don't know if I should say it or not."

"What?"

"If I had to guess who the target was, I'd say Mark."

"Why?"

"Don't hold me to this. I didn't know him as well as I knew the other guys. I didn't know much about his friends or his personal life. What I knew was on several of the golf trips he talked about arguments with Kevin."

"His spouse?"

Tom nodded.

"Arguments about?"

"He didn't talk much about the details. I got bits and pieces from his talks with the other guys. Mark owns, owned, a trucking company. It's had good times but like most small businesses hit rough spots. Recently there were more bad than good. Kevin is a pharmacist. He apparently makes a good living and was always pestering Mark to give up on the company and get a job with a steady income."

"You think Kevin poisoned Gary to crash the plane and kill Mark?"

"Yes."

"Why would he want him dead?"

"Insurance."

I knew what he was talking about but was curious about his version. "Life insurance?"

"Sort of. The last time we golfed, Mark was telling Richard he had a key man policy. That's where if something happened to Mark, the company would get the insurance." He hesitated and looked out the window, before turning back to me. "I hate to say this, and I may not have heard all of it correctly. I'm almost certain I heard him say that he was afraid of Kevin; said the taking out the policy may be the death of him."

"Who was he talking to?"

"Gary."

That eliminated a way to verify it. I hesitated to see if Tom was going to add anything. He didn't, so I said, "Do you think he feared Kevin?"

"Yes, but that doesn't mean he killed him."

"It doesn't. Didn't you, Mark, and Richard ride to the airport together?"

"Yes, Gary was already there. We were late. He was perturbed about us not getting there when we said we would. Why?"

"My understanding is the poison was in Gary's drink, a drink he got out of his cooler. How would Kevin have inserted the poison in the drink?"

"Don't know. All I know is the cooler was in the plane when we climbed aboard."

"Did you see anything or anyone who struck you as suspicious when you got to the airport?"

"Like what?"

"Anything. Someone you recognized, familiar car in the lot. Richard mentioned Gary told him he was surprised to see a familiar person in the lot while he was waiting for you to arrive."

Tom scratched his cheek and said, "Not really. You might ask Warren. He was there."

"Warren?"

"Warren Marshall. He's an airplane groupie. He hangs around the airport. In and out of the hangars, in the waiting room. I think he's mildly autistic. Nice guy."

"Describe him."

"White, in his fifties, thin, always smiling, probably knows more about planes than the engineers over at Boeing." Tom looked at his watch again. "Sorry, I need to run."

He walked me to the door, before saying, "Sorry I snapped at you. This whole thing has me upset." He shook my hand with a firm, overly firm, grip and hesitated before saying, "I'm not sorry I told you and your friends to lay off Alyssa. She didn't do it."

I told him I understood how he would be upset. What I didn't say was Alyssa would be off limits.

28

With nothing on my agenda and a glimmer of a clue provided by Tom Kale, I called Charles.

"Ready to go?" I asked when he answered. This was the kind of greeting I often received when he called.

"Where?"

"Airport."

There was a slight pause before he said, "We flying to Tahiti?"

"Wrong airport, the Charleston Executive Airport."

"Ah, it's beginning to make sense. That's where the lucky two, unlucky two golfers took off."

"Pick you up in a half hour."

I hung up knowing the exhilarating feeling my friends must have when they did that to me.

Charles was standing in front of his apartment when I pulled in his parking area. He was wearing tan shorts, his Tilley, and a long-sleeve, navy blue T-shirt with Air Force Academy in white on the chest with Fighting Falcons down the sleeve.

The Charleston Executive Airport was fewer than five miles from Folly as the crow or plane flies, but because the pesky Stono River blocked vehicular traffic between Folly and the airport, we had to drive to Maybank Highway to cross the waterway. That added ten miles to the trip which Charles filled by asking me seven ways what I expected to learn at the airport. I answered each inquiry with a two word answer. *Don't know.* I shared what I'd learned from Tom about a regular at the airport who might've seen something.

I didn't think it was a good sign the turnoff to the airport was immediately past a cemetery. That was after we passed a sign for the Cottage Aroma Bella Day Spa, when Charles said, "Think we should stop and get some spa treatments?"

"We got a mud bath in the marsh when the plane attacked us. That's enough for me."

"Just asking."

It didn't warrant a response.

The rest of the way looked more like farmland than an airport as we drove to a large parking lot in front of the single story Atlantic Aviation building. There must be a lull in activity. A handful of vehicles were in the lot. Ten single-engine aircraft and four private jets were neatly parked on the large concrete pad behind the building.

The waiting room had an earth-tone colored tile floor covering most of the surface. A carpeted seating area was off to the left with a sofa and three chairs. Two men were in deep conversation on the sofa. They glanced our way.

"Can I help you?" said the older of the two.

I would've bet the answer to my first question was the fifty-something year old man seated beside him wearing a red plaid, long-sleeve shirt, and jeans. "We're looking for Warren Marshall."

The man who asked if he could help said, "You've come to the right place." He nodded toward the other man.

I stuck out my hand to shake the hand of the man in plaid. "Warren, I'm Chris and this is my friend Charles."

The man stood. "Oh, hi. I'm Warren."

"Nice to meet you," I said. "Do you have a few minutes?"

"Sure, Brady and I were talking planes. Do you have a plane, Chris?"

"No."

He turned to Charles and pointed at his T-shirt. "Cool shirt. You go to the Air Force Academy?"

"Afraid not, Warren."

Warren frowned. "Oh. You have a plane?"

"Can't say I do," Charles said. "I'd like to. Do you have one?"

That was the first I'd heard of Charles's desire for an airplane. I suspected it was his effort to bond with Warren.

"No. Sad, but no."

The older gentleman interrupted to tell us he needed to get back to work. He headed out the door at the side of the room.

Warren watched him go. "Brady's a nice man. He gets to work with planes all the time." He then turned to us. "You really wanted to talk to me?"

"We do," I said. "Let's have a seat."

"Okay." He sat then turned to Charles. "Charles, what kind of plane do you want?"

"I'm not certain, Warren."

Not certain, I thought. It was more like not even approximate. I sat back to watch Charles get off the topic.

Warren smiled. "I know three for sale. Charles, I could get you the number of the owners. One's cool. It's a Gulfstream G550. 2013 model. They're asking thirty-five million, but I bet you could get it for less."

Charles gulped. "Warren, that's a bit more than I'm thinking about spending."

Warren smiled again. "It is steep. There's a Malibu Mirage sitting out there. Only $876,000. Great plane."

Charles returned Warren's smile and said, "That's closer to what I was thinking."

Around $875,000 from being in his price range, I thought, and decided it was time to move on from Warren trying to broker an airplane deal.

"Warren, do you spend a lot of time here?"

"Yes, mostly in the hangars. That's where I got to know several pilots, got to know their planes. You could say I'm an airplane addict." He chuckled. "Chris, you said you don't have a plane. That right?"

I nodded.

"So, why are you here?"

"We're friends with some of the guys who were in that unfortunate plane crash near Folly Beach." I said and guessed, "Someone said you were here when they took off."

Warren closed his eyes before giving a slight nod. "Cessna 182 Skylane, 2006 model, all-metal, mostly aluminum alloy, built in Wichita, Kansas."

He was right about being an airplane addict. "That's the one."

Warren shook his head. "It was terrible what happened. Mr. Isles was one of my favorite pilots. We talked a lot about planes."

"It was terrible," I said. "Was he here often with his wife?"

"Mrs. Isles was with him sometimes. She didn't like flying. I remember a while back where he nearly had to drag her on the plane." Warren chuckled. "I thought she was about to punch him in the nose. She's not as nice as Mr. Isles."

Interesting, I thought. "Warren, did they argue other times?"

"Don't recall arguing. She didn't look like a happy person. Why?"

"Interested, that's all."

Warren turned to Charles. "Sure would like to show you the planes that're for sale. I know you'd like them."

Charles smiled. "Maybe another time."

I said, "Warren, did you see the other guys get in the plane with Gary?"

"Let's see, I was over at the hangar where Mr. Isles was prepping the plane." Warren chuckled. "Mr. Isles was sort of pissed, whoops, sorry, he was angry because the others were late. He said they were going up to Myrtle to play golf. Mr. Isles thought they'd be late for their game, or whatever you call playing golf."

Charles leaned closer to Warren. "Did you see anyone with him?"

"People were coming and going on the other side of the hangar, but I didn't see anybody talking to Mr. Isles. To tell the truth, I didn't like the language he was using when talking about the guys who weren't there. I went outside to talk to Mr. Jamison. He was getting ready to take off in his Piper PA-46 Malibu. It was built by Piper

Aircraft, down in Vero Beach, Florida." He snapped his fingers. "Charles, I think Mr. Jamison might be interested in selling it. Want me to call him?"

"Not now, Warren. Tell you what, I'll let you know if I want to meet him."

I glared at Charles and turned to Warren. "Got another question, Warren. Did you happen to see Gary, umm, Mr. Isles' drink cooler the day of the crash?"

Warren looked at the floor and toward the door. "Didn't see it, but Mr. Isles was standing by his plane. He remembered he left it in his car and went to get it. He asked me to watch his plane while he was gone." Warren smiled. "Didn't have to watch it too hard. It wasn't going to fly away without Mr. Isles."

I said, "You were there when he returned with the cooler?"

"Sure. I was watching his plane."

"Did he say anything?"

"Now that you mention it, he did say something about seeing someone he thought he knew in the parking lot."

"Thought he knew, or someone he knew?" Charles asked.

"Don't know. It was more like he saw someone. That person reminded him of someone."

That was a confusing clarification. "Did he say who he thought it was?"

"If he did, I didn't get it. It must not be a regular here because he seemed surprised seeing, or think he saw, someone. Something like that."

I said, "Warren, did you see the other guys arrive?"

"No, I was with Mr. Jamison. Charles, sure you don't want me to call him? He's a nice fellow. I know he'd give you a good deal."

Charles thanked him then declined.

"Okay. Let me know if you change your mind."

"Mr. Isles' buddies?" I said to get Warren back on the runway.

"Oh yeah, Mr. Isles and his golfing buddies. Like I told you, I didn't see them get here but I saw them take off. That's all."

I said, "Warren, can you think of anything else about that day?"

"Let's see. It was a pretty day. And, oh yeah, Mr. Lionel landed in his Learjet 45. Mr. Lionel is a UPS pilot. He got his own Learjet from his father who passed last year. The Learjet 45 is supposed to be a competitor in the super-light business jet category, a rival to the Cessna Citation Excel/XLS. I personally don't think it's as good as the Cessna. Anyway, Mr. Lionel lets me go aboard and sit in his seat. Of course, he won't let me fly it."

"Warren," I interrupted. "Do you remember anything else about Mr. Isles or his passengers?"

"No sir, afraid not."

"We appreciate your time." Charles and I stood to leave.

"Stop by anytime. If I'm not in here, I'll be down at the hangar, the one closest to here."

We headed to the door when Warren said, "I think it was a woman."

"Who was?" I said.

"The person Mr. Isles may've known."

"Why do you think it was a woman?"

"I could have it wrong, but I think he said spouse."

"Anything else?" I asked.

"Nope. Oh yeah, Charles, if you want me to introduce you to Mr. Jamison, his plane would be perfect for you."

Charles once again said he'd let Warren know. We headed to the car.

Charles patted me on the arm. "Want to go in with me on buying the Malibu Mirage? I could pull together a couple hundred dollars, you'd only have to pony-up the other $875,800."

I met his proposal with silence.

29

We decided three things on the way home. First, if we combined our worldly resources, we'd fall well more than three-quarters-of-a-million dollars shy of buying the Malibu Mirage, regardless how good a deal Mr. Jamison would give us. We'd have to live without an airplane. Second, Warren was less than helpful when it came to identifying the person, but he verified that someone other than Gary Isles would've had access to the cooler, someone who could've poisoned Gary's energy drink. Third, we were hungry. More importantly, we needed an adult beverage. Cal's was our next stop.

Not many others felt the same need. It was early afternoon and Cal's was five customers shy of empty, that was counting Charles and me. Cal was standing behind the bar wearing his Stetson, an orange Folly Beach T-shirt, looking bored or irritated.

He leaned on the bar and motioned us over. "Finally, friendly faces. First drink's on me if you'll sit a spell."

That was a nice gesture, although the phrase there's no such thing as a free drink popped in my head.

Charles smiled. "Cal, old buddy, that's mighty generous. What kind of deal you offering if we want a burger with the drink?"

"Michigan, old buddy," Cal said as he tipped his Stetson toward

Charles, "add fries to that and I'll throw in all the catsup you can slather on."

The drink was all we were getting out of Cal. I told him it was a great offer and for him to fix each of us a burger, fries, beer for Charles, white wine for me.

"Fine choice, Kentucky. I appreciate your support and presence for a couple of hours this afternoon."

I hadn't thought "sit a spell" would take that long. What I did think was Cal had something to tell us. It became clearer when he pointed to a table on the far side of the room. "Why don't you head over there. I'll take your order to my executive chef."

Charles tilted his head, looked at Cal, and mouthed, "Executive chef?"

Cal nodded, again pointed to the table where he wanted us to sit a spell then walked the short distance to the kitchen entrance.

"Chris," Charles said as he plopped down in the chair, "Now what? I'm at a loss. How're we going to figure out who poisoned Gary?"

I was about to share I was equally lost when Cal arrived with our drinks. Instead of heading back to the bar, he pulled a chair from the adjoining table, sat, and set his Stetson on the table.

Charles repeated what he'd mouthed to Cal earlier, "Executive chef?"

"Junior said he'd be glad to help out his old man. He added calling him anything less than executive chef would be an insult to his expertise, or something along those lines. I didn't have to buy him business cards or one of those expensive chef coats with his name and title sewed on it, so he could call himself whatever he wanted."

I looked toward the door to the kitchen. "Did you have your talk about the changes he'd hit you with?"

"Sort of, pard."

Charles said, "Sort of?"

Cal rubbed his chin. "Let's see, I told him I wasn't comfortable borrowing money to expand the kitchen." Cal nodded like he was finished.

I asked, "What'd he say?"

"I was being shortsighted, not looking at the long-term profitability of the establishment. Told him I was approaching three-quarters of a century on this here earth, my long term was next weekend."

This time Charles said, "What'd he say?"

"He used ten big words to say I was a foolish old man. I told him that was my point. I was an old man. He added a couple more ways of saying it as he stormed out."

A loud bell dinged from the kitchen.

"That's the executive chef telling me your food's ready." Cal pushed the chair back and headed toward the sound.

Charles watched him go. "We here two hours yet?"

I watched Cal return with our burgers, fries, and two bottles of catsup. He set them in front of us then headed to the customers waving for their check.

I didn't realize how hungry I was until I took the first bite. I also didn't realize how much better the burger tasted prepared by an executive chef than from others I'd eaten in Cal's fixed by Cal or his part-time cook. Charles must've agreed since his only comment after taking two bites was, "Yummy."

The other customers exited as Cal returned.

I said, "I gather Junior came back after your tiff over expanding the kitchen."

"You gather right." Cal again looked toward the kitchen. "Surprised the heck out of me when he came back the next day apologizing for his outburst." Cal smiled. "He reminded me of me when I was his age. My temper got me in more fixes than a toad frog in a gaggle of geese. That's ancient history. He was sorry, said he'd be glad to help me out. We could discuss his other ideas later. Later ain't got here yet."

"Discuss what later?" Junior said as he stepped behind Cal's chair. The executive chef wore a black-and-white checked chef's baseball cap, black slacks, and a short-sleeve, white chef's coat with *C. Richardson, Executive Chef, Best Burgers* on the breast.

Cal jumped at the sound of his son. "Hey, Junior. Let me introduce you to two of my best friends, Chris and Charles."

Charles interrupted the introductions, and said, "Junior, we met one of the first times you were in here. We were at the bar."

"I remember. Think you were with him, Chris."

Charles smiled like he'd been recognized by the Governor of South Carolina. I told him he was right about me being with Charles.

Junior pulled another chair to the table. Sat uninvited, and said, "Glad you're here. How're the burgers?"

Charles said, "Yummy," I added, "Fine." The last thing I wanted to say in Cal's presence was that they were the best we'd had here.

Junior smiled. "Great. Now that you're here and are good buddies with Dad, let me bounce a couple of ideas off you to get a customer's perspective."

"Junior," Cal interrupted. "The guys may want to eat in peace."

That'd never stopped Cal from interrupting our eating.

"That's okay, Cal," Charles said like a shark circling a pool of fish preparing for lunch. "We've got time."

"Wonderful," Junior said. "Dad, gee, it sounds strange saying that word. Anyway, he and I've been talking about changes we could make in the restaurant."

I looked at Cal when Junior said *we*. Cal's expression slipped from nervous to frustration, to irritation.

Junior didn't notice or decided to plow ahead regardless. "Things like fixing the place up, getting new equipment in the kitchen, new tables and chairs, expanding our menu and drink offerings. What do you think?"

Charles went first. "Interesting ideas." He turned to me. "What do you think, Chris?"

Thanks, friend. I took a sip of wine then said, "Junior, I agree with Charles. The ideas are interesting. Maybe you could work with Cal and figure out ways to make some of them happen." I hesitated as I thought about what to say next. "During the decade or so I've been on Folly, restaurants have come and gone, some switched ownership, a few opened, closed, reopened with different concepts. I'm sure your Dad's told you this used to be a rock-and-roll bar so it's not immune to change."

Junior interrupted, "See Dad, Chris agrees we should change."

"Junior," I said, "that's not what I'm saying."

Junior stared at me; his eyes narrowed. "What're you saying?"

"Some minor changes might not be bad." I waved my hand around the room. "Cal's is a classic country-music bar. Your Dad's customers come for drinks, mainly beer as you can see, a good burger, and the feel, smell, charm of a calmer, friendlier, better time. If they want a modern bar, or one playing today's music, or somewhere to buy a margarita, there are excellent choices on Folly." I patted Cal on the back. "Nowhere else on earth can they find someone like your Dad. Junior, he's a country legend. Cal's is great the way it is."

Cal rubbed his fingers along the Stetson's brim and grinned. "Thanks, pard."

Junior glanced at his Dad and turned toward Charles and me. "I asked for your opinion, so I should've been ready to listen to whatever you said."

"I'm not saying changes can't be made. Is the kitchen large enough for you to fix burgers and fries? That's all customers want to eat here. They can get limitless choices elsewhere."

"I guess."

"Junior," I continued, "these tables and chairs might not look like much, but they've held up a long time. They have a lot of life left in them."

"Been in here since the Civil War," Charles said. He hated to be left out of a conversation.

"Son," Cal said, "these guys ain't gangin' up on you. They speak for most of my customers. Sure, I could make a herd of changes, a few more folks might mosey in, but that's expensive. I do agree about the old place needing a coat of paint. I have enough cash stocked away to do that."

Junior nodded. "That's great, Dad. One more thing, let me share something I've learned from being in the restaurant business. Most customers are creatures of habit when it comes to their drinks. I'll concede that liquor and some of the fancier drinks may not work, but when it comes to beer, I think expanding the selection could help."

"No craft beers," Cal said. He didn't know what they were, yet he was firm about not adding any.

Junior sighed, "Okay, but why not add Coors, Michelob, or Busch?"

"Suppose we could do that. It won't break us."

I zoned out of the fascinating topic of beer brands and focused on something Junior had said about customers being creatures of habit when it came to drinks. Was that true of the men in the plane? Gary's poison was in his energy drink. Hadn't Cindy said that Mark had a Mountain Dew? What drinks were in the cooler for Richard and Tom? If neither drank energy drinks, then the killer knew what Gary would be drinking.

"Chris, where are you?" Charles said and shook my arm. "Don't you think that's a great idea?"

"Umm, sure," I said, having no idea what the idea was.

"Then it's decided," Charles said. "Chris and I'll be here Monday morning to help you paint."

That'll teach me to agree without knowing what I'm agreeing with. I hate painting.

Two customers came in, told Cal they wanted burgers and beer so Junior and Cal left to do their thing. I looked over at Charles and said, "Tom or Richard?"

Instead of asking what I was talking about, Charles tapped his beer bottle on the table, smiled. "You're getting gooder and gooder sounding like me. I'm proud of you."

It also felt *gooder* and *gooder* returning the kind of statements he'd made countless times. "Well, which one?"

"Tell you what. Give me a hint about what you're talking about, then I'll answer."

"Which one of them are we going to ask what other drinks were in the cooler. We know Gary had an energy drink; Mark had a Mountain Dew."

Charles scratched his temple. "Why is that important?"

I reminded him what Junior had said about customers being creatures of habit before adding, "If the only energy drink was Gary's, the killer knew who'd drink it. If there was more than one energy drink in the cooler, one of the other guys could've been poisoned. If Tom or Richard had taken a sip and collapsed, Gary might not have consumed any. Three of them would be alive today."

"Richard."

"Why?"

"Because Tom's pissed at you for nosing in police business. Might as well get Richard pissed too."

Not the best logic, but it made sense. We decided that since tomorrow was Saturday, he might be home. A casual visit to see how he was doing, might not arouse too much suspicion. We hoped.

30

Richard's house, located on the marsh side of the island, wasn't as large as the other two Folly residents' homes. He answered the door and if he was surprised to see us standing on his elevated front porch, it didn't show. He wore blue shorts and a white T-shirt with a photo on it of the USS Yorktown, the decommissioned World War II aircraft carrier that serves as a museum ship at Patriots Point in Charleston Harbor.

"Cool shirt," Charles said instead of something traditional like hi or hello.

Richard looked down at the shirt like he didn't know what he had on. "Oh, yeah, thanks. I like yours, too."

Charles had on a long-sleeve University of Hawaii T-shirt. Richard didn't comment on my green polo shirt promoting nothing.

Now that Charles and Richard had bonded, it was time to move the T-shirt discussion to the rearview mirror. "Hope we're not interrupting anything. You have a few minutes?"

Richard stepped aside and invited us in. He was more gracious than I would've been seeing us at the door. He said he'd brewed a pot of coffee and asked if we wanted a cup. Charles answered for both of us when he said we'd love some. We followed Richard to the kitchen.

The house was relatively new. The kitchen was filled with black appliances, concrete countertops, and a window with an impressive view of the marsh and a narrow walking pier leading from the yard to the Folly River. The host handed each of us a mug as he asked if we wanted to join him out back.

The view from the oversized deck was more spectacular than the one from the kitchen. The bridge off-island was to our left, to the right we could see the river weaving its way through the marsh. Instead of appreciating the magnificent view, it reminded me of the fateful day we'd met Richard. I shuttered at the thought. I also wondered why Richard hadn't expressed curiosity about why we were here.

He wasn't wearing the sling, so I asked, "How's your arm?"

He waved it over his head. "Almost good as new."

I said, "Great. It could've been much worse."

Charles sipped his coffee, looked around the deck, then nodded at two colorful, plastic toys in the corner. "Richard, it's mighty quiet. Don't you have twins?"

Richard laughed. "Two-year-old twins. They make a jet-ski sound like a feather hitting the floor."

Charles's head bobbed. "I know what you mean."

Words spoken by a man who'd never been around kids, much less twins.

Richard said, "It's quiet because Charlene Beth took them out on the boat a little while ago. They like to look for dolphins in the marsh. I like the silence. It's win-win for all of us." He took a sip, set his mug on the arm rest, and said, "I don't suppose you stopped by to ask about the kids."

I took a deep breath. "Richard, this may seem like a strange question. Do you remember what drinks were in the cooler Gary had on the plane?"

His hand gripping the mug began shaking. He looked toward the marsh then back at me. "Why in heaven's name would you ask that?"

"The police know Gary was poisoned by something in his drink, so I was wondering how the person who put it there knew Gary would be the one drinking it."

"Why aren't the police asking instead of you?"

Great question. "I'm sure they're following up on everything. The drinks were something I've been thinking about. I understand if you're uncomfortable talking about it."

I was preparing to be evicted. Instead, Richard said, "We've been going on these golfing trips a few years now. We know each other's good and bad habits, what foods each like, what drinks. To answer your question, it was a small cooler, only held four or five drinks. Gary was hung up on energy drinks. We teased him that if he had any more energy, he could flap his wings and fly to Myrtle Beach without a plane. Anyway, that was his preferred drink. Mountain Dew was Mark's. I often joked saying it tasted like rotten oranges." Richard hesitated as he rubbed the bridge of his nose. "I won't be teasing him again."

I said, "We're sorry to be dredging up bad memories."

"That's okay. It's always on my mind."

Charles leaned closer to Richard. "What about you and Tom?"

Richard looked at him like he didn't understand the question, then said, "Oh, our drinks. I always have Diet Coke. Tom's another story. We picked on him nearly every trip because he never knew what to order when we were on the course. One time he'd want Pepsi, the next time root beer, sometimes energy drinks. I don't know what he had in the cooler. Gary was such a nice guy, such a gracious host, I'd wager he called Tom to ask what he wanted."

"You don't know what was in the cooler for him?"

"I didn't look. If it's that important, I suggest you ask Tom. Does that help?"

I said it did without adding *almost* before changing the subject. I didn't want him thinking too much about what I'd asked. We talked about the weather, the topic most people talk about while sitting on the deck on a beautiful spring morning. Charles, who'd never owned a share of any stock, asked about recent market fluctuations. He was rewarded with a lecture about international influences on the

United States market. All I understood were the words China and steel.

Richard ran out of words to confuse me, so I said, "Richard, we've taken enough of your time. Thanks for the coffee."

He stood. "Sure you don't want to stay to hear how loud twins can be."

We declined.

* * *

"What did we learn other than twins are loud?" Charles asked as we pulled out of Richard's drive.

"Richard is a more gracious host than I'd be if two strangers knocked on my door. We came close to learning that Gary was the intended poison victim."

"Until Richard said Tom may've had an energy drink in the cooler. If he did, it could've been Tom who was supposed to die."

"Yes, though that doesn't make sense. What would've been the advantage of poisoning Tom on the plane?"

"Because they were in the air, they couldn't get help, no chance of saving his life."

"Charles, my understanding is there wouldn't have been anything they could've done to help him if he'd ingested arsenic."

"Maybe the killer didn't know that. If he did, I suppose there's no advantage for poisoning him in the air. So, are we going to do what Richard suggested?"

"Ask Tom what drink he wanted?"

Charles rolled his eyes. "No, go back to see how loud the twins are."

"When do you want to visit Tom?" I asked, certain what the answer would be.

"Now."

Charles hadn't disappointed. I wasn't as enthusiastic about dropping in on Tom as I was interrupting Richard's morning. I'd left Tom's house on civil terms after the last visit but remembered the hostility he'd showed before we declared peace. Charles was right, so I headed out East Ashley Avenue to Tom's oceanfront abode.

The Range Rover was in the drive, so I figured he was home. I rang the doorbell then paced in front of the door.

Charles said, "Ring it again. His car's here."

I did and could hear the chimes in the house. Then I heard Casper barking on the other side of the door. Still, no Tom.

Charles, who has as much patience as Richard's twins, said, "Again."

"Charles, he isn't deaf. He must not be here."

I turned to leave, had taken three steps off the porch when the door flew open. Tom stared at us. He was wearing a long-sleeve white shirt with the sleeves rolled up to his elbows, dress slacks, and was barefoot.

Casper was cradled in his arm appearing to smile at us. Tom's glare was anything but friendly.

"What now?" the homeowner said.

"Hi, Tom," I said, putting on the friendliest face I could under the circumstances. "We were talking to Richard Haymaker a little while ago. He said we could stop by to ask a question."

Tom rubbed Casper's head as he continued to scowl at us. He said, "You saying Richard told you to come out here?"

It was sort of what he'd said.

I started to repeat my opening when a familiar voice coming from behind Tom said, "Tom, who is it?"

Tom pulled the door partially closed, turned, and said, "It's nothing. I'll be right there."

Charles was doing everything but standing on one foot while leaning through the partially opened door to see who was behind it. He needn't have, the door swung open and Kelly Isles was standing behind Tom. She was wearing a colorful sundress and barefoot like Tom.

She said, "Oh, Tom, it's Charles and, umm …"

"Chris," I prompted.

"Yes, Chris. Tom, don't be rude. Invite them in."

He looked at Kelly, then back at us. "Sure, come in."

I didn't detect a glimmer of hospitality, but it didn't stop us from following him.

Kelly gave each of us a sisterly hug then asked if we wanted something to drink. Tom stood back, didn't say anything, as he continued rubbing Casper's head.

"Thanks for asking," I said. "We're okay."

"Water would be nice," Charles said, ignoring my answer.

We followed Kelly to the kitchen. Tom brought up the rear after he set Casper down.

Kelly opened the refrigerator and said, "Sure water's all you want. We have beer, energy drinks, root beer, white wine. Anything else to offer your guests, Tom?"

"No," he said, slamming the door on other options.

"Kelly, water will be fine," I said, hoping Charles would let it go.

Kelly handed us a bottle of water. Tom pushed the refrigerator door closed before saying, "What's the question?"

This wouldn't be an appropriate time to start a conversation about the weather or anything else strangers talked about during uncomfortable times.

"We were wondering about the drinks in the cooler on the plane. Do you remember what Gary put in it for you?"

"You what? You came here, bothering us to ask that?"

I said, "Yes."

"You couldn't have called with that stupid question?"

Charles took a sip of water then said, "We could've called, but we were heading to the old Coast Guard property to take photos of the Morris Island Lighthouse. Lo and behold, we were driving by your house when Chris suggested we stop."

Not a bad reason, I thought, although this was the first I was hearing it.

Tom's hostility lessened a tad. He said, "Phones work out there."

"I apologize for the interruption," I said. "We won't take up more of your time."

"Don't be silly," Kelly said as if she hadn't noticed Tom's irritation. "We weren't doing anything, were we Tom?"

He smiled at Kelly and turned to me. "Why were you wondering what drink Gary had for me?"

I was trying to figure the best way to ask with Gary's widow staring at me, when Charles said, "Richard said it was either root beer or an energy drink. If it was the energy drink, there's the possibility the poison could've been for you."

I was looking at Tom but heard Kelly gasp.

Tom shook his head. "If it hadn't been for the two of you, all four of us would be dead. Why would anyone have targeted only me? Please don't start pointing fingers again at Alyssa. I thought I cleared that up your last visit."

"Tom," Kelly interrupted as she put her hand on his arm, "all they're trying to do is see if you were the person someone tried to kill instead of …" She hesitated then looked at the floor. "Sorry, instead of Gary."

Tom put his arm around her waist. He scowled at me. "See what you've done. You happy?"

"Tom," I said, "nothing about this is happy. It was a tragedy. Two lives were lost. All we want to do is find out what happened. Hopefully we can help the police bring whoever is responsible for poisoning Gary to justice. Isn't that what you want?"

Tears were rolling down Kelly's cheek and Tom kept his arm around her. The silence was deafening.

Charles did one of the things he does best when he said, "How old's Casper?"

Only he could get away with that transition, that distraction.

Kelly wiped her cheek then bent to lift Casper. "A year old next week. He's a cutie, isn't he?" She smiled for the first time since we'd entered the kitchen.

Tom looked at Casper in Kelly's arms, and said, "Root beer."

It took me a few seconds to realize he was answering the question that brought us here.

All eyes, all except Casper's whose eyes were still on Kelly, turned to Tom who continued, "Gary called the night before asking what I wanted. It didn't matter to me. Hell, I never understood why we had to have drinks on the short flight. It was a big deal to Gary. He said everyone else was easy, he didn't have to call them since he knew their preferences."

I nodded. "Did anyone else know what you told him?"

"I don't know, well, umm, Kelly, did you know?"

She stroked Casper's head, glanced at Charles and me, then looked at Tom. "I heard him on the phone. We were sort of unhappy with each other at the time. The only reason I was in hearing range was that I was on my way to the deck. I didn't hear anything about drinks. I remember him telling you when you were leaving."

Charles leaned over and patted Casper's head before saying, "Did you hear Gary talking to any of the other guys, maybe to tell them the time they were heading out?"

"No. I took a walk on the beach. It was a great night. Pleasant temperature, nice sea breeze. I was out there an hour or so."

Tom had been watching the exchange as well as his watch. "Guys," he said, "I don't mean to sound rude, but I promised Kelly I'd go with her to the Charleston Crab House for a late lunch. We need to be heading out."

Kelly smiled. "Casper likes to ride in my boat and will be happy in it while we eat on the restaurant's deck."

The restaurant was on Wappoo Creek and one of the nicer casual dining spots in the area. I again apologized for interrupting their day then told them to have a good lunch. Charles had to give Casper a good-bye kiss on his way to the door. Kelly thanked us for stopping by. Tom didn't second it.

After we were safely back in the car headed toward town, I asked Charles the same question he'd asked me after we left Richard's house. "What did we learn?"

"Casper's got a big birthday coming up. Umm, Tom and Kelly are mighty close for her being a recent widow. Both barefoot. How about how she said *we* have beer in the refrigerator, rather than saying *he* has. If she was an actress auditioning for the part of grieving widow, she wouldn't get it."

"That's true, but—"

"Whoa, I'm not done. What's with Tom defending his ex? If I were her and knew my hubby was playing footsie with a neighbor, I'd give serious thought to killing him, even if I had to bring down a plane of golfers to do it."

I glanced over at him. "May I speak now?"

"If you must."

"His ex has more reasons to want him dead than Kelly has, especially if Tom and Kelly had something going before the crash. On the other hand, if Tom and Kelly weren't seeing each other, she could've had other reasons to poison her husband. She was unhappy about not being able to practice law. You heard her say she and Gary were *sort of unhappy* with each other the night before the crash. It could've been far worse than unhappy. She could've easily known what drinks were in the cooler. She, of all people, had the best opportunity to poison him."

"Chris, how are we going to prove any of this?"

I shrugged.

31

The routine events of life overshadowed thoughts about the murder the next few days, that is except Monday when I'd let Charles commit me to painting Cal's. We'd spent three hours finishing one wall. Cal decided we could attack the other walls another day. I decided to listen more closely to what Charles was committing me to. The next three days, Charles helped a local contractor with a room addition on the west end of the island. My friend wasn't good at building anything other than rapport with people and canines but provided the contractor an extra set of hands to haul lumber and other materials. I thought a few times about returning to Cal's to see how the owner and his son were coexisting, yet that was as far as my good intentions went. I started thinking about the crash more than a few times but knew I didn't know enough to draw conclusions. I called Chief LaMond once to see if she knew anything new about the investigation. She was consumed with a rash of break-ins and didn't take time to insult me for calling, so I knew not to bother her further.

Heavy raindrops bouncing off my tin roof woke me a little after sunrise. I barely had time to pad my way to the kitchen to start a pot of coffee when the phone rang. Virgil's name appeared on the screen;

his voice came from the speaker. "Did you forget about your assistant detective chilling out in a lumpy hospital bed?"

"Good morning, Virgil. How're you feeling?"

"Like the bonds have been removed from my body. Like birds are singing to welcome me back to the world of the living. Like my detective partners deserted me."

That'll teach me to ask. "You've not been deserted. I've been busy, so has Charles." I hoped he didn't ask busy doing what.

I looked out the window and saw a steady stream of water cascading off the roof, so I figured Charles wouldn't be working with the contractor. "Are you up for visitors?"

"Oh Lord, my prayers are answered."

I took that as yes. I said I'd call Charles to see if he's up to a trip to the hospital. Virgil thanked me three times before I got off the phone.

Charles didn't surprise me when he said he'd work it in his schedule, yet did surprise, no, shocked me when he asked what time I wanted him to pick me up. I could count on one hand the number of times he'd offered to drive. I said ten o'clock and was ready when he arrived at nine-thirty.

"Why'd Virgil call?" Charles asked before we were out of the drive.

I told him I didn't know although he sounded lonely. I left out the words *assistant detective*. I also questioned the wisdom of driving to the hospital in a rainstorm after Charles slammed on the brakes twice and swerved around puddles the size of lakes covering the road. The jog from the parking lot to the entry added to my questioning the visit. We were soaked as we headed to the floor where Virgil had set up temporary residence.

Our new friend looked drastically different than the last time I'd seen him. He'd shed his mummy look; the only cast remaining was on his lower leg. He was also seated in a chair beside the bed. He greeted us with a smile as he slowly stood, grabbed the crutches leaning against the chair, and balanced himself on them.

He looked at his visitors. "You look like soaked cats. Forget to disrobe before taking a shower?"

Charles looked down at his blue and white Duke University long-sleeve T-shirt like he didn't know it was wet. "Virgil, old buddy, it's storming out there."

"Great," Virgil said, "my detective partners don't have enough sense to come in out of the rain." He laughed which prevented me from smacking him with my soaked Tilley.

I pointed at the crutches. "Are you able to get around?"

"Get around, you bet. They've got me entered in the hundred-yard dash tomorrow." He laughed louder. "Come on, let's go to the waiting room. I could use a change of scenery."

Virgil wasn't ready for a hundred-yard dash but managed to maneuver us through the corridors to a vacant waiting area where he took a chair. Charles and I sat on the sofa opposite him.

"How much longer are you going to be here?" Charles asked as Virgil dropped his crutches beside the chair.

"A few more days. I asked if I could move in permanently since it's a lot nicer than my apartment. A cute little nurse gives me sponge baths. Food ain't bad either." He sighed and shook his head. "They said they'd love to have me, but the tightwads at the insurance company frowned on paying my rent." His smile disappeared. "Enough about that. What've I missed in the real world? Caught the killer?"

I summarized what new had happened, a summary that didn't take long since it consisted of nothing had happened.

"Sounds like you need me back on the job," he said as he scratched his leg under the top of the cast.

I smiled instead of commenting. Charles wasn't as vague, when he said, "Virgil, it looks like the cops need all the help they can get."

"My thoughts exactly," Virgil said like he'd won a victory. "I've been thinking on it." He laughed. "That's about all I have to do. The docs haven't asked me to help them operate on anybody. Heck, I even offered to help housekeeping mop the floors. They said I'd be too slow. Can you believe that?"

I was afraid to ask what he'd been thinking. I didn't have to.

He continued, "I'm about ninety-five percent certain Tom's ex, Alyssa, poisoned the pilot. It's a crying shame. The only thing the pilot did wrong was fly the guys to the golf course. He and Mark Jamison didn't deserve to die because Tom's ex was pissed."

"Virgil," I said, "what makes you so certain?"

"I told you all of this when we broke bread together in the Dog. She was fighting him about dividing up their money, she wanted custody of Casper. Tom still has that adorable poodle, so Alyssa wasn't winning that battle."

Did Virgil think Alyssa caused two deaths over the dog? I said, "Virgil, those could be reasons, but from what we know, the other three spouses have the same number or more reasons. That doesn't count suspects we don't know."

He held his hand up like he was either asking permission to go to the restroom or wanting me to stop. I guessed the second reason. "What?"

"I'm still a novice at this detective stuff, not pros like you two. That's my best thinking."

Charles looked around the empty room then moved closer to Virgil. "Those are good thoughts, my friend. Did you and your wife have a boat?"

Virgil didn't appear as confused as I was about Charles's off the wall, or off the water, question.

"Did we ever," he said shaking his head. "Had a forty eight foot Ocean Yachts Super Sport. Loved that boat. Cruised at twenty-six knots—"

Charles interrupted, "Chris, a knot's about 1.151 miles per hour."

I said, "Thanks, Mr. Trivia. Virgil, go on."

"Slept six in three staterooms, two heads. Master stateroom had a queen berth, color TV, stereo system. Should've seen the main salon. Entertainment center, Corian countertop, large L shaped sofa, intelligent 1-5 SAT TV." He shook his head a second time. "Loved it."

Charles, please don't ask about the SAT TV. We could be here all day.

"Virgil, it sounds great."

"It is. It was. I lost it three months before I lost the house." He smiled. "Got to keep the fifteen-foot jon boat. The only head it had was when I pissed over the side."

Charles said, "Sorry to hear that."

Virgil glanced down at the crutches before turning to Charles. "Why'd you ask about the boat?"

I was wondering when he would get curious. I knew I was.

"No reason," Charles said. "Thought you must've had one. Is the jon boat at your apartment?"

Virgil laughed, not quite the reaction to Charles's question I anticipated.

"I can see me hitching a trailer to my scooter to haul a fifteen-foot boat to the river. Nah, gave it to someone I know who lives backed up to the marsh. He can get some use out of it."

"That's too bad," Charles said.

"Not really, but I can borrow it whenever I want." He rubbed his thigh and grimaced. "Guys, this has been fun. Think I need to get back to my luxurious bed so I can stretch out my leg."

We followed him to his room at about half the speed, maybe one knot, we took to get to the waiting area.

Before we left, he said, "Guys, would it be asking too much if I could hitch a ride with one of you back to my apartment when they evict me?"

Charles smiled. "Holler and it'll be done."

"Much appreciated. Oh yeah, one more thing. Could you take a gander in my apartment to make sure everything's okay? Wouldn't want the mice to invite their friends to move in while I'm gone."

Charles said, "It'll be done."

On the elevator ride to the lobby, I said, "What's with the question about a boat?"

"I was curious about what kind of countertops he had in the salon."

"Funny. Need I ask again?"

"No. It was something you'd said before about Virgil asking so many questions about what the cops knew about the crash. You were hinting he may've been responsible, so he could get closer to Charlene Beth. It's a weak reason, but it still counts. Someone took the cooler plus the other stuff out of the plane, someone needing a boat to get there."

I nodded. "So now we know Virgil has access to one."

"Yessiree."

"And remember, Kelly Isles was taking Tom out on her boat. Charlene Beth had the twins out on their boat when we visited Richard. Add to that, there're places where you can rent boats near Folly. Finally, imagine how many boats in the area are owned by private parties."

Charles rubbed his chin. "Yeah, so how are we going to find out if Kevin Robbins and Alyssa Kale have boats." He snapped his fingers. "We could head to Mt. Pleasant, saunter up to Kevin Robbins's pharmacy counter, then say something like 'I've got a cough. What do you recommend and, oh yeah, do you have a boat?'"

"That's an idea. A stupid one. The fact is everyone we consider to be a suspect either has, or could easily get, access to a boat."

Charles pulled onto Folly Road and said, "You're no fun. I think you might be right about Virgil. He's too interested in the killing. Too interested in sucking up to us to see what we know." He scratched his cheek. "Besides, he's too happy, seems content with his situation. How would you feel if you had a mansion, a big-ole boat with Corian countertops, then poof, it was gone? Yep, the boy's too happy to have all that bad stuff happen to him."

I didn't agree or disagree. We made the rest of the trip in silence and pulled in front of Virgil's apartment building, a one story, concrete block structure with five parking spaces for the four units. Virgil's scooter was parked in front of a faded green wooden door with a rusting, six-inch high number 2 beside it.

"Not quite a mansion overlooking the Battery," Charles said in a rare understatement.

32

The lockset was so loose I had to hold it in place to turn the key.

Charles stood back and said, "We didn't need a key. I could've picked it with my elbow."

The door swung inward, and we were accosted by heat that'd built up. The first thing I did was check the thermostat. It'd been switched off, most likely to save money, so I left it off and looked around. Other than being hot enough to bake cookies, everything seemed okay, to my surprise, neat and tidy. I headed to the kitchen, Charles to the bedroom. Everything in the kitchen was neat. A box of corn flakes was beside a clean, empty bowl on the table that wasn't much larger than a dinner plate.

Everything appeared in order so I turned and headed back to the living room when Charles said, "You might want to stop in the bedroom."

He was staring at the twelve-inch, clunky, tube television on the dresser. More accurately, he was staring at a six by nine inch piece of paper taped to the TV screen. Neatly typed on the paper was a note that read, *Mind your own business or the next time you won't be so lucky.*

Charles said, "I'm taking Virgil off my suspect list." He was saying something else, but I didn't understand what. I was busy punching in the Folly Beach Department of Public Safety's number on my phone.

I'd told the dispatcher it wasn't an emergency, so I wasn't surprised when it took several minutes before a patrol car pulled into Virgil's parking lot. Officer Trula Bishop stepped out, adjusted her duty belt, checked out the surroundings, then came over to Charles and me. We'd moved outside so we wouldn't disturb anything more than we already had.

"Mr. Chris," Bishop said, "what've you stumbled into now?"

I'd known Officer Bishop for a few years. She'd always been helpful and friendly.

I explained how we'd been asked by Virgil Debonnet, the apartment's hospitalized resident, to check to see if everything was okay. We led her to the bedroom where I pointed to the message on the television.

She read the note, then said, "Would that be the Virgil Debonnet who had the unfortunate contact with a motorized vehicle a while back?"

As we headed back outside, I said it was. She asked if we knew what the note was referring to or who might've put it there. I shared how Virgil had taken an unusual interest in the plane crash, that he'd known the Haymakers and had talked to one of the other survivors since the crash. I omitted Virgil's self-proclaimed assistant private detective title.

Our conversation was interrupted when Chief LaMond pulled in the lot beside the patrol car. She shook her head as she approached.

"Lovely afternoon, Chief," Charles said.

She glowered at him like he'd called her a slimy slug. "I was peacefully sitting in my luxurious office dreaming about vacationing in the South of France when I heard about a call from one of my senior citizens, a guy named Landrum, who could use the services of my fine public safety department. Knowing how much trouble the caller often causes, I took a break from daydreaming to see what trouble he'd blundered into this time. So, yes, Charles, it is a lovely afternoon. I'm anxious to see how you, along with that geezer, standing beside you are once again going to ruin it."

The geezer wasn't Officer Bishop. I shared with Cindy the same information I'd given Bishop. Instead of griping about us being there or nosing where we shouldn't be nosing, Cindy asked how Virgil was recuperating as we headed to the bedroom. Charles shared Virgil's current condition as she stared at the note.

Charles finished his medical update. Cindy turned to me. "What do you think Virgil did to deserve this?"

"He's been asking around about the plane crash. I know little about him, so it may have to do with something other than the crash."

The Chief turned back to the note. "You don't believe that, do you?"

"Not for a second," Charles answered for me.

Cindy sighed, as she turned to Bishop. "Officer, give a holler to Detective Callahan, key him in, see if he wants to send over crime-scene techs. I doubt they'll find anything, but you never know. Don't tell him who found the note. He'll have a fit if he learns these two snoops are involved." Before she turned to walk out the door, she said, "Also throw the riffraff out of the apartment then wait for whoever shows up from Charleston."

Officer Bishop chuckled and said, "Riffraff, you heard the boss lady. Disappear."

We headed to the car, happy to get out of the hot apartment. There were a dozen people standing on the other side of the police vehicles. I wasn't surprised since police activity was a spectator sport on the island drawing locals and visitors. What did surprise me was seeing Junior Richardson in the group.

He waved at us as Charles motioned him over saying, "Hey, Junior, what're you doing here?"

He pointed to the door two apartments down from Virgil's. "I live there. It's not the Ritz, but it'll do until I find a house to buy. What's going on? Nothing's happened to Virgil did it? Isn't he still in the hospital?"

I didn't know which question to answer first. Charles didn't have qualms. He started telling Junior the chain of events leading us to standing here. Some of the looky-loos began inching closer to listen, so I suggested we take our conversation to air-conditioned comfort in Charles's car. We moved to the car where Charles assured Junior that Virgil was recovering nicely, that the police were at his residence because of a note.

"Good," Junior said. "He's a nice guy."

I said, "How well do you know him?"

"Not that well. We talked a few times since we're both new to Folly and are having, let's say, an interesting time adjusting to island life."

"He say anything about having enemies?" I asked.

Junior looked at Virgil's door. "Like someone who would want to run him over?"

Charles said, "That'd qualify."

"Not that I've heard. He was always in a good mood. Frankly, if I'd lost everything like he had, I'd be madder than a one-wing parakeet. Not Virgil. He's a nice guy who didn't deserve everything bad that's happened."

"Junior," I said, "someone has it in for him. Do you recall anything he said that could help the police figure out what's going on?"

"Help the police, or help you? Dad says you're disaster magnets, like playing detective. Said you're good at it."

"Yes," Charles said, "we're—"

I interrupted before he went into his story about being a private detective, "That was the Chief who just left. We're friends so if you know something to help learn who's endangering Virgil, we'll tell her."

I hoped I sounded more convincing to Junior than I had to myself.

Junior adjusted the air-conditioner vent and nodded. "Let's see. The last time I talked with him was, well actually, it was the night before he was hit." Junior smiled. "We were laughing about how he'd been rich, how I'd owned several restaurants. Now we're living in this building that's more fit for chickens than for a king. I found it funny because I was here temporarily. I don't know why Virgil found it funny, except that he acted like a burden had been lifted off his shoulder after losing his wealth. Admirable, yet weird."

Interesting, but not what I had in mind. "Junior, did he say anything about looking into the plane crash?"

"He spent time talking about the people he talked with about it. I don't remember any names since I didn't know who he was talking about. As far as I know, unless some of them are customers in Dad's place, I didn't know them."

Charles said, "Remember anything about them?"

"The ones he mentioned were gals."

"How do you know?" I asked.

"Because he kept saying she this, she that."

Virgil had talked to Kelly Isles, Alyssa Kale, and of course, had spent more time with Charlene Beth, so that hadn't told me anything new.

I said, "Anything else?"

"It did worry me a little at the time, worry that proved to be well-founded."

"Worried about what?" Charles said.

"He told me he asked each of them a bunch of questions about the crash and how they thought the pilot was poisoned. It sounded like he was playing cop. If I happened to be the killer and someone kept asking me questions like that, I'd be worried."

Charles said, "Don't suppose he told you who he thought it was, did he?"

"Charles, I'm no detective. If Virgil told me who he thought did it, don't you think I would've started with that?"

After Virgil told me he talked to the wives and the ex-wife about the crash, it entered my mind he may've raised too much suspicion by nosing around—enough suspicion to get him in trouble. I felt that more strongly now after what Junior shared.

"Junior," I said, "have you seen anyone going in or hanging around Virgil's apartment since he was hurt?"

He scratched his chin then shook his head. "Don't think so. We get a lot of people walking by. With my odd hours at Dad's place, I keep the blinds closed so I can sleep during the day. I don't see who's here. If you want, I'll ask around."

I told him that could be helpful. Officer Bishop tapped on the window with a notebook. Charles lowered the window. She looked at Junior. "Sir, do you live around here?"

Junior said he did as he pointed toward his door. Officer Bishop asked if he could step out of the car to answer a couple of questions. He exited and stood beside the officer. Charles, being Charles, left his window down so he could eavesdrop. Bishop asked Junior his name and phone number, before asking if he'd seen anything unusual around Virgil's door or if he'd seen anyone enter. Charles tapped me on the shoulder and smiled because it was the same question I'd asked.

Junior gave her the same answer he'd given me. She asked if any of the other residents were standing in the group watching us. Junior looked at the group and said one of the two remaining residents was there. She got the name, thanked Junior, leaned on Charles's windowsill, and said, "Guys, the crime scene techs can't get here for a couple hours. The Chief told me to lock the apartment. She also asked me to get Virgil's key and drop it at the office for the techs to pick up."

I handed her the key. She said she'd get it back to me when the techs were done. She left to talk to the apartment dweller standing outside. Junior said he had to get to Cal's, that it was nice talking to us.

That left Charles and me with one fewer suspect and a stronger case the murderer might be one of the three women. How to prove which one, if in fact it was one of them, was anyone's guess. I was also left with the realization that if Virgil was run over because he was asking questions, where did that leave Charles and me since we'd been doing the same thing?

33

I was getting ready for bed when the phone rang. I let it go to voicemail since friends knew not to call this late and the screen read *Unknown*. If it was important, not a robocall, the caller would leave a message. Thirty seconds later, the phone dinged indicating a message. Two clicks later, I heard, "Chris, this is Junior, you know, Cal's son. I talked to the neighbor in my building who wasn't there when the hubbub happened today. She told me things I figure you'd want to know." There was commotion in the background and Junior said, "Cool it, Dad. I'm working on it. Umm, Chris, I'll tell you some other time." The message ended.

It was a little after ten o'clock and I didn't have anything to do or anywhere to be in the morning, so why not walk to Cal's? A couple of reasons came to mind; both related to me being lazy. Besides, the walk would do me good, or so I was trying to convince myself. It must have worked, since I entered Cal's fifteen minutes later. I was met by the comforting smell of frying hamburgers and the sounds of Patsy Cline singing "Sweet Dreams." Roughly twenty customers were enjoying the music, conversation, and beer.

Junior was at the grill flipping a burger, Cal was behind the bar pulling two beers from the cooler. He turned to set the drinks on the bar in front of two men dressed in starched shirts and dress slacks, which most likely meant that they were staying at the Tides. Cal wore his ever-present Stetson, a yellow golf shirt, and even though I couldn't see below his waist, I'd guess shorts.

I took the stool two seats from the men. Cal glanced my way, did a double take, then looked at his watch.

"Lordy, Chris, what brings you out in the middle of the night? Sleepwalking?"

I assured him I was awake.

He said, "Vino?"

"Vino?"

Cal shook his head. "I'm practicing being a classy-joint owner. Junior's influence." He tilted his head toward the kitchen.

I said yes to his drink suggestion, then added, "How's it going with you two?"

He walked to the cooler to grab the wine bottle, poured my vino, set it in front of me, and said, "Much better. Much better until this afternoon."

I took a sip while waiting for him to continue. He didn't, so I asked what happened.

He looked to make sure Junior wasn't near. "You'll never guess what the youngster ordered to make burgers with. Never in a million years."

"Sawdust?" I said, to let him know I was paying attention.

"Near as bad. He ordered bison burgers, then to top it off, ordered veggie burgers, and turkey burgers, yes, turkey burgers. Can you believe that?"

More quickly than I could believe sawdust. "Why'd he do that?"

"Said it'd draw the healthy crowd."

"What'd you say?"

He again looked toward the kitchen. "Told him it ain't Thanksgiving, told him where he could stuff his turkey burgers. Then reminded him veggie burgers ain't really burgers, they're, umm, well, they're vegetables. Finally, I had to point out one of the most important facts of life."

"What might that be?" I asked, enjoying Cal's tirade more than I should have.

"Beer guzzlers can't tell the difference in the taste between a good ole' beef burger and a potted plant. We ain't going to spend a penny more than we have to for the meat we slap on the bun." He shook his head. "Chris, I don't hold out much hope for this to work. Every day something pops up that causes a ruckus. I'm trying, I'd love it to work, but—"

"What ruckus?" Junior said as he slipped behind his dad. The front of his white chef coat was stained, sweat rolled down his cheek.

Cal glanced over his shoulder at his son. "Was telling Chris about the unruly customers a couple of nights ago. Thought I was going to have to call the cops."

"Right," Junior said, not buying it.

Patsy Cline was singing her version of "Faded Love," and a table of four waved for Cal's attention. He headed their way and Junior said, "Get my message?"

I nodded. He motioned me to follow him to the kitchen. There were two burgers, hopefully beef burgers, on the grill so Junior flipped them before saying, "I talked to Rebecca. She stopped for a drink after work."

"Rebecca?"

"Rebecca Holland. She's the woman who lives next to Virgil who wasn't home today when the police were there. Remember, I said I'd see if she knew anything about the note-leaver at your friend's apartment."

"Did she?"

"Hold on," Virgil said as he slid the burgers on the bun, plated them, and headed to a table on the other side of the room.

He returned with four empty beer bottles and dropped them in a large trash container by the door. Cal was still with the other customers. Junior said, "Yep."

"Yep, what?" I said.

"Yep, Rebecca saw something, actually she heard something more than seeing it."

I was determined to wait him out.

He scraped the grill then said, "Rebecca heard noises coming from Virgil's apartment two days ago. The building's so cheap the walls are as thin as wrapping paper, not the good stuff but the paper you get at dollar stores. She said she didn't think anything of it until she was in bed that night when she remembered Virgil was in the hospital. It couldn't have been him."

"Is that it?"

"Maybe, maybe not."

"Explain."

"Rebecca said while she was in bed, she started putting two and two together. She remembered seeing a woman walking away from the building a few minutes after she heard the noises from Virgil's."

"Did she know who it was?"

Junior lowered his head. "If she's to be believed, no. Rebecca only saw the back of her. Said she had a sweatshirt with a hood pulled over her head. She thought the person was young, could've been tall, not thin or fat."

"What do you mean by if she can be believed?"

"Nothing," Junior said sharply.

I started to pursue it, but figured he'd said all he was going to about it. Instead, I said, "How'd Rebecca know the person was young?"

Junior smiled. "I asked her that. She said young people walk different than old folks. Faster, more confident."

I watched Cal heading back to the bar. Rebecca was right.

"Did she say if the woman was black or white?" I asked, thinking of Tom Kale's ex-wife, Alyssa.

"Didn't mention one way or the other."

"Anything else about her?"

Junior put two more patties on the grill before saying, "Not really. Rebecca said she wasn't paying attention since folks are around there all the time. She didn't put any of it together until she was in bed."

"Did she tell the police?"

"Nope. She wasn't there when the cop lady talked to us. Nobody came back to question her."

"I'll share this with Chief LaMond. She'll want someone to talk to Rebecca."

"Sounds like a plan."

"What's the plan?" Cal said as he stuck his head in the kitchen.

Junior smiled. "Chris was telling me the health inspector was going to shut us down. That way, you could sell the building to McDonald's, so they could tear it down, build a Mickey D's."

Cal said, "Funny."

Junior thought it was. He was laughing as he patted his dad on the back. Cal started to respond when my phone rang for the second time during my no-call hours. It was Bob Howard.

With his booming voice, he said, "Didn't wake you up, did I?"

"No. In fact I'm at Cal's."

"Well, crap. I was going to get a kick out of shaking you out of your sugar-sweet dreams. What in the hell are you doing out this time of night?"

"What are you doing calling this time of night?"

"I already said. To irritate you."

"That the only reason?"

"Hell no. Got some gossip you'll be interested in."

"What?"

"Not tonight. You're probably sleepwalking and won't remember it when you wake up. Head to Al's around lunchtime tomorrow. Bring your shadow, as if I could stop him from showing up. Thy rumor will be disclosed while you're savoring the best cheeseburger in the universe."

He'd hung up before I could let him know I'd either be there or not. He knew me well. It'd take a natural disaster for me not to show.

34

It took Charles fewer than ten seconds to say he'd go, and that included him asking where, when, and of course, why. I answered two of the three questions before we'd pulled out of his lot. The answer to the remaining question would have to wait until Bob told us why I'd been summoned.

Traffic was heavy, so it took twice as long to get to Al's than normal. That wasn't bad, since it gave me time to call Chief LaMond to share what Junior said Rebecca Holland told him about the noise from Virgil's apartment, then seeing a woman walking away. Cindy asked for the description and huffed and puffed while I told her the mysterious woman was young, could've been tall, not thin, not fat, black or white.

"Hot damn," the Chief said, "I'll put out an APB. My guys won't have trouble snagging someone with that description. A few dozen."

The phone was on speaker. Charles leaned close to it and said, "I have confidence in you, Chief."

There was a moment of silence before Cindy said, "Chris, your voice has turned stupid."

"Charles is with me."

"Duh," the Chief said in police-speak. "Chris, not you Charles, did Junior happen to say anything that can be the least bit useful?"

"No."

"Anything beyond that spot-on description?" Charles added.

We ignored him. "Chief," I said, "has Detective Callahan learned anything?"

"About as much as Rebecca Holland. There weren't prints on the apartment's door. The paper was as common as no-see-ums over here, the message could've been made by seven-thousand printer models. To be honest, he's stumped."

"Chief," Charles said, "Thomas Jefferson said, 'Honesty is the first chapter in the book of wisdom.'"

"Cindy LaMond says, what in hell does that have to do with anything?"

I agreed with Cindy but waited for Charles to honestly share some wisdom.

Charles said, "Chief, just thought I'd add a dollop of wisdom. If we all admit we don't have anything worth talking about, there's a chance some wisdom will show through then we can figure out who poisoned the pilot."

Cindy sighed. "Charles, I spend, oh, roughly thirty seven hours a day shoveling pachyderm poop after my guys dump it in my office. Now you throw camel crap on top of it."

Time to guide the conversation back to civil. "Cindy, I'll call if we learn anything."

"I'll be waiting with bated breath. In the meantime, I'll have my guys pick up every young female who could be tall, not thin, not fat, black, or white."

She hung up as Charles was telling her that was a great idea.

I found a parking spot on the street around the corner from Al's. Instead of getting out, I took a deep breath and turned to Charles.

"Charles, you were right, you—"

"Of course, I was," he interrupted. "Umm, right about what?"

"Whether I want to or not, whether it's our business or not, we've got to help the police."

Charles's head jerked my direction. "Whoa, you sound like me."

"Two people perished in the crash; two others were fortunate to have survived. We nearly lost our lives. Someone tried to kill Virgil, most likely because he knows something about the poisoning. The police are stumped. And, what's to say we're not next on his or her list?"

"Chris, I agree. There's one tiny problem. How?"

I wish I knew. Instead of sharing my doubts, I said, "We're going to start by hearing what Bob has to tell me—tell us."

Charles smiled. "Then why are we sitting out here?"

I opened the door to Kenny Rogers singing "Lucille" from the jukebox and Al sitting at his welcome chair. He slowly stood, gave each of us a hug, and said, "Charles, it's good to see you, my friend. It's been too long since you've visited."

Charles seldom visited. His wide smile told me that he was pleased to not only be recognized but being called friend. He thanked Al as I looked around the dark room. Three tables had customers, a fourth had Bob munching a fry.

Al glanced toward the owner and said, "You'd better get back to his throne. He doesn't like me keeping folks from spending money."

Willie Nelson was crooning "Always on My Mind" when Bob reinforced Al's comment and yelled "Old man, get out of the way. Let the paying customers order."

Al mouthed, "See?"

We gave him another hug then headed to the cheerful, friendly owner. Before we slid in the booth, Bob turned toward the kitchen and yelled, "Hey, what's-your-name goofing off back there, get these old farts cheeseburgers, a beer for the one with hair, one of those fruity-tasting, box white wines for the bald one. Chop, chop!"

Bob's atrocious management style was only surpassed by his abundance of rudeness, yet Lawrence chuckled and said, "Yes, master."

"He's the greatest," Bob said through a mouthful of fries. "Don't know what I'd do without him."

I said, "Can't imagine him wanting to work anywhere else."

"Smart ass," Bob said, showing that he treats both customers and employees with the same level of respect.

Charles asked how Al was doing. Bob turned serious and gave an abbreviated update on Al's condition which could be summarized by no worse, no better. He then used the same words to describe how business was since the change in ownership. Lawrence delivered our drinks while Bob rambled on about the excessive cost of beef, beer, and Lawrence's astronomical salary.

He shifted direction and said, "Enough restaurant talk. Repeat this and I'll squash you like a termite." He looked around to see if anyone was spying on him. The CIA, FBI, the ASPCA must've had more important things to do than listen to Bob's nonsense. He continued, "You amateur sleuths are rubbing off on me."

"There you go," Charles said. "Proof you can teach an old dog new tricks."

I said, "Bob, what's that mean?"

"Yesterday I met with Alyssa Kale. Charles, she's my stockbroker. My portfolio has been getting broker. Get it, stockbroker, broker?"

Charles nodded; I groaned; Bob continued, "I wanted to see why she was letting me go broke. Her worthless answer was something about declining international stocks, unrest in the electronics sector, corrections in pork bellies, or pork chops in Great Britain, or something like that, and blah, blah, blah. Bottom line was for me to hang on, things will be okay in the long run. I told her to look at my ample stomach, gaze at my birth certificate, then tell me what the odds are on me being around for the long run."

Charles asked, "What'd she say?"

Lawrence delivered our cheeseburgers, Bob glanced at our food and told what's-his-name to fix him another heaping helping of fries. As Lawrence headed to the kitchen, Bob said, "Hell, I didn't ask you here to talk about my financial health. I remembered how Alyssa was about her ex-hubby the last time I talked with her. She acted like she'd be sadder if a housefly died than she'd be if Tom kicked the bucket. Yesterday, I tried to be sympathetic-like, to say something again about how glad I was he survived the crash."

Charles repeated, "What'd she say?"

Bob stared at him. "I'm getting there. You may not believe this but being sympathetic-like is not one of my strengths. I may not have pulled it off like you, Chris. Alyssa stopped looking at my portfolio on the computer and looked out the window. I waited for her to say something like, 'I poisoned the pilot so he'd wreck the plane to wipe out my jerk of an ex-hubby.'"

Charles said, "Did she?"

"No. She did say she wished he had been."

"She really said that?" Charles asked.

"It was like she didn't mean to say it out loud. She started apologizing, said she shouldn't have said it, that she shouldn't be sharing personal stuff with a client. It threw me off. Not many people feel comfortable telling me stuff. I don't bring out the damned ooey-gooey, touchy-feely stuff in people, so I didn't know how to react. I told her it was okay, whatever the hell that meant. I added she could tell cuddly Uncle Bob anything. It worked. I asked why she felt that way about her ex."

Charles said, "What'd she say?"

"Charles," Bob said, "You have the patience of a drunk waiting for the liquor store to open. The distressed chick said she and her ex were going to court next Tuesday to come to an agreement about splitting the money. I figured if Tom died in the crash, they wouldn't be meeting. Alyssa said that even with the divorce she was still his sole beneficiary."

Charles was persistent. "She say anything else?"

"Yes."

Charles leaned toward Bob. "What?"

"She said, 'Let's sell 500 shares of Marathon Oil.'"

It would be futile to ask if she said anything else about her ex-husband. I said, "Bob, do you think she poisoned Gary?"

"Absolutely."

"Why so certain?" I asked.

"Can't put my finger on it. I'm not much at detecting things. With that said, it was the way she talked about how sorry she was about

Gary and Mark's death. It was like she regretted they died while her ex survived."

Charles said, "Like she was sorry she killed the wrong people?"

"Like, I don't know, Charles. It was a feeling."

Al made his way to the table. "What're you talking about, Bob? You don't have feelings."

Bob looked over his shoulder at Al. "I feel you're meddling in a peaceful conversation we're having."

"Peaceful, bull hockey. I came to save my young friends from you ruining their lunch."

"Then why are you standing there? Park your bony butt."

That was Bob's way of telling Al he'd love for him to join us. Al had known Bob since the beginning of time, so he could hear past his friend's bluster. "Don't mind if I do." I pulled a chair from the next table and Al slowly parked his bony butt.

Lawrence brought Al a glass of water and asked if he wanted anything to eat. Al declined then patted me on the forearm. "How's your friend Vernon?"

I was going to ask how Al knew about Virgil, when Bob said, "Damnit old man, I told you it's Virgil."

That answered my question. Al corrected the name and I shared that Virgil should be released from the hospital this week. Al said good, he hoped he could get to meet our new friend. I wouldn't have gone as far as saying that Virgil was a friend but told Al I'd see if it could be arranged.

Al smiled. "Good. Did Bob tell you about the guy who threw his beer bottle at the jukebox?"

"No," I said as I turned to Bob.

He took the handoff. "You're not going to believe why the troublemaker hurled the bottle at that fine music-playing machine. Ricky Van Shelton was singing "Life Turned Her That Way" one of my favorite country songs by the way. One of Al's Afro buds thought Ricky should be doing a Marvin Gay imitation singing 'Heard It Through the Grapevine.' Unbelievable, right?"

"Abominable."

Bob smiled like he'd won the trifecta at Gulfstream Park.

Charles said, "What happened?"

Bob nodded toward Al. "Old Mahatma Gandhi here told the bottle hurler if he cleaned up the glass, the next drink was on the house."

Al said, "He did. We did. Another race riot caused by blustery old Charmin-white Bob averted."

"Al's generous with my beer."

"Boys," Al said, "The poor man's in the middle of a divorce. Two of his three kids are hooked on drugs. He thinks he may be the next person laid off from the factory. He needs all the breaks he can get, yes he does."

"Speaking of divorce," Bob said, "I saw where Walter Middleton Gibbs was getting one from his long-time sweetie."

I thought rather than divorce, we'd been talking about the customer who didn't share Bob's opinion of country music.

Al must've thought we'd talked enough about it. "Bob, if you're going to be talking about some rich guy, I'd better get back to the door. Chris, Charles, great seeing you."

He slowly made his way to the door, leaning on chairs along the way.

I said, "Bob, why'd you mention Walter Middleton Gibbs?"

"You're nosy, Charles is nosier. Figured since I told you about the alleged affair Gibbs was having with that double name gal, you'd be interested."

"Charlene Beth," Charles said.

Bob frowned at Charles. "That's what I said."

I said, "Is that all you know about it?"

"Crap, Chris, I ain't wicked-o-pedia. It may have something to do with double-name gal, or good old Walter's wife may dress up like a pansy and hang out in gay bars. Who knows?"

I thanked him for conjuring up that disturbing image as he started in on the super-sized orders of fries Lawrence had delivered.

35

Three days later, the ringing phone disturbed my morning coffee. Charles was on the other end with, "Ready to go?"

"Where?" I asked, a perfectly logical question, I thought.

"Duh, to pick up Virgil."

"Sure."

"Good. I'll be there in fifteen minutes."

A horn was blowing in the drive five minutes later, so I joined Charles in his Toyota.

"I didn't know today was the day."

Charles smiled as he pulled out of the drive. "He called last night, said the docs did all they could do. The hospital and Virgil's insurance company said he was being kicked out of the resort. I said I'd pick him up. I'm bringing you as a bonus, or if he needs help getting around."

"Did you tell him about the break-in?"

"Nope. Though that'd be a good conversation starter."

Virgil was in the lobby sitting in the insurance-required wheelchair. Crutches were balanced across the arms of the chair. The cast on his leg wasn't nearly as large as the one he wore during our last visit. He had a Gucci shoe on the non-casted leg, the other shoe in his lap.

"Boys, you don't know how glad I am to see you. If that car didn't kill me, I was sure the hospital would if I spent another night here. The rent's cheap, the food, not bad, but a funeral home is more fun than spending that long inside these walls."

We got Virgil in the car and started to pull out of the parking lot when he said, "Want to see where I hung my hat BB?"

Charles said, "BB?"

Virgil chuckled. "Before broke."

Charles said, "We'd love to."

Virgil told Charles to head south on Lockwood Drive instead of staying on the road to Folly. The road turned left and became Broad Street where Virgil gave turn-by-turn directions through streets filled with magnificent homes until we reached South Battery. He had Charles pull across the street from a large, white, two-story mansion with porches across the front on each level. The house sat behind a black, decorative, wrought iron fence leading to a curved walk surrounded by sculptured landscaping. It oozed wealth.

"My new front yard's easier to take care of," Virgil said, with a glimmer of humor. "Look at the view the other direction."

White Point Garden, a six-acre public park, sat immediately between Virgil's former home and where the Cooper and Ashley Rivers met forming the Charleston Harbor. The public park is filled with oak trees, statues, and cannons dating from the Civil War. Virgil, and countless thousands of tourists had a view of Ft. Sumter from the seawall and promenade in the area called the Battery.

We told him how incredible the view was. In a moment of truth, he sighed. "I hated to lose the house, and especially walking out the front door to this view." His sad face turned into a smile. "Oh well, it is what it is. Besides guys, the people on Folly are nicer than my neighbors here."

Charles said, "Except for the one who tried to turn you into roadkill."

"Ah, the exception," Virgil said.

While we were on the topic of his clash with a moving vehicle, we should tell him about the break in.

"Virgil, while you were in the hospital, someone broke in your apartment."

"You're kidding. What kind of lowlife breaks in an apartment of a poverty-stricken, unemployed, bum stuck in a hospital bed? They didn't steal my television, did they? It's the most valuable thing I have. Hell, I paid twelve bucks for it."

Charles patted him on the leg. "The good news is they didn't steal the TV. The bad news is they left a note taped to it."

"An apology for breaking in?"

I shared the contents of the note. Virgil started to say something but stopped with his mouth open.

Charles asked if Virgil had any idea who it may've been.

"That's easy, the person who put me in the hospital."

Charles said, "Can you be more specific?"

"No." Virgil whispered. "Police have any ideas?"

I told him what Rebecca Holland said, adding the police had that information, but nothing else.

"Oh great," Virgil said. "I wouldn't trust Rebecca with my trash, much less her word about what she saw."

That got my attention. "What do you mean?"

Instead of answering, he said, "Let's get out of here. It's depressing looking at what I've lost."

Charles turned at the next street and began weaving his way back to the road to Folly. At the first traffic light, he turned to Virgil. "What about Rebecca Holland?"

"I haven't had much contact with her. I heard she's been in prison."

The light turned green, Charles turned his eyes back on the road, and said, "What for?"

"Stealing cars, maybe embezzlement. That's the story going around, don't know for sure. She didn't happen to mention it during our conversations."

I said, "That why you wouldn't trust her?"

"Not really. I've seen her looking in windows of other apartments. The walls at the apartment are thin, and I've heard her going in and out all hours of the night. Don't know what she's doing. These are only gut reactions."

Charles said, "Do you think she could've been the person who ran you down then broke in your place?"

"Wouldn't put it past her."

I said, "It probably didn't have anything to do with the plane crash if it was her."

"Does she have a car?" Charles said.

Virgil didn't respond at first, then said, "I've never noticed one. A woman picks her up for work."

"Where does she work?"

"Printing plant in Charleston. That's all I know."

Charles said, "Probably prints counterfeit money."

I didn't think that was likely and figured that was all Virgil knew about Rebecca. I said, "Virgil, do you know Junior Richardson?"

"Sure, he lives in my building on the other side of Rebecca. Seems like a great guy. Why?"

I asked him if he knew Junior was Cal Ballew's son.

"He mentioned it. Why?"

I explained our friendship with Cal then lightly touched on how Cal didn't know he had a son until Junior appeared on the scene.

"I know he's chef at his Dad's place but didn't know the rest of that."

We pulled on the island where Charles turned left on East Ashley Avenue. A block from Virgil's building, we saw two police cars and an ambulance pulled off the side of the road.

"Crap, not again," Charles said.

36

The entry to the parking lot was blocked, so we drove past it and pulled over in the front yard of a rental house. We walked; rather Charles and I walked, Virgil hobbled on crutches to the patrol car blocking the entry. In addition to police cars and an ambulance, a coroner's van was in the lot. A Folly Beach Public Safety officer I didn't recognize stopped us with a stern look saying we had to stay behind his car.

I stepped in front of Charles and Virgil, pointed to Virgil, and said, "Officer, this is Mr. Debonnet. That's his apartment." I pointed toward Virgil's door. "What's going on?"

Virgil's door was closed, but the door to Rebecca Holland's apartment was open. An EMT and a public safety officer were coming out.

"I'm sorry gentlemen. I can't let you past this spot. The scene should be cleared in an hour or so."

I repeated, "What's going on?"

"Sir, I'm not at liberty to say."

I saw Trula Bishop coming our way, someone who could share what'd happened. She tapped the other officer on the shoulder. "Officer Smyth, I'll take care of this." She motioned for Charles, Virgil, and me to follow her to the adjacent yard.

The four of us stood in the shade of a live oak and Charles dragged a lawn chair from the house's patio over for Virgil. I introduced Virgil to Officer Bishop.

Trula shook Virgil's hand. "Mr. Debonnet, it's good seeing you're doing so well. The last time I saw you, nobody gave you much hope. Isn't that your apartment back there?"

He thanked her, said Charles and I sprung him from the hospital, then asked how she knew where he lived. She said she was the first officer on the scene after someone left a love letter taped to his television.

Charles wasn't going to let the conversation drift too far from the here and now. "Officer Bishop, what happened?"

She turned to Virgil, glanced at a note in her hand, and said, "Do you know your neighbor, Rebecca Holland?"

Virgil shared what little he knew about her. He left out the part about not trusting her. He asked why.

"I hate to tell you, she's dead."

Charles said, "What happened?"

Officer Bishop gave him a dirty look. "I was getting there, Mr. Charles. She was stabbed multiple times, dead when we arrived. That's all we know."

I asked, "Who found her?"

Bishop looked at the note again. "Cynthia Lawrence, one of her co-workers at S&H Printing. She came to take Ms. Howard to work this morning. Apparently, she picks her up each day. The co-worker knocked. Not getting a response, she tried the knob. The door was unlocked. She opened it a little to yell for Ms. Holland. Her rider was never late, always in the apartment, so when she didn't answer, Cynthia went in and saw Ms. Holland on the floor leading to the kitchen. It was obvious her rider wouldn't be going to work today, or any other day. She called us in a panic."

Officer Smyth moved his patrol car so the coroner's van could exit. We silently watched it go, then I broke the silence with, "Trula, any idea who did it?"

"Detectives from the Sheriff's Office are in there now. From what I heard, nothing stands out. It looks like it happened overnight. We're canvassing the area, but so far, no one answered at the apartment on the other side of Ms. Holland. Of course, Mr. Debonnet was in the hospital."

Virgil said, "When can I get in my place?"

Trula glanced toward the apartment. "It'll be two or three more hours. If you need anything, I'll get it for you."

He said he didn't. I offered that Charles and I would babysit him until he could get in. I asked Officer Bishop if she'd let me know when Virgil could return. She said she would, and the three of us headed to Charles's car.

We piled back in the car before Virgil said, "Got two questions. First one's what in the hell is going on?"

Great question, I thought. Charles said, "What's the second question? It's got to be easier than question number one."

"Know what I haven't had since I got smacked?"

"That's not much easier," Charles said.

"It's a two-part question. The second part is do you know where this bent, folded, near-mutilated hospital escapee can get a cold brew? The answer to the first part of the question is I haven't had an adult beverage since I was holed up in Charleston. Seeing what's happened in my building makes me not want a drink. Guys, it makes me need one."

Rather than answer Virgil, Charles drove to Cal's and parked in a spot that was crutch-aided walking distance from the door. The number of customers doubled when we entered. Reginald, one of Folly's personable locals, was seated at the bar nursing a Bud Light, a middle-aged couple was finishing an order of fries at the table near the stage.

Cal saw us in the doorway and said to sit anywhere. I chose the closest table, so Virgil wouldn't have to hobble far. This was one of the few times I'd been in Cal's without music playing. The eerie silence was broken when Cal delivered us two beers and a glass of white wine.

"Hope this is what you want," he said as he set the drinks on the table. "You look like you need something to wet your whistle."

"You got that one right, Cal," Charles said. "You met Virgil?"

"Haven't had the pleasure. Saw him in here and heard a lot about him." Cal turned to Virgil. "Glad you survived the run-in with the car. They know who did it?"

"No." Virgil said. "Thanks for being concerned. Cal, did you know your kid lives two doors down from me. Nice boy you have there."

"Thanks, pard. He's cleaning the kitchen. I'll tell him you're here."

"Let who know who's here?" Junior said as he headed our way. "Oh, hey, Virgil. Didn't see you."

Cal stepped aside and said, "Don't suppose I'll have to let him know you're here. I've gotta see if Reginald needs anything."

Junior sat in the other chair at our table and turned to Virgil. "Didn't know you were getting out of the hospital this soon. Good to see you, buddy."

Virgil spent a few minutes sharing his medical condition and Junior talked about how much he enjoyed his job. It was refreshing we weren't having to speak over loud music.

I'd had enough of their reminiscing. "Junior, have you heard about your neighbor, Rebecca Holland?"

"She been arrested?"

Interesting question. I thought about what he'd said the other time we talked about his neighbor, something about if she could be believed. "Why ask that?"

Junior said, "I don't like speaking poorly of anyone, but I wouldn't trust her farther than I can throw her. I figured she finally got caught doing something illegal. What'd she do?"

"Got herself stabbed to death," Charles said.

The room got even quieter. Junior stared at Charles before Virgil broke the silence, "Junior, my buddies here brought me home from the hospital. Our parking lot was full of cops and the coroner. It seems someone killed our neighbor."

"When?" Junior asked.

Virgil said, "Overnight."

Junior tapped his fingers on the table and said, "Who?"

Virgil shrugged. "The police don't know."

"Junior," I said, "when we were talking the other day, you said something about if she could be believed. Now you say you wouldn't trust her. What's that about?"

"Couple of things. It's okay to say it now since she's, umm, gone. I caught her peeking in my window. Caught her twice. Virgil, I saw her doing it once at your window."

"You caught her," Charles said. "What'd she say?"

"Claimed she heard a strange noise coming from inside, said she was looking to see what it was."

Charles said, "Twice at your apartment, once at Virgil's?"

"She was lying so I didn't waste time pressing her about it. After that, I made sure my door was always locked. The window frame's been painted so many times, no one could get it open. Besides, there isn't anything in there worth stealing."

Nothing as valuable as Virgil's twelve-dollar television, I wondered. "Is that the only reason you wouldn't trust her."

"Mind you, this is only a feeling," Junior said. "She was living there when I moved in. I saw her outside a time or two and asked a few questions."

"Times other than when she was a peeping Tomette?" Charles interrupted.

"Yes."

Charles said, "What kind of questions?"

"Simple stuff. Like where can I do my laundry? Restaurants she'd recommend. It wasn't like I was asking her to divulge secrets. She answered, but the whole time, I had the feeling she was fishing for information."

"What kind of information?" Charles asked.

"Like when I told her I was working for my Dad, she asked how successful the business was, said she'd bet Cal's takes in a lot of cash. Like she wanted me to tell how much. Don't you think that's a strange question to ask someone you just met?"

Charles said, "Sure is."

Not that strange if she thought about stealing it, I thought.

Junior said, "Virgil, how well did you know Rebecca?"

"About the same as you did. I saw her once looking in windows. Thought she was nosy, no more, no less. I heard she had a record. The jail kind, not a recording like your Dad. I didn't trust her."

Marty Robbins singing "El Paso" broke the musical silence and Cal returned to the table, turned the nearest chair around, sat, then folded his arms over the backrest.

"Only so much quiet these old ears can take," he said, I assumed to justify waking the jukebox. "What'd I hear you say about someone being dead?"

Junior told him what he'd learned about his next-door neighbor's death. He asked if his Dad knew her.

"Doesn't ring a bell. When did it happen?"

"Overnight," I said. "Junior, the police will probably be around asking if you know, saw, or heard anything."

"Doubt I'll be much help. Didn't get out of here until two this morning. Think I was half asleep walking home. Someone could've stuck a gun in my face, and I wouldn't have known it. I didn't see anything. I was back here early this morning. Nothing unusual happening around the apartment building when I left."

Ferlin Husky's version of "Wings of a Dove" filled the room, and something Virgil said reminded me of something he'd said the last time we talked about Rebecca Holland.

I said, "Virgil, didn't you say you heard Rebecca had been in jail for embezzlement?"

"That's the rumor."

"And for stealing cars," Charles added.

Virgil asked, "Why?"

I looked at Reginald, still sitting at the bar, then back at the group at our table. "Let me get your reaction. Junior. You said Rebecca gave you a vague description of the person who was in Virgil's apartment."

"It was could've-been-anybody vague," Junior said.

"What if she recognized the person?"

Charles said, "So?"

"Rebecca would know the person she saw was the one who left Virgil's note; most likely, the person who ran him down."

Charles repeated, "What would she have to gain by not telling the police?"

I pointed at Virgil then at Junior, "Both of you have bad feelings about Rebecca." Both nodded. "What if Rebecca found the person she saw and tried to blackmail her or maybe him?"

Junior nodded. "Found her, said something like she saw the person leaving Virgil's apartment and to give Rebecca money or she'll tell the cops."

Cal rubbed his chin. "After that, the person Rebecca was going to blackmail goes to Rebecca's apartment and pretends she's going to pay her. Instead of handing over money, she kills her."

"I wouldn't put it past Rebecca to do something like that," Virgil said.

Junior added, "Me either."

Cal said, "I only see one itsy-bitsy problem with that."

I nodded. "The problem being we still don't know who the person is who ran down Virgil, the person who probably poisoned Gary Isles."

"And the person who knew got herself hauled off to a slab at the coroner's office," Charles added.

Cal leaned forward in the chair. "It seems there may be one other person who knows."

Charles said, "Who?"

"The guy who just got out of the hospital," Cal said, "The one who got a note trying to scare him off."

"Fellas," Virgil said, "if Chris's theory is right, the person who killed Rebecca, tried to kill me, and left me the note, must think I know who it is."

The rest of us nodded.

Virgil shook his head. "Friends, let me tell you right now, I don't know who it is. I assuredly don't."

37

We each consumed another drink while talking in circles about who the killer might be, before deciding someone needed to tell Chief LaMond our theory about Rebecca's failed blackmail attempt. I was nominated and elected. I was the sole dissenting vote. Charles said he'd stay with Virgil until his apartment was released for occupancy. I could walk home to call the Chief. I suspected he didn't want to be witness to the barrage of grief Cindy would give me for nosing in police business.

I considered putting off the call. I wasn't certain what the Chief could do with our speculation other than lambast us for thinking it. Despite my misgivings, I called to get the lecture out of the way, or to prevent another lecture from Charles if I'd failed to make the call. Cindy took our playing detective better than I expected, she even asked how Virgil was recuperating. I didn't mention Junior or Cal since it would've been bad enough saying Charles and Virgil had been speculating on the murder. I asked what happened to the Cindy LaMond who'd scold me if I said anything that crossed into her bailiwick. She said she was too tired to give me grief, adding she was frustrated with the lack of progress on the poisoning case, the investigation of Virgil's hit and run, and now the stabbing death of

Rebecca Holland. She said there would be one additional death if I shared what she was going to say next. I said I wouldn't repeat whatever it was.

"Chris, the Sheriff's Office and my guys are getting nowhere fast. If you, and yes, I'm going to say it, you and Charles can do anything to put an end to these deaths, go for it. Just promise you won't get killed trying."

"You'll be the first to know if we learn anything. I doubt it'll help, but if you or someone from the Sheriff's Office want to talk to the neighbor on the other side of Rebecca Holland his name is Junior Richardson. He's the chef at Cal's."

Cindy laughed. "Cal has a chef?"

"Not only a chef, the chef is his son."

"Well I'll be a pickled pelican."

"There you go with police lingo again."

"Does Cal really have a son?"

I gave her the abbreviated version of Cal's family history then told her I'd already talked to Junior without getting much information other than what I'd shared with her. She repeated what kind of pelican she was before she said she'd head to Cal's.

That night I couldn't shake thinking Virgil must know something that has the killer worried; worried enough to try to kill him. Who had he talked to about the crash and what could he have learned? He knew Richard and Charlene Beth Haymaker long before the plane went down. They'd had a meal together to celebrate Virgil's sale of his house, plus he'd talked to them since the crash. There's no way Richard had poisoned the pilot since he would've gone down with the plane. What about Charlene Beth? Did she have motive? I remembered Richard's comment at the reception held for Charles and me. It had something to do with her gaining weight. Is that or her alleged affair enough to risk killing four people over?

There's Kelly Isles, grieving widow of the poisoned pilot. What motive would she have? She was unhappy about Gary not letting her work even after she'd been employed at the law firm. I suppose his death would allow her to rejoin the firm. Was that enough motive to kill her husband and risk the lives of three others? Barb had said at the reception Kelly didn't appear sad about her husband's death. Then I remembered Virgil told Kelly he was trying to figure out who poisoned Gary. Was that enough for her to run him down? It didn't seem likely unless he'd said something when he talked with her for her to fear he was getting close—close enough to kill him.

What about Kevin Robbins, Mark Jamison's spouse? He was a pharmacist, would possibly have access to, and know how to use cyanide to spike Gary's drink. He wasn't happy about Mark's failing trucking company which could have syphoned much of Kevin's income to keep it afloat. Was that reason to kill? That by itself may not have been until I remembered the key man insurance policy Mark carried which would make him worth more dead than alive. Did Kevin know Virgil? If he didn't, why would he have tried to run him down? I didn't think he knew him, yet I needed to verify it.

That leaves Alyssa Kale. She'd told Bob she and Tom had a highly contested divorce, were in a battle over money. Money, as any law-enforcement official would say, is a powerful motive for murder. Not only did she tell Bob, she'd shared it with Virgil. What did Virgil tell her about investigating the crash? Was it enough for her to try to kill him?

I then started thinking about the cooler removed from the plane after the crash. Whoever took it had to reach the wreckage by boat. Who among the most-likely suspects had boats? Richard and Charlene had one. She and the twins had been enjoying a day on the water when Charles and I had visited Richard. Add Kelly who told us that Tom Kale's dog Casper enjoyed going out in the boat. I didn't know about Kevin Robbins or Tom Kale's ex, Alyssa. Even if they didn't own one, it would've been simple to rent or borrow one. Finally, Virgil reentered my thoughts when I remembered that he had access to a jon boat he saved while on his trip from wealth to poverty. Could he still be a suspect? If so, why the note in his apartment? Charles and I had already eliminated him, so should I put him back on the list?

Before I went to sleep, another thought popped in my head. What if the murderer was someone we either haven't thought about or someone we don't know? There could be countless people who may've had a grudge against Gary. It was no wonder the police were getting nowhere fast. I knew I was.

* * *

Rays of sun peeking through the blinds awakened me the next morning. I had slept later than usual and attributed it to overusing my brain last evening. It could also have something to do with three glasses of wine at Cal's. Water puddled in the back yard, so it must've rained overnight although the sky was clear. I couldn't remember everything about the crash I'd pondered last evening, but I was certain the evening ended with more questions than answers.

Two cups of coffee later, I started thinking about what I did know. Warren Marshall, the airplane junkie, had talked with Gary Isles while the pilot was waiting for the others to arrive. Warren had heard Gary say something about seeing someone he knew there that morning. Warren hadn't seen the person but remembered Gary using the term spouse. Four spouses were at the top of my suspect pool: Kelly Isles, Charlene Beth Haymaker, ex-spouse Alyssa Kale, and Kevin Robbins. Gary wouldn't have been referring to his wife when he told Warren he'd seen someone he knew at the airport, so I marked her off the list, at least for now. Warren may not have associated someone he'd seen that day with Gary, but that didn't mean he hadn't seen the person. It may be another dead end, but I felt the need to talk to Warren one more time.

I called to ask Charles if he was ready for another trip to the airport. This time he didn't ask our flight destination. He asked if we were going to buy a Piper PA-46 Malibu. I told him no, instead of sharing I was impressed he remembered the kind of plane Warren thought we should buy. He also asked when we were leaving. I said I'd be there in thirty minutes, which gave me time to Google the grocery where Kevin was a pharmacist. Fortunately, the store's website had photos of the store manager, the employee of the month, and its three pharmacists. I printed Kevin Robbin's photo, and found a photo of

Charlene Beth on her realtor's website. I couldn't find a photo of Alyssa.

"If we're not going to buy a plane, why are we going to the airport?" Charles said as he slid into the seat.

I shared my thinking and my plan for today.

"That's a sad excuse of a plan."

"I agree, although we don't—"

He waved his hand in my face. "A sad excuse is better than any I came up with."

On that ringing endorsement, we continued our drive to the airport. We parked in the Atlantic Aviation parking lot where there were fewer cars than had been there during our first visit. We were again greeted by the older gentleman who'd been with Warren the first time we visited. He said we looked familiar and I told him that we'd been there to talk to Warren. He reminded us he was Brady then said he hadn't seen Warren all morning, but we should check in the nearby hangar.

A man was pulling a twin-engine, red and white plane out of the hangar using something that looked like a lawn mower attached to the plane's front wheel. There were two single-engine planes parked in the large structure and Warren was standing in the door watching the man. He wore the same red plaid shirt he had on during our first visit.

He saw us approach and smiled. "I recognize you two." He focused on Charles and held out his hand for Charles to shake. "You're, umm."

Charles grabbed Warren's outstretched hand. "Charles, and that's my friend Chris."

"Sure, I remember," Warren said. "Have you come back to buy the Piper Malibu? I told Mr. Jamison about you. He said he'd give you a deal."

"Not today," Charles said.

I said, "Warren, I've got a question."

Instead of asking what it was, he said, "Do you have a plane, Chris?"

It was the same question he'd asked during our first visit. "No, afraid not. I do have a couple of pictures I'd like to show you." I took the photos out of my pocket, unfolded them, and showed him the one of Charlene Beth. "Warren, did you see this lady out here the day Gary Isles and his friends took off?"

"Does she have a plane?"

"I don't think so."

"Oh," he said. He looked closely at the photo. "She's a nice-looking lady. I see a lot of people around here. I may've seen her."

"The day Gary Isles left on the golfing trip?"

"Don't think so. Who is she?"

"The wife of one of Gary's friends with him on the plane that crashed."

"Is her husband the other man killed?"

"No, he survived."

"That's good," Warren said. "His wife looks nice."

I took Charlene Beth's photo from Warren then handed him the one of Kevin Robbins. "Was this man here that day?"

"Does he have a plane?"

"No," Charles said, losing patience.

"That's too bad. If he ever wants one, I know some for sale."

I glanced at Charles hoping he wouldn't respond. He didn't, and I said, "I'll tell him."

"Did he know someone on the plane?"

I didn't know where the conversation would go if I told Warren that Kevin was Mark Jamison's spouse, so I said, "He's a friend of one of the passengers."

"Is he a doctor?" Warren said.

"He's a pharmacist," I said.

"Oh, I saw the white doctors' coat and thought—"

Charles interrupted, "Warren, was he here that day?"

"I don't recognize him. There were several men, so he could've been."

I was beginning to think our trip to the airport was a waste. I didn't have a photo of Alyssa Kale, and held out little hope that asking about her would get us anywhere.

"Warren, there's one other person I'd like to ask you about. Do you know Alyssa Kale?"

"She doesn't have a plane," Charles said to head off Warren's next question.

"You have her picture?" Warren said.

"No. She's African American, probably in her late forties."

"Let's see." Warren looked around the hangar like he thought she might be hiding in a corner. "Umm, there're two black gentlemen who have planes. One's a new Cessna Turbo Stationair T206H, it's a nice plane. The other's a Commander 114TC."

I said, "Warren, did you see anyone who fit the description of Alyssa Kale the day Gary Isles took off with his friends?"

"No."

Charles looked at me and rolled his eyes.

I silently agreed. "Warren, it's been nice talking with you. Let me give you my phone number in case you think of anything else about the day the plane crashed." I jotted my number on the back of an index card and handed it to him.

He looked at the number. "Want me to give this to Mr. Jamison? He'll give you a good deal on his plane."

Through gritted teeth, I declined.

38

"Sure you don't want to buy a plane?" Charles asked as we drove past the graveyard. "I know where you can get a good deal on a Piper Malibu."

The phone rang before I could tell Charles where he could stick his Piper. Bob Howard's name appeared on the screen.

"Good morning, Bob."

"What time are you getting here?"

"Where and why?"

"Where do you think? Al said we needed more diversity in this joint. Equal rights for whites and all that."

Since we had to go out of our way to get to the airport, Al's was closer than Folly and it was nearing lunch time. Besides, Bob wasn't calling just to invite us to lunch. "Half hour," I said and hung up on him. It felt better than it should have.

Charles's only comment was, "You buying?"

Traffic was light on Maybank Highway, so we reached Al's sooner than anticipated. Parking was another matter. Al's didn't have a parking lot and depended on-street parking for customers arriving in vehicles. Many were local so they walked. Two blocks later, I managed to squeeze in a spot between an old Pontiac Firebird and a much-newer Kia Sorento.

Al greeted us at the door with hugs, adding a warning that Bob was surlier than normal. I doubted that was possible but thanked him for the warning.

Bob proved me wrong when he yelled over Fats Domino's "Blueberry Hill" blasting from the jukebox, "Get the hell over here and order some food. Got to make enough to pay Lawrence his astronomical salary."

"Sure you don't want to go back and buy a plane?" Charles said as we made our way around three empty tables to Bob's booth.

I ignored Bob's "cheery" greeting and Charles's offer and slid in the booth opposite the burly owner. Lawrence, who normally spent most of his time in front of the grill, joined us as we got seated to ask if we wanted cheeseburgers and our usual drinks.

"Of course, they do," Bob said. "Get frying."

Lawrence resisted knocking Bob's drink in his lap before heading to the kitchen.

"Damned fine cook," Bob said. "His waitin' on tables skills could use some work. Need to train him better."

Bob training Lawrence *waitin' on tables* skills would be like a Chihuahua training fighter pilots.

I glanced back at Al who'd returned to the chair by the door then turned to Bob. "How's Al doing?"

"Wish I could tell you he was great, but he's far from it."

Charles said, "He still showing up every day?"

"Yes, but he's not staying as long."

"Sorry to hear it," I said.

"Me, too," Bob said as he looked at Al. "Me, too."

Lawrence returned with our drinks; Bob told him he needed to get back to the kitchen to make sure our cheeseburgers didn't burn. Lawrence had been a short-order cook long before high school students had been born, probably before most of their teachers. Bob had never fried a burger, cheese or otherwise, in his life. That didn't stop him from giving Lawrence directions.

"Yes, boss," Lawrence said and left.

Bob said, "Caught the killer?"

I wasn't ready for the transition from frying burgers to catching killers. "No."

"You're slipping in your old age. Fortunately, your good buddy Bob has a clue for you." He leaned back in the booth then grinned.

Instead of applauding what he considered to be a clue, I said, "Going to share it?"

"I learned from a friend of a friend who got it from his cousin that the Real Estate business of one formerly successful realtor is sucking wind."

I was stuck on Bob having a friend. Charles wasn't hung up on that. He said, "Who's the formerly successful realtor?"

"Double first-name Haymaker. My source says she hasn't sold anything worth more than an anthill in the last six months."

"Is that the clue?" I said.

"Part of it."

Charles said, "Do you think she poisoned Gary Isles so he'd crash and kill her husband because she hadn't sold anything recently?"

"Charles," Bob said, "if you'll keep your trap shut, I'll tell you the other part of the clue."

Charles kept his trap shut, not because Bob told him to, but because Lawrence had returned with our food. Charles had stuffed his mouth with cheeseburger, then motioned Bob to continue.

"My friend also told me his friend who happens to be a lawyer said he knew from a reliable source that Richard has a prenup saying if Charlene Beth divorces him she gets zero, *nada*, zilch. Now I'm not a detective like Charles, and sometimes you, Chris, but that sounds like what you detectives call a big-ass motive."

"How would your friend's friend, or friend of your friend's friend, know about the prenup?"

"Crap, Chris. I'm not a lawyer, not a friend of my friend's friend, not a psychic. I have no idea. The point is there's one. Unless your brain is fried from old age, you should remember I'm the one who told you Walter Middleton Gibbs filed for divorce. And, I'm the one who told you the rumor that he's having a fling with the double-named hussy. Do I have to do all your work?"

Bob was right. Those reasons were more motive than Richard's comment at the reception about his wife gaining weight, more accurately, her negative reaction to his comment. I told him about our conversation with Warren at the airport.

"There you go," Bob said as he grabbed a fry from Charles's plate. "A slam dunk. All the credit goes to me. Charles, sign me up to your detective agency."

Charles said, "Bob, I don't—"

Bob grabbed another fry off Charles's plate, waved it in Charles's face, and turned toward the front door. He yelled, "Al, call the sign company. Order us a big-ass sign for out front. I can see it now. *Al's Bar and Detective Agency.*"

Fortunately for us, unfortunately for sales, there were no other customers, so Al treated Bob's declaration like he did most of his others. He ignored him.

I also ignored it. "Bob, Warren didn't say he saw Charlene Beth at the airport that morning. He said he may have. Walter Middleton Gibbs may've filed for divorce, may be having an affair with Charlene Beth, and her business may be off. None of that proves she poisoned the pilot while trying to kill her husband."

"Chris, what more do I have to do?" Bob said. "I've got it. Why don't I call her and have her show me a trillion dollar-house? I'll say, 'Charlene Beth, I'll take it. Write it up. While you've got a pen in your hand, why don't you write a confession telling my good friend Chris Landrum you poisoned the pilot?'"

Charles stifled a smile and said, "Bob, get it notarized."

Bob did have good points—about Charlene Beth, not about the new sign or the confession. I reluctantly told him so. He was less helpful when we discussed how to prove Charlene Beth was guilty. Al joined us, and we turned the discussion to his family and how they were doing. We finished eating and I was paying Lawrence for lunch, when the phone rang. I didn't recognize the number and started to let it roll over to voicemail, when Charles grabbed it and answered for me. He had as much patience as a hungry baby chipmunk.

He handed me the phone. "It's for you."

Duh, I thought. "Hello."

"Chris, this is Brady at Atlantic Aviation. Warren was just in here. He said you'd showed him pictures of people who might've been here when Gary Isles took off the day of the crash."

I told him yes, that Warren wasn't sure about seeing any of them.

"One of them sounded familiar from Warren's description. I could look at the photos to see if I'm right. I'll be here another hour if you could come now."

I told him where we were and were ready to leave. We'd be at the airport within the hour. I told Charles, Bob, Al, and now Lawrence who'd been on the phone and what he wanted. I asked Bob if he wanted to go with us.

"Nope, I'm the brains behind the detective agency. You underlings do the legwork."

We left on that delusional note.

The trip to the airport took longer than I'd hoped. A wreck on Maybank Highway forced traffic to detour through a housing development. By the time we arrived, I was a nervous wreck. It didn't help that Charles kept tapping his fingers on the console while mumbling something about me driving faster. We were pushing the outer limits of the hour when we parked. Brady was lounging on the chair where we'd first met him. He stood and glanced at his watch.

"Thanks for waiting for us," I said.

"Have the photos?" he said, clearly in a hurry.

My hand was shaking as I unfolded the pictures. The image of Kevin Robbins was on top and Brady looked at it for no more than two seconds before shaking his head.

"It wasn't a guy. Warren said you had a picture of a gal."

I slipped the photo of Charlene Beth over Kevin's.

Brady tapped the photo and smiled. "That's her."

"You sure?" I asked.

"Yep. I don't forget a pretty gal."

Charles stepped closer to Brady. "You're certain she was here that morning?"

"Yep. I didn't pay much attention to it until a little later."

"What made you pay attention then?"

"About the only folks who come around here are pilots, passengers, an occasional salesperson. Once I thought about it, I realized she wasn't here to fly anywhere. Struck me as odd."

I said, "Where was she?"

"Out by the hangar. I wouldn't have seen her if I hadn't gone to the car to get some papers I forgot to bring in."

Charles said, "Don't suppose you saw her around a cooler Gary had with him?"

"Nope. She was on the opposite side of the building from Gary and his plane."

I said, "Was she here after the others arrived and the plane took off?"

"Don't know. I only saw her when I was outside. After I came in, I didn't see her, or Gary, or the others again." He lowered his head and his voice when he added, "Gary was a good guy. I'll miss seeing him around here." He looked at his watch. "Guys, I've got to go."

I thanked him, and Charles and I started to the door, when I remembered one more question. "Brady, did the police talk to you about any of this?"

"Nope. I wasn't here the day after the crash. My better half convinced me I needed to go with her to visit her sister up in Georgetown. My sister-in-law had back surgery, so my wife wanted to see how she was doing. The poor women had three surgeries in two years, and—"

Charles interrupted, "So the police didn't talk to you."

Brady looked at his watch again, glared at Charles, and shook his head, "No, they talked to Warren. You may've noticed he's a little slow on the uptick. Get him started talking about airplanes or aviation and he'll talk your ears off. Anything else, well, you know."

We certainly did. "Did he tell you what they talked about or what he told them?"

One more glance at the watch, then Brady smiled. "Yep. None of the cops wanted to buy a plane."

Brady was close behind us as we left the building. We watched him pull out of the lot and called Chief LaMond to let her know what we'd learned.

She answered with, "Chief LaMond. How may I help you?"

It wasn't an insult or her asking how I was going to ruin her day. I knew she couldn't talk so I asked how long she'd be tied up.

"This budget meeting should be over in an hour or so. May I get back with you then?"

I said yes. She said she'd meet me at the Surf Bar. I told her I'd be there.

Charles watched me set the phone on the console. "Chris, we know who the killer is, so what do we do now?"

"I take you home. Then I'll go home and pace the floor until we meet Cindy at the Surf Bar."

"That's all? There's a killer out there and we know who it is."

"That's why we tell the police and leave it in their capable hands."

Charles sighed. "I guess."

39

After leaving Charles at his apartment, I started thinking about what we'd learned. I was certain Charlene Beth had poisoned Gary. I was tempted to drive to City Hall, barge in the budget meeting while yelling I knew the name of the killer. Sure, the Chief would be tempted to shoot me, but wouldn't it be worth it? A few seconds of rational thought led me to conclude waiting a little longer to tell her would be okay. A bit of paranoia seeped into my head as I realized Virgil's life was still in danger. The killer, now known as Charlene Beth Haymaker, had made one attempt on his life. What was to stop her from trying again?

Instead of going home or barging in on a budget meeting, I drove to Virgil's apartment in hopes of finding him safe. I pulled in the parking area and was relieved to see him sitting on a concrete bench at the far end of the property. He was leaning back against a table and was on the phone. His crutches were leaned beside him keeping him company. He waved me over while still talking on the phone. It was in the upper seventies and partly cloudy, so I was content to join him and enjoy the glorious March day.

Virgil suddenly moved the phone away from his ear, stared at the device, and said, "That's funny."

I didn't know if he was talking to me or the person on the phone. He slid the device in his pocket making me think he'd addressed his comment to me. "What's funny?"

"That was Richard."

"Richard?"

"Richard Haymaker. I was thinking more about the crash. I asked him to tell me again everything he remembered. Charles would've been proud of me. I'm catching on to this detective stuff."

"What'd he say?"

"Nothing I didn't know. I suppose part of being a detective is running into dead ends."

"What'd he say that was funny?"

"He was talking when the phone cut off. Dead air."

"Was he in the car? There're several dead spots where phone service cuts out."

"Could be it, except he isn't in the car. He's on his boat."

"By himself?"

"Charlene Beth is with him."

It hit me hard. Virgil wasn't the only person in danger. After all, Charlene Beth caused the crash to kill her husband.

"Where were they?"

"Don't know; didn't ask. He yelled early in the conversation at Charlene Beth to be careful of the oyster bed, something about them being sharp, could scratch the boat. Does that help?"

"Sounds like they're in the marsh. What exactly was he saying when the phone went dead?"

"He wanted to meet me tomorrow."

"He say why?"

"No. He sounded like it was important, though. I was asking him when and where then the call cut off. Why's that important?"

I realized I'd been holding my breath. I exhaled. "Because Charlene Beth poisoned Gary."

Virgil jumped up, then returned to the bench. "You're kidding. How do you know?"

I told him about Brady's identification.

"Chris, what if Charlene plans to kill Richard? Today. Kill him in the marsh. What if—"

"Virgil, we don't know anything. Let me call Chief LaMond to tell her what just happened."

The call went directly to voicemail. I left a brief message for her to return my call as soon as she could. I said I knew who the killer was, that she might be getting ready to strike again.

"Let's try to find them," Virgil said as he jumped up a second time. This time he grabbed the crutches.

"Virgil, we don't have a boat. Besides, even if we did, there are countless places out there where they could be."

Virgil smiled, not the reaction I had expected. "I can get a boat. Let's try."

If Richard wasn't already dead, he could be long before Cindy called back. Against my better judgment, I said, "Where can you get a boat? Your jon boat isn't fast enough."

"Met a guy in the bar before I had the run-in, slam-in with the car. He lives near the end of East Ashley Avenue on the marsh side. Has a fifteen-foot Boston Whaler he keeps behind his house. Has a little dock. Says he doesn't use it as often as he used to since he travels with work. Told me I could borrow it whenever."

Ten minutes later, we pulled in Virgil's new friend's drive. I asked if the man was home and Virgil said his truck wasn't there, so he was probably out of town. Virgil added he knew where the key was hidden. He went to find it as I stood on the dock and stared at the attractive, blue and white striped hull with a white interior. My fear of water kept me from stepping off the land-bound dock onto the boat. I took a deep breath and told myself the boat was more stable than the kayak I'd been in on my last trip to the marsh.

Virgil waved a key in my face and said, "Let's go."

We managed to get the engine started and the vessel untied when I silently said a prayer. I tried Cindy's phone again only to receive the same recording. I then called Detective Callahan and had better luck. I told him what'd happened. He told me to go home, he'd take care of it. I said it was a good idea. I didn't tell him home wasn't my destination.

We headed west to where it didn't take long to realize there were numerous creeks, and narrow waterways weaving through the marsh. It was high tide which made it even more difficult. Some of the narrow streams weren't navigable at low tide, but at high tide they opened to more possibilities. More possibilities to miss the boat.

We had to make several go-left or go-right decisions which made me realize the futility of trying to find the Haymakers. They could be anywhere, if they were even out here. We rounded a bend when I spotted a decent-sized vessel stopped. I'd never seen the Haymaker's boat so didn't know if it was them. Virgil slowed then asked me what we should do. I asked if he knew what the Haymaker's watercraft looked like.

"No. What now?"

The question was answered when I heard a child squeal and saw a dolphin surfacing beside the stationary watercraft. A woman's laugh filled the air. It wasn't Charlene Beth. I told Virgil to approach and stop when we were beside the other boat.

The child who'd been delighted by the dolphin smiled at us. She waved as her mother put her arm around her daughter. The mother said hi.

We returned her greeting adding, "Have you seen another boat out here?"

"A couple of skiffs, oh yeah, an Alumacraft 1860 Bay."

I asked if she noticed who was on the Alumacraft.

"Didn't pay much attention. It was a man and woman. Why?"

I told her I was looking for a friend and asked where she'd seen the other boat. She pointed in the direction where we were headed then said for us to take a left where the creek split. I thanked her adding for them to have a great rest of the day. I hoped that would be true for us.

40

I didn't know what an Alumacraft looked like, but figured it'd probably be the only boat in the direction she'd sent us. Virgil was careful to stay in the middle of the channel and asked me what our plan was when we found the Haymakers.

Sounding like Charles, I said, "We'll figure it out when we get there."

Virgil steered with his left hand as he pointed a crutch at something he saw around the curve. "We can start figuring. I think that's it."

I looked where he was pointing. The boat was white with a red stripe on the side. It was a few feet longer than the craft Virgil had commandeered. I had no idea what to expect. Virgil said he was going to pull even with it on the starboard side.

We edged closer to the side where I had an unobstructed view of most of the deck. The only person I saw was Charlene Beth standing behind the wheel. She had on black shorts, a light-yellow linen blouse, and tennis shoes.

"Wow!" Virgil said. "Is that you, Charlene Beth?"

I thought he'd pulled off the surprised look. Charlene Beth must not have been as convinced. She looked at him with a stoic face then glanced at me. "What're you doing here?"

"My friend Chris wanted to show me where the plane crashed. The boat belongs to a friend." Virgil looked over the side of Charlene Beth's boat. "Where're Richard and the twins? Thought they'd be with you on such a nice day."

Charlene Beth smiled for the first time. "The twins are with our neighbor. She was taking her toddler to the mall, asked if she could take the twins."

Virgil pulled a few inches closer to the other boat so I could see the entire deck. He then said, "What about Richard?"

"He came but one of his clients called needing a printout of his portfolio. Took him back to the house so he could go to the office to get it. I'd better be moving along."

I didn't see Richard but a large red spot on the deck looked convincingly like blood. A splatter of the red was also on the gunwale by the front port cleat.

Virgil reached over to pull our boat closer when Charlene Beth turned her head, catching me looking at the stain. She muttered a profanity. Before Virgil reacted, she reached down and pulled a five-foot-long boat hook from the deck. She grabbed his collar with the curved brass hook at the end of the pole.

Virgil was off balance when Charlene Beth yanked the pole dragging my friend with it. His shoulder hit the gunwale as he reached for the aluminum railing. He missed and toppled into the saltwater. I leaned to help Virgil when she reached under the steering wheel and pulled out a pistol.

My *figure it out when we get there* plan was woefully inadequate.

"I should've done this when you started nosing around about the crash," she said before firing two shots my direction. Her marksmanship skills weren't as good as her boat hook maneuver. A bullet punctured the gunwale, the other ripped through the back of the seat. I didn't give her a chance to succeed on the third shot. My fear of water was surpassed by my fear of a bullet. I dove overboard then treaded water while the boat provided a barrier between Charlene Beth and me.

Instead of another gunshot, the roar from her Evinrude filled the air. I glanced around the side of our boat to see Charlene Beth speeding away. I then remembered Virgil on the other side of our craft.

I held onto the boat and slowly moved around it. "Virgil, are you okay?"

Garbling sounds were followed by, "Can't swim." Then more garbled sounds.

I hurried around behind the boat and saw the top of Virgil's bobbing head. In much of the marsh, the streams were shallow enough to touch bottom. This wasn't one of those spots. He was eight feet from the boat. His flailing arms slapping the water propelled him farther away. I yelled for him to stop struggling, but doubted he heard me. I pulled myself up on the side of the boat enough to grab two life vests from under the rear seat.

There wasn't time to put one on, so I pushed it under my chest and dog paddled to Virgil. He'd stopped struggling and was floating face down. We were six feet from the jagged shore, pluff mud, and oyster shells clinging to the edge. The boat had drifted much farther than that from us, so the best chance to save him was to push him to the uninviting mud and marsh grasses.

My feet finally touched bottom so I could push Virgil up enough to keep his head above water. I caught my breath then shoved him toward a more solid piece of earth. I sank up to my shins in the mud. It felt like I wasn't going anywhere. Was he alive?

I struggled to push his unmoving body to firmer ground. It took me three tries to get him out of the water. I barely had energy to pull myself up to dry land. If there was any chance of him making it, I'd have to perform CPR. Time was critical, but if I didn't have the energy to lift my arms, I'd be useless. I put my head down and took two deep breaths to garner the strength to help my friend.

Virgil was on his side. I flipped him onto his back, then … then what? I'd taken a CPR course forty years ago. I racked my brain to remember what to do. I put my ear near his mouth and listened for breathing. My heart was beating so fast I couldn't tell if I was hearing him or me. His chest wasn't rising and falling so I guessed he wasn't breathing. I put two fingers on his neck to find a pulse. Nothing. I took another deep breath, placed the heel of my hand on his chest, covered it with my other hand, then began rapid compressions. I knew I should press a certain number of times a minute but couldn't remember how many. Was I helping or were my efforts futile?

My question was answered when I felt his arm move against my leg. He coughed. I turned him on his side as he coughed up water. He tried to speak. I told him to remain still, that he'd be okay. Was I right? The only other sounds I heard were my breathing and birds squawking in the distance.

Virgil turned his head toward me then mumbled, "Am I alive?"

I assured him he was before exhaustion overcame me. I collapsed beside him. I looked at the clear blue sky and gave thanks for both of us surviving. I reached for my phone only to find it wasn't in my pocket. It's probably at the bottom of the stream. Virgil asked what happened to Charlene Beth. I told him how she'd left us in the water. I asked if he still had his phone or if it was in the boat.

"Was in my pocket." He patted each pocket. "Not now."

"That's okay, mine's gone too. It doesn't matter, they'd be waterlogged, useless."

He asked if I could see our boat. I sat and looked around. Our way out of the marsh was about thirty yards behind us, nosed into the mud on the opposite side of the waterway. I felt strength returning to my legs, so I told him I'd try to get the boat. This time, I put on the life vest before swimming back to our ride. It took two efforts before I mustered the strength to pull myself up out of the water enough to climb on board. I looked around to make sure neither of our phones had landed in the boat before we hit the water. All the search yielded were Virgil's crutch and sunglasses. He'll be pleased.

Virgil moved better than I would under similar circumstances. He was waiting for me on the edge of the solid ground as I edged the boat close enough for him to step aboard. He thanked me for saving his life, thanked me for finding his sunglasses. I couldn't tell which he was happier about.

He was moving better, but in no condition to pilot our ride. I wasn't certain how to retrace our voyage to the dock, but thought I recognized the dense marsh at the spot where the plane crashed. If I were right, I thought I could find my way to the Folly River Boat Ramp, so I headed that direction. Besides, I figured it was safer than going the direction that Charlene Beth had exited.

I showed him the spot where the plane crashed.

He nodded then suddenly pointed to the left. He yelled, "What's that?"

I slowed the boat and turned to see where he was pointing. It appeared to be part of a red raft caught in the marsh grasses. I turned the boat and moved closer to the object. I was shocked to see the red was a shirt, a shirt worn by Richard Haymaker.

Virgil was reaching down to pull the body to the boat before I brought our craft to a complete stop. It took both of us to pull the six-foot-two body up enough to get it onboard. Virgil lost his footing and slipped under Richard as they both flopped down on the deck.

Virgil slid out from under the lifeless body and said, "Is he dead?"

Richard's soaked hair was matted, his shirt had what appeared to be a bullet hole below his shoulder. I pushed the sleeve up exposing a clean entry wound and a not-so-clean exit wound on the other side of his arm. Water had washed the blood out of his shirt and off his arm, so I couldn't tell how much he'd lost. I felt his neck for a pulse. It could've been my imagination, but I thought I detected a slight movement. The boat was rocking, so I couldn't be certain if it was a pulse or the movement of the boat. Richard's eyes popped open. It startled me so much that I fell back, coming inches from smacking my head on the gunwale.

"Hey, Richard, how're you doing?" Virgil said as if he'd run into Richard in the grocery.

I laughed when Richard mumbled, "Huh?"

The wound began bleeding. Clearly, he wasn't doing well. I pulled my shirt off then told Virgil to press it against Richard's arm. I told Virgil to stay with him while I piloted us to the dock to find help.

I began thinking we were lost until I saw houses on Folly that backed up to the river. Five minutes later I crossed under the bridge to the island and approached the Folly River Boat Ramp where a pickup truck was pulling a boat out of the water. I yelled for the two men with the truck to help as we hit the side of the ramp. One grabbed our bow, the other looked at Virgil then Richard and asked what happened. Instead of answering, I asked him to call 911 to request both medical assistance and police.

I shut off the motor and moved beside Virgil. Richard was able to hold my shirt against his arm. He appeared more alert than he'd been earlier.

I said, "Richard, what happened?"

Instead of answering, he said, "Where's Charlene Beth?"

We shared what little we knew then again asked what happened.

"She said she wanted us to take a pleasant ride through the marsh. The weather was nice, the kids were with a neighbor. I thought it was a good idea. I was talking to Virgil when we lost cell service. Then we were near where the plane crashed. I said something about how strange she'd been acting since that day."

"What do you mean?" I asked.

"She's been distant. Saying little. I'd heard a rumor about her and some guy in Charleston. Since we were out with no distractions, I figured I'd share the rumor with her. You know, saying how silly it was, knowing it couldn't be true."

He pulled the shirt away from his wound, grimaced, then looked at it. The bleeding had slowed. He returned the shirt to his arm.

"What'd she say?"

"Nothing, not a damned word. She pulled a gun out from under the wheel, pointed at me, pulled the trigger. Chris, I didn't even know she had a gun. Thank God she wasn't a good shot." He pointed at his arm. "Got me here. It knocked me out of the boat. Thought I was a goner. Honest to God I did."

Sirens from emergency vehicles headed out way. Officer Bishop was first to arrive.

"What happened, Mr. Chris?"

I told her Richard's wife shot him, that she was the person who poisoned Gary Isles. I said they might catch her at the house then added the twins were with a neighbor. Bishop got the address from Richard, then radioed for someone to go to the house. She asked Richard what Charlene Beth was driving. He told her a white Lexus SUV but didn't know the plate number.

One of Folly's fire trucks arrived next and two EMTs rushed over. One asked if I was okay. I told him yes, so he went to check on Richard, while the other one tended to Virgil. A crowd had begun to gather. A man I'd seen in Bert's a few times offered me a T-shirt he had in his truck. I accepted and felt like Charles when I noticed the University of South Carolina logo on the front.

I smiled, not only because of the shirt, but more because I was alive.

41

Charles said, "I can't believe you didn't take me on your peaceful boat ride through the marsh."

It was at least the fiftieth time he'd said it, or similar words, in the six days since I docked the bullet riddled boat at the boat ramp. We were on our way to a party at Tom Kale's house. This time, to celebrate me saving Virgil and Virgil and me saving Richard. I didn't think a party was necessary but didn't have the heart to say no to Tom, especially after he told me he'd already invited several others.

The party was also to celebrate the capture of Charlene Beth Haymaker by a Columbia, South Carolina, police officer two and a half hours after she picked up her kids from the neighbor's house. She'd been pulled over for speeding. Thank you police vehicles with on-board computers.

Tom's drive was full when we arrived, three cars were parked along East Ashley Avenue. We were greeted at the door by Kelly Isles carrying Casper. I gave Kelly a peck on the cheek, Charles kissed Casper. Kelly said the party was in full swing, for us to follow her up to the deck, the same spot of the earlier reception for Charles and me. I was surprised to see Cal, standing behind his antique mic and strumming the opening to "Farewell Party." He wore his Stetson, an orange Folly Beach T-shirt, and black jogging shorts.

Tom was in deep conversation with Bob Howard, so he didn't see us arrive. Virgil did see us. He was down to one crutch, but I don't think it hit the deck as he rushed to greet us. He had a beer bottle in his other hand. His Gucci shoes had lost much of their luster after their trip through the marsh. His sunglasses were bent.

"Here's the hero," he said as he gave me a hug. I was pleased when he also hugged Charles. That probably kept my friend from fuming the rest of the afternoon.

Bob moved away from Tom and stood in front of Cal and mouthed the words to "Chiseled in Stone," the song Cal was singing. Cal finished, saw me standing with Charles, tipped his Stetson my direction, and said, "Guys and gals, our guest of honor has arrived."

I turned several shades of red as everyone broke into applause. Virgil put his arm around me. Bob pushed his way through three people standing close together and tapped me on the arm. "Where's beautiful Barb? I'd much rather see her than your ugly mug."

What's not to love about Bob, I thought. "She's at work, Bob. Isn't that where you should be?"

"Hell no. I couldn't pass up free booze and those little sandwich-thingees you have to eat a dozen to equal a sandwich. Besides, since I'm the one who figured everything out and helped you nearly get yourself killed saving two guys, I had to be here to make sure you didn't take all the credit."

"Thanks, Bob. I needed that."

He tapped me again on the arm, pivoted, then headed to the bar.

I spotted Junior leaning against the railing watching his Dad begin another song. I walked over to say hi. He smiled and nodded toward Cal. "I love Dad's enthusiasm. I only wish I'd known him years ago. He's a great guy."

"Have you told him that?"

Junior smiled. "Couple of days ago. I apologized for being such a pain in the ass. We decided to leave Cal's the way it is, except for finishing the paint job. It's his life, his love. It's keeping him young."

"That's great. I know he feels good about you being here."

Cal announced that he was taking "a pause for the cause," set his guitar on its case, and ambled over to Junior and me.

"Welcome to the shindig," Cal said.

I told him I was surprised he was here and not at the bar.

"All the drinkers will wait for me to open in a couple hours."

Chief LaMond was next to arrive. She was off duty and wore a green blouse and tan shorts. She came over, looked around, then said, "Any dead bodies?"

I told her I didn't know of any.

"That's a surprise. Can you handle being around all living folks?"

"I'll manage."

She looked around again, then said, "Where's Richard?"

That was one question I knew the answer to. "Home. He wanted to stay with the kids. They're too young to understand where their mom is. He said he'd feel bad about leaving them."

Cindy smiled, "Here's a phrase I don't often get to use. Smart man."

"Funny," I said.

"Did you hear Charlene Beth's attorney is trying to work a deal with the district attorney? Leniency if she admits to poisoning the pilot, killing Rebecca, and trying to knock off her hubby, twice."

"What are the chances of that happening?"

"About as good as me winning Miss America. I'd better say hi to the host." She left me standing at the rail where Virgil spotted me.

"Virgil, how much trouble are you in with the guy who owned the boat? He probably didn't appreciate the bullet holes."

"Wrong, my friend. Oh, so wrong. He thinks they're wonderful. Said it gives him a great conversation starter, gives his boat character. He said I could use it any time. Want to go out on the marsh with me?"

I smiled instead of shouting, "Never!"

SEA FOG

A FOLLY BEACH HALLOWEEN MYSTERY

BILL NOEL & ANGELICA CRUZ

Copyright © 2021 by Bill Noel

All rights reserved.

No part of this book may be reproduced in any form or by any electronic or mechanical means, including information storage and retrieval systems, without written permission from the author, except for the use of brief quotations in a book review.

Front cover photo and design by Bill Noel

Author photos by Susan Noel

ISBN: 978-1-958414-18-7

Enigma House Press

Goshen, Kentucky 40026

www.enigmahousepress.com

BILL NOEL'S FOLLY BEACH

SOUTH CAROLINA

1 Rita's
2 Dude's surf shop
3 Sand Dollar
4 Haunted House
5 Loggerhead's
6 Snapper Jacks
7 St. James Gate
8 Surf Bar
9 Cal's
10 Mr. John's Beach Store
11 Landrum Gallery/Barb's Books
12 The Crab Shack
13 City Hall/Public Safety
14 Sean Aker, Attorney
15 Planet Follywood
16 Woody's Pizza
17 The Washout
18 Post Office
19 Pewter Hardware
20 Lost Dog Cafe
21 Bert's Market
22 The Edge

* From my imagination to yours.

1

The last time I visited a Halloween haunted house I was thirteen, maybe fourteen. It's hard to remember exactly how old since it was more than fifty-five years ago. What I do remember was the female classmate I went with screaming from the spider-webbed entry until we exited the darkened house between two skeletons grabbing at our arms. True, there were scary scenes in the house, but to impress the girl squeezing my arm enough to cut off circulation, I acted like I regularly sauntered through dark corridors with axes swinging overhead and ghosts waving their translucent hands in my face. The other thing I remember was that she refused to have anything to do with me the remainder of the school year as if I was responsible for her traumatic adventure. I would've been wiser convincing dad to drop us off at the ice-cream shop rather than the haunted house. Live and learn.

Fast forward a few decades, when my best friend Charles Fowler called to suggest it'd be fun if we relived some of our youth and attended a haunted house being staged in a large, white frame house adjacent to Loggerhead's Restaurant. I said no, perhaps louder than a simple no, then reminded him we didn't know any young people we could escort through the exhibit.

He said, "What's that have to do with anything?"

"Nothing other than we're old enough to be mistaken for mummies."

Charles laughed. "Speak for yourself. I was talking to a couple of guys at Planet Follywood last night. They said they went through it and had a good time. Said there were a bunch of older people doing the same thing."

"Older people?"

"Yeah. Some were in their thirties."

"You do know that's less than half our ages."

Charles is two years younger than me.

"Picky, picky, picky. So, what time you meeting me there?"

Arguing with Charles was like arguing with a rabid raccoon, so I said six-thirty, hoping it was before the crowd arrived.

***

BEING THURSDAY, I figured attendance at Folly Beach's answer to Lizzie Borden's House would be light with fewer people around to laugh at us for taking in the attraction, so I waited for him in Loggerhead's parking lot forty-five minutes before the time we agreed to meet. For those who might not know Charles, thirty minutes early was his definition of being on time and it was easier to adjust to his idiosyncrasy than to convert him to reality.

Ten minutes later, he skidded around the corner on his classic Schwinn bicycle, nearly colliding with a Ford pickup truck travelling the correct direction on the one-way street. Charles was breathing heavily as he parked his bike while looking at his bare wrist where normal people wore a watch, his way of indicating he was on time. Years ago, he'd confided to owning a watch, but I'd never seen it.

"Whew," he said as he took a deep breath. "Almost late. Know why I'm wearing this?" He pointed to his gray, long-sleeve sweatshirt with Michigan State in green letters on the front.

"You're cold?" I said, knowing it wasn't the answer he was fishing for.

He shook his head; a motion people often resort to after listening to Charles for a period. "No, silly boy, they offer a course called 'Surviving the Coming Zombie Apocalypse.'"

"You know that how, more importantly, why?"

"Ghost-hunter Google told me. Figured it's appropriate for our adventure through the haunted house."

"Oh," I said, often a reaction to his insightful comments.

"Knew you'd be impressed. Ready to get the heebie-jeebies scared out of us?"

I didn't get a chance to say no since he left his bike leaning against the wooden bench facing the street and headed toward the large tent erected in the attraction's side yard. A large white sign with ENTER AT YOUR OWN RISK painted in blood-red block letters was taped above the tent's open flap.

It was a half hour before sunset but the strobe lights on each side of the tent's entry bounced orange, and black ghost-shaped images off the tent's sides. A half-dozen high-school-aged teens were lined in front of a table where a man dressed like a farmer wearing bib overalls was selling admission tickets. I didn't know whether to laugh or roll my eyes at the faux arrow sticking out of his head. So far, to my relief, no one recognized me. That was until someone tapped me on the shoulder.

"Well if it isn't my good buddy, Chris Landrum," Stanley Kremitz said as he put his arm around my shoulder. "You're a sight for sore eyes."

Charles said he'd get our tickets. I chalked it up as his wanting to avoid Stanley rather than being overcome with generosity, a rare occurrence.

Stanley was an acquaintance I'd run into several times a year ago when he provided information and was for a time a suspect, in a murder I'd become more involved in than I wanted to be. He was a nice, friendly man but had never met a cliché he didn't like, and repeat.

He wore black slacks, a black sweatshirt with a skeleton on the front, and a ballcap with *Staff* on the crown.

"Working the haunted house?" I asked. A safe guess considering his attire.

"A win-win, my friend. I enjoy getting out of the house and feel like I'm helping the wonderful charity benefitting from this shindig." He chuckled. "Besides, Veronica says me doing stuff like this helps keep her sane. Out of sight, out of mind, you know."

Veronica was Stanley's wife, or his better half in Stanley-speak. I understood what she meant about him not being home.

"Oh."

Stanley looked around like he just noticed me standing by myself. "You taking a youngster through?"

Yes, it's Charles, but I didn't share that with Stanley. "No. How're ticket sales?" I said to avoid the next logical question he might ask.

"Selling like hotcakes."

"Good to hear it."

I looked around to find Charles and a possible rescue. He was at the side of the elevated house avoiding eye contact with Stanley.

"Better get in, Stanley. Good seeing you."

He smiled. "Good luck in there. Not everybody gets out alive, you know. You can take that to the bank."

I would rather face a house full of ghosts, goblins, serial killers, and a psychopath or two than spend more time with the cliché king.

"Thanks for that information."

It wasn't hard to figure out where we were to go next. A four-by-eight-foot sheet of plywood was painted white and attached over a window on the side of the house. The structure was less than a block from the ocean, so I suspected during hurricane season, the wood was used to protect the window from storm damage. COFFIN ISLAND HAUNTED HOUSE was written on the plywood in red paint which ran down each letter looking like blood or simply a poor paint job. During its early history, Folly was dubbed Coffin Island.

I joined Charles where a staff member at the bottom of the steps stamped our hands with the image of something that looked like a spider. We headed up the steps. Metal arches were over three of the stairs with artificial spider webs draping down enough to brush against our heads. If it were darker, visitors would get an eerie feeling with the webs touching them.

"What were you and Stanley shooting the breeze about?" Charles laughed at his use of a cliché.

"Funny."

A man on the landing at the top of the stairs emoted screeching sounds as he waved his arm toward the door. I didn't speak screech, so I didn't know what he was saying, but his motions indicated he wanted our tickets and waved us into the pitch-black hallway. The non-profit organization sponsoring the event must've gotten a good price on strobe lights. Everywhere I turned, the flashing, distracting lights disoriented me, achieving their intended goal.

The amplified sound of rattling chains drew our attention to a door leading to a large room where a coffin was lightly illuminated in the corner. I heard screams coming from a couple of the teens who preceded us into the house. I hadn't seen anything to get that level of fear but wouldn't be surprised if something terrifying was coming around the next corner or two.

Before I gave more thought to what was coming next, someone dressed like a mummy slipped up beside me. No, I didn't scream, but will admit to coming close. The creature, man, woman, whatever put its arm around mine and led me to the coffin. Out of the corner of my eye, I saw Charles following at a safe distance.

Fake fog began to fill the area around the coffin and the mummy nudged me closer to the prop—what I assumed to be a prop. Sinister laughter coming from several different voices reverberated off the walls.

The top of the coffin suddenly flipped open and someone dressed like Chucky sat up wielding a knife. I'd never seen the Chucky movies about a serial killer and voodoo practitioner who, after being shot, somehow became a child-sized doll, but did have to take a giant step back after spotting the lethal weapon. Okay, yes, I'm a coward, but, hey, who wouldn't be faced with someone sitting up and staring at you from inside a coffin. Charles's laugh was louder than those coming from the sound system. I didn't want to go Chucky on him, but revenge wasn't far from my mind.

The top of the coffin closed as quickly as it had opened. A howling sound pierced the air and a spotlight's beam penetrated the artificial fog as it reappeared in the room. The light shone on a door at the side of the room revealing a sign reading *Blackbeard's Bedroom*. The tour-guide mummy waved us to the door then stepped aside as the door slowly creaked open. There were no strobe lights, fake fog, or strange creatures within sight. This time, Charles took the lead and stuck his head in the door and looked around. I figured the mummy hadn't led us to an empty room, so I stood behind Charles to wait for the next fright. After all, Blackbeard's bedroom wasn't designed to give visitors a warm, fuzzy feeling. Edward Teach, aka Blackbeard, the scary pirate from the early 1700s had once resided on Folly and was known for putting smoking fuses in his long, stringy black hair to frighten his victims.

Folly's Blackbeard incarnation wasn't quite that frightening, but when he put his hand on Charles's shoulder, my friend jumped higher than I'd ever seen him levitate. I didn't laugh, but came close, as Charles quickly backed out of the room.

The mummy then nudged us into what was the kitchen although there were no appliances, and only one of the cabinets had been installed. Before I looked around to see what frightful site we were supposed to see, someone screamed. It was loud, scary, and not recorded.

Instead of hearing recorded laughter or other sound associated with a haunted house, someone on the far side of the kitchen yelled, "Get the lights!"

Overhead lights came on temporarily blinding me. The door leading from the kitchen to the back porch swung open and two men wearing the same kind of black sweatshirts and hats Stanley had worn rushed into the room, looked at Charles and me, then headed into a large, walk-in pantry where two teens were backed against the shelves. One of the teenagers had his hands over his face, the other pointing to something on the floor.

Charles and my visit to Folly's haunted house quickly became a nightmare as we stepped in the pantry and stared at a body on the floor.

2

The phrase *running around like chickens with their heads cut off* came to mind as a staff member yelled for everyone to leave the house. He didn't have to say it twice to the two teens who were out the back door as quickly as a cheetah. The older man waved for Charles and me to leave, then stared at the body before rushing out to start herding those who followed us into the house to the exit. The other man held his hand over his mouth. I was afraid he was going to lose his latest meal. He took two deep breaths, appeared to regain composure before glancing in each corner of the pantry like he was afraid someone wielding a knife would jump out at him, then rushed out of the room.

Despite being told to leave, Charles motioned me closer to the body and knelt near the unmoving person.

"Know who he is?" Charles said as he looked up at me.

The man's head was turned at an odd angle, so I couldn't get a clear look at his face. He was in his forties, white with light-brown hair, and wearing jeans with raveled cuffs and a black, long-sleeve sweatshirt. He didn't appear to be one of the actors in the house but could've had a behind-the-scenes role.

"Don't think so. You?"

The recorded music and haunting sound effects came to a screeching halt and were replaced by the sound of sirens from Folly's police and fire vehicles approaching the house.

The gruff voice of the older of the two staff members barked, "I told you to leave."

"On our way," Charles said although he was still bent over the body.

"Now!"

Before the man physically evicted us, Officer Trula Bishop barged into the room. I'd known Trula for four years since she began working as a Public Safety Officer in Folly's Department of Public Safety, more commonly known as a cop in the police department. She was professional, competent, and someone I'd trust in the most difficult situation.

She glanced at Charles and me, nodded at the worker, before walking over to the corpse, bending to get a better look at his face, then saying, "Anyone know who he is?"

Instead of answering her question, the staff member again told Charles and me to leave.

"Sir," Bishop said, "I'm speaking to these gentlemen as well as to you."

I was glad Charles didn't stick his tongue out at the bossy staff member.

I said, "Officer Bishop, I don't recall seeing him before tonight."

"Me either," Charles added, not to be left out.

Two firefighters who double as EMTs entered the room and immediately went to the body, ignoring Officer Bishop and the rest of us.

Bishop glared at the staff member. "Sir, what's your name?"

"Lester, ma'am. Lester Holmes."

Bishop jotted it down in a small notebook she pulled out of her pocket. "Mr. Holmes, do you know who this is?" She pointed to the body like he wouldn't have known who she was referring to.

"Umm, no officer."

Bishop looked back at the body and then at Lester. "He didn't work in the haunted house?"

"I don't believe so."

"You're not sure?"

"Not really, ma'am. There are a lot of people involved in the project. Actors dressed like ghosts, skeletons, Blackbeard, serial killers; then the technical crew running the lights, sound, fog machine, and other special effects. I don't see everyone. My job is to make sure once guests finish the tour, they leave down the back stairs."

"You don't see everyone working here?"

"No. I don't get here until right before we open. Leave as soon as the last guest is out the door."

"Okay, Mr. Holmes, please go out the back door and wait at the bottom of the stairs. A detective will want to talk with you once he arrives."

Folly is in Charleston County, South Carolina, a stone's throw from beautiful and historic Charleston. Its small police force isn't large enough or trained to handle murder investigations on the island so that's delegated to the Charleston County Sheriff's Office.

Lester started to say something, but apparently thought better of it, before saying, "Yes ma'am." He gave a tentative salute to Officer Bishop and back peddled out of the room.

Bishop rolled her eyes as he left, then turned to Charles and me. "Okay, Mr. Chris, Mr. Charles, what do you two know about what happened?"

"Trula, I'm afraid not much. Charles and I were going through the exhibit when someone, probably one of the teenagers who went through ahead of us, started screaming. We came in here, saw the two teens and the body. Charles, anything to add?"

"That's about it, Trula," Charles said, one of the few times he was at a loss of words.

"Then I've got another question," Bishop said, "Why in holy hell were you two alleged adults, senior-citizen adults, walking through a haunted house?"

Excellent question, I thought. I turned to the instigator of our visit to respond.

"Thought it'd be fun to see what scares kids nowadays," Charles said, then smiled.

This time Trula didn't hide rolling her eyes in front of the intended recipients.

One of the EMTs moved beside Bishop before she could humiliate us more. He cleared his throat to get her attention, then said, "Officer Bishop, he's deceased."

I was surprised when she didn't roll her eyes at his massive understatement.

"Call the coroner's office. I'll call the Chief and the Sheriff's Office." She turned to Charles and me. "Guys, sure you don't know anything else about what happened?"

I assured her we didn't.

"Then head out the back door and join the others who were here. Don't leave the property."

It would've taken a tsunami to get Charles to leave before learning more about what had happened.

We walked down the back stairs where a cluster of people was herded off to the side by a couple of police officers. We reached the bottom of the steps and were directed to the gathered group by an officer I didn't know.

The group was interesting to say the least. The mummy, Chucky from the coffin, Blackbeard, and two other actors dressed like witches I hadn't remembered seeing in the house were clustered together. It was just after sunset, so they didn't look as scary as they had in the dark, fog-filled house. Two men in their twenties and one slightly younger woman were dressed in all black including caps that looked appropriate for bank robbers were near the scary actors. I assumed they were the special effects team. Two other casually dressed men were standing near the actors and staff.

Standing a few feet apart from the cast and crew, I recognized the two teens who'd been in front of us, and six others, four teens and two youngsters roughly ten years old, were huddled together.

Fortunately, the temperature was mild for late October and while a couple of those gathered were shivering, it wasn't because of the weather. A police officer I did recognize was interviewing two of the teens and taking notes. Officer Allen Spencer had been new to the force when I moved to Folly nearly a dozen years ago. He and I'd talked countless times since then.

Allen noticed Charles and me as we joined the group, gave a doubletake, and looked to see who was with us.

He finished his interview with one of the teens and came our way.

"Chris, Charles, you playing fossils in the house or taking youngsters through?"

"Funny, Officer Spencer," I said.

Charles said, "I'm the youngster Chris was escorting."

Allen smiled. "Charles, I didn't mean mental age."

"Funny, Officer Spencer," Charles said.

Spencer looked around to see if anyone was listening. Seeing no one, he said, "Just kidding, Charles. What happened? I got stuck out here and have no idea what's going on. That is, except for the contradictory stories I'm hearing from the folks who were in there."

"Allen, I'm afraid we can't add much." I shared what little we knew, then asked if anyone he had interviewed knew the identity of the victim.

"No one claimed to have seen him before, but only the two teenagers over there saw the body." He pointed to the two who had been in front of us in the house.

Charles rubbed his chin. "You're telling us no one in that group even saw the body?"

"Correct. The staff member said the pantry where the body's located isn't part of the exhibit, or whatever you'd call the haunted house parts of the house. The two who found it didn't wait for the mummy tour guide and rushed ahead and opened a door they weren't supposed to open. The staff member said it should've been locked. The kids said it wasn't. They figured they were supposed to open it and be scared by something. Don't think they thought it'd be a real horror."

Add Charles and me to that group.

3

"What are you two troublemakers doing going through a haunted—oh crap, never mind," Chief Cindy LaMond said through gritted teeth as she pulled us out of the group like a sheepdog herding two recalcitrant sheep out of the herd and escorted us to a detached garage in the rear of the property.

I'd known Chief LaMond since my second year on Folly and considered she and her husband Larry good friends.

"Chief," Charles said as Cindy opened the garage door and shooed us in, "I thought Chris would like to see how great a job some of your local folks did providing a wonderful adventure for your younger citizens this Halloween season."

Cindy closed the door after we were in the garage. "Charles, I'm from East Tennessee; grew up around farm animals of all kinds; shoveled you-know-what until my arms felt like they were falling off and my nose screamed for an air freshener."

Charles nodded. "So?"

"Glad you asked. I went into law enforcement to escape that. Then lo and behold, here I am with you spreading more crap than I ever ran across in the barnyard. Since I'm Chief and know everything, you dragged the old guy you're with through the house to be nosy, which happens to be your biggest vice, and something you do better than anyone I've ever known. How am I doing?"

"Chief, Abraham Lincoln said, 'It has been my experience that folks who have no vices have very few virtues.'"

"Cindy LaMond said you just added another clump of crap to the pile."

Enough, I thought but didn't say or quote anyone saying it. "Chief, is there a reason we're here instead of out there with the others?"

"Yes. I don't know many of the folks from the house we've corralled, and the three I know, aren't known for reliability. Despite the pain in my rear you two cause, you're reliable and observant."

"You're a wise lady," Charles said.

"Don't forget the part about you being a pain in my posterior."

Over the years, Charles and I had stumbled upon a few murders and despite not having law enforcement training or experience, had managed to help the police bring some killers to justice. In fact, Charles is a self-proclaimed private detective. In the process, we'd inadvertently interfered with police investigations, incurred the wrath of numerous law enforcement officials, including Chief LaMond, and had come close to being killed on more than one occasion. Despite that, Cindy had learned to trust our, or at least my, judgement and had even sought our help. She would deny it regardless of the kind of oath she would be put under. I didn't blame her. I often questioned my judgment and that of Charles and a few of our friends who've gotten into things we shouldn't have.

"Chief," I said, "what do you want to know?"

"Your version of what you saw, experienced, and your gut reactions about what went on in there." She nodded the direction of the house.

We alternated telling her everything beginning with arriving at the tent then ending when Officer Bishop arrived. The Chief asked if we saw anything unusual during our time in the house.

Charles smiled. "Anything unusual?" He rubbed his chin. "You mean other than a mummy grabbing my arm, a clown sitting up in a coffin waving a knife in Chris's face, and, oh yeah, Blackbeard scaring the, well, stuff out of me?"

"Let me rephrase, anything other than what you'd expect to find in a Halloween haunted house?"

"Not really," I said. "It was early, so I doubt many people had been through before us. The only two I saw ahead of us were the two teenagers, the ones who found the body."

Cindy shook her head. "That's all?"

Charles said, "Afraid so, Chief."

I nodded.

"Crap."

"Chief," I said, "let me ask you something."

"Could I stop you? Never mind, go ahead."

"Who owns the house?"

She removed a small notebook from her pocket. It was like the ones Officers Bishop and Spencer were using.

"Fred Robinson. He's new to the area; bought it a few months ago."

Charles said, "Who's he?"

"Don't know much. He's a dentist with an office on James Island; think it's one of several offices in a practice out of Savannah. I talked to him once. Jotted his name down since he was new here. He was meeting with his contractor in the front yard. Said he was fixing the house up. Not sure if he planned to live in it or use it as a rental. He didn't offer additional information. Not a very friendly fellow. Why?"

"Curious," I said. "Wondering if the body could've had something to do with the owner."

Officer Bishop stuck her head in the door. "Chief, Detective Adair's here."

I'd met Kenneth Adair with the County Sheriff's Office three years ago when he was lead detective on the murder of a college student. He'd focused on a friend of mine as the prime suspect. Detective Adair and I weren't on the friendliest terms since I nosed into the investigation and helped prove my friend innocent. It mattered little to him that I also helped catch the murderer. Go figure.

Cindy said, "I'll be right there."

Bishop left to relay the message, and Cindy said, "Guys, let me know if you learn anything that may be helpful." Before she left, she added, "Now get your butts back out there and stay with the group from in the house until Adair talks to you."

Charles turned to me after Cindy had left. "Chris, you hear that?"

"What?"

"She wants us to find out who killed the guy."

That wasn't my interpretation, not by a long shot.

That'd never stopped Charles. I had a hunch this time would be no different.

We returned to the group still huddled near the steps leading from the house. Officer Spencer was talking to one of the teenage girls while another officer I didn't know was in deep conversation with one of the witches. We received a couple of curious stares from others in the group, most likely because we'd been singled out by Chief LaMond. Someone had distributed bottles of water to the assembled group and two of the crew members were off to the side puffing on cigarettes.

Chief LaMond was near the tent at the front of the property talking with Detective Adair. The detective was in his late thirties, roughly six-foot-one, thin, and sporting a buzz cut. He wore a white shirt, navy blazer, slacks with a sharp crease, and highly polished wingtips. He looked like he could've come from a corporate board meeting, although I doubted it since he was dressed like he'd been each time I'd seen him during our previous encounters.

Adair and the Chief finished their conversation and approached. He whispered something to Cindy, then turned to the group.

"Ladies and gentlemen, I'm Detective Adair from the County Sheriff's Office. I apologize for you having to be here so long and know this has been a trying evening. Chief LaMond and I will be talking to each of you one-on-one over by the garage. I know you want to get out of here, so we'll be as quick as possible. I'll be back momentarily."

He and Cindy went up the back stairs and entered the house.

It was well after dark and Charles and I were the last to be interviewed, so I learned *as quick as possible* was two hours, twenty minutes.

I apparently drew the short straw and had the privilege of being interviewed by Adair; Charles lucked out with Chief LaMond. We were a few minutes into the interview before Adair remembered me from previous encounters. From his body language and sighs during some of my responses, his recollections weren't any more positive than mine. Once he figured he couldn't learn anything significant from me, he gave me his card, told me to call if I remembered anything else, then said I could leave. He didn't say anything about me not nosing around. I didn't know it for a fact but would put money on Chief LaMond telling Charles not to.

Charles headed for his bike; I started home when I noticed a crowd of onlookers standing on the sidewalk across the street from the house. The group was in front of the Charleston Oceanfront Villas, an expansive, four-story, oceanfront condo complex. Police and fire activity are a spectator sport on Folly, drawing crowds of locals and visitors. It was dark so I couldn't get a good look at the faces, but thought I recognized Preacher Burl Costello as he was illuminated by the red and blue strobes from two emergency vehicles. I'd met Burl a few years ago when he arrived on Folly and founded First Light, a nondenominational church that meets most Sundays on the beach. With his five-foot-five-inch height, portly body, milk-chocolate colored mustache, and balding head, he would've been hard to miss.

The preacher was standing with his arm around the shoulders of a young lady, around ten years old, although I'm terrible at guessing ages, so she could've been a couple of years on either side of ten.

I would've crossed the street to talk to Burl, but after telling my version of what I knew and saw more times than I would've liked to, I wasn't ready to repeat it. Instead, I stayed on the same side of the street as the haunted house and walked four blocks to my cottage.

I was tired when I got home and plopped down in bed hoping sleep would follow quickly. It didn't. Every time I started to drift off, visions of Chucky, Blackbeard, a mummy, a couple of ghosts popped in my head. I could handle those images. My confidence evaporated when I kept seeing the body from the pantry.

4

Morning came earlier than usual after a restless night of mummies, Chucky, pirates, ghosts, and yes, a real dead body. Knowing the state of my kitchen pantry, going next door to Bert's Market for breakfast seemed like my best, possibly only, option to stop my stomach from an all-out revolt.

Bert's was usually quiet this time of day, so I hadn't expected to see anyone I knew; all the better after the event-filled evening and restless night. Of course, what we plan is seldom what we get.

I was halfway down the aisle when from across the room I heard the familiar voice of Burl Costello say, "Good morning, Brother Chris, how's this fine morning treating you?"

"Morning Preacher, wasn't expecting to see you this morning."

"I was going to give you a call. I saw you last night leaving the haunted house and wanted to touch base."

"I thought I saw you, but it was dark, so I wasn't sure."

He nodded. "I'm not one to stick my nose in something that doesn't concern me but in a way this does. Being a shepherd, I need to keep my flock safe."

I smiled. "Preacher, I'm sure nothing is going to come out of the haunted house and steal the souls of the good people of Folly."

"Brother Chris, perhaps we should speak about it," he said as his eyes darted around the room.

Something was on his mind; something best not discussed in public.

"Want to go over to the house for coffee and donuts?"

Burl smiled. "A splendid idea. My favorites: donuts and good conversation."

"I'll get the donuts and try to come up with some good conversation."

I grabbed a box of prepackaged powdered sugar-covered donuts. We each drew a cup of complimentary coffee from the large urn, then headed to the counter. As I paid, I glanced at Burl, wondering why he was interested in last night's event and who the young girl was with him.

The short walk to the house was quiet with Burl matching me step for step but not saying anything. Strange, since he's usually talkative. I ushered him into the seldom-used kitchen where he attacked the box of donuts like he hadn't eaten in days. I ate two donuts to keep up with my guest. After all, I didn't want to be rude, or so I rationalized.

After he wiped flecks of powdered sugar out of his mustache, I said, "Preacher, what's on your mind?"

The question hung in the air as much as the smell of our coffee.

Burl reached for a third donut, then pulled his hand back. "Brother Chris, what do you know about the deceased individual? Know his identity?"

I leaned forward. "Charles and I stumbled into the situation. We were walking through the house and were startled like everyone else when we heard a scream that was more than someone frightened by a fake ghoul. There was a bunch of shouting and on the floor a body." I paused and waited for Burl to say something. He didn't, so I continued, "That's the end of the story. As far as I know, I'd never seen him and wish I hadn't last night." I again paused, but Burl remained silent. "Preacher, what's your interest? Do you know something about the death?"

Burl stirred his coffee as he looked at the donuts. He took a deep breath, then said, "It's about the young lady I was standing with when I spotted you. Do you know her?"

"Don't think so. I couldn't see her face that well, my eyes aren't as young as they used to be. Besides, at my age, I don't know many young people."

Burl chuckled, then said, "Brother Chris, I can appreciate that, the age part."

"Does she have something to do with what happened in the haunted house?"

He smiled, took a bite of donut, then said, "No, she was simply curious about what happened. Her name is Roisin. She moved to Folly from Minnesota with her family in May. We've become close in the last couple of months." He hesitated, then said, "She has a different way of looking at the world and is wise beyond her eleven years."

Not knowing what to say, but wanting to encourage him to talk, I said, "Does she and her family attend First Light?"

"No, I met her when she literally ran into me one afternoon in front of the Post Office. She was picking up her family's mail and flipping through a magazine when we collided." Burl chuckled. "Remember almost word-for-word what she said. 'So deeply sorry, sir. Didn't see you standing there. Please forgive my lack of observation.' She was more adult than many adults I know."

"It sounds like it."

"We stood there and spent nearly an hour talking about everything." Burl hesitated and laughed.

"What's so funny?"

"After she told me she was from Minnesota, she asked if I knew Minnesota has three times more white tail deer than college students. Of course, I didn't. I started to ask if she was related to Charles, the trivia collector."

"She sounds interesting."

"Quite. I met her mother, Shannon, the same day. I walked Roisin home to let her parents know where she'd been for so long."

"Oh," I said, not knowing what else to say.

"Brother Chris, the family follows a different spiritual path." He slowly took a sip of coffee, then added, "They're practicing Wiccans."

Visions of witches flying around the house on brooms or a witch with a group of flying monkeys flashed through my mind.

As if Burl could read my thoughts, he laughed. "It's not what you think. Wiccans are not the bad guys so many have made them out to be. While it's not Christian, it's a peaceful, nature-based religion."

"I'm not that familiar with the religion, Preacher."

"Not many are. Perhaps I could introduce you to Roisin and her family. Shannon owns Red Raven Herbs and Readings, a small business she runs out of their home. The dad's a lawyer."

"I'd like that."

A loud knock on the back door nearly brought me out of my chair.

Before I got to the door, Charles opened it, stuck his head in, and said, "Chris, have any suspects in our case?" He hesitated, looked at Burl, then as if nothing were unusual about me sitting in the kitchen sharing donuts with the preacher, said, "Hi Preacher. Didn't know anyone else was here."

Charles walked in the ever-shrinking kitchen, sat next to Burl, and looked at me for an answer.

"Charles, we don't have a case. We're aged citizens where one convinced the other to go to a haunted house and things that have nothing to do with us happened. End of story."

Charles said, "Ronald Reagan said, 'Facts are stubborn things.'"

"Gentlemen," Burl said, "I'll leave you to your discussion."

Charles said, "Preacher, you don't have to go."

"Brother Charles, if I don't prepare my sermon, I'll have an entire flock trying to stick me in the coffin that I hear is in the haunted house." He stood and looked toward the door. "I'm already a day behind."

I took his hint, thanked him for joining me for *breakfast*, and escorted him to the front door.

Leave it to Charles, aka the fount of presidential quotes, to be up bright and early itching to get started on an investigation, a preacher telling me there are witches among us, and here I am trying to peacefully have a donut and coffee after little sleep.

There's seldom a dull moment on Folly.

5

After Burl left, Charles looked at the few remaining donuts, then to the empty counter near the sink, and said, "Man cannot live on donuts alone."

"Did a President say that?" I thought I knew the answer, but knowing Charles's penchant for quoting United States Presidents, I wouldn't put money on it.

"Probably, but I don't know who. You avoiding my question?"

"Which question?"

"You have any suspects?"

I was afraid that was the one. I started to respond when he held his hand in my face. "Hold that thought. Let's take a walk."

My back ached from tossing and turning all night, so it may have been one of Charles's better ideas. It was in the low sixties so I grabbed a light jacket and followed him out the back door, then toward Center Street, aptly named since it was the figurative center of the six-mile-long, half-mile-wide barrier island, and the center of commerce housing most of the island's restaurants and shops.

We reached Center Street when Charles said, "Well, suspects?"

"Charles, first, whatever happened is a matter for the police, not us. Second, even if there was the slightest chance it did involve us, how would I know anything about suspects? You were with me the entire time I was there. We left as soon as Detective Adair and Chief LaMond dismissed us."

We turned right on Center Street. Charles said, "Know where we're going?"

"The Dog."

"Wow, you're on your way to being nearly as good a detective as me. How'd you know?"

That was a much easier question than identifying suspects. "You said man, meaning you, couldn't live on donuts alone, so I figured you were hungry. The Dog is your favorite restaurant."

The Lost Dog Cafe, known by most residents and many vacationers as the Dog, was not only Charles's favorite restaurant, but mine as well. I'd eaten countless more meals there than in my cottage. The food was excellent, the atmosphere refreshing, and more importantly, they always had food, something that couldn't be said for my kitchen.

"Not bad. Now, how about suspects?"

"Charles, I said—"

"I know, I know, you don't have any. Wanted to give you a chance before I told you who I'm suspecting."

I'd have to wait until we were seated. We were escorted to a table in the center of the restaurant. It was often packed with people waiting for a table this time of day, but late October wasn't its busy season.

Amber, a server who'd been at the Dog since I moved to Folly, greeted us with a smile, a mug of coffee, and a question about what we wanted to order.

Charles returned her smile. "Dear, sweet Miss Amber, why don't you guess?"

"French toast for Chris, Loyal Companion for you."

No, Amber wasn't psychic. Those were the items we ordered roughly ninety-five percent of the time we were there for breakfast.

Charles smiled and said, "Excellent guess, Miss Amber."

Another no, neither of them consulted me on my menu choice. Sadly, I admit, they were right.

Amber left to put in our order and Charles returned to the topic I wanted to avoid.

"Chris, you know John or Bri Rice?"

"No. Who're they?"

"The J and the B of J&B Renovations. Husband and wife team."

"Okay, so what's J&B Renovations?"

"Mr. Unobservant, didn't you see the J&B job sign leaning against the haunted house?"

"Umm, no. Should I have?"

"Of course. It was there plain as day, right by the hose rack on the side of the house, turned so the words faced the house. How could you miss it?"

Could be because it was against the side of the house with the words facing the house so I couldn't read it. It would've been futile to say that, so I said, "Do you know them?"

"Nope."

"How do you know about them? I'm guessing since their sign was at the house, they had something to do with the renovations."

"You're catching on."

Before I asked what I was catching on, Amber returned with our meals and a question.

"Did you hear they found a body in the haunted house last night? A real body."

Charles looked at his plate, then at the server. "Miss Amber, glad you asked. Not only did we hear about it, we were there when it was discovered."

She shook her head. "Why doesn't that surprise me? What were you two geezers doing in the haunted house?"

"I was showing Chris what everyone's been talking about this Halloween season. Thought he needed to see what scares youngsters like you and me."

Amber had recently turned fifty, so I wouldn't put her in the youngster category, although she wouldn't hear that from me. Charles was nearly my age, so no comment was needed.

"Charles," Amber said, "since the customer is always right, I won't tell you what I think of your comment about us being youngsters. Sounds like you two stumbled into a horrible situation—again."

Charles said, "Amber, hear who the body belonged to?"

"Not yet. Nobody I've heard from has even said for certain what caused his death."

Charles said, "Any theories going around?"

She chuckled. "Old Mr. Musgrave said he must've been scared to death by a ghost in the house. Sally Denton figured it was a heart attack. If you ask me, they were guessing. None of our regular cop customers have been in, so I don't have an official version. You mean you don't know?"

"Not yet."

Two men at a table across the room waved in Amber's direction, so she headed their way.

"J&B Renovations," Charles said, answering the question I asked before Amber brought our food, "is in Mt. Pleasant. They do big and small jobs in the Charleston area. Hired by Dr. Robinson, the new owner of the house. It didn't look too bad on the outside, but from what I've heard needed a lot of work inside. Was taking longer than the owner thought it should, pissed him off royally. They're now supposed to be done November 1."

"Charles, if you didn't know the couple, how'd you learn about them? I doubt all that was on the side of the job sign facing the house."

"Last night after the senior citizen I was with went home to get his beauty sleep, I figured I couldn't learn anything about what happened holed up in my apartment, so I turned my trusty Schwinn around and peddled back to the haunted house. Stanley was getting ready to head home until I cornered him. A hundred clichés later, he told me everything I told you."

"Stanley didn't happen to know what happened to the guy did he?

"Nope."

"Did he know who he was?"
"Nope."
"Learn anything else from Stanley or anyone else there?"
"Nope. That's what our job is."
I thought, but didn't say, *nope*.

6

Charles left the Dog to go to his apartment and get his bike so he could deliver a wetsuit for our friend Dude Sloan, owner of the surf shop. Charles's surf shop deliveries were limited to Folly and nearby areas since they were made on his bike. These deliveries along with helping a couple of restaurants clean during tourist season, and lending a hand to contractors who needed unskilled, seriously unskilled, help were ways Charles made enough money to live modestly.

Amber asked if I needed more coffee, but since I was about to float out the door, I declined. She also asked if I was okay after my trip to the haunted house. One of Amber's many attributes was her deep concern for people she'd friended over the years. After assuring her I was, I knew she wasn't convinced, but she was perceptive enough not to push.

She looked around to see if she was needed elsewhere in the restaurant, sat in the chair Charles had vacated, then said, "Jason and his girlfriend of the week went through the haunted house the night before you-know-what was found. What if he'd been the one to stumble on the body?"

Jason was Amber's twenty-one-year-old son who I'd first met

when he was about the same age as Burl's friend Roisin. Amber and I'd dated a couple of years and she'd broken it off when Jason happened to walk in an apartment the same time I'd discovered a murdered woman. She was afraid I'd expose him to other dangerous situations. I'd thought that unlikely but understood her concern; a concern she was expressing now.

I explained how the body was in a room that wasn't part of the haunted house experience and reminded her Jason most likely wouldn't have seen the body even if he'd toured the house the night I was there. The look she gave me indicated she wasn't swayed by my explanation. A customer at the table behind us waved for the check, so Amber cut our conversation short to take care of the customer. I left money for my, and yes, Charles's breakfast on the table and told Amber I'd see her later.

Amber hadn't known the identity of the body, but if anyone did, it'd be Chief LaMond. So instead of heading home, I walked three blocks to the Folly Beach Department of Public Safety located in the salmon-colored City Hall. The Chief was sitting at her desk and partially hidden behind a stack of multi-colored folders. I stood in the doorway but was tempted not to disturb her since her expression reminded me of someone who'd watched their house get blown away in a hurricane.

The decision was made for me when Cindy looked up, saw me lurking, shook her head, then waved me in.

"Catch you at a bad time," I said, stating the obvious.

"Hell, Chris, why would you think that? All I'm doing is sitting here looking at photos of one of our cruisers. One that's two feet shorter than it was when Officer Dampier decided to chase a speeder out your road, then decided to swerve to avoid hitting a dog, then unintentionally, or so he said, decided to try to move a giant oak out of his way with the front of the car."

"Is Dampier okay?"

She tapped her finger on the photo. "He's much better than the tree and our newest patrol car. With that cheery image out of my head, what are you going to do to add more grief to my day?"

I smiled, hoping it'd be contagious, and said, "No grief, Chief. Thought I'd stop by to see how you were doing."

My smile wasn't contagious.

"Don't suppose you honestly think I believe that pile of crap?"

Instead of kicking me out, she motioned me to move two boxes off the chair in front of her desk, then to have a seat. I took it as a good sign.

"So, why'd you really come up here? Most sane citizens avoid this office."

"Curious what you've learned about the body in the haunted house."

"Anyone tell you what curiosity does to cats?"

"Sure, Chief. Glad I'm not a cat."

She stared at me. "Todd Lee."

"Todd Lee?"

"My first reaction to your curiosity comment was to tell you I didn't believe you, that you and probably Charles were nosing into something that's police business and none of yours. You would say of course you weren't nosing in, that you were there when the body was found, and simply curious. I'd tell you that was a crock. You'd give me that innocent smile you've perfected and wait for me to tell you what I knew."

"Chief, I'm—"

She leaned forward and waved her hand in my face. "I'm skipping all that. Todd Lee." She sat back in her chair and folded her arms across her chest.

It finally made sense. "Todd Lee was the victim."

"Wow, no wonder you claim to be a private detective."

"That's Charles, I'm merely a curious citizen."

"Right."

"So, who's Todd Lee?"

"Just told you. He's the body in the haunted house; the one that wasn't in a coffin."

Time to try another tact. "How'd you find out who he was?"

"Superior detective work."

"And?"

"Georgia driver's license in the wallet in his pocket."

"Excellent detective work."

"Smart ass."

"Yes ma'am. What else did you learn about Todd Lee?"

"Remind me why it's any of your business."

"Merely curious."

"I repeat, right."

I gave her one of my *innocent smiles* I wasn't aware I had and waited.

This time, she returned my smile. "Todd Lee turned forty-three nine days ago. Don't know how he celebrated his last birthday among the living."

"If his driver's license was from Georgia, what was he doing here?"

"Good question. In the condition he was in, he couldn't answer it, and no one else there knew him. So, no clue. The address on the license was in Savannah. Detective Adair is contacting police down there to see what they can find."

"Cause of death?"

"Hole in the heart, according to the coroner. Won't know for sure until the autopsy."

"Shot?"

"Nope."

"Knife?"

"Nope."

"Cupid's arrow?"

"Nope, wrong holiday."

I was out of options. "Then what?"

"No more guesses?"

"Nope."

She smiled. "I deserved that. You wouldn't guess it anyway. Ice pick."

"You're kidding."

She smiled again. "Nope."

"How long had he been dead?"

"Several hours before you showed up, so you're not a suspect, although if given time, I'd come up with something to charge you with."

Over the years, Cindy had threatened to have me arrested for everything from harassing a police chief, to being a pain in her rear. I ignored her comment.

"Was he killed in the house or put there after he was murdered?"

"Lividity would indicate that's where he took his last breath. If he was moved, it wasn't far, probably dragged."

"Did he have any connection to the haunted house?"

"No idea."

"Anything else?"

"Yeah, get out of here before I do something I could be arrested for."

I took the hint, thanked her, and left.

7

Charles was perched on his bicycle at the entry to the Folly Beach Department of Public Safety when I exited the building.

"What took you so long?" he said as he looked at his wrist, where, of course, no watch resided.

I ignored his comment. "What're you doing here?"

"Delivered a wetsuit to a man from France. He and his family are spending three months at Iguana House. Saw you heading in and figured you were interrogating the Chief about the dead guy. Found time in my busy schedule to wait for you."

The Iguana House is a rental property a block past the entrance to the Department of Public Safety. The house has an eclectic 1940s cottage look with a brightly colored exterior, not unlike many houses on the quirky island.

"Glad you could work it into your busy schedule," I said with a touch of sarcasm. "If you delivered a wetsuit, why is one in your basket?"

"Excellent question, resident of a land far from France. My new acquaintance looked at the wetsuit, held it up, and exclaimed something in his native tongue. I don't have to understand French to know he wasn't admiring my delivery."

"So why is it in your basket?"

"Apparently, it's the wrong size and for some reason beyond my understanding, he said I should have known that. I have the privilege of exchanging it for a larger size, a much larger size."

"Sorry. That where you're headed?"

"Nope. His condescending attitude didn't quite inspire a quick return with a suit that'd fit his ample belly. Know where I was headed next?"

I didn't ask how he thought I'd know. "Where?"

"Haunted house. Want a ride?"

I was much larger and heavier than any package he'd delivered for the surf shop, so I declined and said I'd meet him there.

I took the beach access path to West Ashley Avenue then the short walk to the haunted house. Charles had already parked and was talking to a man who appeared to be in his late forties, tall, maybe six-foot-six or taller, muscular, with dark brown hair. The image of Paul Bunyan came to mind.

"Chris, you know John Rice?"

"Don't believe so," I said, and extended my hand. "John, I'm Chris Landrum."

We shook hands and he said, "Pleased to meet you."

Charles said, "John owns J&B Renovations. They're doing the work on the house. I was telling him how we were here when the body was found."

John said, "Rough."

"Did you know the dead guy?" Charles said.

He was beginning his fishing trip.

Don't know," John said. "Who was it?"

I said, "Todd Lee."

Charles glared at me, no doubt because I hadn't told him what Cindy had shared.

"You're kidding," John said. "You sure?"

"I heard it from the Chief," I said, and added for Charles's benefit, "a few minutes ago. You know him?"

John waved at one of his workers entering a door to the lower level of the house. "Reggie, go ahead and fix the door. I'll be there in a few." He turned to Charles and me. "Sorry. What were you saying?"

"Did you know the dead guy?" Charles asked before I repeated the question.

"Umm, yeah. He came around looking for a job. I met him near where we're standing now. I needed help so I hired him. He worked about a week." He shook his head. "Not a good fit."

Charles said, "Why?"

"Don't get me wrong. He was a good worker but didn't take kindly to being told what to do or how to do anything. I couldn't have that, you understand. Told him I didn't need him any longer. Gave him an extra week's pay. I could tell he was borderline homeless. Felt sorry for the guy, but again, couldn't have his attitude on the jobsite, you understand."

Charles said, "When was the last time you saw him?"

John rubbed his chin. "Let's see. Must've been five, six days ago. Came to pick up his check. You sure it was him?"

"Afraid so," I said. "Is the haunted house interfering with your work here?" I asked to move the topic off the dead man.

"You know Fred Robinson, the owner?"

I shook my head and Charles said no.

"You're lucky. He hired my company to do an almost total renovation of the house. He said the house was perfect for him and his wife but needed work. Boy, did it ever. To be honest, it needed more than Robinson and I thought. We started and according to Robinson, we were so slow he took his wife on a European vacation just so he didn't have to fume about how slow we were progressing. Guy's a dentist and like most docs thinks he knows everything. We got in an argument or two early on." He smiled. "I told him he may know how long it takes to pull teeth and put on a crown but nothing about how long it took to renovate a house."

I said, "How'd he take that?"

"He bitched and moaned but took the hint. We came to an awkward agreement. I wouldn't pull teeth and he'd stay out of my way so I could get the job done. That and the haunted house."

Charles said, "What's that mean?"

Someone yelled for John from the door his worker entered earlier. "Hang on, I'll be back."

He didn't know it would've taken a herd of elephants to pull Charles out of the yard when John had more to share.

Charles watched the contractor enter the house, then turned to me. "I think he killed the guy."

"Why?"

"Someone did. He's the first person we've talked to who knew the dead guy."

"Wow! What more proof do we need?"

"Smart ass."

"Too late," I said. "Cindy already called me that."

"Well, then—"

"Sorry guys," John said as he returned. "Where was I?"

Charles was quick with, "Telling us about the haunted house."

"When I was a little whippersnapper growing up in Charleston, I loved visiting Halloween haunted houses. Were some good ones, especially knowing the history of hauntings in Charleston. Led to other interests." He pointed to the house. "Anyway, first time I saw this house, I knew it'd make a perfect haunted house."

Charles said, "The dentist let you turn his future home into a haunted house?"

John chuckled. "Yes, course it helped that I promised a completion date the first week in November and reduced the price."

"Money talks," Charles said.

"It also gave me a chance to give back to the community and told him I'd do it in Dr. Fred Robinson's name. All the proceeds go to local charities. Think the good doctor saw dollar signs for his dental practice in the good publicity the house would get him."

Charles said, "Win, win."

John looked back at the house. "Don't know about the doctor winning considering there was a dead body found in there."

True, I thought.

"I'd better get back to work before I have a rebellion on my hands.

Nice talking to you. If you need any renovation done at your places, give me a call." He handed each of us his business card then left us standing in the yard.

Charles held his hand in front of John. "Let me ask one more question."

"Sure, what?"

"The body was in the pantry."

"That's what I heard," interrupted John.

"We were told the pantry was locked and off limits to folks touring the haunted house. Any idea how it got there?"

John glared at Charles. "You accusing me of putting it there?"

"No, sorry, that's not what I meant. Wondering how the killer got in. Also, when we were going through the house, the kids in front of us were in the pantry. They found the body."

John slowly nodded. "The door had an old lock on it. Could've easily been opened with a credit card or a good shove. It's on the list of things we're upgrading."

"Oh," Charles said. "Makes sense. One more thing, did you provide all the scary stuff in the house like the fog machine, sound system for the spooky noises, other things?"

"Collected it over the years. Everything was mine except the coffin. Didn't have one of them laying around the house. Borrowed it from a funeral home in Mt. Pleasant." He looked at his watch. "Guys, I really have to run."

8

I walked beside Charles as he pushed his bike to the sidewalk across the street before turning toward Center Street. Once the haunted house was no longer in sight, he pulled off the sidewalk, glanced back in the direction of the worksite, and said, "Need any renovations done at your house? I know where you can get a good haunted house creating contractor."

His question didn't deserve an answer, so I said, "What'd you think of John?"

Charles glanced back toward the house again before saying, "Seemed okay. Thought it was a great idea doing the haunted house. It gave kids something to look forward to." He shrugged. "Who could find anything bad about giving the money raised to charity, especially the local charities. Admirable." He again glanced back.

"But?"

"But what?"

"You have that look on your face. Something's bothering you about John other than fifteen minutes ago you thought he was the killer?"

"Can't put my finger on it. If I heard for the first time that a man who'd worked for me a few weeks earlier just so happened to turn up dead in my project, I wouldn't react calmly saying, 'Umm, yeah,' when asked if I knew him. He didn't act more shocked or traumatized than he would've if he learned someone stepped on a dandelion in his yard. Don't you think that was a serious underreaction?"

"Like he already knew the identity?"

"Yes, or was the guy who turned Todd dead. Seemed strange to me, that's all."

"Charles, we all react differently to bad situations. We don't know the man well enough to gauge his reaction."

"Why do you think I said I couldn't put my finger on it?"

"Anything else about him bother you?"

"Not really." Charles said. "What do you think he meant when he was talking about growing up visiting haunted houses and said something about how it led to other interests?"

"Don't know. Why didn't you ask him?"

"Was too surprised the dentist let John turn his new place into a haunted house."

"Sounds like the discount was too good to turn down."

"Whatever. Anyway, I still think there's something odd about John. Don't know if it's enough for him to kill Todd. Not ruling him out. Suppose I'd better get this itsy bitsy wetsuit back to Dude. Don't want to cause an international incident by not getting the Frenchie a chubby-sized one."

Charles was overestimating his influence in starting an international incident, but I didn't want to keep him from his "job."

He peddled off after saying he'd talk to me later.

* * *

LATER CAME QUICKER than I would've guessed. Charles called as I was taking the first bite of my "home-cooked" meal of a bologna sandwich, two slices of apple, and the plate colorfully adorned with a stack of Cheetos.

Instead of something normal people might say like, "Hey Chris," the first words out of his mouth were, "Bet you can't guess what Dude told me."

He was right, although, I'd wager Dude wouldn't have used a complete sentence telling him.

"He didn't have a wetsuit large enough for your French friend."

"No, I mean yes. He didn't have one large enough. He's going to call the guy, so I won't have to get yelled at in French. That's not what I'm talking about."

"Don't have to guess again, do I?"

"You're no fun."

"I agree, so what'd Dude tell you?"

"He asked if I knew who the dead guy was."

"Let me see if I have this right. You returned the wetsuit saying it wasn't large enough for your new friend, and Dude said, "Know who the dead guy was?""

"Not exactly. I told him about the wetsuit, and he said it took me a long time to get back. I told him about us visiting the haunted house, then talking with John. That's when Dude said, 'Who be dead bod?'"

"And you told him it was Todd Lee?"

"Duh, of course. Guess what he said."

I guessed, "Who be Lee?"

"Nope."

"Then what?"

He let out an audible sigh. "Have I told you lately you're no fun?"

Finally, a question I could answer.

"Yes, so what did Dude say?"

"Said, 'Be kidding. Me know Todd L.' He said it like he was shocked because it was someone he knew, unlike John's bland reaction."

"How'd Dude know him?"

"Said he came in the store asking if they were hiring. Of course, Dude didn't use all those words, but that's what he was trying to say."

"Don't suppose Dude hired him."

"You suppose right. Dude said Todd seemed nice, not pushy, not knowing everything like John said."

"People act different when they're trying to get a job. It doesn't mean Todd wasn't like John said he was once on the job."

"True."

"What else did Dude know about him?"

"Said he was sorry Todd be dead bod."

I didn't recall John saying that.

9

After a sleepless night followed by a day of running around, my body decided a visit to bed would be the best bet to avoid the haunting characters that'd visited me in my sleep the night before. Tonight, sleep came quickly and uninterrupted.

The phone was my alarm clock and I wasn't pleased.

"Brother Chris, how's this lovely morning treating you?"

"Fine I think, Preacher. What's up?"

"I was curious if you'd like to go with me this afternoon to visit Red Raven Herbs?"

"Who, where, when, what?" Jarred awake brain fog must've sent my vocabulary back to grade school.

He chuckled. "Guess I was vague. Red Raven Herbs is Shannon Stone's store. Remember, she's young Roisin's mom? You mentioned you'd like to meet the young lady and her family."

"Sounds good. Should I meet you there?"

"Unnecessary, Brother Chris. I'll swing by and pick you up around one."

With most of my friends I was the designated driver. It was pleasant having someone else offer to drive. I thanked Burl and said I'd see him then.

Walking next door to Burt's to get my morning coffee and unhealthy breakfast woke me enough to get my mind focused on meeting the Stone family. To my knowledge, I'd never known a Wiccan. I suspected what I'd seen on TV weren't the most accurate portrayals of the religion.

"That all you need?" asked Roger, one of Bert's personable clerks, as I took my cinnamon Danish to the register.

"Enough for now. I'll be back if I decide to fix supper."

"No reason to be rash on the supper fixin'. Enjoy a meal out; no cooking, no paper plate to throw away."

"Excellent suggestion," I said, as if there was a chance I'd cook a meal at home.

A weekly, okay, monthly cleaning while waiting on Burl kept most of my thoughts occupied. I didn't like going into a new situation with preconceived ideas, but I suppose it's human nature no amount of cleaning was going to sweep away. Burl wasn't a proponent of always early Charles's time schedule, so I was sitting on the porch a couple of minutes before one, when the preacher's Dodge Grand Caravan pulled in the drive.

"Are they expecting both of us?" I asked as I slipped in the van.

As Burl backed out of the drive, he said, "Yes, I talked to Shannon and Roisin this morning. Roisin is excited to meet you; suppose I've talked you up enough to impress a preteen."

"Thanks, I think."

"Shannon told me she and the kids will be happy to talk with us. Her husband is in Charleston and won't be back in time." He hesitated before saying, "These are good people, Chris. I know you'll go in with an open mind."

"I will, but what I don't understand is where you stand. Aren't their beliefs against God's teaching?"

"Brother Chris, meet them and after that if you still have questions, we can discuss it."

"Fair enough."

The remainder of the short ride was quiet except the music from a gospel CD with Burl humming along to "Amazing Grace." The house on East Huron Avenue was bordered on each side by large oaks and several shrubs isolating its residents from the neighbors. The small, concrete block, pre-Hugo single story cottage was painted an eye catching bright blue. The yard was impressive with flowers and plants everywhere. Even this late in the year it reminded me of a Monet painting.

We pulled in the drive when Burl said, "Brother Chris, not everyone treats others fairly. People can be quite cruel and ignorant. The Stones have had some issues—"

A raucous bark coming from a horse sized dog looking straight into my eyes through the passenger window interrupted Burl. I like dogs but I'd never seen one this large with so many big teeth—big teeth inches from my face.

Burl said, "That's Lugh."

"What's a Lugh and is it going to eat us?" I began to wish we'd brought Charles since there's never been a dog he didn't fawn over. At the least he would make a nice snack while Burl and I escaped.

A woman appeared on the front porch and yelled, *"Eist liom!"*

The massive canine loped to her and sat beside the attractive red headed woman. She smiled toward the van as the dog stared at her.

"It is safe," she said. "He will not harm you. He wanted to greet you his special way."

I said, "You sure?"

"Of course, if he wanted to harm you, he'd sneak up on you quieter than a speck of dust floating to the ground, then bare his teeth announcing displeasure. This is his cheery greeting. Shall we go have a pleasant conversation and a spot of tea?"

"Shannon, I'd like you to meet Brother Chris Landrum."

She gave a mini curtsy. "Good afternoon, Mr. Landrum. Welcome to my home. This big baby is Lugh. He's an Irish Wolfhound."

"Nice to meet you and Lugh. Please call me Chris."

"Come in out of this humidity. I'm still not used to this weather." She smiled. "Not sure I ever will be."

Stepping into the house was like walking through the door to a bygone era.

"Please have a seat in the parlor. I have a kettle on for tea."

"Roisin, our company is here," she said in the direction of what I assumed to be a bedroom.

Shannon left the *parlor* as if floating on air, Lugh followed her to the door then plopped down blocking the doorway.

Burl and I sat in what appeared to be antique wingback chairs. I said, "How often have you been here?"

"This is my third time at the house, it doesn't look like anything like you would think from the road."

I looked around and whispered to Burl, "Was thinking it doesn't look like anything from this century. The wallpaper is like something you'd see in England." I nodded toward the opposite wall. "That tapestry looks like it's over a hundred years old, same with the furnishings."

Burl glanced at the tapestry depicting a colorful garden scene. "Brother Chris, nature plays an important role in their lives, especially Roisin."

"You talking about me?"

I hadn't seen or heard our youngest hostess enter the room like magic as she appeared next to me.

In a quiet voice, she said, "Hello, I am Roisin. It's okay to stare, I know I'm a mini version of Mom."

"Nice to meet you, Roisin. I'm Chris," I said, hopefully covering being startled by her arrival.

Burl said, "Little Sister, how have you been? Where's that brother of yours?"

"Desmond is out back. He'll be in shortly." She rolled her eyes. "He likes to make a grand entrance."

Shannon appeared in the doorway to the kitchen. "Roisin, please help serving. Chris, would you like a scone with your tea? I know Burl enjoys them."

"Yes, please."

Burl took a cup of tea off the silver platter and put a scone on a matching saucer, then said, "I brought Chris so he could meet your family and learn about your beliefs. He has an open mind; unlike some you've encountered."

Shannon set the platter on a table in the corner of the room, took a seat on an upholstered Victorian sofa, and said, "Burl, any friend of yours is welcome here. We have had a few issues but that's nothing new. Being Wiccan, we're occasionally viewed as evil people worshiping the devil or practicing the Dark Arts."

I said, "I admit, I know nothing of Wiccan beliefs."

Shannon took a sip of tea, glanced around the room, before saying, "If you look around you will see objects that may seem strange or out of place. These are a few of the implements used in our religion." She looked across the room. "On the table against the wall are candles, salt, incense, water, herbs, and crystals. It's the family altar."

Roisin said, "Mr. Chris, those things represent the four elements. Wicca is the love of life and nature. Everything in nature should be treated with the utmost respect." She smiled. "People see me walking around talking to animals and things in nature. They look at me like I'm crazy. Mom says they are out of touch with things our natural world can offer." Her smile turned to a frown. "They lack the respect that should be given. I have been taught everyone has the right to their ideas and beliefs."

Shannon said, "That's my eleven-year-old, going on thirty. She can get a bit overzealous when someone shows interest, but her words are true."

I smiled. "Shannon, Roisin, Preacher Burl tells me Red Raven Herbs is your online store. What do you sell?"

"Herbs, crystals, and bath salts online and by word of mouth over here." Her voice lowered. "While I know it's prohibited on Folly, I occasionally do card readings, by appointment, and only for people I know. Spells are also performed if requested."

"Spells, like curses?"

An uneasy giggle broke out from Shannon and her mini me daughter. I wasn't sure if it made me feel better or worse. Nothing witty came to mind to defuse what I might have started so I took a bite of scone and waited for what would come next, praying it wasn't a curse.

Shannon shook her head. "Curses, no that would be going against what we practice, harm none and the law of threefold. "The spells I was referring to would be for love, health, peace, and so on."

"I didn't mean to offend."

Shannon leaned forward and patted my arm. "No offense taken. This is how people learn about others, asking questions and being open to the answers. We were aware of the challenges that might arise when moving here from Minnesota leaving the community that was like family. That is life and life is everchanging."

I said, "I would never have guessed your accent was Minnesotan."

She surprised me with a full throated laugh. "Yes, by way of Kilkenny, Ireland. I moved to Minnesota in the late nineties. I met, fell in love with Mike, the rest is history."

I said, "Why Folly?"

"Mike received an excellent job offer from a law firm in Charleston that he'd heard about from a friend from law school. They needed a medical attorney. The company offered us access to a nice house in Charleston, but I couldn't see the family being at peace in the big city. Folly seemed so inviting and laid back. We could not resist. Found this house our first day on the island. The Goddess blessed us, and here we are."

Burl said, "Brother Chris, that sounds like how most of us got here. You, me, now the Stone family. Folly has benefited from our diverse presence."

"You are very kind, Burl," Shannon said.

"Kind, and a weaver of bologna. Folly is more eclectic than anything we can provide."

We shared our experiences discovering Folly and the weather in October, then I said, "Shannon, Roisin, thank you both for your hospitality. We won't take up more of your afternoon. The scones were great as well as the conversation."

Burl patted his stomach. "Good food and conversations are this preacher's vices. As usual, I've had a wonderful time. Sister Roisin, we still on for our walk to the marsh this week?"

"Of course, don't forget your notebook so I can teach you more fauna."

Lugh rose and walked over to the chairs before I was fully standing. For his size, I was amazed how quietly he moved. Burl petted the dog as I shook Shannon's hand and smiled at Roisin.

On the way to the door, a room to the left caught my eye. On a small round table in the middle of the room there was a lit candle and a variety of metal and wooden tools including an ice pick. I would've sworn the door to the room had been closed when we passed it upon arriving.

On the way to the van, Burl said, "Brother Chris, I believe that went well. Did you enjoy yourself?"

"Yes, but I thought Roisin's brother was going to come in."

"Desmond has a way about him."

Turning to walk to the passenger side of the car I nearly ran into a young Ozzy Osbourne look alike. He was dressed in black but wasn't giving off the good vibes of Johnny Cash.

The young man, roughly sixteen, I would guess, said, "Sorry I'm late, had something that needed to be done. Did you find out everything you wanted to know about the freaky family living there? He pointed to the house, his house. "Sorry there were no coffins or dead goats. Guess it was boring."

"Desmond, this is Chris Landrum, a good friend of mine," Burl said, ignoring the young man's snarky comments. "We wanted to visit; missed you not being there. We have a few minutes if you'd like to talk."

"No. I'm sure you have all the answers to your questions, besides your friend looks a little pale."

We pulled out of the drive and Burl went back to humming gospel and my mind processed the afternoon's events. Shannon seemed pleasant and I saw why Burl adored Roisin, but I couldn't shake the feeling of dread when looking into Desmond's crooked smile. He looked out of place in the beautiful garden in front of the little blue cottage. He'd look more at home in a mausoleum or yes, a haunted house.

10

"Have I got a deal for you," Chief LaMond said to begin her early morning call.

"Morning, Cindy," I said in an attempt to add a glimmer of civility to the conversation. "And what might that be?"

"Head to the Dog and I'll let you buy me breakfast."

I smiled and said, "Wow! How lucky can a guy get?"

"Wise reaction. You on your way?"

I told her I'd be there in ten minutes, knowing Cindy had something to share or wouldn't have called.

It took me closer to fifteen minutes, but Cindy wasn't as anal about being prompt as Charles, so I didn't worry about being castigated for being late. The fog was so thick on the drive over, I could barely see fifty feet in front of me.

Cindy was at a table near the front of the restaurant tapping on her phone and sipping coffee. She saw me enter, placed the phone face down on the table, pointed her coffee mug at me, and said, "Get lost in the sea fog?"

Okay, she was slightly time sensitive, still far from Charles's level.

Amber was quick to the table with a mug of coffee. She chuckled.

"Chief said to get you anything you want. Said you were buying her breakfast so to treat you nice."

"Thanks, Amber. Chief LaMond is sweet like that. Think I'll have French toast."

Cindy said, "Told you so, Amber."

"That's why you're Chief," Amber said and headed to put in my order.

Since Cindy extended the *generous* invitation, I took a sip of coffee and waited for the reason for the invite.

"So, aren't you going to ask what I've learned about the murder?"

"Figured you'd tell me when you're ready."

"Okay, here goes. This is everything I know about the murder." She held up her right hand and touched her forefinger to her thumb forming a circle, or more accurately, a zero.

"Nothing?"

"Correct, Mr. Senior Citizen. I know nothing more than I did the last time we talked. I had a worthless call this morning from Detective Adair. He'd contacted police in Savannah in an attempt, feeble attempt, to find out where the late Todd Lee lived. They found no record of anyone by that name ever living in their historic city: no speeding tickets, no parking tickets, not even cited for jaywalking. Add to that, none of my officers recall having contact with Mr. Lee." She shook her head. "Chris, I'm beginning to believe Todd Lee was another one of the ghosts in the haunted house."

"Didn't his drivers' license list an address?"

"Excellent point. Yes, it did."

"So why couldn't the police have learned he lived there?"

"Another excellent point. They probably could have if it weren't for the fact the address on his license belonged to an empty lot. Empty now, apparently there was a small building there at one time, a building demolished in the 1940s, long before Todd Lee was born. See what I mean about him being a ghost?"

"Yes. Sorry, Cindy. Anything else about Lee?"

Amber arrived with my breakfast before Cindy responded. I

slathered syrup on the French toast and waited for the Chief to enlighten me as to why I was there.

"Chris, I'm from the mountains of East Tennessee; didn't pay much attention in school. I'm not big on history and all that old stuff, but I seem to recall some famous guy saying something about folks who fail to learn from the past are condemned to repeat it, or something like that."

"Chief, I'm impressed. Think it was George Santayana."

"Thought that was a rock band."

"That's Carlos Santana."

"Damn, Chris, you're getting worse than Charles."

"That's a low blow. Remind me again of your point."

"Haven't told you the first time. My point is history tells me you, Charles, and possibly a few other misfits you hang with, have a way of nosing into things that aren't your business. So, I'm learning from the past that you're going to do the same thing when it comes to the untimely death of Todd Lee. How am I doing?"

I smiled. "Chief, I wouldn't call it nosing into his death, but there are a couple of things we've learned that you and Detective Adair might not be aware of. A couple of days ago—"

She interrupted, "I love being right."

I took a sip and waited for her to finish gloating so I could continue.

"Okay, I feel better. What did you learn?"

I told her about meeting John Rice and what he'd said about Todd Lee working for him a week, why he'd been fired, and how Todd had returned to get his paycheck. Cindy started to give me grief about visiting the haunted house and, in her words, interrogating John Rice. She stopped mid sentence saying it wasn't worth her breath telling me I shouldn't have done it.

She jotted a couple of things in her notebook before asking if I thought Rice could've had something to do with the death.

"Nothing that was apparent. He didn't appear upset Lee was dead or that the body was found in the house he was renovating, but we each react differently to things, so it could mean nothing."

"I'll share that with Adair. He'll probably want to talk to Rice again. Anything else?"

"Not about the murder, but do you know the Stone family?"

"Blue house, East Huron?"

I nodded.

"What about them?"

"Preacher Burl took me to meet them yesterday."

Cindy took a sip of coffee, looked at the front of her phone, and said, "So?"

"Late for something?" I asked, noticing it was the second time she'd glanced at her phone.

"Yeah, but don't change the subject. Why ask if I knew the Stones?"

"Thought they were interesting."

"Because they're witches?"

I sighed. "Wiccans."

"Witches, Wiccans, whatever."

"What else do you know about them?"

"Mom runs an Internet herbs company out of the house. Dad's an attorney."

"Anything else?"

"About three months ago, the dad, think his name's Mike, called to file a report. Seems some jackass left a broom leaning against their front door with a note saying something like, 'Hop on this and fly out of town. Your kind ain't wanted here.'"

"What'd you do?"

"Officer Bishop caught the call, took the note as evidence, apologized to the head witch, excuse me, Wiccan, and said we'd keep a closer eye on the house."

"How'd he react?"

"He's an attorney. Told Bishop he knew there was nothing more she could do and thanked her for coming. He was a hell of a lot nicer than I would've been. Bishop said she apologized again for them having to put up with some narrowminded jackass. Don't think she put it exactly like that but should've." Cindy took another sip, stared at me, before saying, "See if I have this right. You asked if I knew them because they were interesting?"

"Yes. I thought of them because Preacher Burl was outside the haunted house the night the body was found. He was with the Stones' young daughter Roisin. That's all."

"Interesting. Hmm, if you say so. Regardless, I'm late for a fun filled meeting with his honor the Mayor."

I wished her luck with the meeting; she said she'd need it.

After she left, I wondered if I should've mentioned the ice pick at the Stones' cottage.

11

I was finishing my coffee while wondering why I didn't have something better to think about than a murder, when a shadow fell across the table. Looking up from my mug, I was greeted by the smiling face of John Rice.

"Chris, right?"

"Correct, Mr. Rice."

"Call me John. Mind if I join you if you're not too busy?"

I smiled. "Too busy, no. I'm retired so I've no place to rush off to."

Amber noticed the addition to the table and returned to clear the plates and ask John if he needed a menu.

"No menu," he said with a smile. "I'd like a bagel with cream cheese, bacon, and iced tea, if that wouldn't be too much of a burden on such a pretty lady."

Amber rewarded him with the kind of smile people use when faced with a nice yet back handed comment. She picked up my plate and pointed to my mug. I nodded before she headed to the kitchen.

John said, "Other than my crew, I don't know many folks on the island. Some days eating alone isn't much fun."

"If you'd arrived a couple of minutes earlier, you could've met another Folly resident, Chief Cindy LaMond, our number one crime fighter."

"I saw her leave."

His tone was more like he was waiting for her to leave before he came in, or I could be looking for ulterior motives where none exist—in other words, becoming Charles. Laughing to myself, I thought about the belief that couples start to look and act alike after being together for a long period. My internal monologue must've lasted too long when I realized the room was eerily quiet.

I said, "Maybe you can meet her next time. How's the renovation coming?"

"Little behind schedule but that's expected since there was so much rot and damage we couldn't see when estimating a completion date. Still think we'll make it on time." He looked toward the door before turning back to me. "If you don't mind, I'd rather not talk shop."

I nodded. "No shop talk it is."

Amber arrived with John's food, drink, and my refill. She smiled at me, then headed to another table without a word.

John took a bite, a sip of tea, then looked at me like it was my turn to speak.

I took the hint. "The other day when Charles asked why you promoted the house to the owner as becoming a haunted house you said something about liking them as a child."

He smiled. "Halloween was my favorite time of year. Went to a bunch of haunted houses, a haunted forest or two. Those were in my younger, much younger days."

"I think you said it led to other interests."

He looked at me like I'd asked a trick question, before saying, "Paranormal activity, my true passion besides my wife. Luckily, she's into it as much as I am."

Casper the ghost floated up in my mind, not the friendly one, but a headless version. Halloween was becoming my least favorite time of year.

"Paranormal, like ghost hunting?"

"You might say that. Growing up in Charleston with its prolific afterlife community either gets a youngster interested or repulses him." He chuckled. "I'm in that former group. Bri is from Savannah, another paranormal hotbed, so we immediately hit it off."

"Interesting," I said, although not very.

"We host ghost tours and paranormal activity research, founded Lowcountry Paranormal Investigations."

"Oh," I inarticulately said. "Sounds like a fascinating business."

"Yes, Charleston is filled with paranormal activity from the old slave market to many of the historic downtown buildings, not to mention nearby plantations."

"I'm not originally from here, so I wasn't reared knowing much about it."

"Ah, it's everywhere, my friend." He pointed his glass at me. "The dead don't hurt you. It's the living, although Bri and I've come across some instances where the dearly departed weren't so dear. Oh well, just curiosity on both parts, the living and the dead."

He smiled as he took a large bite. He looked at me like he was trying to get my take on the strange direction our conversation had headed. I was never a believer in the supernatural or hauntings, so sitting across from someone who did and talked about it like others did about the weather seemed odd.

"Interesting," I repeated. "I guess you don't think a ghost killed Todd Lee?"

John laughed so loud customers at a table behind us looked our way to see what was so humorous.

He lowered his voice. "We've seen little evidence of ghosts in the Robinson house, so my guess would be it wasn't one of them that took his life. Was stabbed if the rumor going around's true."

"You'd said he was a pain to work with. Did he have conflicts with anyone on your crew or was he close with someone? I was wondering since he was back in the house after you'd let him go."

"Not sure if he got along with any of my guys. If I had to pick one who had the most beefs with him, it'd be Nathan Davis, one of my carpenters. He and Todd had a few heated words." He took another sip before continuing. "Todd tried to tell Nathan the best way to measure lumber, something stupid and none of his concern. Nathan has been a carpenter all his life and had worked for me for years."

"Nathan didn't like the newbie telling him how to do his job."

"Would you?"

"Did it ever get physical?"

"Pretty sure it would've if I hadn't stepped in. Funny though."

"Funny?"

"Nathan called him a world class pain in the ass. Todd went off like he'd been slapped in the face. He was ready to stomp on Nathan."

"Was Todd just bullying someone smaller than he was?"

"Nope, Nathan is a big, burly guy. I was concerned about my new hire getting his clock cleaned. Can't have that on my jobsite."

"Fired him after that?"

"Next day. I wanted to give him a second chance, but he came in the next morning more pissed than the day before." John shook his head and stared at the table.

Could he be wishing he could've done more for the late Mr. Lee? I had a feeling our conversation was about to end, and I wasn't sure where I'd hoped our discussion had been headed in the first place. What I did have was the name of another person who knew the victim; not only knew but had run ins with him. The pool always seems to get deeper and deeper the harder you look. For good or bad, I had someone else Charles could claim was the killer.

My thoughts were interrupted when John said, "I've got to get back to work. Sorry to have invited myself to breakfast."

"No need to apologize."

As he left money on the table for his meal and headed to the door, I couldn't help thinking he seemed like a genuinely nice person. Unusual interests, but nice. He runs two businesses with his wife, donates to charities and is concerned about his employees, and even about a man who worked for him a week, one he didn't particularly like. So, why was I feeling he's holding something back?

Then what about Nathan Davis? Could he have something to do

with Todd's demise? With so many questions bouncing around in my head, I should leave before someone else decides to join me.

The drive home cleared my head enough to realize I'd have to tell Charles what I'd learned. He'll belittle my interrogation skills, but that's okay, all in a day's work for one retired citizen who happens to have a friend named Charles Fowler.

12

That evening, a three block walk to Cal's Country Bar and Burgers, commonly called Cal's, might get my mind off the haunted house and who might've killed Todd Lee. Besides, it'd been a few weeks since I visited the bar's owner. I'd known Cal since he settled on Folly nearly a decade ago after spending most of his seventy five years traveling the South singing his brand of country music at any venue that'd have him. I was honored to call him a friend. We'd gotten better acquainted earlier this year when he learned he'd fathered a child fifty plus years ago. To put it mildly, Cal was traumatized when the son he didn't know he had, moved to Folly to be closer to his dad. I'd become Cal's sounding board.

I entered the bar to the sound of Patsy Cline singing "I Fall to Pieces" from the classic Wurlitzer jukebox. The jukebox wasn't the only classic thing in the room. The tables, chairs, flooring, walls, and Cal would all fit that definition. Mid October wasn't peak season and only two of the dozen tables were occupied, plus two people seated at the bar along the right side of the room.

Cal was behind the bar setting a beer bottle in front of each of the nearby customers. He was wearing a Stetson that's been with him since Lyndon Johnson was President, a long sleeve sweatshirt with an image of Hank Williams Senior on the front, and a wide smile when he saw me at the entry.

He held up an empty wineglass, I nodded, he turned to grab a bottle of Cabernet off the backbar, filled the glass with a heavy pour, and pointed to a vacant table near the front of the room.

"See Charles on your way in?" Cal said as he folded his six-foot-three, slim body in the chair opposite me.

"No. Was he here?"

"Trying to find you. I wanted to remind him he had one of those modern day inventions called a cell phone that'd probably be easier finding you than traipsing all over town."

"Cal, you just learning you can't tell Charles anything?"

"You betcha."

Before Cal elaborated, my phone rang with Charles's name appearing on the screen. I pointed the phone at Cal so he could see who it was, then answered.

"You know you're not at home, Loggerhead's, Cal's, Rita's, or Planet Follywood?" Charles said instead of hello.

"Wrong."

"Wrong, what?"

"I'm at Cal's enjoying a glass of wine and talking to Cal."

"You weren't, oh, never mind. On my way."

The phone went dead.

"Cal, how about grabbing a Bud for Charles."

He tipped his Stetson and headed to the bar.

Roger Miller was singing "King of the Road" when Cal returned with Charles's beer.

"Hear you and Charles were playing like you were kids going through the haunted house when the stiff got himself discovered."

"Who said that?" I asked, although not surprised Cal would know.

"One of the kids named Charles. He also said the two of you were going to figure out who killed the guy."

I shook my head. "It's in the capable hands of the police."

Cal laughed then said, "Of course it is. Then I guess you wouldn't be interested in talking to the guy sitting at the end of the bar."

I glanced at the bar. The person Cal was referring to was in his mid forties, long black hair, burly, and appeared tall, although I couldn't tell for sure since he was seated.

"Who's he?"

"Name's Nathan Davis, works on the crew renovating the house that's temporarily haunted."

The name sounded familiar, but it took me a few seconds to remember he was the person John Rice said had conflicts with the murder victim.

"Why would I want to talk to him?"

"Charles said no one knew why the guy was killed in the house. Nathan, prefers Nate, is here most days after work. Nice fellow, doesn't get loud or obnoxious, pays his tab, doesn't pick fights, but is a world class bitcher."

"He say something about the body?"

Charles came in the door; Cal waved him over, then said, "I'll leave you two Hardy Boys to detectin'." Cal tipped his Stetson toward Charles then headed to the bar before answering my question about Nathan who prefers Nate.

Charles took a long drag on the beer, not asking if it was for him, set his Tilley on the corner of the table, and said, "So, where were you when I was in here a little while ago?"

"Hiding from you under the table."

His eyes narrowed. "You're kidding, right?"

"Yep. Was hiding behind the bar. Why were you looking for me?"

"Funny. Haven't heard from you in a couple days. Wanted to confab about our plan to catch a killer."

Before we could *confab*, there were a couple of things I had to share then brace for a ton of grief he'd give me for not telling him sooner. I took a deep breath, a sip of wine, then began sharing about my visit to the Stone family. As predicted, Charles stopped me with a hand in my face.

"Why wasn't I invited?"

I repeated what I'd already said about Burl inviting me since I'd expressed interest in meeting them the day after the haunted house fiasco. I didn't think I needed to point out the invitation was to me, not Charles and me.

He sighed before saying, "Go on. What else did I miss—miss because I wasn't invited?"

I got as far as mentioning Lugh before he interrupted with a barrage of questions about the dog's name, breed, and size. It took the rest of Charles's beer before I reached the end of the story.

"What'd the Stone family have to do with the murder?"

"Probably nothing, although it was an interesting coincidence that Todd Lee was killed with an ice pick and that there was one in their house."

"Like there is in most every house or garage on Folly."

"That's why I said it was interesting, not necessarily relevant."

He made a couple more *feeling sorry for himself for not being invited utterances* before calming. I knew it was temporary then began telling him about meeting with John Rice and what he said about being a paranormalist and how one of his employees, Nathan Davis, had conflicts with the dead guy.

Lightning might not strike twice in the same place, but volcanos can. So can Charles. I thought he was going to fly out of his chair, before pounding his beer bottle on the table, rolling his eyes, and nonverbally doing a volcano erupting imitation.

I sat back, listened to Johnny Horton singing "Sink the Bismarck" and waited for glimmers of sanity to reenter Charles's body. It was an uncomfortable but necessary wait.

Charles finally calmed, quicker than usual, a sign of maturity, or possibly lack of energy attributable to aging. Regardless of the reason, I was pleased.

He took another sip, then said, "Other than not thinking about your friend while galivanting all over town investigating the murder, anything else you haven't shared?"

"Only one more thing, see that guy sitting at the end of the bar?"

Charles pivoted toward the bar. "Yes."

"Know who he is?"

"No, who?"

"Nathan Davis."

The former volcanic eruption morphed into a laser guided missile. Charles was out of his chair and headed to the bar before I could ask what he was doing. He pulled the barstool closest to Davis and started talking to the unsuspecting interviewee. Two minutes later, Charles, along with his new friend were headed to my table.

"Chris, meet my new buddy Nate Davis. Would you believe Nate is working with J&B Renovations, that's the company fixing up the haunted house?"

I could believe it since it's what I told Charles five minutes earlier. I shook Nate's hand and Charles pointed for him to join us.

"Chris, I told Nate you were buying the drinks. That okay?"

"Sure," I said, as if I had a choice.

"Thanks," Nate said, "Charles told me you were in the haunted house when someone found Todd."

I nodded. "You know him?"

I could play Charles's game.

"I guess. He worked with us about a week before John, he's the company's owner, wised up and canned him."

Charles leaned closer to Nate. "How come?"

Nate began peeling the label off his beer bottle. "Because he's a first class asshole."

Charles said, "Sounds like you didn't get along."

Nate glared at Charles. "No, but I didn't kill him."

Charles smiled at Nate. "Of course not. Just wondering why you think he was an asshole."

"He was a know-it-all. Knew everything about construction. The rest of us were idiots, unable to operate a screwdriver, according to him."

"Sounds like a prince to work with," Charles said.

"You can say that again. Not only did he know everything, he kept telling me how he wouldn't need his crappy job much longer."

"What'd that mean?" Charles asked.

"Don't know; didn't like him enough to ask. He'd tap his head with a finger and say something about a secret he knew that was going to make him rich." He looked around the room then said, "Fellas, I may've killed him myself, if somebody didn't beat me to it."

Cal moved beside Charles. "Anything else for you guys?"

"Another beer for my friend here?" Charles said as he pointed at Nate.

"Anything else?"

"Not yet, Cal. Chris is picking up the tab."

Cal left to get Nate another drink and increase my indebtedness.

Charles turned his attention back to Nate. "Any idea who killed him?"

"No."

"Know why he was killed in the haunted house?"

"Nope. He had no business being there."

"How long have you worked for J&B?" I asked to move the discussion away from the murder.

"Going on five years. Good company to work for; pay's good. John's a little rough on his employees, but Bri's a doll, can swing a hammer with the best of us although you couldn't guess it seeing her blond ponytail sticking out behind her pink hardhat." He smiled.

"Sounds like a good job," I said, not knowing anything to add.

"Biggest problem is clients, always wanting the job done faster than possible, wanting us to slash costs."

Cal arrived with Nate's beer, and again asked if we needed anything. I said no; Charles shook his head. Cal left to see if the couple at a table by the small bandstand in front of the room needed anything.

"How's—umm, what's his name, Chris?"

"Dr. Robinson," I said, assuming he meant the haunted house's owner.

"Yeah, how's Dr. Robinson to work for?"

"I'd put him in the pain in the ass category, although I don't have to deal with him directly. John has that pleasure."

Charles said, "What's his problem?"

"Let's just say, I wouldn't want him working with a drill in my mouth. The boy's got a temper combined with a snooty attitude."

Charles said, "He know Todd Lee?"

"Lee was only there a week, thank goodness. Let's see. Don't know about the damned dentist knowing Lee, but think his wife, believe her name's Erika, may've been in the house once that week. Why?"

"Curious," Charles said.

Also known as nosing around, trying to catch a killer. Hopefully, Nate didn't know Charles well enough in the few minutes since they'd met, to figure that out.

Nate looked at his watch. "Wow, where does the time go? Fellas, I've got to be at work early in the morning. Umm, thanks for the beers, Chris."

He pushed his chair back, thanked me again, before heading to the door.

Charles watched him go, turned to me, and said, "See, Chris, that's why you need me with you when you're trying to catch a killer."

"What do you think about Nate?" I asked, ignoring his critique.

Charles took a sip, nodded, then said, "Think he's got a thing for a blond with the pink hardhat. Think he wasn't president of the Todd Lee fan club. Think he's not adding the Robinsons to his Christmas card list."

"Think he killed Todd Lee?"

"Hell if I know."

And that's why I need him with me when trying to catch a killer?

Johnny Cash's distinct voice filled the air with "Oh Lonesome Me."

13

It'd been several days since I'd seen Barbara Deanelli, the lady I'd been dating for a little over two years. She owned Barb's Books, a used bookstore on Center Street. After a lazy morning around the house, it was time to rectify that situation. The temperature was in the upper end range for late October and the store was two blocks from my cottage so I couldn't come up with a good reason not to walk. The store was housed in a space I'd rented when I had a photo gallery, a lifetime dream that'd become a nightmare when I learned photos weren't as popular to the buying public as food, medicine, and lottery tickets.

Although used books were vastly more in demand than my photos, other than Barb, I was the only person in the attractively decorated store. Barb was my height at five-foot-ten, thin with short black hair. She greeted me with a smile, a kiss, and an invitation for a drink of my choice, if it was a soft drink, water, coffee, or wine. I followed her to the small backroom and said coffee sounded good. She grabbed a pod from a stainless steel rack and plopped it in the Keurig machine before getting a bottle of water for herself.

"What brings you out?" she asked, knowing it wasn't to buy a book.

"Hadn't seen you for a while so I thought I'd stop by and enjoy your company for a few minutes."

"That's sweet if I believed it."

"It's true."

"Okay," she said with a skeptical look. "Then have a seat and enjoy the coffee and my company."

She rolled her chair close to the door so she could see customers venturing in.

I took a sip and said, "Hear about the dead body found in the haunted house the other night?"

"Aren't there always dead bodies in haunted houses?"

I smiled. "This was a real one."

"I know," she said as she continued to look to the front of the store. "Was joking. I'd be a poor example of a Folly resident if I missed hearing something like that."

"Did you hear Charles and I were there when it was found?"

Her head jerked in my direction. "You've got me there. I hear when men get old, really old, they regress to their childhood. That what you and your buddy were doing?"

I didn't remind her she was a mere two years younger than I. "No. Charles wanted me to experience what kids enjoy nowadays."

"And it just so happened on the same night a body was visiting?"

"Afraid so."

"Why doesn't that surprise me?"

"Bad luck."

"Speaking of bad luck, know what happened, who he was, and who killed him?"

"Can answer two of the three. Name was Todd Lee, killed by an ice pick through the heart. Ever hear of that?"

She shook her head. "I've had the privilege, speaking sarcastically, of knowing a few murderers in my day, but never one using an ice pick. Who's Todd Lee?"

Barb had been a successful defense attorney in Pennsylvania before moving to Folly a little over two years ago after going through a divorce.

"Don't know much about him, nobody appears to. He worked for a week on the crew renovating the structure they're using for the haunted house. Don't know where he lived or why he was killed. Do you know John or Bri Rice?"

"Don't believe so. Who're they?"

I shared what little I knew about the contractors.

"Do they know anything about him other than he worked for them a short period of time?"

I shook my head and added, "Don't know Nate Davis, do you? He works on the J&B crew and had argued with the dead guy."

Her gaze narrowed. "You and Charles sticking your noses in police business again?"

"Not really."

"Not to parse words, but *not really* isn't the same as no."

"We have no reason to butt in."

"Again, not the same as no."

Time to change the subject.

"Do you know Mike or Shannon Stone?"

"Finally, a question I can answer. Don't know Mike but Shannon comes in occasionally; so does their son, believe his name's Desmond. Then there's little Roisin. She's something else. How do you know them?"

"Burl Costello took me to meet them the other day. Mike wasn't home, but I met the rest. They seem like a nice family."

She grinned. "Burl the minister took you to meet a Wiccan family?"

I laughed. "Seems Roisin friended Burl. What did you mean by she's something else?"

A customer came in before Barb responded. She went to see if she could help and I leaned back, enjoyed the coffee, and a piece of Halloween candy from a bag on the table. A few minutes later, Barb returned.

"Can you believe I didn't have a single book on the Samburu tribe in Northern Kenya?"

"I can't believe someone was looking for one."

"Well, she was; I didn't and lost another customer. Where were we?"

"Roisin Stone."

"That young lady is as sharp as some of the attorneys I worked with; more inquisitive, too. She comes with Shannon and regardless which section Shannon goes to, Roisin darts the other direction and starts pulling books, parks herself on the floor, and flips through them like she's reading whatever they're about. She came in once with her brother who's as different from her as a tree to a turnip. If I had a Goth section, that's where he'd hang out."

"I only talked to him for a minute but you're right. Burl said Mike was a medical lawyer. How's that different from what you practiced?"

"Attorneys can't specialize in specific areas while in school, but as you know, many find a niche in which to focus when making a living. The ones who gravitate toward medical law often represent plaintiffs who've been injured due to alleged malpractice or hospital errors. Of course, in the wonderful world of law where there are at least two sides to everything, they go against other medical attorneys defending the docs or the hospitals."

"Any attorney can claim to be a medical attorney?"

"Yes. That's why potential clients should check an attorney's track record before signing on as a client."

"Makes sense, but isn't that easier said than done?"

"Therein lies the problem. Most clients have no idea how to screen potential attorneys. I could claim to be an immigration lawyer, but most people needing an attorney to help with immigration issues wouldn't know if I had extensive experience, little experience, or no experience in that field. You plan on suing a doc?"

I smiled. "No. Curious, that's all."

She took a sip of water, started to say something, when another potential customer entered the store.

"Work calls," she said as she stood.

"I've taken enough of your time. How about grabbing supper tomorrow?"

"Sounds good. Want to meet at Rita's?"

"Perfect. Six?"

She nodded and went to greet the latest arrival, and I grabbed a box of Milk Duds from the plastic pumpkin on the counter.

14

One of my favorite activities is taking early morning walks along Center Street. Most of the stores and restaurants are closed, the sidewalks empty. A vehicle occasionally passed as its sleepy driver navigated his or her way to work. The sun heightened the saturation of the brightly painted buildings on the west side of the street. Today, as I often did, I ended my walk on the iconic Folly Beach Fishing Pier where I looked back at the island from the thousand foot long structure over the Atlantic then turned and looked out on the seemingly endless ocean. The peaceful view often put my life and thoughts in perspective. How little everything appears when staring at the great expanse of the Atlantic.

After spending twenty minutes watching seagulls floating on air above the water, a hot cup of coffee from Roasted, the Tides Hotel's coffee shop, was just what the doctor ordered. Yes, I occasionally paid for coffee rather than bumming free cups at Bert's Market. Making my way into the warm coffee shop adorned with Halloween decorations on the counter made me realize how chilly I had gotten while daydreaming on the Pier.

I smiled at Penny, the shop's manager, who looked like she had her hands full with a well dressed middle age couple who appeared upset.

I sat at one of two small, round tables in the center of the room to wait for Penny to finish with the only other people in the shop. The couple finally stomped away from the counter and took the remaining table. From the look on their faces, neither Penny nor coffee alleviated their irritation.

I moved to the counter, smiled at Penny who rolled her eyes while nodding at the unhappy couple, ordered, then grabbed a copy of *The Post and Courier*, Charleston's daily newspaper, someone had left on the counter by the window overlooking the ocean. Taking up real estate among the news stories were multiple ads for pop up Halloween stores offering discounts on costumes and candy, various ghost tours, and, of course, area haunted houses. In all my years, I never paid much attention to the October holiday; this year had become a tragic exception.

Penny handed me my coffee, I paid, as I told her to have a good day. She whispered it couldn't get worse. I returned to the table, not five feet from the couple.

The woman wearing a white dress with large colorful flowers on it looked more like she was going to a cocktail party than having coffee at the beach. She pointed her coffee stir stick at the man and said, "Fred, calm down. It's not worth blowing up over such an insignificant issue."

"Insignificant!" the man blurted. "They lost our reservation. That's not the way to run a business. Don't they know they can't treat people like us that way?"

Pretending I couldn't hear their debate that probably could be heard by people in Wales, I buried my head in the newspaper like I was intrigued by a *Giant Sale* on Halloween candy at Harris Teeter.

"Fred, the manager is resolving the issue as we speak. Besides, you know there's a good chance your receptionist failed to make the reservation."

"Miscommunication, my ass," he said in his grating voice. "Erika, sometimes you're so naive."

The woman looked past the man and saw me studying the newspaper. It was like this was the first she'd noticed me seated five feet away.

"Sir, I'm sorry for the disturbance. Didn't see you there."

"No need to apologize," I said, although I suspected one was due Penny.

"Well, it's not neighborly to display one's dirty laundry in public."

The man with her mumbled something followed by a profanity. With his wavy jet black hair, black sports coat, gold Rolex, and heavy jowls, he reminded me of a Mafioso boss.

I smiled at the lady. "I hope your vacation gets better."

"Thanks, but we're not on vacation. We're moving here next month. Came over from our apartment in Summerville for a couple of days to check the progress on our house. It's being renovated."

"Welcome to the island, I'm Chris Landrum."

"Mr. Landrum, I'm Erika, this handsome man is Fred, my husband."

Fred glared at me like I was interfering with his delightful morning, then said, "Dr. Fred Robinson."

I faked a smile. "Please call me Chris. It's quite a coincidence, but I've been through your house. Great property."

Erika said, "When it was for sale?"

Fred added, "You know I won the bidding war."

Duh! I thought.

"No, Dr. Robinson," I said, with an emphasis on Dr. "A friend and I went through the haunted house."

Erika looked like she'd seen a ghost as she twisted a napkin between her hands before pushing her mid length, black, curly hair out of her face. "Oh."

"Chris, pull up a seat," Dr. Robinson said as he pointed to my chair.

How could I resist since I'd been wondering how I'd meet the house owners?

Fred appeared to have put his foul mood on the back burner as he said, "You were at the haunted house, so you know about the issue we're having."

I didn't think the fate of Todd Lee was Fred's issue, but why not jump in with both feet and see what the owners have to say about *their* issue.

"A friend and I were there when the body was discovered. Not the scare we were looking for."

Erika said, "Fred, what're the chances we'd run into someone who was there when a deceased gentleman was found in our house?" Her face formed a smile that more closely resembled a grimace. "Not the introduction to the community we wanted."

"Did either of you know Todd Lee, the victim?"

After a long pause, Fred cleared his throat and said, "Why would we know some dead guy?"

"What Fred's trying to say is we don't know anybody on the island, so there's no reason to know the victim."

"I only thought that since Mr. Lee was killed in your house, there's a chance you might've known him."

Fred said, "We've not moved in. The house is ours in name only. If I were you, I'd speak to John Rice about the guy. He's doing the renovation and is on site daily, or he's supposed to be. I'm paying good money for the house to be in tip top condition and so far have seen little progress."

I didn't see reason to tell them I'd already talked to Rice. Instead, I said, "Have you visited the house recently?"

Fred said, "Several weeks ago. My dental practice has been keeping me busy. Today is my first trip since then." He turned to Erika, "How do you like the progress so far?" He glanced at me. "My wife is the creative mind behind the renovations."

She said, "I haven't been there in several days, but thought John was making good progress."

"We'll see," Fred added.

"Hope when it's finished, it meets your expectations. It's in a great location and the people on Folly are extremely welcoming."

Erika smiled, seemingly sincere this time. "Thank you, Chris. It'll be nice to finally put down roots."

"You from around here?"

"New Jersey," Fred said. "Moved to Savannah to be a partner in a large dental practice. Opened the office in Charleston."

"Will you be opening an office on the island?"

"No, I'll remain at my practice in Charleston. More money, upscale clientele, you know."

The temperature in the room dropped several degrees with that statement, so I figured my welcome had better come to an end before I told him what I thought of his upscale clientele or their dentist. After all, I didn't want to alienate the charming Dr. Robinson.

"I must be going," I said. "It was a pleasure meeting you. Again, welcome to Folly."

Erika said, "It was nice meeting a local, hope to see you around town."

Dr. Robinson stood and offered his hand. "Pleasure, I'm sure."

Everyone has a right to his opinion.

15

I was on the screened in porch finishing my cup of coffee when the sound of a bike coming in the drive broke my peaceful morning.

"Hey, Chris, narrowed down our suspect list?"

"Morning, Charles," I said, wondering if he had a normal greeting in his vocabulary.

"Guess that's no to suspect narrowing. Want to head to the Dog where we can talk about what we know."

I said, "You buying?"

"Penny saved is a penny earned. Your idea, so you buy."

I'd have more luck arguing the facts with a magnolia leaf, so I might as well have a meal and see what my friend has up his long sleeve sweatshirt with what looked like a deranged weasel in a baseball cap staring at me.

I pointed to his shirt. "Nice weasel."

"Weasel, ha! I'll have you know this is the mighty Minnesota Golden Gopher."

"Weasel, gopher same difference."

"Chris, I don't know what to do with you."

Charles started pushing his bike toward the road. That answered how we were traveling to our favorite restaurant. I wasn't sure if the gentleman with the weasel/gopher on his shirt would want to be seen with such an uneducated zoologist, but I took my chances and followed.

The temperature was comfortable, so we accepted a table on the front patio. Amber arrived smiling and shaking her head.

"Haven't seen you two in days. Want the regular or are we going to be adventurous?"

Charles returned her smile. "Surprise me with the usual and whatever His Highness wants."

Amber left with our orders leaving me to be interrogated by Charles.

He said, "I'm not sure we're closer to finding out who killed Todd."

"Nope."

"What're we going to do about it? Shouldn't we be narrowing down suspects instead of adding to the list?"

"First, we should mind our own business. It's not our job. Second, we know near nothing about Todd Lee, so how could we have a list of suspects, that is, if it was our business."

"I agree, it's not our job. This is our passion, something we're good at."

Guess he missed the part about it not being something we should be involved with, regardless if it's a job or a passion.

Amber arrived with our food and asked if there was anything else we needed before heading to the only other occupied table on the patio. We said we were fine.

I took a bite of French toast and started to tell him about yesterday's conversation with the Robinsons when I noticed Shannon Stone heading to the entry. She reminded me of a gypsy in her long, colorful skirt and a flowery blouse. Lugh trotting beside her reminded me of a horse.

She nodded, smiled politely then stuck her head in the door, I assume to request a table on the dog friendly patio. Lugh didn't bother acknowledging me. Shannon and her massive canine walked to the side entrance to the patio where Amber met her and pointed to a large, round table at the front corner.

Before Amber returned to Shannon's table with a bowl of water for Lugh and to take Shannon's order, Charles was petting and carrying on a conversation with his new canine friend.

I took a few steps to their table and said, "Shannon, nice seeing you again and of course you too, Lugh."

I introduced Charles, although Lugh had been Charles's new friend for thirty seconds or so. Charles pulled away from his lovefest, wiped Lugh's slobber off his cheek, then asked Shannon about her dog. No more than three minutes later, we'd learned Lugh was from Ireland, was a present from Shannon's grandmother to remind her of the old country, and is a baby, only a year old. I'm sure there was more, but that's all I remembered.

Shannon looked at our table and at the three empty chairs at her table, before saying, "Would you like to join us."

I said, "Don't want to impose."

As I could've guessed, Charles said, "We'd love to, and Lugh thinks it's a good idea."

Charles grabbed the chair next to Lugh. I got our plates and drinks from the nearby table and pulled out the seat across from Shannon. This could get interesting quickly, not knowing what Charles might say, or how Shannon would react.

"I don't recall seeing you here before," I said to reenter the conversation.

"Lugh and I come once a week or so after a beach walk. We collect shells. It's our day to enjoy each other's company away from the house."

"Sounds nice," I said.

Shannon turned to Charles, "If I am not being overly forward, Charles, I sense you're wishing to ask me something."

Maybe she could tell fortunes, or at least read minds. I took a deep breath and waited. I'd never known anyone who'd welcomed Charles's interrogation.

Amber noticed we'd moved. She brought us two new drinks, refilled Shannon's and quietly walked away.

Charles whispered something to Lugh before turning to Shannon. "Now that you mention it, I do have a question or two."

"Charles, perhaps we should let Shannon eat in peace."

Shannon smiled. "That's okay, Chris."

Smirking at me, Charles said, "Told you."

I took a sip of coffee and waited.

Charles said, "Do you know about the body in the haunted house?"

"Yes, Roisin told me about it the night it was discovered."

"Did you know him or how he died?"

"I didn't even know it was a male. I do not read the papers and we don't possess a television."

Before Charles bombarded her with questions, I said, "Shannon, the gentleman was Todd Lee. He was stabbed."

Shannon's face paled more than it naturally was. She lowered her head and mumbled something before slowly raising her head, taking a sip of water, while looking at Lugh. The dog sensed her gaze and thumped his tail on the patio floor.

She finally said, "You certain it was Todd?"

I nodded. "You know him?"

"Yes and no. He was passing our house a while back and saw me in the yard weeding. Asked if I needed help."

"That was kind," I said, thinking it didn't sound like the man others had described.

"Todd has, umm, had a damaged soul; the two halves were conflicted. I saw this and thought I could help."

Charles said, "How?"

"Todd assisted with weeding and herb gathering, then he came inside for tea. We talked for a time."

"Interesting," I said. "He tell you anything about his life?"

"Not much. He had a rough time for several years; couldn't find a place he could relax and call home. Unfinished business stalled his progression."

Charles said, "Did he say what the unfinished business was?"

I added, "Shannon, we're trying to figure out why someone would want to harm Todd."

Charles looked at me with an expression that screamed, see, I told you you're trying to catch the killer.

Shannon didn't notice. "I did not ask, simply let him talk. The more he talked the more relaxed and peaceful he seemed, so I didn't want to push him. That's not my way."

"Did Lugh like him?" Charles asked as if it was a logical question.

"Lugh welcomed Todd in the house but did not leave my side. He showed no aggression, or I would not have invited Todd in. One should always rely on their canine companion's instincts."

Lugh, hearing, his name sat and looked Charles eye to eye. Charles rubbed his ears and spoke to him in the language only the two of them understood.

"Sorry we're asking so many questions," I said. "Not many people here knew Todd. You're giving a different perspective. Did you only see him once?"

"A week later, I was in the parlor doing a card reading for a neighbor and glanced outside. Todd was in the garden. When my session was over, I went out to speak to him, but he was gone."

Charles said, "He didn't stick around to talk?"

"He was gone but had picked sage and left it on the steps along with an amethyst."

I said, "Are those significant?"

"Yes, amethyst calms fears, allows peaceful dreams and spiritual growth to name a few. Sage is used to cleanse, to banish negative energy. It can also be used to give strength."

"Why would he leave them for you?"

"I took it as a sign he was preparing to face whatever was bothering him and to make a new start." She looked at her watch. "Sorry, but we need to head to the house."

I said, "We enjoyed the chance to talk."

As Shannon stood to leave, she said, "One last thing, I gave Todd my husband's business card in case what was disturbing his life required a lawyer."

"Did they ever talk?"

"I don't know."

After they were gone, Charles said, "We now have more answers."

"A few, but way more questions, Mr. Detective."

I started to tell him about talking with the Robinson's when we arrived, but Shannon's visit stopped me. Time to get it over.

"Guess who I had coffee with yesterday morning?"

Charles was usually the one who asked questions I couldn't possibly know the answers to. It felt good being on the asking end.

"Wasn't me."

"That your best guess?"

"That's not a guess, it's a fact."

"Erika and Dr. Fred Robinson."

He glared at me. "And when were you going to tell me?"

"When we got here, then Shannon arrived."

"How many hours was that after you had coffee with the Robinson's yesterday morning?" He stuck out his lower lip.

"Want me to do math or tell you what we talked about?"

He sighed. "What did you talk about?"

I told him about the strange conversation, my negative reaction to Dr. Robinson, and the cheerful dentist telling me to talk to John Rice if I wanted to know about the body.

"Chris, you think he killed Todd Lee?"

"What could be his motive?"

"Nary a clue. How about obnoxious people do obnoxious things? Killing Lee would qualify."

"You'll need to do better than that."

"Okay, how about … umm, no, wait, how about … I'll go back to nary a clue. Why do you think?"

"Charles, to quote a friend, I have *nary a clue*."

16

I was on the way home with a TV dinner from Bert's, when Officer Spencer pulled in the lot between my cottage and the store.

Allen stepped out of the cruiser, chuckled, then said, "Been to more haunted houses?"

I didn't share his glee. "Don't remind me."

"Heard the latest?"

Another impossible question to answer.

I shrugged.

"Sheriff's Office made an arrest in the haunted house murder."

"Who?"

"Don't know his name, some homeless guy."

"How'd they catch him?"

"You know as much about it as I do. Heard it this afternoon." He looked toward Bert's door. "Gotta grab something to eat then back to work. Good seeing you."

I told him the feeling was mutual before heading home to stick supper in the microwave.

As I ate my "home cooked" meal, my mind drifted to what Allen had shared. He might not know anything else about the arrest, but I knew someone who would.

"Cindy, did I catch you at a bad time?"

"In fact, Mr. Pest, you did. Dear, sweet hubby and I were sitting down to an exquisitely prepared, sumptuous meal of hot dogs, slathered with the good mustard, not that cheap yellow stuff, and Pringles. Can I fix a gourmet meal or what?"

I held back a laugh then told her I was sorry to interrupt their meal and asked her to call me while it was being digested. She mumbled a response through a mouthful of her gourmet meal before hanging up. I assumed she'd been saying she'd be thrilled to call me back.

She returned the call an hour later with, "Thought I'd call while Larry was watching *Wheel of Fortune*. He goes ballistic if I disturb him during *Wheel*. The little perv claims the show stimulates his mind, but if you ask me, he's watching Vanna White. Don't ask what she stimulates. Woe, that's way more than you need to know. What do you want?"

"This afternoon I heard the Sheriff's Office made an arrest in Todd Lee's murder."

"Yep," she said before the phone went dead.

I called her back.

Cindy answered, "Vanna White fan club."

I smiled. "Tell me about the murder suspect."

She sighed. "Name's Jeff Hildebrand, mid thirties, homeless until yesterday when he was given a luxury cell in the Charleston County Cannon Detention Center."

"What led them to him?"

"Beverly Kosfeld."

"The elderly lady who rides around town on an adult trike?"

"Chris, yes, if you mean an oversized tricycle like you geezers ride."

"How'd she lead you to him?"

"She shuffled in my office day before yesterday saying she just heard someone got killed in the haunted house. She lives in the Oceanfront Villas, in a unit directly across the street from the murder site."

"Didn't she hear or see all the commotion the night the body was found?"

"Excellent question, fledgling detective. Sweet Beverly hears about as good as a squid, which in case you're interested, can't hear at all. She, Beverly, not the squid, has come close to getting herself squashed by a car more than once because she couldn't hear them coming. She—"

"Got it. She didn't hear anything."

"You want to know what happened or not?"

"Cindy, of—"

She interrupted, "After she learned of the murder, she remembered seeing Todd Lee going into the house late at night after everything was shut down. She didn't think anything of it; figured he worked on the crew getting the house ready for its haunting or worked in it after it closed."

"How'd she know it was Todd Lee?"

"She nearly ran into him with her tricycle a week earlier, slammed on the brakes, then began apologizing. She told him who she was, he told her who he was. That's how. Follow me so far?"

"Yes, so how'd she know who the Hildebrand guy was, and why'd she think he killed Todd?"

"Said she saw some guy going in the house with Todd two or three times. She didn't know who he was. Apparently, she didn't almost run him down to get his name."

"How'd you all identify him?"

"Beverly sees better than she hears. She described him, down to the black Lynyrd Skynyrd sweatshirt he was wearing. I asked around and Officer Bishop remembered seeing someone with that description hanging around the Folly River Park a couple of nights earlier. We found him later that day and turned him over to Detective Adair. The rest is history."

"Don't suppose he confessed."

"You don't suppose correctly. While he didn't solve the murder, he did solve one mystery."

"That being?"

"Where Todd Lee hung his hat several nights. That is, if he had a hat. According to suspect Jeff, he and Todd stayed nights in the haunted house. When Todd worked for the renovation company, he made a key to the house; then on colder nights, he went in after hours to crash. After Todd was fired, he couldn't afford a place to stay and ran into Jeff Hildebrand on the street."

"Cindy, I didn't see anything, but did the detectives or their techs find evidence Todd was staying in the haunted house?"

"Another excellent question. This is where it gets interesting. Hildebrand claims he came to the haunted house about two o'clock the day the body was found. Said he had a lead on where he and Todd could get a cheap room. He thought if they combined their worldly resources, they might be able to scrape up enough to pay rent." Cindy hesitated before saying, "Yes, Larry. I'll fix popcorn when I get off the phone. Umm, sorry about that Chris, my wifely duties are never done. Where was I?"

"Hildebrand came to find Todd."

"Oh yeah, he found him all right, but claims Todd was dead when he got there. Says he panicked, grabbed everything there belonging to him and Todd, and skedaddled."

"Don't suppose Detective Adair believed him."

"Not for a second, but the problem is that pesky thing called proof. He ain't got none."

"Is Jeff still in jail?"

"Currently charged with evidence tampering. Won't have to prove that since he confessed to it. That's a misdemeanor, so if convicted Hildebrand could get up to a year at taxpayer expense. That may give Adair time to find more evidence. Or so he hopes."

"Why may?"

"Adair says even the greenest public defender could get Hildebrand out on bail since evidence tampering, especially in this case, isn't serious enough to hold him until trial."

"Does Hildebrand have bail money?"

"He could. Adair said it wouldn't take much."

"Think he killed Lee?"

"Beats Blackbeard or Chucky doing it."

17

October gifted Folly Beach with another mild morning. Not wanting to be cooped up in the house, I grabbed my windbreaker in case my walk took me to the beach, then grabbed a cup of coffee at Bert's. Among the many nice things about the off season is the lack of vacationers which makes walks serene and less crowded, especially along Center Street. With all the twists and turns I've experienced through the last decade, Folly feels more like my hometown than where I grew up in Kentucky. The island has offered me a fantastic although eccentric group of friends and interesting adventures. As I walked, I realized how lucky I was to have landed in this community.

"Brother Chris!" A booming voice broke the morning air like thunder as I passed Center Street Coffee. I hadn't noticed Preacher Burl sitting at a small table at the side of the small shop.

"Preacher Burl, sorry I didn't see you."

"It's no wonder, you looked like you were in never never land." He laughed. "I've been told I get that look when I'm working on sermons."

"I was daydreaming, not sermon writing."

"Brother Chris, I bet you'd have no trouble writing a good sermon."

"Preacher, Lugh would have a better chance writing a novel than I would penning a sermon. I'll leave the words of wisdom and hope to you. Enjoying the weather?"

"I just left young Roisin after one of our nature walks. That young lady is going to make sure I recognize all the fauna and flora on the island."

"One of us has to learn it since I apparently don't know the difference between a weasel and a gopher."

"Meaning?"

"It's a Charles thing," I said, knowing that'd be all I needed to say since Burl knew most of Charles's quirks. "How's Roisin?"

"She's good, excited her dad's taking time off the next couple of weeks to get ready for All Hallows Eve, Halloween to you and me."

"Didn't realize there was that much to do for Halloween."

Clearing his throat while putting on his best teaching face, Burl said, "According to Roisin, Halloween or All Hallows Eve, Samhain is one of their most important Sabbats."

"Preacher, that's a couple of words I'm not familiar with."

"Brother Chris, me too. I'm spouting off what I learned today, hoping it'll help me remember some of it better."

"Humm, okay, enlighten me."

"Wicca celebrates eight different holidays they call Sabbats, and Samhain is another name for what Christians refer to as Halloween."

I thought how only a few days ago I was blissfully ignorant of this unique way of life. I was equally surprised how a preacher of the Christian faith was so embracing of a religion that seemed so different.

Burl smiled, "Enough learning for today unless you want to acquire knowledge about the Carolina anole."

Finally, something I knew about.

"No, I'm good," I said, thinking how those little lizards have a party on my porch daily. They're some of God's little critters you get used to in the Carolinas. They're everywhere. Fortunately, they eat ants which are unwelcomed visitors in any cottage.

"Lesson over, but I'm glad I ran into you. There is something else regarding the Stones."

"What?"

Burl looked around to see if anyone was near, which I thought strange since the road was void of life except a black and white cat walking up the middle of the street like he owned it.

"Brother Mike called this morning to let me know Roisin was running late. He also asked if I would be comfortable setting up a meeting with us. Was going to call you when I got home."

"Us, like you and me?"

"Yes."

"Why?"

"Not sure, but he thought it best I invite you instead of approaching you directly since you'd never met. Are you willing?"

"Sure, when?"

Burl looked at his watch, then said, "This afternoon, if you're not too busy."

I wondered if Burl knew how not busy I was most days?

"That'll work. He in a hurry?"

"I wouldn't say urgent, but something in the way he asked made me think it'd be better sooner rather than later."

"What time and where?" I asked, hoping not at Mike's house. I was in no hurry to see Lugh or Ozzy, aka Desmond.

"I'll check with Brother Mike to nail down the time but let's say one o'clock unless that won't work for him. We can meet at First Light." He smiled. "I'll even provide lunch."

I cut my short walk shorter and headed home wondering why Mike Stone wanted to meet. Then again, how bad could it be since I was getting a free lunch. It'd be a pleasant change since I normally got stuck with the check. The black and white cat escorted me most of the way home. I was ready to tell him he wouldn't find Friskies at my house when he trotted past me without a backward glance, then ran behind Bert's.

I spent the next two hours flipping through photo magazines and wondering what Mike Stone could want. I also must've fallen asleep since the next thing I remembered was the clock revealing I had twenty minutes to get to the meeting.

Most First Lights' services are held on the beach near the Folly Pier. The location of today's meeting was in a building that was used as a foul weather sanctuary and a base for Preacher Burl to meet with individuals or small groups from his congregation, or as he refers to them, his flock. The building isn't what most people think of when visualizing a church. It's next to Barb's Books and faces Center Street. It has no stained glass windows or a steeple, but more important than those physical features, it has a dedicated flock and a caring minister.

A block before I got to the First Light, I noticed a man exiting a turquoise 1965 Mustang Fastback in front of the church then entering the sanctuary. I used my detective skills and deduced it was the person I was to meet. I walked in and was greeted by the aroma of hamburgers. Over the years, I've learned most kids love hamburgers, then as they grow up, the love changes to a simply they're okay. When people reach their second childhood the love of burgers returns. Okay, by most kids, I'm referring to yours truly.

"Brother Chris, glad you could make it," Burl said as we shook hands. It struck me as odd since the preacher is always polite, but seldom shook hands. I wondered if this was his way of showing I was no threat to the witch, or was it warlock?

I finally got a better look at Mike Stone who'd been standing behind Burl. The newcomer was slightly taller than me and perhaps twenty pounds heavier. He was wearing a red polo shirt and jeans. Clearly, Desmond didn't get his fashion style from his dad.

"Glad to be here, you must be Mr. Stone," I said.

We shook hands. He gave me what appeared to be a sincere smile that seemed nothing like the one given by some lawyers I've met.

"I'm only Mr. Stone in court, please call me Mike."

Burl led us to a table across the room before saying, "Let's sit, break bread, and have a pleasant conversation."

Silence filled the room as we each grabbed a burger and an iced tea. Burl joked that the food came from the Crab Shack and not his kitchen so we wouldn't have to fear food poisoning.

After a few bites, and an uncomfortable silence, Mike said, "Chris, I guess you're curious why I wanted to meet."

"I admit, I was surprised when Burl mentioned it."

Mike smiled. "You've become a topic of conversation at my house."

I find it strange anyone would be sitting around the house talking about me.

"Why? I'm not that interesting."

Mike continued to smile. "Oh, but you are. Roisin thinks you are a nice man who is open to new ideas."

"I've always been a good listener. Your daughter is brighter than some adults I know."

"Roisin is an old soul, not her first go around." The smile across Mike's face was beyond a proud dad, more akin to pure admiration. "Shannon tells me your aura is peaceful and shows you're trustworthy. Not a common reading nowadays."

I glanced over at Burl to see his take. No reaction.

"I'm not sure what to say."

"I understand. Trust me, I'm normally not forthcoming with our personal beliefs. Were you reared on Folly?"

"No, I'm a transplant from Kentucky."

"I'm sure Shannon told you, we moved from Minnesota where I attended University of Minnesota Law School. That's where I found the love of my life and earned a law degree."

"Was Shannon in law school with you?"

Mike's warm laugh made me feel like I was one of his best friends. "Sorry, what's funny is she hated my career choice. Said it'd be the last degree she'd ever want. Hers is in agricultural. Apparently, she didn't find me as untowardly as my career choice. We met and were married thirty-seven days later."

Burl wagging a fry at the attorney. "Brother Mike, I had no idea you were so impetuous."

"I'm not, simply couldn't see my life without her by my side. One might say our stars aligned."

I said, "You're a lucky man."

With the meal a few bites from finished, I was certain the reason for the meeting hadn't come up, that is unless Mike was curious about my aura.

"Very lucky. Chris, shall I get to why I asked Burl to get us together?"

I nodded.

"Shannon told me you were asking about Todd Lee."

"Did you know him?"

"I talked to Mr. Lee twice, once by phone then at Loggerhead."

"Do you mind if I ask what you talked about?"

"Chris, not sure you know, attorney client privilege remains even after death."

I nodded. "Todd was a client?"

"Not a paying client, but yes, he told me what was on his mind and I gave him advice with regards to the law. Technically, he didn't hire me, simply needed someone to listen to. Doing that, I could also provide legal advice if he needed it."

"Don't mean to pry but did it seem he was going to take your advice?"

Of course, I was prying. Charles wasn't here so how else would I get answers?

Mike stared at me, briefly glancing at Burl while rubbing the back of his neck. "With him ending up dead, I'm guessing he didn't take my advice. Not surprising, Todd didn't strike me as being genuinely nice."

"Shannon told me he was troubled. Did you get a different impression?"

"Let's just say after our meeting at Loggerheads, Mr. Lee knew I didn't want him at my house." He hesitated before saying, "Chris, I wanted to let you know I knew Mr. Lee, that he appeared more than troubled, and was no longer welcome at my house. I can't tell you more."

"Have you talked to the police?"

"Not yet."

"I don't know the Sheriff's Office detective that well but know Cindy LaMond, Folly's Chief. If you know anything you can share that could help them find his killer, I'd suggest you talk with her."

"I'll take that under advisement."

Since Todd wasn't technically a client, I didn't see why Mike couldn't tell Cindy, but I didn't get the impression I'd convinced him.

We spent the next fifteen minutes talking about the weather, restaurants along Center Street, Folly's proximity to Charleston, and other things strangers discuss. Sensing our discussion nearing an end, instead of pushing him about Todd Lee, I said, "Mike, it's been a pleasure meeting you, and Preacher, your company is always welcomed."

Burl said, "Brother Chris, will I see you Sunday?" Burl's smile showed he already knew the answer.

At best, I was an irregular attendee at First Light.

"I'll see."

As Mike and I walked out into the brisk October air, I couldn't shake the feeling there was something he wanted to tell me away from Burl.

To keep the conversation going, I said, "That's one nice ride, Mike. You don't see many classic Mustangs over here."

"My dad bought her off the showroom floor. Everything's original. She's been taken care of better than most children."

"Is she your daily drive or just for special occasions?"

"If you see me, Banshee will be close by."

"Banshee?"

"Dad named the car, so who am I to change it? I want to extend an open invitation to the Stone house anytime you would like."

"I appreciate that."

I watched Mike open the driver's door, then hesitate as if he wanted to say more. Other than, "See you later," no words came. As the car pulled from the curb I was left wondering if I just read more into peoples' actions, thanks to Charles noisy influence, or was it something else.

18

Over the last few years, I've been trying to lose weight and get in better shape. I've failed miserably, but that hasn't stopped me from telling myself I was trying. Experience has taught me that walking through soft sand on the beach is more strenuous than on paved surfaces. Other than a better cardio exercise, walking along the ocean does much for my spirit, the earlier in the day the better.

Today I headed to the beach, then turned toward the sun wishing me a good morning as it peeked its head over the Atlantic. The temperature was already in the upper sixties, high for this close to Halloween. The only life I noticed was a colony of seagulls searching for breakfast at water's edge.

I don't know what I'd been thinking, but it must've been time consuming. I looked up and saw I'd already walked nine blocks from Center Street. I also was oblivious to the thick fog rolling in off the ocean. Before I became oblivious to walking into the surf and drowning, I turned and headed back toward the center of town. Fortunately, I had the coastline to guide me toward the Pier since the view in front of me was of nothing but thick, gray fog.

It was a couple more blocks before I saw life other than seagulls. The vague image of two people walking toward me came into focus,

SEA FOG

almost focus. Fifty yards closer, I recognized the images as Roisin and Desmond Stone. Roisin wore a long skirt, bright red blouse, a backpack, and was barefoot. Her brother had on black jeans, cuffs rolled up, a black T shirt with Black Flag plastered across the front, and black, hiking boots.

Roisin said. "Hi, Mr. Chris, out for a walk?"

While I thought it was obvious, I said, "Yes. Good morning, Roisin, Desmond." She smiled; Desmond looked at me like he'd seen a sea monster. "Going somewhere in particular?"

Roisin's smile increased. "Enjoying Mother Nature's glorious gifts." She chuckled. "That is until she dumped fog on us."

"Sea fog," Desmond said. His sour look unchanged.

"What's Black Flag?" I asked to offer something he might want to talk about."

"Punk rock band," He shook his head and said, as if who wouldn't know that.

Clearly, I didn't. "Oh."

Roisin twisted her feet in the soft sand and said, "That's okay, Mr. Chris, I didn't know it until my punk rock brother told me fifteen times."

I saw why Preacher Burl thought so highly of the young lady.

Desmond sneered at his sister before turning to me. "Sea fog. Stories about it have been around for centuries. Ghost ships, boats disappearing in it never to be seen again. Sea monsters grabbing crew members right off the deck during outbreaks of the fog."

"Mr. Chris," Roisin said, "you don't have to pay attention to him. His brain works different than yours or mine."

What to say to that?

I didn't have to say anything. Desmond said, "You've heard of the Bermuda Triangle, haven't you?"

"Sure."

He pointed toward the ocean. "It's nearby, right out there. Countless ships floated into it; many never came out. Airplanes flew into it; bunches of them were never seen again."

Roisin kicked sand at her brother, then rolled her eyes. "How many times do I have to tell you the Bermuda Triangle is nowhere near Folly Beach. It's down south."

"Like you know everything," Desmond said. "Bermuda is right out there, and the triangle goes from it down to Puerto Rico then to Florida. Look it up." He turned to me, "Not all the mysteries of the sea happen out there." He pointed to the ocean. "Mister, see how the sea fog also covers land?"

I nodded; Roisin rolled her eyes again; and Desmond pointed toward town, before saying, "Bad stuff happens there." He stared at me; his eyes narrowed. "You're the guy that saw the stiff in the haunted house. Cool."

"Desmond," Roisin said, "nothing's cool about it. The man was killed."

Desmond ignored his sister. "Me and little squirt here went through the haunted house the night after the dead guy was found. That preacher man was going to take her the night before, but death killed that plan." He rolled his eyes. "Anyway, we had to get there early because so many people wanted to see where the dead guy was." He laughed, an emotion I hadn't seen from him. "Scared the crap out of sissy here." He nodded toward Roisin.

"You were scared too when that clown sat up in the coffin."

"Wasn't," Desmond said before turning to me. "You hear about the broom some bozo left on our porch?"

I thought Charles could change directions on the head of a pin. He could learn from Desmond.

"I heard it somewhere. Why?"

"Wondering. Some people think we're weird."

Roisin said, "Everyone thinks you're weird."

"Sis, you know I meant because we're witches."

"Wiccans," she said.

"No difference to the ignorant," Desmond said. "Stupid people think all of us fly around on brooms. Everybody knows brooms can't fly." He nodded his head slowly then said, "Chris, if I may call you that, we're modern witches. I fly on a Eureka Mighty Mite vacuum cleaner. Some witches prefer Bissell, but the Mighty Mite has more power."

Roisin said, "Mr. Chris, you have to overlook things my brother says. Most of his fog's in his head. His brains were sucked out long ago, probably by a Bissell vacuum cleaner."

I thought her comment was humorous but didn't want to upset Desmond. "I'll keep that in mind, Roisin."

"Mr. Chris, Dad said he met you yesterday."

"Yes, we had a nice talk. He's a nice—"

Desmond interrupted, "He tell you he knew the stiff?"

Roisin shoved her brother. "Mr. Chris, we need to get home. Mom worries when I'm out too long with Desmond. She's afraid he'll be a bad influence." She leaned close to me and whispered, "Mom's a smart lady."

That I could see. I could also see how the conversation about the late Todd Lee was over. "Nice talking to both of you."

Roisin said she looked forward to it. Desmond wasn't that positive, but did say, "Remember, I'll be the one flying the Mighty Mite."

"How could I forget?"

They headed to the dunes line and I continued toward the Folly Pier.

The fog was lifting so I was less afraid of disappearing, being confronted by a sea monster, or buzzed by a vacuum cleaner riding witch.

19

Thoughts of Todd Lee swirled in my head all morning, so I decided I needed to think about something else. Food seemed like a good option. I hadn't been to Loggerhead's in a couple of weeks, so it fit the bill. Mother Nature was still blessing us with warm weather making it another day to give my car a break and to motivate my exercise rationale. I was a block away when I realized the real reason I was headed to Loggerhead's wasn't only the food, but where it was located. Dr. Robinson's house, aka the last haunted house I hoped I'd ever attend, was adjacent to the popular restaurant. I wanted to see what if anything was happening there. The haunted house didn't look too haunted in daylight or it might've been all the activity going on around it. Construction trucks filled the driveway and workers were everywhere. I spotted Nate Davis lugging a sheet of drywall up the front stairs.

I waited for him to set the heavy load on the landing, then said, "Nate, what's going on?"

He looked around before spotting me at the bottom of the stairs. "Hey Chris, come to help?"

I assumed, hoped, he was joking. "You working upstairs? What about the haunted house?"

"It's history."

"Meaning?"

"Dr. Pain In The Ass shut it down."

"What happened?"

He shrugged. "Boss man's out back; he has the answers. I need to get back to work. Maybe I'll catch you at Cal's."

I watched him maneuver the drywall through the front door, then headed around back. The first thing to catch my attention was a petite woman with a blond ponytail wearing a pink hard hat operating a table saw. With my faux detective mind in gear, I deduced she was the B of J&B. I stopped ten feet in front of the action so I wouldn't startle her and cause an OSHA investigation.

She switched off the saw, removing her ear protection, and bounced over to greet me. She reminded me of a cocker spaniel puppy, full of energy and cheer while doing more manual labor than I've ever done.

She said, "What can I do for you?"

"Sorry to interrupt. I was looking for John?"

"Oh lord, what's my husband done now?" Instead of waiting for me to tell her what her husband had done, she turned and surveyed the backyard until she spotted her target. "He's leaning against that tree looking important. I figure he's thinking about lunch."

"Thank you."

As I walked over, I heard the saw start up and what I thought was singing but wasn't sure.

John spotted me.

I said, "You look like a busy man."

"Chris, what a surprise. Busy, no just thinking about lunch."

"A man after my own heart. I was on my way to Loggerhead's when I saw Nate hauling drywall upstairs."

"Yeah it sucks." He shook his head. "Dr. Robinson."

"That's what Nate said. He told me you were the man with the depressing details."

"Sure am, but since you were on your way to lunch and I need a break, why don't we make it a luncheon pow wow."

"Sounds good."

John pushed away from the tree, set his hard hat on an overturned bucket, walked to the table saw where I'd previously stood, and tapped his watch.

The woman ignored John, turned to me, and said, "Told you he was thinking about lunch."

John said, "You two know each other?"

"Yes," she said, "known each other two whole minutes. He was looking for you, so I told him whatever you did illegal, I didn't know anything about it. I added where to find you."

"Sounds like something you'd do," John said, then turned to me. "Chris, I'd like to introduce my lovely, crazy wife Bri."

"Pleasure to meet you, Bri."

"You as well," she said then tapped John on the arm. "So boss, where are you taking our new friend and your lovely, not crazy, wife to lunch?"

"Going to a land far away." He nodded toward Loggerhead's.

Bri chuckled and turned to me. "You'll learn to take what you can get from this big bear." She pointed her hard hat at John. "Shall we walk or should I expect a limo."

"You wait for the limo. Chris and I'll walk."

Bri set her hard hat, gloves, and ear protection on the saw table and in one quick motion, pulled off her long sleeve, plaid shirt revealing a pink tank top. She locked arms with John as we headed to lunch.

It took no more than a minute to make the limo less trip to Loggerhead's then up the stairs to the entry. John asked the hostess for a table on the deck overlooking the former haunted house. It was a good choice considering a warm, late October day couldn't be taken for granted. Decorations were still hanging from every vertical surface from the restaurant's annual Halloween Costume Party held last evening. Since Costume was in the event's name, I wasn't in attendance. I also wasn't qualified for the restaurant's Halloween Pet Costume Party that was advertised on as poster by the door.

We were one of three occupied tables, so a server was quick to arrive, told us she was Doris, and asked what we wanted to drink. We each requested iced tea.

Doris headed inside and I said, "Bri, you've chosen a career most women wouldn't consider."

"That's what my parents said when I left home."

John leaned my direction. "Bri is one of the best construction workers I've worked with, stronger than many of the guys." He laughed. "That's even if she needs a ladder to reach the truck bed."

"Funny," Bri said. "That's why I married a man the size of an oak."

"I'm only six-five, but to a woman who's shorter than a hobbit, well, you get the picture."

I was at a loss for a response, but fortunately I didn't need one. Doris returned with our drinks and asked if we were ready to order. John and Bri went with cheeseburgers. To not slow things down, I said the same.

John watched Doris leave then said, "Chris, you had questions about the haunted house closing?"

"What happened? I heard it was bringing in good crowds."

"Not good, great. Was the best venture we've done. All the proceeds were going to charity and the locals loved the entertainment." He shook his head. "A huge loss all around."

"Damned shame," Bri added.

I said, "So why close?"

John took a sip, slammed his plastic glass on the table, and said, "Dr. Robinson blew a gasket with the large crowds and a lack of progress on the renovation."

Bri said, "John assured him we were on schedule and described the benefits of keeping the haunted house open."

I said, "It didn't matter?"

"Do you know the good doctor?"

"Had the pleasure of meeting him once. A real charmer."

"Don't know the half of it," John said. "In my business, I deal with lots of different people and some are difficult, but none as disagreeable as Fred."

Bri put her hand on John's shoulder. "Boss man tried to convince

Doctor-Feel-No-Good, but the jerk wouldn't budge even with the offer of another discount."

"That didn't sway him?'

John said, "It ticked him off more."

"Interesting."

"He was fixated on people calling his house the murder house, ruining his good name, he claimed. Wanted the murder forgotten."

"I talked to his wife," Bri said. "Thought a woman to woman conversation would help and to remind her all donations would be in their name. That's what the community would remember."

"Her reaction?"

"Not good, really not good."

"What'd she say?"

"The look that crossed her face, made me take a step back. She proceeded to tell me how her husband owned us, and we needed to do what he said. She said a lot more, but I'm too much of a lady to repeat it."

"Seems strange she got so upset," I said as Doris slid our plates in front of each of us.

"Bri told me the full conversation when we got home. Was smart on her part. No way will I have anyone talking to my wife like that. Furthermore, no one owns me."

"I understand."

"We were grateful for them allowing us to host a haunted house. We didn't want to bring any negativity. The customer is always right, but it was disappointing for all involved."

"The community will miss the entertainment, but at least they had it a couple of weeks."

I took a bite of burger, glanced at the former haunted house, and said, "Bri, what was your impression of Todd Lee?"

"That's a strange question."

"Honey, I've heard Chris is trying to put the cops out of business."

Not the direction I wanted the conversation to head. "Nope, simply curious."

Bri smiled but it quickly faded. "Didn't like him. He was an arrogant know-it-all who thought women should be barefoot and pregnant with no place in a man's world."

I said, "I've heard some things about him but that's new."

She continued, "Met him a year ago in Charleston on a jobsite. He came around asking for work, but John was offsite. He was rude, crude, and made a pass at me. Not the best way to get a job, if you ask me."

John's head pivoted toward Bri. "I had no idea he was that guy. You never told me his name. Bri was out of town when I hired him over here."

Bri tightened the grip on her drink. "Was my first day onsite in a week or so. I was bringing in props for the haunted house and ran into him. Was shocked to see him again. The jerk grabbed my arms and made a comment, one I don't feel comfortable saying in public."

I said, "What happened?"

"Nate walked in the room, saw what Todd was doing, yelled at him. I left to find John."

"I fired him and escorted him off property. End of story."

And it was. The rest of the lunch was filled with talk about their favorite vacation spots and how good the food was. John noted workers had arrived back on site, so he said they'd better get back to work. They paid the tab, including mine, before heading next door.

Leaving Loggerheads, I had more questions than answers about J&B. The story they shared differed from what John had told me earlier about firing Todd.

20

I waited until mid morning before calling Charles, not because I was afraid if I called earlier, I'd wake him, but I wanted to finish breakfast and coffee before being subjected to his version of the Spanish Inquisition. The weather was more appropriate for this time of year with a light chilly rain enveloping the area. Spending the day inside discussing motives for a haunted house homicide seemed fitting. I took a deep breath and made the call.

"Morning, Charles."

"Who's this? It couldn't be my long lost friend, Chris, could it?"

"Funny, how're you doing?"

"Well, you'd know if you'd bothered to call in the last two months."

"Months? How about the last few days? You suffering a memory lapse?"

"Nope, neglect."

"You know that thing you're talking on can make calls, don't you?"

"Picky, picky. You're the neglector."

I was jumping down a rabbit hole, so I changed the subject. Not fast enough.

He said, "Catch the killer?"

"You know I can't do that without you."

"Precisely."

"Charles, if you're done griping, I thought you might wonder why I called."

"Calling because you're feeling guilty about not calling for two months."

"Charles."

"Okay, why are you calling?"

"Better. To see if you'd like to come over to talk about the murder."

He was gone. I was certain the weather had nothing to do with the silence or the lack of phone etiquette from my neglected friend. I smiled, refilled my coffee mug, then waited on the porch for my guest whom I hadn't seen in somewhere between two days and two months.

Three sips later, Charles was pedaling wildly down the rain soaked streets looking like Almira Gulch in *The Wizard of Oz*.

He jumped off the bike, stepped on the porch, shook water off his Tilley and off the shoulders of his blue and gray, University of New Hampshire long sleeve sweatshirt with a snarling wildcat on the front, then said, "Couldn't you have picked a nicer day?"

"Thought we needed some old fashioned October weather, hence the reason I ordered rain."

"Didn't know you could do that?"

"You don't know everything about me. Iced tea, water, coffee, or Diet Coke?"

"Don't put yourself out," he said as he headed to the kitchen.

I sat in the living room and waited for him to return with his drink of choice. Apparently, today it was iced tea since he was taking a large gulp from a bottle of tea as he flopped down in the chair across from me.

"Enough of the pleasantries," he said. "Let's get started."

"Where do you want to begin?"

"At the beginning, Chris, at the beginning."

"Todd Lee."

"What do we know about the late Mr. Lee?" He leaned in waiting for my revelations.

"He was relatively new to Folly, homeless for the most part. He wasn't liked by most we know who knew him. Also, remember how your new friend Nate Davis told us how Lee kept bragging about striking it rich?"

"A dream of many homeless folks. How many actually find a pot of gold at the end of a rainbow?"

"Zero," I said. "If he kept saying it, he must've had something in mind."

"Like robbing a bank or winning the lottery?"

I shrugged. "Don't know."

"But who'd want to kill him?"

"Could be someone he was scheming with or somebody he was going to get the money from. Who knows?"

Charles mirrored my shrug and said, "Not me."

Since he didn't bring me anything from the kitchen, I left to refill my mug. Truth be told, it was more to delay the grief I would receive from what I was going to share next.

I returned to my chair before saying, "Yesterday I talked to John and Bri."

He leaned forward nearly knocking his bottle of tea off the arm of the chair. "Without me?"

"Wasn't planned, ran into them."

"Where?"

"The haunted house, well, former haunted house."

"Wow, just happened to run into them at the house where you knew they'd be working. What a surprise." He hesitated, tilted his head, and said, "Former haunted house?"

"Dr. Robinson shut it down."

"You're kidding."

"Afraid not."

"That's just not right for the youngsters." He shook his head. "Not right."

"John and Bri were upset."

"I understand. There aren't that many Halloween activities here for the kids. No trick or treat, now no haunted house. You have to admit it was fun before the corpse showed up."

Don't recall ever thinking *really wish we could've finished this fun filled adventure of getting the stuffing scared out of us, instead of staring at a dead body, a real one.* Charles was looking at me waiting for agreement, but I refused.

I said, "I learned Bri had a past with Todd, not a good one."

"Not good?"

I shared what John and Bri had told me about Todd.

"Don't you find that strange since it wasn't mentioned in other conversations with John?" Charles took a drink.

"Yep."

"Now we're getting somewhere. She can be number one on the suspect list."

"Charles, having a past with someone doesn't mean she killed him."

His fingers tapped on the armrest. "I know, but it doesn't hurt."

"Moving on, let's get back to Nate Davis since he didn't like Todd."

Without coming to any insightful conclusions, we discussed Nate's relationship with Todd.

Charles smiled. "Dude told me a homeless man's been arrested for something about the incident."

"Dude? Didn't realize he was part of your detective agency." I didn't add *using the term detective agency loosely*.

"Nope, but he knows the homeless man. His name—"

I interrupted, "Jeff Hillebrand."

"How'd you know?"

"Cindy told me."

He glared at me. "When were you going to tell me?"

"Now."

He sighed then said, "Police think he did it?"

"Yes, but they have no proof. What's Dude's take?"

"Hillebrand's a guy down on his luck with a temper."

"Seems to be a theme."

"Hillebrand could've killed him, but why?" Charles scratched his head in what I translated as either deep concentration or head lice.

"Cindy said he and Todd spent some nights in the haunted house, but because you share a space with someone doesn't mean you have a reason to kill him. From what we've learned, they had tempers." It was my turn to scratch my head wondering how to find out more about Hillebrand.

Charles stood and headed to the kitchen. Since he still had tea in the bottle, I had a hunch I knew what he was looking for; something he wouldn't find since I hadn't been to Harris Teeter recently on one of my rare grocery shopping adventures.

He returned empty handed. "No chips. Really? You expect me to use my brain power without nourishment?"

"Didn't know your brain needed chips to function. That explains a lot," I said, smiling at my friend standing in the doorway looking unamused.

He shook his head. "I'll be back."

Charles grabbed his Tilley and walked out the door before I responded. I took the alone time figuring how I was going to tell my brain starved friend about the other conversations I've had without him. Hopefully, whatever he gets will sooth his bruised ego.

He returned with two bags filled with goodies. I was glad I didn't have a tab at Bert's, or it would've increased from Charles's brain food purchase.

"You're a crappy host, so I brought refreshments to get us through," he said as he headed to the kitchen.

"Kind of you. When you're done in there, I'll tell you who else I've talked with."

He returned to the living room carrying chips and salsa and said, "More secret meetings?"

"Charles, they weren't secret anything," I said looking at his sad puppy dog face.

"Then, non secret meetings with?"

"Mike Stone, Shannon's husband."

"Lugh's dad?"

"You could say that. Mike knew Todd. Spoke with him twice."

That stopped Charles mid chew. "What'd he say?"

"Mike talked with him once on the phone, once in person, Todd was asking for advice."

Charles had moved to the edge of his seat like I had all this helpful information and he couldn't wait for me to continue.

"Advice about what?"

"Don't know."

"What kind of investigator are you?"

"I'm not one," I said, reminding him for roughly the billionth time. "Mike couldn't say because of attorney client privilege."

"That's all?"

"Well no, he told Todd never to return to his house."

"Seems odd, unless Todd said something to upset Mike. And if he did, could've it been a reason for Mike to kill him?"

I said, "It's as good as any."

"What'd you think of Mike? He a good or bad witch?"

"Not sure which witch, but he seems like a man who won't take crap from anyone. He's protective of his family."

"The plot thickens. Moving on, what about the house owners?" Charles eyes narrowed.

"Not sure. They don't seem personable, but." I shrugged.

"You talked to them, talked to others about them, so you must have thoughts on Dr. Ass and his wife?"

"He seems like a condescending jerk; so, I agree with the others. When I talked to Erika, she seemed calm, like she was trying to fix everything."

"What Bri said about her, makes one wonder."

"Yes, it does, Charles, and raises more questions."

Charles stuffed a handful of chips in his mouth and mumbled, "So, who killed him?"

"Heck if I know. You're the detective, who do you think?"

"Heck if I know."

Finally, we agreed.

21

The cold rain that covered the area yesterday was still around giving me an excuse not to venture out. After too much coffee, a bowl of Rice Krispies, and rehashing Charles and my discussion yesterday, I realized I knew little more about who might've killed Todd Lee than I did when we stumbled on the body. So, why was I thinking about it? Neither Charles nor I knew Todd Lee. We didn't know anyone who would've even considered him a friend. True, seeing him on the pantry floor left an indelible impression. Was that reason enough to be racking my brain for a way to learn the identity of his killer? On a rational level, the answer was clearly no. So, why was I sitting here on a rainy morning thinking about it? On the other hand, what harm would it do if I asked questions of the people who knew Mr. Lee?

Who did I know who might have known one or more of the potential suspects who might've had reason to kill Lee? The police believed Jeff Hildebrand was the killer. He spent several nights sleeping in the haunted house as did the victim. He admitted removing evidence from the house that would've proven he'd been there. I didn't know Hildebrand nor anyone who knew him well. He was by far the lead suspect.

The only people I knew who knew Fred Robinson and his wife

beyond a casual knowledge were John and Bri Rice. After the good Dr. Robinson shut down the haunted house, John and Bri were angry with them. Did they know more than they'd shared? Regardless what John and Bri knew about the Robinsons, what motive would either of the Robinsons have for wanting Lee dead? After all, his death hurt Fred Robinson's reputation, or so he thought, bothering him enough to shut down the popular attraction.

Thinking of John and Bri, did they have reason to want Lee dead? Even if one or both had reason, killing him in the house where they were working wouldn't have been wise. He'd worked for them a week on top of his previous exchanges with Bri in Charleston. There was bad blood between the Rices and Lee. It was a long shot, but my friend and former Realtor Bob Howard might know the couple since they had a renovations' business. A quick call could answer that question. Any answer was better than the ones I had no answer for.

"Bob," I said when he answered the phone with the country sounds of Mel Tillis playing in the background. "How's the world of a bar owner?"

Bob retired from a successful career as a realtor to buy Al's Bar, a rundown restaurant and bar owned by Al Washington, Bob's unlikely friend. Bob knew as much about running a bar as an elephant does about entering a spelling bee but bought the business because his friend was in poor health.

"Couldn't be better. Hell, there were seven people in yesterday for lunch. Damned gold mine."

I coughed back a laugh. "Great."

George Jones replaced Mel Tillis singing in the background, and Bob said, "You ain't with the freakin' IRS, so why are you pestering me about business?"

"Do you know John and Bri Rice, they own J&B Renovations?"

"Yes."

"What do you know about them?"

"Chris, you sound like you need a cheeseburger."

"Sounds like a good idea."

"Good, if you hurry, I can hold off the crowd enough to save you a seat."

I took the subtle hint—subtle for Bob—and said, "See you in a little while."

Al's Bar is in a concrete block building it shares with a Laundromat a block off Calhoun Street near downtown Charleston. Both businesses have been in continuous operation longer than most college students have been alive.

Al met me at the door. He was in his early eighties with short, gray hair, coffee stained teeth, and skin between dark brown and light black. He pushed out of the ancient chair stationed by the door so he could greet guests without taxing his arthritic knees. After Bob bought the business, Al agreed to stay on and function as greeter so he would have somewhere to go, and to serve as peacekeeper between the mostly African American customer base and Bob, whose skin color would make a marshmallow appear gray.

"Thank goodness, you're here," Al said as he gave me a hug. "Your buddy's been moaning and groaning, wondering if you'd ever show. He's been pestering the lunch crowd about it for the last forever." Al pointed to the "lunch crowd," consisting of four men seated at a table beside the window. Bob was at his table near the back of the room. I knew it was *his table* because he'd installed a plaque announcing its vaulted status.

"Get back here and stop gabbing with the hired help!" Bob bellowed, drawing the attention of the *lunch crowd*.

Bob was in his late seventies, six-foot-tall, burly, saying it kindly, wearing a Hawaiian flowery shirt, and most likely shorts, although I couldn't see his legs stuffed between the table and his chair.

"About time you got here," he said in his best customer unfriendly voice. "Hey, you behind the grill, fix my friend a cheeseburger, two helpings of fries, and a glass of cheap wine."

Lawrence, Al's part time cook and person Bob knows the name of as well as he knew mine, said, "Yes, Master Bob."

"Great guy," Bob said as his attention drifted to me. "Don't know what I'd do without him."

"I'm sure he knows how much you appreciate him," I said, oozing sarcasm.

"Smart ass."

I smiled.

"You and your quarter wit friends trying to catch who killed the stiff that wasn't supposed to be part of that haunted house over your way?"

"Why ask that?"

"Let's see. First, I read in the paper about a body found in a haunted house on your little island. Then, you call asking if I know the guys who own J&B Renovations, the company that happens to be fixing up the house where the stiff was found. Finally, you and your eighth wit friend have a way of snooping into things you shouldn't be snooping into. How am I doing so far?"

Lawrence arrived with my cheeseburger, wine, and more fries than I could eat at one meal, although I knew Bob didn't order the double helping for me. I thanked Lawrence and being the wise man I knew him to be, he headed back to the kitchen before Bob could shower him with more love.

"Well," Bob said as I took a bite of burger, "how was I doing?"

"I met John and Bri at the house the other day and was curious if you knew them. I figured since they did renovations, you might've met them during your successful career in real estate. Nothing more."

Bob grabbed one of my fries, stuck it in his mouth, and said, "What a crock. You forget you're talking to old Bob, the guy who saved your bacon more than once when you stuck your nose where it didn't belong?"

"What do you know about them?" I said, skipping over the crock comment.

He smiled like I'd agreed with his assessment about why I was asking about the Rices. "The last two McMansions I brokered the sale of before I became a restaurant magnet needed extensive work. I'd heard good things about J&B, so I recommended them to the homeowners. Because I was such a brilliant and successful realtor, the homeowners asked me to meet with John and Bri to make sure they were legitimate." He grabbed another fry and yelled for Lawrence to bring him another beer.

"What did you learn about John and Bri?"

"From them, little. They told me they were well respected, had a brag book filled with photos of successful, beautiful, functional, blah, blah, blah renovations they'd done. I didn't see any photos of them killing anyone in one of their renovated houses."

"Disappointing."

"Smart ass."

Over the years, I'd convinced myself that was one of Bob's terms of endearment, so I ignored it. "You said, you learned little from them, implying you learned more from others?"

"I can't sneak anything past you."

I grinned as Charlie Rich sang "Behind Closed Doors" from the jukebox.

The song selection was one of several sticking points between Bob and his customers. As a concession to their friendship, years ago, Al salted the jukebox with many of Bob's favorite country songs, or according to Bob, the only kind of songs. They may be the only kind of songs to Bob's ears, but to most of Al's customers, they wouldn't reach the top million in songs they'd play.

"The references John and Bri shared gave glowing comments about the company, their work, on and on."

"Bob, before we die of old age, could you get to the point?"

He sighed. "Being as brilliant as I am, I'd never limit my reference checking to the names given to me by the person I was checking on."

"Brilliant idea."

"Smart ass. Anyway, I called a couple of professional acquaintances to see if they knew of J&B. They didn't have anything bad to say about the company's work, but they both said John was weird. Only one of them knew Bri, but he used a similar description plus a few other things about her."

"Weird?"

"Seems that renovations aren't their only business. Lowcountry Paranormal Investigations is what they really love doing. Seems the renovators are obsessed with the paranormal. Ghosts, things that go bump in the night, dead people returning to haunt us normal folks."

"Bob, a lot of people are into the paranormal. How does that make the Rices weird?"

He stuffed two more fries into his mouth, washed them down with beer, then leaned my direction. "Now I'm not one to judge others," He laughed. "Hell, yes I am. Whatever, apparently the Rices claim to find ghosts where no one else has. One of my acquaintances told me he heard they killed a goat and stuck it in someone's attic, so they could find it and say the former homeowner was a goatherder and his ghost must've killed the animal."

"You believe your friend?"

"Acquaintance, not friend, but hell, who knows. John Rice claims he's a paranormalist, but if you ask me, he's a paraabnormalist."

"Bob, do you think John or Bri could've killed the man in the haunted house because they caught him squatting in there when they were hunting ghosts?"

Bob took another drag off his beer, looked toward Al at the door, turned to me, and said, "I think that'd be one stupid reason to kill someone, but anything's possible. What do you think?"

"Seems unlikely, but possible."

"There you go. Your good buddy Bob solves another murder you're sticking your nose into."

"Don't know how I could do it without you."

"Smart ass."

I agreed.

"One more thing," Bob said, "Not that this is proof of anything, but if you ask me, anyone who'd kill a helpless goat then stick it in someone's attic, has a screw or two loose. Anyone with a screw or two loose can kill a person. You can put money on it."

"You said one of your friends, umm, acquaintances said more about Bri. What about her?"

Bob smiled. "Said she was one hot, blonde, renovating chick."

I finished my cheeseburger, Bob finished the mound of fries, and Tammy Wynette finished "Stand By Your Man." Bob added if I wasn't going to spend any more money, I'd better get back to catching a killer. He said I was taking up a chair that could be holding someone's rear end; someone who could be putting money in Bob's pocket. I didn't point out that there were roughly thirty empty chairs in the room.

Before I left, Bob said, "Try not to get yourself killed trying to catch the killer."

Bob could always be counted on for helpful advice.

On the drive home, I wasn't trying to catch a killer, but trying to figure out if he'd said anything helpful, when the phone interrupted my thoughts.

Chief LaMond responded to my "Hello," with, "Catch you at a bad time?"

"No, was on my way home from Al's."

"Crap, I wanted to catch you at a bad time. You a cheeseburger heavier?"

"Yes, anything else you wanted to know?"

"That's more than I wanted to know, but I called to tell you Jeff Hildebrand was released on bail this morning."

"There's nothing to hold him on the murder?"

"Other than Detective Adair being convinced he did it, no. Again, that pesky concept of proof evades the Sheriff's Office. Hildebrand's evidence tampering trial won't be held for a couple of months. Since he already told Adair he did it, even our imperfect court system will have a hard time getting that wrong."

"Where's Hildebrand now?"

"Who knows. He was told not to leave the country, which was a joke. A homeless man with no wallet, probably doesn't have a passport or the bucks to fly off to Tanzania."

"Cindy, thanks for letting me know."

"You know I live for telling you stuff that's none of your business."

She hung up before I could echo Bob and call her a smart ass.

I was pulling in the drive when the phone rang again.

"Is this Chris Landrum?"

I said it was.

"Chris, this is Mike Stone. Did I catch you at a bad time?"

Wow, two civil conversation beginnings during one car ride. I assured him it wasn't.

"Good. Is there a chance you could meet me tomorrow? Something I'd like to talk to you about."

"Sure."

"Can you stop by the house around two?"

"Yes, is there anything I need to know before then?" I asked, rather than blurting out, *Why would you want to meet with me?*

"Umm, no. We can talk about it tomorrow."

22

Puzzling dreams and unsettling periods between sleep and being awake filled the night. I couldn't put my finger on anything specific, but it was far from normal. My guess was the uneasiness was caused by the pending meeting with Mike Stone. But why? The Stone family was pleasant. Desmond was strange but from my brief encounters with him I couldn't tell if he was simply being a rebellious teen or something more sinister. Today at two, I agreed to enter the lair of the witch, correction four witches, and, oh yeah, a dog bigger than a Fiat. Aren't witches supposed to have cats, cats that can't put your whole head in their mouth? Enough! If I keep on this path, I'll cancel the meeting. I'm being ridiculous.

Heading to Bert's for coffee and human interaction will force me back to reality.

As soon as I entered the store, I was greeted with, "Morning, Chris."

"Roger."

He looked out the door then at me. "I'm standing here waiting for the storm."

I didn't remember asking him what he was doing. "Storm?"

"Chris, head to the Pier and look at those storm clouds rolling in." Roger nodded towards the door.

"Sounds like a plan, but first, coffee."

I drew a cup then walked toward the Pier. Off in the distance, I saw what Roger was talking about. Thick black clouds filled the space the early morning sun normally occupied. Instead of venturing on the Pier, I leaned against the railing overlooking the massive structure. Three fishermen headed my way, probably with little to show for their efforts. The wind had kicked up and the distant skies were so dark it made me think of Halloween. I stood watching the thunderheads rolling my way and was mesmerized by the life the clouds took on. When lightning appeared closer than I was comfortable with, I headed home.

By the time I reached my cottage, the rain arrived, deafening thunder vibrated in my ears. It was fortunate I hadn't walked to the far end of the Pier. October had finally shown its natural colors with a vengeance. I couldn't have picked a better setting to meet a witch than a stormy afternoon in late October.

My lack of sleep must've caught up with me since the next thing I remembered was waking up in my chair in the living room with ten minutes to get to Mike's house. I headed to the car and was surprised the rain had stopped; however, thunder was still protesting and the petrichor of rain still filled the air. Roger should get a second job as a meteorologist since he predicted the storm when today's weather gurus had called for partly cloudy with a zero percent chance of precipitation.

On the short drive, I continued wondering what Mike wanted to share. Surely, he wasn't going to breach attorney client privilege and tell me about his conversations with Todd Lee. Or was he?

I pulled in the Stone's drive and parked behind Banshee. I sat in my car a minute admiring Mike's classic ride, then realized I couldn't stall any longer. On the way to the front door, it entered my mind that I should've brought a bone for Lugh. I smiled wondering where I could get a Titanosaurus bone, one that's big enough for the Irish Wolfhound.

I'd passed the front of the classic Mustang when something caught my eye. I slowly turned to face the car where I saw Mike sitting in the driver's seat.

"Mike, I didn't see you there."

He didn't answer. I returned to the open driver's side window, bent down to say something, when the words stuck in my throat. Mike leaned to the left; a thin stream of blood ran down the side of his face.

I stepped back, tripped over one of the large rocks lining the edge of the drive, and landed on my shoulder in Shannon's flower garden. Not bothering to stand, I grabbed my phone and called Cindy.

She answered with, "Didn't I just talk to you yesterday?" She laughed then added, "What do you want now?"

"Cindy, Mike Stone's dead. You need to get here."

"You sure?"

"Dead certain."

"Where?"

"His house, in the driveway. He's in his car."

"I know where it is. We're on our way. Are you alone?"

"Think so."

"Don't touch anything. Sit in your car and wait for the cavalry. You hear me, don't do anything."

Cindy didn't have to tell me twice. I pushed myself up off the wet ground, looked at Mike one more time, and on wobbly legs, returned to my car. I got in and locked the door. I fought the urge to slam it in reverse, head home, while trying to block out the sight of seeing Mike in his classic car, one he'd never drive again.

I was jolted out of my grim thoughts by sirens heading my way. Cindy wasn't joking about the cavalry. It seemed like the entire police force and fire vehicles were lining the street in front of the house. Cindy approached my door, pulled the handle, but finding it locked, tapped on the window.

"Hop out and come with me."

I stepped out slowly, making sure my legs would hold me. Cindy grabbed my arm and led me to her pickup truck.

She said, "Stay here."

The Chief and two of her officers looked in Mike's vehicle. Cindy shook her head then told one of the officers to stay with the body while she and Officer Spencer headed to the house with firearms drawn. When they reached the door, Officer Spencer turned the knob while the Chief stood on the opposite side of the entry. It opened and Lugh loped past them and bolted for the Mustang. The huge dog stuck his head in the window nudging Mike, then sat and let out a mournful howl. I was watching Lugh and missed seeing Cindy and Spencer enter the house.

Moments later, Spencer came out with Desmond. Cindy followed. Desmond showed no emotion as he looked towards the Mustang. Spencer lightly gripped the boy's elbow and turned him away from the car before escorting the emotionless young man to a police cruiser parked at the street.

Cindy joined me. "Up to answering questions?"

I nodded.

"Let's start with, what in holy hell's going on?"

"Mike called yesterday asking me to meet him. We agreed to meet here at two o'clock. I showed up. You know the rest."

"And lo and behold, you find another body, your favorite pastime."

I closed my eyes and shook my head. My stomach churned.

"Sorry, bad joke," she said and patted my arm. "Did you know Desmond was here? Do you know where the rest of the family is?"

"No to both questions."

Lugh's bark, roughly the same volume as the earlier thunder, drew our attention to the driveway. Two paramedics were trying to get to Mike. Lugh was standing guard, teeth bared, not letting anyone near the car.

One of the paramedics yelled. "Chief, what do you want us to do?"

"Chris, do you know the dog well enough to get him?"

"No, ma'am. I'm in no hurry to meet my maker. His name is Lugh if that helps."

"It doesn't." Cindy looked around as if she were searching for the perfect dog wrangler.

Before someone was chosen to be sacrificed, I heard a familiar voice and phrase from behind Cindy's vehicle.

"*Eist liom!*"

Lugh turned toward the voice then ran to Shannon's side as she stared at the Mustang. Roisin peeked around from behind her mother.

My heart sank. Their world was about to be forever changed.

Cindy approached the new arrivals to block their view of the car. "Mrs. Stone, I'm Chief LaMond. I need to speak to you over here." Cindy tried to turn Shannon away from the yard and driveway.

Shannon wasn't having it. "Chief LaMond," she said in a strong, seemingly emotionless voice, "please allow me to go see my husband."

"I don't think that's a good idea. Let them take care of Mr. Stone."

Thinking a friendly face may be some solace, I walked over to help Cindy move the ladies from the awful scene.

Offering the best smile I could manage under the circumstances, I said, "Shannon, Roisin, I think it'd be best if you go with the Chief."

Shannon glared at me, stared at the sky, then said, "You're right, Chris. Chief, where would you like us to go?"

"Mrs. Stone, it would be best if we go to my office. You and your daughter can ride with me."

"Please call me Shannon," she said as she stroked Lugh's head. I would rather drive; besides, I don't want to leave Lugh here."

"I don't think you should be driving. I can have an officer drive your car." Cindy looked around to see who was available.

Shannon looked at me. "Chris, would you drive us to Chief LaMond's office?"

Before I answered, Cindy said it was a good idea and suggested we head out and let everyone do what needed to be done at the house. Officer Spencer had already left with Desmond.

I followed mother and daughter to their red Ford EcoSport. Roisin opened the tailgate and Lugh stepped in and laid down. I got in and waited for Shannon, who stood looking at the driveway until Roisin touched her arm and they both entered the SUV. The ride to Cindy's office was silent except the haunting notes of a pan flute coming from the speakers.

I parked near the entry to the Department of Public Safety, handed Shannon the keys, and said, "Shannon, I'll head home now. If you need anything, please call." I started to give her my number.

"Please go with us, Mr. Chris. Please," Roisin said as she looked at me in the rearview mirror.

Shannon said, "I hate to ask, Chris, but I'd feel more comfortable if you came with us."

"Of course."

We looked like a mismatched foursome heading into Cindy's office with Lugh leading the way, followed by Shannon, Roisin, then me. Cindy smiled at me as she closed the door behind us.

The Chief's office was large but with all of us packed in it felt cramped, especially with Lugh taking up the space of three large adults.

"We asked Chris to be here, Chief LaMond," Shannon said. "Hope you don't mind."

"Shannon, that's fine."

"Chief LaMond, please tell me what happened to my husband?"

"We're not sure. I'm so sorry. Shannon, I know this is a terrible time, but I need to get some information. Could you answer some questions?"

Shannon nodded.

In a soft voice, Cindy said, "When did you leave the house today?"

Shannon lowered her head and put her hands over her face. Roisin sat with one hand on Lugh's head, her other hand wiping away tears. I didn't think Shannon was going to answer until she jerked her head up and said, "We left for Charleston around ten-thirty; went shopping for herbs and Roisin wanted to find some crystals."

Cindy said, "I know this is hard, Shannon. What about your son? Did he go with you?"

Shannon said, "Desmond doesn't go shopping with us if he can get out of it."

Roisin chimed in before her mom continued, "He was going to the lighthouse with some guys."

Shannon reached for her phone. "I need to call him, so he doesn't go home."

Cindy held up her hand. "Shannon, your son is with one of my officers. He was in his room when we arrived at your house." Cindy waited for Shannon's response.

"He knows?" Shannon said, then stared out the window.

Cindy said, "Yes."

"Shannon," I said, "did you know I was going to meet Mike today?"

Cindy gave me a sideways glance I translated as *I'm doing the questioning*.

"Yes, he told me last night, but didn't say why. I assumed it was about Todd, umm, the dead man from the haunted house."

Cindy's look my direction now became a *what have you done now?* She then turned to Shannon. "Was your husband home when you left for Charleston?"

"Yes, he was going to run to Harris Teeter and the post office but wouldn't have been gone long."

Cindy said, "Do you know anyone who might have wanted to harm Mike?"

A tear rolled down her cheek, and in a voice barely above a whisper, said, "No, he was a gentle soul, never crossed anyone."

"Not even at work?" Cindy said, and jotted something on her legal pad.

Cindy's phone rang before Shannon answered. "Yeah," she said into the mouthpiece. I could hear the faint voice of the other person on the line but couldn't make out what he was saying. Cindy said, "Fifteen minutes, conference room," then returned the phone to the desk before turning to Shannon. "Sorry, you were saying?"

"Law was Mike's profession. He did it well, but he made no enemies. Again, he's a gentle soul." Shannon's hand went to Lugh's head. The protective canine had risen when her voice grew louder.

Roisin placed her hand on her mother's hand then locked on the Chief. "Chief LaMond, do you have more questions, or can we go?"

Cindy appeared stunned by the question posed by the youngest person in the room but smiled at Roisin. "Detective Adair from the

Sheriff's Office will be here in a few minutes and needs to talk with both of you. Let me take you to a room where you'll be able to talk."

Shannon slowly stood.

"Shannon," I said, "do you want me to drive you somewhere after you're done here?"

"Chris, you have done more than enough. We'll be fine, thank you."

Shannon, Roisin, and Lugh left with Cindy. I remained in the office and waited for the Chief to return.

Ten minutes later, she returned, flopped down in her chair, then said, "Ok, what do you make of all that?"

I didn't answer fast enough.

"Chris."

"Sorry, didn't know where to start. Didn't even know if you wanted my input."

"I never want your input but has that ever stopped you?"

I smiled. "I found it strange she didn't ask anything more about Desmond, things like where he was, why he wasn't in the room with the rest of us?"

Cindy said, "That was strange, but I don't know how someone should act after learning her husband, the father of her two kids, was dead." She stood and added, "Let's go, I'll take you to your car."

"Thanks, but I'll walk."

Cindy smiled. "Don't think for a second I'm going to let you go back to a crime scene without adult supervision."

I thought it best not to mention that I was almost old enough to be her father. I quickly fell in step beside the Chief on the way to her truck. The ride to the Stone house was almost as quiet as the ride from the house to Cindy's office, only static from the police radio broke the silence. Cindy pulled up behind my car where I saw crime scene tape around Mike's car and the house. A crime scene tech from Charleston was carrying two large aluminum cases from the van toward the Mustang.

Cindy said, "Get out, go home, rest. That's an order from your wise Police Chief."

I saluted. "Yes, sir."

"Smart ass."

As I left the latest homicide scene on Folly Beach, I found myself with more questions and more sadness.

Then the sky unleashed a torrential downpour.

What could happen next?

23

My legs were still not hike worthy when I arrived home. I grabbed a bottle of tea from the nearly empty refrigerator and moved to the living room. Unfortunately, Mike Stone wasn't the first dead body I'd run across since I'd moved to Folly. In fact, it wasn't the first in the last couple of weeks, but it was the first of someone who'd asked me to meet with him a few hours before his last breath. And, seeing the traumatized, grieving look on Shannon and Roisin's faces, his death struck me harder than the others.

Thinking of Roisin's pain, I knew there was someone I had to call to let him know what had happened, that is, if he didn't already know.

The phone rang five times without an answer, so I was afraid I was going to get voicemail, until a breathless Preacher Burl said, "Hey, Brother Chris, give me a second to catch my breath." The second turned into a minute before Burl said, "Sorry, I just returned from Harris Teeter and was carrying in groceries. To this old preacher, these steps get higher each time I climb them."

"Want me to call back?"

"No, no, let me throw this milk in the refrigerator and I'm all ears." He laughed. "Well, all ears and an out of shape body."

"I know the feeling, Preacher."

He laughed again then said, "What did I do to have the honor of your call?"

I knew my next words would erase all humor from my friend.

"Preacher, Mike Stone was killed today."

"Oh, my Lord, please tell me you're not serious."

"Afraid so. I found him in his car at their house."

"What happened? Was Roisin there? Umm, and, of course, Shannon and Desmond?"

I told him where the family members had been and about what I assumed to be a fatal gunshot wound to the head.

"Brother Chris, anyone know what occurred? Who did it? Why?"

"Preacher, at this point, I don't think there are answers. The family is meeting with the detective from the Sheriff's Office at City Hall. I assume they'll go home after that." I hesitated before saying, "I don't know what kind of spiritual guidance you could offer, but Roisin feels close to you, so you may want to call or visit."

"Brother Chris, regardless of beliefs, we all grieve. Sister Roisin is a sensitive young lady who is quite vulnerable. This will touch her deeply. I'd like to be there when they return, so I best head that way now. Roisin and the family need a friend even if we don't have the same spiritual guidepost."

"Preacher, I know she'll appreciate it. Please let me know if there's anything I can do to help."

He said he would.

I didn't know if it was still storming but knew that unless I informed Charles immediately, I'd incur a torrential downpour of Charles. I was also hungry.

My friend was quicker to answer than Burl had been. In the spirit of if you can't beat them, join them, I took a page out of Charles's phone conversation playbook and began with, "Mike Stone's dead. Meet me at Cal's."

"What? How?"

I hung up with those questions unanswered, for now.

* * *

IT WAS EARLY for Cal's bar crowd. Three tables were occupied, and two men were in deep discussion as they leaned against the bar. From the jukebox, Don Gibson was sharing his version of "Sweet Dreams;" Cal was sliding a bottle of beer to one of the men at the bar; and Charles was standing by the door wearing a cherry red, long sleeve sweatshirt with the University of New Mexico in small letters under what appeared to be an angry dog like animal.

Charles's mouth imitated the creatures snarl when he glanced at his wrist before saying, "What took you so long?"

I didn't think fifteen minutes from the time I hung up was that long, but I'd be wasting my time sharing that observation.

"Glad you could make it, Charles."

He turned to Cal. "Bring my tardy friend a glass of your finest red wine. We'll be at that table by the wall unless Chris gets lost on the way."

I arrived at the designated table the same time Charles made the long twenty-five-foot walk, thirty seconds before Cal set my wine in front of me and handed a beer to Charles.

Charles pointed to the creature on his sweatshirt. "It's a lobo, that's Spanish for wolf, in case you were going to ask."

I wasn't and stared at him.

"Spill it," he said after giving me a second to absorb the Spanish lesson. "Mike Stone. How do you know he's dead? What happened? Who killed him? How's Lugh?" Charles took a breath long enough for me to hear Connie Smith singing "Once a Day," before adding, "Did I already say spill it?"

That was my cue to begin—begin until he interrupted countless times. I started by telling him how Mike had called to ask me to meet him. Charles's first interruption came when he demanded to know why I hadn't invited him to the meeting. Because Mike had asked me was my obvious response, but knew it wouldn't fly, so I skipped saying it and proceeded to tell him what had happened and what little I'd learned from being there finding the body.

After going over the story and assuring him Lugh was fine, he said, "Think it had something to do with what he was going to tell you?"

"That's possible."

"Who knew you were meeting him?"

"Shannon."

"What about the kids?"

"Don't know, probably."

"And Desmond wasn't in Charleston with his mother and sister?"

"No, as I said, he was at the house when I found the body."

"In the house where you saw an ice pick, an ice pick like one that stabbed Todd Lee."

"An ice pick you pointed out like one that could be found in most any house here."

"He was at the house, the others were shopping in Charleston, while his dad was killed in the driveway, feet away from where he was. Super sized coincidence if you ask me."

"What motive would Mike's sixteen-year-old have for killing his father?"

"Don't know, but it wouldn't be the first time a teenager bumped off his pop."

"Okay, I'll concede it's possible."

"How're we going to prove it?"

"We've been over this. I don't know."

Cal returned to the table and asked if we needed anything else. My stomach reminded me that food was the reason I wanted to come to Cal's in the first place. I told him a cheeseburger and fries. Charles asked if I was buying. I nodded and he said he'd have the same. Charles watched the owner head to the kitchen, tapped me on the arm, and said, "Isn't that Nate Davis heading to the bar?"

I twisted around to see who he was talking about. "Yes."

That's all it took for Charles to jump up, rush to the bar, and return with Nate by his side.

"Chris, guess what? Nate said he could join us. I ordered him a burger and told Cal to put it on your tab."

Lacking an ice pick to stick in my friend, I smiled and welcomed Nate.

"Nate," Charles said, "you know Mike Stone?"

"Don't think so. Who's he?"

"An attorney who lived over here. He was killed today."

A cheerful way to start a conversation, I thought.

"Oh," Nate said. "Who did it?"

"Don't know," Charles said and nodded toward me. "Chris found the body."

Nate turned to me. "That's terrible. Are you okay?"

I told him I was then noted that was a question Charles hadn't asked.

After I shared with Nate what I knew of the tragic event, Cal arrived with our food and asked if we needed anything else. None of us did, so he returned to the bar. We each took a bite, before Charles said, "Nate, seems the last time we were in here, you were talking about Todd Lee."

Nate took a sip of beer then pointed the top of the bottle at Charles. "Yes. You think the guy murdered today had something to do with Lee's killing?"

"It could," Charles said. "Mind telling us again what you knew about Lee?"

He took another bite before saying, "Think I told you all of it. He was a jerk."

"Didn't you say something about a secret that'd make him rich?"

"He said it several times, and I didn't have much to do with him."

"What do you think he meant?"

"Don't know for sure, mind you, but think it had something to do with him blackmailing someone."

I didn't recall everything he'd told us before but was certain blackmail wasn't mentioned.

I said, "What made you think that?"

"Look, Chris, I don't know about you fellas, but I don't remember everything someone says to me." He nodded toward the bar. "Hell, I don't remember everything Cal and I said to each other when I came in today. The jerk only worked for J&B a week. He said a lot of stuff like guys working together do. Helps kill time, you know."

Charles said, "So you don't remember what he said about blackmail?"

Nate took two more bites as he stared at Charles like *that's what I just said*.

"How's the remodel coming?" I said to move the conversation forward without belaboring what he'd said he didn't remember.

"Fine, I guess. Lately, the Robinsons are hovering over us like that'll get the job done faster. Don't know how John and Bri put up with it. Glad it ain't my company." He glanced at his watch. "Guys, gotta run. Thanks for the food and drink. Maybe I'll run into you again."

After he left, Charles said, "He sure got in a hurry to get out of here. Think he killed the two men?"

"No reason to think so. He probably wasn't a fan of being interrogated."

"Got him a free meal. What more could he want?" He didn't wait for my response. "Think he's right about Todd Lee blackmailing someone? It'd be a good reason to kill him."

"Yes, but who?"

That question remained unanswered as I left Cal's to Johnny Cash singing "Guess Things Happen That Way."

24

After finding Mike's body, going to Chief LaMond's office with the grieving Shannon and Roisin, calling Burl to tell him the horrible news, and, of course, Charles's interrogation, I was looking forward to a peaceful morning at home. If the weather held, I could take my neglected camera for a stroll to get back to some semblance of normalcy.

Of course, as the saying goes, life happens while we're busy making other plans. On the way to the spare bedroom to retrieve my camera, I heard a faint knock at the front door, so faint I doubted my ears, then I heard it again. Grabbing my camera, I went to the door wondering who would be gently knocking since most of my friends who stopped by seemed more irritated to find the door locked and pounded on it.

I opened the door to, "Good morning, Mr. Chris," Roisin said as softly as her knock.

"Roisin, nice to see you," I said, trying to hide my surprise that the young lady was standing on my front porch after yesterday's tragic event.

"I don't want to bother you but knew this was the place I needed to be. Is it okay?"

Before I answered, her gaze went to my camera and I saw a twinkle in her eyes.

"I'm heading out to take some photos along the beach. Would you like to join me?"

Roisin smiled. "I'd love to."

I grabbed my windbreaker and met her in the yard.

"Do you take many pictures?" she asked, her voice stronger than at first.

"Not as many as I used to. It's a passion of mine and one I enjoy when I can get out."

Roisin smiled. "I love going into nature and taking memory photos."

"Memory photos?"

"Mr. Chris, we don't have an excess of material things." She hesitated and tapped the side of her head. "My pictures are stored in my mind."

"That makes sense, until you get my age when the mind will delete the photos before you get home."

My new young friend chuckled. "You're funny." We walked a few more steps before she added, "Guess you want to know why I appeared at your door." She looked down at her sandals as she walked beside me.

"Yes. It's not often that I see such a lovely young lady standing on my porch."

Except for a quick smile, she didn't say anything for a block, so I was about to ask which way she would like to head when the silence was broken.

"I don't get along with many people. I prefer animals and being in nature, that's where I belong. People find me strange, and that's okay."

I found it strange that she hadn't mentioned anything about her dad, but instead of mentioning it, I said, "You aren't strange, maybe just different than others your age. That's a good thing."

"Nice of you to say. Umm, that brings me to the reason I appeared on your porch without benefit of an invitation. Preacher Burl has become my best friend and he brought you into our lives. I find you to be a nice soul, someone I can talk to and not be judged."

I nodded as we followed the footpath to the beach.

"I, umm, we would like you to attend Dad's funeral service. Preacher Burl will be there and a few others, but I need you there." Roisin stopped and looked at me as if she were pleading for a positive response.

"Of course. I'd be honored, but why do you say you need me there?"

"You found Dad. You were the first good person he saw after the evilness that took him."

"Saw?"

"Sorry, I forgot you don't know our beliefs. Death isn't the ending but a new beginning."

"I didn't realize."

"We don't fear death, Mr. Chris. We are forever connected to those who have gone to the afterlife."

"When and where will the funeral be?"

She twisted her foot in the sand. "He's being cremated today. The funeral will be tomorrow morning at eleven." She looked up from the sand and smiled. "In the back garden."

We continued along the shore taking photos of the sea and birds, me, with my camera, Roisin in her mind. She pointed out potential shots I hadn't noticed. It was a pleasant stroll with a young lady who appeared to have a better grasp on life and death than most adults I know. After an hour, my legs reminded me I wasn't as young as I used to be.

"Roisin, I need to head home, besides I'm sure your family is wondering where you are."

"Mom knows I came to see you. She doesn't worry unless it gets dark, and Desmond is not even home."

"Where's your brother?" I asked, wondering when I started sounding like Charles.

She shrugged. "Yesterday, after we left that nice Police Chief's office, Desmond wouldn't speak to Mom or me. We got home and he went to his room, slammed the door, didn't come out all night. Mom went to check on him this morning. He was gone."

"Is that normal for him to disappear?"

"Mom told me he needed time to cope with someone, umm, killing our father. She said he'd be back." Roisin shook her head.

"Don't you believe her?"

"Oh, I guess, but he's been acting strange, okay stranger than usual since we went to the haunted house. Now this."

"Sorry."

I placed my hand on her shoulder. She took a deep breath and exhaled. It was easy to forget she was an eleven-year-old with her entire world in turmoil, with dark days ahead.

We walked back towards the Pier. When we got under the wooden structure, she looked around as if she just realized where we were.

"Mr. Chris, we will part ways here. I must head home. You can finish your planned day."

"I can walk you home if you like. It's no trouble."

"That's kind of you, but I'm fine." She stopped, stared at me, and said, "Mr. Chris, do you know who killed Dad?"

I was so close to escaping without this sweet young lady asking me the question I'd asked myself countless times since yesterday afternoon.

"Roisin, I'm afraid I have no idea."

"I was hoping you knew."

"Why would you think I might know?"

"Not sure. Dad has been in a different place, sort of not his happy self when he talked to Mom. After meeting you it seemed to bring some grounding to his soul."

"Did he explain his mood change?"

"No. It seemed to start after I heard him talking to someone on the phone. He had this, umm, funny sound in his voice. A sound I hadn't heard before. I had a feeling something was not right. I thought you might know something since Dad was going to talk to you yesterday."

"Who was he talking to on the phone?"

Instead of answering, a tear rolled down her cheek. She said, "I need to get home, see you tomorrow. Thank you for the adventure."

She pivoted and walked away.

It seems every conversation I have leaves me with more questions than answers. Looking at my watch and listening to my stomach growl gave me one answer. It was time for lunch. I was already out, so I might as well treat myself instead of slaving over a hot stove, okay, cold slice of bologna.

Amber's smiling face greeted me at the Dog.

She looked past me, shook her head, and said, "Table for one?"

"Yes, thank goodness."

"Have a spat with your bestie?"

She didn't wait for an answer. She took my elbow, ushered me to a table and asked if I wanted the usual. I nodded and she left to put in my order. It's nice when some things are always the same, bringing balance to life, even if that balance is going to lunch.

I pondered the morning while scrolling through the morning's photos on my camera. One was of Roisin staring at the ocean with a look of wisdom and sorrow on her face. Strange, I don't recall snapping it.

"Nice shot, who's the girl?"

I almost dropped the camera. I hadn't heard Amber arrive with my iced tea. Jumpiness seems to be my middle name this month. I'll be glad when Halloween is over and I can concentrate on something positive like, well, like anything but Halloween.

"That's Roisin Stone."

"Any relation to the man killed yesterday on East Huron?" she asked as she continued looking at the camera's monitor.

"His daughter. She came to the house this morning to invite me to the funeral."

"So, besides finding the body you're asked to the funeral. I didn't know you knew the witchy family."

"Amber, is there anything you don't know on this island, beside me knowing the Stones?"

"Don't know who killed Mr. Stone or the guy in the haunted house. That's up to you and Charles to figure out."

"The man in the haunted house is Todd Lee and it's the job for the police to figure out who killed both men."

She grinned. "Keep telling yourself that."

The remainder of my lunch was filled with my sandwich and numerous thoughts. Who was Mike talking to on the phone? Was it Todd, and if so, who were they talking about? How did Roisin hear the conversation? Who might be next to die, and why? What is a Wiccan funeral like? I finished lunch with no significant questions answered, so I decided the best thing to do was go home.

My phone rang as I opened the door.

"Brother Chris, did I catch you at a bad time?"

"No Preacher, what can I do for you?"

"Wanted to let you know tomorrow is Brother Mike's funeral."

"I know, Roisin stopped by today to invite me."

"Oh," He sounded surprised. "That's good. I was at their house most of the morning helping Shannon. I'll see you tomorrow?"

"Was Desmond there?"

"No. Shannon was vague about his location, and I didn't want to appear pushy."

"That's quite unpreacher-like."

"True, Brother Chris, but I had the feeling we should let sleeping dogs lie. Oh, speaking of dogs, Shannon asked me to invite Brother Charles to the funeral."

"Charles will love being compared to a dog."

"Funny, but not what I meant. Shannon thought it would be good for Lugh if Charles were there. Don't ask me why, just doing what was requested."

"See you tomorrow, Preacher. Have fun talking to Charles."

I sat in the chair in the living room waiting for the inevitable call from Charles.

The wait was short.

"Charles, how are you this afternoon?" Instead of waiting for a reply, I added, "Yes, I'll pick you up tomorrow for the funeral; no, I have no idea who killed him."

"Okay."

The phone went dead.

I smiled as I realized it was one of the fastest, most decisive calls ever with Charles. Perhaps, I'm finally getting Folly phone etiquette. By late afternoon, I realized the events of the last week had piled enough on me that bed seemed like the best alternative. It was possibly the first time since I've been an alleged adult, I've gone to bed before the first evening star was visible.

25

I was surprised the sun was starting to show over the ocean. I'd slept through the night even though I'd gone to bed before dark. While well rested, my stomach reminded me a need for nourishment was unmet. A trip next door to Bert's would take care of that. I was pleased the weather looked like it would remain pleasant if not somewhat overcast for Mike's funeral.

I returned home with coffee and an oversized cheese Danish, sat on the front porch, and started sorting the questions in my head. I thought about calling Cindy to see if she had any information, then realized calling the Chief before the sun was fully up would result in me receiving an unwanted message from her sharp tongue and nothing helpful. I'll wait until after the funeral.

Thinking of Mike's funeral, I realized most funerals I'd attended were held several days after the death and wondered if the timing had to do with his religion. My pondering was interrupted by an all toofamiliar voice.

"Morning, fellow detective," Charles said as he stepped on the porch, coffee in hand. "Knew you wouldn't have a cup for me, so I brought my own."

"You're right considering I wasn't going to pick you up for hours."

"What I figured," he said as he tapped his head while looking smug, at the same time offering a small smile.

I'd say Charles's appearance was surprising, but after all these years not much he did surprised me. However, his logo free pale purple turtleneck and light grey slacks, were strikingly different from his normal wardrobe.

He saw me looking at his attire. "I know you're thinking how handsome. Witch funerals are simply a transition in life, so my clothes reflect that."

I didn't laugh at his comment about being handsome, although it was tempting.

"Didn't know you were in tune with the Wiccan ways?"

"Wasn't until yesterday. I have a book about different funeral rituals. Found it under the stack of cookbooks. Didn't know I had it."

Considering the vast book collection my friend had acquired over the years, I would've been more surprised if he didn't have it.

"Sit and tell me why you're here so early."

"What could be better than two famous detectives going over the ins and outs of a case over coffee; coffee I had to bring because you wouldn't have any for me?"

"Famous?" I said instead of rolling my eyes. "Since you brought it up, I have some information."

"And it is?"

"Yesterday, Roisin Stone—"

"Roisin! What happened?"

"Charles, if you let me finish a sentence you'll know."

Charles leaned back like a boy who'd been scolded by the teacher for answering a question before it'd been asked.

"Roisin came to invite me to the funeral. During our conversation, she asked if I knew who killed her dad. I said—"

"What did you—"

"Charles, let me finish. You might want to hear what she had to say."

He sighed. "Sorry, continue."

"That's better. I told her no. Her response was, 'I hoped you knew who it was.'"

Thankfully, Charles had finished swallowing his coffee, or he might have had to change clothes after his huge exhale.

"Why does she think you'd know?"

"She knew her dad was going to talk with me and figured I might know."

Charles stared at the ceiling like he was trying to figure something out. The only sound came from two seagulls fighting over a cigarette on the side of the street. We watched the battle ending with the larger gull flying away with the prize.

Charles softly said, "Don't suppose she knew more?"

"Nope, seemed she was avoiding saying anything else."

"That's where we start, asking her everything she knows."

"You want to interrogate an eleven-year-old at her father's funeral?"

"Not interrogate. I want us to ask the young lady in the nicest possible way questions that'll help us catch her daddy's killer."

Our conversation turned to the weather; how it seemed to get warmer each year. A line from Randy Travis's song "Forever and Ever, Amen" came to mind, "As long as old men sit and talk about the weather." It must be true.

I reminded my early bird friend we couldn't be on Charles time to the funeral. Twenty minutes later, his ant in his pants routine became too much. I caved.

The drive took longer than normal since I didn't want to be first to arrive. Pulling up to the house, an uneasy feeling was growing in the pit of my stomach. I chalked it up to what awaited me at the house two days ago. The driveway was blocked by large potted flowers, so I pulled down the street and parked behind Preacher Burl's van. At least we weren't the first here. We were greeted by a galloping Lugh. I stopped midstride to let Charles take the lead.

Charles was standing upright but the Irish Wolfhound towered over him with its legs over his shoulders. I'd never been so happy to have my friend along.

Charles said, "What a good boy. Miss your daddy?"

Lugh finished welcoming us, turned, and trotted toward the back of the drive, with us bringing up the rear. Preacher Burl stood halfway up the driveway watching the dog's greeting. He said, "Shannon was correct. Lugh needed Charles here. Brother Charles, Brother Chris, glad to see you."

I said, "Nice to see you, Preacher. Any advice on what to expect?"

I wasn't sure what he knew about a Wiccan funeral but was certain it was more than I knew. Besides, I'd rather hear it from Burl than a prolonged description from Charles.

"Shannon and the kids will explain what's going on throughout the service. We're here to show support and celebrate life."

"Kids?" I said. "Desmond's back?"

Charles shot me a look like I'd been withholding information from him—again.

Burl gazed at the house and said, "He got here an hour ago, seemed in a darker mood than usual."

I said, "Darker? Didn't think that was possible."

Charles cleared his throat to get Burl's attention. "Preacher, do you know who's going to be here?"

"Besides us, Shannon, the kids, a couple who own a metaphysical shop in Charleston, Dude. That's all I know."

I said, "Dude?"

"Brother Chris, it seems Desmond knows Dude from the beach. The young man spends quite a bit of time staring at the ocean."

Charles said, "No family?"

"Shannon told me Mike's family will be waiting until Halloween to honor his passing and even then, won't be coming here."

We were still in the driveway when Dude walked up followed by a couple I didn't recognize. From their attire and being the only people I didn't know, I concluded it was the shop owners from Charleston. The couple wore long black cloaks with detailed black embroidery down the front, and crystal pendants.

Dude flourished a bow towards the couple, followed by, "Be my pleasure to introduce the rad Darrin and Stormy."

The man took a step forward while looking at Dude like most who don't know him well do, then extended his hand towards me, "Hello, I'm Darrin, this is my wife Stormy. You are?"

"Darrin, I'm Chris Landrum, to my right is Charles Fowler, and this is Burl Costello."

Charles chuckled. "Darrin, like in *Bewitched*."

I glared at Charles. By the end of this day he might be turned into a toad, then I'd have to carry Prince Charming everywhere.

Darrin took it in stride. From his reaction, Charles wasn't the first person to make the connection.

We were saved when Shannon called to us from the porch, "If everyone will head to the garden we will begin shortly." Her Irish brogue was more pronounced today.

The six of us walked to the garden behind the house. On an ornate wooden table sat a beautiful shoebox size mahogany container with the tree of life etched on the front. Placed in a circle around the urn were clear crystals and stones. To the left and the right of the crystals and stones were candles, along with a goblet, and other items blocked from my vantage point.

Taking the lead from the cloaked couple, the four non Wiccans stood to the left of the table. Shannon appeared at the garden entrance wearing an emerald green robe as she walked forward barefooted. Roisin followed her mother. Her robe was royal purple. She was also barefoot. Desmond was dressed in an all black robe, and like the others, shoeless. The three went to the right of the table, Lugh trotted to his family, ignoring everyone else, and laid in front of the table.

"I want to welcome and cast blessings on each of you for joining us in our time of transition," Shannon said in a voice stronger than earlier.

Roisin stepped forward and speaking softly but with confidence said, "Most of you have never been to a Wiccan ritual. Allow me to explain." She moved to the table then rested her hand gently on the top. "This is the altar. On it, we have items representing the elements, each meaningful in its own way; also the reason we are here today, my dad." Her voice trailed off. Lugh nuzzled against her foot. The young lady looked at Lugh, smiled, then continued, "During our ritual, we ask you to let the moment into your soul." Roisin took a step back next to her brother.

Shannon stepped forward. "I ask everyone to form a semicircle in front of the altar. Desmond, Roisin, Darrin and I will be lighting the candles at the four points around the circle representing north, south, east, west."

I hadn't noticed the large white candles on stands around the perimeter of the garden, thinking it strange since they were some of the largest I'd seen. We formed the semi circle as the four went to their candle saying something I couldn't make out, then lit the wicks. Darrin and the kids joined the circle as Shannon walked to the table and lit a candle on each side of the altar.

"Please join hands to make our circle complete so we can honor Mike." Shannon's voice cracked as her daughter's had. Lugh nuzzled against her foot as he had with Roisin.

We joined hands. I hated to admit I was thankful I was between Charles and Burl. I wasn't in a hurry to see if mini Ozzy Osbourne felt as cold as he looked.

Shannon lifted a large dagger from the altar and held it in her outstretched hand. Slowly turning in a circle, she placed the dagger down. She chanted and said what sounded like a prayer. The words were loud enough but I couldn't make them out. Music was playing in the background. I hadn't noticed when it began. It was both haunting and soothing.

Shannon then turned to us asking if anyone wanted to say final words or pay their last respects.

Burl cleared his throat. Shannon's hand extended. "Burl, please come forward."

He stepped close to the widow and said, "Sister Shannon, I want to say what an honor it was getting to know Brother Mike. He was truly a great and loving man who thought the world of his family. I'm a better man for knowing him."

"Blessed be." Shannon said as she squeezed Burl's arm as he returned to the chain. She turned to her daughter. "Roisin, do you wish to speak?"

The young lady stepped forward. In a low voice, said, "I will miss you, Dad. I know you are with us and this is a new adventure for you. I only wish the adventure here could have lasted longer." Tears streamed down her cheeks, but she held her head high.

Shannon said, "Blessed be, my little nymph. Desmond, want to say something?"

Desmond stood at the other end of the circle from me and shook his head but didn't make a sound.

Shannon turned to the altar and spoke in what I assumed to be Gaelic as she bent to place her forehead on the urn. She then stood, reached for the dagger, walked to each of the four large candles, and with the blade snuffed out the flames. She returned to the altar and said, "The circle is broken. Mingle and be merry."

Shannon asked Desmond, Stormy, and Darrin to help with refreshments.

Charles moved toward the altar, I assumed to get a better look. Knowing Charles the way I did, I went with him to make sure he remained toad free. About three feet from his destination, a loud growl stopped us in our tracks. Lugh was again protecting his master.

"Lugh, you know they mean no harm," Roisin said, as she moved beside Charles then led us closer to the altar.

"Interesting service," Charles said, then reached out to the altar.

Roisin grabbed his hand before it touched anything. "Only family can touch. It's still a sacred place. We will allow the candles on the altar to burn. When they are finished, this part of the ritual will be completed."

I said, "Roisin, I'd like to introduce Charles, my best friend."

She let go of Charles's hand, smiled, and said, "So nice to meet you, Mr. Charles. Mom and Lugh told me good things about you."

Charles said, "Roisin, it's a pleasure meeting you. I'm terribly sorry about your loss."

She lowered her head before saying, "Thank you."

"May I ask a question?"

"Of course."

"What happens if wind blows out the candles? Do you relight them?"

"Mr. Charles, they will not be blown out or desecrated by rain. The Goddess does not allow that during this most sacred ritual."

"Are you going to bury the ashes or scatter them?" Charles asked since he has no brakes on his question machine.

"On Halloween, the family only will complete the ritual by scattering Dad's ashes. All Hallows Eve is our most sacred holiday where we honor our departed loved ones. It's the perfect day for us to complete the ritual."

Charles and I silently gazed at the items on the table, before Roisin added, "Mr. Chris, Mr. Charles, may I ask something?"

"Of course, Roisin," Charles said in a soft voice. "What do—"

She looked around before saying, "Not here. Please follow me to my fairy garden."

Burl apparently noticed that his name wasn't mentioned. He hugged her and said, "Roisin, I shall speak to your mother and brother."

Charles and I followed her to the far side of the house. The side yard was small but quaint and childlike. There were honeysuckle vines hanging from a trellis, a small wrought iron bench below a window, and what appeared to be a tiny village made of mushroom houses and small fairy figurines. A small dragonfly fountain added to the mystical setting.

"This is lovely. Your own little world," Charles said, as he patted the young girl on the arm.

She smiled. "Mom says it's my Zen place."

I hesitated while trying to find the right words to add.

Before I spoke and surprisingly before Charles could speak, Roisin pointed to a window above the bench. "That's Dad's office. It was here where I heard Dad talking to someone on the phone. He seemed, umm, what's the word, umm, distressed. Most days he has the window open so he can hear the fountain. It relaxes him." She looked at the fountain. "Mom says it will always bring him peace."

"Your mom's a wise lady," Charles said as he looked toward the window. "Do you know who he was speaking to?"

"Think his name was Todd."

My turn. "Roisin, did your dad say anything that might help figure out who Todd was talking about?"

"Dad said anyone can be deadly when cornered. He suggested Todd meet dad in person. That is all I remember. Does that help?"

Charles gave Roisin a hug, "Helps a lot."

I remembered something Nate Davis had shared. "Roisin, do you remember if your dad said anything about blackmail when he was talking to Todd?"

She looked back at the window. "Mr. Chris, I'm not familiar with that word."

I keep forgetting she's only eleven. "Roisin, it means someone demands payment from another person because he knows something and if he gets the money, he won't tell what he knows. It's illegal." I realized that was oversimplifying blackmail, but it was the best I could do on the spur of the moment.

She rubbed her chin. "Oh, okay. Thanks for enlightening me." She shook her head. "I don't recall dad saying anything like that. Sorry."

Charles said, "That's okay. You've been helpful. Let's join the others."

"Roisin," I said, "why did you want to share that information about the phone call?"

She stopped and looked toward the bench. "Mr. Chris, I have faith that you, you too, Mr. Charles, will catch the person that took dad away from the adventure he was sharing with me."

I said, "I don't—"

Charles interrupted, "Roisin, we will."

Thanks, Charles.

As we walked to the group gathered around a table with refreshments, someone caught my eye although my view was partially blocked by the shrubbery near the drive. I couldn't swear to it, but it appeared to be a woman with long blond hair getting into a pickup truck. By the time I moved to get a better view, the truck had disappeared around the corner.

26

When I answered the phone early the next morning, Cindy LaMond greeted me with, "I'm disappointed in you."

"Why?" A logical question, I thought.

"It's almost three days since you found Mike Stone's body and you haven't called to harass me about what else I learned from the Stone family or what Detective Adair discovered from his interviews."

"Sorry to disappoint you. What did you and Adair learn?"

"That's more like Chris Landrum, the one taking nosy lessons from Charles. The answers to your questions along with my check for breakfast can be found at the Dog."

"You there now?"

"Yep, getting ready to order a second breakfast. Hurry or I'm going to add lunch to go."

"On my way."

I'm certain she would have said *Great. I look forward to seeing you.* It must've slipped her mind. She'd hung up.

A quick look out the window told me it was a clear, sunny day, so I walked instead of driving to my go to breakfast spot. Ten minutes later, I found the Chief at a table along the side wall. She may've been serious about ordering a second breakfast. Two plates, one empty, one with an order of bacon and eggs were in front of her.

She nodded toward the chair across from her and said, "In the nick of time. Lori said she'd save room on your check so you could order something."

As if on cue, Lori, one of the Dog's college age servers, was at the table setting a mug of coffee in front of me.

Cindy said, "He wants French toast."

Lori glanced at me, I shrugged, and she headed to put in my order. I wasn't certain if it was good or bad when the Chief of Police knows what I ordered for breakfast nearly every time I was here.

"Morning, Cindy," I said interjecting civility to the conversation.

She stuffed a bite of egg in her mouth, washed it down with coffee, and said, "Desmond Stone told Detective Adair he went to the store with his Dad. Came home and had on earphones and playing music, or that's what Adair called the screaming hyenas the kid was listening to."

Yes, my attempt at civility had failed.

"Go on."

"The Goth witch claimed he didn't know anything was wrong until stormtrooper cops did what stormtroopers do and stormed in his room and pointed their guns in his face." She sighed. "Chris, since I was half the stormtrooper force, I'll admit, I did have my firearm drawn. Had no idea who or what I'd find in the house, but never pointed my weapon at young Mr. Stone. He, Desmond, not Detective Adair, then went on a rant about the police state not having respect for the privacy of law abiding citizens in their own homes."

"Did Adair find or hear anything indicating Desmond had anything to do with his father's death?"

"Not really. He attributed most of Desmond's bluster to him being traumatized by learning of the death. Regardless of his hostile attitude, it had to be horrible learning his father was killed a few yards from where Desmond was enjoying stuff he calls music."

"Did Desmond say anything about his father talking to Todd Lee or anything that would tie the two together?"

"If he did, Adair didn't share it."

"What's your gut reaction to Desmond?"

"I'm no shrink, but it seems he's a scared kid hiding behind his Goth appearance and attitude."

"You may not have the degrees, but you're one of the most perceptive people I know."

"Suck up all you want, but you're still buying breakfast, correction, breakfasts."

"Never doubted it. Did Adair learn anything new or important from Shannon or Roisin?"

She took another bite of my purchase, then said, "No. As you know, they were more shook than anything. If he learned more, he didn't think it was important enough to share."

"Did either of them say anything about Mike's contacts with Todd Lee?"

"They knew he'd been in contact, assumed it was about legal issues Lee was having."

I shared what Roisin had said at the ceremony about her dad's demeanor change after talking on the phone.

"When was I going to hear about this?"

"Cindy, it was yesterday and here we are today with me telling you."

She exhaled, rolled her eyes, took another sip of coffee, before saying, "Anything else you're holding back?"

Might as well get it over with, especially since we're in a public place with witnesses in case she tried to shoot me.

"Chief, when you were in Stone's house, did you notice a small round table in a room off the entry?"

"I was there to see if a killer was lurking, not inventorying furniture."

"When Preacher Burl and I were there the first time there were various tools and other items on the small table, among them, an ice pick."

My hands gripped the table waiting for the explosion.

"Crap on a cucumber, Chris. You saw an ice pick like the thing that killed Todd Lee?"

This was a good time to use Charles's logic. "Yes, but there's no reason to think it was the murder weapon. At one time, about every house over here had an ice pick."

"At one time, every house had an outhouse. At one time, there were Bohicket Indians roaming this island instead of vacationers. At one time, there—"

"Got it. I'm simply saying an ice pick is a common tool."

"Not common as a murder weapon, is it?"

"I don't think—"

She waved a hand in my face. "Enough. Did you see it yesterday when you were there for the funeral?"

"We didn't go in the house."

"After I finish this breakfast, order lunch for Larry, get him some dessert as a bonus, and heck, order some for me as well, I'll pay a visit to the Stones to see if they have any murder weapons laying around."

"Good police work, Chief." I smiled, hoping for a similar response.

That was too much to hope for. She shook her head, frowned, and said, "I feel sorry for them."

"Why?"

"Don't know much about the Wiccan religion, hell's bells, I don't know much about most religions, but what I do know is there's a lot of hate, distrust, and confusion about Wiccan. From what little I know about the Stone family, they seem like good folks. They haven't been trouble to anyone I know."

"Except one of them may be a killer?" I added with a smile. Again, an attempt to reduce Cindy's ire.

"That would shoot a hole in my *good folks'* theory, but that's not my point."

"What's your point?"

"We've received calls, anonymous, of course, claiming the witches on East Huron Avenue are sacrificing animals in their back yard. People are afraid their precious pets will be next. One lady called to say she's afraid for her granddaughter, afraid the witches will sacrifice her. You know about the broom on the porch and the nasty note with it, but you probably don't know about the letter, unsigned, of course, accusing the Stones of casting a spell and turning the writer's husband into a turnip."

I smiled.

"Chris, I'm serious."

"Okay, I'll remember the next time I eat a turnip it may be someone's husband."

Cindy forced back a smile and repeated. "I'm serious."

"Cindy, I know. Remember, I was there yesterday for a funeral. I've been to several funerals over the years, several religions. Mike's was unique, but everything said and done made sense."

She looked at her watch. "I understand. I simply wanted you to know, not all people's impressions of witchcraft are based on *Bewitched*. There's an overabundance of hostility and fear out there."

"Thanks for sharing."

"Chris, I need to meet with the mayor. If I believed any of the stories I've been hearing, I'd ask Shannon to cast a spell on him, maybe turn him into an eggplant." She looked around. "You didn't hear that."

I smiled.

"Thanks for the information about the ice pick. Maybe the next clue you get, you can share it with me the same century."

"Good luck meeting with the mayor and ice pick hunting. One more thing, Cindy, did Adair have anything new to report on Jeff Hildebrand?"

"Nope."

"Nothing to tie him to the murder other than what he said about removing his and Lee's possessions from the haunted house?"

"Is there some reason you didn't think *nope* covered that?"

I smiled. "Nope."

"Adair didn't tell me, but one of my officers saw Hildebrand back on our quaint little island."

"Where's he staying?"

"No idea."

"That helps."

"Nope," she said, smiled, and headed to the door, before adding, "Thanks for the breakfasts, Larry's lunch, and two desserts."

27

Lousy October weather had finally arrived, so the next morning was spent piddling around the house. The last several weeks had been a roller coaster, so self isolation was the plan of the day.

After an attempt at cleaning house, I decided getting out for a late lunch would beat isolation. I was sitting in the car in my driveway realizing I had no real plan on where I was going. Minutes later, I found myself parked in front of Cal's, telling myself my subconscious had made a wise decision. What could beat good country music from Cal's antique Wurlitzer, a heart unhealthy cheeseburger, and listening to Cal's stories about the past?

I was greeted by the Statler Brothers on the jukebox singing "The Class of '57" with Cal harmonizing with the quartet while drying a glass with an orange and black bar towel. I took the table closest to the bar when he noticed me and headed my way during the song's last verse. He plopped down across from me.

"How's Chris?"

"Good, and you?"

"Had to beat customers away with a two-by-four. You know how busy this time of year is." Cal smiled as he spread his arms gesturing around the near empty room.

I smiled. "That couple at the bar and the folks at those two tables make it look like you might be over capacity. The fire marshal might come a callin' any minute."

"Been working on your sarcasm?"

"Nope, comes naturally. Besides, you started it."

"Whatever. What can I get you?"

"Martini and a club sandwich."

Cal stood, patted me on the shoulder. "Wine and cheeseburger coming right up," he said before heading to the kitchen.

I scanned the bar and was amazed how businesses on Folly made a profit during the winter months. There are always small groups of vacationers around and locals venture out more during the slow season, but regardless, business was anything but brisk. I didn't recognize any of today's patrons.

It wasn't long before Cal returned with two cheeseburgers, one beer, and my wine.

"Figure you could use some company since Charles ain't here. You mind?"

"Not at all. You need to get some rest before the next big wave of customers arrives."

"Sarcasm! I'd write a song about you and use it but it's hard for this old crooner finding words to rhyme with sarcasm." He smiled, pulled out the chair, then we toasted our good fortune and started on the closest menu item he had to a club sandwich.

Cal leaned back in his chair, looked around the far from capacity crowd, and said, "Seems several people haven't been having good fortune as of late. Two murders on our little island, and you're in the middle of both." Cal chuckled. "No surprise there."

"Not in the middle," I said, then sipped my drink while waiting for what might come next.

"Chris, I've been going around our island for months, heck, years, and haven't come across one dead body. You've gone and found two this month. Sounds like you're in the middle to me."

"Cal, it's a gift."

"Sarcasm. Your good buddy Charles was in last night telling me more than I wanted to know about the murders and how you two are on the trail of the killer or killers."

"Yes, I've found two unfortunate souls, but that doesn't mean I'm involved in doing anything about it."

Cal smiled. "If you say so. All I know is with you and Charles on the case, a killer will be off the streets soon." Cal raised his beer in my direction before finishing it off.

I sighed and said, "I'm sure the authorities can handle homicides much better than Charles and I."

"If you say so," he repeated. "I do have someone you might like to talk to about at least one of the murders." Cal's sly grin beamed from under the Stetson.

"Who?"

"Jeff Hildebrand. He's around here somewhere. I'm having him help out. Nothing much, just some chores to earn a few bucks, plus meals."

"How long has he been here?"

"Since the fuzz let him go. Found him walking down Folly Road during that nasty thunderstorm the other day. Gave him a lift."

"Known him long?"

"Yeah, since way back when I saw him in the storm. The boy was soaked. Gave him a ride back here figuring I could help the guy out. I know what it's like being down on your luck. Been there a time or two myself."

"I'd like to talk to him if you don't think he'd mind."

Cal smiled. "Not getting involved?"

"Curious."

Cal's smile turned into a laugh. "I'm sure he wouldn't mind. Let me see where he is."

Funny how things work out. I was going to mind my own business today and not seek anyone to do a Charles interrogation on and look what fell into my lap. I also wondered why Cal hadn't introduced Charles to Jeff last night, but then again Cal's smart so there must've been a good reason.

Cal returned from the kitchen followed by a man wearing black jeans and a long sleeve T shirt with Led Zeppelin on the front. He was my height, long brown and graying hair in a ponytail and younger by a decade or more.

"Jeff this is Chris Landrum. Chris, Jeff Hildebrand."

I stood to shake Jeff's hand. "Nice to meet you, Jeff."

"You a cop, a cop?" He held his hand down to his side.

"No."

Jeff smiled and extended his hand for the greeting. Cal pointed to the chair he'd occupied and told Jeff to have a seat, said he had to take care of some business, and there was no rush for Jeff to get back to work. Jeff slowly lowered himself in the chair.

He looked everywhere but at me and said, "Sorry about the cop comment. I'm a little gun shy. Cal said you're okay and I should answer your questions about Todd, about Todd." Jeff's eyes continued darting around the room like he was looking for eavesdroppers, or maybe cops.

"Kind of him, I'm looking into some things going on the last couple of weeks. It started with Todd Lee's murder."

Jeff finally made eye contact. "I didn't kill him if that's where you're headed."

"Didn't think you did, Jeff. I know the police picked you up for tampering with physical evidence."

I wasn't sure if I thought Jeff didn't kill Todd, but it seemed to be the right thing to say to keep him talking.

"That's what they got me for. Umm, I admitted it, but that's all I did, all I did." He shook his head.

"Tell me what you know about Todd and what you think happened?"

Jeff stared at the table. I looked around the room and noticed ours was now the only occupied table. The couple at the bar were laughing, and Cal was singing along with the jukebox playing Hank Williams Sr's hit "Lovesick Blues." He caught my glance, so I motioned for a refill. He was quick bringing a glass of wine for me and a beer for Jeff. Only then did Jeff look up from the table, appearing puzzled at seeing Cal and the beer.

"Jeff," Cal said, "you need the drink. Don't worry about anything." Cal patted him on the back and headed to the bar.

Jeff took a sip, then looked at me. "I don't know much about Todd, then again, not sure if anyone knew much about the guy. He had an attitude, thought he was always right, always right. Had a chip on his shoulder the size of Cal's Stetson."

"That's what I heard. Do you know why he was on Folly or who might've wanted him dead?"

"Why are any of us here? He came from Savannah, wanted to be near the beach, he said, but didn't strike me as a sun worshiper. Besides, there're beaches closer to where he came from than having to come this far, this far." Jeff paused, and took a long draw of beer, then continued, "He told me when he was on his last job he found out something that'd make him a lot of money if he played his cards right."

"Did he elaborate?"

He shook his head. "Said people with businesses should pay more attention to the little people and not look over them like they're equipment because those little people see everything."

"Know what business he was talking about or who the people were?"

"No, that was the first night we stayed in the haunted house. Probably in construction since that's what he was doing here." He looked around the room, took a sip, then continued, "He seemed determined to get his money, but things changed."

"How?"

"I didn't see Todd for a couple of days, I then ran into him late one night on my way to the house where he was just standing outside by the bushes looking scared."

"Anyone else around?"

"Not that I saw. The haunted house was closed; the crew was gone for the night. I made a joke about him fearing a ghost, a ghost. Wanted to lighten his mood, you know."

"Did it?"

"Not a bit. He said something about the living are the scary ones, not the dead."

"Did you two spend that night in the house?"

"Yeah, it was too cold to be out and looked like rain. We talked most of the night about life and other stuff but nothing about what scared him or his big windfall. Was like he was avoiding his favorite subject, money."

"Sounds like something was bothering him," I said, attempting to get more without sounding pushy.

"That was our last night there. The next day I met a guy at the hardware store. He needed help building a deck. I offered to help for some cash. Job took three days and he let me stay in his garage." Jeff took another drink of beer. "I finally had some cash in my pocket, so I went back to the house to tell Todd we should spend a couple of nights at a hotel. I never felt good about sneaking in someone else's place." He took a deep breath, closed his eyes, his hand balled into a fist. "That's when I found him, found him."

"That must've been horrible."

"I never seen a dead body before. He was in the kitchen. I dragged him to the pantry and closed the door." Jeff's hands were shaking.

"Why the pantry?"

He shook his head. "I didn't want some crewmember or especially some youngster going through the haunted house finding him on the kitchen floor. That could mess up some kid. I grabbed all our stuff and left so no one would know we'd been staying there."

"Okay," I said, not sure what else to say to this man who was visibly shaken about the experience.

I didn't have to say anything. He offered, "I didn't go to the cops because, well, I'm no angel. I just wanted to forget everything."

"I understand. After you found him, did you see anyone around the house?"

"Didn't see anyone but heard something in the front of the house, But there was no way I was going to the room with the coffin. All I wanted to do was grab our things and get the hell out of there."

"I don't blame you."

He looked at his trembling hands. "Chris, I wasn't always like this.

Sometimes life keeps knocking you down. I'm trying to get back on my feet. You've got to believe me. I'd never hurt anyone, anyone."

"Jeff, it sounds like you're taking a good first step, Cal's a great guy to have in your corner. Thanks for sharing. It was helpful."

Jeff looked around to make sure no one was nearby and said, "If you want it, I still got Todd's stuff."

"The police didn't get it from you?"

He shook his head. "Told them I threw it in a dumpster, just didn't feel right handing over a man's whole life to someone who was just doing a job."

"Do you have his things here?"

"I'm not going all over Folly with a dead man's gear. I can get it to you in a couple of days if you want."

"Jeff, that'd be great."

He stood. "I'll have Cal get ahold of you when I get Todd's things." He attempted a smile. "Thanks for the talk. Made me feel better."

He left the table and disappeared into the kitchen. I was left alone in the bar wondering what I'd agreed to. Does this make me an accomplice to withholding evidence? Cal was nowhere in sight, so I left money on the table to cover my bill and headed to the door to contemplate what to do next and if I should wait to call Charles later or get it over with now.

The sound of Hank Locklin singing "Please Help Me I'm Falling" followed me out.

28

Yesterday's cold, dreary weather that'd limited my activities to a trip to Cal's had made way for temperatures in the low seventies and a clear blue sky. After grabbing a cup of coffee from Bert's, I made my way to the diamond shaped upper level of the Folly Pier. My conversation with Jeff Hildebrand reinforced my belief that he wasn't responsible for Todd Lee's death and that Lee had sights on blackmailing someone. Who and why remained unanswered.

Prior to meeting Hildebrand, my talk with Cindy hadn't revealed anything I didn't know or suspect. At least, she'd check on the ice pick at the Stone's house. While I couldn't imagine any of the Stones killing the family's patriarch, I wasn't as certain about one of them not stabbing Todd Lee. Desmond would be my prime suspect if I had to limit it to a member of the family. Was that simply because of his demeanor, his appearance, his constant scowl, or his apparent dislike for most anyone I'd seen him interact with?

I didn't get to analyze the teenager deeper. I heard Charles's cane tapping on the steps to the upper level before I saw him.

He was out of breath as he reached the top step, but it didn't stop him from saying, "Knew you'd be here."

He was wearing a long sleeve red sweatshirt with Nebraska on the front, jeans with a tear in each knee, a Tilley, and tennis shoes.

"How?"

"I'm guessin' that's not an Indian greeting. I knew you'd be here because you're not at the Dog, not at your house, not at Loggerhead's, not at the Tides, so where else would you be but here?"

That'll teach me to ask.

He plopped down beside me, took two deep breaths, then said, "Herbie Husker."

"Who's Herbie Husker, I said, regretting it before it was out of my mouth.

He pointed to the front of his sweatshirt. "University of Nebraska's mascot, duh."

"You were looking for me to share that?"

"Nope. Wanted you to experience a teaching moment."

"Then why did—"

"Speaking of trivia," he interrupted, "that reminds me. Did you know Skittles are the number one Halloween candy? They're more popular than M&M's, Snickers, and Reese's Cups. Can you believe that?"

"Wow," I said, with a sugary bite of sarcasm, "two teaching moments in one morning. What did I do to deserve such enlightenment?"

"You making fun of me?"

"Yep. Now, why did you go all over town looking for me?"

"I went to the Dog and Lori told me you'd been there yesterday meeting with the Chief. I figured she told you something you'd want to share, but since you didn't call, I knew your phone must be busted. I ate breakfast so I'd have the energy to find you, then here I am."

"You could've called."

"Wouldn't have done any good if your phone's busted. Besides, our detecting skills work best when we're together."

For the three-thousandth time I chose not to remind him we weren't detectives. "Would you like to know what Cindy told me?"

"Yes."

"Nothing."

"Nothing, what?"

"Chief LaMond didn't tell me anything I didn't know or suspect."

"I looked all over town for you for that?"

"Yep."

"Really, she told you nothing new?"

"Correct." I smiled. "Want to hear who I met yesterday"

"Did he or she confess to killing both men?"

"Don't think so."

"Then who?"

"Jeff Hildebrand."

Charles nearly fell off the bench. "When were you going to tell me?"

"Now," I said and smiled once more, hoping to prevent a tirade.

He frowned. "Chris, you met the killer and didn't think it was important enough to tell me until now?"

Yes, I knew I'd regret not calling him yesterday. "Charles, I don't think he's the killer." I then shared as much as I could remember about my conversation with Jeff.

Charles pouted through me telling him and asked a minimal number of questions—minimal for Charles. He then said, "Chris, that makes all of it as clear as day. Cindy hasn't figured it out. The hotshot Sheriff's Office detective is sitting on his hands doing nothing. If Hildebrand didn't do it, it's up to us to find the killer. Clear as day."

"And how are we going to do that?"

"Herbert Hoover said, 'A good many things go around in the dark besides Santa Claus.'"

"Other than mixing holidays, what's that have to do with anything?"

"The answer is right there in the dark waiting for us to figure it out. See, that's why we're meeting. Who are the suspects?"

I'm glad it made sense to one of us. I've learned over the years, moving quickly past something Charles says, is often the best route to sanity. This is one of those times.

I said, "We suspect Todd Lee was blackmailing someone, and if Jeff Hildebrand is right, it's someone Lee met before he got to Folly."

"Good, then it's Fred Robinson."

"Why?"

"Todd Lee lived in Savannah before moving here. Fred and, umm, Mrs. Fred also lived there."

"Erika."

"Okay, Fred and Erika. There you go, one of them did it. Case closed. Go ahead, call Cindy with the good news."

"Charles, other than Fred being a jerk, what reason would he or his wife have for killing Lee?"

"If I knew that, I'd call Cindy myself. If Lee was blackmailing Fred, there must've been a good reason. Jerks do jerky things. Lee could've known about some of them."

I realized I hadn't told Charles about seeing the blond haired woman at Mike's funeral. I moved his cane, aka weapon, out of his reach and shared what I'd seen.

He opened his mouth, closed it, rolled his eyes, then said, "You let me accuse the dentist and his wife when you knew the killer was Bri Rice?"

"Charles, I don't know that."

"Then why was she there?"

"First, I'm not certain it was her, and if it was, she could've been walking in the neighborhood, not there for the funeral."

"I have better odds of being elected President than she had for *walking in the neighborhood.*" He snapped his fingers. "Didn't Hildebrand say Lee was blackmailing someone about something that happened before they got here?"

"Yes."

"Bri knew Lee when they were in Charleston before they got here. See, more proof she killed him."

I reminded him it was the same argument he used moments earlier when he was accusing one of the Robinsons.

"Yes, but they weren't sneaking around the Stone's house at the funeral."

"We also need to consider Desmond as a suspect."

"Because of the ice pick?"

"Yes," I said, "and because he was at the house when his dad was killed. He had opportunity and knew Shannon and Roisin were in Charleston."

"What's his motive?"

"Charles, I don't know. I don't want it to be him, but the ice pick and proximity to Mike's death have to be considered."

"But what about Lee blackmailing someone?"

"Even if he was, it may not have had anything to do with his murder."

"Where does that leave us?"

I smiled. "Enjoying a beautiful October day."

"While being confused about the murder, murders."

"Yes."

29

Other than concluding Todd Lee was blackmailing someone and was killed because of it, our suspect list was weak at best. On that unsatisfying analysis, Charles announced he needed to make three deliveries for Dude and left me on the Pier. I wasn't ready to let the pleasant day go to waste, so I headed east on the beach for some much-needed exercise, not quite on the level of going to the gym, but that was never going to happen.

I looked down the shoreline and the only living things I saw were sandpipers running to then scampering back from water's edge. The little birds reminded me of kids rushing to go in the ocean but as soon as a wave greeted them, they'd scamper back to their parents.

I was so entertained by the birds' antics I wasn't aware of someone behind me until I heard,

"Crazy, aren't they?"

I jumped and twisted around to see what kind of goblin had followed me. There was no goblin, but a witch in the form of Desmond—dark, wicked Desmond.

"You surprised me," I said, trying to act more composed than I felt.

"Sorry, Mr. Landrum." Desmond smirked, but lowered his head.

"I didn't see anyone around."

"I was behind the dunes when you came down from the Pier. Been waiting for you to finish talking to the cane guy."

That didn't sound encouraging. I have a potential killer hiding out, waiting for me to be alone, then following me to where no one could hear me call for help. My internal monologue was still playing as I looked at Desmond then around to see if I could make a quick exit.

"Mr. Landrum, sorry I startled you," he said as he looked me in my eyes. "I need to talk to you."

For the first time, I saw something less frightening from the boy in black.

"Want to go somewhere where we can sit and talk?"

He moved closer and looked around. "I'd rather talk here."

"Okay, what's on your mind?"

"My sister likes you. Lugh trusts you. That preacher brought you to us and he thinks good of you. I figured you're the best person to talk to."

"Roisin is a special young lady." I smiled. "Lugh hasn't eaten me yet, so I guess we're okay."

The prince of darkness returned my smile. For the first time, I didn't feel like I was about to meet Todd Lee in the hereafter.

His smile faded. "Mr. Landrum, I'm not evil. I didn't kill Dad or the stiff in the haunted house." He shrugged. "Maybe I'm different, but I'm not a monster."

"Desmond, I've never said you killed anyone."

"Bet you thought it." His head lowered as he slowly shook it. "It's okay if you did. Everyone else does."

"I have questions, not accusations. Sadly, many people accuse before getting the facts."

He gave a muted grin. "That means the world's full of those people."

"I've met plenty."

He kicked the sand and stared at the horizon. "People think because I have a different way of living, different clothes, different beliefs that I must be evil. My family had some issues in Minnesota but there are a lot more here. The Twin Cities has a larger Wiccan community with more tolerance."

"I bet once people get to know you and your family, feelings will be different. You have to give them a chance to see the real person, not a disguise."

He looked at his foot kicking more sand. "Not going to change who I am to suit people." He turned his gaze to me. "I get your point. Will sort of work on it."

"Desmond, you didn't track me down for advice. What's on your mind?"

He nodded. "Mr. Landrum, umm, I picked up an ice pick from the yard behind the haunted house after Roisin and I went through it."

"The night after Todd Lee was killed?"

"Yeah, the ice pick is a cool old tool. I collect old tools and knives. They're from a simpler time before we had all the electronic stuff. Anyway, I didn't give it a second thought. I find old stuff laying around all the time." He took a deep breath, then continued, "Took it home, didn't know it was used to kill someone." He sighed. "Who ever heard of getting stabbed with an ice pick?"

"True," I said, "never heard of it until the police said Mr. Lee was stabbed with one. Did Roisin or your mom know you found it?"

"No," he said and smiled. "Thought it was a guy thing." His smile disappeared. "After Dad was killed, the police came to the house and took it. So, here I am with maybe the murder weapon. I was home when you found Dad. Mr. Landrum, all I need is to be around one more dead dude and it's three strikes and I'm out. I'll be up a creek."

"Pretty sure that's not how it works, but I understand it doesn't look good. Did you tell the police where you got the ice pick?"

"A hundred times. Had to tell it to the Folly Chief, then to that detective from the Sheriff's Office, then write it all down like it was a school assignment. Then, Mr. Landrum, after all that, the Folly woman took me to the haunted house. I had to show her exactly where I found it." He sighed. "A pain in the, umm, butt, if you ask me."

"That could help them catch the killer."

"Whatever."

I didn't think it was a good time to tell him I was the one who told the police the potential murder weapon was in his house.

He was more relaxed the longer the conversation went on. I began to see him as a young man playing a role to keep out the world. Self isolation was seldom a good thing, but if his way of life was ridiculed, it didn't leave many options, especially for a sixteen-year-old.

"I loved dad. We had our differences, but he was my hero, our family rock."

"All boys have differences with their dads."

"He thought I should be myself and quit putting on the Grim Reaper vibe. He called me out on it, sort of like you just did. Guess it's from the old person playbook."

I smiled. "I'd prefer to say it's from experience. Desmond, does anything stand out to you from the day your dad died?"

He looked out to sea again, then said, "I went to the grocery with him. We were having one of our arguments. When we got home, I went to my room, turned up the volume on my headsets to tune the world out. That always ticks him off, says the noise will hurt my ears."

"Anything unusual happen when you were at the store? Did your Dad talk to anyone?"

"He just talked, sort of yelled at me. To be honest, our fight started when we were shopping." Desmond picked up a shell and threw it in the surf. "I was being a brat about Dad's job. Told him he needed to spend more time with us. Told him he was letting some stupid stiff in a haunted house ruin his time at home."

"You brought up Todd Lee?"

"Dad was supposed to be off work getting ready for Halloween, but he needed to meet with you first. Like I said, I was being a brat. Dad always put Mom, me, and Roisin first."

"He told you he was going to meet me?"

"Yeah, he told me he'd talked to you once but needed to meet you again that afternoon, something about the stiff. Said once it was done, he'd be free to plan for the holiday."

"Did anyone hear your conversation?"

"Could have, we weren't whispering. Actually, I was sort of

yelling." He shook his head. "Stupid me, yelling in the grocery store. I know better; honest I do. Think it startled someone in the next row."

"Why do you think that?"

"Guess I scared her because she dropped a jar then left in a hurry." He kicked sand as he told me.

"Did you see her?"

"No."

"How do you know it was a woman?"

"A cart with food in it was still in the row beside a busted jar of pickles."

"That made you think it was a woman?"

He rubbed his eyes. "Not the cart. Think I know it was a lady because men don't wear perfume. Smelled it strong."

"Desmond, anything else stand out about that morning."

"Nope, we left the store and headed home. Was raining hard. We were still arguing but dad seemed distracted. Could've been the hard rain because he kept watching the mirrors like he was worried someone might run into the back of the car."

"Did you go inside when you got home, or did you help carry the groceries?"

"Went inside. dad was still in the car when I stomped off to the house."

"Why did he stay in the car?"

"Don't know. I was pissed and didn't care." He sighed then avoided eye contact. "Mr. Landrum, the last thing I said to my dad was mean. How do I go on? No matter what I do now, I'll never feel his arms around me telling me it'll be okay."

"Desmond, your Dad knows you were just being a teenager. It was nothing you two wouldn't have worked out."

"Mr. Landrum, if I stayed outside to help with the groceries, he'd still be alive. My family blames me for his death. So do I." Tears streamed down his face making him look like a sad goth clown.

"That's not true. Your family loves you and wants nothing more than to help you through this horrible time. As far as stopping your

Dad from being killed, you couldn't have stopped it. If not then, whoever did it, would've tried again."

He wiped tears from his face and attempted a weak smile. "Roisin is right. You're a good soul to talk to. Hope she's right about the other thing."

"Other thing?"

"She said you'll find who killed Dad and even the stiff, umm, Mr. Lee."

"I'm not sure why she said that, but I'll help with anything I can."

"She is an old soul and knows things, except about the Bermuda Triangle." He pointed to the ocean and his vision of where the Triangle is located.

"Young man, you're more like your father than you know. He told me the same thing about Roisin the first time I talked to him."

Desmond smiled and looked at the churning sea which seemed to get rougher since we'd been standing here. A dense fog enveloped the end of the Pier.

"Thanks, Mr. Landrum. I need to get home. May talk to you later if that's okay."

I told him any time and watched the not so scary Ozzy Osbourne looking young man disappear in the fog as it rolled in from the ocean. Our suspect list was now shortened by one.

I headed home before Desmond's Bermuda Triangle fog took me away. His story kept bouncing around in my head. He'd mentioned a woman. That would knock our suspects down to half the population but in fact not a huge help since the unanswered questions keep piling up. Another brain worm weaseled its way into my head as I reached my door. Desmond said his Dad had mentioned talking to me once about Todd Lee. Did the mystery woman hear Desmond and Mike's conversation?

It was enough to make me look over my shoulder before opening the door.

30

I was awakened the next morning by heavy rain pounding my metal roof and a headache pounding my brain. *Not the most pleasant way to begin the day*, I thought as I padded to the kitchen to start my Mr. Coffee machine and search for a bottle of ibuprofen. Thirty minutes later, coffee had begun to do its thing while the wonder drug had begun attacking the headache. Neither coffee nor ibuprofen had lessened the amount of rain covering my island home so I decided it would be the perfect day to stay indoors, a decision reinforced when I found a three day old box of powdered sugar covered donuts in the cabinet. A breakfast gift from the heavens.

A television commercial plugging a pop up Halloween store reminded me the holiday was rapidly approaching. Instead of the commercial inspiring me to visit the store to buy costumes, pumpkin carving kits, or skull shaped candy bowls, it made me think about Desmond and the ice pick he claimed he found in the haunted house's yard the day after Todd Lee had taken his last breath.

The ringing phone interrupted my less than helpful thoughts.

"Hey, pard, here's a heads up."

Cal had caught some of my friends irritating habit of beginning phone conversations by skipping civil phone etiquette openings.

"Morning, Cal."

"Yeah, okay. Want the heads up or not?"

"Cal, what's the heads up?"

"That's better, pard. Jeff asked me to tell you he'd have the stuff from Todd Lee with him when he comes to work. Said you wanted it. Now I've told you."

"When's Jeff coming in?"

"Don't know for certain. He don't have a regular schedule since he's not a real employee, but I'd guess he'll be here around lunchtime. Free lunches are part of his pay for helping, you know," He hesitated then said, "Gotta go, pard. I'll let Jeff know I gave you the message."

"Thanks, Cal. Tell him I'll stop by this afternoon."

He didn't respond so I assumed he'd gone.

The heavy rain didn't stop until a little after noon, so I didn't get to Cal's until one o'clock. I wasn't the only person deciding to stay home today. Two men were in animated conversation at the bar and three women playing cards were the only occupants of the tables. Vern Gosdin's version of "Chiseled in Stone" was flowing from the jukebox and Cal was waving his arm to the music while he filled the beer cooler. Jeff was nowhere in sight.

Cal spotted me looking around. He pointed to the table closest to the bandstand and as far from the group of women as possible. I took the hint and moved to the table as Cal headed to the small storage room beside the kitchen. Moments later, he arrived carrying a large paper sack, set it in front of me, and asked if I wanted anything to eat or drink. My healthy donuts breakfast had worn off, so I said a cheeseburger and a Diet Pepsi, proof I was serious about losing weight, or so I told myself.

He left the sack and headed to the kitchen. I didn't have to be a detective like Charles to deduce the sack contained Todd Lee's possessions. The men from the bar walked to the exit as Conway Twitty sang about Linda being on his mind. The women at the other occupied table appeared settled in for the afternoon.

I waited for Cal to return before opening the sack. I didn't have long to wait. The soothing aroma of my cheeseburger arrived seconds before Cal put the plate in front of me and his body in the chair facing me.

I took a bite of burger, a sip of Diet Pepsi, then asked about Jeff's whereabouts.

"Clueless. He bopped in, handed me the bag, said to give it to you, then boogied."

"What was his hurry?"

Cal shrugged. "I didn't have anything for him to do and he didn't stay for his free meal." He pointed at the card playing trio. "You can see how busy I am. Jeff acted all jumpy but didn't say why." He looked at the sack. "Ain't you curious about what's in it?"

I nodded. "Didn't want a dead man's stuff to interfere from enjoying this fantastic cheeseburger and the music."

Cal smiled like I'd given him a plaque naming Cal's as having the best burger on Folly, then tilted his head toward the sack. "Why'd Jeff have the dead guy's stuff?"

I shared Jeff's explanation. Cal said it didn't ring true but would take my word for it.

I didn't disagree and continued with lunch. One of the women asked Cal to get her another glass of tea. He smiled, tipped his Stetson her direction, and said, "I'd be honored to get it for you." He looked my way, rolled his eyes, then headed to the bar.

I opened the sack, and the stench of sweaty clothes replaced the cheeseburger's aroma. I was glad I'd nearly finished lunch, as I cautiously removed a pair of well worn jeans, raggedy cargo shorts, two T shirts, underwear, and a mismatched pair of socks from the sack and set them as far from my plate as possible. The only other item was a small, bent notebook with most of its pages torn out. On the first remaining page, *Len S.* and *Joseph H.* were scribbled diagonally across the lined sheet. Nothing else. The next three pages were blank followed by one with *25k* crossed out. The next line had *50k* underlined three times. Nothing else was written in the book.

Cal delivered the tea to the woman then returned to my table.

"That's all that was there?"

I said it was.

"What's in the notebook?"

I showed him the two pages with writing on them.

"Who're Len and Joseph?"

I wanted to say how should I know, but limited my response to, "Don't know."

"Let's try another question. What's the deal with the numbers?"

"Don't know for certain, but Jeff thought Todd Lee was blackmailing someone. The 50k could be the amount."

"Hefty amount. Back home in Texas, that'd be enough dough to choke a porcupine. Must've had something good on somebody. Think good ole Len and Joseph had something to do with it?"

"Could be."

"Who do you think he was blackmailing?"

If I knew that, I wouldn't be here; I'd be talking with the police. Instead of stating the obvious, I said, "Don't know."

"How're you going to figure it out, pard?"

I hadn't been counting, but suspected Cal and I had exceeded a reasonable number of *don't know* or similar responses to each question in a fifteen-minute period, so I said, "I'm working on it."

I finished lunch, Cal left to check on three men who'd arrived and was leaning against the bar, I stuffed Todd's possessions in the sack, left money on the table for my food, then headed to the exit. I heard Cal yell at my back, "You'll figure it out," as George Jones began "I Always Get Lucky With You."

Would I get lucky figuring out who the killer was before he killed again?

I seriously doubted it would result in anything useful, but when I got home, I fired up the computer and Googled the two names from Todd's notebook. A quick search told me I'd have a better chance of finding the Loch Ness Monster in my bathtub than finding anything helpful on the Internet about Len S. or Joseph H., and that was combining the names with Charleston, Folly, or Savannah, the cities where both the Robinsons, the Rices, and Todd had resided or worked.

The numbers from the notebook would be even more difficult, so I didn't try. While nothing was that helpful, it reinforced my belief that Todd was trying to blackmail someone and as Cal had said, for a hefty amount. I chuckled to myself thinking all I needed to do now was connect a name to the killer.

31

Waking without the pounding headache or rain was a plus. I'm getting too old for running around playing boy detective, okay, senior citizen non detective. Either way, it takes a toll on a body. I headed to Bert's for my usual nutritious breakfast. To my relief, no one was there to ambush me or to impart unwanted knowledge. I grabbed a cinnamon Danish, a cup of coffee, and headed home to enjoy a quiet breakfast and to do nothing. I finished breakfast and was still sipping coffee when my quiet midmorning was interrupted by the ringing phone.

"Thank the Gods you're still alive." Charles said. "Was beginning to worry." Charles's less than normal greeting crushed my hope for a telemarketer.

"Sorry, Charles, didn't know I stressed you."

"I'll let it slide."

"Thanks. What's up?" I asked, knowing it wasn't a call to check on my health and wellbeing.

"I was taking a late morning stroll and thought what better place to go than to Loggerhead's for lunch. I was sitting on the deck looking at the humongous fake spider web covering the front of the VW bar when I decided I couldn't eat without my best bud, so instead I decided to walk next door and check out the haunted house."

I waited for the other shoe to drop, but nothing came so figured it was my turn to speak.

"That's considerate," I said, not masking the sarcasm. "Are you inviting me to lunch?"

"I'm standing in front of the house that until a few days ago was haunted. They're about finished with the renovation. I was thinking you could join me for a walk through."

He must've forgotten the luncheon invitation.

"I didn't realize we were purchasing the house and needed a walk through."

"Okay, smarty, John and Bri might be here and there're questions we need answered. Besides, aren't you curious how the house looks."

"You know curiosity killed the cat."

"That's why I'm a dog person. See you in five."

Three minutes later, I pulled in the driveway at the former haunted house to find Charles leaning on the handrail leading to the entry and looking at his wrist. His imaginary watch was apparently telling him I was late. The glories of Charles time.

"You're late and you even drove." Charles left his perch and walked over to the car.

"Sorry, my teleporter is broken."

"Cute. Let's go inside."

The only other vehicle on the haunted house's property was John and Bri's black Ford truck, or I assumed it was theirs since the company logo was on the driver's door and a large ghost sticker was on the back window promoting Lowcountry Paranormal Investigations. I suppose the workers had already finished, so why not head up the stairs to see if one or both Rices were inside?

We approached as a sour taste surfaced from the pit of my stomach. I really need a vacation from retirement.

"Hello! John, you here?" Charles booming voice echoed through the empty house.

"Hey good looking, what can I help you with?" Bri said, as she bopped around the corner and spotted Charles.

"Oh, hi Chris," she said as she saw me behind Charles. She smiled and added, "What are you all doing here?" Her blond ponytail was tied with a pink ribbon. She still reminded me of a bouncy puppy full of life and innocence. I reminded myself looks can be deceiving.

I returned her smile and said, "Guess I'm not the good looking one."

"You're funny. Who's your friend?"

"Bri, this is Charles Fowler."

"Nice to meet you, Charles."

"You, too, Bri," Charles said. "I've heard a lot about you, but your beauty surpasses anything I've been told."

Bri blushed and about that time a voice came from the hallway.

"Chris, Charles, great to see you. What brings you to our project?"

"Charles told me it was almost complete, and we wanted to see how the house looks, if that's okay."

Bri turned to her husband. "You have all sorts of secrets. You knew Charles and never thought to introduce me to such a charming man."

John laughed. "Answered your own question. I don't need the competition." John put his arm around Bri's waist and moved her away from Charles.

Bri said, "Would you like the grand tour or prefer to explore on your own?"

"Bri, John," I said, "we don't want to take you away from your work, but a tour would be great."

Charles nodded.

John said, "We're touching up paint where electricians moved some duplex outlets. A tour will kill two birds. I can show you around while checking to see if anything else needs attention."

The four of us walked through the house with John pointing out what had been done and Bri detailed any unresolved issues. I was impressed how different the house looked from the last time I was here. It had a light, airy beach feel with high end finishes giving it a sophisticated look. There'd be no way anyone could walk through and be reminded of its recent past as a haunted house. The tour ended in the kitchen, but my eyes skipped over the marble countertop and went straight to the pantry.

"Chris," John said as he noticed me looking at the closed door, "like to see the pantry?" He chuckled. "I guarantee no dead bodies."

Charles answered for me. "Of course, we would."

John opened the door and stood to the side so we could look in. I didn't remember the pantry being so large, but then again, the last time I was in it there was a dead guy taking my focus off the rest of the room.

John and Bri remained in the kitchen where Bri said, "So gentleman, what do you think?" Her pride was evident.

Charles said, "It's great. Wouldn't mind living here myself. It'd give me a bit more wiggle room."

About a million times more, I thought, but said, "You've done a fantastic job. The Robinsons are lucky to have found you to do the project. They'll be happy here."

John frowned and shook his head. "The Robinsons will never be happy with anything or anyone. They're the most unhappy, miserable people I've had the displeasure of working with. Made me rethink my business. Perhaps I should deal only with the dead, they're better company."

Bri patted John's large hand. "What John's trying to say is thank you. It means a lot that you think the house turned out well."

"I'm sorry Chris, Charles. Thanks for the complements. We take pride in our work and it means the world when people appreciate our dedication, ideas, and work."

"I understand. From what I've experienced and heard about the Robinsons, they think they're, umm, special."

Charles laughed. "Special is Chris speak for pain in the ass."

I wasn't ready to go down that path and said, "Thanks again for the tour. We've bothered you enough. We'll let you get back to work."

Charles snapped his finger. "Chris, isn't there something you wanted to ask Bri?"

"Thanks, I almost forgot." I hoped my glare at Charles wasn't obvious.

"Bri, I saw someone outside Mike Stone's funeral on East Huron the other day and thought it might've been you."

Bri looked down before answering in a not so cheerful voice, "Yes, I was sort of there."

John glared at his wife but didn't say anything.

I said, "Did you know Mike?"

"Chris, you know John and I study the paranormal and everything involving that realm. I've always had a curiosity about witchcraft. Not the stuff you see on television or in movies but real life practices. I was in Charleston talking to Stormy at her shop and she mentioned the funeral she'd be attending on Folly. Thought it'd be a chance to observe."

"Why didn't you come in?"

"The Stones don't know me. I didn't want to disrespect anyone or impose. That's why I stayed near the street. I was able to see some of the ritual. I left as quickly as I could hoping not to be seen. The last thing the family needed was some uninvited outsider showing up. Figured it'd be my only time to see what a Wiccan funeral was like. Thought you saw me but didn't want to stick around to be sure. Did anyone else see me?"

"Not that I know of, why?"

"I've felt bad ever since then. It was a sacred time and there I was watching out of mere curiosity. If the family had seen me it would've been awful."

John wrapped his arm around her shoulder and said, "Bri would never want to hurt or interfere with anyone." He smiled. "Occasionally her curiosity overtakes common sense."

"No harm done, Bri," I said. "Charles and I really need to get going and let you two finish before the good doctor has a cow about the house."

"He has no reason to. They'll be moving in right after Halloween like he was promised," John said, as he walked us to the door leaving Bri in the kitchen.

As we waved bye to John, Charles said, "Can you give me a ride home? Weather looks like it's going to turn nasty."

As I figured, Charles's Loggerhead's luncheon plan was a ruse to get us invited into the house.

On the way to his apartment, he said, "Do you believe Bri's story about why she was at Mike's funeral?"

"It makes sense considering her interest in the occult and not wanting to intrude on the ceremony."

"Yes, sounds like a perfect excuse to be there but it also sounds like a perfect excuse to be there if you know what I mean." Charles eyes drilled a hole into the side of my head. "You know killers often attend the funeral of guys or gals they've killed."

They do on television shows and in novels, the extent of Charles's investigative training. Instead of pointing that out, I said, "You're right. If she thought I saw her, she had time to come up with a reason for being there."

Rain started pounding the windshield and put a damper on our conversation, I suspected Charles was thinking the same thing I was. Was Bri an innocent woman with unique interests or a killer with the ability to come up with a decent excuse?

32

If Bri was telling the truth about why she was snooping around the funeral, there was a good chance she wasn't the killer, nor would her husband have a motive, at least not an obvious one. That brought me back to square one, or somewhere near that proverbial starting place. Then I remembered Charles saying Dude had talked with Todd Lee, but that was about all he'd said. Why not visit the surf shop to see if Dude remembered more than he'd shared with Charles? Even if he hadn't, the rain had stopped, and a walk would do me good.

The surf shop with no capital letters in the name was on Center Street near its intersection with Ashley Avenue. The single story, wood frame, elevated structure with an exterior displaying many surfboard sized decals promoting surfing equipment was as much a staple on Folly's main drag as was Planet Follywood, the Crab Shack, and the Sand Dollar private club.

I was greeted at the door, using the term greeted loosely, by Stephon, one of Dude's employees who would be the winner hands down if the island ever had a rudest employee competition.

"What?" he said with a smirk after he couldn't ignore me since I was a foot in front of him.

"Dude here?"

Stephon's smirk intensified as he pointed his arm covered with more tattoos than Dennis Rodman has on his entire body toward the back of the store. It was his way of "politely" indicating the store's owner was in his office.

"Thanks, Stephon," I said faking a smile.

He muttered either, "You're welcome," or a profanity before turning back to his more important task of thumbing through an issue of *SURFER* magazine.

Dude's office door was closed so I shook off my rude welcome from Stephon and knocked.

"What?" Dude yelled.

I opened the door, stuck my head in, and said, "Dude, have a few minutes?"

Dude was in his late sixties, looked like a cross between Arlo Guthrie and Willie Nelson, and wore one of his many tie dye shirts featuring a large peace symbol on the front.

"Whoops. My bad, Chrisster. Thought be tatted peep Rudester knockin'." He waved me in.

I'm often wary meeting with Dude without Charles, someone who could translate much of what Dude was saying, although Rudester could only be Stephon.

"Got a question," I said, reducing my words to match the man who never grasped using ten words when two would sort of do.

Dude smiled as he pointed to the chair in front of his cluttered desk. I moved the stack of shirts, sat, and waited to see if he had anything else to say before I asked the question. He didn't, so I said, "Dude, you were telling Charles a few days ago that Todd Lee applied for a job."

He nodded. "Be sitting right here. Pluto be eatin' food beside desk."

I waited for more, but apparently Dude had exceeded his word quota. Pluto was his Australian Terrier that looked like a miniature version of its master.

"Charles said you didn't have anything available."

"Chrisster, this be month ten. Business sucky. Rudester handles peeps surfin' in. No be needin' overstaffing."

Fortunately, I understood all that.

"Did he fill out an application?"

Dude leaned forward. "You be moonlightin' as EEOC cop?"

I smiled. "No, trying to learn more about him."

"In dark ages, had job wanting peeps fill application. Called it doin' Dude diligence." He chuckled then tapped his head with his forefinger. "Waste of time. Job wanting peeps only gave employers who say boss things about them. Past bosses also lied about how good past peeps did jobs. Waste of time." He held his arms out. I assumed indicating how big a waste of time. "Most peeps I hire spent most of life on wrong side of law. Need new chance."

Rudester Stephon came to mind. "I understand. Do you remember anything Todd Lee said that may help me figure out why he was killed?"

"He be all jittery. Can you believe, he afearin' *moi?*"

Yes, I thought, but didn't say it. "Maybe he got nervous about job interviews. That's not uncommon."

Dude nodded. "Pluto jumped in his lap, got him relaxin'. Told me last job he got payroll check was in Savannah, G. A."

"A surf shop?"

He shook his head. "Medical office, but he not be doc."

"What'd he do there?"

"Highlight be getting fired."

"Dude, what was his job before he was terminated?"

He shrugged. "He not bigwig."

I figured that was all I'd get from Dude about Todd's job duties.

"Do you recall the name of the office where he worked?"

"Didn't ask. Not surf shop, so didn't care."

"Do you remember anything else he said?"

Dude smiled, nodded his head, and said, "Be stoked about knowing Pluto."

"I don't blame him. Pluto's a great dog."

Dude's smile covered his entire face, then he pointed to me. "My turn for questions?"

"What might they be?"

"Might be how many peeps live in Tangier, but not. Question one, you know first name of candy corn be chicken food? First box had rooster on front. Believe that?"

"Huh?"

"Halloween candy."

"Oh," I said, like he'd made perfectly good sense. "You learn that from Charles?"

"Nope, television. Be Halloween Eve, Eve. Thought you needed Halloween factoid."

"Thanks."

"Question two, you going to catch slimeball that wiped out Todd and my new, and now dead, friend Mike the witch?"

"Trying to."

"Cool."

Dude asked if I wanted to leave out the back door to avoid Stephon, or that's what I think he meant.

I said, "Cool."

33

On the walk home, I reviewed what Dude had shared about Todd Lee. All I'd learned was that Todd had worked in a medical office in Savannah, Dude no longer checked references, and chicken feed was the original name of candy corn. By the time I reached my yard, I decided there was no reason to be stressing over it by myself. I could get with Charles and between the two of us come up with, umm, come up with something. My kitchen cabinet was as bare as Old Mother Hubbard's Cupboard, so instead of going in the house, I stopped at Bert's for snacks, or as Charles would say, brain food. I left the store with more junk food than needed for a teenage girl's slumber party before calling Charles to invite him over.

"What's wrong? Who died?" Charles said instead of a simple *hello*. My dislike of Caller ID deepened.

"Nothing's wrong. As far as I know, no one died. Want to come over and try to figure out where we are with, umm, the murders?"

"About time you admitted that's what we need to do."

I imagined Charles patting himself on the back for convincing me it was what we needed to do.

"You coming?"

"On my way. Have anything resembling food or should I give you time to go shopping before I show up?"

"I have plenty." The phone went dead. If nothing else, Charles doesn't disappoint.

I put the chips in a bowl on the kitchen table and added a package of Oreos on the table beside the chips, poured Charles a Coke and myself a Diet Coke when I heard the front door open and a cane tapping on the floor heading my way.

Charles removed his Tilley and leaned his cane against the counter before staring at the table. "Wow, buttering me up for something. You have the name of the killer or killers to go with this feast?"

I smiled at his definition of feast, and said, "I talked with Dude. Wanted to see if he knew more about Todd Lee. I remembered you said he'd interviewed Todd for a job, but that was all. As you know, it's hard to get everything from listening to Dude's stories."

"Where did you see Dude?"

"His shop."

"Went on your own, no translator, no me?"

"I understood most of what he said."

"By understanding Dudespeak, you might've attained local status."

"I've lived here more than a decade."

"Yeah, but you weren't born here." Charles tapped his fingers on the table like he'd made a profound statement.

"You weren't either. For that matter, most people I know here weren't."

He sighed, grabbed an Oreo, and stared at me.

Not hearing a comeback, I said, "Charles, you ready to hear why I called?"

"What did you learn from Dude?"

"Todd's last job before coming here was at a medical office in Savannah."

"Which one? What did he do there?"

"Dude didn't know which one or what kind of medical office."

"Hmm, interesting, worthless, but interesting," Charles said as he reached for another Oreo.

"I have more," I said, knowing I was in for grief for not telling him sooner. "Todd had a notebook with two first names in it along with what appears to be a dollar amount."

Charles waved a hand in my face, "You—"

"I'm not finished."

He shook his head, moved his hand away from my face, and said, "Well, what are you waiting for?"

"Jeff Hildebrand left Todd Lee's possessions with Cal who gave them to me. And, before you ask, I googled the two names but came up dry."

Charles glared at me. "You just have the dead man's notebook and didn't think to share that monster clue with the only person who could help you find the killer." He grabbed another Oreo and shoved it to his mouth.

"Charles, I just got the things from Cal." Okay, *just got* was a bit of a stretch, but I wasn't in the mood to be lectured.

"In the spirit of catching a killer, I'll let that oversight, gross oversight go."

"You're too kind," I said, oozing sarcasm.

"So, we think Todd was blackmailing someone before he came to Folly. According to Dude in a meeting I wasn't invited to, Todd worked in a medical office in Savannah. There's a notebook that was left for you at Cal's that you got when you went there without inviting me, a notebook with a dollar amount and first names of guys he may've been blackmailing someone about. That cover it?"

"Wordy but sums it up. What are reasons for blackmailing someone?"

Charles rubbed his chin, looked at the ceiling, then said, "Sex, drugs, rock and roll, murder, lies, embezzlement, deep dark secrets."

"We can take rock and roll off the list, the others, possible."

Charles smiled. "See, we've already narrowed it down. What kind of medical office?"

"I already told you I don't know, and there are probably hundreds in Savannah."

Charles nodded toward my office. "We better start looking."

I knew a computer search was futile, but so was arguing with my friend. We grabbed our drinks, the bag of Oreos, and moved to my computer.

I Googled medical offices in Savannah, Georgia, and to no surprise found numerous listed.

"Okay, Mr. Detective," I said as I looked over my shoulder at Charles, "how do you want to narrow this down?"

"You're the Google finder guy. What do you suggest?"

"I could Google medical offices with best blackmail opportunities?"

Charles stared at me. "So, you have no idea?"

"Yep."

"Then why are we looking at the computer?"

"It was your idea."

"You're thinking it wasn't one of my best."

"Yep," I repeated. "If Todd learned something where he worked, it could be about a patient, someone working in the office, someone who visited the office, someone who cleaned the office, on and on. And, it may not have had anything to do with where he worked."

"Chris, you sure know how to fog up a mirror."

"Yep."

Charles snapped his fingers. "Whoa, why didn't I think of it earlier? Who do we know who worked in a medical office in Savannah, someone who just happens to own the very house where Todd Lee took his last breath?"

I wondered when Charles was going to figure that out. I didn't want to start with that fact since Charles would've proclaimed that solved the case closing out other possibilities. I also didn't remind him he'd already said Fred or his wife was the killer just the other day. I said, "Dr. Fred Robinson."

"There you go. We figured out who killed Todd Lee and I suppose Mike Stone. You better call Chief LaMond, or Detective Adair, or the Charleston newspaper, TV and radio stations and let them know." He pointed to my phone before stuffing another Oreo in his mouth.

My strategy of not mentioning Dr. Robinson's *medical office* in

Savannah had failed "And tell them what? Fred Robinson worked in a dental office in Savannah, so he has to be the killer?"

"No, tell them he's the killer because Todd was blackmailing him because of the names in the notebook and for the amount that was in there. Duh."

"Charles, I must've missed it. What proof do we have? Why was he blackmailing the good dentist?"

"Chris, we can't do everything. Don't you think it's time the police did some of the work?"

"Charles."

He interrupted, "Hold it, you said you Googled the two names from the notebook?"

"Yes," I said, omitting the word halfheartedly since all I had was first names and what I assumed to be a last initial.

"Sure there was nothing?"

"Yep."

Charles shook his head. "So, all those chips and Oreos and we came up with nothing except Dr. Robinson is the killer, but we have no way to prove it."

"Yep."

34

Never having had children to take trick or treating or willingly attending Halloween parties as an adult because I hated the idea of dressing up like someone I'm not, the October holiday was never high on my list of favorite holidays. With Halloween only hours rather than days away, this one topped all the others I've experienced in both horror and nightmares—topped them by far.

My talk with Charles yesterday only uncovered more questions. Was Dr. Robinson the killer? Should I call Chief LaMond to let her know what we suspected? The logical side of my brain overruled the Hardy Boys side. We had no proof, just a bunch of disjointed facts and the coincidence that Todd Lee and Dr. Robinson had lived in Savannah. I was still going over the possibilities when the phone rang.

Before the caller could say anything, I started the conversation with a brilliant and seldom used greeting on Folly, "Hello."

"We're in luck," Charles said, his voice a couple of octaves higher than normal. "I just saw a big ole moving truck at the haunted house. Two guys the size of bull elephants were unloading tables, boxes, and a bunch of filing cabinets."

"Who is this?" I said, hoping to tamper his excitement.

"Funny. Ready to do some grade A snooping?"

"See if I have this right. You're out casing the former haunted house. You see a moving truck and decide to call your friend for some breaking and entering? How'd I do?"

"About sums it up."

"Charles, with all due respect, have you lost your mind? Why would I agree?"

"If Todd was blackmailing Fred about something that happened in the office, I figure the chances are good some information would be in those filing cabinets at his house and not in his office where someone could find it. That's where I'd keep my secrets."

"Did you ever own a filing cabinet?"

Today was let's send Charles over the edge day, primarily to deflect what he wanted to do.

He sighed, then said, "Not the point. You coming?"

"Charles, it's the middle of the morning. What makes you think the house will be empty? What about the movers? Or, what about John and Bri, or, umm, how about the Robinsons, you know, the owners?"

"Well, Mr. Know It All, it's the perfect time. The moving van pulled out ten minutes ago. The only other vehicle here was Erica Robinson's. She drove off when the moving van left."

"Charles, what—"

"Whoa, there's more. Best of all, the fog's so thick nobody would see us going in. Okay, your turn."

"What about Fred Robinson? He could be in the house, and you didn't see him. It's not like you have an infrared camera checking for occupants?"

I knew this was a losing battle. I needed to go to keep Charles from getting himself in more trouble, but that didn't mean I had to give in quickly.

"Infrared cameras. What a great idea for our detective agency. Why didn't you ever suggest that before?"

Out of all the reasons I gave for not breaking into someone's house, Charles focused on infrared cameras.

"Because we are not detectives. This is a bad idea."

"Oh, ye of little faith, it's the perfect idea and time. I called the dental office and according to Mildred, a helpful lady who answered the phone, Dr. Robinson is scheduled to be there all day. Said she was sorry about my aching tooth, but he didn't have a free appointment until late next week."

I'd be wasting words trying to stop him.

"I'll be there in a few minutes. Don't do anything until I get there." I omitted the word *stupid* after *anything* and hung up.

Fortunately, the short drive to the last haunted house I will ever enter was quick. If it'd taken longer, I would've talked myself out of the absurdity of breaking into the private residence of a person who might or might not be a killer. Then again, this entire month has been nothing but one absurdity after another, starting with Charles wanting to relive a childhood memory of attending a haunted house. Now he's on the verge of breaking in a house to live out his adult fantasy of being a detective. Truth be known, I blame him for all this, but a big part of me wants answers as much as he does.

I parked and spotted Charles leaning against the garage in the former haunted house's back yard. He was wearing his long sleeve, black sweatshirt with NYPD in white on the chest.

He smiled and said, "Ready to get the party started?"

"What're the chances of talking you out of this crazy idea?"

"Chris, have I ever led you astray?"

"You really want me to answer that?"

"Umm, no. You know you want answers as much as I do. This is our chance before the Robinsons move in."

It was hard to argue with him since I did want to know. Besides, all we had for the police was a hunch, and that was based on Dude saying Todd Lee worked at a medical office in Savannah and that he may've been trying to blackmail Fred Robinson because, umm, because why?

"Charles, I'm trying to stop you from doing anything stupid, well more stupid than breaking into a house that's not yours."

"The house is nobody's yet. John and Bri have finished work on it and the Robinsons haven't moved in, so it's abandoned. It's fair game." Charles had already headed to the back stairs like that said it all.

I hoped he was right.

35

Charles's less than brilliant idea began to sink in as we approached the house. More accurately, I think we were approaching the house, but I wasn't sure since a dense sea fog enveloped the structure making it nearly indistinguishable from the gray fog.

"Good news, Chris. There's not a chance anyone will see us break in," said my glass is half full friend.

"Good news, right."

"Looks more like a haunted house now than it did when we stumbled on Todd Lee, doesn't it?"

I didn't know about that but was certain my nerves were frayed as we reached the back stairs. I nearly missed the first step when the sound of a vehicle speeding past the house startled me. I was about ready to turn and hightail it home but reminded myself while this ill conceived adventure could turn out bad, it couldn't possibly be as bad as if Charles did it alone. Or could it?

"Keep a watch for anyone coming," Charles said as he bent to see how to get in the back door.

"The fog's so thick I wouldn't see anyone until they were up here with us."

Charles didn't own credit cards, so he was slipping a small putty knife between the door and the frame to push the latch bolt enough to unlock it. I was impressed he thought to bring the tool, but this wasn't a good time to praise his ability to commit a crime.

Another vehicle zipped by, but it didn't startle me nearly as much as the Halloween horror movie squeak the door made as it swung inward after Charles's successful break in.

"See, it's an omen," he said, "it wanted us to come in."

Charles's logic at its best.

It was light outside, but I had difficulty seeing more than a few feet in front of me. I was still looking around, clearly not moving fast enough for Charles, who'd already gone to the pantry, aka the room where we found Todd Lee. He turned on the overhead light and stared at five stacks of moving boxes covering half the floor.

He said, "Think there's a clue in there?"

I didn't think that deserved a response which was fortunate since he'd already started looking for ways to open the top box in the closest stack without disturbing the tape holding it shut. Instead of watching my friend, I kept looking at the spot on the floor where we'd seen Todd. I shuttered thinking of that night.

Charles had managed to loosen the tape without tearing it or the box when I thought I heard the back door squeak. Was I imagining it, was it a ghost, or was someone there?

Then I heard the back door shut. I never thought I'd prefer to see a ghost more than what I saw. Erika Robinson was standing in the doorway to the pantry. What was more frightening was the black handgun she pointed at me.

Charles was focused on the boxes and didn't see the latest addition to the pantry until Erika said, "Couldn't leave it alone, could you?"

Charles pivoted so quickly that I thought Erika was going to shoot him as she twisted in his direction. His hands flew over his head.

Erika smirked and said, "Wise man." She pointed the gun at the floor. "Sit."

I had no doubt she wasn't going to let us leave the house alive, but with the boxes and filing cabinets covering much of the floor and Erika blocking the exit, I couldn't see a way out. If I could keep her talking, there was a possibility she'd make a mistake—a remote possibility, but our only hope.

I lowered myself to the floor and said, "Erika, what happened?"

She started to speak but was distracted by another vehicle passing the house. Unfortunately, she wasn't distracted enough for me to attack.

She turned back to me. "My idiot husband wasn't satisfied being a dentist. We have a good income. He was made partner in an extraordinarily successful dental practice where he could reap the rewards from several offices. That wasn't enough."

Her hand trembled as she appeared to get angrier. Perhaps getting her talking was a mistake, but I couldn't see another way to buy time.

"What do you mean?"

"He figured out he could make more, a lot more, selling oxycodone prescriptions to patients than working on their teeth." She shook her head. "Told him he was an idiot, but no, oh no, he knew better. Know what happened?"

I suspected I did but didn't see any advantage in sharing. It was her story, hopefully a long one, long enough to figure a way out of this mess.

Charles said, "What happened?"

She slowly pointed the gun at my friend. "Two deaths, that's what. Wouldn't you think someone with medical training would've known prescribing oxy to addicts might not turn out well?"

Charles said, "Len and Joseph?"

She sighed. "Knew you busybodies couldn't leave it alone. Where'd you hear about those guys?"

Erika wasn't going to leave loose ends, so if I told her we got Todd's possessions from Jeff Hildebrand I'd be signing his death warrant. "Couple of guys talking in a bar. Don't know who they were."

She uttered a profanity then said, "Fred's going to be the death of me yet."

I didn't see that happening anytime soon, but still needed her to keep talking.

"Why kill Todd Lee?"

She smiled but it appeared more of a smirk. "Who said I did?"

Charles said, "Did you?"

"Know what my idiot husband did after the oxy deaths?"

I didn't detect a confession in there but had no doubt she or her *idiot husband* had killed Todd.

"What?" Charles asked.

"He had one of his office workers shred eight patient files. Told the guy they were old and no longer patients. Fred told me he had the person shred eight files so he wouldn't get suspicious about two of them dying. Idiot."

"Todd Lee?"

She nodded. "Told me Lee was so stupid he'd never put two and two together. Know what Fred did then?"

Charles said, "What?"

"Fired Lee. How stupid is that?"

Figured it was a rhetorical question, so I remained quiet.

"Fred was partially right, I guess. Lee didn't say or do anything about it until we moved to Charleston. How were we to know Lee was here? We ran into him in Bert's one day when we were checking on the house. Quite a shock it was. He called Fred the next day."

Charles said, "Blackmail?"

She shook her head. "Fifty thousand dollars and Fred would never hear from him again. The cash would erase it from his head, so he claimed." She continued shaking her head. "Never hear from him again, he said. Never until he wanted more. How stupid did he think we were? I couldn't have that, could I?" The sound of another vehicle broke Erika's rant. She looked toward the street but didn't let it distract from her outburst. "Know what Fred said?"

I didn't so I remained quiet.

Silence was outside Charles's comfort zone. "What?"

I thought I heard the back door squeak, but after a few seconds realized it was wishful thinking. Where was Chucky or Blackbeard when we needed them?

"Fred said fifty K was more than Todd had ever seen in his life and would be thrilled having it."

I said, "You didn't agree?"

"Not for a second. I told Fred I'd deliver the money, so he would be at work in case anything bad happened. Good alibi, you know. He thought that was a great idea. Idiot."

I said, "You had no intention of paying him?"

"No way."

Charles said, "What happened?"

"Called and told Todd we'd meet him here. The haunted house crew wasn't here in the morning and the contractors were only working two days a week until the haunted house was over. Come to think of it, that was supposed to be tomorrow. Could hear Todd jumping with excitement over the phone." She gave a sinister laugh that would have been perfect in any haunted house. "He came in like he owned the world. Wasn't how he left, was it?"

"Why an ice pick instead of that?" I said as I nodded toward the gun.

"Good question. You're smarter than the man I married. I knew what I was going to do when I got here, but Fred didn't since he thought I was handing the blackmailer a stack of cash." She chuckled. "When he got home from his office, umm, his alibi, I said Lee tried to attack me, wanted to take the fifty thousand and anything else I had in my purse, and no telling what else he wanted to do to me. So, I grabbed the nearest weapon I could find. Said the ice pick was in the kitchen." She chuckled. "Sort of forgot to mention I brought it with me. You see, I had no choice but to stab him."

Charles said, "He believed that?"

"Told you he was an idiot. Yeah, took more than a few tears, but he finally agreed I didn't have a choice. So sad for poor Todd. Know what Fred wanted to do?"

I guessed, "Go to the police?"

"Can you believe that? Well, that wasn't going to happen. Took more tears to get him to agree."

I said, "Why kill Mike Stone?"

"Didn't want to, but Todd told me before he met the ice pick that he'd talked to an attorney. He figured that'd give him leverage. Anyway, I was afraid he told the lawyer about the oxy overdoses."

Charles said, "Did he?"

"Don't know but couldn't take a chance. Took me the longest time to figure out who the attorney was. Todd only referred to him as Mike. Know how many lawyers there are in Charleston named Mike or Michael? If I didn't hear him talking, arguing, with a kid at the grocery, I'd still be looking for him." She looked at the weapon in her hand, at Charles, then at me. "Guess it's time for this little gathering to come to an end. It's been—"

A sound came from the doorway. It wasn't Chucky, Blackbeard, or the police coming to the rescue.

Lugh nearly filled the entire opening. Desmond stood behind him and shouted, "*Greim!*"

The word was barely out of his mouth when Lugh bounded into the room and with his massive jaws grabbed Erika's outstretched arm holding the gun.

I reached the gun before she pulled the trigger. Lugh still gripped Erika's arm. Desmond stood back and watched like it was something he saw every day. He then gave a command I couldn't understand. Lugh let go of her arm, took a step back, and sat.

I looked around to find something to secure Erika and noticed Lugh's oversized leash. I asked Desmond if I could use it to tie Erika. He smiled, one of the few times I'd seen that emotion on his face, as he unhooked the leash and handed it to me. Erika wasn't going to be restrained easily. She twisted and tried to bite Charles's hand as he maneuvered her around so I could get to both hands. Lugh was no more than three feet away from her yet remained still. Erika noticed the dog's eyes following her every move. She wisely stopped resisting enough for me to tighten the leash around her wrists.

After she was secure, it took another thirty seconds before I caught my breath enough to dial 911. Charles held onto the leash making sure Erika couldn't loosen the restraint. Desmond moved closer and put his arm around Lugh's neck.

I went to the front room to open the door for the police, stared at the street, and swore I would never attend another haunted house no matter how much anyone begged. Period.

36

Over the years, I've attended numerous Christmas parades on Folly and had never heard as many sirens as I heard approaching a former haunted house on Halloween Eve. At least three, possibly more, patrol cars were rushing to our location, plus the distinct sound of two fire engines. Fewer than three minutes after my 911 call, the drive, much of the side yard and along West Arctic Avenue in front of the house were filling with emergency vehicles.

Officer Trula Bishop was first up the stairs, asked if I was okay, receiving my assurance that not only I was, but so were the other three people in the house. She either exhaled from excitement knowing I was okay or was trying to catch her breath from jogging up the steps.

Either way, she gave me a police officer's stare and said, "Chris, what pile of manure have you stepped in this time? The last time I was here, you were standing over a dead body."

"Trula, if you'll follow me, I'll take you to the person who stabbed the man whose body I'd been standing over and the person who killed Mike Stone."

Before I could lead her through the house to the pantry, Officer Spencer rushed up the steps, with a hand resting on his holstered firearm. He didn't say it, but from the look on his face, he shared Officer Bishop's sentiments about me. Instead of explaining what'd happened, I led both officers to the pantry filled with filing cabinets, moving boxes, Erika, Charles, Desmond, and Lugh who was occupying the most space. Both officers saw the Irish Wolfhound and stepped back. I suggested that Desmond escort Lugh to the back porch until the officers removed Erika. Bishop said it was an excellent idea.

After the room was one sixteen-year-old and one massive canine lighter, Bishop asked what was going on. Charles and I tag teamed her with the explanation while Spencer told the EMTs who'd entered the house that their services wouldn't be needed. He then helped Erika to her feet and out the door while the rest of us moved to the large front room.

Chief LaMond was next to arrive. She watched Spencer escort Erika to his patrol vehicle then silently listened to Bishop's explanation of what'd happened, shook her head a few times when Bishop told her why Charles and I were here, then asked Bishop to take notes while Charles and I explained everything a second time.

Thirty minutes later, which, I might add, seemed like three hours, the Chief and Officer Bishop appeared satisfied with our explanations and asked us to come to her office the next day to review and verify the events as recorded by Bishop. She added that Detective Adair would be contacting us later today or tomorrow.

I lied and said, "I look forward to it."

Cindy smiled and finally got around to asking if Charles and I were okay.

Charles said, "Fine as frog's hair on Halloween."

Cindy gave him a skeptical look, one he often receives, and said, "Don't suppose a President said that?"

She didn't wait for an answer before turning to me. "You okay?"

This time I was truthful. "I will be."

Two more officers arrived and were dismissed by the Chief. She then said. "Chris, I'll give you and Charles a few more minutes in here to, umm, catch your breath. Can I trust you to lock up on the way out?"

"Of course, Chief," Charles said.

Cindy shook her head one more time before heading to the door.

Desmond and Lugh were still waiting on the back deck. Desmond held his arms around his black Sisters of Mercy T shirt to stay warm. The temperature must've dropped ten degrees since we'd entered the house. I asked if he wanted to come inside where it was warmer. He nodded and led Lugh back in. Lugh stared at the door to the pantry and Desmond who'd watched the recent activity in the house through the back door window assured his canine pal the bad woman was gone. I didn't know how much English Lugh knew, but he moved close to Desmond and sat.

"Desmond, what were you doing here?" Charles asked the question that was also on my mind.

He lowered his head and barely above a whisper said, "You won't tell Mom, will you?"

I couldn't make that promise considering what'd happened. "Not unless I have to."

"I came around the haunted house most nights it was open. Stood across the street or out there." He nodded toward the back yard. "Mom didn't want me to be here, said if people saw me, they'd start associating our religion with bad things haunted houses make popular, or something like that."

Charles said, "Like knife flailing serial killers and pirates?"

"Sort of. Anyway, I'm interested in the occult, mysticism, conjuring, stuff like that."

Charles said, "Because of your religion?"

Charles, let the young man finish, I thought.

"Sort of. I'm also interested in finding out more about Christianity." He smiled. "Even attended one of Preacher Burl's services. Roisin wondered why. I told her not to worry. I wasn't converting. Told her I was scouting the competition."

A sense of humor from Desmond. What other surprises did he hold?

"Desmond," I said, "why were you here today?"

"Mr. Landrum, even when the haunted house wasn't open, I liked hanging around. I've watched the construction guys from back there." He again nodded toward the back yard. "Lugh liked it, too. I don't much, but he likes people. Likes to watch them. Strange, I know. Anyway, days before the guy was killed in there, I saw a woman going in a few times. Thought she must've been part of the bunch working on the house, but whenever she was there, the workers weren't around."

Charles said, "Did you recognize her?"

"Not until today. Lugh and I were back there. Saw you two, umm, break in, then she went up the steps. I didn't know what was going on. Thought she was meeting you, so Lugh and I sneaked up the steps. We weren't breaking in. Honest. The door wasn't closed, so I sort of pushed it all the way open. That's when we heard you talking in that storage room or whatever it's called."

"Pantry," Charles the trivia king interrupted.

"Yeah, pantry. Anyway, I heard her tell you about … about killing Dad." He wiped a tear from his cheek before continuing. "She had that gun and I figured if she killed that other guy and dad, she was going to shoot you two. That's when I told Lugh to attack." He reached down and patted Lugh's head.

I wanted to put my arm around the young man but was afraid Lugh might not take too kindly to it. Instead, I said, "Desmond, we're glad you did. You saved our lives."

He gave a weak smile. "Guess so. Something good came from me snooping around the haunted house all those times. Maybe Mom will be proud of me."

"Desmond, she will be."

He grinned. "Suppose I'd better get home. I don't know what needs to be done, but Mom said there were some things we needed to do to prepare for spreading Dad's ashes tomorrow. Halloween's a special day for us, you know."

I said, "Desmond, before you go, let me ask you something. Did you say the back door wasn't closed when you got here?"

"It was open, Mr. Landrum."

I smiled. "Thanks again for saving us."

Charles added, "You too, Lugh."

I didn't know exactly what would happen tomorrow, but there was no doubt Desmond and Lugh saved two lives on Halloween Eve.

37

Halloween had finally arrived. I was more excited than I had ever been for the holiday to get here. It wasn't because of the normal Halloween festivities, but because I was alive. To many, the holiday was a celebration of death. I was celebrating life.

After two cups of coffee, I decided the best way to celebrate was to have a gathering of friends, old and maybe some new, to remind all of us the importance of living each day as if it's our last. I smiled thinking how absurd it was to start planning a Halloween party on Halloween morning. Then again, the absurd is often normal on Folly. Besides, I'm not big on costume parties or decorating for the holiday, so why not? After all, the most important part of any party was having guests you enjoyed being with.

I couldn't afford to waste time but needed to make a call before going shopping. If I didn't call Charles, I'd never hear the end of it, plus, he can spread the word quicker than any method of communication known to man.

He answered on the second ring with, "Happy Halloween! Been held at gunpoint lately?"

Ignoring his comment, I said, "Was thinking of having a get together later today."

He responded with a loud sigh and, "Nothing like waiting until the last minute to invite me. Thought we were friends."

"You're the first person I've invited. Thought it'd be nice having a small gathering with friends to try to get our lives back to normal."

"I don't do normal very good, but it's not a bad idea. Who's on the list and what can I do?"

"Invite anyone you think would like to come. Before you ask, no, not the entire island, only our friends. Charles, this isn't a big event. One more thing, no costumes."

"No costumes? So, you're not going to the costume contest at the community center?"

"Charles!"

"Okay, okay, sounds like someone doesn't have the Halloween spirit."

"That's right."

Another sigh, followed by, "What time is the no costume Halloween event going to start? I'd vote for four, so it doesn't conflict with the Witches Dance at the County Park."

"Wouldn't want you to miss that event, so four is fine. Remember, no costumes and not the entire island."

"On it."

I made a list of items needed and since I had nothing in the house fit to serve guests, a trip to Harris Teeter was mandatory. On the way, I stopped at Barb's Books to invite its lovely owner to the event. I hoped she hadn't heard about yesterday's traumatic events. She wouldn't be happy regardless, but the blow would be softened if she heard it from me, or so I hoped.

"I was beginning to think you'd vanished in all of this fog of late," she said as I entered the bookstore.

"Vanished, not really. Been busy."

"Retirement must be exhausting," she said with a smile. "Want some coffee?"

"No thanks. I'm on the way to Harris Teeter, which brings me to the reason I stopped by."

"You don't have to get me anything. I can shop for myself, but thanks for the offer."

"Good to know. Next time you can do my grocery shopping. I'm having an impromptu Halloween party this afternoon around four and wanted to personally invite you."

"Then it's after you enter the costume contest at the community center?"

"Have you been talking to Charles?"

"No, why?"

"Never mind."

She smiled. "Well, I have to rearrange my busy schedule and close early, but I can squeeze you in. What do I need to bring?"

"Just yourself. One more thing, it's not a costume party."

"Darn, I was going to wear my sexy zombie outfit." She laughed, grabbed my arm, and gave me a kiss on the cheek.

"My loss."

Now to broach what happened yesterday. I was pleased when all she said after my abbreviated version of the traumatic event was she was glad we caught the killer. This time, she gave me a kiss on the lips. I'd dodged a possible lecture about getting involved. Perhaps, Halloween wasn't so bad after all.

I left the store and noticed the door to First Light open. If Preacher Burl was there, it'd save a phone call.

"Preacher, you here?" I said as I entered the foul weather sanctuary.

"Brother Chris, come in. I was getting a pot of coffee going. Want some?"

"No thanks. I'm having some friends over this afternoon and wondered if you could stop by. I know it's short notice."

"Love to, it'd be nice to get out and socialize."

"My house around four."

"Sounds good. Would you mind if I brought some people?"

"People?"

"Not sure if you know, but today Shannon and the kids will be spreading Brother Mike's ashes. I was thinking it might be nice if they had something to distract them."

"I remembered that's what they were doing. Speaking of the Stones, have you heard what happened yesterday?"

"Guess not."

I gave a shortened version of the happenings in the haunted house.

"Oh, my word. I must contact them immediately."

I told him it was a good idea and if they were up to it, they were welcome at my party.

An hour later, although it seemed like an eternity slogging up each aisle in the grocery and buying enough food and drinks to feed a small army, I arrived home. Whose idea was this party?

Time flew as I straightened the house and put out candy. I couldn't have a Halloween party without candy. I chuckled as I filled two bowls with candy corn thinking about Dude saying it'd originally been called chicken food. I also wondered if that was true. I'll take his word since I didn't have the energy or interest to Google it.

***

BARB WAS the first to arrive which surprised me since Charles is always first to anything.

"Surprised you're here early. You beat Charles."

"That was my plan," she said as she slipped past me and took a grocery bag to the kitchen counter. "I figured this was the first party you've had at your house, so you'd need a woman's touch." She then waved for me to follow her to the door.

On the way to her car, she said, "I thought you'd need help getting ready and I brought a few things you can help with."

Her passenger seat was stacked with trays of fruits, cold cuts, and cookies. If Charles did invite the entire population of the island, we'd have enough food.

As we lugged the containers in, Barb said, "Men and spur of the moment party planning never end well."

I didn't disagree.

We were in the kitchen arranging the platters when I heard the familiar sound of a cane tapping on my front door. Charles was not alone.

He said, "Finally, was thinking we were going to be left on the porch. Chris, I believe you know Cal, Dude and, of course, Pluto." Charles gestured behind him.

"I believe we've met."

If anyone had been watching, they would've thought I was having a costume party. Dude was wearing a tie dyed, long sleeve, multicolored T shirt with a giant glow in the dark peace symbol on the front. Cal had on his ageless Stetson, his rhinestone trimmed coat, and carrying his guitar case, and even Dude's dog Pluto was adorned with a rhinestone covered leash with a white cloth wrapped around his body. Charles was the most muted person on the porch wearing an orange, long sleeve University of Tennessee sweatshirt. All reminders that normal is a foreign concept on my adopted island.

Cal tipped his Stetson. "I couldn't turn down Charles's invite. Always wanted to sing "Monster Mash" at a real Halloween party. Hard to believe, but when I do it at the bar, some people laugh. Can you believe that?"

Yes, but I didn't say it.

Dude and Pluto followed Cal into the house. "Pluto plus me be chillin' when Chucky said there be a party. Here we be."

I put my arm around Charles's shoulder and whispered, "Only two and a pup. I'm shocked."

"Two more will be coming. I invited John and Bri. They're coming later."

"Cal, Dude, Pluto welcome, and make yourselves at home."

Dude lifted Pluto so I could see what appeared on the front of the homemade T shirt around his body. On the front of it was an orange peace symbol. "Know this not be costume party. Pluto and me going to Loggerhead's Dog Costume Contest after boogie from here. Okay he wear here?"

I assured him the no costume rule only applied to people before Cal, Dude, and Pluto made a beeline for the kitchen and Charles said, "I called Burl, but he said you'd already invited him, and that he was bringing Shannon and the kids. That's when I thought of John and Bri. Think it'd be good if they met each other."

"Not sure I follow, but they're more than welcome."

"Bri's interested in Wiccan and the Stones need to meet people who are interested but won't judge," Charles smiled. "Besides, we can't have a Halloween party with just witches. We need to have ghosts or at least ghost hunters."

Everyone appeared to be enjoying each other's company and especially the food. Cal had moved a chair to the side of the room and was singing; Barb was being a much better hostess than I was a host, when a knock at the door got my attention. Burl was on the porch and John and Bri were walking through the yard behind him.

I said, "Come in and join the party."

"Thank you, Brother Chris. Shannon and the kids are on their way. I must've driven faster."

Charles pushed past me, shook Burl's hand, and said, "Preacher, guess that means your car is faster than a broom. Nice to know."

Burl un-preacherlike rolled his eyes.

John and Bri were next to the door. "Chris, hope it's alright that Bri and I came. I tried to tell Charles you might not have wanted the entire population of the county at your house."

"John, Bri, the longer you know Charles, you'll learn it's impossible to convince him of anything. I'm glad he invited you. Come in."

Introductions were made and I went to the kitchen to get drinks for John and Bri. Between Cal's playing and the conversation, I must've missed the knock on the door.

Dude opened the door, took a quick step back, and said, "Chrisster, monster at door!"

I saw Lugh looking around the room like he was wondering which person would be the best choice for dinner. Shannon was standing next to him in an emerald green dress that looked as if it was from another era. Both kids were behind her. I crossed the room to greet the latest arrivals and to save Dude from the monster.

I said, "Welcome, please come in."

Shannon put her hand on my arm and squeezed as she said,

"Thank you for inviting us. We needed to be with, umm, friends and the living."

I smiled and patted her hand. "Today must've been difficult."

Charles magically appeared beside me, bent to put his arms around Lugh's neck. "Lugh, my big baby, Happy Halloween. Want to go out back and stretch your legs? I bet Uncle Charles can find you a snack."

I said, "You have to forgive Charles. People are an afterthought when dogs are around."

Shannon unhooked Lugh's leash and said, "Chris, I understand."

On Charles and Lugh's way out back, Charles invited everyone to join them. The temperature was pleasant, and the house was growing smaller by the minute, so it was a good idea. Everyone followed except the Stones and Burl.

Roisin squeezed past her mom and wrapped her arms around my waist. "Thank you so much, Mr. Chris, I knew you'd find Dad's killer."

"Roisin, I was lucky. If it weren't for your brother and Lugh I wouldn't be here." I glanced at Desmond who smiled. I could be wrong, but it appeared sincere.

Shannon cleared her throat, "Desmond told me all about yesterday. We are grateful to you and Charles for what you have done for us."

Burl walked over and hugged her. "Shannon, how are you? Today must be exceedingly hard on the whole family?"

Roisin moved beside her mother and grabbed Burls hand. "Mr. Burl, it was nice. We spread Dad's ashes in the flower garden. We were going to share them with the ocean but this way he's close to home."

Shannon followed Burl and Roisin to the back yard, leaving me alone in the house with the not so scary Desmond. I asked how he was.

He looked towards the back door and said, "Mom and little sis need me to be strong and help the family."

"You also need them, Desmond. Things will get better as long as the three of you stay close."

"Mr. Landrum, I'm going to take your advice and give people a chance to see who I am."

I put my hand on his shoulder. "If you need anything or just want to talk, you know how to find me."

"Thanks," he said then laughed. "Bet you never thought you'd be friends with a witch."

Dude stuck his head in the door, spotted Desmond and me, and said, "Yo, Sand, join us under the moon."

Desmond said, "On my way."

I looked at the young man and said, "Sand?"

Desmond smiled. "Yeah. First time I met Dude, we were on the beach. He called me Sand Witch."

"Oh," I said articulately.

"It's okay. He's a cool old guy," Desmond patted my arm before heading outside.

He was right. I never thought I'd be friends with a witch or a witch family but there are lots of things I never thought. I headed out to join my ever growing party crowd. Lugh and Pluto were getting to know each other. Dude, Charles, and John, plus the addition of Desmond, supervised the meeting, probably to keep Lugh from devouring Pluto in one bite. Off to the side, Cal was playing his guitar with Burl, Roisin, and Barb listening nearby. Across the yard, Bri was standing by herself and watching the activities.

I made my way across the yard to Shannon and motioned her to follow as I made my way to Bri.

"Bri, I'd like you to meet Shannon Stone. Shannon, this is Bri Rice."

They smiled and shook hands.

Shannon nodded at Bri and said, "I believe you were at my husband's funeral ritual the other day. Am I correct?"

Bri looked as if she wanted to vanish. "Umm, yes. I'm so sorry. I didn't mean to intrude. I was curious."

"Mrs. Rice, it is okay. You were not there to harm but with a true interest. How could I fault you for that?" Shannon's hand went to Bri's shoulder.

"Please call me Bri. Thank you for understanding."

"Bri, call me Shannon, if you have questions, please ask. My kids and I welcome sincere discussions. Chris can vouch for that."

I smiled and said, "Bri, you need to watch Roisin. She's smarter than the rest of us and according to her brother, she's a very old soul."

Shannon said, "You are correct. My little nymph is wise beyond her years." She motioned in the direction of the rest of the party. "I believe it's safe if you leave Bri and me to share a conversation."

I took the hint. When I looked back, the women were sitting on the ground talking like they had known each other for centuries. I made it halfway back to Barb when I saw Cindy standing in the side yard.

"Chief, did someone call in a noise complaint about Cal's singing?"

"An invitation certainly didn't bring me here. Suppose mine was lost in the mail or the owl dropped it."

"Owl?"

"You're not a Harry Potter fan. Anyway, not important."

"I would love it if you and Larry could stop by. This wasn't really a planned thing."

I wondered if it was a crime to not invite the Chief to the party she just crashed.

She smiled. "Messing with you. I finished at the office and wanted to talk to you on my way home. Larry and I always go out to dinner and a costume party in Charleston on Halloween."

"Didn't know you were into that sort of thing."

"You could write a novel on what you don't know about me. I'll leave it at that. The reason I'm here is a preemptive strike on you calling about Dr. Robinson and his wife."

"What's happened?"

"Dr. Robinson has been arrested for selling drugs and involuntary manslaughter with more charges pending further investigation."

"More charges?"

"The investigation just started. I'm not positive about Georgia law, but I've heard of a case where a drug dealer was charged with felony murder when one of his customers died of an overdose. Dr. Robinson is out of my jurisdiction. I only need to help the Sheriff with his case against Erica, the shrill unstable double murderer. That's enough."

"Chief ,thanks for letting me know. Sure you can't stay?"

"Nope, need to get my zombie on and cruise on to Charleston." Cindy turned and headed to her pickup truck.

I watched Cindy go only to hear her yell back, "Hey, old geezer, think you can wait until after Thanksgiving to find another body?"

Charles appeared at my side and said, "Got a question. Before Desmond left yesterday, why'd you ask him if the door to the haunted house was open when he and Lugh saved us?"

"I would've sworn I heard it close before I saw Erika. Must've been mistaken."

Charles slowly nodded. "Or a ghost opened it so Desmond and Lugh could save us."

I waited for him to laugh at his joke. It never came.

"Charles, I'm sticking with being mistaken."

He put his arm around my shoulder. "If you say so."

"Let's head back to the party and be thankful for our new and old friends."

Cal was singing "Monster Mash," country style at the top of his lungs, the atmosphere was becoming more festive, and the horrific experiences of the last month were disappearing just as the sea fog had.

MOSQUITO BEACH

A FOLLY BEACH MYSTERY

Copyright © 2022 by Bill Noel

All rights reserved.

No part of this book may be reproduced in any form or by any electronic or mechanical means, including information storage and retrieval systems, without written permission from the author, except for the use of brief quotations in a book review.

Front cover photo and design by Bill Noel

Author photo by Susan Noel

ISBN: 978-1-942212-58-4

Enigma House Press

Goshen, Kentucky 40026

www.enigmahousepress.com

First Edition

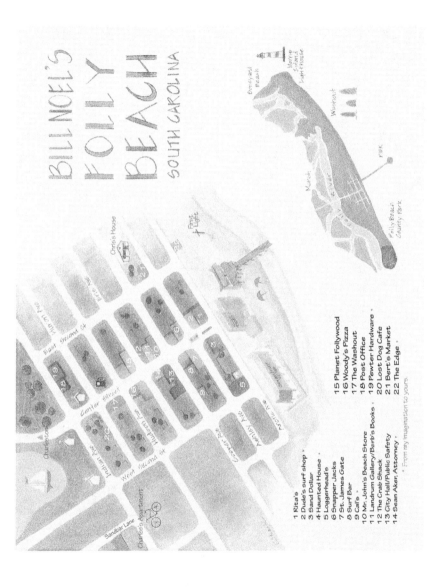

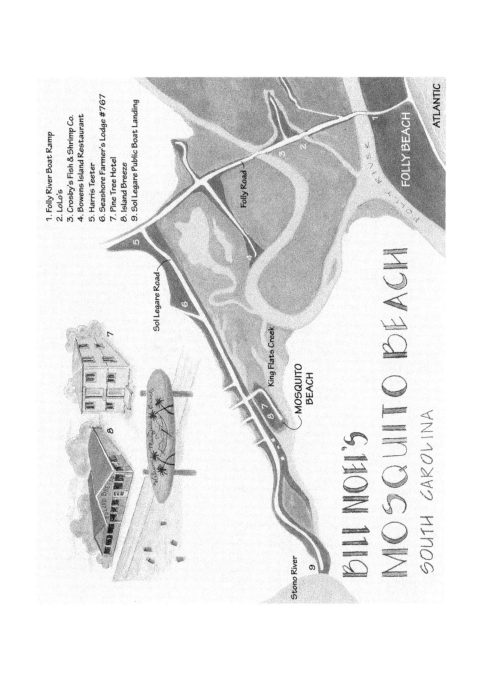

1

"Mr. Chris, this is Al. Did I catch you at a bad time?"

I didn't tell my friend his call interrupted my exciting morning sitting on the screened-in porch watching cars speed by my cottage. What I did was ask if he was okay since during the years I'd known Al Washington, this was the first time he'd called. He also had spent much of his eighty-second year with serious health issues; for a time, it didn't look like he'd survive.

He chuckled. "Sorry to startle you. I'm fine."

I paused giving him time to elaborate but he didn't, so I said, "What do I owe the pleasure of your call?" I thought that was subtler than reminding him he'd never called before.

"Have you heard anything about a body, umm, guess more like a skeleton, found on Mosquito Beach?"

I'd never been to Mosquito Beach but knew it was a quarter-mile strip of land off Sol Legare Road about four miles from my home on Folly Beach, South Carolina.

"No, should I have?"

"Blubber Bob says you know everything bad that happens on Folly. Mosquito Beach is near there, so I figured you might've heard."

Bob Howard, occasionally called Blubber Bob or other unflattering names by Al, is a friend I'd met when I moved to Folly more than a decade ago. He was the realtor who helped me find my retirement home. He recently retired from his successful career and now owns Al's Bar and Gourmet Grill near downtown Charleston, ten miles from Folly. Al's was previously owned by and named after my caller until Bob bought it, most likely preventing Al from dying from worry, stress, fatigue, and a huge debt on the neighborhood bar.

"When do you believe everything Bob tells you?"

"Good point, but I figure he can't always be wrong."

I smiled. Bob and Al had been friends for decades, yet they were as opposite as black and white; appropriate since Al was African American, Bob was as white as an albino polar bear.

"Al, what do you know about the body, the skeleton?"

"Thought I heard something on the news. Wasn't paying attention until the news guy mentioned Mosquito Beach."

"Why'd that get your attention?"

"Spent a lot of time there in the 1950s after I got back from Korea. Mosquito was one of two or three places Negroes, as we were called back then, could go to a beach. The ocean beaches were segregated." He gave an audible sigh. "Had some good times out there, sure did."

There was another long pause which told me there was more to Al's curiosity than he'd shared.

"I don't know much about Mosquito Beach other than seeing a sign for it on Sol Legare Road. What else did they say on the news?"

"Something about a man cutting across a field when he found bones. That's all I got."

"Want me to call Chief LaMond to see what she knows?"

Cindy LaMond was a friend who happened to be Folly Beach's Director of Public Safety, informally known as Chief. Mosquito Beach wasn't in Folly's city limits, but Cindy could use her contacts to learn what was going on.

"Oh, no. Don't bother her. Just thought you might've heard something."

"It's no bother. I'd be glad to ask."

"No need, old man's curiosity, that's all."

"You sure?"

"Yeah. Sorry to bother you. I'm sure you're busy."

"Yes, I'm so, so busy. Retirement's a full-time job, but, Al, I can always find time for you."

He laughed then repeated he was sorry to bother me. I still felt there was something on his mind about the news from Mosquito Beach.

"It's great hearing from you. Let me know if you change your mind. Be sure to say hi to Bob for me."

He laughed again; said he'd rather not incur Bob's wrath by telling him he talked to me. Before ending the call, he suggested I could tell Bob myself the next time I visited Al's.

What I didn't tell him was my next call would be to Chief LaMond.

Cindy answered the phone with, "What are you going to do to ruin my day?"

Since I'd moved to Folly after retiring from a job in the human resources department with a large healthcare company in Kentucky, I'd stumbled on a few horrific situations involving the death of acquaintances. Through luck, being at the right place at the right time, and with the help of a cadre of friends, I'd helped the police bring the murderers to justice. Cindy had more than a few times accused me of being a murder magnet, a pain in her "shapely" posterior, but in weaker moments, a good friend who helped her catch some evil people.

I asked what she knew about a body found on Mosquito Beach.

"Chris Landrum, you're going to be the death of me. Isn't it enough for you to butt in every death my highly competent department led by a more highly-competent Chief investigates, now you stick your nose in things that happened decades ago?"

"Al Washington called to ask if I knew anything about the body. I hadn't heard about it, but knew you, being highly competent, would have more information."

She sighed. "Mr. Suck-Up, why'd Al want to know?"

I explained the little he'd shared then repeated my question about what Cindy knew.

She reminded me Mosquito Beach wasn't in her jurisdiction. All she knew was what was reported in the media.

"I assume it's being investigated by your good buddies in the Charleston County Sheriff's Office. Think you could make a call and see what they have? I don't know why Al is interested, but he'd appreciate learning more."

The Sheriff's Office investigates major crimes in Charleston County which includes Folly and Mosquito Beach.

"Tell you what, I'll cut my afternoon nap short, and because I like Al, I'll call the Sheriff's Office. I'll tell you what I learn; then you'll tell Al. Now pay close attention, you'll not, I repeat, not stick your nose where it don't belong. Deal?"

"I have no plan to get involved."

When I said it, I meant it. Honestly I did.

I hung up from my second call of the day thinking about the Yiddish proverb, "Man plans, God laughs."

2

I spent the next hour on the computer learning about Mosquito Beach. The problem I often have when researching something on the Internet is finding too much information. That wasn't the case when it came to the small, James Island community located on the banks of a tidal creek. I was reminded that Mosquito Beach is the location of Island Breeze, a restaurant that I'd heard about after it'd been damaged by a hurricane that'd swept through the area a few years back. This might be a good chance to learn more about the nearby dining establishment.

Ten minutes later, Barb Deanelli agreed to accompany me to dinner. Three hours later, I picked her up at her oceanfront condo, and we were driving up Folly Road. Barb was three years younger than my sixty-nine years, at five-foot-ten my height, but unlike my slightly overweight body, she was paper thin.

We turned left on Sol Legare Road at the Harris Teeter grocery when Barb, who'd been unusually quiet for the two-mile ride, said, "Don't suppose Mosquito Beach was named after the Mosquito family, and not those pesky, biting troublemakers?"

It wasn't. I smiled. "That'll be a good question to ask at the restaurant."

She glanced over at me, frowned. "That means it was named after the insect most of us try to avoid."

Barb and I had dated a couple of years, so she was familiar with most of my quirky friends plus was game for most adventures. I was surprised by her reluctance to go somewhere named for mosquitos.

I patted her on the knee, smiled, then said, "Remember, you once told me you liked to try new restaurants."

She glanced at a boy riding his bicycle in a front yard, turned back to me and said, "I also would like to go to Paris. Can we do that after recuperating from mosquito bites?"

Another mile up the road, I turned left on Mosquito Beach Road marked by a surfboard with *Welcome to Mosquito Beach* painted on it. It didn't help my case that a mosquito the size of a condor was painted on the sign. A couple hundred yards farther, the pavement took a sharp right turn with the marsh and tidal creek fewer than twenty yards to our left and running parallel to the narrow road. Three small structures looking like they'd survived several hurricanes dotted the right side of the road. Small patches of grass resembled tiny islands in a sea of sand surrounded the structures. So far, the only living creature we'd seen since turning on Mosquito Beach Road was a tabby cat eyeing us with a mixture of fear and curiosity.

The lifeless landscape changed drastically as we came to a brightly painted yellow building. Island Breeze was painted on the front gable in letters large enough to be read from passing airliners. Umbrellas advertising Angry Orchard Hard Cider and Traveler Beer provided partial shade for three wooden, do-it-yourself tables made from cable spool holders. Each table was occupied. Three men leaned against the railing separating the restaurant from the screened-in patio. It was hot for mid-September, so I was surprised to see so many people outside enjoying food and drinks.

I parked across the street on a grass and sand parking area. We shared the parking area with three cars and two pickup trucks that from the dents and layers of dust and dried mud were workhorses used for what trucks were created for. Several vehicles were parked on the far side of the building. We walked across the street to the sounds of Bob Marley blaring from outdoor speakers. Animated conversations from groups seated at the tables mixed with the music. Most of the fifteen or so people appeared to pay little attention to us. A handful glanced at the newcomers. A couple of them smiled, but I didn't recognize anyone. While the Sol Legare area was predominantly African American, several of the casually dressed patrons were white. Four men wore dusty jeans and work boots, most likely having arrived in the pickup trucks.

We went inside and moved to the bar lit by colorful Christmas lights strung along the backbar reflecting in the bourbon, rum, and gin bottles where we were greeted by a woman who told us to sit anywhere. I looked around the crowded room. The walls were painted light blue and the bourbon-barrel tables covered with round pieces of wood were occupied as were the seats in front of the restaurant. We chose bar-height chairs facing the creek at the long, foot-wide wooden table nudging the screened-in porch.

A middle-aged man seated two chairs away noticed me looking around for a menu.

He pointed his beer bottle over his shoulder toward the bar. "Menu's on the chalk board."

I thanked him. Barb and I saw where oxtail headed the menu. I didn't know what that was, so I quickly skipped down the list and decided on barbecue. Barb chose the same.

"They're short on help. Order at the bar," our helpful neighbor offered.

I thanked him again then headed to the bar where the woman who first told us to sit took our order. I waited while she got a beer for Barb, a glass of house wine for me.

Before I could take a sip, the man moved one seat closer to us. "First time here?"

I said, "Yes."

He reached his coal black, thin arm my direction. "I'm Terrell Jefferson." He smiled. He wore black shorts, a black polo shirt with paint stains on the shoulder, a diamond stud earring, and a faded ARMY tattoo on his forearm.

We shook hands as I told him who we were. He said he was pleased to meet us. He glanced at my tan shorts and faded green polo shirt, then at Barb's navy shorts and red T-shirt.

He took a sip of beer, and said, "From around here?"

Barb leaned forward so she could see Terrell past my head. "We live on Folly, if you consider that from around here."

Terrell glanced around, leaned toward us. "Close enough. What brings you to Mosquito Beach?"

I had the feeling Terrell was almost irritated we were here. I shook the feeling off, reminding myself he was the one who initiated the conversation, the one who moved closer to us.

Barb nodded at me to respond.

I said, "Terrell, I've lived on Folly several years. Barb has been there a little over two years. We like visiting different restaurants, so we wanted to try Island Breeze. You from here?"

Terrell said something, but I was having trouble hearing. From the sound system, the Drifters were singing about having fun under the boardwalk. Three men standing near us were having a loud conversation about their boss who apparently was a "jerk." I asked Terrell to repeat what he'd said.

"I live off Sol Legare Road a half mile or so from here but work on Folly. Cook at Rita's. Do y'all work somewhere there?"

Rita's is one of Folly's nicer restaurants. Whenever I'm itching for a hamburger, it's my on-island go-to spot.

Barb turned to face Terrell. "I have a used bookstore on Center Street, my friend here's retired. He spends his time pestering us working folks."

"Barb's Books," Terrell said. "Never been in but have seen it. Got any history books?"

The woman who took our order brought the food in paper baskets then asked if we needed another drink. I told her not yet. She said if we did, we knew where to find her.

I took a bite while Barb said, "I have several. They're not my best sellers, but occasionally have someone looking for them. You a history buff?"

"Hang on," he said and held up his hand, palm facing Barb. "I'll be back."

We watched our new acquaintance head toward the restrooms and Barb took a bite of sandwich.

I said, "Think he'd rather talk to you than me."

Barb grinned. "Who wouldn't?"

"Funny," I said, although it was true.

"Seen any mosquitos yet?" Barb said then smacked me on the arm.

"Funny," I repeated.

Terrell returned carrying another beer. This time he took the chair beside Barb.

She winked at me.

"Started getting into history a few years back after I mustered out of the army. My grandpa got me interested," Terrell said, answering the question Barb asked ten minutes earlier.

Barb smiled, "Any particular history? US, world, ancient?"

"Never gave much thought to any of it until grandpa started telling me stories about the civil rights movement." He took another sip then slowly shook his head. "Grandpa died a year ago. I miss him a bunch."

"Sorry to hear it," I said to reenter the conversation.

"Was ninety-three, led a good life. He lived next to my parents' house, the house I inherited after they passed back before I entered the service." He shook his head. "Enough about me. Did you say if you had books about the 1960s?"

I didn't recall him asking but let Barb answer.

"I'm not sure. Next time you're nearby, stop in. I'll see what I have. Or, if you give me your number, I'll check and call you."

"That's kind of you. I'll stop by."

One of the men who'd been talking about his jerk boss apparently was tired of griping about work. He said, "Heard the body was a Civil War soldier."

His co-worker put his arm around the man's shoulder. "Nah. Wasn't buried that long." The group moved closer to the bar, farther away from us, so I couldn't hear what else they were saying.

I turned to Terrell. "I heard those guys talking about a body. Know what they're talking about?"

Terrell looked at the group, turned to me, and frowned. "A friend of mine stumbled across a body, mostly a skeleton out where the road ends." He pointed toward the far end of Mosquito Beach Road.

"Anyone know who it was?" I asked earning a dirty look from Barb, a shrug from Terrell.

"Depends on who you ask?" he said. "Somebody said it was like from the Civil War. There was a battle near here. A woman said it was a guy who died from some strange disease. People were scared of catching it, so they buried him the day he died." He paused and rubbed his chin. "One old-timer swears he remembers stories a few years back where some white guy was trying to rob a man staying in an old hotel that was here." He nodded to his left. "That's what the boarded-up building next door used to be, was named the Pine Tree Hotel, if memory serves me correct. The hotel guest shot the man as he came through the door. He was afraid the cops would arrest him if they found out, so he buried it. The old-timer said the body was buried out where the skeleton was found. I don't put much faith in that one. The old guy is known for making stuff up." He took another sip of beer then shrugged.

I said, "What do you think?"

"Hell if I know. Tell you what, though, I'd be interested in finding out."

3

I called Al's Bar and Gourmet Grill a little before noon the next morning. The phone rang several times, so I was ready to hang up when Al answered, or I assumed it was Al. He was gasping for breath to where I had a tough time understanding what he was saying.

"Al, this is Chris. You okay?"

"Oh, hi. I'm a little out of breath. Been sweeping the sidewalk."

Even though Bob Howard owned Al's, the former owner volunteered to come in whenever his health was up to it to act like a Walmart greeter. He knew most of the patrons, had known them for years, so he could serve as a bridge between the customers and Bob, whose personality fell short on the customer service skills range. Truth be known, an alligator has more customer service skills than Bob.

"I don't know much more than I did the last time we talked. Barb and I went over to Mosquito Beach last night to eat at Island Breeze. We talked—"

"Mr. Chris, please allow me to interrupt. I hear Bob in back arguing with a supplier about the price of beef. I need to get between them before he takes hamburgers off the menu. Could you call back this afternoon?"

"Sure. Good luck playing referee."

"Don't worry, I'm getting good at it. That's a skill Bob's given me a lot of practice with. Yes, he has."

It was good Al had to go. No sooner had I set the phone on the kitchen table, Cindy called.

"This is your faithful, conscientious, I might add charming, police chief calling to let you know the latest about the skeleton that'd been hanging out on or under Mosquito Beach."

"Thanks for calling back."

"Gee, fine nosy citizen, no need to thank me. I wake up each morning thinking about what I can do to meet your countless demands."

"Thanks anyway. What'd you learn?"

"Not much. The body was found by someone named Clarence Taylor, a lifelong resident of the area. He was minding his business, walking across an area between his house and a restaurant on Mosquito Beach. Let's see." I heard papers rustling in the background. "Here it is, Island Breeze."

It wasn't the time to tell her I ate there last night.

"Anything else?"

"Give me a break. You're getting as impatient as your vagrant buddy Charles. I'm having trouble reading my hen scratches. Okay, got it. The coroner hasn't had time to do a full autopsy, but is certain the person is male, most likely African American. While he can't tell how long it'd been there, the clothing fragments appear to be 1950s vintage."

"Cause of death?"

"If I knew that, don't you think I would've told you before I told you about his taste in sartorial splendor?"

"I assume that means cause of death hasn't been determined?"

"Can't slip anything by you."

Time to fawn. "Cindy, you're wonderful. I appreciate everything you've shared. You're a good friend."

She sighed. "Are you standing in a pile of crap?"

Okay, sucking-up doesn't always work on Folly's Director of Public Safety.

"I'll stick with thanks."

"Better. Now, remind me again how you're going to stay out of whatever's going on."

"Of course, I am."

She hung up laughing.

Showers were passing through the area, so I decided to stay in, fix a peanut butter sandwich, and flip through photo magazines I'd accumulated to kill time until Al's lunch hour was over before calling.

He sounded better than last time as he thanked me for calling back. He reported he'd averted another world war, that Bob and the meat salesman were still among the living. I started to tell him about the visit to Island Breeze.

"Let me interrupt again. Could I ask a huge favor?"

"Of course."

"I've been thinking a lot about the time I spent on Mosquito. Can't get it out of my head. I haven't been there for I don't know how many years. I've wanted to drive over to see how it's changed, but doc says I shouldn't be doing much driving. Would it be too much trouble for you to take me out there? I know it's a lot to ask."

"I'd be glad to. When do you want to go?"

"How about in the morning? Tomorrow's a slow day around here. I figure Bob could probably handle everything without starting a race riot."

"Want me to pick you up there?"

"Umm, be better if you get me at the house."

* * *

I'D NEVER BEEN to Al's house, neither had my vehicle's navigation system, yet it had no difficulty directing me around the sprawling Medical University of South Carolina to Cannon Street then to his address. It was fewer than five blocks from his former bar.

The faded-green, two-story, wood structure looked as tired as did its owner. Shutters on the front windows were missing slats, several roof shingles were broken. All the windows were open. Al's gold, twenty-year-old Oldsmobile was parked in the driveway that was no more than dead weeds and ruts compressed by years of tire wear. The car was covered with a layer of dust and looked like it'd hadn't moved in weeks.

The gate on the front, waist-high iron fence squeaked so loud it rousted a black Rottweiler that'd been sleeping on the porch next door. The dog let out a series of high-pitched barks as it charged to the corner of Al's fenced-in front yard. It was making so much racket I figured I wouldn't have to knock to announce my arrival.

I was right. I walked up the three steps to the front door when Al appeared.

His serious health problems over the last year had taken a toll. His short, gray hair was lighter than the last time I'd seen him. It contrasted drastically with his dark-brown skin.

He leaned on the door frame and smiled. "Morning, Chris. I see you've met Spoiled Rotten."

I glanced at the barking dog. "Spoiled Rotten?"

Al smiled. "Ain't his real name. Gertrude named him some fancy German name I can't pronounce. He's just a baby with a big mouth. She spoils him like he's her only child. That's why I call him Spoiled Rotten. Wouldn't hurt a bug."

"What about hurting a man visiting his next-door neighbor?"

Al laughed. "Well, he hasn't eaten any visitors yet."

I wondered how many visitors Al has. I asked if he was ready to go.

"Come in while I change shirts."

I stepped in the entry and was surprised to see a neatly-made single bed in what would normally be the living room. An aluminum clothes rack was in the corner with several shirts hanging on it. The room was sweltering. Despite the windows being open, it had the musty, medicinal smell that reminded me of nursing homes.

Al saw me looking at the bed. "Bedrooms are upstairs, but doc told me with my arthritis and weak ticker I shouldn't be climbing stairs more than I have to, besides, it's cooler down here. Bob rounded up a couple of my, umm, his customers to haul the bed downstairs." He chuckled. "Bob bitched the entire time although the biggest thing he moved was that lamp." He pointed to a brass lamp on a small table on the other side of the bed. "It ain't the look you'd find in one of those fancy homes magazines, but it meets my needs. Getting old's a pain, yes, it is."

He changed shirts and turned off a portable radio that'd been playing jazz. "I'm ready."

On the painfully slow walk to the car, Al veered to the neighbor's fence to pet Spoiled Rotten. The Rottweiler had stopped barking and leaned against the fence so Al could reach it without bending.

After saying *adieus* to Spoiled Rotten, Al joined me in the car, smiled, then said he was ready to head to the beach. It took him a few blocks before his breathing returned to normal. The weather typically began to cool by mid-September, but today was an exception. Upper eighties with bright sun were in the forecast so I was worried about Al walking around Mosquito Beach. I also knew it was best for me to keep my concerns to myself to maintain his self-esteem. I hoped it wouldn't be a mistake.

4

Al rubbed his hand along the dashboard. "Can't tell you the last time I was in a Cadillac. Smaller than they used to be."

"It's the ATS, smallest car Cadillac makes."

"Nice, but I can remember back when they were the size of a houseboat, had those fancy tail fins. Yes, they were." He stared out the windshield. "The heyday for cars, if you ask me."

We were on Folly Road a couple of miles from the turnoff on Sol Legare Road. All Al had said since leaving his house were comments about cars. I couldn't tell if he was feeling bad or in a quiet mood, something unusual for my talkative friend.

About a mile up Sol Legare Road, Al tapped the passenger side window. "Wow."

"What?"

"Last time I saw the old Seashore Farmers' Lodge it was propped up by long pieces of wood, looked like it was ready to fall over. Hurricane Hugo nearly did it in. Glad to see someone trying to bring it back to its glory days. Looks good, don't it?"

I vaguely remember news stories from shortly after I moved to Folly. A group of locals helped by a reality TV show renovated the building, but that was all I knew about it.

"What's its story?"

He waved his arm around. "In the late 1800s, this whole area was populated by people looking like me. Mostly freed slaves. Now if you were Bob, you'd make some crack about my age. You'd say I knew because I was around back then. Thank the Lord, you're not Bob. Anyway, it was a close community. Everyone supported everyone. The Seashore Farmers' Lodge was started in the early 1900s." He smiled. "No, I still wasn't born then. White folks wouldn't sell us insurance in those days, so the locals formed the group that was sort of an insurance policy for its members. If something bad happened, house burned down, child got sick or died, someone got hurt while working on a shrimp boat, or if someone needed help with crops, everyone came together to support the family that was down."

Al became more animated the more he talked until I turned on Mosquito Beach Road. He shook his head when he noticed waist-high weeds along the side of the road. "Used to be nicer."

I drove to the end of the road so he could see what remained. Once again, he shook his head, but didn't say anything.

I pulled in the grass parking area where I parked when Barb and I were here. A man was sitting on a large slab of broken concrete at the edge of the creek. He looked to be in his seventies and wore denim bib overalls, a long-sleeve shirt despite the temperature hovering in the upper eighties.

"If you're planning on eating, you're out of luck," he said without taking his eyes off the water slowly flowing in front of him. "Don't open until three."

Al moved closer to the stranger, and said, "Thanks, my friend. We're not here to eat. Just lookin' around."

The man finally glanced over his shoulder at Al. "Not much to see."

Al laughed. "Looks that way, don't it?" He was less than a foot from the seated stranger. "I'm Al Washington."

The man stood, brushed dirt off the seat of his pants. He was at least six-foot-three and looked like he'd been a boxer in his younger days. Much of his muscle had turned to fat.

He reached to shake Al's hand. "I'm Clarence Taylor. Al, who's your chauffeur?" He pointed at me then chuckled.

I'd heard his name before but couldn't recall when or why. I stepped closer and held out my hand. "I'm Chris Landrum."

"We're good friends," Al added.

"Pleased to meet you," he said as he shook my hand with a firm grip. "From around here?"

"I live in Charleston," Al said. "Chris hangs his hat over on Folly."

Clarence nodded like that explained everything. "Why'd you choose this little corner of heaven to be looking around?"

Al could field that one.

"After I got out of the army in the early '50s, I spent a lot of weekends here. Think I was only back twice since those days. Wanted to see what it looks like."

Clarence shuffled his foot in the sandy soil. "Korea?"

"Yes, sir," Al said. "Were you there?"

"Born too late for that one," he said as he continued shuffling his foot in the soil. "Got to do my international traveling in Viet Nam." Clarence nodded, again using one of his two body movements. "Don't know about you, but I've had all the sun this old body can take. Want to join me over there in the shade?" He added a third movement when he pointed to a red picnic table beside the closed restaurant.

Al glanced at me. I gave a slight nod. He told Clarence, "Don't mind if we do."

Clarence laughed. "Then you're a heap smarter than most folks from Charleston. From my experience, they don't have enough sense to get in out of the rain or out from under the blazing sun."

Interesting, I thought since it was coming from the man wearing a long-sleeve shirt who'd been sitting in the blazing sun. Regardless, it was a wise decision to move to the shade. I let Al and Clarence take their seats before I sat beside Al.

"You live out this way?" Al said.

Clarence pointed toward the far end of the road. "Live a hop, skip, and jon boat ride that direction. Got an old house on Sol Legare Road. Got it from pop, who got it from my grandparents. I'm the only one left in these parts. Got a sister up north, somewhere in Ohio. Got herself to uppity to come back. Don't rightly know why. All she did was marry a man who owns an underwear making company. Don't reckon that'd put her up there with the Queen of Sheba. I retired from the post office, been a bum ever since." He hesitated then said, "Al, you remember the old pavilion that was out there?"

Clarence made the abrupt transition without any body movements. I waited for Al to respond.

"Spent many Saturday nights at that pavilion. Think it was the main reason I came here. I recall several fine-looking ladies I had the pleasure of dancing with."

Clarence shook his head as he nodded toward the creek in front of us. "All that's left is them wood pilings holding up nothing."

Al and Clarence were silent, I assumed their minds were drifting back to the 1950s and dances at the pavilion.

Clarence broke the silence. "You hear about the skeleton found the other day out at the end of the road?"

That jerked Al back from the past. He shifted on the bench to face Clarence. "Sure did."

Clarence tapped his hand on the table. "I found it."

That explained why his name sounded familiar. Cindy had shared it with me.

"Had to be frightening," I said.

He sighed. "Chris, I've walked from my house, climbed in my jon boat, paddled over here, walked the rest of the way to the bars and restaurants going on fifty years. That was the first damn time I'd ever found a body. Hope it's the last. I'm not too proud to say it scared the, umm, scared me a lot."

"Clarence," I said, "you've walked from your house to here for a long time. Did you do something different that day?"

"Different. I'd say. Found a body. Ain't that different enough?"

I smiled. "True. What I meant was did you take a different path?"

He rubbed his chin. "The last hurricane did a number on the land near the water. Everything got shuffled around. Water now hangs out where it didn't before the big wind blowed through. Mushy soil makes it impossible to walk through it without stilts." He nodded. "I get your point. Yeah, I've had to change my way here since then."

"On the day you found the bones, did you walk a different path than before?"

"Now that you mention it, I suppose so. We had a big-ass rain the night before. I couldn't walk the same way I normally do."

That could explain why he stumbled on the body. Heavy rain may've uncovered some of the dirt or muck that'd covered it.

Al leaned closer to Clarence. "Any idea who he was?"

"No, but I'd say he wasn't new to the sandy dirt. He wasn't skin and bones, like they call skinny folk. He was all bones."

"Could you tell if he was black or white?" Al said.

Clarence smiled. "The bones were white, but so are mine. I haven't seen them mind you, but that's what they say. There wasn't any skin left that I saw, so I couldn't tell what color it would've been. Suppose the medical folks in Charleston will figure that out."

Al nodded. "Any idea how long it'd been there?"

"Al, my friend, from years working at the post office, I could tell you exactly how long it'd take a letter to get from downtown Charleston to Mt. Pleasant or to London, the one in England. Telling how long those bones were planted out there is outside my area of knowledge. I suspect those same folks who'll tell what color he was will answer that question." He looked down at the table and then at Al. "Bad thing about it, at least, from my way of thinking, is someone from over here might've been the one who put the poor man in the ground. I hate to think it may be someone I know, or someone who's related to someone out here."

Al rubbed his chin. "That's a bad thought, isn't it? Hope it's not true."

"Tell you one thing. It's bothering me enough to want to learn what happened."

I said, "How?"

"Don't rightly know, to tell the truth. It won't stop me asking around, especially talking to the folks who've been here forever." He wiped the sweat from his forehead, smiled at us, and said, "Now I don't know about you fellas, but all this talk about bones is giving me the heebie-jeebies. How about talking about something pleasant?"

Al must not have wanted to make his new friend uncomfortable, so he asked about the food at Island Breeze, if there was good fishing in the tidal creek, and when the other businesses that'd been here closed. The conversation slowly came to an end. Clarence said it was good meeting us. If we ever wanted to share a meal with him, he'd meet us and introduce us to the owner of the restaurant. Al thanked him for the offer. Clarence said he'd better get home in time for his afternoon nap. Al said it sounded good, he might do the same. Al's chauffeur agreed.

5

Cindy often referred to Charles Fowler as my vagrant buddy. Through an apparent glitch in the world of logic, I call him my best friend, and he has been since I arrived on Folly. Charles moved to Folly from Detroit at age thirty-four. For the last thirty-three years, he hasn't been burdened with being on anyone's payroll. During the same period, I'd spent most of my adult life working in Kentucky. He occasionally picks up cash helping restaurants clean during busy season or delivers packages for our friend Dude Sloan's surf shop. Charles lives in a tiny apartment, remains single, and walks or rides his bike most everywhere, so his financial needs are minimal.

It'd been a few days since I'd seen my friend, so I called to ask if he wanted to meet for breakfast. He said he thought he could work it into his schedule, so we agreed to meet in the morning at the Lost Dog Cafe. I anticipated a few rough moments at breakfast, since one of his quirks—his many quirks—was giving me grief if I learned something and failed to share it with him within, oh, let's say, the blink of an eye. I wasn't certain if he'd heard about the bones, but I knew he didn't know about my visits to Mosquito Beach.

I decided to walk six blocks to the restaurant, located less than a block off Center Street, Folly's hub of commerce. The Dog was in a former laundromat, but from its colorful porches, attractive entry, and hungry customers waiting outside to be seated, you'd never guess its former life. I'd told Charles eight o'clock, so I arrived before seven-thirty, knowing he subtracts thirty minutes from whatever time we're meeting. Yes, another quirk.

I walked past three couples waiting for a table to be greeted by Amber Lewis. She'd turned fifty, looked younger, was five-foot-five, with long auburn hair pulled in a ponytail. She was my favorite server at the Dog and had worked there since before I moved to Folly. In fact, she was the first person I'd met when I arrived on the six-mile-long, half-mile-wide island. We'd dated for a while then after we decided to go separate romantic ways had remained good friends.

She gave me a high-wattage smile, glanced toward the waiting customers, then motioned me to follow. She took me to a table near the back wall where I waited while she cleared dirty plates and glasses.

"Here's a vacant table. Want it or would you prefer waiting outside until the masses ahead of you are seated."

I chose the perk Amber had reserved for her favorite people then she said she'd get me coffee. I told her Charles would be joining me. She smiled as she asked if I wanted her to tell him he'd have to wait until everyone else was seated.

"Not today."

I looked around the packed restaurant. Two city council members, Marc Salmon and Houston Bass, were in deep discussion in the center of the room. They spent most mornings at the Dog, allegedly discussing city business. Mostly they were collecting or spreading gossip about everyone and everything. I gave a slight wave to Marc who responded with a similar gesture.

I was going to walk over to say hi, when Charles entered, looked around, before heading my way. He was a couple inches shorter than I and twenty pounds lighter. He wore a long-sleeve, navy T-shirt with Penn State on the front and Nittany Lions down the sleeve, yellow shorts, a canvas Tilley hat, and was swinging his ever-present hand-made cane around like he didn't have a care in the world. He's one of the few people I know where that may be true.

He looked at his bare wrist where normal people wore a watch. Normal had never been used to describe Charles.

"Good to see you're on time," he said, then removed his Tilley, put it on the seat beside him, then propped his cane against the chair.

"Good morning."

Amber returned with my coffee plus a cup for Charles although he hadn't told her he wanted it. She had to get food for a couple seated across from us and said she'd be back.

Charles watched her go, then turned to me. "So, what did I do to deserve a breakfast invite?"

I took a sip of coffee, smiled, and said, "Nothing. It'd been a few days since we talked, so I thought we could get together."

"Hmm, if you say so."

Now, to get the thorny stuff out of the way. I told him about Al's call and our trip to Mosquito Beach. I also told him about taking Barb to eat at Island Breeze. Veins in his neck popped, his grip tightened around the mug.

Before he lambasted me for not telling him immediately after it happened, Amber returned to ask if we were ready to order. I silently thanked her, then said, "Yes, French toast."

Amber rolled her eyes. She'd been trying to no avail to get me to eat healthier. Charles said he'd have the same thing. That was a surprise since he normally chose bacon, eggs, and toast.

Amber said, "You sure?"

Charles nodded, then she went to place our orders.

I tilted my head and stared at Charles. "French toast?"

"I can't order something different?" He clunked his mug on the table. "Ronald Reagan said, 'Status quo, you know, is Latin for *the mess we're in*.'"

Add quoting US presidents to Charles's quirk pile.

"Of course, you can. It surprised me, that's all."

He took a sip and looked in his half-empty mug. Without looking up, he said, "It threw me for a loop you didn't think I was a good enough friend that you could let me know about your trip to Mosquito Beach. Oh wait, your two trips."

"You're the best friend I could ever have. Barb and I went out to eat. That happens all the time. Do I tell you about each of them? Of course not. Al and I went yesterday, now I'm telling you about it."

Charles looked up from his mug. "If that's an apology, you need to work on your delivery."

I thought it was more of an explanation, but if Charles thought it was an apology, regardless how poorly done, I'd let him take the victory. I repeated in greater detail about my trips to Mosquito.

Our dueling French toast orders arrived, and Amber refilled our coffee. She asked if we needed anything.

Charles pointed at me. "Ms. Amber, you could teach my alleged friend here how to apologize."

She patted him on the arm. "Charles, I don't do anything wrong, so I never have to apologize. You need to find another teacher. Get someone who's sorry a lot." She snapped her fingers. "Got it. Why don't you teach him?" She chuckled then rushed to a table across the room.

I shrugged then saw Chief LaMond enter. She was in her early fifties, five-foot-three, well built, with dark, curly hair, and a quick smile. She headed our way.

"Morning, thorns in my side. Either of you buying me coffee?"

"Chris is," offered my generous friend.

I motioned her to join us, and Amber set a mug of steaming coffee in front of the Chief before she was settled in the chair. Being Chief has perks.

"Cindy," I said as she took a sip, "learn more about the body?"

She glared at me. "Yep, he's dead."

Charles leaned closer to the Chief. "Learn that from the coroner?"

"I figured it out all by my lonesome. The coroner said it weighed twenty-seven pounds. Hell, my left arm weighs that much, so I figured he was dead."

Charles looked at Cindy's arm. "With or without your watch?"

"What else have you learned?" I asked before the conversation sank deeper in a pile of absurdity.

Cindy moved her arm away from Charles then turned to me. "As suspected, it was a male, African American, probably in his late teens, early twenties."

I said, "Best guess on when he died?"

"The coroner is consulting with a forensic anthropologist who'll run tests this old gal from East Tennessee is clueless about. With luck and some scientific gobbledygook, they may be able to get close to when the person died. The guesses I've heard range from a year to a hundred thousand years ago. I'm no expert, but I'd guess closer to a year than ancient times, unless cave dwellers wore black and white wingtip shoes. Mr. Skeleton dressed well."

"Glad you narrowed it down," Charles said.

Cindy took another sip and pointed her forefinger at Charles. "I know in your fantasy world, you think you're a private detective. Crap on a cucumber, in my fantasy world, I'm Charlize Theron. The point is you ain't a detective. I ain't a movie star. Wait, that was only half of my point, the rest is you and your accomplice sitting across the table need to keep your noses out of police business. Think you can do that?"

Charles gave a stage nod. "Of course we can."

What he didn't say was that we would. Cindy knew not to push.

She glanced at her watch, weight unknown, then said, "Time to go pester my officers who I'm sure are sitting around the office, drinking coffee, telling dirty jokes. My chiefly duties never get a rest."

I thanked her for letting us know what she'd learned about the skeleton.

She had Amber put her coffee in a to-go cup, headed to the exit, stopped, and returned to the table. "Oh, one other thing about the skeleton. He had a hole in his head, a hole the coroner thinks was made by a bullet." She pivoted, waved bye to us over her shoulder, and was gone.

6

I still had the nagging feeling Al knew something about Mosquito Beach he wasn't sharing. Not only something, but something that was bothering him. Late the next morning, I had space in my stomach for one of Al's famous cheeseburgers, and for the previous owner to have another chance to share his concern.

I pulled in a vacant parking space a block off Calhoun Street and directly behind Bob Howard's dark plum PT Cruiser convertible, the un-realtor-like vehicle he'd driven since I've known him. I was a half block from Al's Bar and Gourmet Grill housed in a concrete block building. The building blended with the tired looking neighborhood of wood frame houses, plus a couple of low rent businesses. At some point in ancient history, the building had been painted white. That would be the last word to describe its color today.

I opened the door then waited for my eyes to adjust to the dark interior illuminated by neon Budweiser signs behind the bar. The sounds of Freddy Fender in his Tex-Mex country voice singing about "Wasted Days and Wasted Nights" along with the smell of frying burgers saturated the air. Motown classics and traditional country hits filled the jukebox. Bob was a huge country music fan, much to the chagrin of Al's predominantly African American customers. That was only one of the several clashing points between the customers and the bar's new owner, and the real reason Al was stationed in a chair by the front door.

"Well, Lordy," Al said as I blinked to adjust to the dark. "Look who's here."

He slowly pushed himself out of the chair to hug me. He looked as well-worn as the dilapidated furniture that populated the room. What didn't fill the room was diners. It was past the traditional lunch hour and three men were seated by the plate glass window painted black to block the interior from the street. They appeared to be finishing sandwiches. Lawrence, Al's cook, was facing the grill; the current owner, Bob Howard, was seated at his table near the back of the building.

I told Al I was glad to see him, that I woke this morning with a sudden urge for one of his cheeseburgers.

He started to say something but was interrupted by Bob's bellowing voice, "Old man, stop gabbing with the damn paying customer. Let him park his scrawny butt and order."

Calling my ample posterior scrawny should tell you something about Bob. If it didn't, let me say the seventy-eight-year-old bar owner is six feet tall carrying the weight of someone a foot taller. I don't recall often seeing him with less than a four-day-old scruffy beard or wearing shorts and Hawaiian flowery shirts, regardless of the weather.

I said to Al, "Guess I'd better get back to see my good friend before he runs off all the customers."

He looked at the three men at the table by the window. "Don't worry, they've learned to ignore the profane bundle of lard holding court back there."

"Good. Why don't you join us when you get a chance?"

Al laughed. "I will if there's a lull in the lunch rush."

I'm sure Bob would've stood to greet me if he hadn't been tightly wedged between his seat pushed up against the back wall and the table. Of course, that was only my wishful thinking.

"Good afternoon, Bob."

"What's so damned good about it? See those tightwads sitting over there?" He pointed to the three customers.

I nodded.

"That's today's lunch crowd. Sorry, I'm off by one. Some damned street person hobbled in saying he was starving. Can you believe he wanted me to give him a burger?"

"Did you?"

Bob mumbled, "Yes. If you tell anyone, I'll swear you're a psychopathic, mentally deficient bowl of Jell-O." His hand jerked up in the air. "Lawrence, damn it, don't you see this anorexic white guy needs food. Stop discriminating. Get your golden-brown face out here and take his order."

The three customers turned to Bob while simultaneously shaking their heads.

Bob glared at them. "Lawrence, while you're on your way, take those troublemakers another beer. On me." He turned back to me. "Now, where were we? Oh yeah, you were interrupting meditation hour."

Lawrence dropped off the beers at the other table, then asked what I wanted to order. Al's cheeseburgers were, in the view of Bob, "The best damned cheeseburger in the world," so how could I resist.

"Cheeseburger," I said.

Lawrence nodded. "Good choice."

"Only damn choice," Bob said. "And don't forget to fix him fries. Need to fatten him up, get some extra cash out of him."

"Another good choice, Master Bob," Lawrence said through a smile.

It was good seeing Lawrence adjusting to Bob's charming exterior.

"Smart ass," Bob said. "And bring him a glass of that cheap, fruity, white wine you hide in the refrigerator behind that green stuff you put on the cheeseburgers."

"Lettuce," Lawrence said as he rushed away before Bob could hurl more insults his way.

Bob watched him go and said, "Great guy. I'm lucky to have him."

"I can tell," I said, interjecting an order of sarcasm.

"Smart ass."

I'm sure Bob was still referring to Lawrence. Time to change the subject. "How's Al?"

Bob looked at Al seated by the door. "Glad you asked. He was doing much better with his ailing heart, his severe arthritis until some damned whippersnapper kidnapped him, dragged him out to some isolated strip of land by a creek, made him walk more than he has in the last seven years combined, then made him sit outside with the temperature pushing three-hundred degrees. Nearly did him in."

"I don't think it was that bad. Besides—"

Bob waved his meaty hand in my face. "Hold your defensive excuses. Let me finish. He's still alive, hasn't stopped talking about how much he appreciated you taking him. He said it was the highlight of the year. I thought seeing me every day would've held that honor, but I pretended like I agreed with him."

"He had an enjoyable time."

"After you nearly killed him."

Bob was back to being Bob. I started to ask more about Al's health, when I heard Willie Nelson singing his version of "Crazy" and Al scooting a chair up to the table.

"Couldn't you find anyone else to drag in off the street to spend money to keep this dump afloat?" Bob said as Al lowered himself in the chair.

Al leaned my direction and patted me on the arm. "Thought Mr. Chris needed saving from your griping."

Marvin Gaye joined in the discussion by belting out "I Heard it Through the Grapevine."

"Crap, not that again," Bob said as he put his hands over his ears in case we didn't know what he was talking about. "What happened to the good music?"

Good music equals country music, with no room for variations according to the restaurant's owner who never failed to let everyone know.

Al smiled at the three men at the other table tapping their beer bottles on the table in time to the music.

"See" Bob said and shook his head. "Your music is about to start a riot."

Al and Bob had been good friends for years, would do anything for each other.

Al ignored him, one of his techniques for keeping the friendship alive, then turned to me. "You recall that man's name we talked to at Mosquito? Been trying to remember it all morning."

"Clarence Taylor."

Al smiled. "Yeah, that's it. Bob, Clarence is the guy who found the skeleton."

On the jukebox, Johnny Horton replaced Marvin with his version of "North to Alaska." The three men at the other table joined in with a chorus of boos. Bob glared at them. They pointed their bottles at him and laughed.

Bob's glare turned to a smile. He kept looking at his customers but said to me, "See how happy my music makes customers?"

Al said, "They don't call Bob *the great peacemaker* for nothing."

"Who calls me that?"

"Nobody," Al said. "It was a joke."

A good one, I thought.

"Ha ha," Bob said. "So why does that damned place named after god-awful mosquitos mean so much to you?"

The music war was placed on hold, at least for now.

Al said, "You really want to know?"

"Crap, Al, your trip out there is about all you've been talking about. Figure anything you talk about more than telling me how great I am, must mean something powerful."

Lawrence delivered my order, Bob told him he'd better bring him another beer, saying he'd need it to put up with Al. Lawrence left without comment.

Al said, "In 1950, Communist North Korea invaded South Korea. The US of A was back at war. I'd just turned sixteen but lied about my age, said I was older so I could join up. They needed all the able-bodied men they could get so they weren't checking ages too close. I looked older than I was. Servin' my country was important to me. I was in three years—three danged rough years."

"Came back a hero," Bob added. "Modest Al don't like talking about it, but he saved seven soldiers while he was over there."

Bob had previously shared that point of pride with me.

"Anyway," Al said and probably blushed but both he and the room were so dark I couldn't tell. "When I got back to the states in '53, I couldn't find a decent job in Charleston."

Bob interrupted. "Blacks were good enough to die for our country, but not good enough to eat in most restaurants or get good jobs. Damned segregation."

"Bob," Al said, "you forget who's telling this story?"

I smiled as Bob motioned for his friend to continue.

"I took a job downtown as a porter at the Francis Marion Hotel. I was lucky to get it. It was long hours, hard work, but it was work."

"What's that have to do with Mosquito Beach, old man?"

The phrase *the great peacemaker* popped into my head.

"I worked six days a week, so when I got time off, I wanted to get as far from town as I could. Mosquito Beach was a thriving black community in those days. Several bars, dance clubs, the pavilion were places to be. Yes, they were. Boy did I have a fine time." He closed his eyes, smiled, as he slowly nodded.

Bob remained silent, choosing wisdom rather than his normal MO. Ray Charles was singing "Hit the Road, Jack." The other customers began singing along. Bob didn't fake displeasure with the music, and I continued eating my cheeseburger.

Al's smile faded. "Can't help but wonder what happened."

One of the other customers raised his hand. Bob yelled for Lawrence to get the men their check. Al twisted around to make sure the men were being taken care of. His nostalgic mood was broken.

"Al, what were you wondering about? What happened?"

"Nothing, really," he said, as a couple entered. "Better get back to my post to greet those folks. Good seeing you again, Chris."

He grimaced as he pushed himself out of the chair then slowly moved toward the entrance.

Now, I had no doubt that there was something about Mosquito Beach that Al wasn't sharing.

7

I called Chief LaMond the next morning to see if she'd learned anything new about the skeleton's identity. After putting up with a litany of insults about pestering her before she'd finished her third cup of coffee, and before she'd finished yelling at two of her officers for ticketing a council member's wife's new convertible, she shared that the County Sheriff's Office seemed as interested in investigating the death as they were about learning the whereabouts of Jimmy Hoffa. In other words, it was a cold case. She hung up before I could thank her for the enlightening information.

I was one cup of coffee behind Cindy, so I refilled my cup then moved to the screened-in porch to watch the steady stream of vehicles pass my cottage carrying sad-faced, sleepy drivers on their way to work. Since retiring, watching people heading to work was one of my guilty pleasures.

The phone rang, and Charles said, "I'll pick you up this afternoon at five."

"Where're we going?" I asked, rather than saying something normal like, "Good morning. How are you today?"

"To eat, duh," he said, like who wouldn't have known.

He said he'd pick me up at five, so he'd be here at four thirty. I was ten minutes off. He pulled in my drive at four twenty to be greeted with, "Sorry, I'm almost late. Got talking with my neighbor about the weather. Couldn't get away."

"I was beginning to worry," I said with an overabundance of sarcasm. "Care to share where we're going?"

"Nope."

Five minutes later, the mysterious destination became clearer when Charles turned on Sol Legare Road.

It was Friday and the parking areas around Island Breeze were packed. Charles drove a hundred yards past the restaurant before finding a vacant spot. The temperature was cooler than during my other visits and twenty or so diners were crowded around tables in front of the building. The inside was equally crowded, I was beginning to wonder how long we'd have to wait.

My wonder ended quickly when someone tapped me on the shoulder. Terrell Jefferson was behind me dressed in all black, the same as he'd been when Barb and I met him. He had a smile on his face.

"Hi, Terrell," I said.

"You remembered. I'm impressed."

I didn't know how to respond so I introduced Charles.

"Where's the lovely lady you were with the last time?"

"He's going for brains tonight rather than beauty," Charles said even though Terrell had asked me.

Terrell, like many people who first meet Charles, didn't know how to respond, so he turned to me. "There's a long wait. I've got a table out back, want to join me?"

"That'd be great," Charles said, answering for both of us.

We weaved our way through the crowd to the back door that opened to a large area with several tables. All were occupied. We followed Terrell to a table near the back of the lot. There were three empty seats, a fourth was occupied by a heavyset man with a white curly beard. He was reading a paperback Walter Mosley novel through thick, black-rimmed glasses. Terrell motioned for us to take two of the empty seats.

"Jamal," Terrell said, "This is Chris and, umm, sorry, I didn't catch your name."

Charles said to the man who looked like a black Santa in his late-seventies or early-eighties, "I'm Charles."

"Jamal Kingsly. Pleased, I'm sure," said the reader. His eyes never left the book.

"Pay no attention to Jamal," Terrell said. "He'd rather read than eat."

Jamal looked over the top of the book at Terrell. "Food for the mind."

"I'm a big reader," Charles said.

"He's got nearly as many books as the Folly Beach Branch of the Charleston Library," I added.

That struck a chord with Jamal. He stuck a jack of hearts in the book before closing it, and said, "What do you like to read?"

"Pretty near anything. You?"

"Mysteries like this one." He held up the book he'd been reading. "Some history. These old bones have been around nearly eighty-two years, so now I've got to do most of my living through books."

Their discussion was interrupted when a server appeared asking what we wanted to drink. Charles said beer, any kind. I said white wine.

She left to get our drinks, and Terrell said, "That's how I got to know Jamal. I'm into Civil War history. He lent me a book about it."

"You ain't given it back yet," Jamal said.

"My bad. I'll have it the next time I see you."

"Jamal," I said, "are you from around here?"

He smiled for the first time. "Born, reared, lived my entire life up until now within three miles of this spot." He tapped the table. "Where are you two from?"

I answered as our drinks arrived. The server asked if we were ready to order. Charles and I stuck with barbecue sandwiches plus at Terrell's urging, a side order of pickled cabbage and sauerkraut. Jamal told the server to throw in some Coco bread. I didn't know what it was but didn't want to question our new table mate.

"Is it always this busy?" Charles asked.

Terrell said, "Friday and Saturday."

Charles nodded. "Know who the body was someone found out here the other day?" He asked it like it was the most logical thing to ask after learning about weekend crowds.

Terrell glanced at me before turning to Charles. "Haven't heard anything. If the police know they aren't saying." He turned to Jamal. "Hear anything?"

Jamal sipped his beer, looked around the patio, before turning to Terrell. "No. Whoever it is, it's ancient history. Just what Mosquito needs is someone digging up its reputation for violence." This time he took a large swig of beer.

That got Charles attention. "Reputation for violence?"

Jamal sighed. "Started in the 1950s, around '55 as I recall. A young guy was shot inside an old juke joint. Died smack dab on top of a pool table. Then, there was another murder three years later. Mind you, everything I got about the killings was second hand." Jamal smiled. "That was a little after the pavilion was built on stilts over the water."

Our food arrived, and Jamal told the server to bring another beer for Terrell who was holding an empty bottle.

Charles took a bite of sandwich, wiped sauce off his upper lip, then said, "Think the body they found could be someone from those days?"

Jamal said, "No. It's probably somebody's elder parent. Funerals were expensive. Many of the folk living around here weren't rolling in dough."

The late-afternoon sun peeked through the clouds; the temperature was warming to near uncomfortable levels. Charles removed his Tilley, fanned his face with it. "I hear he was shot in the head."

Jamal and Terrell turned to my friend.

"Who died?" came a voice from behind me.

Jamal looked over my shoulder. "Hi, Eugene, nobody died, not recently anyway. We're talking about the skeleton."

I twisted around in my seat and saw a man roughly six-foot-tall, white with gray hair, and eighty or so years under his belt looking down at us. He was thin with the posture of a Buckingham Palace guard. I was starting to think we were eating at a senior citizen center.

He glanced around the table. "Jamal, who're your friends?"

Since Charles wanted to know every human on earth, he stood, stuck out his hand, and told Eugene who he was as well as introducing me.

Eugene shook Charles's hand, patted me on the shoulder, then turned back to Jamal. "No need to waste anyone's time talking about an old bag of bones that probably was buried out there for a hundred years. Probably some bum."

"Mr. Dillinger," Terrell said, "Is that any way to talk about the dead? He was someone's son, could've been a dad, could've been anyone."

Eugene, whose last name apparently was Dillinger, ignored Terrell's remark. He asked Charles where he and his friend were from. Charles told him we lived on Folly.

"I'm building a house over there. Just came from the job site."

Jamal said, "Eugene's a builder."

"Best in the area or was when I was doing much of the work myself. With my arthritis, I lean on my crew to do everything now," Eugene said. "My current project is oceanfront, on East Ashley past the Washout. You know the one I mean?"

I didn't. Neither did Charles who asked the address.

Eugene told him. Charles said it sounded interesting, that he'd look for it the next time he was out that way. Eugene smiled, the marketer in him seeping out. He probably thought Charles could use a new house. He didn't know Charles would have to rearrange his budget to buy a pencil.

There was an empty chair at the table beside us that Jamal or Terrell could've told Eugene to pull up if they wanted him to join us. Eugene glanced at the empty chair, but not hearing an invitation, said he'd better be going. He added it was nice meeting Charles and me, especially Charles, since he handed him his business card. His arthritis didn't stop him from marketing. He nodded bye to Jamal and Terrell before heading to the gate leading off the patio.

Jamal watched him go and mumbled, "Asshole."

That explained the lack of an invitation for Eugene to join us.

Charles needed a more detailed explanation. "Jamal, doesn't sound like you're buddies."

"Wouldn't trust him as far as I could throw him," Jamal said.

Terrell said, "He's not that bad."

"You're too young to know better," Jamal said. "That honky—no offense Chris and Charles—has been screwing over black folks since he started his homebuilding business in the 1950s. He was just out of high-school when his pop kicked the bucket. Eugene inherited a fledgling remodeling business, ripped off some customers before starting building houses. A lot of Negroes were desperate for work. Eugene promised jobs. Minimum wage back then was seventy-five cents an hour. Dillinger Executive Homes, the damned self-important name he called his business, came out here, picked up labor for fifty cents an hour, sometimes less. Lord, that was for fifty hours a week. We didn't have much choice back then."

Charles asked, "Does he still do that?"

Jamal chuckled. "Hell no. Now he hires guys who can't speak English so no telling how little he pays them. Let's just say that the African American community could use a lot fewer Eugene Dillingers."

Terrell said, "Aren't his foremen black?"

"Two of the four," Eugene said. "They've been with him twenty-five years or more. I suspect they make good money, but that don't make up for the years he took advantage of us."

If what Jamal said was accurate, I was surprised Eugene showed his face on Mosquito Beach. "Where does he live? Does he come here often?"

"Hell," Jamal said, "he lives somewhere on your island. I don't go over there. Don't know where it is. He spent a lot of time in the juke joints here when he was getting his business going. He was one of the few white faces around in the '50s. He hired some of us, so we put up with him. Work was hard to come by."

I asked Terrell and Jamal if they wanted another beer. They quickly said yes, and I added it was my treat.

Charles said, "Me, too."

Jamal got the server's attention. The conversation took a kinder, gentler turn as Jamal started regaling us with stories of the bands that had performed at the pavilion and how Mosquito Beach had been such a popular gathering spot even after the Civil Rights Act of 1964 outlawed segregation.

"We were all friends, felt like we were one large family," he added.

I suspected that there was one man who didn't feel like that—the man whose bones are at the coroner's office in Charleston.

8

Over the next several days, in a moment of weakness, I painted the bedroom. It'd been a decade since a paintbrush touched anything in the interior of my cottage, and even then, the bedroom escaped new paint. Besides, the outside temperature hovered ten degrees above the average high for September. Staying inside was appealing; appealing until it took me two days, numerous twists of my already weakened back, and spilling nearly as much paint as made it to the walls. I hadn't given a second thought to Mosquito Beach during the painting ordeal.

I finished the arduous task, yelled, "Hallelujah!" to the empty, newly painted room, then walked to Barb's Books to see if I could elicit a modicum of sympathy and praise for my hard work.

"Hello, stranger," Barb said as I left the humid, late-summer heatwave to step in the attractive, air-conditioned bookstore. "It's been so long since I've seen you, I figured you skipped town with a young floozy."

I smiled. "You're reading too many of the romance novels you sell."

"Eww. You know I can't stand romance novels."

"They're still your best sellers, aren't they?"

"Back in the day when I was practicing law, I had a few clients I couldn't stand. They paid the bills, so I tolerated them. Same with romance novels. Want something to drink?"

I told her "yes" then followed her to the small back room. Until four years ago, I had a photo gallery in the space housing Barb's Books. In those days, the back room served as a storage room plus a gathering place for my friends. The room had been sloppy, held a yard-sale table and chairs, a refrigerator stocked with wine, beer, and soft drinks. Barb has the space looking like a professional office with a sleek, modern desk, a Bose sound system, and a Keurig coffeemaker. Fortunately, her new, black refrigerator held a six-pack of Diet Cokes. She handed me one, fixed herself a cup of coffee in the high-tech coffeemaker then pointed to one of the chairs. I sat as she pulled another chair closer to the door so she could see if customers ventured in.

I hinted for a sympathetic shoulder to lean on while telling about my painting experience.

She responded with, "It's about time."

The front door opened before she could elaborate. Barb left me at the table so she could greet the new arrival. She was gone a couple of minutes when I heard a vaguely familiar voice, so I peeked around the corner to see who it belonged to.

Barb was showing Terrell Jefferson the selection of history books. He saw me standing in the doorway. "Oh, hi, Chris. I didn't see you there."

He had traded his all-black clothes for black and white striped chef's pants plus a white chef's jacket.

"Chris," Barb said, "you remember Terrell, we sat with him when we went to Mosquito Beach."

"I do. In fact, I ate with Terrell a week ago at Island Breeze."

"You did?"

Terrell said, "With your friend, Charles, right?"

I nodded.

Terrell continued, "They were there last Friday. The place was packed. They looked lost, so I asked if they wanted to join my friend Jamal and me."

Barb smiled. "Chris and especially his friend Charles often look lost." She turned to me. "Terrell was looking for history books that cover the 1960s."

That was depressing since I didn't think the years of my late teens, early twenties should be in history books. I didn't say anything.

Terrell shared he was early for work at Rita's, so he stopped by.

Barb pulled a couple of tomes off the shelf while Terrell and I were talking. She flipped through the table of contents, shook her head, then re-shelved them.

"Terrell, I'm afraid we don't have what you're looking for. Check back in a week or so. We get new books all the time."

"I'll do that. Oh, by the way, Chris, remember how we were talking about the body found out my way?"

"Sure."

Barb stared at me, probably because I told her I wasn't getting involved.

"I gave it a lot of thought after you left. Grandpa Samson told me stories about being around in the '50s up through the end of the civil rights movement in the '60s."

Barb ended her glare and turned to Terrell. "I remember you telling us something about him when Chris and I met you. Didn't he die a year ago?"

"Yes. If I remember it right, he told me several times about a friend, actually it was more like someone he knew, not a friend. Grandpa was in his late twenties in those days. He told about some of the young guys who were always raring for a fight. Always talking about equal rights, wanting good jobs. That was in the early '50s, before the civil rights movement. Anyway, the guy he talked about was leading other youngsters in fighting segregation. Got a bunch of folks riled up. A lot of the blacks got behind him, a few didn't like what he was doing. They said he was bringing too much attention down on them; making enemies because of it."

I said, "What happened to him?"

Terrell shook his head. "No one knows. Grandpa said he was there one day, gone the next."

"You think it's his body?"

"That came to mind after you left the other night."

"What was his name?"

Terrell rubbed his chin then looked at the floor. "All I remember is his first name was one of those old-time Bible names. Grandpa told me, but for the life of me I can't remember. Next time I'm at Island Breeze I'll ask around. A lot of old-timers hang out there and I'm certain some will remember. It's interesting. I'd like to know what happened to him." He looked at his watch. "I'd better get to work."

Terrell started toward the exit, stopped, and said, "Chris. I want to apologize for how Jamal acted. He's got a lot of anger about what happened back in the old days. Most of the time he hides it good, but as you saw, it's not far under the surface."

"It sounds like he has reason to be angry at Eugene after how he treated African Americans."

"True," Terrell said. "It's not only whites, Jamal was royally pissed—excuse me, Barb—irritated at many people of color back then."

I asked, "Why?"

"Some of them were, how shall I say it, umm, rocking the boat. They were pushing, pushing hard for things to change, like I was saying about the guy Grandpa told me about. The laws may've been changing but words on paper don't change what's in people's hearts. That brought a lot of heat down on everybody. Some cops didn't take a liking to troublemakers. The Klan was also active in the Charleston area. Was a bad time all around." He smiled. "Didn't mean to go off on a tangent." He glanced at his watch again. "Gotta go."

"I'll keep an eye out for the kind of books you're looking for," Barb said as Terrell headed out.

She turned to me as Terrell closed the door. "Anything else you'd like to share about your trip to Mosquito Beach?'

I told her about being there with Al.

"You're not going to leave the mystery alone, are you?"

I again told her I had no intention of getting involved. She shook her head, once again giving me her best skeptical look.

Perhaps I should have stayed home and painted the living room.

9

"Chris, I've got an idea," Charles said after his call woke me out of a sound sleep.

I glanced at the bedside clock and realized I'd slept an hour past my normal seven o'clock waking time. Painting had taken its toll.

"What is it?" I said, knowing little good could come from whatever it was.

"Over my morning cereal, I was reading an article online. It gave me a brilliant idea. Ready for it?"

I had serious doubts about its brilliance but gave the only acceptable answer. "Yes."

"DNA," he said like that explained everything.

"DNA what?"

"You still asleep? DNA. That's how they can tell who the skeleton belongs to."

"The guy's been dead a long time. Even if they checked his DNA, there wouldn't be anything to match it to. DNA databases are relatively new."

"That's where my early-morning research while you snoozed paid off. You're right, there probably isn't a way to figure out who he is by finding his DNA anywhere except on the body. This is where genealogical DNA comes in."

"Explain?"

"Okay, here goes. You awake?"

I sighed. "Yes."

"You know those TV ads where you spit in a little tube then stick it in the mailbox? They tell what country or whole bunch of countries you came from."

"I've seen them. How does that help learn the body's identity?"

"Millions of folks have used those DNA sites. When they get the skeleton's DNA, they can see if he has any genotyped relatives in the data bases. Then his kin can say who he was. Simple, right?"

My knowledge of anything scientific is slightly greater than anything a frog knows about cliodynamics.

"Doesn't sound simple to me."

"Doesn't have to. All you have to do is share the brilliant idea with Chief LaMond. Let her run with it."

"Don't you know Chief LaMond?"

"Sure."

"You have her phone number?"

"Yes."

"Why don't you call and share your *brilliant* idea?"

"Two reasons. First, she thinks I'm a moron. Second, she takes things you tell her serious. Don't know why, but she does. Like those hip dudes on TV say, you've got creds."

"I'll think about it."

"Hurry. I'm sure she's waiting for you to enlighten her so she can figure out who the poor guy is."

"I don't think there's a hurry. He's been dead decades. What difference will a few more days make?"

"Won't know until you tell her."

I did the only thing that'd get Charles off the phone short of hanging up on him.

"I'll tell her your idea."

"Not idea, brilliant idea."

***

I was in no hurry to call Cindy to share Charles's idea. An early-morning walk on Folly's Fishing Pier would be a good way to put off the call. I went next door to Bert's Market, grabbed a complimentary coffee, bought a pack of sugar-coated donuts, then headed two blocks to the Pier. The temperature was in the mid-seventies, perfect for the walk. I wasn't the only person who thought visiting the iconic location was a good idea. There must've been fifteen men, women, and a couple of teenagers dangling fishing rods over the side of the thousand-plus foot-long structure. Walkers made up the rest of the crowd. I recognized a couple of the men and shared pleasantries before continuing to the far end of the structure. I sat on a bench, looked back at the nine-story Tides Hotel and the Charleston Oceanfront Villas, a long condo complex adjacent to the hotel's parking lot, while thinking how fortunate I was to live in an area where people from all over the country vacation.

My phone rang, interrupting my feelings of contentment. For the second time in forever, it was Al.

"Chris, did I catch you at a bad time?"

"No."

"Good. I hate to call so early, but something's been bothering me since we were together. I had to get it out of my system."

"What is it?"

"I don't like talking on the phone. Never have. Could we, umm, is there a way we could talk in person? I hate to ask you to come over here, but—"

"Al," I interrupted, "what do you think about us going to Island Breeze tonight for supper?"

There was a long silence before he said, "That sounds wonderful, but I'm sort of afraid to leave Bob alone at the restaurant. You may not believe this," he hesitated then laughed. "He rubs some of my, umm, his customers the wrong way."

"Not loveable, personable, open-minded Bob?"

He chuckled. "That's the one."

"Won't Lawrence be there? He can protect your customers from you-know-who."

Again, he chuckled. "I'm more worried about Bob than I am the customers."

"He'll be fine."

"You convinced me."

We made plans. I continued to look toward shore and watched a line of surfers off the side of the Pier. Instead of thinking how fortunate I was to live here, I tried to figure out what was bothering Al. It didn't take long to realize I'd have to wait until tonight to find out. I also couldn't figure out exactly what to tell Cindy about Charles's idea, so decided that it could wait until tomorrow. Avoidance was one of my favorite activities.

10

During the decade I've lived on Folly, I'd never visited Mosquito Beach. In the last two weeks, I was pulling on the out-of-the-way strip of land for the fourth time, the second with Al Washington. Most of the ride we talked about our mutual friend, Bob Howard, and how much Al appreciated the blustery, obscene, overweight owner of Al's former business. Al shared a couple of humorous stories about the cultural clash between his customers and the wealthy, white owner, who couldn't let a day—correction, hour—go by without insulting someone. I shared some of my experiences with Bob, including how after the rental house I was living in was torched with me in it, Bob dragged me out of the hotel where I was staying after the fire then insisted I move to the cottage I eventually purchased. Bob swore it was so he'd make a commission on the sale. I knew better. His heart exceeded the size of his obscene vocabulary, which was gigantic.

It was Wednesday so Island Breeze wasn't nearly as crowded as during Charles and my Friday visit. A table in front of the building was vacant, so I asked Al if he'd like to sit outside. He said it'd be a welcomed relief after spending most daylight hours in the dark confines of the bar.

A server arrived and Al told her a cold brew was what the doctor ordered. She joked saying for him to call her nurse Judy, then told him his prescription would be right out. I stuck with white wine so Judy didn't see anything to joke with me about.

Al stared across the street at the tidal creek. "I can still picture that wonderful pavilion. Folks dancing, smooching, hanging out, enjoying time away from work, worry, life's challenges."

All I could see was a handful of wood piles sticking out of the water—piles that once supported the pavilion.

Judy arrived with our drinks and asked if we wanted anything to eat. I deferred to Al who told her maybe in a little while. He said he wanted to enjoy the drink before eating.

He took two sips as he leaned back in the chair. "Chris, I appreciate you bringing me here. I don't get out often, probably don't have many years left. I suppose looking back makes me feel like time on this earth is longer than it really is."

"You've got a long life ahead of you."

Al smiled. "Bob lies to me all the time. I expect it. Don't make me start putting you in that boat."

I returned the smile. "That hurt. Besides, there isn't enough room for anyone else in a boat Bob's in."

"True." He took another sip, glanced at me, then down at the beer bottle as he peeled off the label. "Chris, you asked me a couple of times the other day if there was something bothering me. I wasn't ready to get into it. I apologize for not answering your questions."

"No need to apologize. My friends don't answer my questions all the time." I smiled, hoping to put him at ease.

He nodded. "Back when I was spending weekends here, must've been the summer of '53, I made friends with Elijah Duncan. We hit it off, but Elijah was a hell raiser, a troublemaker." Al smiled, as he pointed to the piles. "I see him as clear as day. He'd be out there leaning on the railing like he owned the place. He was a sharp dresser, even wore one of those stylish double-breasted suits that were big back then. Everyone else was dressed for the weekend, casual like, then there was Elijah lookin' like he was headed uptown."

"He sounds like a character."

Al turned back toward the water, took another sip, and slumped down in the chair. "He was that, my friend. He sure was. Chris, I think the reason we became friends was before I went off to Korea, I was Elijah."

"In what way?"

"The problem with youngsters today is when they see old folks, they think we were born old. They can't see past the gray hair, wrinkled face, stooped shoulders. No, they can't."

I was tempted to say something, but knew Al wanted to make a point but was having a hard time with it. I sipped my drink.

"I haven't told anyone this," he said, hesitated, then continued, "ever. Hell, I can't tell any of my kids. Heaven forbid I say anything to Bob, or I'd never hear the end of it." He took a deep breath before continuing, "Before I went off to Korea, I was as big or bigger hell raiser than Elijah. In school, I drove my poor teachers nuts. I was a pistol." He chuckled at the memory. "Chris, I smoked cigarettes, umm, and pot. I drank too much." He took another sip of beer then glanced up from the bottle at me. "One of my friends was a little slow at thinking things. Know what I mean?"

"Yes."

"We were out one night, ran into his two older brothers. Those boys were trouble with a capital T. My friend, Benjamin was his name, and I were out walking. His brothers pulled up in a shiny green, 1948 Buick Roadmaster Sedanet." He shook his head. "I remember that car like it was yesterday. They waved us over. Benjamin begged them to take us for a ride. We hopped in the back seat. The driver peeled out like we were at a drag strip. I tell you, that car could move. Yes, it could."

Judy returned to ask if we were ready to order. That shook Al out of his ride in the Buick. I said another drink first. She said our wish was her command.

"Where was I?" Al said.

"Riding in the Buick."

"Did I mention it was stolen?"

"No."

"Benjamin's brothers had scrapes with the law for as long as I knew them. I didn't recognize the car but figured they must have bought it since I'd seen them last. That's what I told myself. I knew better. We weren't zipping around the city more than a few minutes, when I saw a car I did recognize. I heard a siren, turned, looked out the back window. There was a black and white Ford with a big red light on top. It was after us."

"What happened?"

"Benjamin's brothers weren't as slow in the head as he was but not far from it. The one behind the wheel stomped on the gas. The Buick had a big engine. It managed to pull away from the cop car. But, like I told my boys when they were growing up, cop cars are like rabbits. Where there's one, there're more. You may outrun one, but another will catch up with you. Yes, it will."

"What happened?"

"Benjamin's brother pulled in an alley. We bailed. His brothers ran one way, Benjamin and I took off the other direction. We were lucky. The cops went after his brothers while Benjamin and I managed to hide behind a row of bushes. We were there forever before we had the nerve to come out."

"Did the police catch the brothers?"

Al shook his head. "Sort of."

"Meaning?"

"In those days, the stupidest thing a Negro could do was to run from the law. They caught one of the brothers." He hesitated. "Killed the other one." He shook his head again. "It could as easy have been me. It sure could've."

"I'm sorry."

"I knew not to get in the car. I knew Benjamin's brothers couldn't afford a car, especially one that new, that pretty. I can still hear the cop's gun. Pop! Pop! Chris, I was a fool, could've been shot as easy as my friend's brother."

"Al, you were a kid. That was nearly seventy years ago. You were lucky, but you didn't get your friend's brother killed."

"I know." He shook his head. "I know."

I wondered what his story had to do with Elijah. I was about to ask, when I saw Jamal Kingsly coming across the street. He was leaning heavily on a cane and carrying a paperback book in his other hand. He did a double take when he saw me, like he thought he might know me but wasn't certain.

I stood, smiled, and said, "Hi, Jamal. I'm Chris, we met the other night when I was here with a friend."

"Yes, sir, I remember. Your friend's a reader."

"Jamal, meet another friend, Al Washington."

Al slowly stood and shook Jamal's hand.

"Al, you live over on Folly like your friend here?"

"I live in Charleston."

"What brings you out? Sure ain't the weather."

I waited for Al's response.

He glanced at me, then turned to Jamal, "I spent time here in the '50s. Wanted to see what the old place looked like now."

Jamal pointed over his shoulder at the creek. "Guess you were here when the pavilion was hoppin'."

Al gave an exaggerated nod. "I was here most every weekend the year it was built."

Jamal stepped closer to Al then looked at him like he'd inspect a diamond ring. "We were here at the same time. You don't look familiar, but hell, I wouldn't recognize myself either since this old haggard, fat body don't look anything like it did back then."

Al looked toward where the pavilion had been. He shook his head. "Those were the days, weren't they?"

Jamal followed Al's gaze. "Al, our memories make those days better than they were. Sure, we had good times over there, but age makes us forget there was no air conditioning, no work, no respect in any store that wasn't owned by someone like us. No offense, Chris."

"None taken," I said then waited for Al to respond.

"Jamal," Al said, "were you heading here to eat?"

"No sir, just hankerin' for a beer after a long day of doing nothing."

Al pointed to an empty chair. "Care to join us?"

Motown sounds filled the humid air.

"Don't mind if I do. These old legs don't move as well as they used to," Jamal sat and put the Walter Mosley paperback in the empty chair. It was the same book he'd been reading during my previous visit.

The server appeared behind Jamal's chair.

"Nurse Judy," Al said, "get my friend here whatever he wants to drink."

Jamal twisted around. "Judy, when did you go back to school and get your nursing degree?"

She put her hand on Jamal's shoulder. "Jamal, if I was a nurse, do you think I'd be out here waiting on old farts like you and begging for measly tips?"

"Well excuse this old fart's mistake."

Judy laughed and hugged Jamal. "Al, Jamal is one of my favorite customers."

"Judy," Jamal said, "are you going to get me a beer or stand and gab all night with these newcomers?"

She continued hugging Jamal then turned to Al, "You all ready to order something?"

I felt like I was a potted plant sitting on the table.

Al pointed to the building. "You got some good wings back there?"

Jamal answered for her, "The best on Mosquito Beach."

"The only on Mosquito Beach," Judy added.

"Chris," Al said, "want to start with some?"

Thank goodness, someone noticed I was still here. "Sure."

Judy said she could round up a few in the kitchen then headed inside.

"Jamal," Al said, "did you know Elijah Duncan back in the day?"

Jamal's eyes narrowed, he tapped his fingers on the table. "Smart dresser. Chip on his shoulder the size of a damned shrimp boat. Always preachin' for Negro rights years before it was safe to do. That Elijah Duncan?"

I thought he was going to pound a hole in the thick wood tabletop.

Al nodded. "That'd be the one."

"Al, that goes back a long way. Sure, I knew him. Everyone did. Why are you asking?"

"We weren't close, but the two of us got along. I saw him on weekends so don't know what he did the rest of the time. I was wondering what happened to him."

"Depends on who you ask."

Judy returned with Jamal's beer and said the wings would be out soon.

Al waited for Jamal to set his bottle on the table then said, "What's that mean?"

"Different ideas about what happened." He blinked a few times. "Let me rewind my memory. Remember, that was about a thousand years ago. Let's see, there was a story going around that Elijah ran off with Preacher Samuel's daughter. The child was barely in her teens. Preacher Samuel left for Illinois shortly after. No one asked him about his daughter, or if they did, I didn't hear about it. Then, the story was Elijah was killed by a jealous husband who dumped his body in the ocean for shark food. None of the husbands around here took credit." He snapped his fingers. "Oh yeah, how could I forget? I heard he was hanged by a group of Klan members because he was stirring up a pot of trouble, too uppity for his own good."

I said, "Jamal, what do you think happened?"

"Course I don't know for certain. He was here one day, then he wasn't. There were as many rumors out here as there were mosquitos. I tend to think he got tired of being here. Left on his own. Probably headed north where a lot of the younger guys went to find work, to live happily ever after."

Al said, "Down deep, he was a good kid."

"Except when he was drinking," Jamal added.

Al nodded. "Except when he was drinking."

"Which was most all the time," Jamal said, then took another drink.

"Hey, Jamal," came a voice from behind me.

"Hey, Robert," Jamal said.

I turned to see a tall, thin man with long gray hair pulled in a ponytail. He wore tan slacks, a red polo shirt, a Charleston RiverDogs gold, white, and blue ball cap, and a huge smile.

The newcomer pointed at Jamal's book. "See you're still reading. Some things never change."

"No reason to stop now," Jamal said. "Besides, these old eyes are about the only thing on me still working."

"I'm a couple of years older than you, so I know what you mean. Who're your buddies?"

Jamal pointed to Al. "This here's Al Washington." He nodded my direction. "That's Chris, umm."

"Landrum," I said.

"Yeah, Landrum," Jamal said. "Al's from Charleston, Chris from over on Folly. Guys, meet Robert Graves. Him and me go back to the '50s. He lived up by where the Harris Teeter is now and sneaked over here when musicians were playing in the pavilion."

"Best music anywhere," Robert said. "We do go back, don't we, Jamal?"

"Guys, Robert was the first white guy I ever had much dealing with."

"If it weren't for Jamal, I probably would've been run off."

"I think the only thing that kept you safe was because your dad worked for that tobacco wholesaler. You'd sneak cigarettes out here and share them around."

"That too. Those were interesting days."

"You meeting someone?" Jamal asked.

"No. Thought I'd get a drink and have an excuse to get out of the house. Gets pretty boring sitting there watching stupid television shows while listening to Sandra gripe about, well, about everything."

"Want to join us?" Jamal said.

Robert smiled as he took the remaining chair.

Judy reappeared and set our order of wings in the center of the table. "Sorry it took so long guys. The kitchen's backed up."

Al told her we weren't in a hurry. She asked Robert what he wanted to drink. He said a Budweiser. The rest of us said we were okay, for now.

Al took a bite of chicken wing and turned to Robert. "Back in my younger day, I spent some time here. If I'm not mistaken, I remember seeing you."

Jamal pointed at Robert. "Would've been hard missing him. He was one of the few white faces here."

Al smiled. "Then, Robert, it's good seeing you again."

Robert nodded, as Judy set his beer in front of him. He took a sip, looked at each of us, then said, "You guys hear who belonged to that skeleton?"

I shook my head and Jamal said, "Nothing for sure. They say it's been buried a long time. Nobody's claimed it or confessed to planting it."

"Jamal," Robert said, "I'm disappointed. You've always known what's going on."

"Those days are long gone. Hell, I have trouble knowing what's happening in my own head."

"Jamal, I don't believe that for a second. You've always known more about what's happening here than anyone else on Mosquito. I heard the poor soul had been shot. That true?"

"I heard the same thing. Enough about ancient history. Let's sit back, enjoy our new friends, and the great weather."

That wouldn't have been possible if I'd been with Charles. He'd be playing detective while asking a million questions. Al chewed on a wing, bobbed his head to the Bob Marley songs playing through the sound system, and enjoyed the easy banter between Jamal and Robert. All in all, we had a great evening.

* * *

AL WAS both hyped and exhausted by the time I pulled in front of his house. On the ride back, he'd shared memories from the dances at the pavilion, how crowded it got on Saturday nights, and how many restaurants there had been "in the day." The entire time he was talking, he leaned back against the headrest with his eyes closed, his hands unmoving from their crossed position in his lap. I wasn't certain he knew we were at his house.

Finally, he opened his eyes, looked at his house, but he made no effort to open the door. "Chris, you don't know how much it meant being there tonight. You're a loyal friend to put up with this old man."

"I enjoyed it."

He closed his eyes again. "Remember what I told you about being a hell raiser when I was young?"

"Sure."

"Korea changed all that, yes it did. I saw evil, true evil, how it hurt and changed even the best people. It wasn't that I stopped having bad thoughts, Lord knows I'm not perfect. What it made me think was what I did, what I said touched other folks." He slowly shook his head. "I know I'm not making sense. I'm trying to say when I got back from that war, I started seeing how bad folks treat other folks. My eyes were opened. Think that's why I spent time with Elijah and wanted to be his friend. Like I said at the restaurant, he was a good kid, but misguided." He hesitated, then said, "No, not misguided; was more like he wanted things to be right but didn't know how to get it across without pissing people off."

"I hope he appreciated what you were trying to do."

"I suppose he did." He sighed. "When he wasn't drinking. After a few, nothing could get through to him."

"You think the body was Elijah, don't you?"

"Hate to say it, but I truly do. Everything fits."

"You could be right. There's just as good a chance it's someone else."

"You heard what Jamal said about Elijah having a chip on his shoulder, preaching equal rights before it was a smart thing to do. Remember, he said everyone knew Elijah, knew the problems he was causing."

"I'm not saying it wasn't him, but Jamal also said there were stories about Elijah running off with a preacher's daughter. He could've left the area."

Al tilted his head my direction. "He also said there were stories about a jealous husband killing him, or he was hanged by the Klan."

I thought about Charles's idea that the bodies could be identified through familial matches with their DNA.

"Did Elijah have family?"

"Suppose he did. He never talked about kinfolk. I thought that was strange. He lived close to Mosquito, yet never mentioned kin. Why?"

I shared Charles's idea about DNA familial matching,

"Don't know about scientific stuff, but if he still has kin in the area, they might know what happened to him. Think I'll have Tanesa do one of those Google searches to see if any Duncans live nearby. That's a good thought, Chris."

Tanesa was an ER doctor in Charleston and one of Al's adopted nine children. She's his only child living in the area. She's been a tremendous help with Al's medical issues and giving him the support he needs to live alone. She also drove him to work most days.

I suspected there'd be several Duncans in the Charleston area. Al would have his hands full trying to run down relatives of Elijah. Regardless, he was enthusiastic about trying. It was great seeing Al excited about something.

He barely had strength to push the car door open, so I went around to help. The walk from the car to his door was painful to watch. He leaned on me the entire way. When we got to the door, I asked if he wanted me to help him in. He said he could make it. He reminded me that was why his bed was on the first floor.

"Thanks for one of the best days I've had in years," he said as he closed the door.

I was pleased Al had such an enjoyable time but worried it may've been too much on his deteriorating body. I also started thinking about what Jamal had said about Elijah Duncan's disappearance and the possibility the bones were his. Something else was forming in the back of my brain. What was it Terrell Jefferson had said about his grandpa talking about someone on Mosquito Beach who was always wanting to fight; someone in his early twenties; someone who got people riled? And, someone who was there one day, gone the next. Terrell speculated the skeleton was that person.

What else had Terrell said about the person who disappeared? Got it. He had an old-time Bible name; a name Terrell couldn't remember. What were the odds that name was Elijah? I wonder if he's working tomorrow? There's one way to find out. Even if he wasn't at work, it was about time to get one of Rita's great cheeseburgers.

Rather than tell Charles everything later, why not have him there to meet Terrell? I called my friend as I pulled in my drive. After asking me three times what the occasion was, my telling him three times he would have to wait until tomorrow to find out, it took him all of two-seconds to accept the invitation.

11

Rita's would be busy during lunch hour, so I'd asked Charles to meet me at one-thirty, knowing he'd arrive by one o'clock. Rita's was on a prime slice of Folly Beach commercial real estate. It was across the street from the Folly Beach Fishing Pier, cattycorner from the oceanfront Tides Hotel, and across Center Street from the Sand Dollar private club.

The temperature was a comfortable seventy-five degrees, so I requested a table on the patio and had been seated when Charles entered the restaurant. He wore his Tilley hat, navy blue shorts, a long-sleeve, black and gray T-shirt, with the head of a tiger in orange on the front. He tapped his cane on the floor as he approached the table.

"Go ahead, ask," he said as he put his Tilley and cane on the corner of the table.

"Ask what?"

He pointed at his chest. "About the shirt. Duh."

Charles has one of the largest collections of T-shirts and sweatshirts, most of them sporting college and university logos and nicknames, found outside a sweatshop shirt factory in China. They were interesting but I tried to ignore the shirts to avoid a lengthy monologue about them.

"Okay, what about it?"

He smiled. "That's better. Idaho State University, they're the Bengals."

"Why do I want to know that?"

"You don't. Just wanted to say it's in Pocatello, Idaho. I love saying Pocatello."

See why I avoid asking about his shirts?

Britany, one of Rita's personable servers, arrived at the table. I ordered a Diet Pepsi, Charles said the same. We told her we'd wait to order food when the drinks arrived.

"Okay," Charles said. "I have a hunch you didn't ask me here so I could tell you about Pocatello. What's up?"

"Last night I was at Island Breeze with Al when—"

Charles's hand flew my direction and stopped a couple of inches from my face. "Whoa! You didn't think to invite me?"

I explained that Al had asked me to take him. I didn't think he needed anyone else going. Charles huffed another minute before asking what the trip had to do with lunch.

Drinks arrived before I shared the connection. I asked Britany if Terrell Jefferson was working. He was, so I asked if she could tell him Chris Landrum was here and wanted to have a word with him when he had a chance. We ordered cheeseburgers and Britany said she'd relay the message.

Charles said, "Who's Terrell Jefferson? Why do we want to talk to him?"

I explained how I'd met Terrell when I was at Island Breeze with Barb, saw him again in the bookstore, how he'd told us about his grandfather telling him about a man who disappeared from Mosquito Beach in the 1950s.

Britany returned and said Terrell was busy but would get a break in an hour if we wanted to wait. I told her we would.

Charles spotted Chief LaMond walking by the patio. He waved then pointed to the empty chairs at our table. She rolled her eyes, but instead of continuing her walk, opened the patio gate, talked to a couple seated near the entry, then made her way to our table.

"You two vagrants planning a crime?"

I smiled.

Charles said, "Not now that you're here."

Britany returned to ask Cindy if she wanted anything. She looked at Charles. "You buying?"

He nodded my direction. "Chris is."

Cindy laughed. "I'll have a Pepsi and whatever food they ordered."

"Excellent choice," Charles said as Britany headed to the kitchen.

Charles took a sip, and said, "Chief, Chris wanted to talk to you about a new scientific breakthrough he was reading about. Tell her, Chris."

Revisionist history was another of Charles's "endearing" quirks.

I explained the breakthrough *I'd been reading about* the best I could considering I'd heard all of it through Charles's filter, plus I'm scientifically challenged.

After my enlightening explanation about something I knew next to nothing about, Cindy took a sip of Pepsi Britany had delivered during my lecture on biochemistry, rolled her eyes for the second time in five minutes, and said, "First, I didn't know you could read so your statement you were reading about whatever that was, struck me as absurd. Second, many of the words you just spouted sound surprisingly like something that'd be coming from the mouth of someone else at this table—hint, not me. Third, you probably won't believe this, but I, an old country girl from the mountains, actually know what you were talking about."

"You're not that old," Charles said.

"Compared to you and Chris, coal ain't that old. May I continue?"

Charles motioned her to continue.

"Whenever I get tired of hubby reading me 'fascinating' specs on the latest sump pumps and fiberglass insulation, I actually read police journals."

Cindy's husband Larry owns Pewter Hardware, Folly's tiny hardware store.

Charles leaned forward. "Can I have them when you're finished?"

"No. May I make my point?"

"Of course, Chief," I said.

"Using DNA if there isn't any on file for the bad guys by comparing it to family members is used in twelve states. Guess what, South Carolina isn't among them."

Charles said, "Why not?"

"It gets into those pesky concerns about privacy. You know how much easier my life would be if we didn't have to worry about privacy, or those danged amendments giving bad folks all those rights? And don't get me started on that Ernesto Miranda fella who got a warning named after him. If it wasn't for all that, we could beat confessions out of bad guys, knock doors down anytime we want, arrest you and your buddy Chris and charge you with giving me hemorrhoids." She leaned back in her chair. "Oh, the good old days."

I smiled, knowing she didn't mean any of it, except maybe the part about arresting Charles and me.

Before Charles hijacked the conversation further, I told Cindy about taking Al to Mosquito Beach and his theory a friend of his from the 1950s was the skeleton. Charles stared at me. I knew he was fuming because this was the first he was hearing it. The Chief asked a few questions then said she'd let Detective Callahan know.

Charles said, "Learn anything new about the body?"

It was as if what I'd told her wasn't enough.

Our food arrived, Cindy took a bite, then said, "Remind me again why it's any of your business?"

Charles looked at me, and turned to Cindy, "Because Chris's good friend Al is worried sick. He thinks it could be someone he knew back in the day. Cindy, how could you possibly deprive the poor old man of learning if it was his friend? You know he doesn't have many years left on this earth. Poor Al." He bowed his head.

I stifled a chuckle before turning to Cindy.

"Charles," the Chief said, "remember me mentioning a few minutes ago that I'm an old country girl?"

"You're not that old," Charles repeated.

"Not the point. Know what there wasn't a shortage of when I was growing up?"

Charles tilted his head. "Do I need to take notes?"

Cindy sighed. "There was no shortage of cow manure, horse manure, and chicken manure."

"Eww," Charles said.

"I thought I'd never come close to being around that much crap after I moved here. I was wrong. You spew more bullshit than I thought possible."

"I don't—"

"Charles, I'm not done. Eat your burger, keep you trap shut."

"Can't do both."

"Eat, don't talk."

He took a bite.

"Chris, not Charles, you can tell Al the experts are saying the skeleton belonged to a black male, height, five-foot-seven or eight, probably younger than twenty-one, and yes, probable cause of death, a gunshot wound to the head, or he could've died of a heart attack watching the bullet heading toward his head. No way of knowing for sure."

So far, it was consistent with Al's theory.

I asked, "Any idea when he died?"

"That gets harder. From what he was wearing, they guessed sometime in the 1950s, or he could've been going to a Halloween party in the '60s or '70s dressed like a pimp from the '50s."

"If he died in the 1950s, it matches what folks are saying about Elijah Duncan's disappearance."

"That's what the Sheriff's Office is looking at. Al might be right."

"Cindy," I said, "how hard are they looking? You said before you didn't think they were taking it seriously."

"If you ask the Sheriff Office's public relations hack, she'll say they're not letting any stone go unturned, pun intended. Will spew they're following all leads."

Charles tapped her on the arm. "Chris asked you, not a PR hack."

"Charleston records more than four hundred violent crimes a year.

How much time do you think they'll spend chasing down a murderer from 1950-whatever? They'll send someone to Mosquito Beach, he or she will interview everyone who happened to be in the area during that time frame and will come back with no hot leads. End of investigation."

I shook my head. "Perhaps Al will get some solace knowing what happened to his friend."

Cindy took the last bite of her cheeseburger then glanced at her watch. "Sorry I don't have better news for Al. Now I need to get to City Hall and act like I'm doing chiefly stuff."

She left the patio after I thanked her for the information, she thanked me for the food.

Charles watched her go and said, "Wow, did you hear that?"

"What?"

"She said since the cops weren't going to, we have to find out who killed Al's friend."

Before I could remind Charles he wasn't a private detective and I wasn't one with a death wish, Britany returned with the check. She also said Terrell would meet us behind the building.

12

Rita's backed up to a large, gravel public parking lot that during vacation season overflowed with vehicles most every day. Terrell was seated on an overturned milk crate near the back door talking with another employee. The men were puffing on cigarettes while waving their hands in animated conversation.

Terrell stood when he saw me, told his colleague he'd see him inside, and greeted us. I introduced Charles. Terrell wiped his hand on his food-splotched shirt, dropped his cigarette on the ground, putting the burning tobacco out with his foot, before shaking Charles's hand.

He looked around. "Let's go behind the dumpster where we can talk. It gets busy here with employees coming and going through the door."

We were shaded from the sun by the dumpster enclosure and stood close to each other to stay shaded.

"Thanks for meeting us," I said.

"What's up?" Terrell asked then lit another cigarette.

"When we talked in Barb's Books, you said your grandpa told you stories about someone who was missing? You thought that person could be the skeleton."

"Sure. What about him?"

"You couldn't remember his name, but it was something out of the Bible."

Terrell nodded.

"Could it be Elijah Duncan?"

Terrell snapped his fingers. "That's it. How'd you know?"

I told him a little about Al's experiences on Mosquito Beach in the 1950s.

"Did your friend know what happened to Elijah?" Terrell said before taking another drag on his cigarette.

"Nothing other than he had a reputation as a troublemaker, then disappeared."

Charles couldn't stand being left out of a conversation. He stepped closer to Terrell. "Chris and I are going to figure out what happened and who killed him."

Terrell's head jerked back. "What makes you think so?"

Good question, I thought.

"Terrell," Charles said, "I've helped the police a few times catch bad guys. I'm known over here as a private detective. Got a pretty good success rate. Chris has helped me a time or two."

Charles has a tough time keeping his fantasy world to himself.

"We've been fortunate," I added.

Terrell took another puff, looked down at the gravel by his feet, and turned to me. "Gentlemen, I've lived on Sol Legare all my life. Heard about all the good that's happened out there. Heard about all the bad. Know pretty much everyone. No offense, but you two have a big handicap when it comes to getting close to folks out there."

"We're white," I said.

He nodded. "That's part of it, but the main reason is people don't know you. Don't matter what color you are, you're outsiders. I'd have a much better chance learning what happened. Grandpa talked a lot about Elijah. I knew it bothered him when he disappeared without anyone knowing what happened." He took another puff. "I owe about everything I have, everything I know to him. After we talked the other night, I told myself I owed it to grandpa to solve the mystery of his missing friend. Don't mean to offend you, but for the life of me I can't see how you could figure any of it out. I think I can."

Charles took a step closer to Terrell. "Chris and I've solved harder problems than this one. You don't know—"

"Terrell," I interrupted, "you're probably right. We don't know what happened sixty or more years ago, probably wouldn't be able to. There's one thing we've learned over the years, people who kill won't hesitate to do it again, especially if they're cornered. If the body belongs to Elijah, the reappearance of his bones changes things. Not only were his bones brought to the surface, but so was the fact he was murdered. Whoever did it thought he's gotten away with it, has for decades. From what everyone says, Mosquito Beach is a tight-knit community with everyone knowing everyone."

"Chris," Charles said, "what's your point?"

"My point, Terrell, is if the killer is still alive and in the area, he's a danger to anyone snooping around. You need to be careful."

"I appreciate your concern, but like I said, I owe it to Grandpa to find out what happened. Don't worry, I'll be careful."

The restaurant's back door opened, and someone yelled for Terrell.

"Guys, I've got to get back to work. Let me have your phone numbers in case I learn anything." He handed me a pen and a Rita's bar napkin.

I wrote both numbers on it. He said it was nice talking to us, for me to say hi to Barb.

"He's an interesting fellow," Charles said as we headed to the sidewalk in front of Rita's. "Let's go to Barb's Books to tell the lovely owner that Terrell said hi."

"Yes, and okay."

"Yes, and okay, what?"

"One of these days you're going to listen to what you say. I was responding to you."

"Ye of little faith, I suppose the 'yes' was to me saying he was interesting, the 'okay' was for going to the bookstore."

Maybe it was only other people Charles didn't listen to. We were two blocks from Barb's when a silver Range Rover with a Dillinger Executive Homes logo on the front passenger door honked its horn. It parallel parked a half block in front of us where Eugene Dillinger got out and waited for us.

He was dressed in what must be the uniform of builders. He had on a light blue shirt, khaki slacks and boat shoes.

"I thought that was you, Charles and, umm, Chris. I was thinking about you yesterday Charles. I remembered you were interested in the house I'm building out East Ashley."

"Good to see you again," Charles said. "The house is oceanfront, right? It sounds great."

"Tell you what, I have some free time. Hop in, I'll give you a tour."

"That's okay," I said. "We don't want to take your valuable time."

Clearly, the "we" didn't include Charles. He moved toward the Range Rover and waited for Eugene to unlock the door.

"Nonsense," Eugene said, "I always have time to show my houses."

Three minutes later, we were enjoying an extraordinarily smooth ride on East Ashley Avenue, Folly's longest street, heading away from the center of town. Charles had already commented how much he enjoyed the comfortable seats, bragged on the infotainment screen, and the vehicle's new car smell. Eugene soaked it all in, certain, I'm sure, he had a potential homebuyer sharing the front seat with him. It took all my willpower to keep from laughing.

We passed the Washout, the narrowest part of the island, a place where surfers swear they could find "boss waves," when Eugene pointed to a mustard-colored, wood-frame house on the right. A construction trailer in the drive featured the same Dillinger Executive Homes logo that was on the Range Rover.

Eugene pointed to the house that appeared nearing completion. "We tore down a pre-Hugo tiny concrete block house to make room for this magnificent structure."

He should've added *if I say so myself*.

"Nice," Charles said, one of his few understatements.

"It's sold, but I have another lot a little farther up the road. I could build you a home like this one for a mere 1.9 million."

Charles couldn't have afforded the tiny concrete block teardown even if it had been in, well, been anywhere.

"Something to think about," Charles said as Eugene pulled in the drive and ushered us toward the front door.

Eugene said something to a rebar-thin African American gentleman in work clothes, a white hard hat, and carrying himself with the confidence of someone in charge. After a brief conference, the man headed to a couple of Hispanic men working on one of the windows, barked orders in Spanish, then saluted in Eugene's direction signaling whatever Eugene told him to do had been accomplished.

"He's my foreman. A good man," Eugene said before continuing his sales pitch.

Somewhere around the time he was telling Charles about the hardwood floors, granite countertops in the kitchen, the six-person jacuzzi on the patio, I'd heard all I wanted to about the *magnificent structure*. "Eugene, Jamal told me you've been in this business since the 1950s. You must've seen countless changes."

His eyes narrowed as he glanced at me. He wasn't fond of me interrupting his sales pitch.

"I've been fortunate. Homebuilding has had peaks and valleys over the years, but I've managed to keep the quality up, kept customers clamoring for my homes."

Another *if I say so myself* moment.

"Jamal also said many of your employees came from the Sol Legare community."

"Some of my best workers came from there. That's why I go back whenever possible. Many of the residents consider me a friend. Some of their family members were on my earlier crews."

That wasn't the impression Jamal had given, but Eugene was telling the story, so I didn't see reason to challenge him.

Charles said, "did you know the person whose bones were discovered the other day?"

Eugene stopped and stared at Charles. "I haven't heard who it was. Do you know?"

"I haven't heard either. I figured since you know so many people out there you may've heard."

Eugene moved a piece of paneling from the floor, yelled to get his foreman's attention, and walked toward him. He was back in less than a minute.

"Guys, I'd love to show you more, but there are a couple of things I need to do at the office. Unless you have specific questions, let's head out."

He dropped us where we'd met him then sped off to his office to get a couple of things done.

Charles watched the Range Rover speed away, and said, "I sure know how to break up a great sales pitch. I was getting ready to write him a check for a deposit on the other house."

I said, "Unless you're in medical school, talking about skeletons will dampen most conversations."

"I think it was more than that, don't you?"

"Yes."

13

One of the first people I met on my initial visit to Folly Beach was William Hansel who lived next door to the house I'd rented. He'd greeted me in the drive before I carried my suitcase into the house. William teaches in the hospitality and tourism program at the College of Charleston and has been a Folly resident for nearly thirty years, a widower for twenty. His graduate education and teaching experience were in travel and tourism, but his true passion was history. He's been a dedicated member of a group raising funds to preserve the historic Morris Island Lighthouse visible from the east end of Folly. In recent years, he's become interested in the Civil War and its impact on South Carolina.

It'd been several weeks since we'd talked, so I thought it was time to right that wrong. Besides, I'd be interested in what, if anything, he knew about Mosquito Beach. Most late afternoons he could be found in his garden. He took it as a personal affront if a weed had the audacity to pop its head out of the soil in proximity to his vegetables. A low cloud cover and a temperature in the upper 70s encouraged me to walk instead of driving—that combined with the fact it was only three blocks away.

As I guessed, my friend was standing in his garden, leaning on a hoe, staring at something growing. My knowledge of gardening exceeded my knowledge of stratigraphy, but not by much, so I had no idea what he was focused on. I figured since he wasn't decapitating it with the hoe, it was something that was supposed to be there.

"You look busy," I joked.

"Ah, my friend," he said in his bass voice, "you've come to rescue me from laboring over my cool-season vegetables."

William is three years younger than I, my height, although thinner, and African American. He also has a way of speaking that takes getting used to. It often resembles a professor giving a lecture rather than a conversation.

"I have no idea what that means, but if my presence rescued you from anything, I'm glad to help."

He took off his gloves, dust flying as he tapped them together, leaned the hoe against a nearby tree, then neatly placed the gloves on the ground beside the implement.

"Shall I prepare us a glass of tea?"

I'm not a tea drinker, but William's hospitality made consuming the drink tolerable.

"That would be great. Can I help?"

"Absolutely not, you are my guest." He pointed to two chairs under the oak tree in the corner of the yard. "Repose thyself. I shall return shortly."

What'd I tell you about his speech?

Ten minutes later, William returned. He'd exchanged his sweaty shirt for a short-sleeve, white polo shirt. He was carrying a silver platter holding two tall drink glasses, a white ceramic sugar bowl, and napkins. Cloth, of course.

We each took a sip before he said, "What brings you out this fine day? I surmise it isn't to watch me eradicate weeds."

"As exciting as that may be to watch, I did have something to ask."

He laughed. "Then don't hold back."

"Are you familiar with Mosquito Beach?"

William took another sip of tea and nodded. "Familiar, slightly, although I've never been there. Most of my knowledge about the predominantly African American enclave comes from a gentleman I met a few years ago. He's worked at several jobs around town." William chuckled, "James Brown is his name; he lives off Sol Legare Road. To hear him talk, he's spent a lot of time at Mosquito Beach. When I feel industrious electing to walk around Folly, I occasionally run into him. As you know, I'm reserved. Mr. Brown isn't. To anyone who knows both of us, we would appear to be strange acquaintances. Ah, neither here nor there. What precipitated your inquiry?"

"Have you heard anything about a body found out there?"

William's eyes narrowed; his head tilted. "Christopher, please don't tell me you're embarking upon another quest into areas better relegated to the police."

The year I retired to Folly, a friend of William drowned; the police thought it was a suicide. William convinced me his friend had a fear of water. Even if he'd been intent on taking his life, he wouldn't have chosen drowning. He was convinced his friend was murdered. To make a long story much shorter, I, along with Charles, managed to catch the murderer. William was also familiar with other times I'd stuck my nose where it has no business venturing.

I told him I wasn't and shared some about Al's and my visit to Mosquito Beach.

"Enlightening," he said.

"You have an interest in the history of the area, so I thought you might've heard stories about those living in the Sol Legare community."

"I'm familiar with how segregated the beaches had been, including here." He waved his hand around to let me know he was describing Folly. "If African Americans wished to be near water for a respite, they were limited to places like Mosquito or Riverside Beach on the Wando River near Mt. Pleasant. Neither location had what we now would call a beach but were the best available locations for African Americans to gather near water."

"Anything else?"

"I'm afraid not. Certainly, the times prior to the passing of the Civil Rights Act in 1964 were extraordinarily difficult for citizens of

African descent." He shook his head. "Even then, things didn't change quickly."

"I appreciate you sharing."

"I'm afraid I didn't share much beyond a glass of tea."

"Spending time with you is always a delight. The tea and information about the beaches were bonuses."

"And you accuse me of speaking professorially."

I laughed.

After fifteen more minutes of discussing everything from the weather to how difficult today's college students are to communicate with, William said he'd better get back to weed eradication.

I thanked him for the tea and conversation.

"Chris," he said as I started to leave, "you've piqued my interest in Mosquito Beach. James has said if I ever want to go to the restaurant there for supper to let him know. He'd meet me there. I think I'll take him up on the offer."

I told him it was a good idea then headed home. My phone rang as I was crossing Center Street.

"Chris, this is Cindy, have a minute?"

She was never that courteous, normally started a conversation with an insult, so I knew something was wrong.

"Yes," I said and moved to the alley behind Snapper Jack's Seafood Restaurant so I could hear better.

"Thought I'd tell you before you heard it from someone else and you called pestering me about it."

That had my attention. "What?"

"There's been a murder on Sol Legare Road, just past the turnoff to Mosquito Beach."

"Who?"

"Clarence Taylor."

I closed my eyes. "What happened?"

"You know about as much as I do. Detective Callahan's caught the case. Because Folly's so close to Sol Legare he called to tell me. He said a neighbor found the body in the vics yard early this morning. That would be a neighbor who didn't see or hear anything unusual next door, well, except finding Taylor with two bullet holes in his chest."

I've known Detective Michael Callahan for three years. He was the detective on the murder on Folly where he'd accused one of my friends of committing the crime, a crime he hadn't committed.

"Anything else?"

"I had a bagel for breakfast," Cindy said.

"About the murder."

"If there was, wouldn't I have shared it before telling you about breakfast?"

"I know. It's just I'm shocked. I met Clarence when I took Al to Mosquito Beach. He seemed like a nice man." I paused waiting for Cindy to respond. She didn't. "Who'd want him dead?"

"No idea. I'm glad it's not up to me to figure out. Now I must go play nice with the Mayor. Seems my department has blown the top off its budget. The way things are going with the price of gas, I'm afraid my folks will have to start chasing speeding cars on skateboards."

It took me a few seconds to shake that image out of my head, before responding. "Thanks for letting me know. If it'll help, you can tell the Mayor you were on the phone with a citizen who called to tell you how great a job you're doing."

She laughed and hung up. I leaned against the fence behind the restaurant, took a deep breath, and continued home.

* * *

I SPENT the next hour slowly sipping a glass of Chardonnay, watching a steady line of traffic drive past my cottage, while trying to figure a connection between Clarence and the skeleton. Knowing near nothing about Clarence didn't help. My only contact had been during the trip to Mosquito Beach with Al. If the skeleton belonged to Elijah Duncan and if he died in the early 1950s, Clarence would've been a child, not yet a teenager. On the other hand, hadn't Clarence said his family lived on Sol Legare Road for several generations? Even if he didn't know Elijah, his family would have. Now that the skeleton had been uncovered, could that have reminded Clarence of something a family member told him leading to whoever committed the murder? Did yesterday's murder indicate whoever killed the person whose remains Clarence found was still around. And, was that who killed my new acquaintance? If it was, why now? The original crime happened decades ago. Had Clarence told Al and me anything indicating he knew something that'd be a problem for the murderer now that the bones had been discovered? Not really.

After an hour asking myself questions, questions I had no answers for, all I concluded was I hated someone I knew, albeit slightly, had been murdered. The identity of the murderer and why were unknown.

Should I call Al to see if he'd heard about Clarence's death? I'd rather he learned it from a friend rather than being shocked via television.

I picked up the phone to call, when it rang. It startled me so much I dropped the device. I picked it up and saw a number I didn't recognize displayed on the screen. Great, another robocall.

It wasn't. I was surprised to hear a vaguely familiar voice say, "Is this Chris Landrum?"

I said it was.

"Chris, this is Terrell Jefferson. Is it okay if I called? You gave me your number when I met you and your friend behind Rita's."

I told him it was good hearing from him. I didn't know if it was or not, but I wanted him to feel comfortable calling.

"Good, I don't know if you've heard, but there's been a murder out here. You're interested in the skeleton and this is weird, so weird. I hope it's okay for me to tell you."

I told him it was.

"You're not going to believe this. Clarence Taylor, the man that found the body, was shot in his yard last night or early this morning. His neighbor found the body. Is that weird or what?"

I didn't tell him Cindy already shared the information.

"Any idea what happened or who did it?"

"Hell if I know. It's scary. This is a tiny community. We all know each other. I don't know who did it but seems to me it must've been someone that knew him."

"Why?"

"I hear he was shot in the chest at close range. That says he knew and trusted the killer. Folks out here don't take too kindly to strangers. Old Clarence wouldn't have let someone he didn't know get close enough to stick a gun in his chest."

I didn't tell him Clarence hadn't hesitated to talk to Al and me or get close enough to invite us to sit in the shade with him.

"Any other reason you think he knew the person?"

"Chris, I'm working an early shift tomorrow. Should get off by four. Think you could meet me somewhere? There's something else, you should know."

"Why don't you let me buy you a drink after work?"

"Sounds good." He chuckled. "Anywhere but Rita's."

That I understood. "How about Pier 101?"

"Sounds even better. Let's say four-thirty."

I told him I'd see him there. Now there was one more thing I needed to do, to do quickly. I called Charles to invite him to Pier 101. He asked why. I told him if he'd show up, he'd find out. Of course, he said he would.

With tomorrow afternoon planned, I made one more call, the one I'd planned to make before Terrell's call.

Al answered, and I heard Conway Twitty in the background singing about what happened "Fifteen Years Ago."

"Al, this is Chris. You at work?"

"No, I love to put old Conway on my record player at the house. Makes me think of Bob."

I laughed and reminded myself how funny Al could be when he wasn't dodging Bob's insults.

"I was wondering if you'd heard news today about what happened on Sol Legare Road?"

"Unless Hank Williams Senior sang about it, I ain't heard it today. I've been here since ten this morning listening to Bob wail along with his country friends on the jukebox and some of my, umm, his, regulars bitching about the music."

I told him what'd happened. He didn't respond for so long that I thought something had happened to him.

Finally, he said, "Oh, my Lord. He was such a nice man. Who would've had anything against him?"

I said I didn't know, and heard Bob's booming voice in the background yell, "Al, damnit, get off that freakin' phone. Smile at that handsome couple who just stepped in. Where're your customer service skills?"

Another textbook example of the pot calling the kettle black.

"You heard the boss," Al said. "Better go. I'd hate to get fired from this job that pays nothing, although Bob makes up for it with his love for his employees, paid or otherwise."

I told him we'd talk later.

14

Pier 101 was on the Folly Pier with a panoramic view of the beach and the Atlantic. In addition to the views, it had a varied menu plus a well-stocked bar. What more could one ask for in a restaurant? There was a low cloud cover with the temperature hovering in the low eighties.

I figured Terrell who'd been cooped up in Rita's kitchen all day would prefer sitting outdoors, so I requested a patio table. Two young women pushed strollers along the Pier, three men stared at their fishing poles waiting for an elusive bite, and a dozen walkers added colorful shirts, blouses, and bathing suits to the mix.

Charles peeked his head around the corner. He wore a long-sleeve, navy blue T-shirt with Xavier University proudly displayed on the front, tan shorts, and a wide smile.

"What's the smile about?" I said as he put his Tilley on the adjacent chair before leaning his cane against his chair. The brisk breeze off the ocean mussed his already unruly hair.

"Glad you're outside. I was afraid you'd wimp out, want to be in the air conditioning. I've been stuck in the apartment most of the day."

"Stuck doing what?"

"Google stuff."

He never hesitated to share his never-ending fount of trivia, so I figured he'd eventually tell me what *stuff* he'd been Googling.

I'd have to wait. Terrell came around the corner of the building and saw us. He smiled then headed to the table. He'd changed out of his chef's coat and was wearing a black T-shirt with a large Nike swoosh on the front. He still had on chef pants.

"Aha!" Charles said. "I'm beginning to see why you invited me. Knew you wanted to catch the skeleton killer."

"He called, wanted to meet. I don't know if it had anything to do with the murders."

"Murders? Like more than one?"

I didn't have time to tell him about Clarence before Terrell took the remaining seat and made the mistake many who don't know Charles make when he said, "You go to Xavier?"

"Nope. Like the big X on the front."

"Oh," Terrell said, a common reaction to my friend.

A server arrived before Charles told Terrell all the other schools he didn't attend. She told us her name was Shelly then asked what we wanted to drink.

Terrell looked at me before turning to Shelly. He told her a Budweiser would be nice. Charles said the same, I stuck with white wine.

Terrell's eyes hopped from Charles to me to the surrounding tables. His fingers tapped on the table.

"First time here?" Charles said, noticing how nervous Terrell appeared.

"Yeah. Guys at work talk about how good the food is, but most of the time when I get off work, I want to get as far from restaurants as I can."

Terrell looked at two grackles fighting over a French fry one of them grabbed off the floor after a giggling young girl "accidentally" dropped it. Drinks arrived, and Shelly asked if we were ready to order. Terrell grabbed the menu and scanned the offerings. He looked at me and shrugged, so I told her to give us a few minutes.

Terrell had called, so I didn't want to distract him from saying whatever he had to say. I took a sip of wine.

Charles, who had the patience of a chipmunk, said, "Chris tells me you called."

Terrell turned to Charles. "Yes. Do you know about the man killed yesterday near my house?"

Charles shot me a dirty look before turning to Terrell. "What man?"

Terrell said, "Clarence Taylor, he was—"

"Whoa," Charles said as his head jerked in my direction. "Isn't that the guy you and Al talked to, the one who found the skeleton?"

I told him it was which earned me another evil look.

"Sorry to interrupt," Charles said. "My friend must've forgotten to tell me. What were you saying?"

"I was going to say Clarence was shot in his yard, shot twice. No one knows who did it."

I said, "Were you close?"

"We weren't best bros, but close. I've known him forever. I can see his house from mine. He was a lot older than me. I liked it when he'd talk about the old days."

Charles said, "You have any idea who might've killed him?"

He shook his head. "Everybody liked Clarence. He didn't have kin in the area, so he spent most nights at Island Breeze talking to everyone." He shook his head again. "Everybody liked Clarence."

One person didn't, but I didn't remind Terrell of the obvious.

"I Get Around," the Beach Boys classic, played from the speakers along the restaurant's pergola.

Charles was more focused on Clarence's demise. "If everyone liked him, why do you think someone shot him?"

Shelly returned to the table to ask if we were ready to order. I motioned for Terrell to go ahead.

He pointed to an item on the menu. "I'll have the smoked jumbo wings."

Charles went with a fried grouper sandwich; I said the same.

As soon as our server left, Charles returned to his question. "Why do you think he was killed?"

Terrell took another sip. "That's why I called Chris. I think it has to do with the body Clarence found."

"But why kill him?" I said. "All he did was stumble on the remains."

Terrell shook his head. "If that's all he did, I think he'd still be alive."

Charles said, "What's that mean?"

Terrell ignored Charles's question. He was staring at two men being seated three tables away. He then lowered his eyes and whispered, "Crap."

Charles turned in the direction Terrell had been staring. "What?"

"See the fat guy with black hair?"

I slowly turned, trying to get a better look at the men without being conspicuous. One was thin, wore a short-sleeve white T-shirt with Def Leppard in red on the front. The other man was obese, with long black hair, wearing a black T-shirt. Both appeared in their sixties.

Charles said, "What about him?"

"Name's Andrew Delaney. He's in the KKK."

Charles said, "Ku Klux Klan?"

"Yeah, but they're trying to sound classier. His group's called the Loyal White Knights of the Ku Klux Klan." He mumbled something I couldn't understand.

I said, "How do you know?"

"A white guy I work with knows him. Says he's trouble. Told me I'd do myself a favor if I stayed clear of him. I've seen him in Rita's a couple of times. Rumor is he and his buddies have been cruisin' Sol Legare, but I've never seen him there."

The breeze had picked up. It may've been my imagination, but I felt a chill in the air.

Charles glanced toward the men. "Why would he be on Sol Legare?"

"Only reason I think of is to cause trouble. My friend that told me he saw him out there said Delaney was in a pickup truck with two other white dudes. They were driving slow. My friend was walking along the road when the pickup sped up and passed real close. Said the truck nearly hit him."

"Was that the only time your friend saw them?" I asked.

"Yes, but he told me another guy saw two other trucks a couple of days earlier. Delaney was in one of them."

Charles glanced at the men again. "How do you know his name?"

Good question, I thought.

"A few months ago, there was a picture in the Charleston paper showing three guys waving a big Confederate flag down at the Battery. One of them was named Andrew Delaney. The day before the picture was in the paper, he was in Rita's; got in an argument with the server. Something stupid about his credit card. It really shook the server. She told all of us in the kitchen about it, kept repeating his name." Terrell smiled. "Course she surrounded it with profanities. We all looked to see who she was talking about. It was the guy over there." He nodded his head in the direction of the other table. "My friend on Sol Legare also saw the picture in the paper. That's how he knew the guy in the truck and told me about it."

Charles said, "Know who the other man is?"

"No, he wasn't with Mr. White Knight in Rita's."

Our food arrived, the Byrds version of "Mr. Tambourine Man" filled the air, and immersed in silence, we each took a bite.

A few awkward minutes later, Terrell said, "Sorry to change the subject, let me get back to Clarence. I was saying if all he did was find the skeleton, things might've turned out different."

Charles said, "How?"

"Clarence was a talker. Suppose after spending all that time in his house by himself, he had to say a lot of words to catch up. When he was in Island Breeze or at any of the picnics folks had on Mosquito, Clarence talked up a storm. Not only talking."

I waited for Charles to repeat, "What's that mean?" Instead, he said, "Talking about the skeleton?"

Terrell nodded. "Nearly every second since he found it. He wasn't just talking, he more like was quizzing everyone old enough to be around Mosquito in the 1950s, early '60s. He wouldn't let anyone off the hook. Asked them if they knew Elijah, if they hung with him, if they knew if he had enemies, on and on."

"Terrell," Charles said, "do you think he was killed because he was asking too many questions?"

"No," Terrell said, and looked around at the nearby tables. "Think he was killed because he got answers."

"Elaborate," I said.

"Clarence didn't look like much in his tattered bib overalls, his wrinkled face, but I'll tell you one thing, he was smart. He was a sharp old man." He chuckled.

Charles said, "What's funny?"

"I remember Clarence once told me old-timers said the way to find out if someone was lying, they'd get a Bible, open it up and have the person tell the story again. Said if the person was lying, the pages would flip without anyone touching them. He said it'd scare the shi—umm, scare them enough to tell the truth. Wouldn't be surprised if he didn't try that trick on people he suspected of the killing."

"Terrell," I said, "think he figured out who killed the man?"

"Yes sir."

I said, "Did he tell you that?"

"No, but that's why I'm telling you. Like I told you before, with you being outsiders, I doubt you could get close enough to folks to learn much, but you never know. You said you were good at helping the police. Figured you could help again."

I didn't remind him Charles had said it, not me. I didn't have to, Charles said, "We'll do our best."

Terrell took another bite, watched a dozen or so seagulls off the edge of the Pier squawking about something, looked at me, then turned to Charles. "Don't know what you can do, but I'll tell you what I'm going to do. Clarence was more like my pop than a friend. He didn't deserve to die for asking questions. Fellas, if it's the death of me, I'm going to find out who killed Clarence, maybe who killed the buried body."

I was afraid that was where he was going with the conversation.

"Terrell, like I told you before, whoever killed Clarence won't hesitate to kill again if he feels someone is getting close to finding out what happened. It could be dangerous. You need to stay out of it, leave it to the police."

He said he'd think about it. I wasn't convinced. Now to change the subject. "Have plans been made for his funeral?"

Terrell looked out to sea and I wondered if he'd heard my question. Finally, he said, "No funeral. Police found a note on my friend's bulletin board. One of the cops I know let me copy it." He took a folded piece of paper out of his pocket, unfolded it, and handed it to me. Charles leaned over to read it along with me.

This here's my final request. Pay attention, I mean it. I've been to too many funerals in my life. I don't want to go to another one, especially with me in the box. I want someone to take what money I have left in my checking account and have me cremated. You all can spread it anywhere you want. I don't care. What I do want is for you all to throw a big celebration of my life. Hold it at Island Breeze. If I had any money left in my account, buy the drinks. If not, sorry, you're on your own. If there are any tears, I'll come back and haunt you. This is a party, a celebration.

Charles said, "When's the party?"

"It'll be in a few days. No one wants to celebrate yet. I'll let you know."

From the restaurant's speakers, Jan and Dean harmonized on "Dead Man's Curve."

15

The next morning, I woke up thinking about Terrell's theory on why Clarence Taylor was murdered, also how Terrell was determined to uncover who killed him. I was also thinking about how good French toast sounded for breakfast. I couldn't do anything about Terrell, but a walk to the Lost Dog Cafe would meet my breakfast need. It wasn't yet seven-thirty so there were several vacant tables. Amber was behind the counter waving for me to sit anywhere. I headed for my favorite booth along the back wall when I noticed Marc Salmon at a table in the center of the room. He was often seated where he could be the center of attention along with Houston, his fellow council member.

I smiled at Marc. "Where's your buddy?"

"Running late. He called a plumber last night, something about a leak in the kitchen." He glanced at his watch. "The plumber's there now."

The last time I needed a plumber, it took three days then was a given a four-hour window for him to arrive. "How'd he get a plumber to his house this early?"

"Played the council member card. It doesn't work as good as playing the mayor card, but it beats being Joe Average Citizen."

Whatever, I thought. "I'll let you get back to eating."

"Why don't you join me? It'll be a while before he gets here. He and I've got important business to discuss. You know, we're looking at new regulations on property owners who rent houses to vacationers. The question being, does the city need to inspect them? We're also hot and heavy in trying to stop building close to the shore. For some reason a few of our citizens think if they build a house near the beach, it'll be there forever. Mother Nature has a way," he chuckled, "or wave, of proving them wrong."

Those were hot-button topics the council had been grappling with, but I suspected most of Marc and Houston's restaurant conversations centered on the latest rumors and gossip swirling around Folly.

"Why not."

Amber was quick to the table. She looked at my normal booth then at Marc. "Morning Chris. You lost?"

"Miss Amber," Marc pointed at me. "I thought Chris here needs to learn more about the governance of our city."

She shook her head. "You mean you want to see if he has any gossip."

Marc patted her arm. "You know me well."

Chris," she said, ignoring his comment. "Can I recommend our fresh fruit parfait?"

"Of course you may. I'll have French toast."

She put her hand over her chest. "Bring out the defibrillator. I think my heart's done stopped."

Marc held up his coffee mug. "Amber, don't die before you get me a refill."

She smiled at the council member. "Here are two rumors for you. Marc Salmon is an idiot. The guy sitting with him is going to be the death of me yet."

Marc laughed. "Amber, say it all again slower so I can take notes." He pretended he was writing on the table.

She rolled her eyes then left us to discuss city business or the latest rumors. I didn't have to wait long for Marc's preference.

"So," he said, "what's new?"

"Not much. I heard about someone getting killed on Sol Legare Road. Know anything about it?"

"I didn't hear about it until Mrs. B. came home from the beauty shop."

Mrs. B., for Bridget, was Marc's wife and angel-in-training to put up with him.

"What'd she say?"

"Nothing more than a man was found shot dead in his yard. Why?"

I didn't want to get in a long discussion about the murder, the skeleton, or the people I'd met at Mosquito Beach. I limited my answer to, "I'd recently met the man who was killed."

I was being overly optimistic if I thought that would end it with Marc.

"Where'd you meet him?"

I told Marc I took a friend to Mosquito Beach after he told me he'd spent time there in the 1950s. He wanted to see the place again, and we'd met Clarence Taylor on our visit. The best way to slow Marc's questioning was to give him a chance to expound on something he knew.

"Marc, you know Eugene Dillinger?"

"Sure. Big time builder. Built some of the larger houses over here. In fact, he's building one out East Ashley. Why?"

"Somebody told me he had less than a stellar reputation. I figured if anyone knew anything about him, it'd be you."

A little sucking-up goes a long way with Marc.

He looked around to see if anyone was listening before turning to me. "These are only rumors, mind you. I heard a few years ago, maybe more than a few. I think it was in the 1970s." He shook his head. "Time flies, doesn't it?" He didn't wait for a reply. "Dillinger got in trouble with our friends at the Internal Revenue Service."

"What happened?"

"Don't know for certain but heard it was a big stink. The feds don't take kindly to people not paying taxes. Go figure. He paid a large fine, they confiscated some of his properties. He was building a strip center, also some cheap houses in North Charleston in those days.

Heard he lost it all. Now I don't know that for a fact. Rumor, you know."

"Isn't he—"

Marc snapped his fingers. "There's more. Another story going around was he got in trouble with the Department of Labor. Minimum wage in the '70s was a hair over two bucks an hour. Dillinger was paying his workers fifty-cents less."

That was consistent with what I'd heard about him underpaying the employees he got from the Sol Legare area.

"How'd he get from all those problems to building upscale houses at the beach?"

Amber returned with my breakfast, a coffee refill for Marc. He told her he was glad she was still alive. She told him I wouldn't be for long if I kept eating French toast every meal. Marc said that wasn't his problem. All he cared about was her remaining among the living to keep his coffee flowing. She left on that high—low—note.

Marc took a sip then pointed his mug at me. "Chris, I've known you ever since you moved here back in the dark ages. I've known your buddy Charles since prehistoric times. The only time you two ask questions like the ones you've been laying on me is when you're nosing in police business. Do these questions about Eugene Dillinger have something to do with the murder on Sol Legare?"

"Marc, I'm curious. I heard he hired a lot of his workers in the 1950s and '60s from the African American community on Sol Legere. I met him one night when I was over there eating. That's all."

"Hmm."

I escaped having to answer more questions when Houston arrived at the table saying, "Have I been replaced?"

I grinned. "You're irreplaceable."

I'll let him figure out how I meant it. My regular table was still vacant, so I started to take my breakfast to it.

"One more rumor," Marc said. "Hear he also got in trouble for using substandard building materials. I wouldn't trust him as far as I could heave Houston."

***

After my life-threatening French toast, I stopped by Barb's Books to see how the owner's morning was going.

I was greeted with, "You again."

I assumed it to be a term of endearment, so I smiled. "Good morning my favorite bookstore owner."

Fortunately, she returned my smile. "I assume you're not here to buy anything, so can I interest you in coffee?"

I'd reached my limit but didn't want to appear unappreciative. "Sure." I followed her to the back room where she fixed each of us a cup.

"Your friend Terrell was in yesterday."

"Why?"

"Unlike some people, he actually likes books rather than simply drinking my coffee."

Of course, she wasn't referring to me. "Did he buy anything?"

"Yes. I called him a couple of days ago to tell him I got a book in about the Civil War in South Carolina. He asked if I'd hold it for him, said he'd get it on his way to work"

"What'd he have to say?"

"You mean after he thanked me profusely for holding the book?"

I rolled my eyes. "Yes."

She smiled. "I didn't tell him the only other customer who has any interest in the Civil War is your friend William. Terrell didn't say much since he was running late for work. He did say one thing that bothered me. He's looking into who killed the man the other day. Suppose the decedent was Terrell's neighbor."

I told her about my conversation with Terrell at Rita's and how he said the victim was a friend, or more like a father figure since he was much older than Terrell.

"I hope he has enough sense to leave police work to the police." She tilted her head as she glared at me. "I wish everyone I know had that much sense."

"I do, too."

My phone rang before Barb asked if that included me. Charles's name appeared on the screen.

"I've got a hankering for chicken wings, maybe a barbecue sandwich for supper. Want to go with me tonight?"

I didn't have to ask Charles where.

I told him it sounded good then was surprised when he said he'd drive, would buy, and would pick me up at the house at five o'clock.

Barb either knew it'd be futile trying to discourage me from getting involved in things that were none of my business or had forgotten what we'd been talking about before Charles's interruption. She asked if I wanted to go with her Monday afternoon to an art gallery in Charleston. She said she needed to get out of the store and Mondays were slow. It wouldn't have been on my list of things I wanted to do, but the chance to spend time with Barb trumped my lack of desire to see paintings. I said I'd love to.

16

The temperature was in the upper 70s, and combined with the low humidity, it felt great outside. I was waiting for Charles on my front step when he arrived thirty minutes before the time he said he'd be here.

"On time, great," he said as I slipped in the passenger seat.

Charles was wearing his ratty, tan shorts, and a navy blue, long-sleeve T-shirt with *Fisk Bulldogs 1866* on the front.

I didn't comment on the shirt or his on-time remark. As if I didn't know, I said, "Where're we going, if it's not too much to ask?"

"Not too much to ask," he said and pulled out of the drive, turned on Center Street to head off-island. I sat back in the seat enjoying not having to drive for a change. It wasn't too much to ask but appeared to be too much to answer.

"Aren't you going to ask again where we're headed?"

"Nope."

He turned on Sol Legare Road, reinforcing what I suspected.

I wasn't the only person who thought it felt good outside. Cars were parked across the street from Island Breeze, and for a hundred yards on either side of the lively dining spot. All the tables in front were taken plus several customers standing nearby. We stepped in the crowded restaurant where there wasn't a vacant table to be had. I suspected the area out back was equally crowded.

Jamal Kingsly and Robert Graves were leaning against the bar with a beer bottle in front of each.

Jamal waved me over. "Chris, it is Chris?"

I smiled and told him it was.

"And Charles."

Charles said, "Right again."

"Guys, there's an hour wait. We've been here near that long, so we should have a table soon. If you want, you can join us." He shrugged. "If not, no hard feelings."

Charles moved beside me, smiled, and said, "We'd love to."

Jamal introduced Robert to Charles then asked where the man I'd been with the last time was. I told him about Al's Walmart-greeter-like job in Charleston and that he doesn't often get away from the bar. Robert said he enjoyed talking to Al, said not many old-timers are left. I told him I'd try to bring Al the next time.

A college-age employee came over to Jamal to say his table was ready. She had a diamond stud in her nose and was wearing a white T-shirt with a large *C* on the front with the word *Charleston* through it. We followed her out the back door to a table along the side of the property.

Charles pointed to her shirt. "College of Charleston?"

She gave him a wide smile. "I'm a junior." She pointed at his shirt. "You go to Fisk?"

He smiled. "No."

She started to respond, but like many who encounter Charles for the first time, didn't know what to say. She retorted with, "A server will be with you shortly."

"Ain't Fisk a black school in Tennessee?" Jamal said.

Charles smiled. He could spew trivia to a new audience. "Yes, Nashville. Founded in 1866 as an all-black school. Its student population is now about eighty-percent African American."

"Interesting," Robert said with as much enthusiasm as Mick Jagger at a ballet.

We were saved from an extended history lesson about Fisk when a tall, middle-aged gentleman with a goatee and a full head of stringy black hair arrived. He announced he was Isaac and would be serving us. I silently thanked him for the interruption as we ordered drinks.

The bubbly reggae beat of Bob Marley's "Waiting in Vain" bounced from the sound system mixing with the conversations from the crowded dining area. Jamal leaned forward so we could hear him over the music. "What brings you to our hotbed of ethnic culture?"

Charles looked around the patio. "President Gerald Ford once said, 'The three-martini lunch is the epitome of American efficiency. Where else can you get an earful, a bellyful, and a snootful at the same time?' We wanted to savor some of the best Caribbean cuisine in Charleston County, imbibe in beer, meet new friends."

Jamal stared at him with a look created by awe, or gas.

Robert smiled at Charles. "My wife Sandra looked at me a couple of months ago. She said, 'Robert, you can't shit a bullshitter.' Charles, I think she was talking about the wrong man."

Jamal laughed so loud that the couple at the neighboring table turned to look at him. Robert joined in the laughter. To Charles's credit, so did he. I never thought Charles was that funny but to maintain peace at the table, I laughed along with them.

Isaac returned with our drinks and asked Robert what was so funny.

Robert tipped his RiverDogs hat to the server and said, "Politics."

Isaac set a new beer in front of Robert and said, "Ain't that the truth?"

Instead of responding to Isaac, Robert took a long draw out of the bottle while Isaac gave each of us our drinks then asked if we wanted to order.

Jamal asserted himself as the king of the table when he said, "How about bringing a couple orders of wings?"

Isaac told us he knew where he could find some and headed out on the quest. Bob Marley continued working his way through his greatest hits with "Three Little Birds," as the chatter from diners increased in volume.

For the next few minutes, the conversation covered the typical talking points when strangers were thrown together. The weather, size of the crowd, how we liked the music, and more talk about the weather filled time until Isaac returned with our wings.

Charles's true reason for wanting to visit Mosquito Beach began to emerge when he said, "Did I hear something about a man getting killed somewhere over this way?"

"Clarence Taylor," Robert said as he shook his head. "He was one of the nicest people you'd want to meet."

"Was everyone's friend," Jamal added.

Charles said, "Anyone know what happened?"

"Suppose the person that shot him knows," Jamal said.

"Jamal," Robert said, "you know everyone better than I do. Anybody have an idea who did it?"

Jamal shook his head. "Don't know about the police, but nobody I talk to is sharing names."

Charles snapped his fingers as he turned to me. "Chris, didn't you tell me it was Clarence Taylor who found that skeleton?"

Since that was the reason Charles wanted to come tonight, I didn't think he deserved an answer. For our new friends benefit, I said, "Yes."

"Wow," Charles said in the direction of our table mates. "Think finding the skeleton had anything to do with someone shooting him?"

"Don't see how it could," Robert said. "I was talking to Clarence a couple of days before he died." He bit his lower lip. "We were right out there by the creek. Such a nice man. He didn't say anything about finding the skeleton. Nothing seemed to be bothering him." He turned to Jamal. "Do you think it had something to do with the skeleton he found?"

He shook his head. "All Clarence did was stumble on bones. How could that have anything to do with it?"

Charles bit meat off one of the wings, took a sip of beer, then said, "Chris knows this, but you fellas wouldn't. I pride myself on being a private detective. I've helped the police over the years; helped them catch bad guys. There's something I learned a long time ago, something the police taught me." He nodded and took another sip. "Know what it was?"

"I'm not good at guessing," Jamal said. "Why don't you tell us?"

Jamal didn't know he couldn't stop Charles if he'd stuck a billiard ball in his mouth.

"Guys," Charles said, "there's no such thing as a coincidence."

Of course, there was. Fortunately, neither Jamal nor Robert challenged him.

Robert said, "Are you saying Clarence was killed because he found a bunch of bones buried out there, bones that'd been buried forever?"

"Yes."

Jamal shook his head. "Man, that don't make sense."

"I agree with Jamal," Robert said. "Charles, since you're a detective, how're the two related?"

"That's a good question. I didn't know Clarence. I don't know anything about the skeleton, so it'd be hard for me to answer."

Time to move on, I thought. "I'm sure the police will figure it out."

Jamal said, "Wouldn't count on it."

"Why not?" I asked.

He pointed at Robert, then at Charles and me. "You all can't understand what it's like being black, especially in the South. It ain't your fault, you just can't. They're better now than they were in the old days, but the police still don't take crime in the black community as serious as in white places. Oh sure, they give lip-service to doing their job, investigating crimes, working on catching bad guys. Hell, sometimes they're successful." He stared at his beer bottle. "Sometimes."

Bob Marley got a break. The Four Tops were singing "It's the Same Old Song," the boisterous crowd continued to get louder. Our table fell silent.

Finally, Robert said, "Jamal, this ain't the old days, the Klan doesn't cause trouble anymore, there are plenty of excellent white and African American cops. Don't you think they want to catch the person who shot Clarence?"

"You may be right, but I ain't holdin' my breath."

Robert mentioning the Klan reminded me of Terrell pointing out Andrew Delaney at Pier 101.

"Jamal, Robert, either of you know Andrew Delaney?"

Robert shook his head as he leaned back in the chair.

Jamal glared at me, gripped his beer bottle so hard I was afraid it would break. Through gritted teeth said, "Why?"

I took that as yes. "Robert reminded me of something I heard the other day from someone else who lives over here, Terrell Jefferson. I was talking to him when he saw Andrew Delaney. He told me Delaney was a member of the Ku Klux Klan and had been riding up and down Sol Legare Road. He didn't know why."

Jamal continued to strangle the beer bottle, then said, "How'd Terrell know the bastard?"

"He said someone at work knew him and told Terrell to stay clear. Said Delaney is bad news. Jamal, I figured since you knew everything that goes on here, you'd know him."

"The Klan has been strong in Charleston, not as much now as in the past, but still around. A few years back, they got all hot and bothered when some of the wiser politicians pushed to have Confederate monuments removed from public places. That got the Klan riled up. Hell, it probably got them more attention with more people joining. Bad always comes out of good." He chuckled. "You can probably guess we don't share afternoon tea and crumpets. Yes, I know who he is."

Isaac returned to see if we needed anything else. Again, Jamal spoke for us. He said two more orders of wings would be perfect. Marvin Gaye was singing "What's Going On," and Robert said, "Anybody have something good to say about anything?"

Charles must have a different definition of something good. He said, "Anybody know yet who the skeleton belonged to?"

"Nobody's proved it yet," Jamal said, "but I'd put money on Elijah Duncan."

That was the same thing he'd told Al and me.

"I thought he ran off with Preacher Samuel's daughter," Robert added.

Jamal said, "He was trouble around here. Let's move on. Let the past be gone."

Robert looked at his watch. "Fellas, you'll have to eat wings by yourself. If I don't get home soon, Sandra will be burying my body out here." He threw a twenty on the table saying he figured it'd cover his share of the food.

"Thought you were going to buy my beer," Jamal said.

"In your dreams, old man."

Jamal reminded Robert that he was four years older than Jamal then gave him a man hug before he headed home to Sandra.

Our wings arrived quicker than the first time. Jamal patted his stomach. "Now that Robert's gone, that's more for us. Eat up, boys."

17

We'd finished the wings and socializing with sunset still a half-hour in front of us. Charles asked if he could see where Clarence found the skeleton. He'd driven, so I didn't have much choice. I told him to drive to the end of Mosquito Beach Road. We passed a cyan-colored building and pulled in a small, rutted, sandy parking area under a large live oak. The tidal creek was on our left, a wide swath of marsh to our right. The tide was out and a couple of jon boats rested on pluff mud. It would've been difficult for a boat to dock during low tide. Roughly four hundred feet across the marsh, I saw cars on Sol Legare Road and the back of houses.

Hidden behind one of the oaks to our left, a short piece of yellow crime-scene tape was tied to the trunk of a small tree. The loose end flapped in the light breeze. Straggly grass, weeds, and sand had been trampled by what looked like a herd of buffalo or many law enforcement officials. This must be where the body had been. Charles headed to the spot where the ground had been excavated.

He looked around then said, "Chris, I can't see the other buildings from here but have a clear view of the houses across the water. There wouldn't have been much privacy to bury someone."

"True now, but I wonder how many of those houses were there

when it was buried. Look how deserted it is out here now. If he was buried after dark, I doubt anyone would've been close enough to see anything."

Charles nodded toward the three houses closest to where we were standing. "Think one of those belonged to Clarence?"

"Could be. He told me he lived a short jon boat ride from where we are. Come to think of it, he said he inherited his house from his father who inherited it from his father."

"Meaning, he probably would've lived there when the guy was buried." He looked back at the houses across the water. "Young Clarence could've seen what happened."

"Maybe," I said. "If the skeleton belongs to the man Jamal and Al thinks it is, he was killed in the early 1950s, making Clarence ten or so at the time. Don't you think he would've said something then about what he saw?"

"If he understood what he was seeing. Just trying to figure it out," he said then walked around the trees, pushed some brush aside with his cane, and stared at the ground like he'd find a written confession stuck in the sandy soil. Finally, he looked up. "Don't think there's anything else to see."

* * *

I WAS SCHEDULED to meet Barb at seven at Loggerhead's Beach Grill located directly across the street from her condo in the Charleston Oceanfront Villas. Like the night before at Island Breeze, the weather continued its moderate temperature with low humidity, both rare for September. It was perfect for sitting outside at the restaurant's large elevated deck. On a less positive note, I knew the exceptional weather would bring out more patrons than seats at the popular venue, so I arrived forty-five minutes before Barb was to get here hoping I could get a table. Ed, the restaurant's owner along with his wife, Yvonne, said he was glad to see me as I reached the top of the stairs. I looked over the packed deck. Ed put my name on a list saying there should be something available before Barb arrived. I thanked him and managed to find a vacant stool at the outside bar when a couple was told their table was available, giving up their seats.

I ordered a glass of Chardonnay from the harried bartender and listened to my favorite island entertainer, Teresa Parrish, aka Sweet T, sing "Jolene," from the raised area in the corner of the deck. My wine arrived, and I glanced around the crowded deck and realized how fortunate I was to live where so many people from other parts of the country want to spend their hard-earned vacation time and dollars.

Teresa transitioned into "Smile, Smile, Smile," one of her self-penned songs, as a vaguely familiar man pushed his beer belly up to the bar taking the stool next to mine. It took me a few seconds to remember it was the alleged KKK member Terrell had pointed out. He wore a black T-shirt like the one he'd worn the other time I'd seen him.

I didn't see Mr. KKK order, but the bartender set a plastic cup of beer in front of him. He took a sip, turned toward the stage, and bumped my arm. Beer sloshed on my shorts.

He said, "Crap! Sorry, man."

I told him it was okay and hesitated. To talk or not to talk, that is the question. I decided to do a Charles imitation.

"Are you Andrew?"

He looked at me like he couldn't recall seeing me before, a legitimate expression since he probably hadn't.

He finally smiled. "Andrew Delaney, at your service. Let me buy you a drink to make up for my clumsiness."

I told him he didn't have to, that my shorts would dry.

"I insist." He looked at my face again. "Have we met?"

I told him who I was then added, "Someone pointed you out to me the other day at Pier 101." I didn't want to give him time to ask who, so I added, "Live over here?"

"James Island, just past Harris Teeter."

"What brings you to Loggerhead's?"

He must've thought it was a trick question. He narrowed his gaze. "Why?"

"Curious."

"A couple of friends live over here. They like to hang out at a few of the outdoor bars so I thought I might run into one of them."

"They're not here?"

"Not yet. Even if they don't show, the beer's good. Let me order that wine."

I again told him it wasn't necessary, but it didn't stop him. I hoped the bartender was slow since my glass was still half full.

"Past Harris Teeter," I said, "That's near Sol Legare Road, isn't it?"

"Close, why?"

Why must be one of his favorite words.

"Since you live out that way, I was wondering if you heard about the murder on Sol Legare Road."

I waited for why.

"Who hasn't? Why?"

I figuratively patted myself on the back.

"What'd you hear?" I asked ignoring his predictable use of the three-letter word.

"Only that it was an old black man." A frown appeared on his face. "Excuse me, I should've said African American. Got to be politically correct, you know. Heard he was shot in his yard, probably by some other, umm, African American. Black-on-black killings are the way most go down. What did you hear about it?"

It may've been in the upper-70s, but I was skating on thin ice. "Not much more than you've heard. I met him once. Seemed like a nice man."

Andrew stared at me like I'd grown horns. "Where'd you meet Clarence?"

The victim had gone from being an *old black man* to Clarence. Interesting.

"A friend and I were on Mosquito Beach a while back and met him. How'd you know him?"

My second drink arrived. I was beginning to think just in time. I watched Andrew's expression change from a frown to glimmers of anger. Had I said too much?

"I may've met him years ago. I worked for a landscape company back then. My boss hired quite a few, umm, African Americans from out Sol Legare. His name sounded familiar when I saw it in the paper." He lowered his voice. "My friends and I don't have, don't want to have, contact with black folks, if you know what I mean."

After hearing what Terrell had said about him, I suspected I knew, but he didn't need to know that. I shook my head. "I'm not sure what you mean."

His eyes shot daggers my direction. Yes, I'd gone too far.

"You a bleeding-heart liberal?"

I forced a smile. "No way," I said, hoping to lower his blood pressure, mine as well. "I was curious what you meant about you and your friends. It sounded like you might be a member of a white supremacist group. Just curious."

He returned what most likely was a forced smile. "What if I am? Have a problem with that?"

I had several but expressing any of them would surely bring an abrupt end to our conversation. I shook my head.

That appeared to appease him. He said, "I've got my own opinion about blacks, but in my line of work, have to get along with everyone. Enough said."

I thought of something the famous politician and legislator, Sam Rayburn, once said, "No one has a finer command of language than a person who keeps his mouth shut." I followed that sage advice. Charles would've been proud of me. Not for keeping my mouth shut, but for being able to quote someone, even if it wasn't a president.

He tapped his empty beer bottle on the counter then looked at his watch. "Don't look like my friends are going to show. Better head out."

His friends are probably at a Klan rally.

Andrew started to slide off the stool, turned, patted me on the back, and said, "Be careful out there. Never can tell what might happen to you out Sol Legare."

18

Barb hadn't arrived, but good to his word, Ed told me a table was ready earlier than he thought it'd be, then escorted me to a spot along the railing overlooking the street and Barb's condo building. The live music had ended, and numerous conversations floated through the air sprinkled with bursts of laughter.

I replayed my conversation with Andrew as I waited. He hadn't said much I didn't know or would've guessed. I was pleased he didn't get too defensive or angry when I asked if he was a white supremacist. It clearly irritated him, but he kept his anger under control. He also didn't deny it. One thing stuck out. He knew Clarence's name and said he may've met him years ago. He was also interested in how I knew Clarence. Did that mean anything beyond the obvious. Probably not, yet it struck me as interesting.

Barb saved me from reading more into Andrew's comments. She weaved her way around the tables. She wore a red blouse, tan shorts, and a smile that made me forget Andrew.

"Sorry I'm late," she said as she sat on the other side of the small table. "Had a rush of customers as I was locking up."

That was something I'd never experienced during the years her building housed Landrum Gallery. In fact, not only did I not have a rush of customers as I was trying to close for the day, I never had a rush of customers, period. That's a big reason why my former gallery space is now a bookstore.

"You're worth waiting for."

She pointed at my wine. "How many of those have you had? You're sounding like some of your weird friends."

"This is number two. I like to think my friends, weird or otherwise, are beginning to sound like me."

"You wish."

A server arrived before our conversation regressed further. She said she was Lorraine and asked what Barb wanted to drink. Barb told her she would have what I was having. She added she would probably need more to put up with me. Lorraine didn't offer an opinion.

"So, how've you spent another day in retirement?"

It didn't take many words to say until I arrived at Loggerhead's, I hadn't done anything since greeting the morning. I then mentioned Charles and I spent time yesterday on Mosquito Beach. Barb's wine arrived, and our conversation began to feel like an interrogation by a defense lawyer, which was what she'd been before moving to Folly. She began by asking why we had gone there. I told her it was his idea.

She stared at me. "Did Charles handcuff you, throw you in his car, force you to go with him?"

"No."

"Did he want to visit Mosquito Beach because there wasn't anywhere to eat on Folly?"

"Another no."

"Are you two playing detectives again?"

"Of course not."

Barb smiled, shook her head, then held up her wine glass before saying, "Knew I'd need more of these."

Lorraine must have seen Barb's gesture. She returned to ask if we wanted to order. Thank you, Lorraine.

Barb said, "Crab cakes plus another glass of wine."

I went with the flounder dinner but made a point of not ordering more wine.

Barb watched Lorraine go, then turned to me, "Now that you and your shadow aren't playing detective, did you learn anything out there that if you happened to be playing detective you would've found enlightening?"

"No. We talked to Jamal Kingsly and Robert Graves," I explained who they were. "They knew the man killed the other day."

"Did either of them confess to killing him or tell you who did?"

I smiled. "We must not be as good at being detectives as Charles thinks. We didn't ask. They did have something interesting to say about the skeleton. Jamal thought it was Elijah Duncan, the man Al knew back in the 1950s. He told Al and me the same thing when I took Al to Mosquito Beach."

"Why does he think it's Elijah?"

"Nothing concrete other than Elijah ruffled feathers about race relations in the days when it wasn't the wisest thing to do."

"Did they both think it was Elijah?"

"Only Jamal. Robert thought Elijah had run off with a preacher's daughter."

"What proof did Robert have?"

"None. To be honest, I don't think either man knows what happened. They're sharing stories that've been going around for decades."

"Speaking of stories going around for years, your new friend Terrell was in the store again. He's still trying to find books on the civil rights movement. The last time he was in, I told him I'd call if I got any." She chuckled. "He's as patient as Charles."

"Interesting you should mention Terrell. When Charles and I talked with him after work the other day, he pointed out a man sitting near us saying he's a member of the Ku Klux Klan. The guy's name is Andrew Delaney." I took a sip of wine.

"And?"

She also was becoming as patient as Charles. There's hope for her.

I nodded toward the bar. "Before you got here, I was waiting at the bar for the table. Guess who was sitting beside me?"

"Andrew Delaney."

"Charles needs to add you to his detective agency."

"Funny. I suppose there's a reason you're telling me."

"We started talking. He told me he lives off Folly Road near where it intersects Sol Legare. I asked if he'd heard about the man getting shot. Not only had he heard about it, he knew Clarence by name."

"Wasn't the name all over the news?"

"Yes, but he said he may've known him years ago."

"Don't tell me you're leaping from *may have known him* to killing him."

"Not necessarily. I found it interesting that a member of the KKK knew the man who was murdered."

"Did Delaney tell you he was in the Klan?"

"Not directly, but from everything he said, it was clear he either is or was a Klan sympathizer."

"You think that'd be motive enough to kill Clarence?"

"Don't know."

Our food arrived, distracting Barb for a few minutes, but not enough to change the subject.

"Chris, that's quite a stretch. I'd tear a prosecutor to shreds if he tried to convict a client of mine with that feeble evidence."

"I know it's not much, but I think I'm going to share it with Chief LaMond."

Barb smiled. "You're going to share it with the Chief then step aside?"

"Of course."

I pretended I meant it. Barb pretended she believed me.

19

The next day began with me walking next door to Bert's for coffee and a cinnamon Danish. After all, breakfast is the most important meal of the day. I then walked two blocks to the Folly Beach Fishing Pier where I ate at the far end of the structure. I remembered my promise to Barb and started to call Chief LaMond when the phone rang. I was surprised to see the Chief's name on the screen.

"Morning Cindy, how'd you know I was getting ready to call you?"

"I'm Chief. I know everything."

"Good, so you know why I was calling."

"Okay, perhaps there are a couple of things I don't know. Where are you?"

I told her. She said she'd see me in five minutes.

The sun was breaking through low, dark rain clouds off the coast and heading away from shore. Other than a few fishermen, the Pier was unusually quiet, with a handful of walkers nearby.

The Chief wasn't off much. She was headed my way, then stopped to talk to two men leaning against the railing and staring at their fishing rods. They said something, she laughed, and patted one of them on the back before continuing toward me.

She sat beside me, reached over, pulled off a corner of my Danish, put it in her mouth, then mumbled, "We meet again on the edge of the edge."

Folly was nicknamed *The Edge of America* because of its location and because so many people gravitate to it when they are at the edge of their careers, existence, or wit.

"Morning, Cindy. How's your world?"

"Gee, you can be civil when none of your weird friends are around," she said as she picked off another slice of pastry plopping it in her mouth.

"One's around now."

"Cute. Why were you going to call?"

I leaned toward the Chief. "You first. You called me, remember?"

"True. Our friend Detective Callahan called yesterday. He was full of no information."

"He must've had some or you wouldn't have called."

She held her forefinger an eighth of an inch from her thumb. "This much." She leaned back on the wooden bench.

"You waiting for me to ask what he told you?"

"Yep."

I motioned for her to continue.

"Okay, you beat the confidential information out of me. Callahan said without DNA to compare and only estimates from the forensic anthropologist, the range of time of death of the skeleton is between 1940 and 1960, give or take a few leap years. He wasn't a skeleton back then, just recently dead."

"Didn't you say they found black and white wingtip shoes with him?"

"Wow! Unlike most people I encounter, you pay attention to what I say."

"Always."

"Don't push it. Yes, the shoes were a model produced in the late 1940s. There's no way of saying when the victim wore them, but it's consistent with what Detective Callahan found from interviewing a handful of folks who would've been around in the early '50s. It's also consistent with what your friend Al said. Elijah Duncan disappeared around 1953. According to a couple of men Callahan interviewed, he was a snazzy dresser, one who'd wear two-tone wingtips."

"I don't suppose any of the folks interviewed had much insight into what happened to Elijah?"

"Nothing worth hanging a murder charge on. Seems he simply disappeared. I know that's not what your buddy wants to hear. To be honest, I'd be shocked if we ever learn if the body belongs to Mr. Duncan. He didn't put it this way, but Detective Callahan considers the case cold, from his perspective, closed. Sorry."

"That's too bad. What about Clarence Taylor's murder?"

"Technically, I suppose, the Sheriff's Office knows more about his murder than they do about the one in the '50s. They know who he was and when he was shot."

"And?"

"That's it. No suspects, no motive."

"Don't you find it strange that Taylor finds the skeleton then is murdered?"

Cindy looked toward the beach then back at me. "Strange, definitely. Connected, no clue."

"But—"

"What about *no clue* did you not grasp?"

"Sorry. I'm just frustrated. He seemed like such a nice man."

"Frustration noted. Detective Callahan shares that feeling. He's working the case. I'm hopeful he'll get to the bottom of it, but with the clue pool empty, it won't be easy." She tapped me on the leg. "Now, since you're about as old as a diamond but not nearly as valuable, I know your brain cells are dying off as we speak, so I doubt you remember you said you were going to call me. Think you can find the reason somewhere in your deteriorating gray matter?"

"What do you know about white supremacists in the Charleston area?"

"Not much. From bulletins we receive from the feds, there's an uptick of Klan and other white supremacist groups activity in a bunch of states including South Carolina. The only real contact I've had with any of them was when some white supremacists thought it was a clever idea to wave the Confederate flag around a few locations on Folly. I thought it would have been a better idea if they'd wrapped themselves in the flags and jumped in the ocean." She pointed to the railing at the end of the Pier. "But hey, free speech is a strange and powerful thing. It makes us what we are as a country. Why the interest?"

Do you know Andrew Delaney?"

"Name's not familiar. Describe him?"

I did. I also explained how he'd been pointed out to me at Pier 101 as being a member of the Ku Klux Klan, then how I happened to be seated next to him at Loggerhead's last night.

"Why are you telling me this?"

"We started talking."

"Did you ask if he was in the Klan? If he was, where he got his white robes?"

"Not directly. He didn't come out and say it but left the distinct impression he was a member of an extremist group."

"That's not illegal. What about him bothered you?"

"I've heard that Klan members have been riding up and down Sol Legare Road. It's bothering some residents."

"I can understand that but it's a free road, out of my jurisdiction, I might add. What do you want me to do about it?"

"Nothing. There's one more thing about him. I asked if he heard about the murder the other day. He brought up Clarence Taylor's name saying he may've known him years ago. Don't you find that interesting?"

"You're adding one plus one and getting three. Delaney might be a member of an extremist group; he may have known Taylor years ago; therefore, he murdered him. In my undersized brain, that doesn't compute."

"I'm not saying he did. It seems more than a coincidence."

"Tell you what. I'll pass it along to Detective Callahan. He'll probably think I'm making a big deal about nothing. When he does, I'll give you all the credit."

"That's what friends are for."

She laughed and abruptly changed the subject by telling me about one of her officers who was showing his kid how he'd skateboarded when he was young. He's no longer young. He ran off the road with the skateboard going one way, the officer going another landing on his left arm. Now instead of wearing a uniform he's wearing a cast. Cindy thought it was way funnier than she should have.

Her expression turned serious.

"How's Al doing? I know you're worried about his health."

"Thanks for asking. He's slowing quite a bit. He's eighty-two, an age I thought was ancient when I was young. I know several people his age who are in much better shape. All his years spending day and night at Al's, plus raising nine kids, has taken a toll. He's not spending nearly as much time in the bar now than he did after Bob first took over. He's also spending more time thinking about the past. I suspect that's why he wanted me to take him to where he had good memories after returning from Korea."

"He's lucky to have friends like you, even Bob. If you tell your hefty, blustery friend I said that, I'll arrest you for...hell, I'll find something."

"Your secret's good with me."

"Enough chitchat." She started to stand, then added that unless I was going to give her a recording of someone confessing to killing Clarence Taylor, she had to get to the office to pester her officers.

I had a theory but no confession, so I thanked her for listening. She said it was more fun listening to me than to the drunks and irate citizens she spends time with. I repeated that's what friends are for.

I didn't have to go to an office, pester anyone, or be pestered, so I leaned back on the bench and watched three dolphins a hundred yards off the back of the structure. I've always been amazed by how graceful the aquatic mammals glide through the water, unlike most humans who think smacking the water is swimming. It's also possible, likely, I dozed.

My phone's ringtone jarred me out of my reverie. Al Washington's name was on the screen.

"Good morning, Al. Is everything okay?"

He chuckled. "You don't have to ask that every time I call. If something isn't okay, I'll let you know."

"You're right. I'll stick with good morning."

"Good morning to you, my friend. The reason I'm calling is to ask a huge favor. If the answer is no, I certainly understand, I sure do."

"Tell you what, why don't you ask then I'll determine how big a favor it is?"

"Fair enough. Ever since we were at Island Breeze, I've had a powerful desire for more good Caribbean food. After eating them every day for let's say a hundred years, I'm tired of my burgers, yes, I am. That's even if Bob says they're the best in the galaxy."

"Al, what do you say we go back to Island Breeze?"

He laughed. "If you insist."

"When?"

"How about tonight?"

"Umm, okay. Think Bob can get along without you there?"

"Think so. He's learning how not to offend every customer coming in the door."

"That's progress."

20

The weather veered from good to *good grief* as I was on the way to get Al. Waves of torrential downpours covered Charleston, flooding several streets. I detoured around barriers the closer I got to his house. Fortunately, there was a parking spot in front of his gate. He must've been watching for me. He came out, opened a large red and green golf umbrella before motioning for me to stay in the car. I leaned over to push the passenger door open while he closed the umbrella, shook water off, put it in the footwell, then slid in the seat.

"I know how to pick nights to go out eatin', I sure do," he said as a greeting. "Think we need to try another time?"

"The rain will end soon," I said like I knew what I was talking about. "Besides, there shouldn't be too big a crowd."

He smiled. "Sure wish my glass was half-full like yours, yes I do."

"Don't be silly. You're one of the most optimistic people I know."

"It's getting harder. These old bones remind me every day how they're nearing the end of their run."

I didn't respond.

We took another detour to get to Folly Road. The rain stopped as quickly as it had begun, and the rest of the ride was uneventful. When

I parked, Al said he was taking his umbrella in with him in case it was raining when we were leaving.

Al's old bones must have been screaming in pain. I was afraid he wasn't going to make it across the narrow road to the restaurant's entrance. I saw the real reason he brought the umbrella when he leaned on it with every step.

I was right about rain keeping customers away. There were only five diners. I recognized two from restaurants on Folly where one was a bartender, the other a server. If they were surprised to see me, it didn't show. The woman behind the bar was the same person I'd seen on my previous visits. She pointed to three vacant tables, told us to sit wherever we wanted.

Al pointed to a table in the corner in front of a colorful tapestry adorned with Bob Marley's smiling face. Painted beside the tapestry were the words "One Love," referring to Marley's song by the same name. The sound system was quiet. The lady behind the counter pointed to the menu board as she asked what we wanted to drink. Al said Ting. I had no idea what that was, so I stuck with Diet Coke. A college age server brought our drinks and asked if we were ready to order. Al squinted at the menu board. I told the server to give us a few minutes.

Al watched her go to the next table. "Thank you. I have trouble reading the fine print this far away. Would you mind telling me what's on it?"

There were only four items. One was jerk chicken. Al said that he left the only jerk he knew minding Al's.

I smiled and he said, "Let's wait a few minutes to order. I'd like to sit and soak in the atmosphere, I sure would."

I told him to soak all he wanted. The sounds of Bob Marley singing "No Woman, No Cry" flowed out of the sound system. Al smiled as he took a sip of his drink.

The rain had returned, and two men rushed in the door, flung water off their ball caps, then moved to the table beside us. I recognized both from previous visits, Robert Graves and Eugene Dillinger. Eugene waved toward the lady behind the bar and said, "Two beers."

Robert looked at Al, then at me. "Met you two in here before, didn't I?"

Eugene snapped his fingers and reached his hand out to me. "Didn't I see you here with another guy? I remember now. You and him visited a house I'm building."

They both were right. I reminded them who I was then introduced Al to Eugene.

"You're becoming a regular," Eugene said in my direction.

I told him Al had spent time on Mosquito Beach when he got back from Korea in the early '50s.

Eugene shook his head. "Korea, one hell of a mess. Glad you made it back safe, Al."

"Eugene, were you in Korea?" Al asked. "You look about the right age."

"No, thank God."

Robert tapped Eugene's arm. "Let's let these guys drink in peace."

The server returned to ask if we were ready to order.

I started to say not yet, but Al said, "How about a couple of orders of wings. We'll split them with my new friends here." He pointed to Robert and Eugene.

Robert said, "Al, you don't have to do that."

"Don't have to, want to."

The server left to put in our order. Al asked if Robert and Eugene were regulars.

"Eugene's in all the time," Robert said, "I'm here about once a week. Sandra says I—"

"Chris," Eugene interrupted, "while I'm thinking about it, tell your friend Charles I got an option yesterday on an oceanfront lot out West Ashley. If he's still interested in me building him a house, he'll love this one. It's going to have a fantastic Atlantic view from the deck."

I saw Al give me a strange look. He knew Charles, so I didn't blame him. I told Eugene I'd give Charles the message then changed the subject before Al commented.

"Either of you hear anything new about Clarence Taylor's murder?"

Robert glanced at Eugene and said, "It a crying shame, if you ask me. Clarence was one of the nicest men out this way. I'd known him for ages. If he had enemies, I never heard about them. How about you, Eugene?"

"I don't think I ever mentioned it to you, Robert, Clarence worked for my construction company for a few weeks back in the 1950s or the early '60s. That was before he went off to Viet Nam, then came back to get that good paying job at the Post Office." He laughed. "Old Clarence was skinny in those days."

Al said, "Did you two stay close all those years?"

"Not really. I think I pissed him off more than once when he worked for me. If he could get out of doing hard work, he would."

Our wings arrived, the server put an order on each table. I ordered another diet soda, Al, another Ting, the other guys asked for their second beer.

Al took a bite, wiped his mouth with a paper towel from the roll on the center of the table, then said, "Eugene, I think I remember Robert from over here in the 1950s. Were you here much then?"

"Not as much as my boy Robert here. I was growing my home building business. I was over occasionally trying to hire workers. Most of the time I was on James Island throwing up houses as quick as I could. Business was booming. Why?"

Al nodded. "Was wondering if either of you knew Elijah Duncan? He was here around 1952 or so."

"Elijah Duncan," Robert said and shook his head. "I recall him, but don't know much about him. How about you, Eugene?"

"Was he a sharp dresser, thought he was God's gift to woman, always itching for a fight about civil rights?"

Al laughed. "That'd be Elijah, yes it would."

"Why ask about him?" Robert said.

"We were friends about the time he disappeared. No one seems to know what happened to him."

Robert rubbed his chin. "I remember hearing about someone

turning up missing. That could've been your friend. I heard he ran off with a preacher's daughter."

I said, "I heard a detective from the Sheriff's Office has been asking about Elijah. There's speculation that he could've been the body."

Eugene leaned my direction. "Where'd you hear that?"

"A friend of mine is Chief on Folly. She heard it from a Sheriff's Office detective."

Robert shook his head. "No one's talked to me, how about you Eugene?"

"Nope. No reason to, I don't know anything about it."

Robert said, "Al, if it was your friend, I'm sorry to hear what happened."

"Me too, I sure am."

"Guys," I said, "do you think Clarence's murder could have anything to do with him finding the body?"

"I heard he was asking everyone about who might've murdered the guy he stumbled on," Eugene said.

"Even if he was," Robert added, "I don't see how it could have anything to do with him getting shot. My money's on an outsider."

"Why?" I asked.

Robert looked at Eugene, turned to me, and said, "Rumors have been going around that there are some, how shall I say it, outside agitators trying to stir up race issues around here. Could easily have been one of them getting in an argument with Clarence, ending with a bullet. The Clarence I remember had a quick temper. It could've gotten him killed."

"Chris," Al said, "think I'm ready for some curry chicken."

He was done talking about murder. I motioned the server over, ordered curry chicken for Al, a barbeque sandwich for me. I asked Robert and Eugene if they wanted anything. Robert said he had to get home to Sandra, Eugene said he wanted to check on his construction site on Folly. They thanked us for the wings and conversation then headed to the bar to pay for their drinks.

Al watched them go. "Nice men."

"Compared to Bob, you're right."

Al laughed before turning serious. "Are the police really asking folks over here about knowing Elijah?"

"That's what Cindy said."

"Good."

"She also told me to say hi the next time I see you."

He smiled.

Jimmy Cliff's smooth reggae sounds of "The Harder They Come" filled the room.

21

Barb called the next morning to remind me I'd agreed to accompany her to a gallery opening that evening. I said of course I remembered, that I was looking forward to it. The opening must have been somewhere in my memory bank, but until she called, it'd been misfiled. She said she'd pick me up at three o'clock and hinted since it was being held at one of Charleston's classy galleries it might be wise for me not to wear shorts. I asked if I should leave my chewing tobacco at home. She laughed before saying she knew I didn't chew tobacco but if I wanted to, she'd get me some so I could leave it at home. I told her it wouldn't be necessary; I'd even wash behind my ears before she picked me up. She responded with the same response I often get from Charles. She hung up.

Unlike Charles, she pulled in the drive at the time she'd designated. The temperature was in the upper 70s, so she had the retractable hardtop down on her new, cardinal red, Mercedes SLC roadster. She'd recently traded her Volvo for the Mercedes and said she wished she had more opportunities to drive. This was one of those opportunities. Who was I to argue? I slipped in the beige, soft leather passenger seat and kissed her cheek. She wore a red silk blouse, tan linen slacks, and tan open-toe sandals. I felt underdressed in my navy, short-sleeve, button-down shirt and gray slacks.

"What's the deal about the art exhibit?" I asked as she pulled out of the drive.

"It's the opening of an exhibit by a young Colorado painter. I read about it in the paper, thought it'd be a good chance to get away from the bookstore. Besides, it's a wine-and-cheese event. Hard to turn down."

We headed up Folly Road to the turn off to downtown Charleston. Her Sirius XM radio was on the '60s channel and Chubby Checker was blaring out "The Twist." I sat back enjoying the air blowing through my thinning hair. Barb's short black hair was going several directions. One of the many things I admired about the woman next to me was she didn't worry about appearances or what others thought of her. That is, except not wanting me to wear shorts tonight.

The road we were on became Broad Street and we drove several blocks through residential neighborhoods before reaching the intersection of King Street where Broad turned from primarily residential to commercial, an area dubbed gallery row because of several art galleries lining the historic street. The opening was in Mary Martin Gallery on the corner of Broad and King.

Parking is always an issue in this area, so Barb drove several more blocks before finding a spot on the street. That wasn't a problem since it was perfect walking weather, so we enjoyed gazing at some of the cities most beautiful residences on Tradd and Meeting Street before reaching King for the block-long walk to the gallery.

I didn't feel quite as underdressed when I saw the wide variety of attire of the twenty or so people milling around the room. Two men wore seersucker suits and bowties, another couple had on ironed jeans and bright red and green tops. The others wore everything in between. An attractive elderly lady met us at the door, with a British accent, welcomed us to the exhibit, handed each of us a glossy, full-color brochure highlighting the featured artist, then told us to mingle, visit the refreshment table, and meet Lawrence, the artist. The man she pointed out was at the side of the room talking to a woman about one of his paintings. He was roughly five-foot-four, thin, with short curly brown hair. Despite his diminutive height, he would've been hard to miss in his white, flowing long shirt and red slacks. We thanked her, skipped meeting the artist who continued an animated conversation with a potential buyer who had an ear-to-ear smile, then headed to the wine and cheese.

A college-age caterer greeted us at the drink table and offered us a glass of white wine. I took two glasses after slipping two dollars in a glass tip vase located by the cocktail napkins.

I handed a glass to Barb who was studying the brochure. She said, "Lawrence apparently doesn't have a last name or thinks we all know who he is like Oprah or Elvis." She pointed to one of his paintings. "The brochure says his paintings are reminiscent of works by Georgia O'Keeffe, recognized as the mother of American modernism."

"Oh," I said, not having a clue what that meant. What I did say was, "It's refreshing that most of his paintings are landscapes of mountains. So many of the paintings I see on the coast are seascapes."

Others arrived. We kept moving so we wouldn't block Lawrence's paintings from those who were studying them like they were the most fascinating works they'd ever seen. I spent most of the time studying the price tags ranging from five to seventeen thousand dollars. I liked his work, but his mountain scapes were too steep for my budget. Barb had drifted to the other side of the gallery where she was talking to a woman about a painting with a stream in the foreground, a sun drenched mountain in the background, when someone tapped me on the shoulder. I turned to see Lawrence smiling as he pointed to the painting I was viewing.

"That's my favorite," he said. "I simply loved the light that spring morn."

"It is incredible," I said, figuring that would be the appropriate response. What I really thought was incredible was the eleven-thousand-dollar price.

"Are you a collector?" he asked with a smile.

"No, but I am a photographer, so I appreciate the challenges of light and shadows you've captured masterfully," I said, pushing my limit on sounding artistic.

His smile lessened, probably after he figured I wasn't a potential buyer. "Are your works in nearby galleries?"

"Not currently."

He looked around the crowded gallery. "I'd better continue mingling."

He could have added, *since I can't sell you anything*. I said it was nice meeting him and wished him well with his work.

As no-last-name Lawrence headed toward a couple gazing at a canvas, I noticed his black and white wingtip shoes, reminding me of the shoes found with the skeleton on Mosquito Beach. This was the first time I'd thought of it since Barb picked me up. I also realized the painting the couple was looking at was of a cow's skull over the door of a rustic cabin with a majestic mountain range towering over it, one more reminder of the murder years ago. That depressing thought combined with the realization that even if I wanted to purchase one of these paintings I'd have to sell my house to afford it, made me lose interest in the exhibit which wasn't difficult since I had little interest to begin with. Now, how do I convince Barb we should leave?

She was talking to a couple in their thirties who appeared mesmerized by Lawrence's painting of a closeup of a flower. I heard the man with a wineglass in one hand, the woman's hand in his other hand say, "Stunning, absolutely stunning." The woman with him said, "Truly." Barb nodded, turned to me as I approached, and rolled her eyes. She patted the woman on the back, whispered something, then grabbed my elbow to lead me away from the stunned couple.

"Chris, don't we have to be somewhere? Like anywhere."

I didn't have to try hard to convince her to leave.

We left the gallery, walked one block up Broad Street, then turned right on Meeting Street. I did a Charles imitation when I asked Barb if she knew why the intersection was called the "Four Corners of Law."

"Sure. After all, I'm a lawyer. I know stuff like that. Charleston's City Hall is on one corner, the County Courthouse on another, then there's the

Federal Courthouse." She pointed at the church at the remaining corner. "Finally, St. Michael's Episcopal Church. Four corners, four buildings representing laws, including the church representing ecclesiastical law."

"Not bad. Now, do you know who coined that phrase?"

She looked at the buildings on each corner and shook her head. "No."

"Robert Ripley."

"The Ripley's Believe It or Not guy?"

"One and the same."

"There you go, channeling Charles again."

"Sorry, couldn't help it."

"If the trivia lesson's over, can we go?"

We started walking toward the car. I put my arm around her waist. "Do you ever miss practicing law?"

"Not for a second. Why?"

"Seeing those buildings made me think of it."

"Now I have a question. Other than being in a hurry to do your Charles imitation, why'd you want to leave the opening?"

"I started thinking about the skeleton found on Mosquito Beach, then Clarence Taylor's murder."

"Let's see," she said as she squeezed my hand, "would those be the murders you're not getting involved with, the ones you're leaving to the police?"

I returned her squeeze. "Yes."

She stopped. "You're not going to do that, are you?"

"I don't want to get involved. To tell you the truth, I don't know how I can."

"Yet that's not going to stop you."

I whispered, "No."

"What do you know for certain?"

"Clarence found the skeleton. Now he's dead. I'm fairly certain the skeleton is Elijah Duncan who went missing in 1953."

"What's the connection between Clarence and Elijah?"

"None really. Clarence was a decade younger than Elijah, so they probably weren't acquainted even though they grew up within a mile of each other."

"So, there's no connection."

"I've heard Clarence was asking questions about Elijah."

"What kind of questions?"

"Trying to learn who might've known him. There're still a few old-timers who go back that far."

"Did he learn anything?"

"Don't know."

"Are you thinking the person who killed Elijah killed Clarence?"

"Possibly."

We reached the car. Barb leaned against the fender. "Two things. First, that seems like a farfetched theory. Second, if it happens to be true, there couldn't be too many people around who might've known Elijah. Needless to say, 1953 was a long time ago, so anyone who's still around would most likely be in his or her eighties or older."

"I've met some of them."

"I suspect the police have also talked with them."

I nodded.

"You're not going to let it go."

I shook my head.

She surprised me when she stepped in front of me, kissed me, then said, "Please be careful."

Few words were said on the ride home. I was comfortable with the silence. It appeared Barb was as well.

22

After hanging with the upper crust, wine-and-cheese crowd last night, I wasn't ready to face another large group at a restaurant, so I headed to Bert's for breakfast. I grabbed coffee and settled for a cinnamon roll before heading to pay when someone called my name. Actually, the person said Christopher, so I knew before turning it was Virgil Debonnet. I preferred Chris for two reasons. First, it's easier to say, shorter to write. Second, I didn't like the name Christopher. Why? Just because. Virgil was slow to catch on.

I'd met Virgil six months ago a few days after Charles and I were kayaking only to be nearly decapitated by a single-engine airplane crashing in the marsh within feet of us. Four men were in the plane, two survived. The pilot had been poisoned causing the crash. To make a much longer story shorter, I met Virgil which eventually led to the two of us becoming the target of a killer. We survived, barely. Since then, Virgil and I had run across each other on several occasions.

I pivoted, smiled, and said, "Hi, Virgil. How many times do I have to tell you to call me Chris?"

He returned my smile. "I suppose more since I'm still calling you Christopher."

Virgil was in his forties, my height, with slicked-back black hair, and always wearing sunglasses.

I shook his hand while asking how he was doing.

"Amazingly well for me."

Two years ago, he owned a mansion overlooking the Charleston Harbor, a yacht, had a blue blood wife, a lifestyle bordering on one for the rich and famous. Drugs, drink, gambling, horrible stock investments combined to cost him his fortune, house, yacht, plus his wife after she told him poverty wasn't in her genes. He now lives in a small apartment on Folly. From what I could tell, he was far happier than anyone should be after his downward spiral into poverty.

"Any luck on the job search?"

He'd burned all bridges in the financial industry where he'd previously worked. To my knowledge, he spends most of his days walking around the island or frequenting bars, sharing drinks and tall tales with those around him.

"My gainful employment hiatus is still in effect, although, my landlord allows me to remain in residence if I preform maintenance tasks on the apartments in my current domicile."

"Good," I said, not knowing what else to add.

"A roof over one's head is a valuable commodity." He smiled again. "Enough about me. The rumor mill has been milling stories of one Christopher Landrum, aka Chris, who apparently is taking more than a cursory interest in a skeleton recently uncovered at a nearby venue. Care to elaborate?"

"Where'd you hear that?"

He chuckled. "Enlightening what one hears while bending elbows with some of this enchanting island's fellow imbibers."

If the answer was in there somewhere, I missed it. "Who told you?"

"Let's see," he said as he looked down at his resoled Guccis. "Oh yeah, Macy at Planet Follywood shared what he'd heard from someone who works at Rita's. Macy's acquaintance, whose name he didn't relay, said one of his fellow employees knew you, that you were helping him determine the name of the person who is now merely a skeleton. He also said in its previous life, the skeleton had been murdered. I figured you and Charles are better at catching killers than are the police, so you'd be seeking whoever murdered Mr. Skeleton."

"Have you heard anything about a more recent murder on Sol Legare Island?"

"No, but the last few days, I've been working on fixing the plumbing in two of my landlord's apartments. No time to visit my normal hangouts." He shook his head then squinched up his face. "You wouldn't believe what people flush."

I hadn't eaten, so I didn't want details. "The man who found the skeleton was murdered."

"Coincidence?"

"Don't know."

"You going to find out?"

"That's up to the police."

"I recall you saying that before. Believe it was before we had a few intimate moments with a boat hook and a bullet." He tilted his head, tapped his foot.

"Ancient history."

Virgil smiled. "You can convince some folks, but remember, I'm part of your crime-fighting trio."

When Charles and I first met Virgil, he tried to convince Charles that since he knew some of the people involved in the plane crash he could be part of my friend's private detective agency. No was a word Virgil couldn't seem to wrap his head around.

"Virgil, you do know there's not an agency outside Charles's mind?"

He smiled. "Semantics. The next time you run into Charles tell him all he has to do is call. I'll put unstopping toilets in my rear-view mirror to do whatever he needs me to do to catch the bad guys."

"I'll share that good news with him," I said, with a pinch of sarcasm.

"With that out of the way, got a question. Are you planning to head to Harris Teeter anytime soon?"

And I thought Charles was good at changing directions on the head of a pin.

"Probably. Why?"

"My scooter is under the weather, needs a part."

"They have scooter parts at Harris Teeter?"

"No, but I didn't figure you had reason to go to the cycle shop on Folly Road past Harris Teeter."

"Virgil, would you like me to take you to get the part?"

His smile widened. "Would you, fine sir?"

With my calendar blank for the next, umm, forever, I figured I could work it in.

"Yes, when?"

He looked at his watch, nodded his head left, then right. "Now?"

Five minutes later, I was munching on the roll, sipping coffee, and steering, so I left most of the talking to Virgil who excelled at filling dead air with words. I learned more than I wanted to know about the advantages of PVC pipe over cast iron in plumbing, how he was picking up a few dollars a week dog walking two Irish setters for a lady two block from his apartment, and making serious efforts to cut back on drinking. He was cutting back because he wanted to plus lacked finances to maintain his habit. We arrived at the cycle shop before he shared more of his innermost feelings. He'd called ahead so they were holding a flywheel for his scooter. He paid, and we headed home. I asked if he knew how to install the part.

"Sure, that world-renowned scooter mechanic Mr. Greasy Hands Google said it's easy-peasy."

Fortunately, I didn't have to respond. The phone rang.

"Chris, this is Terrell, you know, from Rita's."

"Sure, Terrell, what's up?"

Virgil wasn't like Charles who'd be gesturing for me to put the phone on speaker so he could hear. He stared out the window, probably replaying Mr. Google's easy-peasy instructions.

"I know you've been over at Mosquito several times lately. Are you going to be there anytime in the next couple of days?"

"Why?"

"I've got three days off, been working on my house. I thought if you were nearby, you might stop in."

I didn't figure it was to help with the work. Did he have something important to share? "Terrell, I'm with a friend, we're on Folly Road near Harris Teeter. If it's okay with my friend, we could stop by now?"

Virgil must have started listening. He nodded.

"Umm, sure, I guess."

"If it's inconvenient, I could make it another time."

"No, that's not it. Things are a mess here. I didn't want to … never mind, now is perfect." He gave me directions and I said we'd be there in a few minutes.

I set the phone on the console and Virgil said, "What'd I agree to?"

I told him who Terrell was.

Virgil smiled. "So, meeting him doesn't have anything to do with you figuring out who killed Mr. Skeleton?"

I shrugged.

23

I followed Terrell's directions and turned on the first road past where Mosquito Beach Road intersects Sol Legare Road then turned in the third gravel drive. The house was a single-story wood frame structure that had withstood numerous storms and hurricanes over the years. The front porch and steps looked new and were in drastic contrast with the rest of the structure. Scrap lumber matching the porch leaned against the side of the house and a rusting, green Ford pickup truck with two pieces of lumber in the bed was parked at the far end of the drive.

Terrell was quick to the door. He had on a white, paint-splattered T-shirt and black shorts, held a paintbrush in one hand, a lit cigarette in the other. He pushed the screen door open with his elbow.

"Welcome to my humble abode." He waved us in with the paintbrush.

The living room was to the left and was obviously the canvas for his painting. Tarps covered the sofa and what appeared to be a couple of chairs or possibly a table. Blue and green flowered wall covering was still on two walls with the edge closest to the ceiling curled from age. The other two walls had been stripped of the wall covering;

newly applied light-gray paint covered one of them. The walls with the flowery wall covering had a coating of nicotine stain over most of them. The spot where the sofa had been against the wall was cleaner than the rest of the wall. The ceiling which had once been white was covered with a layer of nicotine stain. The smell of cigarette smoke and paint was overwhelming.

I introduced Virgil to Terrell who suggested we move to the back porch. He said the smell of paint may be distracting. After living in the house for years, I suspected he was oblivious to the stench of cigarette smoke. I hadn't had the foresight to bring a gas mask, so I quickly agreed to go outside. We walked through the kitchen on our way to the porch. The appliances and counter were old, but clean and neat. The floor looked new.

Terrell saw me looking and said, "Installed it myself."

"Looks great," I said.

Terrell said, "Thanks. I've been saving everything I can, trying to bring this old house up to snuff."

A large cardboard crate sat in the middle of the floor with the word Wolf stenciled on each side.

Virgil wasn't looking at the floor but was rubbing his hand across the top of the crate. He said, "Had one of these bad boys in my house."

Terrell looked at him with new admiration. "Best stove anywhere. You a chef?"

Virgil smiled. "Not a chef. Heck, I'm not even a homeowner anymore."

Terrell waited for Virgil to elaborate. He didn't, so Terrell said, "I've been coveting one of those since I learned to cook. It arrived this morning."

"Need help installing it?" Virgil said.

"Nah. Thanks for asking."

I'd had enough chef talk. The smoke and paint smell still polluted the air. "Ready to head out back?"

Virgil patted the stove container one more time then followed Terrell and me outside.

The back porch was much older than the front steps and in the shade. While it was in the eighties, it was comfortable.

Terrell motioned us to sit in brown resin plastic chairs lined against the railing.

"Walmart special," he said with a smile. "You're the first to break them in."

"I'm honored," Virgil said as he rubbed his hand along the arm of the chair.

Terrell didn't appear to know how to take Virgil's comment, so he turned to me. "Thanks for coming. As you can see, I'm in the middle of stripping wallpaper and painting the living room. I should've done it when I got the house but work always got in the way." He lit another cigarette and took a long draw. Thankfully, he turned his head to blow the smoke away from his guests. "Terrible habit, I know. Tried stopping several times." He shook his head. "You can see how successful I was."

Virgil leaned forward in his chair. "Know what you mean."

Terrell said, "You smoke?"

"No," Virgil said. "My bad habits were distilled spirits and hard drugs."

"Oh," Terrell said.

He still appeared not to know how to take Virgil. He had my sympathy since I knew the feeling.

Virgil smiled. "Nice house. Lived here long?"

Terrell gave him the same story he'd shared with me about inheriting the residence. He ended by saying, "It's not much, but it's all mine. Now that I'm getting able to fix it up, it'll have the best memories from my folks, and my touch. Best part about it is no mortgage."

"I had one once—house, not mortgage," Virgil said. "Ah, those were the days."

That was the second time Virgil had mentioned his house. Again, Terrell was left without a comment.

I needed to move the conversation to why Terrell had asked me over, rather than getting into a lengthy conversation about Virgil's life, regardless how interesting I knew it to be.

"Terrell, we don't want to keep you from painting. What did you want to tell me?"

He pointed in the direction of Sol Legare Road and said, "Can't see it from back here, but from the front porch, I can see Clarence Taylor's house. Loved that man." He slowly shook his head.

"Who's Clarence Taylor?" Virgil asked.

"A friend who was recently killed."

"Oh, I'm terribly sorry. What happened, an accident?"

Terrell looked at the floor. "If two bullets in the chest is an accident, yes."

This time Virgil was without words. I gave a brief explanation about who Clarence was and about his untimely death.

"Terrell, I'm terribly sorry," Virgil said.

"Me too," Terrell said and turned to me. "I called the number your friend Charles gave me. I didn't get an answer. Didn't want to leave a message. That's when I called you."

Other than coming in second, that didn't tell me why I was here. "I'm glad you did."

"Charles said he was a detective, that you helped him sometimes. That's why I called."

Virgil leaned forward. "They're both great detectives. Six months ago, Chris and I were in the marsh when—"

"Virgil," I interrupted before he sucked the wind out of Terrell's story. "Let's let Terrell finish."

He leaned back in the chair.

I said, "Terrell, go on."

"I haven't thought about anything but poor Elijah Duncan since Clarence found his body rotting out there in the ground. I told you before how my family goes back generations on Sol Legare Island. Grandpa Samson knew Elijah. From what he said, they were friends." Terrell pointed to the back door. "Grandpa left this house to my parents, they left it to me. I figured since it didn't cost me anything, I need to repay Grandpa. Only way I know how is to find out who killed his friend." He shook his head. "Now somebody killed my friend. I know as certain as I'm sitting here it was because Clarence figured out who murdered Elijah."

He'd shared all this earlier, so I still didn't know what precipitated a call.

Virgil didn't know any of it. "Why do you think your friend's death had something to do with the, umm, skeleton of, what's his name again?"

"Elijah Duncan," Terrell said. "You didn't know Clarence, but I did. Known him since I was a toddler. One of the best people I've ever run across. He didn't have enemies. He was loved by all, so he couldn't have been killed because someone didn't like him."

Virgil said, "What about things like him being killed for money he owed someone, or over a woman? I hear lots of murders have to do with love. I came close to that a couple of times with my ex." He stared off into space.

Terrell lit another cigarette, looked in the direction of Clarence's house, and waited for Virgil to continue. Once again, he didn't so Terrell said, "My friend didn't have more than a few dollars to his name. Before his government check came every month, he couldn't pay for anything. Was always borrowing a few dollars to buy food. And, don't even think he was killed because he didn't pay it back. He paid his debts with a smile and words of appreciation. Always."

"What about a woman?" Virgil said.

"Not Clarence."

It was time to take Virgil out of the interrogation. I said, "What're you thinking, Terrell?"

"I've been doing a lot of digging into who would've been around Mosquito when Elijah was killed. Wanted to bounce some of it off you and Charles."

"Go ahead."

"There aren't many old-timers left who were around in those days. Hell, I doubt there're over six or seven still alive who were about the same age or older than Elijah. I've talked to a few of them in the last few days." He smiled. "Most said they didn't recall much about him but the ones that did said Elijah was nothing but trouble. Said he dressed all neat and fancy, but his hell raising was anything but fancy. Boy did he stir up the race issues they faced back then."

Virgil said, "What's that mean?"

Terrell stared at him. I was afraid he wasn't going to say anything, at least, anything nice.

He took another puff on his cigarette before saying, "Elijah said, some say shouted, what other African Americans were thinking or talking quietly about among themselves. Virgil, you're younger than I am, so you weren't around during the civil rights movement in the early 1960s, much less what was going on with total segregation when Elijah was young in the 1950s. People my color were treated like second-class citizens, if that good."

"I've read about it," Virgil said.

"Virgil, it's not your fault, but you were born white, probably didn't pay much attention to what you were reading. I'd wager you didn't have many black friends, probably knew little to nothing about what was really going on back then."

"True, my friend. Sad to say, but true."

"Anyway," continued Terrell, "Elijah not only stirred up whites with his loud opinions, he bothered many blacks because they thought he'd bring bad things down on them. The less pot stirring the better."

"Did anyone say anything helpful?" I asked to redirect Terrell's comments.

"Not much. Every time I brought Elijah up, most wanted to leave it alone. What's past is past was their attitude. I don't understand. Why weren't they more interested in finding out who killed someone they knew?"

"Maybe they didn't want to relive what must've been bad times for, umm, blacks," Virgil said. "That was what, sixty or so years ago?"

"Segregation was bad but out here there was a thriving African American community," Terrell said, "Folks looked out for each other. It wasn't all bad. In some ways it was better than it is now."

"Something went bad for Elijah," Virgil said.

"Terrill," I said, "Who'd you talk to?"

"Chris, you've already met a couple of them, Jamal Kingsly and Eugene Dillinger. I saw Robert and Sandra Graves Friday and said I wanted to talk to them about Elijah but didn't have time that day. There are two other old-timers who don't spend much time here like they used to when Mosquito was in its heyday. I'll be knocking on their doors next week."

"What did you want Charles and me to do?"

"Nothing really. Figured since you're detectives you'd be able to tell me if I was barking up the wrong tree or if I was on target. Hell, I'm a cook, when I want to sound important, tell folks I'm a chef. I ain't no detective."

I didn't think it would do any good to remind him Charles and I aren't either. What I did feel the need to remind him again was the danger of asking questions.

"Terrell, you still need to be careful. Asking the wrong person questions can be dangerous. Whoever killed Elijah won't hesitate to kill again."

"Terrell," Virgil said, "seems like there's a good chance whoever killed Elijah is no longer among the living. He would be eighty or older. You may be wasting your time chasing a ghost."

Terrell glared at Virgil. "I can't prove it. Not yet anyway but I know as certain as I can be the person that killed Elijah, regardless how many years ago it was, killed Clarence."

Virgil asked, "What makes you so certain?"

"Because that's the only thing that makes sense. Clarence was nosing around trying to find out who killed Elijah. He must've found out. It cost him his life."

I didn't know what Charles or I could do but thought a good time to be here to talk to some of the folks who were around in the 1950s would be at the party Clarence wanted.

"Terrell," I said, "has a date been set for the party Clarence requested?"

"No. Some of the guys are debating when would be the best time. My guess is that it's a few days off. I'll let you know as soon as I hear."

Terrell dropped his cigarette butt on the deck, put it out with his foot, then glanced at the door.

I took the hint; said we'd better let him get back to painting. He thanked us for coming, said it was good meeting Virgil. I wasn't certain he meant that about Virgil.

24

On the return trip to Folly, I said, "Virgil, what do you think?"

"I think when he gets all the nicotine off the walls and ceiling, the house might collapse."

"I was thinking more about Terrell's thoughts about the person who murdered the man in the '50s."

"I knew what you meant. I was pondering everything he said but it's easier saying something about the house collapsing. Know what I like about that boy?"

It's interesting that Virgil referred to Terrell as a boy since he was younger than Terrell. I hoped he didn't mean it as a derisive term.

"What?"

"His respect for elders. That's something in short supply these days. When he talked about his grandpa, he did it with such reverence. I could see love in his face. The love wasn't because his grandpa gave the house to his parents who gave it to Terrell."

"I agree. He talked about his relatives the same way the last time he'd mentioned them."

"And, did you hear how reverential he spoke about the man who was recently killed?"

"Clarence."

"Yeah. They weren't related but it didn't make a difference. Besides, I liked that cute little diamond earring in his left ear. He's a man after my weird heart."

I shared how Terrell had expressed interest in books about the Civil War and the civil rights movement. How the past meant something to him, how he wanted to learn as much about it as possible.

"You know I'm not a detective like you and Charles, although I suspect I'm more of one than Chef Terrell, so this question may not have anything to do with anything."

I wasn't going to argue who was or wasn't a detective. "What's the question?"

"When you two were talking about whoever murdered Mr. Skeleton, even when the recent murder was mentioned, both of you kept saying he when referring to the killer. Could it be a she? Just asking."

I hadn't thought about it that way, but Virgil had a point. Most likely, Elijah's grave wasn't dug deep or it wouldn't have been uncovered as easily if it'd been buried for decades. There's no reason why he couldn't have been shot by a woman, the same could apply for Clarence.

"Good point. Yes, it could've been a female."

"Wonder how many of those people Terrell hasn't talked to yet are women?"

He mentioned one, Sandra Graves. He still needed to talk to her and her husband. But that was all. I picked the phone off the console to redial the number Terrell's call had come from.

I didn't think he was going to answer. I pictured him on the ladder ripping paper off the wall. He sounded out of breath when he finally answered. I apologized for calling while he was working. I asked if there were any women he wanted to talk to who were around in the 1950s?

"Two, maybe three, why?"

I told him Virgil's theory. He seemed skeptical but said he'd keep it in mind when he was running down others. I encouraged him not to overlook anyone, man or woman, who might have known Elijah. He said he wouldn't.

Virgil smiled like he'd solved the mystery.

* * *

I dropped Virgil at his apartment after he profusely thanked me for taking him to get the flywheel. I asked if he needed help installing it but wasn't disappointed when he said he could do it himself. My mechanical skills were slightly better than my skill reading Sanskrit.

I pulled in the drive when my phone rang with William Hansel's name on the screen. I could count on one hand the number of times he'd called in the more than a decade I'd known him.

"Good afternoon, William."

"How did you know? Oh, I keep forgetting, caller identification. A good afternoon to you as well. You're probably wondering about the nature of my call. I wished to enquire if you would happen to provide an old man a respite from eradicating unwanted interlopers from his modest garden?"

It wasn't Sanskrit, so I had a vague idea what he was talking about.

"Is that an iced tea offer?"

He chuckled and said, "Correct."

"Tell you what, I don't know where I could find an old man, but if the offer of tea is from someone I know who has a garden, I'd be glad to be of assistance. Would now work?"

"That would be wonderful."

"I'll be there in ten minutes."

I wasn't a detective like Charles, but I didn't have to be to know William had something more on his mind than someone to provide a respite from weed slaughtering. I pulled in his drive and noticed that he'd started his respite. He was seated under the live oak tree and sipping from a tall drink glass. The silver platter from my earlier visit was on the chair next to him. It held a second drink glass, a sugar bowl, a spoon, and two cloth napkins.

"I see you started without me," I said as I moved the platter to the ground. I took a sip from the second glass.

"You kindly said you didn't know where you could find an old man, but I'm acutely aware one resides in this aging body. I'm getting too old to continue the never-ending battle against these insidious weeds." He sighed before taking another sip of tea.

I smiled. "Yet, you're never going to stop, are you?"

He shook his head. "No. While my muscles might disagree, the therapeutic value of this exercise exceeds its drawbacks."

William loved teaching but had often shared his occasional run-ins with his dean or the high number of mind and butt-numbing meetings drained much of his enthusiasm for the job. He used time in the garden to decompress.

"I'm sure it does."

He took another sip before turning toward me. "I've been giving a lot of thought to our recent conversations about Mosquito Beach and my experiences earlier in life with, well, the best way to say it would be growing up African American. You and I have never spent much time on the topic. As you are aware, I loathe sharing personal experiences or feelings."

He hesitated like he was waiting for a response.

"That's something we have in common."

He nodded. "As odd as it may seem, that's why I feel comfortable sharing things with you I wouldn't reveal to anyone else. Does that make sense?"

Sort of, I thought. "Yes."

"I believe I shared the last time we met under this tree that I'd become acquainted with a gentleman who works around town."

"James Brown."

"You remembered."

"An easy name to remember," I said, and motioned for him to continue.

"He's several years younger than I, but we spoke a time or two about our experiences being in the minority on Folly. He doesn't live here, but spends many hours working on Folly, has for years. I found it interesting in that when we were growing up, most of those individuals around us were of the same race that he and I share. I had surmised our experiences with others, particularly Caucasians, would've been similar. I spent my formative years north of the Mason-Dixon line; James spent his in the South. It wasn't until I moved here some thirty years ago that differences began to stand out. James reinforced that I wasn't imagining the dissimilarities."

"Like what?"

"I had the good fortune to not have been born when slavery was a legal institution in the United States. I was twelve when the Civil Rights Act was passed in 1964, nearly a hundred years after the abolition of slavery, so I have few memories of the times before that momentous event. The schools I attended were integrated by the time I started the first grade. It was much later than that in South Carolina. Even then, subtle segregation continued." He hesitated, looked at my glass, and said, "Let me go inside and get more ice."

Before I could say it wasn't necessary, he'd headed to the house leaving me to wonder where he was going with the story. He returned with a stainless ice bucket, dropped two cubes in my glass. He must've sensed my confusion about the direction of his story.

"I've gotten off track, allow me to summarize. I possibly read about it in history books during my younger days, but until I moved here, I didn't realize how a matter of a few hundred miles could render attitudes so differently. When I was growing up, I had a vague awareness of the Ku Klux Klan, but that was all. I didn't have direct contact with the organization beyond what I heard in the news. I'm not saying there weren't Klan groups where I was living, I later discovered there were. I also haven't had direct contact with any of the groups here, although I've learned there are some in nearby counties." He took another sip, smiled, and said, "I continue to drift, and appreciate you letting this old man stray from his point."

I didn't know what his point was, so I couldn't tell if he was straying. "William, I'm in no hurry. Keep plying me with tea, and I'll sit here all day."

He laughed. "That won't be necessary. Last summer I was coerced into attending a picnic at work. My preference would have been coming home and pulling weeds, so you can see how much I didn't want to attend the gathering. It was hot, a day much warmer than today. One of my students was there wearing a sleeveless shirt, something I'd never seen him do. I noticed a tattoo on his upper arm—the Odin's cross, a white supremacist symbol." He shook his head. "I wouldn't have said anything, but he saw me looking and said something to the effect that yes, it was what I thought it was." William shook his head again. "I told him it was none of my concern. It was the last day of the term, so I had little desire to converse further with the gentleman. I turned to leave, when he said, 'Not all Klan members wear sheets.' That's a direct quote."

"Why do you think he felt the need to tell you anything?"

"Excellent question, my friend. To this day, I'm not certain. I'm not naïve enough to think people who affiliate with the Klan wear distinctive garb all the time. They look like you and, well, not me, when they're at work, in stores, in restaurants, or in my class. The more I thought about what he said, I concluded he was implying it is not always possible to tell a hater from anyone else when contact is made in public."

"I agree."

"With that said, do you think the officials who are looking into the demise of the man whose skeleton was found on Mosquito Beach are considering all options, including the murderer might not have had anything personal against the poor man other than the color of his skin?"

"I hate to say this, but I don't think anyone is spending time looking for the person responsible for killing Elijah Duncan. They're giving it lip-service, but it appears that's all."

"Elijah Duncan?"

I shared what was known about Elijah and why it was thought he was the victim. I also told him about Clarence Taylor's murder, that Clarence had been asking questions about the skeleton. He asked me again if I was sticking my nose in whatever was going on. I didn't deny it.

He said he needed to get back to his weeds he swore had grown an inch since we'd been under the tree. I thanked him for the tea and conversation.

I left to his final words, "Please be careful. Who else would shoot the breeze with this old man."

On the way home, I realized that what I failed to share was what I knew about Andrew Delaney and his affiliation with the Klan.

25

I answered the phone to Charles saying, "Ready to go?"

"How about a hint about where you're going?"

"Fishing."

"Then no."

"I'm not talking about fish fishing. Gotta go. I'm almost late. Be there in five."

A minute later, Charles was in my drive blowing the horn, in three more minutes we were driving out West Ashley Avenue. A block past the road that led to Sunset Cay Marina, I saw Eugene Dillinger's silver Range Rover parked in an empty oceanfront lot beside an Island Realty sign with SOLD printed diagonally on it. Charles pulled in beside the SUV and Eugene stepped out to greet us.

"Sorry we're late," Charles said as he bounded out of the car. "I had to wait for Chris."

Eugene looked at his Rolex or Rolex knock off. "You're a few minutes early."

Late in Charles time.

"Glad you could meet us," Charles said. "After Chris told me about the lot, I had to see it."

It was becoming clear what kind of fishing faux detective Charles had meant. I stood back to let him throw out the line.

"I'm glad you did," Eugene said. "It won't be long before I'm building on this slice of heaven. You're a wise man to show early interest. Shall we walk around?"

"You bet," Charles said.

As we walked, Eugene spewed facts about the size of the property, how the house on each side was owned by full-time residents, meaning they weren't on the rental rolls with a constant turnover in tenants, and how it was two miles from the center of town, the center of crowded, vacation central. In other words, we were standing on a property surrounded by peace and quiet. Charles nodded with each statement.

I followed, wondering when Charles was going to bring out the fishing gear.

Like a good salesman, Eugene saved the sizzle for last. After sharing way more than I wanted to know, he led us to the back of the property where a steep drop-off led to the beach.

He waved his hand toward the surf. "Picture the wide steps I'll build from where we're standing down to the pristine beach. Now look up and down the beach." He hesitated to give us time to follow his direction, then continued, "How many people you see cluttering the area?" He didn't wait for an answer. A mistake around Charles. "Compare that to—"

"Five," Charles interrupted.

That knocked Eugene off his sales pitch.

Eugene said, "Five?"

"Five people on the beach."

"Oh, yes, umm, think how many there'd be in the same amount of space near the center of town around the Fishing Pier."

He didn't put it in the form of a question. Perhaps he was gaining insight about Charles.

"Eugene," Charles said, "there's no doubt that this is a perfect property. The price range you mentioned on the phone appears fair."

"Charles, will you be financing the lot or the construction?" He held his hand in front of Charles. "I ask because I have contacts with lenders, could fix you up with those having the best rates. They look favorably at my construction and, as you can see, this site is magnificent."

"No, I've been fortunate enough to have inherited, umm, enough not to need a mortgage."

Eugene's posture, already near perfect, straightened even more, a wide grin appeared on his face. I turned my head so he couldn't see my eyes roll.

"Excellent. Shall we start looking at a variety of floor plans to meet your needs? I've also got photos of houses I've built showing possible options."

"Not yet," Charles said.

Not yet, not ever, I thought.

"Oh," Eugene said, his posture slumped.

"I need to meet with my financial advisor to see what needs to happen to free up the money."

"That sounds prudent," Eugene said, then started walking toward his SUV.

"Oh, while I'm thinking of it," Charles said, "have you learned more about the skeleton found on Mosquito Beach?"

Eugene looked at Charles. "What's that have to do with this property?"

Good question, Eugene.

"Nothing," Charles said, "I remembered the first time we met, we were talking about it. You said you had friends out there, so you might know something new."

Eugene shook his head. "Not really. I think it was some old bum who died of natural causes. No one knew what to do with the body, so they stuck it in the ground. Cost, zero. Besides, that's ancient history."

"That could be it," Charles said. "I also heard a young guy out there is asking around about the body. Name's Terrell Jefferson, I believe. He's been talking to some of the old-timers who would've been there around the time the person was killed. He thinks it belongs to, umm, Chris, what's the name?"

"Elijah Duncan."

"Yeah, that's it. Has Terrell talked to you?"

"He has, couple of times in fact. He came to my East Ashley job site asking a bunch of questions. The second time was here on Folly the other day. I was heading to St. James Gate for lunch, Terrell was on his way to work at Rita's. We talked a couple of minutes, no more. He was running late."

"What'd he say?" Charles asked.

"Not much, as I recall. Same things he asked at the job site. He asked if I remembered anyone gone missing back in the 1950s. I may have but it was a long time ago. I didn't remember anyone." We were at Eugene's vehicle, where he added. "Charles, sure you don't want to look at floor plans?"

"Not yet."

Eugene nodded. "Tell you what, I have photos of other projects in here. Why don't you take them with you so you can look them over?"

"Good idea," Charles said. "You sure Terrell didn't say Elijah Duncan's name when he was talking to you?"

If Eugene got dizzy from Charles's abrupt transition, it didn't show.

"Don't recall. He may have but was in a hurry to get to work. I had a roofing issue I was trying to solve in my head, I didn't catch everything he was saying." He grabbed a large envelope from the front seat and handed it to Charles. "You can keep these, I have more. After you talk to your financial advisor, give me a call so we can get together to go over potential plans." He waved his hand in the direction of the ocean. "Picture yourself stepping on your wide deck, leaning back in a comfortable chair, sipping on a cold drink, looking at that glorious view."

Charles and I stood beside his vehicle watching the Range Rover pull off the property and head toward town.

I said, "Private detecting pay better than I thought?"

Charles smiled. "You'll have to ask my financial advisor."

"Would that be the clerk at Circle K who sells lottery tickets?"

He snapped his fingers. "I forgot to share that with Eugene."

"Get any bites on your fishing line?"

"Couple of nibbles. He said he talked with Terrell about the skeleton. From what he said, he didn't confess to Terrell he killed the man."

"I would've noticed if he had."

"Tell you one thing I figured out. Did you catch how fast the old boy decided he had to leave when I started asking questions about the skeleton?"

"Yes, it was nearly as quick as he cut the tour short of the house he was showing us when you brought it up."

Charles said, "I caught it. Don't forget, he said the body was probably some bum. He said the same thing at Island Breeze. It's like he didn't know anything about it. I don't believe him."

"I don't either but that isn't enough to accuse him of the 1953 murder."

"I was about to ask him if he knew anything about poor old Clarence's murder."

"He probably wouldn't have confessed to that one either. Besides, I'd hate for it to be Eugene. Who would you get to build your oceanfront house if he's locked up?"

Moving away from Charles's fantasy world, I told him about Virgil and my visit to Terrell. After catching grief about not telling him sooner, he expressed the same concern I had about Terrell's safety. I told him I tried to warn the cook, but doubted it took hold. He's determined to find out what happened.

"I hope he takes your advice," Charles said. That was something that Charles had seldom done.

On that note, he dropped me at my house.

26

Uneventful would've been the best description of the next two days. I spent several daylight hours walking around the island taking photos of colorful houses, lawn ornaments, sea oats, and dunes. Since closing Landrum Gallery, I haven't had an outlet to sell my photos, but my love of photography, my habit of photographing places and things on Folly hadn't lessened. Many retirees gravitate to golf, some of the more fit retirees lean toward surfing to relax. I'd tried both and was as good at each as I was at swimming to Ireland. Photography was my thing.

I was sitting on the porch sipping a Diet Coke while watching traffic pass by the house when I noticed I'd missed two calls. That didn't make sense until I realized I must've accidentally muted the phone. The first call showed a number I wasn't familiar with. After a long pause on the recording the person ended the call without saying a word. The second call again popped up with the same number and came seven hours ago.

This time there was a message: "Chris, this is Terrell, you know, from Rita's. I've been talking to the old-timers that were around Mosquito in the '50s. The more I dig, the more I find that're still alive. Remember, I told you I was going to find out who killed Elijah way back then, maybe who killed my friend Clarence? Umm, since you and Charles are detectives, I need to tell you what I found. You won't believe it, but I'm pretty sure I know who it was. And get this, if I'm right, the person killed both men. If after you hear what I found and why I think I know who did it, umm, well, after that, if you think I'm right, maybe you could go with me to the police. They'd believe you before me. Give me a call when you get this. Oh yeah, before I forget, Clarence's party is Saturday night."

I called the number Terrell had given me. No luck. There was no answer, no machine to leave a message. I called Rita's and asked the woman who answered if Terrell was working. She said she could barely hear over the crowd. I repeated the question. She told me to hang on while she checked. I was beginning to wonder if she'd forgotten me, when she returned to say he was off today. I tried his number once more and received the same result. I thought about driving to his house but figured if he didn't answer his phone, he probably wasn't home. I'll try again in the morning.

Three hours later, the phone rang when I was getting ready for bed. My friends knew not to call this late and I didn't know what CCSO meant that popped up on the screen. I was ready to let it go to voicemail, when it struck me what the initials stood for. I answered.

A vaguely familiar voice said, "Mr. Landrum?"

I said it was, then realized who was on the other end. I was right about the meaning of CCSO.

"This is Detective Callahan with the Charleston County Sheriff's Office. We've crossed paths on a few occasions."

"I remember."

"Do you know Terrell Jefferson?"

I took a deep breath, barely above a whisper said, "Yes, why?"

"Could you tell me how you know him?"

I gave the detective a brief rundown of my contacts with Terrell. He asked when I talked to him last. I told him and repeated, "Why?"

"Mr. Landrum, umm, Chris, Mr. Jefferson was found dead late this afternoon. I'm sorry for your loss."

I was stunned. After catching my breath, I managed to mumble, "What happened?"

"He was murdered. Found in his house with two bullet wounds in the back."

"When?"

"The coroner's best guess is sometime early this afternoon. Why?"

I didn't answer, but said, "Why'd you call me?"

"Mr. Jefferson had paper in his pocket with your name and number on it. His phone shows he recently made two calls to your number. After that there were two calls from your number to his phone."

"Detective, Terrell left me a message earlier today."

"What did it say?"

"Rather than trying to repeat it, I think you need to hear the message."

"Are you at home?"

I told him I was and gave my address. He said he was at Terrell's house and would come over within an hour.

Our call ended, I slumped in the chair, and put my head between my hands. I pictured my new acquaintance holding a paintbrush while getting excited about improving his house. Improvements he'll never complete.

I must've drifted longer than I thought. The next thing I remembered was Detective Callahan's unmarked Ford Explorer pulling in the drive. Callahan is in his forties, with short hair. He was wearing a navy sport coat and gray slacks. I met him at the door and motioned him in.

"We meet again, Mr. Landrum."

"Please call me Chris."

He and I had shared a few tense conversations since we'd met four years ago but had learned to trust each other as a result. He'd endeared himself to me after one lengthy discussion when he'd referred to a retired detective from his office whom I'd developed a rocky relationship with as a COF—Cranky Old Fart. He couldn't have been more accurate.

We sat at the kitchen table.

"Again, Chris, I'm sorry about Mr. Jefferson."

"Me too. He seemed like a nice man."

Callahan nodded toward my phone on the corner of the table. "The message?"

After the message played, Callahan stared at me, shook his head, and said, "I can't believe this is happening again. What in the hell are you and your friend doing playing detective? Playing detective again."

"We're not playing detective. A friend of mine, Al Washington, spent time on Mosquito Beach after he returned from Korea in the early 1950s. He asked me to take him over there since he hadn't been back in years. When we got there, we met Clarence Taylor, the man who found the skeleton, the skeleton you're investigating. Al might've known the victim, someone who disappeared decades ago. The man's name was Elijah Duncan. It appears it was Elijah, and as you know, Clarence Taylor was recently murdered."

Callahan tapped his fingers on the table like a hummingbird with ADHD, jotted a couple of notes, then resumed staring at me. "Help me understand how you're not playing detective."

"The last two times I talked to Terrell, he said he'd been close to Clarence, had known him his whole life. Terrell was determined to find out who killed him. I told him to be careful, to leave it to you and others conducting the investigations. If someone murdered twice, there was little to stop him from making Terrell number three."

I didn't mention I'd heard as far as Elijah's murder was concerned, it was a cold case, that Callahan was the cop who was treating it that way.

"Chris, it irritates the hell out of me that amateurs are going around acting like it's their calling to solve crimes. You know first-hand how dangerous that can be."

"I agree, but—"

"The only but is me telling you to butt out. Do you understand?"

I nodded. I understood, but it wasn't going to stop me from getting involved. I didn't know much about Elijah, but I knew Clarence and Terrell. I liked both men. Now they're dead.

"With that out of the way, I want you to do two things. First, email that voicemail to me. Second, tell me anything you know that could help me catch the person or persons responsible for the two deaths."

"Three, counting Elijah?"

He nodded. "Three."

I'd never emailed a recorded call and asked Callahan how to do it. He took the phone and said, "And you think you're bright enough to catch a killer."

"Not if he uses a voicemail app as a murder weapon," I said, hoping to lighten the mood.

Callahan smiled, but it lacked sincerity. He tapped a few commands, typed something, then handed it back to me. "Done. Anything else I need to know?"

I told him the names of three people I'd met on Mosquito Beach who were old enough to have killed Elijah. I didn't share anything about Charles and my visit to Eugene's house under construction or the visit to the empty lot. I didn't need him scolding me again for butting in. Callahan said he'd talked to them, and to two others I didn't mention. He didn't share their names. I also told him about Andrew Delaney's connection to the Klan. He asked if Andrew was old enough to have killed Elijah. I told him no.

"You're trying to hang two murders on him because he's a member of the Klan?"

"Not really. I thought you needed to know in case you want to talk to him."

"Anything else?"

"No."

"Then once again, I'm sorry about Terrell." He hesitated. "And Clarence."

"Thank you."

"I'd tell you to be careful, but both of us know I'd be wasting my breath."

27

I waited until morning to tell Charles about Terrell, the message he'd left, and Detective Callahan's visit. As I could've predicted, he gave me a hard time for not letting him know as soon as Callahan was out the door. I explained I was so shaken I couldn't talk to anyone. He said he understood, but it shouldn't have stopped me from calling. Also, and equally predictable, he asked what our next move was to find out who killed Terrell. He didn't say it, but I knew he meant find out who killed Terrell, Clarence, plus Elijah. He ended by telling me to meet him at the Lost Dog Cafe for lunch, he was buying. His uttering that rare offer told me he understood how much the murders were affecting me.

    I walked to the Dog to try to clear my head of depressing thoughts about Terrell. I wasn't successful but at least got some much-needed exercise. The temperature was in the mid-seventies, so I wasn't surprised to see Charles on the front patio. He wore a long-sleeve, blue T-shirt with Peru State Bobcats in white letters on the front, tan shorts, and was sipping coffee. He saw me approach, set the coffee down, then glanced at his bare wrist to remind me I was late. Of course, I wasn't, but that had never stopped my friend's obsession with time, incorrect time.

I walked to the side entrance of the patio. As soon as I pulled out the chair opposite Charles, Amber was at the table.

"Let's see," She looked at her wrist where she actually wore a watch. "Too late for French toast," she said. "What artery clogging item do you want for lunch?"

I smiled and said, "Charles is buying. Surprise me."

"Crap, we're plum out of chocolate-covered gravel. How about a mahi salad?"

"Something cheaper," Charles said. "Didn't you hear him say I'm buying? Sure there's no more gravel?"

Amber patted Charles on the head. "How about a hot dog with home fries?"

"Perfect," I said.

After Amber headed to the kitchen, Charles looked around to see who was close enough to hear.

He leaned closer. "You okay?"

"To tell the truth, no."

"Thomas Jefferson said, 'Honesty is the first chapter in the book of wisdom.' You know Terrell's death isn't your fault."

I nodded although I wasn't sure I meant it. Would Terrell still be alive if the first time we'd met I'd discouraged him from trying to learn the identity of the skeleton? Would he be alive if he didn't talk to everyone he knew old enough to have been around when Elijah was murdered? Would he be alive if after Clarence was murdered, I'd pushed harder for him to leave it to the police?

"Earth to Chris," Charles said, tapping me on the arm. "Did you hear what I said?"

"No," I said, honestly. Thomas Jefferson would've been proud. "What?"

"Same thing I asked on the phone. What's our next step in finding the killer?"

I told him what Detective Callahan said about me, about us, staying out of police business.

"That ever stopped us?"

Amber arrived with my lunch and a refill on Charles's coffee before I responded to his question. She also arrived with a question of her own.

"Can you believe what I just heard in there?" She tilted her head in the direction of the dining room.

Charles said, "You heard Folly's two handsomest men are sitting on the patio."

She laughed, and looked around, probably to see where they were. "Don't you mean funniest?"

"Amber," I said, "what did you hear?"

Her laughter faded. "One of the cooks at Rita's was killed yesterday."

"Who told you?"

"Marc Salmon."

No surprise, I thought.

Charles said, "What else did he say?"

"Not much. Said the man was found at his house off Sol Legare Road."

I said, "Did Marc say who he was?"

"No."

"How'd he hear about it?" Charles asked.

"One of the local cops." She looked at me, her focus narrowed. "Chris, you don't look surprised. Did you know?"

I didn't want to get in a lengthy discussion, but if I didn't tell her before she found out from someone else, she'd do a Charles and be on my case.

"Yes, I met Terrell Jefferson when Barb and I were eating on Mosquito Beach. A county detective told me about the murder last evening." I hoped that was enough to prevent trouble with Amber down the road.

"Oh," she said. "I'm sorry."

Two women seated at a table at the other end of the patio motioned for Amber to bring their checks. She gave them a salute then headed inside.

Charles said, "Now that Marc knows, within hours, everyone on Folly, heck, everyone in the US, Canada, and probably Uruguay will know."

I said, "I don't know what we can do. I keep coming back to what Terrell told us. The Sol Legare community is a tight-knit group. We're outsiders."

"Terrell was from there, lived there his entire life, and that's why he thought he'd be able to discover the killer or killers."

I looked at my half-eaten plate of food, then at Charles. "Look where it got him."

"More reason for us to get involved," Charles said.

It didn't make sense, but I knew what he meant. "What do you think we should do?"

He took another sip of coffee, then said, "Wonder when his funeral will be?"

"He only died yesterday. It'll be at least a couple of days."

"You'd better find out. We don't want to miss it. What do you think will happen now to Clarence's, umm, death party?"

I could see wheels spinning in Charles's head. Where better to nose around and talk to people who knew Terrell and Clarence. Possibly talk to a killer.

* * *

I CALLED AL THAT EVENING. I'd hoped to catch him at home, instead I could tell from the country music in the background he was at the bar. He said there had been an unexpected late rush for beer in the neighborhood. Bob asked him to stay to handle crowd control.

Al added, "Most likely, Blubber Bob figured he was outnumbered ten to one. He needed me to keep him from getting whupped."

I had a hard time hearing him for the music and asked him to repeat what he'd said.

He did, and I said, "You've done your good deed for the day."

"I've got a suspicion you didn't call to see how business was doing."

"I'm afraid you're right. There's been another murder near Mosquito Beach."

"Oh, my Lord. Who?"

"Terrell Jefferson. He's the first person I met the night Barb and I want to supper at Island Breeze."

"Did I meet him?"

"No, he wasn't there when you were."

"What happened? Did it have something to do with Clarence Taylor's death?"

"No one knows. I think it did because it's too big a coincidence both being murdered after trying to find Elijah Duncan's killer."

"What do the police think?"

"All I know is Detective Callahan caught both cases. He's good so if anyone can solve it, he can."

"Don't want to throw water on your optimism," Al said after a long pause. "Is the detective you're talking about white?"

"Yes."

"Don't know for sure about Sol Legare now, but back when I was hanging out there, it was a closed community. Didn't take kindly to outsiders. Thought it could take care of its own problems. Outside cops, especially white ones, didn't have much of a chance, even if they cared, which some didn't."

"I hope it's not as bad as it was then."

"Wouldn't put money on it."

"I hope you're wrong."

"I do too, yes I do. What'll happen to the party Clarence wanted them to hold?"

"It was scheduled for Saturday, but with Terrell's death, I don't know."

I heard voices in the background and Al's muffled voice like he'd put his hand over the phone. Finally, he said, "Chris, think I'd better go save Bob. He just told one of his best customers that if he played one more Motown song, Bob was going to throw him out on his rear. He didn't say rear."

"Sounds like you're needed."

"Yes, sir, I sure am. Will you let me know when the party will be? I'd like to be there."

"Want me to take you?"

"If you don't mind."

"I'd be honored," I said and ended the call.

I was curious if a decision had been made about Clarence's last-wish party. I didn't have phone numbers for anyone I'd talked to at Island Breeze, so I called the restaurant. A man with a Caribbean accent answered with, "Island Breeze. May I be of assistance?"

I asked about Clarence's party. He said it was still on for Saturday.

I then did the wise thing and called Charles to give him the news. For the second time tonight, there was loud background noise that made it difficult for me to hear.

"Where are you?"

"Loggerhead's. Outside bar. Why?"

"I'm having a hard time hearing you."

"You've got ancient ears. Listen gooder."

There was no future disagreeing, besides, there was some truth to his statement. I said, "I'm letting you know the party at Island Breeze is still on for Saturday."

"Say that again. It's loud here. I couldn't hear you."

No, I didn't tell him he had ancient ears. Instead, I repeated it.

"Great," he said, "I'll see if Virgil can go with us."

"Why would Virgil want to go?"

"He's with me. We've been talking about the murders. He wants to learn more about the folks out there."

"Why?" I repeated.

"It's your fault. You took him to meet Terrell before he went and got himself killed. Virgil now has a stake in finding out who killed him. Isn't that right, Virgil?"

I hadn't realized that this was a three-way conversation. I heard someone in the background. I assumed it was Virgil. Charles said, "Oh, right, I'll tell him. Chris, Virgil wanted me to remind you about a few months back when he saved your life on the boat."

That wasn't how I remembered the incident. In fact, it was the opposite, but with Charles's alternate reality, and now I suppose with Virgil's, the best course of action was to ignore the discrepancy.

"What's his point?"

He mumbled something, I assumed to Virgil. Then I heard him say, "Virgil, you tell him."

"Yo, Chris, this is Virgil, how're you doing?"

"Fine."

"You ought to be here with us. Did you know if you tell a guy sitting next to you on a barstool, not Charles, but on the other side, how much you like his shirt, he'll buy you a beer?"

It sounded like Virgil had bragged on several shirts. "I didn't know that."

"Yessiree, it's true. Hey, thanks for letting me go with you all to that party."

How'd I miss extending the invitation?

"Glad you can go."

"I can help you two figure out who the killer is, or is that killers are? Come to think of it, there could be three killers. One guy killed Mr. Skeleton; one killed that Clarence guy. Some dirty, rotten bastard killed my new friend Terrell. Anyway, Charles, and even you, have taught me a bunch about being a detective. I'll help. Won't charge you a penny. Course, you could buy me a beer sometime. Talking about beer, Chris, I'd talk longer but my glass is empty. Gotta tell the guy next to me how much I like his shoes." He lowered his voice. "They aren't as nice as my Guccis, but hell, whose are?"

I was beginning to regret saying I'd go to the party, and it was still two days away.

"You still there?"

"Afraid so. How many beers has Virgil had?"

"Only two since I've been here. Why?"

"He sounded like he's over his limit."

"He did say he'd been here an hour before I showed up. Didn't see any iced tea glasses nearby. What time are you picking me up for the party? I'll tell Virgil, although I doubt he'll remember much about tonight when he falls out of bed tomorrow."

I told him what time then added, "You may want to make sure he makes it to his apartment tonight."

"I'll peel him off the barstool in a few minutes before Virgil tells the generous, well-dressed beer buyer that he likes his underwear. Nothing good could come from that."

I'd planned on calling Al after getting Charles off the phone, but after the three-way conversation with Charles and Virgil, my ear hurt. Al's call could wait until tomorrow.

28

Al was waiting at the front door when we arrived to take him to the party. He wore black dress slacks, a purple short-sleeve dress shirt, a black driver cap, and shoes nearly as shiny as Virgil's. He also carried an equally shiny black cane. My friend was ready to party.

Charles gave up the front passenger seat so Al could have more legroom.

Al shook his head, smiled, and said, "Charles, thanks for the kind gesture, but let me sit in back. Before I meet my maker, I want to be chauffeured around in a Cadillac by a white man."

Charles held the back door open for Al and said, "Want to let the chauffeur borrow your cap?"

Al shook his head before he noticed the other passenger in the back seat. Virgil smiled. "Hi, fine sir, I'm Virgil Debonnet. I'm amazed your driver didn't bring the Rolls for someone as important as you."

Al returned Virgil's smile. "I've heard my friends in the front seat talk about you." He laughed. "You're as full of BS as they said you were."

Virgil's smile turned serious, then back to a smile, before becoming a full-throated laugh. "My sterling reputation precedes me."

Al returned the laugh, patted Virgil on the shoulder, and turned to me, "Driver, to the gala."

Twenty minutes plus several of Virgil's jokes later, we pulled on Mosquito Beach Road to be greeted by more vehicles than I'd ever seen there. They were parked on every piece of flat ground not covered by water, trees, or a building. The temperature was in the mid-seventies with a cloudless sky. That was fortunate because there wouldn't have been room inside for the people who spilled across the front of the building. From what I could see, the crowd also filled the back-dining area. So Al wouldn't have to walk far, I let him and Charles off at the door, then drove nearly to the spot where Clarence had found the body before finding a parking spot. Virgil had refused to get out with Charles and Al saying he'd stay with me in case I needed help walking. I sarcastically thanked him.

Aretha Franklin's "Chain of Fools" blared from the outdoor speakers as we approached Island Breeze. The sounds of a loud, enthusiastic crowd greeted us as we entered the packed restaurant. I didn't see Charles or Al, but Eugene Dillinger was standing inside the back door waving in my direction. The builder wore a white shirt that looked like silk, navy slacks, and held a colorful drink.

"Your friends are at my table out back. They asked me to point you in that direction."

Great. Nothing like having to listen to a sales pitch for a beach-front property with Charles pretending to be rich. I smiled and introduced Virgil to Eugene who didn't skip a beat before asking if Virgil lived on Folly, quickly followed by asking if he was in the market for a new house. On the way to the back door, Virgil said yes, he lived on Folly but wasn't currently looking for a house. He made the mistake of mentioning he'd owned one overlooking the Battery and Charleston Harbor. Eugene put his arm around Virgil's shoulder then said, "Drinks are on me."

Virgil didn't even have to tell Eugene he liked his shirt.

Eugene's table was two large cable spools pulled together on the right side of the property near a large American flag. In addition to

Charles and Al, Robert Graves and a woman I assumed to be his wife were seated closest to Charles, with Jamal Kingsly on the other side of the tables. Eugene motioned for me to take the chair beside Jamal, for Virgil to sit between Robert and Charles. Eugene took the remaining seat before sharing the names of everyone at the table. Sandra, Robert's wife, was the only person I hadn't met. It wasn't quite as loud as inside, but not much quieter. Bob Marley's heavily accented voice shared his thoughts on "Bad Boys" as two women standing across from us swayed to the music.

Robert leaned toward me to say, "Bob Marley and Aretha Franklin were Clarence's favorite singers. You'll be hearing a lot from them tonight."

A college-age server tapped me on the shoulder and asked what my friend and I wanted to drink. Charles and Al had already ordered. I said white wine, Virgil asked if they had Blue Hawaiis. She asked if it was a brand of beer. He said no, that it was a drink with light rum, blue curacao liqueur, and pineapple juice.

"Rum we got. No pineapple juice. I don't know what curacao is."

Virgil nodded at her. "How about a Budweiser?"

She smiled. "That we've got."

Charles said, "Eugene, thanks for letting us share your table. Looks like a packed house."

"Clarence had many friends." He looked around the crowd. "Most folks here wouldn't have missed it. There're some who never met Clarence. They're here because it's Saturday night with good weather."

"He was a prince," Sandra said.

Virgil said, "I didn't know Clarence. Until tonight, I didn't know anyone at this table except Charles and Chris so I'm not speaking from personal experience, but it seems not everyone thought your man Clarence was a friend or a prince."

That silenced his table mates.

Robert put his arm around his wife. "My friend, I assume you're speaking about the person who took his life."

Virgil nodded.

"The person who shot Clarence couldn't be from here. Everyone loved the man." He removed his RiverDogs cap, placed it over his heart, bowed his head, and continued, "He was one of the nicest people I ever knew. God rest his soul." He returned the cap to his head, apparently his sort-of prayer was over. "Sandra and I go way back with him."

Sandra added, "Virgil, you're right about one thing. You don't know any of us. I challenge you to find one person here who has a bad word to say about our friend Clarence."

Virgil held both hands up, palms facing Sandra. "Dear lady, I apologize if I said something that offended you. All I meant was someone shot him, shot him twice as I understand it. That's not an act associated with love."

I needed to change the subject before Virgil dug a deeper hole.

"Sandra, Al tells me there were some wonderful times out here back in the 1950s. Were you around then?"

She smiled. "Sure was. Lots of handsome men were too. Now if you ask my parents, I was never here. They said self-respecting white girls didn't hang around where there were Negroes." She leaned over and kissed Robert's cheek. "What they didn't know, didn't hurt them, or me."

"She flirted with all of those handsome men," Robert said as he squeezed her hand.

Al smiled. "Not with me. I would've remembered someone as lovely as you."

Sandra blushed. "Such a sweet talker."

Al tipped his cap in her direction.

Jamal leaned closer to Sandra and said, "Robert's wrong about one thing. Things were different back then. Most of the guys here were black. If they showed interest in a white lady like Sandra, they'd be asking for trouble. Hell, it wouldn't have had to be anything more than a smile. Sandra's parents were right about the attitudes."

The server returned to ask if we wanted anything to eat or more drinks. Eugene said another round of drinks, that it was on him. Jamal said she'd better get us a couple of servings of wings. He didn't say it was on him. She left to the sounds of Aretha Franklin singing "Natural Woman" and laughter from a nearby group.

Al, who hadn't said much, said, "Jamal, that night you and I were talking out here about Elijah Duncan, you said you thought he'd left and headed north to find work. Have you heard anything else since they're fairly certain the skeleton was his?"

Elijah's death was heavy on Al's heart, but I'd hoped he wouldn't bring it up tonight. We were here to celebrate Clarence's life.

"No. Suppose I was wrong about him leaving." Jamal looked at Robert, Sandra, and Eugene. "All you guys knew him, didn't you? What do you think happened?"

Sandra said, "I think whatever happened to him is buried just like he was. Everyone here knew he was trouble, speaking out about wanting everything us white folks had. Elijah was right, but the early '50s were the wrong time to be shaking-up the laws and those who controlled them."

Jamal nodded. "You're right. He nearly got me beat up once when we were together. He started mouthing off to a white police officer about him always stopping blacks for speeding while letting white folks speed but never doing anything about it. I thought for sure we were heading to the hospital or the cemetery."

Charles said, "What happened?"

"The officer got a radio call about a bad wreck on Folly Road. He gave us one last snarl then rushed off to the wreck." He shook his head. "Never thought I'd be happy to hear about a wreck." Jamal turned to Eugene. "Eugene, didn't Elijah work for you?"

"A little while. We're not here tonight to talk about Elijah. Clarence was one of a kind, wasn't he?"

I wasn't certain but thought that when Charles and I were touring Eugene's construction project on Folly he said he didn't know Elijah. I'll ask Charles later. Eugene was right about one thing. Tonight was about Clarence.

I said, "Jamal, why was Clarence so special?"

"Chris, I suppose everyone who knew him could tell you stories to explain it." He looked around the table, but no one offered any. "Eugene and Sandra, I don't know if you remember. Clarence worked for the Post Office. At least twice I know of, probably times I don't know about, when someone who was short on money or was having home problems brought in a package going to someone who lived in the area, instead of putting it though the system, he'd deliver it himself after work. Didn't charge the customer anything. It wouldn't have cost that much to mail, but he knew every penny counted for his customers." Jamal smiled. "He probably would've lost his job if the boss man found out."

Sandra added, "Saw him several times in our neighborhood sticking packages in mailboxes. I knew that wasn't his job. I suspected he was doing what Jamal said."

Aretha Franklin was spelling "Respect" from the sound system. Jamal pointed to the speaker and said, "Respect. That's what Clarence was all about."

Al waited for the song to end, and said, "Anyone think Clarence's death had anything to do with Elijah?"

He wasn't ready to take the discussion of his friend off the table.

"How could it?" Robert said. "It'd been what, sixty-five years between the two."

"It wasn't connected unless you believed Terrell," Jamal said.

I was surprised that it'd taken this long before Terrell was mentioned.

Charles asked, "What's that mean?"

Jamal glanced at Robert and Sandra, before saying, "Terrell had a stick up his butt about the deaths. He went around asking everyone old enough to know Elijah to tell him everything about the man. He then spewed his theory that the murders were done by the same person. He wouldn't let it go. Robert, Sandra, he talked to you, didn't he?"

Sandra said, "He ran into me at Harris Teeter, cornered me in the produce department then started asking questions about Elijah. I told him I went out with Elijah once." She smiled. "Well, we didn't go out, it was more like he stopped me one day asking if I was going to be at the pavilion that Friday night. I said yes, we met, danced a few times, that was all. He never asked again, which was okay. Robert came along a few months later and swept me off my feet." She leaned over and hugged him.

Robert said, "When I saw them talking at the store, I figured Terrell was talking to Sandra about the improvements he's making at his house. He's mighty proud of it. That new large front porch, painting all of it, that fancy new stove, adding new tile in the kitchen and bathroom. The house never looked better."

Sandra said, "I didn't think I was ever going to get out of the produce section."

Eugene laughed. "I can do one better. Terrell came out to the house I'm building on Folly, followed me around for what must've been thirty minutes. It was a hundred degrees or so. He was wearing his chef's outfit. The boy was sweating up a storm."

Charles asked, "What'd you tell him?"

Our wings arrived before Eugene answered. Everyone at the table was more hungry than curious about what Terrell said. Everyone except Charles, of course.

"Well?" He said while Eugene reached for a wing.

Bob Marley was singing "Redemption Song," a couple behind us was singing along, and Charles stared at Eugene chewing the meat off the bone.

Eugene took another bite then pointed the bone at Charles. "Told him I had no idea who killed either man but was sorry they were dead. Clarence had been asking the same kind of questions. That's all."

I doubted that was all since Terrell had been with Eugene a half hour. He hadn't said anything tonight that he hadn't mentioned when he'd taken us to see the house he was building. I doubted I'd learn more if I pressed.

Charles must've figured the same thing about Eugene. He said, "Robert, was Terrell pestering you like he pestered your wife?"

"Pestered, no. He was persistent though. I knew little about Clarence other than he was liked by all, including me. Terrell was talking to all us old-timers who might've known Elijah. You already know what I told you about Elijah."

Charles took a sip of the beer the server set in front of him, looked at Jamal then at Robert. "Did Terrell tell any of you that he knew, or thought he knew, who'd killed Clarence?"

Sandra shook her head.

Robert said, "Not to me. I wouldn't be surprised if he didn't have suspicions. He was a sharp fellow who was like a laser-guided missile once he had a target in his sights."

"I agree with Robert," Jamal said as he stuffed a wing in his mouth.

Eugene said, "I already told you what he said at the construction site."

Virgil held his new beer in the air. "I propose a toast." He waited for us to put down our food and raise our drinks. "Here's to Clarence, a friend to everyone who knew him. And take a sip for Terrell, too. May they rest in peace."

I was pleased that Virgil didn't say everyone who knew him except one.

The party was still going strong when Al said he hated to but needed to get home. I told my riders I'd get the car and pick them up in front of the building. Before I reached the car, I spotted a familiar face sitting in a blue pickup truck backed into a spot on the creek side of the road.

"Andrew, remember me, I'm Chris?"

He looked to see if anyone was nearby. Seeing no one, he stepped out of the truck, shook my hand, and chuckled, "Sure, I remember everyone I spill beer on."

"What're you doing here?"

"You mean what's a Klansman doing in this brown part of the world?"

I wouldn't have put it that way, but yes. I nodded.

"That's a good question. I heard there was going to be a party honoring Clarence Taylor. Was working up the nerve to go in to pay my respects."

"I believe you told me you may've worked with Clarence."

"You have a hell of a good memory. Yes, we worked together. Not many people know it." He rolled his eye. "Especially my Klan brothers." He looked around again. "Chris, have you ever had your friends tell you how horrible someone was, then when you got to know the person, you liked them?"

"Yes."

"I was that way with Clarence. At first, I didn't go out of my way to pay attention to him at work. He took the lead, talked to me every chance he got. Then, when he was working at the Post Office, I saw him most every time I was in there." He shook his head. "Damn, I didn't want to like him. He was a ni … umm, black. I was a card-carrying member of the Klan. He was a nice guy who didn't deserve getting himself killed. That's why I wanted to be here."

"Are you going in?"

He shook his head. "Thought about it but couldn't bring myself to cross that racial line. I'm paying my respects out here." He looked around again to see if anyone was near. "Know what really pisses me off?"

I told him I didn't.

"I'm a member of a group that thinks blacks shouldn't have a lot of the jobs they have, stealing work from whites, a bunch of other bad things." He sighed. "Now I'm sitting out here and the person who killed my friend Clarence, my black friend, is sitting in there having a good old time."

"How do you know?"

"Don't for certain, but Clarence must've trusted the person who shot him. He never would've let someone he didn't know get that close. This is a small community where everyone knows everyone. So, I'd bet a bunch of money everyone who knew him well is in that party. Am I right, or am I right?"

He didn't wait for my answer. He said he'd better move on before word makes it to any of his Klan brothers. I said it was nice talking to him.

If he'd waited, I would've told him he was probably right about everyone who knew Clarence being at the party. The question he didn't ask, and I couldn't answer even if he'd asked was did Charles, Virgil, Al, and I just spend two hours at the same table with that person?

I picked up my friends in front of Island Breeze to the sounds of Aretha Franklin singing "Amazing Grace."

29

"Okay, fellow detectives," Charles said after we dropped Al off at his house, "What'd we learn tonight?"

Virgil raised his hand like he was in school, except he didn't wait for the teacher to call on him, "That was the most fun I've had at a dead person's party."

I knew Charles wouldn't let it go. "Virgil, how many dead person's parties have you attended?"

"Went to three wakes for people who lived near me when I lived at the Battery. The wakes were for guys I don't recall ever seeing smile. To carry that through to death, the wakes were—pardon the pun—dead. Plenty of booze but none of the laughter going with it."

"Virgil," Charles said, "did you learn anything that could help us catch the killer or killers?"

"Oh, umm, let's see, everyone was friendly. Friendlier than anyone I know would be to strangers. Offering us seats at their table. That was kind. Oh yeah, Eugene is quite a salesman. I nearly grabbed my checkbook and wrote him a bad check for a house. I didn't, but it got our tab paid."

Charles interrupted, "Virgil, anything useful?"

"They don't have Blue Hawaiis at that restaurant, although—"

Charles said, "Virg—"

"I know, I know," Virgil interrupted Charles's interruption. "Everyone there loved Clarence, but even after they said Terrell talked to each of them about Clarence's death, no one said much about Terrell. Hell, he was dead, too."

"The party was for Clarence," Charles said.

Virgil looked out the window before turning to Charles. "How many times did someone say Sol Legare was a tight-knit community? Don't answer, Charles. It was several. If that's true, why so little talk about someone who was murdered out there less than a week ago?"

It was a good question, one for which I had no answer. "Charles, what did you learn?"

"Clarence's favorite singers were Aretha Franklin and Bob Marley."

Wasn't it only seconds ago Charles was on Virgil's case for mentioning things that weren't related to the death of the three men?

Virgil said, "Charles, what's that have to do with the murders?"

I stifled a giggle while keeping my eyes on the road.

"Nothing, it popped in my head. Let's see, we didn't know it before, but Sandra was out on Mosquito in the early fifties when Elijah was killed. She was quite a charmer back in the day."

"And she dated Elijah," Virgil added.

Charles said, "Not really a date. Met him one time, and that was in the pavilion to dance. Not a date in my book."

"That's all she admitted to," Virgil said. "She was sitting with her husband when she said it. Since he swept her off her feet a few months after that, I figured she didn't spend much time talking to him about Elijah."

"Chris," Charles said, "what'd you learn?"

"You've already covered most of it."

Charles said, "Most?"

I told them about my encounter with Andrew Delaney.

Charles said, "You were gone so long I thought you left us."

Virgil said, "Do you think Andrew was right about the killer or killers being at the restaurant?"

"Don't know. It makes sense, but that doesn't narrow it down much."

I let Charles off at his apartment; did the same for Virgil.

I pulled in my drive and repeated what I'd told Virgil about not knowing if the killer was in Island Breeze. What I did know, it was my fault Terrell wasn't there.

* * *

"THOUGHT I'D FIND YOU HERE," Charles said as he lumbered up the steps to the second level of the Folly Beach Fishing Pier. I figured it was his cane tapping on the steps before I saw or heard him.

"Why?"

He wore a long-sleeve, purple T-shirt with Carroll Saints on the front, tan shorts, red tennis shoes, and his summer Tilley. He bent at the waist, put his hands on his knees, and then waved for me to move over.

He sat beside me on the picnic table then pointed to his chest. "It's Carroll College in Helena, Montana. Knew you'd be interested."

"I asked why, not what."

"Why what?"

Why did I even ask, I wondered? "Why did you know I'd be here?"

He rubbed his chin. "Let's see, you weren't at the Dog, Amber said you hadn't been in. You weren't home, or if you were, you were either dead or didn't want to talk to me. Neither option struck my fancy. Then it came to me in a moment of brilliance. Where else would you be if you wanted to think, ponder something, or just hang out to pretend you were thinking when you were snoozing?" He waved his hand around. "Here you are."

For the second time, I wondered why I asked.

"Did any other insightful nuggets come to you in that moment of brilliance?"

"Nary a one. I figured you'd have one or two to share after last night's visit to the Breeze."

Charles was more intuitive and sensitive than he'd like others to believe. Additionally, after him knowing me more than a decade, he knew my moods.

"I was thinking about Terrell, how he'd be alive if I hadn't let him go on and on about finding the person who killed Elijah and Clarence."

Charles removed his Tilley, set it beside him, and wiped perspiration off his brow. He watched two men untangling their fishing lines at the edge of the lower deck, then glanced over at me. "Knew that's what you'd be pondering."

"How'd you know that?"

"Hey, I don't call myself a detective for nothing. That's the way you are. After we left there last night, I could tell it was bothering you. Don't ask why. I knew because it was also bothering me. It didn't bother me enough to keep me awake all night, like I bet it did you."

I started to deny it. No need to lie to my friend. "You caught me."

On the railing behind us two white and black seagulls were squawking, probably laughing at our discussion.

"Know what I figured out, didn't have to stay up all night to do it?"

I probably would regret asking, but he was going to tell me anyway. "What?"

"Terrell's death is not your fault. It's not."

"Maybe, but—"

"No but. Let me finish."

I nodded for him to continue.

"Did you encourage him to nose into their deaths?" He held his hand in front of my face, palm facing me. "No, you didn't. Clarence was Terrell's friend. He'd known him his entire life, looked up to him, was a father figure to him. His death hit Terrell hard. Hard enough to do everything he could to find out who killed him. Could you have stopped him if you tried? No."

"I could've tried."

"Sure, you could have, but you would've failed. I saw that in Terrell's eyes when we met him behind Rita's. Remember, then we were only talking about finding who killed Elijah sixty something years ago, a man Terrell never met. He was going to get involved because his grandpa knew Elijah. Think how much it had to be tearing his inside out when Clarence was killed."

"True, but—"

He pointed his cane at me. "Want to know something else I remembered about that meeting?"

"Of course."

"I heard you tell him without mincing words that whoever killed Elijah wouldn't hesitate to harm anyone trying to dig up the truth after the skeleton was dug up. I also know you enough to know even though I didn't hear you, I bet that wasn't the only time you told him."

Crap, he was good. "I did warn him again after Clarence was killed."

Charles held out both arms. "See, more proof it wasn't your fault."

"You may be right, but it doesn't make me feel better."

"Know what would?"

I took a deep breath, glanced at the seagulls continuing their conversation, then turned to Charles. "Catching the person who killed him."

Charles smiled. "Finally, you got something right."

30

Charles had decided over the years that some of our best thinking came when we were walking and talking; therefore, a walk on the beach would be our best chance of figuring out who killed Terrell, Clarence, and possibly Elijah. I had serious doubts, but the temperature was mild, and we were graced with a blue sky peeking through puffy white clouds. This was the perfect combination for a walk on the beach, something we'd done many times.

Sundays in mid-September were not normally the busiest days on the beach, but you wouldn't know it today. It seemed every square inch of sand was occupied by vacationers of all ages, locals on their daily walk weaving around carefully to not kick sand on the outsiders, kids doing their seagull imitations by flapping their arms while squealing. There were several surfers plus two paddle boarders avoiding the crowded beach by staying a hundred or so yards offshore. I didn't know if we could solve any murders, but the feel of the beach, seeing hundreds of folks and hearing their enthusiastic voices about being on Folly buoyed my spirits.

Before we'd made our way to the steps leading from the Pier to the beach, Charles stopped three times to talk to men fishing off the structure, twice to pet three dogs accompanying their owners. While my spirits were lifted, I knew we couldn't have a serious conversation when surrounded by hundreds of people who'd gathered in front of the Pier or the Tides Hotel, so I motioned for us to head east where there were fewer distractions.

We'd gone a couple hundred yards before either of us spoke.

Charles broke the silence. "Do you think the same person killed all three guys?"

"Makes the most sense. Elijah's body turns up. Clarence made it known to everyone who'd listen he was going to find out who killed him. And don't forget, Terrell left me the message saying he thought he knew who killed both men."

"Couldn't there still be more than one person doing the killing? Terrell said he thought he knew who it was. He could've been wrong; heck, even if he was right, someone else could have shot him."

"You're right, but it makes more sense one person did it all."

"If true, the person is probably in his eighties."

"Yes."

"How many people who live on or near Sol Legare are that old?"

"Several, I suspect. Many of the residents have been there generations, lots of older folks are still around. Also remember, the killer could live anywhere."

"True, but if he lived far away, he probably wouldn't have known about Clarence or Terrell trying to find him."

We passed a group of five couples sitting in folding chairs arranged in a circle. Six of the chairs had orange backs with VOLS in large white letters. Charles pointed his cane their direction. "Want to yell Roll Tide Roll?"

"How many of them can you outrun?" I asked the master topic changer.

He glanced back at the group. "Zero."

"Then, no."

He shrugged. "Who've we met in their eighties from Sol Legare or nearby?"

I said, "The guy who's going to build your house. Then there's Jamal Kingsly, Sandra and Robert Graves, umm. I guess that's all."

"What about your buddy the triple-K guy?"

"Andrew Delaney. He could've killed Clarence and Terrell, but he's in his sixties so wouldn't have been old enough to have shot Elijah. What would be his motive?"

"Did you forget the KKK part?" He snapped his fingers. "Or, one of his relatives, one still alive, killed Elijah and Andrew killed the other two who were getting close to figuring it out before they revealed a family member as the killer."

"He's a suspect, but I doubt he did it."

"How about anyone you've met when I wasn't around?"

"Can't think of anyone."

"Okay, now we have a suspect list, what next?"

"Think back to last night. The place was packed. Other than those at our table, how many other people did you see who could've been in their eighties or older?"

Charles stopped, closed his eyes, and shook his head. "A half dozen, maybe more."

"The killer could've been any of them. Plus, Terrell told me there were a few others he needed to talk to who would've been in that age range."

Charles smiled. "Chris, the other day I was talking to Benny Hilton, he's a big golfer. Said he'd rather golf than eat. I don't believe it since he weighs about five pounds less than a papa elephant. Anyway, I ran into Benny in front of the Crab Shack when he started jabbering about playing the Country Club of Charleston the day before. He was laughing at Shannon, don't know his last name, who's one of his playing partners. You know Benny, don't you?"

"No. Your point is?"

"Touchy today, aren't we?"

"Charles."

"Okay. Benny said whenever Shannon hit a ball into the rough, something he does a lot according to Benny, he drives on the cart path through the rough. He expects his ball to always be sitting there waiting for him. He never thinks it could be somewhere in the rough where there isn't a path."

"The point of the story?"

"The point is we don't know any of those other senior citizens who were at Clarence's party last night, so we have to start our search by the cart path."

"With the suspects we know."

"You're catching on. After I teach you how to be a good detective, maybe I'll teach you golf."

From earlier conversations, I knew Charles had never played golf, nor indicated he'd wanted to start.

"For sake of argument, let's say one of the people we know killed Elijah Duncan in the early 1950s, buried him on Mosquito Beach, never to be found. If it's someone we know, he stayed in the area and remained under the radar until Clarence discovered the skeleton. Then Clarence took it upon himself to dig into the killing hoping he'd learn who killed Elijah."

"A fatal mistake," Charles added. "Then our new friend Terrell took it upon himself to see if he could learn who killed Elijah, simply because his grandpa told him about his friendship with the guy years before Terrell was born."

I nodded. "Then snooping into his friend Clarence's murder was Terrell's fatal mistake."

Our conversation had taken us across from the Folly Beach water tower. Charles pointed his cane at the structure standing taller than any surrounding building and asked if I was ready to head back. I was, so we pivoted to begin the long trek back.

"Okay," Charles said, "we don't know for certain, but the odds are both Clarence and Terrell were killed because they were getting close to learning who killed Elijah."

"I agree."

"To figure it all out, don't we need to know why Elijah was killed? Who'd he piss off enough to bump him off?"

"I don't remember exactly what each of them said about Elijah, but the overall feeling was he was a troublemaker. Even Al, his friend, called him a hell raiser. I think Jamal said something about his having a chip on his shoulder, Terrell hinted that his constant speaking out about African American rights caused problems for blacks. It got whites stirred up and put blacks in their sights. Don't forget Sandra knew Elijah, even danced with him. She could've known him better than the men."

Charles said "Those are pretty weak motives. There must be more. Know what I keep thinking about?"

"What?"

"I keep coming back to how quickly good old Eugene ended our two meetings when we brought up Elijah's name. That fella wants to sell me a house as much as he doesn't want to talk about Elijah."

"True."

"I'd put him at the top of our list. I'd bet others on Sol Legare would too. Eugene thinks folks there like him, but they don't. He took advantage of them with low wages when blacks couldn't speak out for their rights."

"Elijah did."

Charles stopped and said, "That's what got him killed."

31

After the beach walk with Charles and still exhausted from last night's party at Island Breeze, I thought sleep would come quickly. Wrong. My eyes failed to stay closed while my mind kept drifting back to the murders.

I wasn't as confident as Charles about Eugene being the killer, but he was as good a suspect as any. So what? There was no evidence to indicate any of the people I'd met were responsible.

I felt I owed it to Terrell to see what I could do to help the police but realized how handicapped I was. In recent years, some of my friends and I had been lucky enough to help the police. The task was made easier because we knew Folly Beach, were familiar with many residents, plus we had connections with the police. People trusted us so they'd share things they wouldn't tell others.

I had none of those advantages when it came to Sol Legare Island and Mosquito Beach. I was an outsider. The men I knew best from there were dead. Even then, I didn't know them well. With Island Breeze being the center of the tight-knit community, it was the only place I could go without appearing to be nosing around.

With that working against me, why did I feel I had to do something? Wouldn't the easiest, possibly safest thing be to leave it to the police? Then, why was I tossing, turning, and thinking about what had happened on Mosquito Beach?

The answer came down to two words: Al and Terrell.

Al Washington is a friend, has been for years. He's a friend who'd sacrificed most of his eighty-two years, while raising nine adopted children, risking his life, and becoming a hero in the Korean conflict, and experiencing health problems that would've been the end of most people. Add to that, he's put up with Bob Howard for decades. That's suffering personified. Because Al is a friend, I feel an obligation to help him learn what happened to Elijah Duncan, the young man he knew in the 1950s.

It's three-thirty. Sleep, where are you?

I owe it to Terrell because, regardless of what Charles or anyone else says, I feel responsible for his death. I could've discouraged him more than I had. Would it have worked? Would it have prevented his death? I'll never know. What I know is I must do something.

Still no sleep.

Before Charles headed home, he wanted me to call Detective Callahan to tell him ... tell him what? Charles, who seldom runs low on ideas, said I'd come up with something to tell the detective. He may seldom run low on ideas, but some aren't worth the energy it takes for him to share them. I told him this was one of those times. Callahan had already talked with many people about the deaths, including some if not all our "suspects." The Detective had the voicemail Terrell had left me. There wasn't anything else I knew that could be helpful. Of course, that didn't stop Charles from saying I should tell him about Eugene ending our conversations when Elijah's name came up.

I'd left Charles with, "I'll think about it."

And here I was, in the middle of the night, thinking about it, thinking about the other murders, then thinking about Al.

Sleep, please hurry.

A glance at the clock told me it was seven forty-five. I'd finally drifted off after sleepless hours trying to put my arms around the happenings on Mosquito Beach. As promised, I'd thought about

Charles's suggestion for me to call Detective Callahan. I rejected it. There was nothing I could tell him he didn't know. I wanted to see if the detective had learned anything leading him closer to the killer, or killers, but knew it'd be foolish to ask. The next best thing would be to see if Chief LaMond had news. I tapped her number on my speed dial.

"Cindy, this—"

"Meet me, the Dog, twenty minutes."

I hated Caller ID. No need to respond, she was gone.

Fifteen minutes later, I found Cindy on the side patio sipping coffee.

A server saw me at the table and set an orange mug of coffee in front of me without me asking for any.

I took a sip and asked Cindy, "Why'd you hang up on me? How'd you know I'd meet you?"

"What else do old retired guys have to do at eight in the morning? Besides, I hung up in case someone was holding you for ransom and calling me to pay to get you released. I'd hate to tell them no way, Jose."

I deserved that after calling so early. "Good point."

She smiled. "I don't suppose you called to wish me happy Monday."

"I always want you to have a happy day, but there was something else I was wondering."

"Duh. Who would've guessed?"

"Charles, Al Washington, Virgil and I were at a party at Island Breeze Saturday."

"Who'd be desperate enough to invite you to a party?"

I explained it was Clarence Taylor's last wish.

She stared at me. "Clarence Taylor wanted a party after he was dead?"

I nodded. "He left a note saying he'd been to too many funerals, didn't want one for himself but wanted his friends to throw a party."

"And why were you, Charles, Al, and since I only know one Virgil, that the fourth was Virgil Debonnet, invited?"

I explained how Al had met Clarence, so he wanted to honor his life by attending. Virgil was more difficult to explain since he was relatively new to Folly and as far as Cindy knew, didn't know anyone on Sol Legare.

"Okay, now that I know you didn't call to invite me to the party, why'd you ruin my perfectly pleasant Monday?"

"I was wondering if Detective Callahan had any leads on the cases over there."

"So, instead of calling Detective Callahan who would've laughed you off the phone or threatened to have you arrested for nosing in his business, you called me."

I smiled. "Excellent summary."

"You think I don't have enough to do maintaining law and order on this island where there are, oh, let's say, a zillion clowns who love to get drunk, throw beer bottles at vacationers peacefully walking down the street, drive a hundred miles an hour over the speed limit, see how many ways they can nearly drown in that big pond out there?" She pointed toward the Atlantic. "Do you think I have enough time to take care of all that, then add whatever is going on in the rest of Charleston County to my to-do list?"

"No one could do it better than you, Chief LaMond."

She rolled her eyes. "Go get me a refill while I sit here, soak up that praise, and pat myself on the back."

She was on the phone when I returned. I set her coffee in front of her then stepped off the patio to give her privacy. She motioned me back after ending the call.

"Detective Callahan says the coroner didn't find anything unusual on Terrell or Clarence's bodies, that is other than bullet holes. There were no unidentifiable prints in Terrell's house, and, of course, no witnesses to either shooting. The bullets were from the same gun, verifying what everyone suspected; the same person probably shot both men. There's no physical evidence the person who killed Terrell and Clarence is the person who killed Elijah Duncan. Callahan assumes it is. That's why he's interviewing everyone in the area old enough to kill all three."

"He told you all of that while I was getting your refill? I'm impressed."

"Callahan talks fast, doesn't beat around the bush like you do. He's like that guy on that old TV show that started with, "Dum—de-DUM-DUM.""

"*Dragnet.*"

"Yep. You geezers know all that worthless trivia."

She was kind enough to check with Callahan, so I ignored her insult. "Did he learn anything from the interviews?"

"He learned everyone loved Clarence, thought highly of Terrell."

"Someone didn't."

"Therein lies the problem. Now that I've done my good deed for the day, did you and your motley bunch of amateur detectives—I'm being generous calling you amateur, but couldn't come up with a word that meant less than amateur—learn anything at the party to help the real police?"

"Not really. Charles thinks it's Eugene Dillinger, he's a builder who lives over here."

"I know him. Seems like an okay guy although he's accumulated a passel of parking tickets. Why does Charles think it's him?"

I told her about our conversation at the house he was building, then at the empty lot. When I mentioned that we were there because Charles had told Eugene he was interested in a house, Cindy laughed so hard that coffee spewed out her nose. Fortunate for the Chief, I was the only witness.

She regained her composure then asked if that was all I had.

I nodded.

"I spend way more time than I should telling a handful of our locals not to jaywalk across Center Street. Telling them doesn't mean a thing. They're going to continue until one of them becomes road kill. I tell them anyway."

There was a point coming. I wondered if it would arrive before I finished my coffee. I motioned for her to continue.

"Whoever killed Clarence and Terrell is still out there. He has nothing to lose if he kills again. I'm telling you, and by extension, your friends, to be careful."

"Cindy—"

"I'm not telling you to leave it to the police. I'd be wasting my time. All I'm saying is be careful."

"Thank you for caring."

"Hell yeah, I care. Who'd buy my coffee if you were dead?"

32

I was crossing Center Street—yes, jaywalking—heading home from the Dog when a blue pickup pulled in a parking spot in front of me. Andrew Delaney stepped out wearing a black T-shirt and light-gray shorts.

"Well if it isn't my bleeding-heart liberal friend," he said with a smile.

Hadn't I denied that characterization when we talked at Loggerhead's? Regardless, I said, "Morning, Andrew."

"I apologize, I forgot your name."

"Chris."

"Chris, got it. I'm off today, so it's a good morning."

"You live out near Harris Teeter, don't you? What brings you to Folly?"

His gaze narrowed. "This is still a free country even though it's getting less free every day. I can be here if I want to be."

Wrong question!

"Whoa, I was simply making conversation. Didn't mean to offend you."

"Sorry to snap. I'm frustrated about what's happening to my country. Seems like I have to be careful about what I say, where I go, who I hang with, what I do with my own free time." He shook his head. "Don't get me started." He hesitated, looked at me, then chuckled. "Suppose I already got started. Sorry."

I didn't know what to say so I nodded like I knew what he was talking about.

"I came over to wake up my friend to see what he's doing. He's always telling me I should go surfing with him. He's off today and says he has an extra board. I thought I'd give it a go." He smiled. "Can you picture this beer-bellied body on a surfboard?"

I started to laugh but held back. I didn't want to get snapped at again for saying or doing the wrong thing. I said, "Looks like a good day for surfing."

I expected him to say he had to go so I could continue home. Instead, he pointed at the Tides Hotel. "They still sell Starbucks in there?"

I nodded.

"It'd be silly to wake my friend this early. Let me buy you coffee. I promise not to spill it on you, may not even lecture you about anything."

I had exceeded my coffee limit for the day but figured there must be something on his mind besides caffeine.

"Sure."

We entered the Tides and followed the corridor to Roasted, the hotel's coffeeshop.

Andrew looked around. "I've only been in here once." He looked out the large windows facing the ocean. "Great view."

I agreed as he stepped to the counter and asked what I wanted.

I wanted an explanation of why we were here. Instead, I said black coffee. He ordered two cups, paid, handed me mine. We moved to a small, round table in the center of the room. Other than the clerk, we were the only people in Roasted.

Andrew slowly sipped his drink, set the cup on the table, then said, "How well did you know Clarence Taylor?"

"Not well. I met him once when I took a friend to Mosquito Beach so he could see where he spent time in the 1950s."

"Oh, when I saw you at that party, I figured you two were friends."

"Why'd you want to know if we were friends?"

"I think I told you outside the party I'd known Clarence a long time. As unlikely as it was, we were sort of friends."

Something had been bothering me about Andrew from when we'd talked at Loggerhead's. Do I risk asking about it and getting coffee thrown in my face? Why not?

"If I remember correctly, when we met for the first time at Loggerhead's outside bar—"

He smiled and interrupted, "When I shared my beer with you?"

I returned the smile. "Yes. I asked if you heard about a murder on Sol Legare. You were vague when you said all you heard was that it was an old black man."

His smile vanished. "So?"

"A little later you asked where I'd met Clarence. You went on to say you may've worked with him at a landscape company."

Andrew shook his head. "I was hoping your memory wasn't that good. Yeah, I sort of lied."

Sort of lied, I thought. "Why?"

"I'd known you for what, thirty seconds? I didn't know if you were a cop or a crusader set out to blame white guys for everything bad happening to, umm, black people." He smiled. "Besides, I'd had a few too many, if you know what I mean. Hell, it's no telling what I said."

"I understand."

"Yes, I knew Clarence. Like I told you before, I didn't want to, but I liked him. When I saw you at his party, I thought you might have an idea who killed him."

"Did you know Terrell Jefferson?"

Andrew closed his eyes and then shook his head. "He that other black guy killed after Clarence was shot?"

"Yes. He was a good friend of Clarence, had known him most of his life."

"I heard a rumor the same person shot both guys."

"Yes."

Andrew looked in his coffee cup then at the ocean. "There's also a story going around the cops think the Klan did it."

"Is that possible?"

He looked up from his cup and glared at me. "If it was, would I have been asking you if you had an idea who killed them?"

The word no was not anywhere in there. "Not really."

"Look, Chris. Let me be honest. I'm a member of the Klan. I'm not ashamed of it. The guys I know in it don't like black people. Hell, they don't like brown people, or red people. But, killing those who don't look like us ain't something I condone. Neither do my friends. I can't speak for every Klansman, but I can speak for me and my buddies. None of us killed Clarence or that Terrell guy. Period." He swirled the coffee around in the cup. "I asked if you had any idea who killed him or them for two reasons. First, the last thing the Klan needs is to be accused of killing two black men in Charleston County. Second, Clarence was a friend."

"I understand. While I hardly knew him, he seemed like a nice guy."

"Let me ask you something else. Do you know if there was someone at the party named Jamal?"

"Jamal Kingsly?"

"Don't know for sure. If Clarence ever said his last name, I don't remember."

"Jamal Kingsly was a friend of Clarence. He was at the party."

"Thought it may be the man Clarence talked about but wasn't sure. I only saw the guy Clarence called Jamal twice. That was a bunch of years ago. I remembered him being heavy with a white beard. When I saw someone who looked like that go in, that name popped in my head."

"What'd Clarence say about him?"

"Said he was always reading books. Not much else I remember except once Clarence was telling me about growing up on Sol Legare, about the pavilion out there, and the fights he had with some of the other people." He chuckled. "Think it was always over gals."

"Do you think Jamal killed Clarence?"

Andrew shrugged. "Why not? Someone did. It sure as hell wasn't me. Chris, I'm being honest. It wasn't any of my friends."

I started to respond, when Andrew looked at his watch, gulped the last of his coffee, then said, "Time to go wake my buddy. As he'd say, waves are awaitin'."

I wished him luck surfing. I remained seated as he headed out.

33

"Okay, you got me," Charles said when I answered the phone. "Your car's at your house, but you ain't. You're not at the Dog, not on the Pier, not walking aimlessly down Center Street. Where are you?"

"Good morning, Charles. Nice day, isn't it?"

"You forget the question?"

"Did you forget to start the conversation with something a normal person might begin with, something civil, maybe even polite?"

"No. Where are you?"

Once again, I wondered why I tried to introduce Mr. Fowler to civility.

"The Tides, sitting in Roasted enjoying a cup of coffee, some peace and quiet. That is, I was until the phone rang."

"On my way."

Peace and quiet was ending soon.

Three people who appeared to be staying at the hotel came in the coffeeshop, ordering drinks, were looking at Tides T-shirts, and picking through the Folly Beach post cards, when Charles bounded through the door. He looked at the vacationers then motioned me to follow as he exited as quickly as he'd arrived.

He didn't say anything until we'd walked up the steps leading to the Folly Pier.

He pointed to the far end of the structure. "We need to have a meeting of the Charles Detective Agency in our Atlantic office."

Over the years, Charles had given his business several names, and so had those of us who knew him. I leaned toward calling it imaginary, while others preferred names ranging from delusional to hilarious. I didn't recall him ever mentioning the Atlantic office. I didn't question him about it more than I was going to ask about the University of Florida long-sleeve T-shirt he was wearing.

Apparently, the imaginary office was on the upper level of the Pier. He sat on a picnic table facing the shore, took off his Tilley, set it beside him, and propped his cane against the table. I waited for him to call the meeting to order.

The wait was short.

"I spent hours last night thinking while you were wasting your time sleeping. Know what I figured out?"

"What?"

"Nothing."

"Wow!" I said. "To think, I wasted all that valuable thinking time asleep."

He glanced at me. "You making fun of me?"

"Yep."

He sighed. "I deserved it."

"Yep. If our meeting has started, might I ask what you were thinking about while I was asleep?"

He sighed again, shook his head, and said, "Did you forget we're trying to solve three murders?"

"Since you mention it every time we talk, I don't see how I could forget. I also don't see how we know enough to figure out anything."

He smiled. "That's why we're meeting. Let's talk about what we know, not what we don't."

"Good plan, Mr. Detective. No doubt that'll be easier than talking about what we don't know. You first."

"Terrell and Clarence were killed by the same person."

"Killed by the same gun," I said. "Not necessarily the same person."

"Close enough. We know, okay, not know but suspect they were killed by the same dude who offed Elijah back when we were in kindergarten."

"I agree."

"Finally," he said. "Now we're getting somewhere. Whoever it is has to be old."

"And, a current or former resident of the Sol Legare area since everyone says it's a small close-knit community. Outsiders would've had a hard time knowing all three men."

Charles rubbed his chin. "I got that far in my last-night pondering."

He also had gotten that far when we last talked.

"That all you have?"

"Close, but not all. Motive becomes the big bugaboo in figuring it out. We think the reason the person killed Clarence and Terrell was because they were snooping around trying to catch the killer."

I added, "Don't forget, Terrell thought he knew."

"So, if true, it's probably someone he talked to. Someone who decided freedom meant more than getting locked up and decided to kill Terrell after he'd already bumped off Clarence. That means it's someone among the living since I doubt Terrell talked to the ghost of whoever killed Elijah."

"True."

"That's where my figuring ran into a dead end. Three dead ends." He tapped me on the leg. "Now I'll turn the agenda over to you. Who are your most-likely suspects?"

"Your good buddy and your future home builder Eugene Dillinger, Jamal Kingsly, Robert Graves, and then I would guess a handful or more other people who either live on Sol Legare or nearby who would be old enough to have killed Elijah."

"Don't forget Robert's wife."

"And Sandra. Plus, I wouldn't rule out Andrew Delaney."

"I'm not great at math, but if my cyphering is correct, he's not old enough to have killed Elijah."

"He isn't, but he could've shot the other two. Want to know why I was at Roasted when you called?"

"Hiding from me?"

I sighed then shared my conversation with Andrew.

"Let me see if I have this right. He told you neither he nor his friends killed anyone, so you think he did it. Why?"

"I doubt he did, but it struck me strange how much he went out of his way to deny it. Also, he brought Jamal into the conversation hinting he may have something to do with the murders."

"Okay, I'll put Andrew on the B list of suspects. Could he be right about Jamal?"

"We don't know any of them well enough to do more than guess. We know Jamal has a temper. Terrell even apologized to me after Jamal went on a mini-rant about Elijah when he said Elijah had been causing trouble for the black community by pushing hard for equal rights." I paused then remembered something else about Elijah. "The first time I met Jamal he said the skeleton was probably some old-timer who died whose family didn't have enough money to have a proper funeral. He also said the murder was ancient history. I had the impression he didn't want to talk about it."

"Didn't Jamal say he thought Elijah ran off?"

"Yes."

"When we were talking to him, he said he'd put money on the body being Elijah. That'd be a safe bet if he killed him."

"The more everyone learned about the skeleton the more they were convinced it was Elijah."

"Yet, the only proof, if you can call it that, is those fancy shoes."

"Shoes, age of skeleton, how Elijah had disappeared," I said.

"Think Jamal killed all of them?"

"I don't know. I wouldn't rule him out."

"I'd put him on the A list, high up on it. At the top, I still come back to slick Eugene. When we were at that house on East Ashley talking about the skeleton, he said it was probably some old bum, that it was ancient history."

"That's not much different than what Jamal said. Why do you put him above Jamal?"

Charles looked at the Tides, glanced at three surfers off to our left, before saying, "He's sleazy. You said he wasn't liked by the folks on Sol Legare. Back around Elijah's time, Eugene hired a lot of guys from out there and underpaid them. Didn't you say that the only reason they put up with him then and now was because he hired guys from there?"

"Yes, but—"

"Hold on," he interrupted, "there's more. Remember how quick he wanted to get away from us whenever I mentioned the murders?" He snapped his fingers. "Chris, remember when we were at Clarence's party, and I believe it was Jamal who asked Eugene if Elijah had worked for him back in the day?"

"Eugene said something like he had for a while."

"Yes, Eugene then said we weren't at the party to talk about Elijah then changed the subject. That's Eugene changing the subject every time Elijah's name popped up."

"When we were touring Eugene's construction project, he said he didn't know who the skeleton belonged to."

"Then changed the subject. That's all he said about Clarence but remember at the party he said Terrell came to his construction site to ask what Eugene knew about Elijah."

"Eugene said he told him he had no idea who killed either man. That's hardly a confession."

"I'll give you that," Charles said then looked toward the shore. "Remember what he also said?"

"No."

"Terrell was at the house for a half hour. How long do you think it takes to say you don't know who killed either man?"

"Not that long."

"I repeat," Charles said, "Eugene is suspect number one."

"What about Robert?"

"Other than being old enough, what reason would he have?"

"I don't think he did, but he's the only other person we know who's old enough to have killed Elijah."

Charles picked up his Tilley and waved it in my face. "Wrong, wannabe detective. Don't forget Sandra."

"Okay, what motive would Robert or Sandra have?"

"Didn't they say Elijah dated Sandra. Jealousy has to be right up there on the list of reasons to kill someone."

"She said he met her once at the pavilion where they danced. That was it. And, she said Robert wasn't in the picture until months later."

"Swept her off her feet. Did it enter your mind that Robert could've killed Elijah, so it'd be easier to sweep her?"

"That's a possibility," I said, more to get Charles to move along rather than it making sense since Robert and Sandra didn't know each other at the time.

"Glad you agree. He's on my list," Charles said as he scribbled an imaginary word in the bench with an imaginary pencil. "He's sharing equal billing with Sandra."

"What's her motive?"

"Heck, who knows. Maybe Elijah wasn't satisfied with one night of dancing. She thought one night was enough, so when he kept pursuing her, she ended his courtin' with a bullet."

"Going back to your golf ball near the cart path story, the only suspects we've talked about are people we've met. There could be others." I kept coming back to what Terrell had said about Charles and I being outsiders.

"Think it's time for you to call your favorite police chief and tell her what we know. She'll pick out the best parts and share them with Detective Callahan. He can put it all together. *Voila*. We've helped the cops catch another killer." He clapped then pointed to the pocket holding my phone. "Meeting adjourned."

The meeting may've adjourned, but that didn't stop Charles from insisting I call Cindy. That was the only thing I could do to get Charles off my back, so I picked up the phone, punched in her number.

I was rewarded with voicemail. Since I didn't know what I could tell her that'd be helpful, I breathed a sigh of relief and left a message for her to call when she got a spare minute. Charles huffed as if Cindy intentionally ignored my call. Her phone had caller ID, so he could've been right, but I didn't share that thought.

He stared at the phone, then turned to me. "How long do you think it'll be before she calls?"

"Charles, I don't—"

"I know, I know," he interrupted. "You don't know and don't want to sit here waiting until she calls. Call me after you talk to her."

I promised I would. Our after-meeting discussion ended when he headed off the Pier, his cane tapping on the wooden surface with each step.

34

Spare minutes were few and far between for Folly's Director of Public Safety, so I wasn't surprised she hadn't returned my call. The only calls I received between leaving the message and nine-thirty that night were two from Charles asking if the Chief had responded. His calls weren't as irritating as robocalls telling me that the IRS was going to knock down my front door in the next two hours if I didn't call immediately, but they weren't far off.

The phone rang at ten o'clock and to my surprise it wasn't Charles. It also wasn't Cindy.

"Chris, this is Al. I hope I didn't call too late."

I told him he hadn't and started to ask if he was okay until I remembered how he'd said I didn't have to ask each time he called.

"I've been giving a lot of thought to what's happening on Mosquito. Do you think you could spare a few minutes for this old man to talk about it?"

"Of course. What's on your mind?"

"Chris, umm, I hate to ask, but could we talk in person? I ain't my best when talking on the phone."

I chuckled. "Me either. Want me to come to the bar tomorrow?"

"Tomorrow's a light day. None of the suppliers are scheduled to stop by. I figure Bob can handle whatever happens, so I told him I was taking the day off."

"What'd he say?"

Al laughed. "He said he wasn't giving me a paid day off. I told him he wasn't paying me when I was there. He grumbled about me starting a damned greeters union, then added before he knew it, I'd be demanding a salary for doing nothing but sitting by the door."

"I'll meet you at your house unless you're afraid you may get fired from your nonpaying job."

"Sounds like a plan, my friend, yes it does."

We agreed on a time then I headed to bed without hearing from the Chief, another call from Charles, or the IRS.

* * *

AFTER A QUICK STOP at Bert's for coffee and a Danish, I was on my way to Al's when Cindy called.

"Please tell me you called to take Larry and me to Halls Chophouse for a steak dinner."

Halls was one of Charleston's finer restaurants.

"Sorry, Cindy, reservations were last night. You didn't call back, so I cancelled."

"I didn't get to be Folly's head police honchette by believing all the crap some of our fine citizens or vacationers hurl at me. Why'd you call?"

I spent the next ten minutes telling her what Charles and I'd talked about. She mostly listened, listened between overblown sighs, a couple of giggles, a handful of profanities. In the middle of one of her profanity-laced tirades, I missed the turn to Al's house and had to go around the block to get back on track.

Cindy never got off track. She ended the call with a simple question. "In all those words did you say anything that could help the police, you know, the people trained to investigate murders, learn who killed any or all of the men?"

I admitted if there was anything, I didn't know what.

Cindy ended the call; I ended my wayward drive. The parking space in front of the house where I'd parked the last two times wasn't available, so I drove around the corner before finding a space.

Spoiled Rotten announced my arrival. The Rottweiler's barks weren't as hostile as they'd been during my first visit, although I wasn't ready to risk life or limb by going over to pet him.

I knocked three times before Al opened the door. He was barefoot, wearing navy blue pajama bottoms, and a thin, white tank-top undershirt.

He stepped on the porch, said hi to his neighbor's dog, waved me in, then said, "From the sound of his barks, Spoiled Rotten likes you."

"I'm glad."

"Up for coffee?" Al said, then shuffled to the back of the house before I answered.

I followed. The kitchen was spotless, much neater than the rooms we passed along the way. A chrome and black Hamilton Beach coffeemaker and two white mugs were the only things on the counter. He'd planned for my visit. Al poured me a cup, refilled his, before taking a seat on the opposite side of the small table.

"Hope you don't mind my clothes. You caught me in my lounging duds. You don't know how good it feels for this old man not to have to get dressed on my day off."

I told him I did know as he took a sip and stared in his mug.

"I appreciate you coming over, I truly do. I know it's out of your way."

"Glad to come."

"Nobody mentioned it at the party, so I was wondering if there was a funeral for Terrell."

"Sorry, I thought I told you. He told his neighbor when he died, he wanted to be cremated with no funeral service like his friend Clarence. He said he was going to put it in his will, but, as you know, he was killed long before his time. He didn't have a will. The neighbor told the police and the coroner what Terrell wanted. He didn't have any known next-of-kin, so they honored it."

"I've got it in my will I want a funeral, want a chance for everyone who knew me to take a look in my coffin, see me smilin'." He laughed. "Maybe not Bob, but everyone else."

He was kidding about Bob.

He took another sip then turned serious. "That wasn't the reason I asked you over. I suppose you're wondering why."

I smiled. "It crossed my mind."

"Mr. Chris, I don't have many years left to look forward to, so I spend most of my idle time looking back." He chuckled. "I'm not talking about looking back at yesterday or the day before when Bob's fighting with his customers, days where I'm having to listen to Conway Twitty on Bob's jukebox. I'm talking back to the days when I was full of energy, enthusiasm, learning my way around the world. I've told you before some of my best memories are of the times I was out on Mosquito, yes they were."

I nodded, again.

"Anyway, a lot of those memories came back to me when I thought about you and me talking to Clarence when we were out there looking to where the old pavilion used to be. More memories flooded back at Clarence's party."

"You appeared to have a good time."

"My hearing ain't as good as it once was. There were a lot of folks out back making noise." He smiled. "That ain't counting Aretha Franklin and Bob Marley booming over the speakers. I didn't hear everything said, no I didn't."

"I didn't either."

Al took another sip, set his mug on the table, gazed in it, then looked at me. "Chris, before I start telling you something, remember I'm recalling something that happened sixty-five years ago. My memory could be playing tricks. And, heaven forbid, I couldn't raise my right hand and swear on a Bible what I'm saying is the truth, the whole truth, nothing but the truth. No, I couldn't."

"It was a long time ago, so I understand."

"At Clarence's party, Sandra was talking to Jamal. They were sitting at the other end of the table, so I couldn't hear what they were saying. Truth be told, I wasn't trying to listen because I knew it was too loud to hear them. I was sitting there staring at Eugene and for a moment I drifted back to 1953, yes I did." He closed his eyes and slowly nodded. "One Saturday night, a scorcher as I recall, I was in the pavilion talking to Elijah. See it clear as day. Then….Chris, forgive this old man, here's where it gets fuzzy. Elijah looked up the road, said something about having to talk to a man. He told me to wait in the pavilion. He walked in the direction of a man leaning against a car, an old black Dodge, as I recall." Al stopped and looked at my mug. "Let me get you more coffee."

I started to say I was fine, when he stood, grabbed my mug, and headed to the coffeemaker.

"Want a cookie? I've got Oreos."

"No thanks."

I didn't know where the story was going, but Al was in no hurry to get there.

"While I wouldn't swear on a Bible about it, I'd almost swear to you that Elijah went to talk to Eugene."

"That was decades ago. What makes you think it was Eugene?"

He shook his head. "First, the man was white. You've heard me say there weren't many whites on Mosquito in those days. My eyesight was better then, so I know the man was thin and stood straight as a flagpole. I noticed the same thing about Eugene the other night."

"Did you get a clear look at his face?"

"Not clear. It was dark, but I got a quick look when a car drove by. Headlights hit the man and Elijah."

"Did Elijah come back to the pavilion after talking to the man?"

"Before he left to talk to the man, he was in a great mood. We'd had a few beers. I remember him laughing, having a gay old time. When he came back, he brought a dark cloud with him."

"Did you ask about it?"

"I don't know for certain, but I can't imagine not being curious and asking him, especially since his mood shifted so much."

"Did he seem angry?"

Al shook his head. "Angry, no. Chris, my gut said he was scared."

"Al, do you think Eugene killed Elijah?"

"I only saw Elijah one more time after that. Must've been the next Saturday. I can't tell you anything he said but can tell you one thing. He wasn't the same Elijah I knew before." He shook his head again. "Do I think Eugene killed my friend? Don't know if he did or didn't. I'll tell you what I do know. My friend was spooked by something Eugene said, he sure was."

"Do you remember anything Elijah said before that night about Eugene? Did he ever mention wanting to work on one of Eugene's construction crews, or anything about other people he knew working for Eugene?"

Al looked back down in his mug then closed his eyes like he was trying to relive the past.

"Don't recall him saying anything about Eugene, but he often spoke about white men taking advantage of Negroes. That was one thing that got him pissed more than anything else he talked about."

"Did he talk about specific, umm, white men?"

"That was a long time ago. If he did, I don't recall. Sorry."

"No reason to be sorry, Al. I'm just trying to figure it out."

He smiled. "Good luck with that."

"Would you mind if I told Detective Callahan what you remembered?"

"Don't guess it'd hurt, although I'd hate to get Eugene in trouble if my memory is wrong." He shook his head. "A lot's gone on in this old head since way back then. No telling how far off I could be."

"If Eugene is innocent, he'll be okay."

"Mr. Chris, I reckon I didn't ask you over for you to do nothing. Do what you think is best."

35

I thought about calling Detective Callahan when I got home but decided to get it out of the way. I pulled over and dialed his number before leaving Charleston. He answered on the second ring and I told him who I was.

"How may I be of assistance, Mr. Landrum?" he said in a tone the warmth of an iceberg.

I shared what Al told me about thinking he saw Elijah with Eugene; how he felt that his friend was afraid of the builder.

Callahan paused when I finished. I wondered if he was still on the phone.

Finally, he said, "Mr. Landrum, I hope you appreciate how patient I've been with your interference, your theories over the years. Chief LaMond thinks highly of you, and you've occasionally garnered information before we were able to."

"Chief LaMond is a good friend. She's told me on more than one occasion you're an excellent detective."

"Neither here nor there. I appreciate you thinking what Mr., umm, Washington told you was important. My problem is he's talking about something that occurred before I was born. Let me ask you, do you think you could identify someone you saw two years ago? How about one year?"

"It depends, I suppose, on how well I knew the person."

"Okay, I'll give you that. But what about someone you saw thirty, forty, fifty or more years ago? How well did Mr. Washington know this Eugene Dillinger?"

"Detective, I get your point. Al had only met Eugene a time or two."

"He saw someone across a dark parking lot, and thinks he remembers who it was? Give me a break. It's not possible."

"You don't know Al like I do. He has an excellent memory. He wouldn't have said anything unless he was certain. Besides, the person he remembers seeing was white, a rare sight on Mosquito Beach in those days."

"Let's assume for sake of argument your friend is right, that he saw Eugene Dillinger talking to Elijah Duncan. What's there to say he killed him?"

"Nothing from that brief encounter."

"Correct. We're now faced with no evidence from all those years ago. There wasn't even a missing-person report. There was no reason for the police to look for Elijah. As I suspect you know, I've talked to several Sol Legare residents old enough to remember Mr. Duncan. When he disappeared the thoughts on what happened to him ranged from him running off with a preacher's daughter, him just running off, to him being killed by the Klan. Nothing specific, little the police at the time could've followed up on."

"But—"

"Let me continue, Mr. Landrum. Considering all that, we're still not certain the remains are Mr. Duncan. The time of death is consistent with his disappearance, the bones are of a black male approximately Mr. Duncan's age. From everyone I talked to who was around Sol Legare in 1953, Mr. Duncan wore shoes like those found with the remains. I don't think anyone doubts that the skeleton belongs to Mr. Duncan, but no proof can and probably ever will be found."

"It appears the recent murders of Clarence Taylor and Terrell Jefferson are related to Mr. Duncan's murder. Wouldn't you agree?"

"It makes sense, but again, other than both men taking a strong interest in learning who killed Mr. Duncan, there's nothing tying them together."

"My understanding is they were doing more than taking, as you say, a strong interest. They were talking to everyone who was around in those days, and don't forget, the voicemail Terrell left me saying he knew who killed both Clarence and Elijah."

"Mr. Landrum, did you forget your friend Chief LaMond said I'm a good detective? The murders of Terrell Jefferson and Clarence Taylor are mine to solve. They're not the only homicides on my plate, but they're at the top. I appreciate you sharing what you consider important information about the death of Elijah Duncan. Now let me share something that's important. The deaths are a matter for the police. Step aside, let us do our job. Do you understand?"

I told him I understood. I didn't tell him I'd step aside.

* * *

I STARTED the next morning with a pack of mini-donuts, coffee from Bert's, and a nagging feeling I'd let Al down. I'd shared his recollections with Detective Callahan yet knew Al wasn't certain he'd seen his friend talking to Eugene. Even if Al was one hundred percent correct when he saw Elijah talking to someone, there was no proof Eugene killed Al's friend. Unless someone confessed to murdering Elijah Duncan, it'd remain unsolved. Terrell thought he knew who killed both Elijah and Clarence. Now he's dead.

That got me wondering what Terrell could've possibly learned to lead him to the conclusion he knew the identity of the killer. He wasn't alive in the 1950s, so it couldn't have been anything he had direct knowledge of. He'd heard stories about Elijah from his grandfather but when he talked to me, he'd never said anything about his grandfather knowing what'd happened. I assumed he'd learned something from one or more of the old-timers he'd talked with.

Even if Terrell was right, how could that help? As he hadn't hesitated pointing out, I was an outsider to the Sol Legare community. What excuse would I have for nosing around?

The phone interrupted as I was working hard figuring out nothing. I didn't recognize the number.

"Is this Chris Landrum," said a vaguely familiar voice.

I said it was.

"This is Jamal Kingsly from over on Sol Legare. Did I catch you at a bad time?"

"Hi, Jamal. No, it's fine."

"You gave me your number when you were at Clarence's party. I hope it's okay to call."

"Sure."

"Good. I'm calling to let you know a few of us were talking last night about the party we had for Clarence and wanted to do the same for Terrell. Him and Clarence were good friends, so we were feeling bad about having a big shindig for Clarence but nothing for Terrell. The last time I talked to Terrell, he said some nice things about you and your friends Charles and, umm, Vernon, so we wanted to invite all of you. I only had your number."

"His name's Virgil. I think it's a kind gesture. When?"

"Tonight. Sorry about the late notice. We only decided last night. If you think you can be here, could you ask the other guys?"

I told him I'd love to be there and would ask the others. He told me what time, then again apologized for the late notice.

My first call was to Charles, who took approximately a nanosecond to say he'd go. Virgil took a little longer.

"Hey, Chris. Guess where I am?"

And I thought I only had to play this game with Charles.

"Zurich, Switzerland."

"You been drinking?"

"No. Where are you?"

"On the Pier watching—wow! There goes two. Almost jumped plum out of the water."

I sighed. "Dolphins?"

"No, mermaids." He laughed. "Just kidding. Been out here an hour watching a flock, herd, or whatever you call a bunch of dolphins horsing around, no, dolphining around close to the Pier. Boy, are they cool."

"A pod."

Charles would be proud of me for knowing that bit of trivia.

"Huh?"

"A group of dolphins is called a pod."

"Silly name. Anyway, you should be here. They're fantastic."

"I was talking to Jamal from over on Sol Legare. He told me about a party tonight for Terrell and wanted to see if you, Charles, and I wanted to attend."

"Tonight? That's almost here. I'll have to check my social calendar. Also need to see how much longer this pod—still think it's a silly name—will be swimming around." He hesitated then continued, "Whoops, where'd they go? Umm, guess I'm available. What time?"

I told him and he said he'd see me then, before saying he was walking to the other side of the structure to see if the pod was over there. I didn't wait for an update.

Jamal hadn't mentioned Al, but I'd invite him anyway. I wasn't as lucky with Al. He said he'd love to go, but this was one of the bar's busiest nights. He'd told Bob he'd work. He asked me to let him know how the party goes and told me to say hi to his new friends.

I hung up and stared at the phone. "Thank you, Jamal." I now had a reason to be nosing around.

36

On the way to Island Breeze, I told Charles and Virgil what Al had said about possibly seeing Elijah talking to Eugene.

"Holy, moly," Virgil said from the back seat. "Does Al have a photographic memory?"

Charles said, "Eidetic imagery."

Virgil leaned between the front seats. "Huh?"

"The name for photographic memory is eidetic imagery," said the walking, talking trivia collector.

"Porpoise pods, eidetic whatever. Do you guys sit around reading the encyclopedia?"

Charles turned to Virgil. "Chris doesn't read anything deeper than road signs. I'll admit to reading most of the encyclopedia. Skipped the x words. Virgil, did you know the word mosquito in Spanish means little fly?"

"The encyclopedia translates Spanish?"

"Nope. Aquilino at Snapper Jacks told me. Since we're headed to Mosquito Beach, thought it'd be a good nugget to know."

In a transition that made sense to Virgil, he said, "So, did Al really remember something he saw on a dark night a million years ago?"

I said, "Unlikely, although knowing Al, I wouldn't rule it out."

Virgil said, "If Eugene is there, are you going to ask about it?"

"Not unless it makes sense in the conversation," I said.

Charles's silence told me he wasn't saying no.

The parking areas around the restaurant weren't nearly as full as they'd been during Clarence's party. His event was on a Saturday which could've made some of the difference. With the temperature in the upper eighties, I hoped those gathered for Terrell were inside rather than on the back patio.

We were in luck. In a large room off to the left, Jamal was carrying drinks to two tables that'd been pulled together. The man we'd been talking about possibly being seen with Elijah was at the table. Sandra and Robert Graves were watching a man I didn't know play pinballs on one of the two machines in the other corner. Jamal set the drinks on the table and told Sandra and Robert where they were.

Eugene saw us. "Welcome. Jamal said he invited you. We hoped you'd come."

I think he'd have a different opinion if he knew one of my reasons for being there.

Sandra and Robert returned to the table then grabbed their beers like they thought someone might take them. Jamal was breathing heavily as he shook our hands. He offered to go to the bar to get us drinks. I told him to sit while I went. Charles was already talking to the Sandra and Robert, so Virgil accompanied me.

The lady who'd been behind the bar during my previous visits got us a beer and two white wines. We headed back to the table where there were four vacant chairs so I wondered who else might be joining us.

Jamal said, "Charles was telling us Al couldn't make it. He seems like such a nice man. Sorry he's missing it."

"He is, too," I said.

"I've invited three or four others, but it's iffy if they'll show. Having this on a weeknight probably wasn't a good idea. Youngsters have jobs, you know."

Coming from Jamal, that probably meant guys under seventy.

Eugene said, "Some of us older guys also have to work."

"The rich get richer," Jamal said with a faux smile.

If it bothered Eugene, it didn't show. He turned to Charles, "Talked to your financial advisor yet? The lot's going to go quick. I've already shown it to three couples."

"Got an appointment next week," Charles said. "I'll let you know when I learn something."

Virgil, the man who knew Terrell less than anyone at the table, ignored their conversation, lifted his wine glass, and said, "I'm sure Terrell will know it's the thought that counts. Let's toast to our friend. I didn't know him well but could see he was a fine gentleman with a big heart."

Each of the four people who knew Terrell longer than we three newcomers combined, graciously lifted their bottles to toast. Sandra thanked Jamal for pulling the event together then agreed with Virgil that Terrell would be pleased.

The sounds of Aretha Franklin singing "Spanish Harlem" was playing, but not as loud as it had been on my previous visits. Tonight, I could hear everyone at the table.

"Anything new on what happened to Terrell?" Charles said, not wasting time digging for answers.

"If you mean, has anybody been arrested, not that I know about," Jamal said.

Charles said, "I wonder if the police have suspects."

Sandra took a sip, pointed her bottle at Jamal then said, "I doubt anyone over here shot him. Terrell had a temper and worked on Folly. It's no telling who he may've pissed off."

Robert put his arm around Sandra and said, "That police detective, what's his name?"

"Callahan," Sandra said.

"Yeah, Callahan came to the house to talk about Terrell, but mostly he was interested in what we remembered about Elijah Duncan." He smiled. "Think it was because we're old, old enough to have known Elijah."

Jamal said, "He talked to me, too. Don't know why he cared about something from the '50s when poor Clarence, now Terrell have been murdered, all within a mile of this here spot." He waved his arm around the room.

Eugene added, "He came to my house. We had a pleasant talk, but he didn't tell me anything I didn't already know."

I didn't remind him the detective wasn't there to tell him anything, but the other way around.

Virgil leaned closer to the table. "He probably thinks the same person killed all three."

Jamal looked at Sandra who glanced at Robert who said, "Can't imagine how a killing that many years ago could've been made by the same person."

"Me either," Jamal said.

Sandra added, "No way."

Eugene took another sip and didn't say anything.

"How well did you all know Elijah?" Virgil asked.

Each shared memories and opinions which could be summed up with they didn't know him well. They agreed he was a troublemaker, a spiffy dresser, and disappeared. Sandra repeated the part about him meeting her once at the pavilion to share a few dances. They didn't say anything we didn't know.

Charles turned to me, "Weren't you saying Al told you he thinks he remembers Elijah talking to," Charles turned to Eugene, "Gosh, I guess it was you Eugene."

They don't call Charles subtle for nothing.

I smiled. "That's right. Al was talking about how much fun he had out here after he got out of the service. Said those were some of the best years of his life. Anyway, he thought he remembered a night he was talking to Elijah when his friend saw someone in the parking area he wanted to talk to. He thought it was you, Eugene."

Eugene looked around the table then focused on me. "If Al remembers something like that, he's got a better memory than me. Crap, I can't remember who I talked to last week, much less, what, sixty-something years ago."

I smiled. "He wasn't certain either, but I've known Al a long time.

I've never known him to be wrong, at least not wrong about something important."

Eugene returned my smile. "I don't remember, but it could've happened. Elijah was out here nearly every time I ventured over. I wasn't here often, but I'm sure we talked."

"That makes sense," I said.

Thankfully, Charles didn't mention what I'd said about Al thinking Elijah was scared after talking to Eugene.

"Sandra," Virgil said, "you think it was someone from Folly who shot Terrell. That makes sense. Guys, any of you have other ideas who might've done it?"

Robert said, "I agree with Sandra."

Sandra chuckled. "Wise man."

"I know what side my bread's buttered on."

Virgil said, "Other than being a wise man, and I agree with that, why do you think it's someone from Folly?"

"I don't know people on Folly like I know guys around here," Robert said, "I can't speak about them getting along with Terrell. I know he was liked by everyone here. Since the police say the same gun shot Clarence and Terrell, it couldn't have been anyone I know. Clarence wasn't only liked, he was loved by everyone."

Charles, Virgil, please don't say, All but one.

"I agree with Sandra and Robert," Jamal said. "I don't know about it being someone from Folly. It could be. I don't know many folks there. All I'm certain of, it wasn't anyone here."

"Enough murder talk," Robert said. "Next round is on me while we talk about the good stuff we know about our friend Terrell."

No one argued, especially about Robert buying the next round.

One more round later, this one paid by Eugene, you would've thought from listening to Robert, Sandra, Eugene, and Jamal that Clarence and Terrell were candidates for sainthood. Stories of acts of kindness from the two dominated the conversation. I didn't know either man nearly as well as they did but couldn't find reason to argue with their conclusions. I also couldn't find any hints one of them may've been responsible for either death. I liked the group. On one level I was relieved no one at the table struck me as a murderer. On the other hand, that left me with no clue who may've ended the two, probably three lives.

After several beers, the conversation took a turn that I would've preferred to avoid. Virgil told the locals that Charles and I, along with his assistance, had helped the police catch the person responsible for the plane crash that took two lives. Jamal said he remembered the crash but hadn't kept up with stories about what happened. Eugene said he'd heard more than Jamal remembered; primarily because he lived on Folly he also casually knew the survivors. He asked how we knew so much about the crash to help the police. Charles gave an abbreviated—abbreviated for Charles—version of what'd happened. Virgil chimed in with his contribution that took a murderer off the street. Robert and Sandra appeared more interested in their drinks and music from the sound system. I'd hoped Jamal and Eugene followed their lead.

The party broke up when Jamal announced his hemorrhoids were acting up from sitting too long. That was clearly a party-ending revelation. We took the hint. Eugene, Jamal, and Robert settled their checks, and Jamal thanked us for coming.

Aretha Franklin escorted us out of the restaurant with her rendition of "Natural Woman."

37

During my near seven decades on earth I've received thousands of telephone calls. Of those calls, I couldn't recall a single one coming at six a.m. bringing good news. That's why when my phone jarred me awake, I took a deep breath and feared the worst before answering.

The name Tanesa Washington appeared on the screen. I'd met Al's daughter several times over the years, then when Al had experienced serious health problems, we had daily contact.

"Chris, this is Tanesa. Did I wake you?"

I lied. "No."

"Good. Dad said you're an early bird. He made me wait to call."

Al didn't want me to ask how he was every time he called, but he wasn't calling.

"Is he okay?"

"He will be. Around three this morning, his neighbor's dog awakened her when it wouldn't stop barking and scratching at the window. The neighbor saw smoke coming from Dad's second-floor window. She called 911 before running next door and pounding on his door. It took Dad a long time to answer. She thought he was dead." Tanesa sighed. "He finally answered. Dad's got more lives than a cat."

"You sure he's okay?"

"The neighbor rushed him to the hospital before the fire trucks arrived. He told them in the ER he was fine, that his daughter worked there. I wasn't on-duty, but the nurse knows me and called. Dad wasn't about to spend another minute at the hospital, so I rushed over to bring him to my condo. I gave him something to help him sleep. He's shook, his asthma is acting up, but he's stable." She chuckled. "Before he fell asleep, he wanted me to call you. I asked why. He said, and this is dad for you, he wanted to know about the party you went to last night."

"Do you want me to come over?"

"He'd like that."

"When would be a good time?"

"He's never slept more than a few hours a night in his life, so I suspect he'll be awake by noon. I have to be at work at one, so why don't you stop by around twelve-thirty. I'll let you in?"

I said I'd be there then asked how much fire damage there was.

"There's a firehouse fewer than five blocks from his house, so they got there quickly. Most of the fire damage was limited to the second floor, but there's a lot of water downstairs."

"They know what caused it?"

"If they do, they didn't tell me. I was only there for a minute before picking him up at the hospital. I heard one of the firefighters say they needed to call an arson investigator. I don't know if that's standard procedure or if they suspected something."

Something told me it wasn't standard procedure, but I didn't tell Tanesa.

I DROVE by Al's house on the way to Tanesa's condo. A red Ford Explorer with a Charleston Fire Department Fire Marshall logo on the door was parked in the drive. From a previous encounter with the Fire Marshall Division, I knew it investigated suspicious fires, which reinforced my hunch it wasn't accidental. The fire had burned through part of the roof. Two of the upstairs window frames were flame blackened. It could've been worse, much worse.

Tanesa lives in an up-scale condo development overlooking the Ashley River and adjacent to the Bristol Marina. The building is less than a mile from Al's house and within walking distance to her hospital. The contrast between Al's wood-frame, ninety-year-old house and Tanesa's three-story, brick and glass modern condo building was night and day. I rode to the third floor in the quietest elevator I'd ever been in.

Tanesa greeted me with a smile and a hug. Her bloodshot eyes told me she'd had little sleep, something she was used to considering her erratic hours as an emergency room doctor.

"Thanks for coming. Dad already asked me three times since he got up when you were getting here."

I whispered, "How's he doing?"

"I hear you talking about me in there," came a voice from my left.

Tanesa laughed. "That answer your question? He's in the kitchen. Want coffee?"

I told her that sounded good then followed her through the immaculate condo. The dark, hardwood floors in the entry and living room opened to the white kitchen floor, most likely some Italian, aka expensive, tile.

Al was seated at a small, round table and gripping a mug. He wore blue pajamas. He smiled when he saw me, but not nearly as big as Tanesa's smile when she'd greeted me. Tanesa poured me a cup as I sat. She said she had to get dressed for work and left us to talk. I glanced at the granite countertops and stainless-steel appliances mentally contrasting them to Al's kitchen.

"How do you feel?"

"Chris, know what I'm looking forward to when I'm stretched out there in my coffin?"

I couldn't imagine looking forward to anything. "What?"

He chuckled. "You won't walk in, look at my wax-looking face, and say, 'How do you feel?'"

I smiled. "You're not in a coffin yet, so how do you feel?"

He shook his head. "And Tanesa invited you over. That gal's going to be the death of me yet." He put a hand in front of my face. "Okay, I'm tired, sore all over from having to move so fast getting out of the house. I'm pissed. Chris, I've lived in that house since the beginning of time. It's paid for. I can't imagine living anywhere else. Now it's … I don't know how it is."

"I drove by it on the way over. It looks like the damage was contained on the second floor. I think it can be repaired."

"Whew," he said. "Tanesa said it didn't look too bad, but I figured she was soft-pedaling it so I wouldn't worry. I figured with it being old and all wood, it'd be burnt to the ground."

"It'll be as good as new."

"It hasn't been as good as new since Indians roamed the neighborhood, but it's my house, my home. Tanesa said I can stay here as long as I want." He hesitated then looked at the door to the living room before lowering his voice. "She has it in her mind for me to live here the rest of my days. Chris, it ain't going to happen. I want, no, need to get back to my place as soon as I can."

"I understand. What happened?"

"Wish I knew. I went to bed like I always do around midnight. Was slow to go to sleep, but finally did. Next thing I remember was a horrible pounding on the front door. I opened my eyes, thought I smelled smoke. Figured I was dreaming. The pounding continued. I realized the smoke was real. It took me a long time to get moving, gets longer each day, I'm afraid. I managed to get to the door to see my next-door neighbor standing there in a bathrobe, pink curlers in her hair. That was a sight to behold, I tell you." He smiled, shook his head, then took a sip of coffee. "Chris, what's it like outside?"

"Nice, cooler than it's been. Why?"

He pointed to a door leading to the balcony. "Let's go out there. Since I wasn't sure I'd live to see today, I'd like to enjoy it."

He struggled getting out of the chair. I wanted to help, but knew he needed to do it on his own. He refilled his mug, slowly walked to a large glass-topped table on the patio and lowered himself in one of the four chairs around the table. He was out of breath after the short walk. I took the chair closest to him.

The view was fantastic. The marina was directly in front of us and a large sailboat was maneuvering away from the dock.

"Your neighbor was at the door, then what?"

He looked at the sailboat, bit his lower lip, and said, "She told me what I finally figured out. The house was on fire. Seems Spoiled Rotten was barking up a storm. He woke her up. She looked out, saw smoke, then skedaddled over to save this old man. I've got to get to the store to buy the biggest bone they have for Spoiled Rotten. If it wasn't for him, you'd be looking in my coffin, not asking how I was, yes you would." He pointed his mug at me. "Tell you one more thing, Chris. If my bed hadn't been moved to the living room, I'd be in that coffin even if my neighbor knocked on the door. Not only did moving the bed downstairs save my knees and heart, it saved my life."

"Any idea what started the fire?"

"Chris, that's all I've been thinking about since I got here." He smiled. "Except when I was sleeping. That danged daughter of mine drugged me."

"You needed your sleep."

"Same thing she said. Now to what you asked. Didn't storm overnight so it wasn't lightning. Nothing electric is plugged in upstairs. I wasn't burning any candles upstairs so a mouse couldn't have knocked a candle over. Didn't even have a lantern up there so old Mrs. O'Leary's cow couldn't have kicked it."

His sense of humor was intact, thank goodness. "You don't know what could've started it."

He slowly shook his head.

I told him about the Fire Marshall's SUV at his house.

He tilted his head. "You don't think somebody did it on purpose, do you?"

"Don't know."

His hand trembled as he gripped the mug. "Suppose they'll figure out what happened." He glanced again at the sailboat then turned to me. "Didn't Tanesa tell you I wanted to hear about last night's party, not talk about the fire?"

I nodded.

"So, let's hear it."

Before I started, Tanesa came out, patted Al's arm, said she had to head to work, and asked if he needed anything before she left.

"Yes, my house fixed. A ride home."

"Afraid I can't do that, but I called your insurance agent. He's going to send an adjuster. He'll call me so I can meet him there."

Al said, "You don't need to meet him. I can do that, yes I can."

Tanesa patted his arm again. "Maybe so, but you're not going to. Doctor's orders."

He frowned at his daughter, the doctor. "More like prison guard orders."

She kissed the top of his head, leaned down, hugged me, before heading out.

"Al, you've raised a fantastic woman."

He beamed.

I told him everything I remembered about the party. He listened without moving. I couldn't tell if it was because he was exhausted or paying rapt attention to my fascinating description of events. He asked twice if I'd shared his condolences, how much he'd wanted to be there.

"Chris, I was wondering if you told Eugene I recalled seeing him talking to Elijah?"

"Yes. He said he didn't remember, but it could've been him. They knew each other plus he'd been at the pavilion several times."

"Did you tell him Elijah was scared after talking to him?"

I smiled. "I left that part out."

"Did you tell him I wasn't certain it was him Elijah was talking to?"

"I think so."

"Good. It was a long time ago." He closed his eyes, then said, "Chris, I don't want to be antisocial, but think everything's getting to me. Maybe a nap would do me good."

"Anything I can do for you before I leave?"

"No. My prison guard fixed me a salad, put it in the frig for when I get hungry." He laughed. "Think I would've preferred normal prison food like bread and water instead of salad. Her heart's in the right place."

"Sure there's nothing I can do?"

"There's one other thing, it's a big one. Could you stop by the bar and tell Bob what happened? He expects me to be there later this afternoon. Don't think I'm up to it."

"Consider it done."

38

"The damn dog did what?" Bob yelled.

Roy Acuff's "Wabash Cannonball" blared in the background.

"Flames coming out his roof!" Bob screamed.

The country legend managed to get in a few more words of his song.

"He's running around in his pajamas," Bob moaned.

Roy finished his classic. Silence came from the jukebox.

"Poor, poor old man," Bob broke the silence as he plopped his ample behind at his table. He put his hands over his face.

All I'd managed to say was Al's house had a fire in the middle of the night, his neighbor's dog alerted the neighbor who saw smoke and called 911, that Al was okay and staying at Tanesa's condo. Okay, I must've mentioned pajamas, but I didn't recall saying it. Fortunately, Al's was empty except for Bob and his cook, Lawrence, when I entered and attempted to tell the owner what'd happened.

"Mr. Chris, can I get you something to eat or drink?" Lawrence asked as I sat across from the bar's owner.

"Some water, if that's okay."

I knew Bob was shook because he didn't rant and rave about me not buying anything. That was a first, I might add.

Lawrence set a bottle of water in front of me then asked if I was okay, something that must've slipped Bob's mind. I said I was, Bob asked me to start from the beginning, not to leave anything out.

Johnny Cash's unmistakable bass-baritone voice shared "Love is a burning thing, and it makes a fiery ring." I held my breath waiting for Bob to react to the words from "Ring of Fire" with another rant.

Instead of an outburst, he said, "Tell me everything. I mean everything."

I began with Tanesa's call. The only time Bob interrupted was when I told him about the dog alerting the neighbor.

"The damned dog's named Spoiled Rotten?"

I told him that's what Al called it, it wasn't its real name. That satisfied him for the moment.

"Any idea what caused it?"

"No, when I passed it on the way to Tanesa's place, there was a Charleston Fire Department Fire Marshall vehicle in the drive. They'll determine cause."

Bob rubbed his chin. "I suppose it could've been anything. That house is as broken down as Al, and older. Maybe they'll have to tear it down so Al can move into something nice with a real bedroom on the first floor. The day he moved it downstairs to the living room, he was so embarrassed. He doesn't deserve embarrassment."

"I wouldn't bet on him moving anywhere. He said he's moving back to that house. I mentioned Tanesa wants him to move in with her."

Willie Nelson's "My Hero's Have Always Been Cowboys" broke the background silence.

Bob looked at the jukebox like you'd look at someone who just slapped you in the face, then continued, "Chris, whatever my friend wants is what he needs to get. From my days in real estate I've accumulated enough tradespeople who owe me favors to get the house repaired, get it done fast. Al will never ask me to do it, so you'll have to let me know what it'll take. Thy will be done."

"He'll appreciate it. Something else, Bob, do you know anyone who had anything against Al?"

"You mean someone pissed enough to torch his house?"

"Yes."

"Hell, Chris. I'm the maddest person I've ever seen at Al, and I love him to death. No way anybody could be angry with him. Do you really think someone could've done it on purpose?"

"Al's convinced there wasn't anything on his second floor that could've started the fire."

"It sure as hell wasn't spontaneous combustion. Suppose we'll have to see what the fire department finds. Is there anything the poor man needs, other than his house?"

"I don't think so. Tanesa fixed a salad for when he gets hungry."

"A damned salad! That gal was smart enough to go to doctor school yet thinks a freakin' lettuce and other little green things scrunched together will make him feel better. Is she trying to kill him?"

I told him I didn't think so. I also didn't tell him that he may want to try more of those lettuce and other green things occasionally. I'd already heard enough of Bob's rants for one day.

He pushed his way out of his booth then yelled, "Lawrence, fix me two cheeseburgers to go, throw in an order of fries, no, make that two! I've got to go on a mercy mission to save my friend from drying up and blowing away after eating a damned salad. While I'm gone, drag some customers in here, make them spend money. Tell them that unless they do, I'll have to fire my cook."

Clearly, my conversation with Bob was over. He had a more important mission. I didn't want to stand in his way.

Patsy Cline's "I Fall To Pieces" was playing as I left.

* * *

THE SUN HAD SLIPPED behind the marsh before I finished two slices of pizza I picked up at Woody's Pizza on the way home. Bob's tirade plus my poor eating habits kept me from ordering a Greek salad to go with the pizza.

I moved from the kitchen to the front porch to watch the early evening stream of traffic and to reflect on the day. I didn't know Al as well as I did the bar's new owner, but from my many conversations with him and the way his former customers treated him, I agreed with Bob about no one disliking him enough to burn his house, especially with him in it. I also knew Al enough to know when he said there was nothing on the second floor to start the fire, there was no doubt in his mine. Of course, it could've been ancient wiring in the wall.

I interrupted reflecting to call Charles to tell him about the fire. I was surprised when he didn't go through his usual griping about me not calling him as soon as I heard about the near disaster. Charles knew about Al's health issues, so was quick to ask how he was doing. I assured him he was okay, or as okay as one could be under the circumstances. Charles transitioned to asking what started the fire, to which I gave the same answer I shared with Bob. Unlike Bob, it wasn't good enough.

"You mean you haven't called the arson inspector demanding the cause?"

"Tell you what, Charles. Let me find their number so you can pester the people at the fire department."

"So, you'll let me know the cause as soon as you hang up from the fire folks?"

Why do I even try with Charles?

"I'll make a call. I'll let you know if I learn anything."

"Good," he said, then hung up.

I told him I'd make a call but didn't say it'd be to the County Fire Marshall.

Instead of saying something normal like hello, Cindy LaMond answered with, "Guess what I'm having for supper? Hold it, don't guess, I don't have all night. I'm having a Stouffer's Chicken TV dinner I cooked all by myself because Larry's in Columbia at an incredibly fascinating, his words, hardware store trade show. Know what else I'm having? I'm having a wonderful, peaceful time eating while enjoying the silence." She sighed. "You're going to screw it up, aren't you?"

"Good evening, Cindy. I didn't mean to interrupt your delightful meal."

"Smart ass."

I chuckled. "Yep. Want me to call after you finish your culinary creation?"

"You've already ruined my peaceful respite. Go ahead, ruin it more!"

I told her about the fire. She interrupted to ask how Al was holding up. I shared everything I knew about his condition.

"Why do I have a tickle in my gut telling me there's more to this call than telling me about the fire?"

"You're way too wise, Chief."

"Tell that to the Mayor."

"He knows how good you are."

"Okay, Mr. Charm, what do you want?"

"You're so well connected, so well respected, I thought you could contact the Fire Marshall's Office to see if they know the cause."

"Do you think it was intentionally set?"

I told her Al's thoughts on why it couldn't have been accidental.

"Do you know how many fires there are each year caused by faulty wiring—wiring the homeowners swore was fine and couldn't be the reason their houses were turned to charcoal briquettes?"

"How many?"

"Hell if I know but it's a bunch. Crap, that's why accidents are called accidents."

"You're right."

"Aren't I always?" She laughed. "Don't answer that. I'll call in the morning, will let you know."

"You're an angel."

"Always right, angelic. Think I'll order business cards with that on it."

"Add modest."

"Smart ass."

39

"Hello," was all I said in the phone before Cindy took over.

"If fortunetelling wasn't illegal on Folly, I'd recommend you open a shop to read palms, leaves, shiny yard globes people stick in their garden, the people who think those round things aren't as stupid looking as everyone else does, or whatever else those quacks read before taking their naïve customer's bucks."

"Good morning, Cindy. Care to enlighten me as to what you're talking about?"

"Arson."

"You sure?"

"Unless Al accidentally stuck a ten-foot ladder behind his house, climbed up it on his rickety legs, threw a gas-filled bottle with a burning piece of cloth sticking out through his upstairs window, yes. The brilliant investigator using all his training cyphered it was arson."

The house wasn't air-conditioned. The windows had been propped open when I visited, so it would've been easy to do what Cindy described. What I didn't know was why.

"Did the investigator learn anything from the Molotov cocktail?"

"If you mean did he find a scorched, signed *Thinking of You* note attached to it, no. Actually, he didn't find anything important. The bottle was generic. The ladder was stolen from a house two doors away. The owner said the last time he saw the ladder it was parked beside his garage. The investigator figured whoever was on it was scared off by the rotten dog."

"Spoiled Rotten."

"What ever. That leads back to who and why? You sure Bob or Al didn't know anyone who'd want to harm Al?"

"That's what they said. I don't know anyone who had anything against him, but someone did."

"Duh, Sherlock," Cindy said. "You're nearly as smart as the arson investigator."

I heard someone talking in the background and Cindy said she had to go. Something about if it was okay with me, she had to go make Folly safer. She added, "You know Folly, the place where I have jurisdiction."

I thanked her for calling then wished her well making my island safer.

The call left me with a headache plus an unanswered question: Why would someone want to kill Al?

He'd spent a lifetime thinking of others. He and his wife had sacrificed more than anyone should be expected to while adopting and raising their children. He'd been a war hero. From everything I knew, he was generous, kind, harmless. By putting up with Bob for all so many years without killing him, showed he wouldn't harm anyone. So again, why'd someone want to kill him?

I didn't have an answer, but knew there was one question I could answer, and that was who I'd better tell about the arson.

"Good morning, Charles."

"It's another fine day in paradise," he said, almost laughing out he words.

I was pleased he was in such a good mood, but also surprised by his early morning enthusiasm.

"What're you so happy about?"

"What's not to be happy about? I'm sitting at the Dog, sipping coffee I didn't have to fix myself, talking to the lovely, charming, talented Amber. Thanks for calling to check on my happiness."

"In addition to that, there's something else I need to tell you. I just got off the phone with Cindy. She—"

"So," he interrupted, "you on your way?"

I smiled. "Yes."

"Hurry, you're already late."

Ten minutes later I headed to Charles's table when Marc Salmon waved for me to stop at the table where he was sitting with his fellow council member Houston.

Marc looked around to see if anyone was listening. Then asked me to join them for a minute. I was curious, so I took the vacant chair. Marc looked around again, leaned closer to me, and said, "Remember when you were asking what I knew about Eugene Dillinger?"

"Of course."

"I heard something yesterday. Don't know if it has anything to do with the killings on Sol Legare, but figured you'd want to know."

Amber set a mug of coffee in front of me. I thanked her, while Marc looked around the room once more.

"I didn't hear it firsthand so it may not be exactly the way it happened, but his foreman told me Eugene was out at the house he's building on East Ashley. He threatened to kill one of his workers."

"Was he serious?"

"Don't know. Rumor is he has a short fuse, flies off the handle without much provocation. Apparently, he'd told one of his Mexican workers to do something with a window they were installing. The next day Eugene got to the house and whatever it was hadn't been done the way he wanted. He grabbed the worker by the arm then read him the riot act about not doing whatever it was he was supposed to do. Said if it happened again he'd kill the guy." Marc smiled. "Want to hear the funny part?"

I couldn't imagine what'd be funny about the story. I told him yes.

"Eugene lambasted the wrong man. The guy who was supposed to do whatever wasn't even at the house. Eugene told the guy who told me the story to him all Mexicans looked alike."

I still didn't see the humor in it but smiled to not disappoint Marc. I added, "That's interesting."

"Yeah. The foreman said he thought Eugene was mad enough to harm his worker, don't know about killing him. Thought you'd want to know since you're trying to figure out who killed those guys on Sol Legare. Sounds like it could be Eugene."

"That's interesting, Marc. Thanks for sharing."

"Doing my civic duty. Public service is what I'm about."

Behind spreading gossip, I thought, but kept it to myself.

"I appreciate it, Marc."

Houston spoke for the first time. "Chris, you'd better get over to the table with Charles. He looks like he's about ready to lasso you and drag you over."

I thanked both for letting me interrupt their conversation, took my mug, and prepared to be interrogated by Charles.

"It's about time you got here. My coffee's almost cold."

He was in a better mood on the phone.

Amber appeared, kissed the top of my head, then said, "Glad to see you at the right table."

"Nice to see someone's happy to see me."

She smiled.

Charles said, "I ain't about to kiss your bald head, but I'm happy to see you."

Amber ignored him, a talent she's used countless times to maintain her sanity. She asked if I wanted something to eat. I told her French toast, she faked shock, then left to put in the order.

Charles took another sip before saying, "Two questions, you got off the phone with Cindy, and?"

"She called to—"

"You ain't heard question two. What could've been so important that you parked your butt over there for what, an hour, instead of landing where you are now?"

I told him what Marc had shared.

"See, I told you he killed those guys."

All I saw was Eugene had a temper, had trouble recognizing one man from another. I told Charles it was possible, but I wasn't convinced. He mumbled something as he changed the subject to what Cindy wanted. I told him the arson investigator's findings. He asked the same question I'd asked myself, "Who'd want to harm Al?"

I said I didn't know.

"I do. Eugene."

"Because?"

"Because of what Marc just told you. Your memory slipping?"

"Connect the dots for me."

"Okay, Al was partying with Elijah at the pavilion when Elijah saw Eugene. He went to talk to him. Elijah came back scared. Right?"

I nodded.

"I told Al's story at Terrell's party the other night, you know, the one about Elijah seeing Eugene and talking to him."

"Charles, I heard you tell the story, remember?"

"Making sure. Anyway, I figure Eugene was worried about what Elijah may've told Al, so he started the fire to kill poor Al."

"That's quite a stretch."

"Not really," Charles said while he tapped his fingers on the table. "Eugene killed Elijah. After the bones popped up, Clarence and then Terrell started asking questions. Questions that led them to Eugene which led them to getting themselves dead. Al's the only person left who may know who did it."

I said, "Even though Al doesn't know more than he's already said, Eugene doesn't know that. As far as he knows, Elijah told him what got him so scared of Eugene. Now Al's put two and two together and figured Eugene is the killer. A good reason to want to get rid of Al."

"You're catching on junior member of my detective agency. With that figured out, what're we going to do about it?"

"Detective Callahan knows Al's idea about Elijah talking to Eugene, then quickly discarded it as ancient history."

"But he doesn't know about the fire," Charles said. "He stared at my phone like it'd call the detective if Charles wished it to."

He didn't have to wait for a miracle, I called and got Detective Callahan's voicemail. If I hadn't, Charles would've never let me enjoy my breakfast that Amber slipped in front of me while I was calling. I left Callahan a brief message about what happened to Al. I also suggested he may want to verify the cause of the fire with the Fire Marshall's Office.

My semi-peaceful breakfast ended after sharing with Charles a second time how Al's house looked after the fire; in excruciating detail, what Tanesa's condo looked like; and finally, a second time, that Spoiled Rotten was unhurt by either the arsonist or the fire. He'd milked me for everything I knew before saying he had to deliver a package for the surf shop.

He picked up the check and left the restaurant leaving me in shock.

40

On the walk home, I kept thinking something Marc said was important. I tried to replay our conversation and was so focused on it I nearly collided with Virgil walking the opposite direction.

"Sorry, Virgil. I was daydreaming."

"No apology necessary. I spend most of my wake hours daydreaming. I probably do the same when I'm sleeping." He chuckled. "Suppose that'd be nightdreaming. Glad I ran into you, or you ran into me. Got a few minutes?"

I nodded.

He pointed to a bench in front of the Sand Dollar Social Club. "Care to join me in my office?"

We crossed Ashley Avenue to commandeer the bench. He watched the traffic light change from red to green, or I assumed that's what he was doing since I couldn't see his eyes hidden by his ever-present sunglasses. He turned to me. "Chris, you know I'm not as good a detective as you and Charles, but something's been bothering me about what happened to Terrell."

He hesitated and waited for me to say something. I wasn't about to respond to his detective comment, so I jumped right to, "What's bothering you?"

"Remember when we were at Terrell's house?"

"Yes."

"He was doing a fine job fixing up the place. Anyway, remember that big box in the middle of his kitchen?"

"A new stove."

"Not just any stove, a Wolf stove. I had one like it back when I was rich."

"I remember you telling Terrell. What about it?"

"I'm not certain, but I seem to recall him saying it got there that morning. I asked if he needed help installing it."

"That's what he said. What's bothering you about it?"

Virgil leaned back on the bench, again staring, or so I thought, at the light change colors. Once the excitement subsided over watching green turn to yellow, he leaned forward. "Chris, this is where I'm putting on my detective-in-waiting hat." He pretended to put a hat on. "Remember when we were at the party for Clarence?"

"Of course."

"Someone mentioned Terrell's new stove. Remember who?"

"No. There's a lot I didn't hear that night. It was noisy, the sound system was turned up. You were sitting at the other end of the table, as I recall. Why?"

He looked at his resoled Gucci shoes and said, "It seems to my way of thinking whoever mentioned the stove had to be in Virgil's house after we were there, or the person wouldn't know about it."

"You think the person who mentioned the stove is the killer?"

Virgil nodded.

"You don't recall who said it?"

"No sir, but it narrows it down to Sandra, Robert, Jamal, and Eugene. In my amateur detective brain that's pretty good whittling down the suspects."

"I agree."

"There's hope for me yet in this detective racket. Why not call Charles? See if he remembers?"

Add Virgil to the people who think I'm their personal secretary, or more politically correct, administrative assistant. Either way, he had a valid point.

The phone rang several times before an out-of-breath Charles answered. "I'm on my bike. Hang on a sec, let me pull over."

I hung on. It was way more then a second, but I didn't do what he would've done. I waited without telling him he was taking too long.

"Whew," he said, "Dude has me delivering a humongous box to a house out by the County Park. I'm getting too old for tooling around on my bike." He took a deep breath. "Did you call to see what I was delivering?"

"No. Got a question. When we were at the party for Clarence, do you remember anyone mentioning Terrell's new stove?"

"His stove? That's one of the stupidest questions you've called to ask. What's that got to do with anything?"

"It may tell us the identity of the killer."

"I already told you, it's Eugene."

"Humor me. Do you remember the conversation about the stove?"

"Not really. I suppose it was Sandra Graves. She'd know more about stoves than anyone else there." I heard what sounded like him snapping his fingers. "Tell you what I do remember. When you and I were talking to Terrell behind Rita's, he said he'd talked to a few old-timers about Elijah's murder. He said he still had to talk to Robert and Sandra. Maybe they came to his house and saw the stove."

"Maybe," I said with little conviction.

"Have you checked with Al? He might remember."

"That's my next call. Have fun with your delivery."

I told Virgil what Charles said before calling Al. For the second time this morning, I received a voicemail rather than a live voice. I asked Al to give me a call when he had a chance.

"Well, that's the pits," Virgil said.

I agreed. Before Virgil headed to his apartment, I said I'd let him know what Al had to say.

It was late afternoon before Al returned my call. He said he'd hung around Tanesa's condo as long as he could. He added something about it being so clean, neat, and new he felt he was in a spaceship from the future. He couldn't wait to get back home, his comfortable old shoe. Since moving home was out of the question, he'd convinced Bob to help him escape from the spaceship. He was at Al's keeping the peace between owner and customers.

"Al, I've got a question. Remember when we were at Island Breeze at the party for Clarence?"

"I'm afraid I do remember it. Sad. Clarence seemed like such a nice man."

"Virgil remembers someone mentioning the new stove Terrell got for his house. He didn't remember who said it. Charles thinks it was Sandra Graves. Do you remember hearing anything about it?"

I heard Hank Williams's nasal sounding baritone voice singing "I'm So Lonesome I Could Cry" in the background and a customer moaning. It was good that Al was there to mediate debates about music, race relations, or just Bob being Bob.

"Sure do," Al said. "Don't tell him I said this, but Charles got it wrong. Right family, wrong person. Robert mentioned the stove. I remember because Wolf is a fine stove. I was surprised Terrell got himself one. Why?"

As soon as he said it, I remembered what Marc told me in the Dog that had eluded me earlier. When he shared the story about Eugene's temper, he added that Marc's source said that Eugene said all Mexican workers looked alike to him.

"Al, let me ask you one more question."

"Chris, at my age, you're pushing your luck."

"This one's harder. Back in 1953, when you said Elijah left you at the pavilion to talk to a man and returned scared, is it possible that Elijah went to talk to was Robert, not Eugene?"

There was a long pause. All I heard was Patsy Cline singing "Sweet Dreams." Al finally said, "Chris, in those days, segregation was still a big thing. I doubt there were a handful of white folks who ventured out to Mosquito. Robert and Eugene were two of them. Before you just asked me, I'd swear it was Eugene talking to Elijah, honest to God, I would. I hate being wrong, but you might be right. Robert and

Eugene were both skinny, about the same height. It could've been Robert, yes it could've."

"Al, that was a long time ago. It would've been easy to mistake the two men. It was dark, he was far away."

"And white," Al added.

"Yes."

"Are you saying Robert killed my friend, and the other two men?"

"I think so."

"You going to tell the police?"

"I'm calling them as soon as I hang up."

"Then go. I'm sorry to accuse the wrong person."

"No reason to be sorry. You may've solved the murders."

I didn't have to make the call. My phone rang, and I saw CCSO on the screen. This time I knew what it stood for.

"Mr. Landrum, this is Detective Callahan returning your call. What can I do for you?"

The tone of his voice made it sound more like, "Why are you pestering me?"

I thanked him for calling, then hesitated. Where do I begin? Do I tell him about the fire at Al's or what I learned in the last fifteen minutes?

"Detective, I called to tell you about a fire at Al Washington's house. The Fire Marshall's Office determined it was arson, and—"

"Mr. Landrum," he interrupted, "what's that have to do with me?"

"Maybe nothing but let me tell you what I learned this afternoon." I shared everything that Virgil had reminded me about and the confirmation from Al that it could've been Robert that he saw talking with Elijah all those years ago.

"Mr. Landrum, if I was getting this from any Tom, Dick, or Harry I'd jot down the information then file it in that round container beside my desk, or in a file cabinet across the room that's stuffed with everything from thirty-year-old parking tickets to empty cheese cracker packages."

"But—"

"Hang on, I'm not done. Your Director of Public Safety thinks a lot of you, says it an embarrassing number of times. To show how well our offices can cooperate—rare I understand—I'm going to get Robert and Sandra's address and take a ride out to their house to ask a few questions."

"Thank you."

"Don't get all excited. All I have to confront them with is ancient history and talk about some sort of fancy stove I've never heard of."

"Will you let me know what happens?"

"Don't push it. I'd talk longer but I need to go on a wild-goose chase."

I gave a sigh of relief as I poured a glass of wine and settled in my living-room chair while staring at a mindless television sit-com.

41

I was awakened from a nap I didn't know I was taking by a loud drug commercial on TV. It was almost nine o'clock, so I must've been asleep thirty minutes or so. The next sound I heard didn't come from the television, but from someone knocking on the door. I was still groggy as I reached the door. My sleepy eyes were suddenly jarred awake when I saw Robert Graves, wearing a black T-shirt, black slacks, a RiverDogs ball cap, and holding a black matte, semi-automatic Glock handgun I couldn't help notice was pointed at my stomach.

I tried to slam the door, but he'd put his foot between the door and its frame.

"May I come in?" he said as calmly as if he was selling Girl Scout cookies.

I didn't see an option. "Sure."

I must not have moved quickly enough. He shoved the gun in my stomach. I took three steps back. He stepped in, slammed and locked the door.

"These old bones ain't what they used to be," he said. "Shall we sit?"

Again, I didn't see I had a choice. I motioned him to the chair in the corner while I took my recliner.

He surprised me by saying, "Where's Al Washington?"

"How would I know?"

"Because I hear your buddies think you know everything. You think I haven't noticed you and your friends nosing around Island Breeze? So, cut the bull, where is he?"

I glanced around to see what might be nearby to use as a weapon. All that was handy was my cellphone, no competition for a handgun.

I shrugged. "I don't know where he is. As you know, his house was torched. Speaking of his house, why'd you decide to kill my friend with a fire rather than a gun like you did the other three men?" I pointed at the Glock that hadn't wavered from pointing at me since he'd lowered himself in the chair.

"See, I was right about you knowing too much. You and especially Washington."

"You don't have any reason to leave me alive, so how about feeding my curiosity before you move on?"

"Why would I do that?"

"I figure you'd want to tell someone other than Sandra about it."

"Why do you think she knows?"

"Does she?"

"Maybe, maybe not. What're your questions?"

"Let's begin with why you killed Elijah Duncan."

He lowered the gun a couple of inches, but not enough for me to reach him before I'd regret trying.

He shook his head. "Elijah, Elijah. You heard the stories how he was a troublemaker and stirred up all sorts of rifts about equal rights. I didn't have anything against that, in fact, I agreed with him. I saw how blacks were treated in those days. Like dogs at times." He shook his head again.

The Glock swayed along with his head. Could I get to him now? It was as if he heard my thoughts. He leveled the gun at me.

"You also heard Elijah and Sandra met once in the pavilion. It was scandalous in those days."

"Wasn't that months before you met her?"

"Yes, their date at the pavilion was nearly three months before we met. Huh, if that ended it, Elijah might still be alive." He chuckled. "If he hadn't already died of old age."

"They dated after that night?"

"Dated, no, but he didn't stop trying. There were several lovely gals around then, yet damned Elijah wouldn't give up on Sandra." He shook his head. The pistol didn't shake. "By that time I'd met her, and thought she was the prettiest young lady I'd ever seen. We'd gone out a couple of times before she told me about how Elijah kept trying to get her to go out with him. Don't think anybody else knew."

"What happened?"

Robert closed his eyes. I pushed out of the chair. His eyes popped open. He stood and moved a couple more feet away from me.

"Sit!"

I sat. He remained standing.

"Thought you wanted to know what happened."

"I do."

Instead of returning to the chair, he walked behind me, then to the doorway to the kitchen.

"I confronted him out at the end of Mosquito. It was turning dark. Know what he did?"

I shrugged.

"He laughed at me. All I could see was those bright-white teeth and heard him laughing."

"You shot him," I said, and pointed to his handgun.

He nodded. "Not with this. I had an old cowboy six-shooter I bought off a man who probably stole it. I looked around afraid someone saw or heard what'd happened. No one did. I dragged him behind a big-old tree, got a shovel out of the trunk." He smiled. "Dad always told me to carry one in there. Said I'd never know when I'd need it. Smart man. Anyway, I buried Elijah twenty feet from where he took his last breath."

"Did you tell Sandra?"

My phone rang before he answered. He jumped like a cannon had gone off behind him. I reached for the phone.

"Wouldn't do that if I was you."

I pulled my hand back but saw that the call was from the CCSO. It rang five more times before kicking over to voicemail.

"No," Robert said.

"You didn't tell Sandra?"

"Not a word. I walked around on eggshells the next couple of weeks. Then I started hearing the rumors, best news I could've got. Did I know Elijah left the area? Did I know he was killed by the KKK? Or my favorite, did I know he ran off with some preacher's daughter? I could breathe again. A year later, Sandra and I tied the knot. We've lived happily ever after." He pointed the gun at the floor, blinked twice. "Lived happily until his damned bones jumped up in front of Clarence."

My phone dinged indicating I'd received a message. Robert jerked up from the chair again and pointed the gun at the phone like he was going to shoot it. I thought I was scared and nervous. It appeared Robert had me beat. And, he had the gun.

"I can understand why you killed Elijah, but why Clarence? All he did was stumble on the bones."

He moved the gun to the other hand. "I hated that. Old Clarence was a good man. I really liked him, I really did."

You had a funny way of showing it, I thought. "What happened?"

He glanced back at my phone like he was still considering shooting it. "Of all the people out that way, it had to be Clarence finding the bones."

My phone rang once more. This time Robert pushed out of the chair, grabbed the phone, mouthed *Charles*, and switched off the ringer. He lowered the gun, and I started to dive for it, until he raised the weapon again. It ran through my head that if he heard the phone one more time, he'd go berserk.

He was breathing heavily. I gave a silent prayer this would be a good time for his heart to give out.

It didn't.

Robert said, "Three days before Clarence met an untimely end, he ran into Sandra at Harris Teeter asking if she knew who killed Elijah. She told him of course not, but when she told me about it that night, she said he didn't believe her. I asked how she knew. She said she just did. The next day I went to his house, found him in the yard, said I was there to talk about Elijah. The old coot grinned like he knew I'd done it."

"Did he accuse you?"

"No, but he was going to. I'm certain." He smiled for the first time since he'd arrived. "Now, he can't." He burst into laughter.

Unless I did something soon, I'd be joining Elijah and Clarence. But, what?

"Why kill Terrell?"

"Loose end, my friend. Terrell looked up to Clarence, saw him as a father figure, or so I heard. Terrell told everyone he had to avenge Clarence's murder. He was a lot younger than most of us, full of energy, full of using it to catch the killer." He shook his head. "To catch me. The police weren't doing much. I know they figured whoever killed Elijah was long gone or was dead, besides, they didn't have any evidence. The gun I used got swallowed up by the deep blue sea decades ago. There was no way for the cops to figure it out. None of that was going to stop Terrell, especially after Clarence's death. He'd talked a little to Sandra and me. He wanted to talk more. I went to his house to see how I could help. He met me at the door looking like he'd seen the devil. I figured maybe he had. Somehow, he knew it was me, or had a serious hunch it was. I invited myself in like I did here." He smiled showing no humor. "The boy was doing a good job fixing up the old house. New stuff everywhere. I hated messing it up with his blood. Oh well, he didn't have to clean it up."

"How did he know it was—"

"Enough chit chat. One more time, where's Al Washington?"

"Why do you need him?"

"Next to you, he's the last loose end."

I wondered why he wasn't considering Virgil or Charles loose ends but didn't dare mention their names.

His phone rang. He nearly collapsed. He looked at the screen, answered and said, "Hi, Sandra. What's up?"

He listened a few seconds. "You're kidding. How long ago did he leave?"

He looked at the ceiling and closed his eyes.

I took two quick steps, swatted his arm away that held the gun, then rammed my head in his stomach. He stumbled over the chair, dropped the phone, then tried to pivot so the gun faced me.

I grabbed for his arm holding the gun. I missed. He twisted toward me. I grabbed for it again. His knees buckled. I rammed him a second time. His head hit the floor, the gun slid out of his reach.

I lunged for the weapon. Robert tripped me before I reached it. I turned toward him as he swung at my head. I ducked. His age finally took its toll. He fell and grabbed his chest. I slid over to the gun, grabbed it, and pointed it at the eighty-five-year-old man gasping for breath.

My phone was six feet away. It seemed like miles. I scooted over, punched in 911, told the dispatcher to send the police and an ambulance. I remained on the floor outside Robert's reach until I heard sirens approaching. He hadn't moved since hitting the floor.

When I heard the first patrol car stop in my drive, I pulled myself up with the door handle to greet Officer Bishop, accompanied by a steady stream of first responders. Bishop was kind enough to help me to my chair without making me feel like an old man or an invalid.

An hour later, I'd shared my story with Bishop, Chief LaMond, and a detective I didn't know from the Sheriff's Office. Robert Graves was alive when he left my living room on a stretcher. Barely alive, according to one of the EMTs.

After everyone was gone, I remembered the voicemail message and tapped on the icon.

"Mr. Landrum, this is Detective Callahan. I just left the Graves's house. Robert wasn't home. Sandra claimed she didn't know where he was. I started asking her about the fire at Al Washington's house, then about the deaths of the three men on Sol Legare. She said it'd be wise if she didn't say anything else and called an attorney. I don't think you have anything to worry about, but I wanted to let you know Robert was out there somewhere. You might want to be careful until we find him."

I laughed, pushed out of the chair, and headed to the kitchen for another glass of wine.

EPILOGUE

The smell of fresh paint mixed with a faint aroma of burnt wood greeted Charles, Virgil, and me as we entered Al's house. It'd been seven weeks since the mystery of the three murders on Sol Legare was solved in my living room. It'd been two weeks since Bob's makeshift crew of carpenters, painters, and roofers had restored Al's house to, in his words, a better condition than it had been in since the Revolutionary War. Al wasn't prone to exaggerate, but I suspected that was one of those times.

Tanesa saw us and rushed to greet her Dad's guests to the housewarming party, or as Bob called it, "house cooling party." He didn't think warming was a good word to use after the fire. Written invitations weren't sent, so he could call it anything he wanted.

Tanesa wore a light-blue blouse, tan slacks, and a smile. She kissed each of us on the cheek then thanked us for coming. Charles said nothing could've kept us away. She said the house was too small to hold everyone, that the other guests were in the back yard. As we walked though the house, I agreed with Al. The restoration was impressive. The walls had a new coat of paint and felt fresh. His former living room, now his bedroom, had new furniture that wasn't there on my previous visit. A fifty-five-inch flat screen television was on a low stand opposite the bed. Something told me that Bob was responsible.

Fortunately, the temperature was mild. The high humidity that'd blanked the area the last two weeks was only a memory.

A makeshift bar was near the back fence. A college-age man wearing a white waiter's coat was behind the bar handing a beer to someone I didn't recognize. Two other men who looked vaguely familiar were waiting behind the one being served. If I wasn't mistaken, they were regulars at Al's. I'd wager Bob also deserved credit for the bar and bartender.

Al was seated in a kitchen chair beside the steps leading from the kitchen to the yard. He was patting Spoiled Rotten that had one paw firmly placed on Al's thigh. He saw me and tried to push the dog's paw off his leg. He failed. I told him not to stand. I thanked him for inviting us.

He introduced me to Gertrude, the dog's owner, who said it was nice meeting me, before adding that she needed to get home to take some "God awful" pills.

Al then gave me his full attention. "Mr. Chris, you've got to be kidding. Don't tell me not to stand. I owe you a stand, a salute, and a bow. You've given this old man peace knowing who killed my friend. I'm sorry you nearly died doing it."

"The house looks great," I said, changing the subject.

"Better than I deserve," he said and smiled.

"That's for damned sure," Bob said from behind me. He patted me on the back before he grinned at Al. "Just kidding, friend."

Al smiled.

Charles and Virgil joined us and thanked Al for inviting them.

Two more people arrived before Al responded.

Jamal and Eugene looked around like they were at the wrong party. I went to greet them. I thanked them for coming and escorted them to Al.

Jamal said, "Eugene made me. I don't get this far from home unless I'm kidnapped."

Angelica Cruz is the award-winning coauthor of *Sea Fog: A Folly Beach Halloween Mystery*. Ms. Cruz lives near Elizabethtown, Kentucky, with her husband Hector, two dogs, a bird, two cats, and four chickens.

Learn more about the series and the author by visiting www.billnoel.com.

Printed in the USA
CPSIA information can be obtained
at www.ICGtesting.com
LVHW021402050724
784681LV00001B/8